# BRIDGES

## Leatha J. Patton

Continental
RIGHTS LLC

Bridges
Copyright © 2025 by Leatha J. Patton



*Library of Congress Control Number: 2025909838*

ISBN
978-1-967804-08-5 (Paperback)
978-1-967804-09-2 (eBook)
978-1-967804-07-8 (Hardcover)

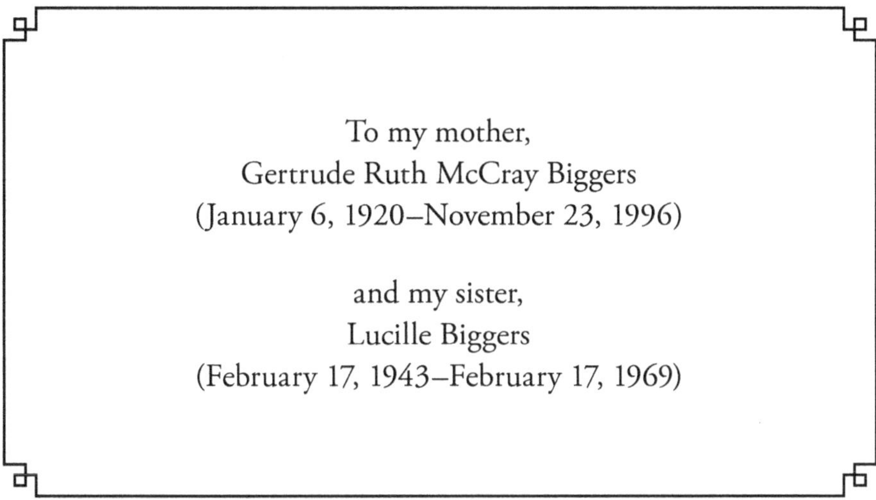

To my mother,
Gertrude Ruth McCray Biggers
(January 6, 1920–November 23, 1996)

and my sister,
Lucille Biggers
(February 17, 1943–February 17, 1969)

# Table of Contents

Part One

# THE BECKFORDS

(1823–1949)

# CHAPTER ONE

Without time to reload his rifle, he took its butt end and, leaning from his horse, slammed it hard against Calvin Beckford's leg. Beckford, large and strong even in his advanced years, did not go down as intended. Instead, the violent act caused his aim to shift from its target, and consequently, the bullet tore into the animal. Beckford snatched away the white hood just as the horse, whinnying, fell heavily to the ground. The dead weight pinned the rider underneath, killing him instantly. Exposing were cold, lifeless eyes in a vaguely recognizable face. Drifting clouds again obscured the moonlight as Beckford stood at the entrance of the forest on the wide strip of land that separated it from the cotton crop. The menacing flames had died, but segments of the destroyed crop billowed with smoke.

"On my own land!" Beckford bellowed, his voice carrying through the woods. "On my own land, God damn it."

To further enrage him were the bodies of his sons, swaying like pendulums in the trees, visible whenever the moon emerged from behind the clouds. He was certain that this dastardly act was in retaliation for all the dead bodies that lay motionless on the ground. He braced himself, expecting that more were coming, but then realized the gunshots he heard were dispersing the remaining trouble into the woods. Once more, the moon's light allowed visibility, and he had to focus. He looked down at the calf of his right leg in the semidarkness and saw that he had sustained a nasty wound that was bleeding profusely; the partly frayed, bloody pant leg lay limp and wet against it. Anxiously he tore away enough of the pant leg to expose the injured calf. With the torn cloth, Beckford tied a tourniquet above the bleeding gash, moaning with pain. His mother had taught him about tourniquets many, many years ago.

"Beckford," a voice called in the darkness. "Beckford!"

He recognized the younger McDermott approaching him beneath a clear night sky in Georgia. Following close behind was Sheriff Getties. All other law enforcement had left. The moon began to steadily reveal itself from behind the clouds, casting light on the ghastly carnage.

Calvin Beckford would carry to his grave the horrendous images of his sons dangling like ragdolls in the trees at the entrance of those woods.

Raleigh McDermott IV's rifle was over one shoulder as he walked toward Calvin Beckford. Approaching the grotesque sight of the lifeless bodies, now motionless, at the mouth of the woods, he suppressed his shocked reaction as best he could. He quickly diverted his attention to Beckford's leg.

"I think that's a nasty wound, Beckford," he said. He then turned to Sheriff Getties, unable to disguise the tremor in his voice. "You'll pass by Blaine's place, won't you?" Dr. Blaine was the one doctor around who did not discriminate against blacks. McDermott wasn't.

"I'll make sure he gets over there," Getties' answer was almost a mumble to conceal his confused anger. "Beckford," Getties continued with a measure of discomfiture, "we need to cut them down."

"Leave them be," Beckford replied with emotion in his voice. "I'm coming back for them."

It was an awkward moment for all three. McDermott kept his head averted as the sheriff appeared helplessly baffled.

"Well, I'm done here," McDermott finally said because his emotions were beginning to betray him. Hurriedly, he left the two men; in a day or so he would assess the damage.

❧

Calvin Beckford watched the younger McDermott as he left the site on foot and in the distance saw his horse, barely visible, waiting patiently. He shifted most of the weight to his unwounded leg, limping with great effort over to his chestnut, Dan, as the throbbing pain intensified his wrath and devastated sorrow.

"I would rather die on my own soil than live off it," he said softly but with fierce conviction because Getties's reputation was well known.

"Now, now, Beckford, there's no need to talk like that."

The main culprits were dead or had been chased off; the worst was now over.

"I have sacrificed two sons," he replied in anguish. "None could be greater, so there's no need to stop now."

"Can you ride your horse, Beckford?" Getties gruffly asked.

Calvin looked down at the wound on his lower right calf. He managed to thwart any assistance and slowly climbed on his horse, with great difficulty.

"Dad," Medgar, his eldest, had teased, "you need to learn to ride." He was fifteen at the time. His response to his father's protest was laughter. "But you are no longer a slave—you're a free man. You don't always want to be bothered with hitching a horse to wagon."

His leg continued to throb with pain. Gently he nudged the animal, and it responded obediently by trotting slowly, carrying him away from the site of death as, fleetingly, he endured an eerie, out-of-body experience. He would never know if the sheriff would have shot him had McDermott not been present. At this point he was beyond caring.

"The doctor needs to look at that leg, Beckford," Getties called out gruffly while Beckford was still within hearing range. "I'll send him."

The bright moon continued to cast its fixed gleam on the horror in the trees as well as that strewn on the ground. Getties, frightfully mesmerized by the monstrous sight, abruptly turned away and momentarily hesitated in his saddle. Down through the years he had infrequently jailed or threatened the incarceration of whites. Years of deception had denied whites the well-disguised information about his origin. Otherwise, his position, which now generated fear and respect, would have quickly dissipated. Perhaps he too would be hanging in a noose from a tree branch. Thankfully, in appearance he had managed to escape his mother's curse—the slight brush of the tar. He felt a pang of regret that in conclusion the world was not a nice place.

Calvin Beckford continued to travel the distance of approximately a quarter mile to his house. He could ride as well as his sons, but Dan had a cold and could not manage the full gallop required, only a trotting gait. Common sense told him that even if the horse had been in top condition, he would have arrived too late.

Getties continued to watch Beckford as he gradually diminished to a tiny silhouette against the horizon of an early dawn. It was in times such as these that he warred with emotions of self-rebuke, incapable of purging mental pictures of the hauntingly sad eyes of his mother. It had been so many years since his abandonment. It was coincidental that he had learned of her death upon his return to this place.

He thought back to the sight of McDermott mounted in his saddle at the entrance of the Beckford property earlier that night, patiently awaiting his arrival, as if daring him not to show up. Once he and his men arrived, they were hampered by a combination of pitch blackness and drifting smoke from the burning crop. The conditions taunted even the law. He barely avoided stepping on a dead body. Finally, after traveling by foot for quite a distance on Beckford land in the variably dense forest, he and his deputized men managed to defuse the remainder of the mob—at least all who had not already escaped. It was doubtful that any of that rambunctious group would have allowed themselves to be jailed even if those deputized by court order had tried. The gunshots permitted all remaining perpetrators to flee like candle wax melting from a flame. As the chaos subsided, McDermott caught up to join him on foot, and then both encountered Beckford.

Getties thought back to McDermott's cold steel gaze as he stood in his living room earlier that evening. "I apologize for coming to your home on business," said McDermott, "but I tried to get to you before you left your office. I won't be long, Jim." He removed his hat, but refused the offered seat with an explanation that he was short on time. "Trouble is brewing in the hinterland, and I know how you are about that type of thing."

Sheriff Getties frowned slightly. "I'm not following you."

"I know how you are about not interfering with things that are unlawful when they deal with 'keeping niggers in their place,' Getties."

Since the McDermotts no longer grew crops, the agreement was that the Beckfords could grow cotton on both properties. Therefore, he didn't mention the significant encroachment on his property.

The culprits were the descendants of Grainger and Burton Kane who were still engaged in maintaining the ongoing feud that had existed since plantation days between them and the McDermotts. During those days Grainger and Burton Kane were considered yeomen farmers. The problem began when McDermott's great-grandfather seized most of the best land. It had transpired long ago and was now irreversible.

Common knowledge was the McDermotts were having a relatively difficult time keeping the mill solvent. No longer was there unpaid labor to pick the crop. Grainger and Kane had concocted a scheme to force the Beckfords to discontinue growing cotton for the mill causing the McDermotts no choice but to pay a higher price for the stuff. What more appropriate time to turn business away from the Beckfords to themselves! No longer would they have to compete on the open market with the other cotton growers as before when the McDermotts had a captive labor force.

"But what's happening is unjustified," McDermott had continued. "It's much like the incident which occurred on your watch about ten years back, remember?" He referenced the random lynching of a free black man, a drifter looking for work. At the time, the cavalry, although not ubiquitous, still occupied much of the South to provide protection for the newly freed black population. Getties, a US marshal in the region at the time, could have assisted county law enforcement in preventing the lynching. The gruesome event was becoming more frequent all over the South. These incidents caused Raleigh McDermott IV unease and led his father to label him a throwback to his great-uncle, Neville.

"Now see here, McDermott, I—"

"Just a second, hear me out," said McDermott quietly. In contemplation he smoothed the brim of his hat, rendering Getties a thoughtful and steady gaze. "You know, my great-grandparents knew the Oglesby family. They remembered when the plantation's patriarch, Andrew Oglesby, had a quadroon for a plaything who was pregnant child when he bought her. It was discovered that this young girl had been cohabiting with the previous overseer and gave birth to a female octoroon. As the story goes, years passed. On weekends this female octoroon after about fifteen years of age was passed around to guests. In time she birthed a son who, born under the Oglesby umbrella, was one-sixteenth Negro. One day that teenage boy left Georgia, just slipped away during the night sometime before the Civil War. A search party was loosely thrown together to look for him for a few days. On occasion his name would come up because we wondered what had become of him. Well, the story intrigued me even more than it did the others.

"When you were assigned jurisdiction over this region, I couldn't quite place the familiar resemblance. I don't think anyone else noticed, but my family and yours were well acquainted for many years. At one time we visited each other. So I recalled the likeness. One day I realized you were more than just under the Oglesby umbrella. There was a likeness. You possessed the signature features of the Oglesby males—the same blue-gray eyes, ruddy complexion, and blonde hair and that very pronounced nose, the Oglesby trademark."

The angry sheriff was taken aback.

"I guess you're wondering how I knew since you're no longer known as an Oglesby, a name that can be traced back to your house slave beginnings. In search of respectability, you carefully changed your name. For a while you resided in another state, but after the legislation of the 1850 Fugitive Slave Act, you were assigned to this region as a US marshal. Keep in mind, my background as a lawyer allows me to methodically track information with critical thoroughness unavailable to the average citizen." He paused briefly. "You allowed your aspirations to run amuck, causing your reputation to precede you." He laughed wryly. "In many slave quarters you were called Marshal 'Hound Dog' Getties. 'I always get my nigger'—that is how you were quoted in the law enforcement community. Chasing your own, searching for your own, lynching your own." He paused momentarily. "They are your own, Getties, because the one-drop rule still applies. Is that why you never married—afraid of risking the price of retribution for past deeds?" He paused with a quiet laugh and shrugged. "I can't say that I blame you. There is that universal law in some form."

Getties appeared petrified, clutching the arms of his chair so tightly his knuckles were visibly white.

"Do your job, Oglesby." McDermott paused, feigning apology. "Excuse me. You're Getties, James Getties." Mocking him, he tipped his hat, placed it back on his head, and offered a sardonic smile. "No more Josiah Oglesby for you, isn't that right?"

Getties's emotions were doing a tailspin. He felt as if he had just been doused with ice water. He was loath to mentally revisit his humble beginnings and have them recalled by himself or anyone else.

"Don't worry, Getties, I will keep the secret. I will keep my end of the bargain if you keep yours. Got it?"

He didn't answer, staring warily. He wanted to ask McDermott why he was so concerned with this nigger.

"Got it?" McDermott repeated pointedly.

"I believe that I do."

McDermott turned and left.

❧

Young Raleigh McDermott IV was a prominent lawyer. His father, Raleigh McDermott, III, was only a part-time judge because of his involvement with the textile mill. One of the three law clerks, almost frightened out of his wits, had passed on the sinister news that pertained to the mill. Everybody knew that the Beckfords, ex-slaves of the

McDermotts, grew the cotton crop. Without prompt relay of upcoming disaster, things would have been much worse.

Because of the prestige of the McDermotts throughout the county and beyond, things were aborted quickly. The court order was implemented at the discretion of a colleague, thus allowing Judge McDermott to avoid a conflict of interest. Getties, with the reluctant local law enforcement and even less enthused court-ordered deputies, arrived to put down an onslaught, which saved Calvin Beckford's life.

To this day, Getties held a mental picture of McDermott's great-uncle, Preston, mounted on his deep brown mare gazing down to greet his nephew and Getties as they played in the front yard of the Jade mansion. Getties still recalled that he had continued to play as he watched the man at short intervals until he was out of sight. He would never forget those cold, steel gray eyes, and he now decided that, yes, of course he too had known. All the so-called Southern gentlemen conversed with one another away from public spaces and their wives. It was the last he ever saw of the Jade plantation. Thereafter, the mistress slipped away without him.

Getties thought again about McDermott's remarks as he left Beckford land. How had McDermott discovered his involvement in that incident? In fact, it had happened only a relatively short distance away in a similarly wooded area. He was only guilty of remaining passive. Weeks afterward, the ancestors had castigated him relentlessly.

The former marshal wondered what the mood of the South and the remainder of the country would be if all blacks had been cut from Beckford's mold. Exactly what was the bond between the McDermotts and the Beckfords? Why did the Beckfords not carry the plantation name as did most freed blacks? He would probably never know. His thoughts drifted to the Haitian Revolution. It had erupted during the latter part of the last century. On that island their slaveholding counterparts had met a tragic end that most never mentioned. Hurriedly those thoughts were discarded.

With the Civil War over, Getties truly longed for a new South with peaceful separation of the races—with him on the white side, of course, according to the blood of his father, whose race would always reject

Josiah Oglesby. With a jolt, other images interjected to add sadness. The strapped Southern gentleman's concubine, his mother, never experienced freedom.

A little less than a half hour later, Sheriff Getties notified Dr. Blaine of the events; Blaine responded by grabbing his medical bag.

Moving on, Getties's forced his mind to dispel all memories of his disturbing, maladjusted, and humble past. He had just performed his very last duty in this place. He was a US marshal again! Another kind of war was being waged out West with the Great Plains Indians. His future beckoned.

☙

The sun was bright and promised a brutally hot day as Calvin Beckford arrived once more at the site. He was freshly bandaged, in pain, and limping badly. Various volunteers, including church members, helped to separate the bodies from the tree branches. Gently, they were lowered to the horse-pulled wagon. A reverent, hushed calm permeated the hot late morning air filled with the smell of death. At the insistence of Pastor Ruben, the bodies were to be prepared at the back of the church for their mother to view, with sacrificed white sheets spread over quilts on the large table used for church suppers. No comments were made that one son had been genitally mutilated. Pronounced rope bruises encircled the necks of both young men. With deft skill coffins were constructed— two crude rectangular boxes—as both bodies were washed and dressed for the burial.

Engrossed in grief, Maude Beckford insisted that Pastor Ruben perform an impromptu eulogy. News of the formal ceremony was hastily and urgently disseminated throughout the black community. The next day, church members and friends would join the Beckford family as they mourned their devastating loss in a formal service.

In solitude, Calvin Beckford wept. The beautiful longleaf pines intermingled with other trees and the many species of fowl peculiar to Georgia alone voiced their presence. Calvin Beckford wondered how a place so very beautiful could render such evil.

Because Medgar and Jule had rushed in without thought or warning, the family had been saved from potentially even worse havoc that led to their deaths. Thus, Calvin agonized over whether instilling his own fervor for the land in those two had been a mistake.

&cs;

Before talking to Beckford, Raleigh IV decided to take a ride through the burned fields. Being the fourth generation of lawyers, he would have loved to put all this behind him and devote the time to his law practice instead, but money as well as time was heavily invested. The textile mill had begun as a dream of his great-grandfather and at this point was becoming a lucrative enterprise. It was needed to save the McDermotts from financial ruin. How many times had he heard the story about Driscoll in the lowlands and the cultivation of those rice fields? Eventually Jade was established to grow cotton. He memorized the story almost verbatim as repeated many times by older family members.

In 1798, Raleigh McDermott Sr. arrived from low country to central Georgia with advance knowledge supplied by his son Preston. Information was shared by Burton Kane, an overseer from a neighboring plantation. He was familiar with the fertile land west of the Ocmulgee River. Preston verified the information from Kane and immediately alerted his father. To the site Raleigh Sr. brought with him from Driscoll (the rice plantation founded by his grandfather) a significant number of African slaves to clear three thousand acres of land negotiated with the Creek Indians. First cleared was one and a half acres on which he could build a great house for Rebecca McDermott, his wife and the mother of their four sons, to allow her to return to Georgia from Connecticut. He named the plantation Jade.

Raleigh Sr. attended the funeral and interment of his father, Warren McDermott, which was held in Boston. His mother cautioned him. "Your grandfather and father were on opposite ends. Your grandfather was only interested in making a profit, and your father was extreme in his devotion to Driscoll, which killed him. Warren McDermott, an old man, had succumbed to malaria; he was seventy-four. Always, his mother's actions spoke loud and clear. Most of her time was spent in Boston or on trips abroad, far away from Driscoll with its ditches, floodgates, and all else that made it profitable. In her opinion, it was an unattractive and dangerous business venture. She detested the rice culture and everything that tediously growing it entailed. Warren often reminded her that it yielded her a lavish lifestyle and, second, that she shouldn't forget that because of him the plantation bore her maiden name. (The grandfather had never bothered to name the place.) She would occasionally scoff in reply, fully cognizant of both ultimate truths. Ten years of attempting to reside there caused her to permanently return to her original home state of Massachusetts. Whenever Warren McDermott wanted the company of the mother of his children (Raleigh had two sisters with families of their own), he would reside there for a reasonable amount of time. It was then back to the rice fields—the rice *swamps*, his wife constantly corrected him.

It was with reluctance that Raleigh Sr., Warren's only son (now with a family of his own which included a namesake), inherited the plantation that would relegate his profitable law profession to part-time status.

From the outset, Raleigh Sr. decided he would use the advice he had offered his father years ago: add to the wealth of rice an income from growing cotton but avoid the problems of constantly revitalizing the soil. That was the primary problem of growing this staple in low country. He had firsthand knowledge of those planters' dogged determination to conquer this adversity, which reinforced his decision to grow cotton in central Georgia. At the time, his ambition was twofold. Like rice, a textile mill, also needed water. However, his dream of reopening an old textile mill (a failed one) on the Ocmulgee River was soon discarded. It became clear that the mills in the east wanted to maintain their stronghold on that lucrative business venture. Well, he would combine the sale of cotton with rice for a more enterprising business venture at home as well as abroad.

Preston, his second son, had been tentatively left in charge of Driscoll. Meanwhile Raleigh Jr. was practicing law in the North, and much to his father's disappointment, refused to have his aspirations even minimally interrupted.

Raleigh Sr.'s wife, Rebecca, Connecticut-born and reared, also disliked Driscoll but for different reasons. She thought that the lives led by enslaved Africans, brought to the lowlands specifically for the purpose of cultivating rice, was an especially dismal existence. Knowledge of its cultivation for thousands of years had proved for these Africans to be a cursed skill in North America. That there was such a high mortality rate among the majority of even the younger slave population saddened her.

After a disastrous fall from her horse, Rebecca temporarily returned to Connecticut to live with relatives— "until I can get away from that dampness," she said about Driscoll. Her actions were justified because residing there did cause additional soreness in her joints and further aggravated the excruciating pain in her lower back. Rebecca McDermott's physical condition was Raleigh Sr.'s primary reason for building the Jade mansion a considerable distance from the Ocmulgee.

Like his father before him, Raleigh Sr. desired to reside in Georgia, but in precautious proximity to Driscoll; he chose to reside at Jade.

Raleigh Sr. had been growing cotton for about six years when a convention was established between the United States and the Creek Nation about opening more of the latter's land to whites. This was the Treaty of Washington, November 14, 1805. Explicitly in Articles I–V, the treaty contained wording in favor of the United States regarding said properties, and for the Creeks it was becoming an uphill battle to retain any of their land. Eventually, all their lands throughout the entire state would be ceded. Ultimately, in 1823, after tirelessly strategizing and exhausting all feasible appeals to reason with the government, the Creeks would receive a final decision from the US Supreme Court: Indians could occupy lands within the United States but could not hold title to those lands. Their "right of occupancy" was subordinate to the United States' "right of discovery."

Long before this Supreme Court decision, all the lands on both sides of the Ocmulgee River had been ceded. Raleigh Sr. did manage to receive an additional three thousand acres to keep expanding the growth of cotton. Years later, after the Supreme Court debacle, some of the smaller yeomen farmers became insolvent, including Burton Kane. McDermott seized this opportunity, forever reversing the favorable rapport between the two families. The result: Raleigh McDermott Sr. owned a total of ten thousand acres on which to grow cotton plus five thousand acres of forestry—lumber! The combined total was fifteen thousand acres. Close to two hundred slaves would cultivate the ten thousand acres of cotton from seed to harvest.

Driscoll also continued to be profitable and well operated. Raleigh Sr.'s reward to Preston for his initial discovery of Jade was to welcome him in making cotton as profitable as rice. Additionally, he wasn't getting any younger, and the father's keen observation was that his youngest son, Donovan, was savvy in the cultivation of rice and could manage without Preston. The forced, unpaid labor necessary to grow it (a subject raised quite often by his wife) was hard enough on the slaves without Preston's harsh, unyielding temperament. However, Donovan was cautioned by his father to always avoid Driscoll's dangerous rainy season.

Eventually, the law practice of Raleigh Jr. proved to be only sporadically profitable at best, which prompted him to ingratiate himself with his father. Raleigh Sr. was a pragmatic man and decided after considerable pondering that his will should reflect his oldest son's misstep.

❧

Raleigh IV abruptly stopped reminiscing and returned his focus to surveying the current devastation because his father, Raleigh III, awaited his evaluation. Together, Calvin Beckford and the younger man assessed the damage. The residue from the destruction was depressing in both sight and smell. Although necessary, the words Calvin wished to use were hard to tactfully construct.

"I got a good deal," young Raleigh was explaining as the pair walked through the fields where the fire had not reached a considerable amount of the cotton on McDermott land. Enough was salvageable to pay a small amount to this man, which could at least sustain his family and livestock through the winter. "There's enough cotton here," he said, in reference to the mill, "to tide us over until we receive the shipment from the next county in a few days."

His father had managed to negotiate an immediate cash sale with one of the cotton growers who usually shipped a sizable amount of bales overseas. These days expedient payment was welcome now that labor was no longer free.

"If you want to use someone else to grow the cotton, I will understand." Calvin's thoughts conflicted with his words.

"You need the money, right?" the younger man replied, none too gently.

No longer ago than yesterday, Raleigh IV had told his father that the only alternative was to close the mill, which he flatly refused because it was starting to yield a profit. "All right then, the decision has been made for us," he'd said. "Case closed."

"Sure, I need the money," replied Calvin Beckford.

"And I need to use the McDermott land that is free and clear," Raleigh IV responded with matter-of-fact sternness, "to grow cotton as cheaply as possible. Beckford, the mill needs to stay out of the red, understand?"

"I understand," he answered. It was an awkward moment.

"This helps both you and me," Raleigh emphasized. There was a reflective pause as he slowly scanned the destruction. "I can assure you they won't be back. We're in a good place because we have enough information to arrest them on sight if another attempt is even rumored, and they know it." Again, he paused, shaking his head in disgust. "They didn't carefully think it through, believe me."

❧

Long after Raleigh McDermott IV had left, Calvin remained in the field, thinking back to just what had brought him to this point.

Calvin's mother, Naomi Beckford, told him that he was born at Jade in 1806. It turned out that Rebecca had returned to Georgia somewhat prematurely. Naomi told him that Rebecca McDermott candidly explained that a white nurse hired to care for her was averse to employment in "such close proximity to so many darkies." Her exact phrase. However, she did agree to stay until the arrival of her replacement.

Neville suggested that his father bring Naomi to Jade for that purpose. Since she had worked closely with him and his wife, he could vouch for her competency as a nurse. She would take excellent care of his invalid mother. Neville, through his knowledgeable sources, had her tracked to the plantation that bought her; Naomi arrived approximately three months prior to giving birth to her child. Neville's intimate interactions with the Underground were knowledge that Naomi would take to her grave.

She was brought to the plantation from the low country when Raleigh Sr. bought her from a neighboring rice plantation near Savannah. Previously, she was free and working as a nurse for Neville McDermott, Raleigh Sr.'s youngest son, (a doctor in Philadelphia). "I got ambitious," she told her son, "I decided that I wanted to help Nathaniel Beckford (Calvin's father) free my sister Julia and her two sons." It turned out badly. His father, Nathaniel Beckford, and Calvin's Aunt Julia, his mother's sister, were killed, while attempting to fight off the slave catchers. Julia's two sons and Naomi were sold to other plantations. That they were captured during "runaway slave business" became deliberately lost in the transaction. The devious slave catcher allowed, for a fee of course, the trader to purchase his human merchandise. Neville managed to find out who bought her, and then his father purchased her; she ended up at Jade nursing Neville's invalid mother. And so, the thing that Neville hated (his reason for leaving Jade) saved Naomi Beckford. However, Neville never told his father that the young woman was once free. All Raleigh Sr. knew was that she had worked in his son's office. In fact, an abolitionist friend covered Neville's story, that she was on loan to him from a colleague who sold her to a trader to satisfy his debt. Pennsylvania had Freedmen, but the state still had remnants of slavery as did other northern states. The shrewd businessman wanted to make his money as soon as possible without entanglements that would undermine the deal. He preyed upon the fact that it was close to harvest time on rice plantations. Replenishment of workers was necessary.

Reminiscing, Calvin Beckford was nudged back in time. It was 1817. He was eleven witnessing in the distance a horse-drawn wagon leaving Jade. The distance kept him from seeing who was in the wagon. Knowledge was immediate when he reached the little cabin where his mother sat on the floor in a corner.

"Who did they sell her to?"

"I don't know," she answered sorrowfully.

Rocking back and forth and shaking her head, she cried softly. She stopped abruptly to become totally motionless, and the two of them sat quietly together for what seemed an eternity.

"Her scars are almost healed," she said with quiet pride, breaking the long silence. "They're still visible, but they don't look too bad. There are less than I thought possible."

Triumph stole into her voice. She had gone into the woods and collected the necessary herbs. Mixing them with the same soothing oil used on Rebecca McDermott, she had dissolved them in their cabin over a low fire until she had created a salve of soft paste consistency. Each day, she would leave the Big House to "tend to Sarah."

"I gave her the rest to take with her," she said, "but she will need someone to apply it." She sighed heavily. "My heart aches for that young woman."

She held Calvin close as he began to cry in uncontrollable anguish. "Hush now," she whispered. "Hush, Calvin," she repeated, attempting to comfort the youth.

Even Naomi couldn't shut out the bleakness now invading the space that Sarah had periodically shared with them for six years. Together they cried fresh tears for her.

"Baby, just keep her in your heart," Naomi said after a long pause, tenderly placing her hand on his chest. "Just keep her right there."

So many thoughts and memories were coming to Beckford now, and it was getting dark. He didn't want Maude in the fields to fetch him, but he couldn't go in just yet.

There was a relatively less remote time. How old had he been? Fourteen, he thought. Late one evening he had overheard a man reciting in his broken English a disturbing and tragic chapter in the African narrative. Whispering, he recounted going to sleep and emerging the next morning from his hiding place to discover the absence of many people he had known all his life. Some in their village had been his playmates. Soon his own fate was to exist as an enslaved African in Georgia. In very broken English, he had talked about the "Drisco swomps" and then being brought to Jade. It was such a frightful story that afterward Calvin had many sleepless nights and would not attempt to eavesdrop again for a very long time.

For many days while he worked in the field picking cotton with the steady crack of the driver's whip keeping everyone frightfully alert, the old African's story coursed through his brain.

Each week, either Saturday or Sunday, Naomi visited the cabin; all other times he saw her only at the Big House because she had been Rebecca McDermott's private nurse for as long as he could remember. During this week's visit he talked to his mother about what he had overheard. She listened for a long time saying nothing, and then began to talk.

"He was explaining a rice plantation," she said slowly. "Driscoll is the McDermott's rice plantation. I've never been there, but I was at a rice plantation—somewhere near Savannah—before Neville's father brought me here to nurse his wife." She paused, collecting her thoughts. "There was one pure African woman I could understand rather well. She told me she knew how to grow rice before she came to America. I never got a chance to ask how they grew rice in Africa, but here the rice stalks are grown in swamp water."

"So how do you pick it?" Calvin asked.

Naomi laughed. "Baby, you don't pick it. You have a rice hook curved like a sickle." She paused. "You know the tool used to saw wood?"

Calvin nodded, saddened as his thoughts momentarily filled with fond images of Gabe. He had taught him carpentry. He recalled how Sarah and Gabe were together at every opportunity.

"Inside the curve is a sharp edge like the teeth of a saw. You cut the stalks of rice by grabbing as much as you can, and with one swoop"— she demonstrated with one arm in a sweeping motion, away from the body. The other was in a crooked position to mimic holding an armful of substance. "You cut as much as you can. Men roll up their pants above the knees. Women pull up their skirts and tie them up with a cord." She paused. "You're barefoot the entire time. Water is up to your knees."

"Mama," Calvin exclaimed emphatically, "that sounds nasty."

"It is," she said softly. "It's awful." She smiled sadly. "All of this is bad," she said, gesturing all around them with her hand. "It's just that growing rice is even more horrible."

Both were silent for a long time. Calvin would never forget; he spoke first.

"What then?"

She sighed heavily as if reliving the entire ordeal. "Then you leave the armful on the stubble you just cut it from for the person following close behind to tie in a bundle." She paused. "You know how you have a long sack to put the cotton in?"

He nodded.

"These stalks—called sheaves—are left all over that rice field." Naomi laughed because Calvin looked rather confused.

"How long does that take?"

"It takes hours, just like picking cotton," she said. "You know how long it takes to pick cotton?"

"A long time," he replied.

"Well, there are rows and rows of those sheaves of rice. All of us were doing the same thing—leaving those bundles containing rice all over the field."

"What do you do with it after that?" he asked.

"Well, to keep the animals—the rice birds and ducks—from eating it, muskets and what are called clappers make noise to keep them away." She paused and took a breath. "It's hot with plenty of mosquitoes. You're always in water. I saw rats," she said quietly. "I never saw one, but I was told sometimes there are alligators too." She paused. "Snakes too.

Right before I arrived a few men has snake bites. Snake bites are rather common."

Calvin tensed and became very attentive. "Mama!" he exclaimed. "Did any die?"

"I don't know," she said somberly. "I was getting to the end of my journey. I never would have made it if Neville's father hadn't come for me." She smiled sadly. "The winnowing house—high up off the ground! It was my next stop. My last!" As she finished, she sounded and appeared spent.

"*…it was my next stop. My last.*" He would always remember those words. They were the essence of her soul and revealed to him why she was unwilling to run. He thought of his mother's sister, his Aunt Julia, and her two sons. Family he would never know!

A few years before the enactment of the Fugitive Slave Act, he and his mother, Naomi, were having a heated discussion. Always a problematic topic invoking passionate opposition. That time she angrily reprimanded him.

"And just how far do you think you will get?"

"We could at least try, Mama," he argued.

"Do you know what happens if you—if *we*—get caught and are dragged back to Jade? That is, if we get back at all."

"You were once free," he argued in a hushed tone.

"Yes," she whispered, "because I was right across the border from Pennsylvania in Maryland. Slaves have always escaped from the border states."

Through the years mother and son continued to have the same passionate discussion about escape. Always it ended the same way. Naomi always won, and both remained at Jade. Where would one go without the other? The only family they had was each other.

He now relived another incident. Becky—that's what Naomi called Rebecca McDermott in private—had been dead for almost ten years. He was married with a family of his own. His mother was spending as much time as she could in her cabin away from the Big House; he often teased her.

"What's wrong with the house that Gabe built?" he would ask jovially. "All those fancy floors and woodwork. It's a mighty fine place you leaving to come to this."

"I don't like that woman, that tattletale, that liar, that suck-up! I watch everything I say around her. Daphne thinks that's going to make them treat her better. Stupid woman, a house nigger!" She paused. "Besides, I have privacy here and don't have to tiptoe."

"Mama," he said with laughter. "My, that's some strong language coming from a nice lady like you."

After Sarah, Daphne—much younger at the time—was Naomi's helper for years. Calvin recalled her as a docile old woman with profound difficulty with life, post slavery, and was forever thankful that she was not "turned out"—her words. He smiled to himself as he vividly recalled other specific endearments his mother had concerning Daphne. He knew some of it was resentment because she remained angry about what had happened to Sarah. Yes, Daphne had been an enigma, a holdover from Jade's past.

In January 1863, Naomi was ecstatic when she heard that Lincoln had signed the Emancipation Proclamation, punishment to all the states that had rebelliously seceded from the Union. Georgia was one of the first, and this act would eventually force that state and all the others back into the fold. Calvin now shared a cabin with his wife, Maude, and their four children. His mother practically breezed in, all smiles.

"It won't be long now," she said. "Your father would have been overjoyed as well."

The Civil War would continue for two more bloody years, and even though the entire country paid a dear price, it was the South that bore the brunt, losing billions in free labor; Georgia was in turmoil.

Naomi Bedford, suffering with congestive heart failure, died peacefully in her in her cabin, where he found her. She never shared with him the good news: the Civil War had ended. With her gone, Calvin was prepared to start a new life someplace else. He was a disgruntled ex-slave with mouths to feed, devastated that he and his mother had never had a chance to celebrate freedom together.

In the present day, Beckford could see that Raleigh III's attitude at the time aligned him with most of the landowners as they plotted an advantage to this drastic upheaval that had altered their way of life. Rumors abounded, specifically regarding "forty acres and a mule." This had been a suggestion of General Sherman and others to compensate the black race for centuries of unpaid labor. As leader of the Radical Republicans, Thaddeus Stevens was on the Congress floor fighting for the same. Yet, amid this confusion were the landowners and others who were finagling and agitating, anxious to maneuver the conditions to regain some, if not most, of their way of life. Maybe they could achieve the end to slavery in name only.

In the center of this turmoil and the promise of a "new day," the younger McDermott came to Calvin with a proposition. "Stay and grow cotton for the mill, Beckford. You could fare well."

"I'd like to start someplace else," he replied, even though he wasn't sure where he and his family would go.

"Beckford," Raleigh IV asked, "where would you go? Do you have a piece of land staked out?" The questions challenged Beckford. "At your age, do you realize how long it would take to start life somewhere new with a family to feed? Time is on their side, but not yours."

Beckford's reply was sudden and almost explosive. "How does your father feel about this?"

Raleigh IV was taken aback and for a moment did not speak. "Well," he finally replied, "I don't think he has much choice." He laughed wryly. "We need to stay in the black! Driscoll's population," he continued with slow tactfulness, "has dwindled almost to none. We are going to have to shut it down." He sighed. "Jade—at least the land—is free and clear and can grow cotton for the mill, which will allow us to keep our heads above water." He pondered for quite some time. "Beckford, it could be a good start for you and your family."

Beckford thought back to how he had allowed his mother to talk him out of leaving, running, years ago—with or without her—after the death of his *first* wife and child, as a young man. It was before Maude, before the birth of their sons and daughter, even before the enactment of the Fugitive Slave Act.

"Beckford, if things work out, you'll accumulate land, a thousand acres, and an additional five hundred that isn't farmable—it's lumber! It's always good to keep some land undeveloped, reserved."

Beckford knew about the densely wooded area of McDermott land, approximately five thousand "reserved" acres; ten thousand acres always had been used for crops.

For days he agonized about what to do and with calculated deliberation finally decided to accept the offer. His farmable land would be partitioned from the ten thousand that had been sown and tilled to grow cotton, and another five hundred acres was lumber. For generations, that ten thousand acres had been cultivated from seed to crop by ancestors, forever unpaid, young and old alike. Both men and women had died with calloused hands, bowed backs, aged beyond their years. It still angered him. He recalled from his youth those who had once lived at Driscoll, the older slaves, told vivid horror stories about those rice swamps. They spoke of sickness, misery, and even death lurking like restless ghosts in both the fields and the bleak, damp shanties. These experiences erupted from their past to still haunt their thoughts, plague their memories.

Some of the slaves were afraid to separate from Jade, and that also angered him. The returnees, the ones who had at least ventured out to test their chances, were the ones he convinced to work with him. None knew the promise McDermott had made him. He tenaciously guarded his secret, even from his wife.

It was a ragtag crew that had been brought together by fear, diffidence, despondency, and hopelessness or perhaps a glint of faith. No rudder to power hope, but like a ship depending on the wind to push it forward to wherever from whatever. Their circumstances meant less than being fully in charge of their own destiny. A selfish, but necessary action. The need to provide for his family.

His mother had recently died, dashing his hope that they would spend at least some time together as free human beings. He knew he would always question whether years ago they should have seized the opportunity to be free. He shoved those thoughts aside to focus on his present family whose lives he wanted to make better.

One member of Calvin's crew mentioned several times this preacher passing by their roadside camp. He told them about a group of newly freed slaves being run off a significant piece of land that they had claimed for themselves. He had spent time at a contraband camp and witnessed horrific devastation there.

During the next ten years, he and his ragtag crew of ex-slaves, the ones who were convinced to stay on after others had eventually left, planted and grew cotton for the McDermott mill. During harvest time Beckford and his men, with a sizable recruit of seasonal workers, brought in a decent quantity of cotton. He was aware of being paid less for the cotton crops than the white farmers received for theirs, but never lost focus on the land needed for his family. The promise of land was his motivation to pass most of the money received from the cotton on to his crew and seasonal workers. He made certain there was food for all, especially his family, by reserving a generous portion of acres to grow vegetables—collards, turnip greens, turnip bottoms, tomatoes, various other fruits and vegetables to sustain them all.

When he first started, he thanked God that Gabe had taught him carpentry skills. He and his helpers hurriedly built a makeshift house of two rooms, which provided crowded conditions at best. These living conditions sustained them for two years. They were up off the ground! Thank God for a wood floor.

☙

So now he owned land—one thousand acres for farming and an additional five hundred of forest—and had paid dearly to keep it.

Many whites did not like Calvin Beckford because, unwavering and unflinching, he looked anyone, white or black, dead in the eye when talking to them, especially after what happened to his sons. So did his remaining son, Hale, and his grandson, Chester. This was what caused Raleigh III mild discomfort. It was after that particularly horrific event that whites began labeling the Beckfords "those crazy niggers" even though they had justifiably defended what was rightfully theirs at such a dreadful cost.

After this horrendous ordeal, Calvin told his wife more than once, "Taking a stand for what's ours is not a right owed black man. If McDermott hadn't needed to keep cheap labor, where would we be? Right after the Civil War was over, they closed Driscoll because they had no choice! Who else was going to wade around in those swamps?"

The two weeks following the ordeal was a period of unease for the Beckford clan. Finally, the progression of time confirmed that the worst was over. It was decided that the Beckford family would live fenced off from the rest of the county. Solely for that purpose, a select group of trees were cut down, with a generous amount donated from the McDermott property. The fence was erected on three sides of their property. Surprisingly, this was suggested by Pastor Ruben, and the church men and farmhands assisted. The only barrier separating McDermott and Beckford lands was the fruit orchard; McDermott land remained totally accessible. The Beckford women and some of the church sisters joined in by providing drinking water, cleanup necessities, and meals. If the men needed supplies that were not heavy, they brought them as well. Soon there was a completed fence. After all, the Beckford farm often fed the poorest among them. The Beckford family even provided supplements for some church members through the winter, especially those who assisted with the planting every spring. Although meat was never provided, plenty of tomatoes, cabbages, beets, greens, and a wide variety of other vegetables were frequently canned at the Beckford farm.

Maude knew Calvin needed help when he began to have sleepless nights. Often, she awoke to an empty space beside her. It was then that she began to worry.

Hale, as always, did the chores of feeding the chickens, the hogs, the few horses, and the small herd of cattle. A stark, grim reminder of his brothers' ultimate sacrifice was that except for burned crops, everything else was left undisturbed, including the livestock.

For months, Calvin Beckford was dogged by thoughts about what might have been had they been passive and not fought back. In the final analysis he knew his family would have been subjected to even more devastating circumstances. He knew stories of blacks who had been driven from their land to end up homeless, whereas others had been forced to flee north or, worse, were subjected to horrible deaths—lynchings! Dealing with diabolical encroachment became a way of life for many. United States Cavalry protection was no more. Often if families escaped death, they became penniless without means of subsistence and thus were relegated to that despised status of vulnerability: sharecropping! Calvin willed himself to rise above such despair. He still had family on this side of the grave to consider—his daughter, Cammie, Hale and Maude. Well, not so much Hale who had his own family—a wife and eight-year-old Chester. All his hypothetical maneuvering and rearrangement of events—what if, what should have been, what could have been, and on and on—brought him back to that very same desolate place: the state of Georgia in the United States of America.

When, where, and how, Calvin now thought as he stood in his field, could a black man gain respect in this country? What was it like to be simply left to one's own discretion with no intervention but that of the good Lord—to exist, fail, prosper, live, and die naturally as determined by God Almighty? A person could then truly know he had been granted permission to be all he could be. Free to plot life's course, to choose this path or examine that fork in the road, to move there or to stay here.

❧

Two months passed before Calvin Beckford was well enough to work on the farm and attend service. This Sunday morning Beckford and his conspicuously reduced family entered the church to occupy their favorite pew. Some offered sympathetic glances while others approached them to extend condolences just as they had during the funeral and repast. From the pulpit the pastor made his descent to warmly greet them. Church began a few minutes later, and, as always, the pastor's wife led some of the hymns with the congregation joining in. Pastor Ruben led them in prayer and verses from the Bible, and then all settled down to listen to the sermon.

"This morning the topic is man's inhumanity to man. First, let us pray for our lost white brothers."

That was all Calvin Beckford heard; he simply could not listen to anything after that. *You pray for them*, he thought. *I sure as hell cannot.* He fled that sermon to inhale the fresh, chilly October morning air and welcome the sunshine. It would be a long time before he could pray for anything other than the precious souls of his sons. His mind was full of reflection as he slowly started out, using the cane to bear the weight of his limp, which was lessening each week with daily exercise. As he walked the half mile home with a heavy heart, he reviewed the turn of events. It seemed like yesterday that they were all sharing jokes at the breakfast table. Calvin had teased his sons with a jovial forecast of upcoming marriages and future babies—their children, his grandchildren. Who would these very likable young women now marry? Most remaining prospects were field hands and sharecroppers hardly capable of sustaining themselves.

Years ago, Calvin had been considered odd because he stayed to himself most of the time. The midwife had done her best for his young wife, who, in desperate need of a medical doctor, had succumbed to complications beyond the midwife's capabilities. So, the years passed. Youth slipped away with the need of a mate becoming his focus. One day he spotted a young lady relatively new at Jade and was pleased that the attraction was mutual. Eventually they jumped the broom to start their family.

When the Civil War broke out, he was even older, with preteen sons and a four-year-old daughter, Camille (everyone called her Cammie), but he decided to risk slipping away to join the bluecoats, a black regiment of course. It was the worst argument he and his mother ever had.

"How irresponsible and sightless," she spat vehemently when he told her of his plan. "You're going to abandon your wife and children to go off to a war that you may never get to or, if you do, may never come back from."

Neville now wrote to her often. He explained the ongoing, horrendous conditions of the camps. Do you know some are being taken at gunpoint to contraband camps for distasteful tasks that the Confederate soldiers do not wish to do, and even the Union Army as well!" She paused. "Death," she said. "Death," she repeated, "is doing a strut through those camps."

(Neville wrote her from a contraband camp in the Washington, DC, area where he and his wife were providing the Union Army as much medical care as they could.)

"Mama," he replied, "you have been holding me back all my life."

"Holding you back? Holding you back! And just what do you think will happen to Maude and your children if you end up dead, Calvin? You could die there or on the battlefield—that is, if you get there! And then what?" She shook her head in disgust, but he didn't miss the fright that had stolen into her voice. "What then?" She shook her head again; she was almost in tears. "No, your war is here."

So, he did not slip away.

The Civil War over and enslavement was over. Jumping the broom was not good enough. His pastor, a man who commanded respect, performed the short, legitimate ceremony for him and Maude. Later that year the minister died suddenly of a massive heart attack. Several months after that, Pastor Nehemiah Ruben was behind the podium.

Presently, Calvin Beckford heaved a regretful sigh. Whenever he was feeling low, his thoughts escaped to Sarah and Gabe, Gabe and Sarah who provided an equalizer. Perhaps he retreated psychologically to a tragedy that allowed some sense of perspective. He often prayed that the woman had found some kind of peace, gleaned as much happiness as possible from a life of bondage. She had been so very pretty, so he thought that she most likely had gone to work in a Big House and bred a passel of half-breeds. In that respect her beauty was a curse. That buffer group invariably and tenaciously clung to the race of their white fathers. He could yet hear her soft, silky laughter floating forward from his past. He hoped she had managed at least a few good moments. Maybe she had escaped to freedom! He heaved a woeful sigh.

Suddenly he felt a sharp stab of anguish. He had entered the yard to be confronted with the two makeshift crosses soon to be replaced by those permanent metal grave markers, compliments of the town blacksmith, Isaac. He thought about Isaac working in the presence of whites, dutifully addressing them as sir, mouthing "yassuh," "nossuh," in the preferable way expected of black men in the South. *If that is what you wish for me*, he said silently to God as he continued to look down on the two graves, *I would rather join them and be at peace.* It was a futile thought, an action his mother Naomi would have categorized as selfish. Suddenly mental images—of Cammie, Hale, little Chester, and dear Maudie—intercepted his thoughts. His three sons had worked long hours. Now there was only Hale. Life was now going to be extremely difficult, almost unbearably hard.

His leg began to throb with pain. He needed to rest it. Grimly, he limped heavily into the quiet house and eased into his favorite chair, attempting to create for himself a mental void as he waited for his family to come home. Even now he was bitter, angry, and filled with an unmitigated rage. He wanted to physically transform into a tangible source of that substance and rend this country asunder for all the pain and suffering perpetrated on black people. He looked over at the Holy Bible he'd purposely left behind this morning. "Aren't you going to take your Bible?" his wife had gently asked as she picked up her own; he didn't utter a word as he simply held the door open for her. There had to be something wrong with a book that taught people to love their enemy and be kind to those who consistently harm them. It did not make sense! He wanted to ask God exactly when he intended to take his vengeance on a people who more than deserved it. Immediately he thought of that kind old lady, Rebecca McDermott. Additionally, there was her son, Neville McDermott, who had befriended his mother. Well, maybe not all deserved it, but a significant number. He attempted to push away thoughts of Sarah and Gabe as they continuously and stubbornly appeared on his mental stage like eerie phantoms. Thoughts of them came at other times too, but those were the pleasant memories: Sarah and Gabe holding hands in one of their rare, stolen moments of brief happiness; Gabe and Sarah sitting on the wood floor of Gabe's cabin when Calvin, in his boyish jealousy, would peek through the small, windowless opening created by Gabe after expressing, "It's stuffy in here!" Gabe bringing her wildflowers and Sarah gently holding them like precious treasures. Both cheerfully chased him away. Those were their brief moments of shared joy. Afterward: Hell!

A few weeks after Calvin abruptly exited the church service, the iron markers, in the shape of a horseshoe, were placed upright on the Beckford sons' graves, bearing their names and years of birth and death. All the family stood at the grave site, surrounded by church members and friends; Pastor Ruben presided over the formal memorial.

For the next two months Calvin was absent from church service. Each week, Maude reported, Pastor Ruben looked expectant, offering a pleasant smile to the Beckford family as they entered the church. Each week he would leave the pulpit to welcome Maude and her diminished family as they entered the church. Always, he would inquire about the well-being of her husband. Her response was consistently favorable to the reverend, but to Calvin she said, "Honey, I can't keep tellin"im the same story."

Calvin's limp, his leg having healed remarkably well, was replaced with a subtle, changed gait that became only slightly noticeable during rainy weather. Justifiably, this naturally good-natured, loving, kind man was now taciturn and somewhat distant. He was never mean because that was not his spirit. He went to the fields early and came back later than usual with his loving wife trying to make him as comfortable as possible by preparing his favorite meals, giving him back massages, and providing all the tender, loving care possible.

As time passed, Calvin made a pragmatic decision, gently ignoring the protestation of Hale. "Hale," he explained firmly to his son, "you work hard enough already."

"Dad," Hale exclaimed, "we don't need to do that."

"You need to be around for little Chester," replied his father. "You're a young man, but death doesn't have a number. You're in the field now from dawn to dusk."

Ironically, Hale had married at the tender age of seventeen. Chester, now eight, was born the very next year when Hale was approaching his eighteenth birthday. Calvin was sixty-four at the time. At seventy-two years of age, Chester was his only grandchild. He recalled how Jule and Medgar had teased Hale of not liking freedom; his response was a good-natured smile.

"We have to figure out a way to pay whoever we hire, Dad," Hale protested gently.

"Hale, let me handle this. Work it out."

The pay was low, but the young men were compensated with a place to stay and two meals a day. Considering the alternatives, it was an attractive arrangement for all. The experience for Calvin Beckford was a reflective, sorrowful one. Still, he was glad to have the physical emptiness filled with two young men close to the ages of his deceased sons. They bore the upstanding biblical names of Joshua and David. Joshua was kind, very soft-spoken, and well-mannered to a fault. David was shy, possessed comparable attributes.

❧

Time trudged on uneventfully through winter, and then came the glorious scents of spring with bright sunshine as the birds chirped their welcome. Calvin Beckford had not been back to church, His wife, for fear of his answer, did not ask his intentions. Maude Beckford often discovered her husband standing adjacent to their home, looking down on the graves of his two sons. She was fearful of what he could be thinking. She wished she had insisted that they be buried with all the others in the cemetery behind the church. Cautiously, she pondered how to approach him. She had a talk with him to draw him out of this mental stalemate.

"Calvin," she said quietly as she went to stand beside him at the grave site, "perhaps you should talk to Pastor Ruben. Maybe you…"

"Why?" he asked, his tone matching her quietness. What he wanted to tell her was that he hoped Pastor Ruben's reputation had not preceded him. He would never forget that crew member's story. He wished he was still here. Ruben had mentioned spending time in a contraband camp during one of his sermons. Calvin considered him suspect because of it, but when he came to pastor their congregation, rumors churned like disturbed dust yet to completely settle. There was no way of confirming the rumors to validate what he had heard. Perhaps he was being unfair to compare Nehemiah Ruben's demeanor to that of their well-liked, late pastor.

"So that he can tell me to pray for those that abuse us, Maudie, to bow and scrape and be grateful for whatever crumbs we get?" Again, he was engaging a mental picture of the blacksmith, Isaac, with all his "yassuh" and "nossuh." To be a man before his time was Calvin Beckford's fate. He looked down at his wife. "All my life I have been trying to figure out when God is going to be on our side." He offered a wry smile. "Can you tell me that? When can a black man live freely and keep what is his along with his dignity while being left alone to live and die like everybody has the right to do? Did God give only white men that right? Can you answer that?"

This moment was awkward for Maude because she did not know what to say or do. This was a side of her husband that she knew could surface. The circumstances, sinister and all-encompassing, were stealing away the life they enjoyed together.

"They were my sons too, Calvin," she said as she began to weep. "I loved them just as much."

The dam broke, and all the pent-up emotions rushed out. Maude sobbed uncontrollably. All he could do was embrace her, attempting to console her, while feeling the residual rage resurfacing in a powerful aftermath.

Time passed, and neither knew how long they stood there at the grave site, her clinging to him as he attempted to console her while dealing with his own inner turmoil. Finally, he heaved a sigh and released her to gently stand a short distance away.

"This should never have been," he said matter-of-factly. "There was no need for any of it." Still standing apart from her, he reached out and caressed her back gently. Then his arms went motionless at his sides, and the strangest look came across his face. "It cannot happen again," he said quietly. "If any sons of bitches come here again, I'm prepared to die. I mean it, Maudie. You will be a widow."

"Calvin," she said fearfully, "don't talk like that." On this particularly sweltering summer day, a momentary chill blanketed her body. Suddenly she was caught up in rash desperation. "Maybe we should leave here and—"

"And go where? Where would we go?" He paused. "Wherever we go represents a fresh start and face the same problems. Do you want to start all over again at our age, especially *my* age, not knowing what is next? You already know how long it took and the sacrifices made to accumulate this much land. This is ours, Maudie. This is our land. As long as I'm breathing, no one is going to run us off it."

She stared at him through a blur of tears, vacillating between feelings of panic and sheer helplessness.

"I am a man, Maudie. No one will take that away from me. I lived as a slave once. It was 'go here,' 'do that,' 'eat now,' 'work longer' even when tired or sick. Never, ever getting paid for any of it while watching others prosper because they were born white. Watching them live in the Big House that was built by us while we lived in shacks and—" He shook his head, gazing at nothing, focusing on his troubled memories. *Shacks with dirt floors*, he thought. "I lived like that once and will not return to that but go to my grave and become a free man."

Distraught, quaking with fright, and with tears softly tracing her cheeks, Maude embraced herself. She prayed, wishing to silence her deep unrest. She wanted to return to an element of calm and peace away from this dreadful place, which was stealthily pilfering away the remains of what they'd once had. She realized restoration had to happen here, in this place, which was exactly why her sons had died. She missed them terribly and mentally clasped to her heart the precious, irreplaceable memories of them. She knew she wished to travel the rest of life's journey with this strong, beautiful man. At that moment her profound love for her husband was stronger than ever before. Fear gripped her like a vice. What would become of her and their remaining children if she lost him?

⁊

Pastor Nehemiah Ruben smiled sadly. What message did he have for this woman who sat before him on the church bench crying softly, looking so very defeated? He remembered all his unfulfilled religious aspirations as a young man. He fearfully asked himself, had the spiritual depth required to assist this woman ever totally resided in him? Inwardly he struggled to grasp even an inkling of that plateau he'd reached when things were fresh and promising. He often wondered whether his belief system had broken down to an unredeemable state because of all the chaos, death, and destruction he had witnessed throughout the years. The trickles of hope he had managed to salvage for a better tomorrow were meager because he had seen too much. Attempting to select the appropriate scripture, he thought of what he had been taught in his ministry. How to aid this woman totally eluded him as she sat before him in justified, painful despair.

"Pastor Ruben, they burned mos' of our cotton; the sky was ablaze. They had promised that they would do it as a warning not to plant anymo' and be in direct rival with'em, and that is exac'ly what they did." She paused. "I tried to talk to Medgar and Jule and told them to wait on they father. He was in the barn cause one of the cows was birthin' a calf. When I went to get him, Medgar and Jule already took off, one on a mule, one on horseback, guns and all." In agony she relived the horrific event, but at this precise time being able to finally release what had been pent up inside for months seemed to be therapeutic for her. "Our older horse, Dan, had a cold and couldn't be pushed too hard, so I'm not sho' how long it took fo' Calvin to catch up to'em. I heard gunshots from way off. Pastor Ruben, I was so'fraid just wonderin' what took place, not knowin' and jus…" Fresh tears were streaming down her face. "My sons, my sons, oh my sons! Lawd, lawdy, lawdy! Poor Hale was comin' from the bahn and I stopped him at gunpoint, I did." I thought of little Chester. She heaved a wretched sigh. "I really wasn't going to shoot him, but…" She embraced herself and rocked back and forth. "Demons, that's what they are, demons!" Now, arms unfolded, she began to slap her thighs with open palms in agonized distress. "Take all the joy out of livin' and leave you with nothin'."

He was tired, but his large hands attempted to calm those of this tormented woman who sat before him. He chose his words carefully.

"Man has always trespassed against his fellow man," he started, projecting a false air of calm. "We must pray for those who—"

"Then what, Pastor Ruben? What then? These are not just any men, but white men who want to keep everything fo' themselves and leave us with nothin'. I'm afraid fo' my husband, fo' us. He's a man, Pastor, and won't allow nobody to make'im less." She attempted to control her sobbing, but the tears continued to flow. Her eyes were now red and her eyelids puffy. "Do you know how hard my husband and our sons worked? Fo'teen hours a day, six days a week, just to keep they heads afloat. They burned most of our cotton crop, Pastor Ruben, all but five hundred acres."

Maude Beckford was distraught to the point of practically shouting while the pastor struggled, waiting for all he had been taught to surface and enable consolation for this woman. Needed was scripture suitable for this situation. Did he lack attributes possessed by courageous men? Deeply regretful that he was now inflicted with the worst kind of impediment. Contrition for a past he evaluated as being without substantial substance.

Recollections pursued him. Somehow, he knew that a few of the members still hadn't totally accepted him, foremost Calvin Beckford. He yet remembered the surprise on Beckford's face the first Sunday when introduced by one of the elders of the church as their deceased pastor's replacement. The committee had not been able to wait until he could attend the meeting to vote on the joint confirmation. As soon as he stepped to the podium for his first official sermon, Calvin Beckford was there. The look on his face indicated his surprise.

❧

Had her vision not been blurred with tears when she left the church, Maude would have been able to physically see the extent of Pastor Ruben's emotional turmoil. Hurriedly trudging down the road, a little before dusk, feeling defeated and dejected, she groped for spiritual solace that never came. Inconspicuously, she had slipped away from the house to speak with her pastor. Calvin and Hale were working with

Joshua and David. Was Calvin right about this man of the cloth who offered nothing even remotely comforting? In all fairness, he had tried to help, but his mind was elsewhere. In fact, she felt at more of a loss than when she'd arrived. In the yard, Maude dampened her eyes with cold water from the yard pump and wiped them with a tear-drenched handkerchief. She slipped into the quiet house, her heart pounding in her chest as she tied her apron, quickly stoked the fire to complete dinner. Almost an hour passed before they came into the smell of a great dinner of fried chicken, steamed cabbage, sliced tomatoes, and crowder peas.

Often Hale had dinner with his mother and father before going to his own place. This evening he simply told everyone he would see them the next day.

She never wanted her husband to know that she had sought solace from Pastor Ruben. She was beginning to wonder if just maybe he was no longer her husband's pastor. It had been months since Calvin had sat beside her in church. Meanwhile, she was mentally rehearsing how to approach him, how to ask him why he no longer picked up the Bible. He prayed at bedtime and in the mornings and evenings. Always, blessed his food before eating. Short of rejoining a traditional congregation, he engaged in all the practices of those who were considered God-fearing.

# Chapter Two

Time passed without incident, and for that Maude Beckford daily thanked God. One day they had a visitor. At first, she attributed the soft rap on the screen door to the beautiful summer day's warm breeze circulating throughout their home. For over a week Calvin had been mentioning the need to tighten those hinges. The second time Maude heard the rapping sound, she turned away from the stove where she was preparing dinner; at the door stood Raleigh McDermott IV. Maude had not heard the horse-drawn buggy pull up. *"How many they's gonna have wit dat name? Must think they royalty or sumpin.* After all these years, that old slave woman's frequent comment still amused Maude. So, the reason for her smile was twofold. She dried her hands to let him in.

"Hello, Maude."

"Hello, Mr. McDermott," she quietly replied. Her brain throbbed with the voice of her husband: "Maudie, we're no longer slaves, so don't you dare call that man Massa Raleigh." Somehow, she had always liked the man because, unlike his father, he had managed to escape most of the trappings of the typical Southern gentleman. Instead, he was basically a genuine human being who tried to be fair, avoiding as much as possible the trends of both the old and new South. It was as though his mannerisms and calm demeanor were subtle indications that he sought pardon for his family's past—well, at least when in the presence of Calvin, since it was his family the McDermotts had held in bondage much longer than hers.

She wanted to thank him for assisting in stopping last year's turmoil. She didn't know exactly how to broach the subject. She could still hear Calvin. "What else could he do, Maude? How else was he going to grow the cotton crop cheap?"

McDermott stood in her spotless kitchen as he removed his hat.

"Maude," she reprimanded herself out loud, "mind ya manners." She went to the kitchen table and pulled out a chair. "Have a seat, Mr. McDermott. I can make ya a cup of tea, if you'd like."

His visits were always for a specific reason, nevertheless congenial. "That would be nice, Maude."

"Calvin should be in shortly," she said, taking a cup and saucer from the cupboard.

It was dusk dark. The sun was setting when her husband, son, and helpers arrived from the fields just as McDermott was finishing his tea. A strained expression came across Calvin's face. He nodded his greeting. Hale spoke.

McDermott arose from the kitchen table with an ever-so-slight smile. "Beckford, could I see you for a few minutes?" He bid farewell to Maude and Hale.

Beckford. He always did call him that, as if it was a compromise, a trade-off to balance the awkward circumstances of the South, for he knew Calvin Beckford would never call him Mr. McDermott but would consistently use his last name. McDermott's youth separated them by more than a generation.

Calvin nodded his consent, and the two men headed outside. The screen door closed behind them as Hale washed his hands at the kitchen sink and offered his mother a perplexed expression; she avoided his eyes. He went to the screen door to look out on an empty front yard and then caught sight of the two shadowy figures in the distance as they strolled to the small family cemetery that held only the bodies of his brothers. He descended the steps to go home to his wife and Chester.

⁂

Calvin and McDermott stood looking down on the graves of the two Beckford sons, refusing to bring up what had taken place barely a year ago. McDermott looked hesitant for a moment and then began to speak.

"Personally, I think… I think you should have been told years ago, but… Well, at least my great-grandfather didn't think it was necessary at that time, so things were just allowed to remain the same. I'm the only one left to tell the story as it was told to me… It really bothered my great-grandmother, so after a considerable length of time, she wrote Uncle Neville and told him what had happened."

Calvin frowned, not knowing exactly what the younger man was saying, but listened intently while he continued.

"I was told that from then on in letters, until his death, Uncle Neville pressured the family to make sure you knew who your real mother was, and he was right. If possible, everyone should know how they came to this earth. Naomi never did, but Uncle Neville thought of it as a travesty to use her in that manner. He always liked Naomi, and perhaps she told you he often wrote to her when writing to his mother."

"She told me." He was perplexed and feeling out of sorts.

"Beckford, remember Sarah?" McDermott suddenly seemed sad. "I was told that you were a young boy but old enough to remember her."

"I remember Sarah," Calvin said quietly. How could he possibly forget Sarah? Not a day passed when he didn't think of that beautiful young woman. Of course, he remembered Sarah—and the awful beating that this man's great-uncle Preston had given her before he sold her. Before subjecting her to such heartless cruelty, in cold blood he had murdered Gabe, the man she dearly loved.

"Well, Sarah was your mother," McDermott continued candidly. The need for tact was gone. "Preston, my great-uncle, did not want his wife to know that he had been going to Sarah's room, but it became evident when Sarah became pregnant. She had never been away from the house long enough for anything like that. She was never in the slave quarters until she became pregnant with you." He paused briefly before continuing. "She was fourteen when you were born. That was around the time Naomi Beckford came to Jade, so it was decided she would be your mother instead of Sarah. From what I was told, Uncle Preston's wife usually said very little, but for years afterward she was adamant about not allowing her in the house. So, she lived in the slave quarters and, finally, in the cabin with you and Naomi. You see, Naomi came to the plantation pregnant, giving birth to a baby girl. I was told the infant survived for only a few hours. This was about three or four days before Sarah delivered you, and then Naomi took over nursing you as her own. As you are aware she was also my great-grandmother's nurse."

Calvin, practically numb with disbelief, could only nod; he lacked any coherent response. So that son of a bitch was his father? That was almost ungodly. The information left him numb, immobile, contrite. Tears stood in the corners of his eyes. Well, at least there was not a pronounced trace of evidence, although his hair possessed more than a slight curl. He was a few shades lighter, but from what he had been told, so was Nathaniel Beckford. Sarah was a pretty chocolate brown. He wondered why now, in death, that rascal wanted to claim him. Well, time often brought about some form of retribution.

After the deaths of his son and then his wife, Preston never remarried. Word disseminated throughout the slave quarters about how he suffered at the end with relentless progression of cancer, how it ravaged his body with a vengeance before he eventually succumbed. His impotency was well known among slave women because of what couldn't be requested from respectable white women. He didn't wish to have such detailed information disseminated within those Macon brothels that he himself had frequented earlier in life. Had such information fallen on the lips of the wrong gentlemen to be spread about, amusing ripples of such news would have swiftly traveled throughout circles in which he was well-known.

"Preston and his father, my great-grandfather—well, it was my great-grandmother's idea, actually your grandmother…" McDermott trailed off. "Anyway, Uncle Preston deposited money in a Beckford family trust fund," he said as he gingerly placed a large envelope in Calvin's reluctantly outstretched hand. "It's all there. You can withdraw on it at any time. In fact, by now I am sure it has probably gained quite a bit of interest." Preston McDermott had been dead for many years. "There are a few other papers as well," he added.

Calvin's silence created an awkward moment.

"Is there anything you would like to say? Perhaps you have questions?"

"I really don't know what to say," he replied, rather unsettled, attempting to withhold the involuntary tremor that stole into his voice. He realized at that moment his cheeks were wet as McDermott became only a blur in the semi-darkness, relieved that the younger man could not totally witness his reaction. "This is almost unreal." Struggling to collect his thoughts, he found he had one question. "Do you know who bought Sarah?" he asked quietly. To his own ears, his voice was almost unrecognizable.

For a few moments McDermott didn't speak, and Calvin read his reaction to the query to be discomfort.

"I was told that Sarah was taken to Driscoll," he stated quietly. "She was not accustomed to that type of climate… the heat, the constant dampness, the insects, the chilling wetness of the rainy season, just the entire environment of the rice swamps." He paused again. "From what I was told, during her third year there she contracted pneumonia. She didn't survive."

There was a long silence as the two men stood together, not actually facing each other, just sharing space. For Calvin the earth momentarily wobbled on its axis. The depth of his despair was beyond description. Mentally, he was transported to a dark and dismal place. He looked to the heavens and the last remnants of a sky dimly sprayed in orange, streaked in red. Calvin imagined those intermingled streaks of red to represent bloody, open wounds for Sarah. The setting sun barely peeked above the horizon. Sudden wind responded promptly to disturb the foliage of the trees. *Poor Sarah*, he thought. *She and Gabe never had a chance.* He wondered just how much the lingering effects of that beating interrupted her physical well-being in the horrible living conditions of Driscoll?

"I know it is on paper, but is there any reason to change anything at this time?" Calvin asked, breaking the deafening quiet. He hoped the impatience he felt did not give him away. "Naomi Beckford, when alive and now in death, has been my mother for seventy-two years. I feel quite strange thinking of Sarah in that manner. Her being so close to me and the woman I knew as my mother made me accept Sarah like an older sister. As far as your Uncle Preston is concerned," he said, faltering, "I find it difficult to think of him as my father." He paused. "This doesn't feel real this late in life. It makes me feel strange."

"No, there isn't any reason to act," McDermott responded. "If you want to deal with it in a more acceptable way, I will understand. There needed to be an explanation regarding the money being deposited in an account for the Beckford estate with my Uncle Preston's name on it. My great-grandfather's signature needs no explanation."

After a lengthy pause in the darkness, McDermott said, "It was my great-grandmother's doing, really. She disliked the whole ordeal. Uncle Preston. What happened to Sarah… Concerning Gabe…" He trailed off again.

The information was being conveyed awkwardly, slowly. *Get on with it!* Calvin wanted to urge. Darkness had moved in stealthily. It swiftly enveloped Georgia, transitioning to nightfall as all the nocturnal insects and animals positioned to phase out the day. In the distance the hooting of an owl joined the unified lament for Sarah; a choir of crickets filled the air.

"As you know," he continued, "my great-grandmother was not from the South and never approved of our way of life. She told Uncle Preston he would have to set things right, so to speak." He paused again. "Plus, you needed to know before receiving the money. It makes you sure-footed and gives you the right perspective."

"I understand," Calvin replied, at an absolute loss for what more to say. *The right perspective*, he thought, examining that phrase, turning it over in his mind. *I was a slave*, he thought. *Sarah was a slave. That's the right perspective.*

"Well, my business here is done," McDermott said. Calvin Beckford nodded in response. In the darkness, they walked from the cemetery to McDermott's buggy hitched to a waiting horse. This defined his persona whenever he was in his lawyer pose, as did his weekly commute by train to Atlanta.

"I'll be seeing you, Beckford," he said as he climbed in the buggy and pulled off. Because he practiced law in both Macon and Atlanta, Calvin assumed he still lived part-time in Atlanta as before. However, that was not the sort of conversation he had with McDermott.

The latest housekeeper was an old Irish woman from Macon. Naomi often talked about a few of McDermott's overseers being Irish and therefore "their own." It was known that Raleigh Sr.'s grandfather had started from extremely humble beginnings—his own roots, Calvin thought regarding McDermott's Irish ancestry. His thoughts briefly settled again on the current housekeeper. His mother had often said, "They understand each other." *Yes, Mama*, he thought with bitter certainty, *she gets paid!*

Calvin never came to dinner. He remained outside sitting in the dark on the front steps. What had his mother said so very long ago? *My heart aches for that young woman.* He tried to imagine the awful anguish and misery Sarah must have felt as a young girl and then as a woman. Not one day had passed that he had not thought of her. This recent revelation explained some other things too. Why Old Lady McDermott had quietly made certain he could read and write, why Old Man McDermott had never interfered, why Preston in the field overlooking the cotton crop while riding his beloved Bay during their unexpected encounters (occurring several times) he abruptly rode off in another direction.

Somehow that evil bastard had possessed a distorted attraction for that black woman. As an adult Calvin could now make the connection. Her preference for Gabe over Preston had been more than the latter could handle even though he himself could not grant her a shred of dignity or respect because of her status dictated by law, determined by the color of her skin. Until now, Calvin had fervently prayed that she had found some small happiness despite living under such a hellish system. He would forever hold steadfast to her memory, her lovely face, her beautiful smile, and her voice. That he now had to abruptly stop visualizing her growing old made his bereavement even more painful and further accentuated the tragedy.

So, Preston McDermott had fathered one son within the rigid, legal bounds of Georgia law and another he could not legitimately claim. It was getting late when Maude came to join him, knowing that often, when troubled, he stayed to himself.

"Calvin, yo' food's cold, but I can heat it up for ya," she said quietly from the doorway. He did not respond as she joined him on the steps.

They sat together for a long time before he finally spoke.

"Let's go inside," he said. And they did. *I still need to tighten those hinges*, he thought. The screen door squeaked shut.

He was still holding a sealed envelope addressed to him as he sat down at the kitchen table. The kerosene lamp burned brightly. "Open this," he said with trepidation. Calvin Beckford was scrawled on the larger, newer envelope, and inside was another older one accompanied by other papers. Without a doubt, the McDermotts had read the contents of the letter addressed to Neville, had screened its contents which, from the envelope's appearance, he guessed had been stored for quite some time. (However, because of the frequent absences of the McDermotts during the latter years of Naomi's life, she had received Neville's mail void the "screening" process.) He recognized the Philadelphia address as belonging to Neville McDermott. His and Naomi Beckford's demise were only a few years apart. No postmark date was on the letter meaning they had withheld Naomi's correspondence that should have been mailed to Neville. For a brief second, he became angry that they had screened the correspondence. *Why wouldn't they?* he thought, no matter how much they had depended on Naomi for Rebecca McDermott, who had grown extremely old and, in the end, totally bedridden. Fifteen years after the death of Rebecca, his mother was laid to rest separated from the McDermott family burial site, consistent with her position on earth. Calvin was saddened only by the fact that she was buried away from her grandsons. Of course, at that time the land was not in his possession. He recalled, with a wry smile, reading the words etched on her tombstone: *Naomi Beckford, Our Faithful Servant.*

Absently, he opened the large envelope, withdrew its contents. He handed the smaller envelope to his wife, momentarily forgetting that she possessed minimal reading skills, that he always assisted her as inconspicuously as possible whenever she read scripture with the congregation. At home, together, they would review the selected scripture.

"I think you should read this yourself," she said quietly, returning it to him. He opened the envelope reluctantly, as if almost fearful of what it contained. He read aloud, sharing the contents with his wife.

> *"Dear Calvin,*
>
> *Every human being on earth should know how he or she got here. This is part of your family history and I wanted to make sure you had it, so I sent it to Neville who I knew would make certain you received it after my death."*

"Maude," he said to his wife, "he never got it. They kept it from him, knowing he thought I had been told about Sarah years before." He continued to read aloud his mother's last words.

> *"I am not the woman that gave you life, but I always loved you just like you were my very own. Everything I have ever told you was truth, so help me God. I never told you about your birth mother. Calvin, your birth mother was Sarah, and your father was Preston McDermott. She told me that at age thirteen she was still working in the Big House when her grandmother died, and that Preston McDermott began coming into her room. He began sleeping with her and she gave birth to you when she was fourteen years old.*
>
> *"Fredonia, Preston's wife, gradually became suspicious that he was slipping into Sarah's room late at night. Sarah, a house slave, never visited the slave quarters, so when she became pregnant, it was a surprise to Rebecca McDermott, Preston's mother, because he was careful not to let her know what was going on. As you know, the McDermott house is*

*very large and where Sarah slept was on the first floor at the very back of the house, away from everyone else. If you recall that room eventually became mine whenever I still had to remain on-call in the Big House to tend to Rebecca McDermott when she needed less care. Otherwise, when she was very ill and in great pain, I gave her bedside care and slept on a pallet beside her bed. So, I know why his mother did not suspect what was happening. Evidently, Preston was absent from his own bed even more than usual, so it finally became obvious to Fredonia that her suspicions were correct. Sarah, now pregnant and showing, was sent to the slave quarters to work in the fields until it was time to give birth. I came to the plantation only two months away from delivering my baby, as was Sarah. My child, a little girl, only lived a few hours and was born three days before Sarah gave birth to a son; that infant was you.*

*"Rebecca McDermott sent me to the slave quarters to find Sarah when one of the old slave women came to her and told her she was in labor without any help. The plantation's midwife was not there at the time, but rented out, and would not be back for a few days. Somehow, although I could never prove it, I think it was planned that way. Since I was a nurse, I was the one that delivered you, cleaned you up, and gave you all the necessary care. I had milk. You needed someone to nurse you and care for you, and that became me. I wanted to. You were such a beautiful baby.*

*"Fredonia was furious, and I think her intention was that you and Sarah would die. However, her son did die. He was born about three months after your birth and lived only a few hours. She had unleashed all her fury on Sarah while her husband was allowed to be without blame. Having just suffered the loss of my own baby, I gladly volunteered to continue to care for you since Sarah was not allowed to*

*provide your needs. You were such a joy. You lived in the Big House until you were almost five years old. I don't know if you remember that, but you did against Fredonia's wishes. Your grandmother, Mrs. McDermott, wanted it that way so she could keep an eye on you. As time went on, most of the slaves that knew you were not my son had died or were no longer on the plantation. All the other plantation owners and McDermott friends knew nothing about this, but just assumed you were my son. Not that it would have mattered since many plantation owners have fathered children by slave women. But these circumstances were a little different.*

*"My little girl was buried quietly without any fanfare whatsoever, without even a marker, and only a few people's knowledge. Fredonia knew that she could not overstep any boundaries set by Rebecca McDermott because that was her mother-in-law, and she was living in her house. None of Rebecca's sons defied her, either, because even though unhealthy, she was a strong-willed woman. Additionally, Mr. McDermott did not tolerate any of his sons disrespecting their mother. However, you became my son, and Sarah was never allowed to be your mother.*

*"Please forgive me, but I found it almost unbearable not to tell you this. God bless you.*

*"I have loved you forever,*

*Mama (Naomi Beckford)"*

Calvin shook his head. "They kept this letter all this time." In explicit detail Calvin recounted to Maude what McDermott had told him. He had previously accounted to his wife years bits and pieces about Sarah, but never in detail about what had happened to Gabe and Sarah.

He now read the letter again, this time silently to himself. Afterward both sat in silence for quite some time. Calvin carefully refolded the letter and broke the silence.

"He raped Sarah," he said quietly, "and then his sleeping with her became a usual thing. I'm sure his wife was alone many nights."

"Calvin," Maude questioned softly. "How do you know?"

There was a lengthy silence, then Calvin spoke. "Once Preston arrived from Driscoll to assist his father, he was often in the slave quarters looking for Sarah." He paused. "I remember when he had been back at Jade about two months—Sarah was with Gabe, you know." Maude nodded as she listened with focused attention. "His excuse was that she was needed at the Big House. So, she left Gabe's cabin and started toward the Big House, and he offered her a ride. Well, she couldn't refuse, right?" Calvin paused, and Maude nodded in agreement. "I was about nine at the time. Now, Gabe had built a cabin for that bastard where he sometimes stayed periodically when he visited Jade, and after he moved back it became a getaway. It was on the far end of the land, near the wooded area. I'd be willing to bet that is where he would take her. You know, I was a boy then, but now as I look back on the situation, I recall that whenever she would return to our cabin it was always late. Every time she would lie quietly beside me, very sad. Maude, I could almost reach out and touch the gloom. There was no talking on those nights. Even as a young boy I could almost touch her misery. Each time, for a few days following those times she and Gabe hardly spoke to each other. Probably angry because he had no control over what was happening." He sighed heavily. "I told you she loved Gabe, didn't I?" Maude nodded and he continued. "Then they would be with each other again. Those nights she didn't come to our cabin."

Calvin shook his head in deep thought. Suddenly he laughed wryly. "I recall Preston McDermott riding up to the slave quarters on Sable— big, beautiful, beaming in the sun, deep dark brown, looked black! This evening Sarah wasn't there when that bastard came looking for her. He stormed off so angry. For a few minutes forgot the exact location of Gabe's cabin! Of course, he found her with Gabe." Calvin shook his head in sorrow. "She was crying, begging, and pleading with him as he dragged her out. Gabe in tow." Vivid and poignant reflection peeled away the years; he was eleven years old again. He couldn't quite make out whether it seemed as though Gabe had raised his hand to try to help Sarah. "Maude," he said with a tremor in his voice. "Preston shot Gabe, murdered him, and then dragged Sarah to that big chestnut tree he always sat under, tied her to it. Beat her bloody. A month later she was gone." He was quiet for some time. "For sure, that evil bastard didn't love Sarah, just hated that she preferred Gabe to him." He paused. "Plain and simple, it was sexual jealousy."

There was a long silence as Calvin continued to think. "Sarah's mother died when she was very young," he continued after a long, thoughtful silence. "I don't know how, but I do know that from the age of seven, she helped her grandmother in the kitchen, learned to cook and serve meals. She was never allowed in the slave quarters. What happened had to be from inside that house. Her grandmother was the McDermott cook and housekeeper for most of her life, first at Driscoll and later at Jade. I knew that much because Sarah told me about her background, but that's where she ended her story.

"Poor Sarah," he said quietly. "He raped her as a young girl. That's as sure as Georgia rain."

"Some story," Maude said. "Some story indeed," she said. Enough ta take ya breath away."

So, Calvin realized, the son he'd thought to be the first for Preston and Fredonia, dying within hours of his birth, was their second attempt. Until the very end she'd tried unsuccessfully to give him a legitimate male heir.

"He and his wife never gave his parents a grandson. See what happens to slaves? Lives are hashed up just as white folks see fit to please themselves, to make the pieces fit so their lives are made more comfortable and damn us because we aren't supposed to have feelings."

"Calvin, all we can do is pray for Sarah's soul, that she is at peace now," Maude replied as she consolingly caressed his arm.

Calvin didn't respond, but he would always cherish his beautiful, limited time with Sarah. Never to another living soul would he reveal what had transpired between her and Preston. Calvin mentally recaptured those nights when as a boy and she lay beside him, talking in her soft, gentle voice, unable to tell him that she was his birth mother. It had to be conflicted misery. Forbidden to express maternal love to him and disallowed to share love with Gabe as a woman. For daring to grasp even an inkling of pleasure in loving someone, banished to the rice swamps. He felt like crying. It was such a thoroughly sorrowful story. Now that he knew she had died as a young woman, he said a prayer for her soul, fervently hoping that she rested in peace.

He thought again of the older slaves and their vivid oral accounts, shared with graphic detail. Runaways who sometimes would be gone for six months, even a year. Inevitably being caught and returned to Driscoll to endure additional punishment for attempting to escape.

During the next few weeks, Calvin thought of Sarah more than ever. What were her last years like. In those swamps? He knew she suffered! Hell on earth. Worse than if she had remained at Jade.

Had this chapter in his life been left undisturbed, the puzzle would have remained unsolved forever once he found out about the money. Especially with Preston McDermott's signature so prominently scrawled along with that of Preston's father, Raleigh Sr.; Calvin would have forever wondered why. The amount of money was somewhat impressive as well as unexpected. The truth was they certainly could use the money now, but he hoped to be able to save at least a small amount to start a fund for educating future Beckfords. Education was the one thing that could never be taken even in death.

A mental rearrangement was in order. He would replace Naomi's dead child with himself as his own method of amending history. He would forever think of Sarah as a young girl who, along with countless others without sanctuary, was forced into womanhood. Now more than ever, he would tenaciously hold steadfast to mental pictures of that beautiful young woman, untarnished and without blame.

Over the next few months, he repeatedly reread Naomi Beckford's letter before refolding it for the final time, allowing it to lay among the other papers from McDermott, including Naomi Beckford's death certificate. One document, Naomi Beckford's purchase for two thousand dollars, he looked for an extended length of time. Never had he seen a document showing payment for another human being. Strange, he thought. Shaking his head in thought, for the last time he looked at the document containing Preston's signature below that of his father, Raleigh Sr. This information would be stored in a safe place. Naomi's letter would be available to following generations to decipher as they wished. However, they would all inherit the name Beckford, not McDermott, because he honestly could see no good in passing on that name.

# CHAPTER THREE

Chester decided that his grandfather, Calvin Beckford, was in biblical terms a man who had lived by the sweat of his brow. Rough hands with calloused palms and a face more than generously loved by the sun's rays. Chester was becoming better acquainted with the mustached leader of the Beckford clan who held many untold stories. He discovered that his grandfather shaved every morning to "keep away the stubble." Hale, his father, described his deceased brothers as "big men like me and your grandfather," he had said quietly, "like you are going to be."

Chester knew he was tall and considered handsome, but he felt that once he matured, his angular frame would fill out proportionately to complement his large hands and feet. There was one certainty: he would always wear gloves to avoid acquiring those rough hands.

He admired the fact that his grandfather, unlike most who were once slaves, read well and could write. Calvin Beckford's mother, Naomi, had been responsible for his learning such skills, with some assistance from Rebecca McDermott.

For as long as Chester had known his grandfather, he had always smoked a corncob pipe. Only twice had Chester seen the deep gash on his right leg. When he asked his grandfather about it, he received no response. Only once, briefly, did his father explain how it had happened. Although Calvin Beckford no longer did daily work in the fields his attire was, as always, bibbed overalls. He still rose at sunrise; he turned in relatively early.

Still puffing on his pipe, he now occupied his only possession—a roomy rocking chair. His daughter Camille (everybody called her Cammie) and her husband had planned on building a better house for themselves. Problem solved, declared Calvin Beckford. What did he need with a house and furniture? Although delighted, Cammie had wanted him to share the home with them, but he knew she would forever fuss over him and not let him be.

Chester was delighted that there were now to be four people in the home he shared with his parents. Whereas previously he and his grandfather, living on the same land but in separate households, had held brief conversations. Only on a few occasions had they engaged in lengthy talks. Now they had time to become fully acquainted, especially since the old man had decided to bequeath to him the family heirloom in oral narrative. So, it began.

"I never told you much about your *great*-great-grandmother," said Calvin Beckford one evening to his grandson, Chester—so far, his only grandchild! "I think I should; everybody should know family history.

"Kate, the one who took Mama under her wing," he continued, "told her she never remembered Bess, your great-great-grandmother, having a flat belly. She was always having babies and working in the field picking cotton until time to give birth." He paused, choosing his words. "Mama said that Kate had given birth to twelve sons, and each had been sold by the age of six or seven. Bess died giving birth to Mama who was about five when the last one was sold. She and her brother got to know each other pretty good. Mama said they were playing together for quite some time and then one day he was gone." Calvin Beckford snapped his finger, "Just like that! Now, boys always brought a better price than the girls because they could be studded and eventually, as men, driven to work harder." He paused with a wry laugh.

"Like animals," Chester offered quietly.

His grandfather nodded. "I'm sure that if Massa Doc had sold a few of his horses he could have made a lot of extra money."

❧

Chester shook his head in disbelief. "And that's an awful lot of babies," he said. He felt profound compassion for a relative he would never know.

"You're right," his grandfather answered slowly. "I think you already know that studs—you know, male horses, stallions—can be used to cause ten mares to have a colt. That is the same way they used black men in slavery, especially after no more slaves were brought in from Africa."

"How old were you then?" Chester asked.

"This was before I was even a heartbeat. Massa Doc—that's what Mama said he was called—had no money to spare for buying slaves. 'Good stock' was what they called a big, strong black man and females of good stock. So, on some plantations more than one black woman could probably be pregnant by the same black man. Then if that devil was not careful with how he used his bucks, brothers and sisters could be walking about on the same plantation and not even know it. Now, some females were not breeders. You see, Bess was not a very big woman but was able to get pregnant without a lot of bedding. Do you understand?" he teased with a wink.

"Yes, Granddad," Chester replied, but he didn't smile. He was attempting to imagine himself with a girl he didn't care for, aware that the old man was engaging in a gentle pry. Chester was *real sweet* on a young girl at church and well aware that his grandfather did not want him getting any young ladies "in the family way." Following the tradition of Calvin Beckford, Hale had talked to Chester at length about *not* sowing wild oats.

"Anyway, your great-grandmother, Naomi, said she had been plucked from the cotton fields like you choose an apple or an orange from a fruit tree. She couldn't say why she was chosen except that she was free of charge, and there was never enough money to pay for help in ole Doc's office. She was trained as a replacement for the Missus, the doctor's wife. She said she knew from the questions they asked that they had thought it through pretty good. They knew teaching her to read was against the law. To work as the replacement for the Missus she needed to know some things. They convinced themselves that just merely teaching her enough about identifying charts to put them away and working out a color-coding system was not like teaching her to read a book. They thought that was good. What the Missus and the good doctor didn't know was that your great-grandmother, Naomi, already knew how to read and write. She had been taught by an old slave named Cecil from the scriptures of a beat-up Bible as early as the age of five. With twigs he had taught her to write on the dirt floor of his cabin, scuffed and smoothed away after each lesson. Over what could be considered an earthen board, he kept a raggedy piece of blanket from the horse stables where he worked. The marks were not deep, just so she could see'em, and then they were smoothed away after each lesson. Your great-grandmother was a fast learner." Calvin laughed. "To protect herself and old Cecil, she pretended to neither read nor write because she said those devils surely tested her—making sure, you know.

"Anyway, with that out of the way, she began to help in the office. Small things at first, like fetching everything but the patient's record and straightening up after each patient's office visit. And so, like I said, by the age of eleven she was keeping the office clean with the help of an old slave woman. By age thirteen she was taking blood pressures and temperatures, assistin' in dressing wounds, and performing all the duties of nursing. Most didn't mind, but sometimes a patient didn't want her to touch'em. At those times Massa Doc would take care of that patient by himself and just let her clean up afterward. One thing he never did was let any of his patients know that Mama could put away the charts, even if it was by matching colors. She was never allowed to pull charts; Massa Doc did that. And she had to wait until the end of the day when all the patients were gone before she could put them away. Then she straightened up and put away the files. She also had to clean the office every night with the help of that old lady so everything would be ready for the next day."

"It was against the law to teach us to read and write," Chester repeated. "I learned about that in school." Chester no longer attended school, but he did possess an eighth-grade education.

"Glad to hear it." Calvin smiled with an approving nod. "When she was twelve," he continued, "Mama started living in the cabin with Kate and her three children because the Missus did not want her staying in the Big House, and Kate didn't think it was right for her to continue sleeping in the cabin with Cecil. Mama said Massa Doc was starting to have his eye on her when she was about fifteen. This was when he and the Missus had started getting along real bad, and he drank a lot. She said some of the time he would stand too close. One time Mama said she heard the Missus tellin' Massa Doc that he was 'breeding her like a nigger.'" Calvin laughed. "She was a busy lady with seven children! So, I guess she didn't want to have any more babies and stopped allowing ole Doc to touch her so much." He laughed again and paused. "The Missus always went with Massa Doc on the house calls and at those times left Mama with the children. Most of the time this happened at night when the children were asleep, or at least in bed, was when Mama stayed in the Big House. When Massa Doc and the Missus returned, the Missus would get her up and send her to the slave quarters. Mama was a handsome woman even when she was older. She was medium brown, not that tall, you know, and even when I was about forty-five or so, she was still good-looking.

"Cecil started worrying about Mama when she was about sixteen because most of the time, she acted afraid. She was beginning to complain and told him everything that happened at the Big House. For the next year she complained all the time, so one day he told her some of the slaves were planning their escape. He wanted her to go with them because all they had to do was cross over into Pennsylvania. Like I told you, the Border States were always losing their slaves, and even when they went after them, the slaves weren't always found. She told me how afraid she was during that time, afraid to leave and afraid to stay. The Missus was acting real ugly toward her even though Mama did everything she was told and did it good, too. Sometimes she would question Mama about what she did in the slave quarters after leaving the Big House. Mama said she had to do something to get away because she was not going to be able to stay there. The Missus began telling her that maybe she and the doctor should never have trained her as a nurse, as if she thought Mama and Massa Doc were seeing each other. Mama said she couldn't be sure, but that was coming up a lot. Often, she was afraid to go to the office to work.

"Well, then the big day came. The overseer always went away once a year—I guess for about a week—to visit relatives in another county. Left a trusted slave in charge, Jute. Massa Doc always gave his okay because ole Jute was a plantation spy, always tellin' everything he knew to tell. Cecil kept after Mama about trying to make a run with his help. He had helped plan it for months, even though he had to stay behind. She and another young girl escaped with three men. Mama told me she was never so scared in her life. She said it seemed as if they were running forever. She said she was out of breath trying to keep up with them, and at one point two of the men grabbed her under the arms to haul her so fast her feet hardly met the ground. Anyhow, they got to Pennsylvania, where some of the Underground folks was waiting to give them a place to stay, feed'em, and send'em on their way—that is, unless they decided to stay in Pennsylvania. Only Mama stayed. The other woman, older than my mama, maybe late twenties, went on to Canada with the men. I think two of'em was related to her, brothers or cousins. Mama told me she was tired from moving so fast and wanted to stay behind to see if there was something for her in Pennsylvania. Anyway, she stayed in Pennsylvania with this family of freedmen who took her in because they were part of the Underground Railroad—this was a network of people who moved people out of slavery."

When his grandfather paused, Chester nodded. "Freedmen were the free blacks, right?" he asked.

"Right, not like white folks, but with more rights than slaves." He winked at his grandson. "They had to be careful because a lot of whites were not that crazy about freedmen. Even though those whites with the Underground wanted to free the slaves, most did not want to make them as free as white people were. A black man always had to have a job or could become jailed or even enslaved for not working." Calvin paused to take a long puff on his pipe, which had almost gone out. "Anyway, Mama settled in with the family—a man and his two sisters—and not long after that, she was going to the meetings with them. That's how she met Neville McDermott, who was part of the Underground. Think of it. He left the plantation where his family-owned slaves, went to college and medical school to become a doctor. He then became part of the movement. Going to college was not enough, so he went to medical school because he wanted to do something more, he told Mama. She said he told her that he was not trusted for almost four years while he attended the meetings. There were some things they did not say when he was around. If he walked up on them talking about something they didn't want him to be a part of, they just started talking about something else. He was from the South, and they found it hard to believe that one of the Georgia McDermotts wanted to help get rid of slavery. He told Mama that after the fourth year they began to trust him. He had been giving money to their Underground operations for some time even though he did not know exactly how the money was being used. Anyway, he was a doctor in Philadelphia. One of his nurses went off with her male friend to get married, leaving him high and dry with only one nurse—his wife! Neville had a large practice and two nurses—a head nurse and an assistant. The assistant left." His grandfather chuckled and took a puff from his pipe. "So, when he found out Mama knew nursing, he gave her the chance to work with him and his wife, the head nurse. Mama was very good. He told her that, and so it worked out fine. Mama said she did not know just how well trained she was until she started working with McDermotts.

"Everything was working out just fine." Calvin laughed again. "Then she met my father, Nathaniel Beckford. He came into the office with a bad cold—at least that is what he thought he had. It turned out to be the flu, and Mama kind of nursed him back to health. By that I mean she would take him soup that she had made, make him tea. A few times she made dinner for him. Well, they fell in love and got married. Until this time, Mama didn't know how to join letters—"

"She printed, you mean," interjected Chester.

"There you go," replied his grandfather, clearly glad that this family history was of such interest to his grandson. "My father taught her how to join letters. To write. Nathaniel Beckford was an educated man from Virginia who could read and write real good.

"My father hated slavery and had made several trips into the South—the Border States, his home state of Virginia, also Maryland— to bring slaves to freedom. Well, Mama wanted to free her sister and her sister's two children. Those devils had sold the father of her children—a fine specimen of a man—for over two thousand dollars because he was labeled a troublemaker. Of course, they never told that to the ones who bought him. Mama wanted to go with Nathaniel since she had convinced him to do it. After all, he was risking his life for her sister, so she wanted to help. My mother's sister—my Aunt Julia—and her children had planned to meet them at a certain place, one of the stops of the Underground in Maryland. Now, don't ask me to explain how my Aunt Julia got to Maryland from North Carolina. I don't know. Mama told me they were to meet at a specific place in Maryland and then go on to Pennsylvania. My mother figured she could withstand the trip since they were close enough to Pennsylvania. She was only two months pregnant with me, you see, but she began to have awful pains in the pit of her stomach because they were moving so fast, and she needed to slow down. That's how they got caught: she couldn't keep up and had to be left behind for my father to return there to pick her up. The return was what caused the problem. She told me many times she would always regret not staying behind in Pennsylvania." He paused and sighed. "Mama said she was hidden in a shed with a dirt floor way out yonder from the house. In that shed were mice, and unless she kept moving some part of her body—her foot, her hand, something—they would run over her legs or her arms or her head. She was there for at least a night waiting for my daddy to return. She said she was so scared, didn't sleep all night long. If she had been caught in the home of the family that hid her, they would have been in serious trouble. They could lose everything.

"Meanwhile, slave catchers had been tracking them for quite some time, miles maybe. They lost sight of the family for a while and then picked up their trail again because of the return trip to pick up Mama. Finally, they caught up to them and wanted to know where my mother was because those devils had taken headcount. My father wouldn't tell them and got killed trying to fight the slave catchers because he knew he couldn't get away. They killed Aunt Julia too. She wouldn't tell them where Naomi was either. To keep the children alive and not give away the people who were hiding her, my mother left the shed and came forward. Any free black person helping slaves to freedom became a slave, so my pregnant mother, after gaining her freedom, was again on the auction block as a slave, with me in her belly. They sold my cousins to another plantation—I don't know which one—so my mother lost track of the only family she had left." He paused and shook his head.

"At the time," Calvin continued to explain to his grandson, "Since Mama was not showing it was not known that she was pregnant. She arrived at the plantation at harvest time and never worked on a rice plantation.

"Neville wrote Mama often at Jade, but the letters to her were included with those sent to his mother. Because of what had happened to my father, Mama did not wish to run again, especially with me. Besides, we would have had a difficult time because we were a long way from a state close to the North like Maryland or Virginia." He paused and was momentarily pensive before he spoke again. "Mama and, of course, Gabe had the only shanties with wood floors, but not fancy like those in the Big House." He sighed, returning to his story. "I wanted to at least try, but she begged and pleaded with me, protesting that she did not want anything bad to happen to me. She would always begin to cry and wring her hands about me being all the family she had outside of her nephews, and only God knew where they were." He shook his head sadly. "Anyway, I had cousins I never met. They're most likely dead by now."

Calvin Beckford often interwove into his narratives detailed descriptions of his youth spent in slavery. He also proudly related how his mother had taught him to write and read using the Bible and a few worn books.

"There was a little help from Old Lady McDermott, and of course the books had to be kept out of sight, always staying in the old lady's bedroom. She said that somehow McDermott Sr. didn't react much to Mama and me being able to read and write."

Granddad," inquired Chester, "who was Sarah?"

"She was a young woman," he began slowly, "that I knew when I was a boy." He paused. "She lived in the cabin with me and Mama. She took up with Gabe who was a carpenter. Before that he was a cooper." His grandson looked somewhat quizzical. "A cooper repairs and makes barrels and casks." He paused. "These hold rice and from what I understand when he left Driscoll—the McDermott's rice plantation—a young fella' he had been training for quite some time took over that job." Chester nodded. "Anyway, Sarah sometimes stayed with him in his cabin.

"When McDermott had land cleared Gabe was brought from Driscoll to build his house there. Some of the others told me Gabe was the carpenter that was in charge. He told all the others exactly what to do. He was a *good* carpenter. He built all the cabins—with help of course," he said, and added with pride: "He taught me. His cabin and ours were the ones with wood floors because ol' man McDermott wouldn't let him put floors in the others. All the others at Jade were built with dirt floors."

"Why?" asked his grandson.

"Because he said it would take too long." Calvin paused, thinking back. "I was told that it took Gabe and his help over four years to build the Big House at Jade. Some of his help were pretty good, but not like Gabe."

"What happened to Sarah?" Chester's question cut through the calm, invading Calvin's private reminiscence. Suddenly he wished that there had been no mention of her.

Calvin's account of Sarah was abridged, yet crisp and clear. He had told his wife Maude, now deceased, a version of his true feelings about Sarah. He still held a mental picture of that horrible day. He sorrowfully recounted Preston whipping her after he murdered Gabe, the one she dearly loved. He was silent for a long time, lost in thought about that young woman.

"Some other time," he said quietly, taking another puff from his pipe. He avoided talking about Sarah, especially after his discovery of what happened to her. Finally, he spoke again. "I know one thing—Preston was an ornery cuss. So was that overseer he hired."

"Who's Preston?"

"That was Old Man McDermott's second son. Anyway, then somethin' happened, and the old man fired that son of a bitch. A few months passed before they got a new man." He paused and took another puff. "Preston's wife died in childbirth, and their little son didn't live but a few hours, and the other two children—both of them girls—grew up without a mother."

"What did Preston look like?" Chester asked.

"Not too tall, rather stocky. The others were leaner. None of the McDermott men were very tall. All had light hair and blue eyes, except for Preston—he had cold gray eyes."

"Like Raleigh IV?"

"Yeah, you could say that." He paused. "Preston? Much meaner."

"How many brothers were there?"

"Four," Calvin answered. "Raleigh Sr. had four sons—Raleigh Jr., Preston, Donovan, and Neville, the youngest. Neville left Georgia as a teenager and never came back."

The conversation turned to other topics. Chester had found that his grandfather never used the word "nigger" unless it was during one of his stories. He hated the word and had taught all his offspring to never use it. "That's what you were called when they were beatin', ya," he said when the subject came up on this occasion.

"Were you ever beaten, Grandpa?" Chester's voice was hesitant.

"A few times," he answered, "but the driver—that's the one that did the beatin'—told me to holler as if it really hurt."

"Did it really hurt?"

"Well," it stung, but never broke the skin. It left welts."

Chester suddenly retreated from that line of questioning, more interested in pursuing a previous topic. "Granddad," he pressed, "who was Sarah?"

There was complete silence for a long time and then a ponderous sigh. "Like I said before, I knew her when I was very young," he said slowly, "and then I didn't know her anymore."

That terminated conversation for that evening, like securing the barn door to keep the animals inside. Always his grandfather became fully engaged when the topic was land and ownership that could grant you independence. In fact, it was one of his favorite discussions.

"Be smart, be intelligent and always own land," he said during another talk with his grandson. "Never sharecrop, boy. Never! Worse life on earth is sharecropping. You will never, ever have anything of your own because you will never get out of owing that son of a bitch. They even own the shanty they allow you to live in. Make you pay for that, too. Finagle so that you don't even own the clothes on your back. Keep you in debt no matter how much cotton you plant and pick." He paused and took another puff from his pipe. "Always grow your own fruit and vegetables and kill your own meat. Then you can eat as much as you want when you want and feed your family. That's the kind of man you want to be. Responsible for caring for himself and his family."

"Did you fight in the Civil War?" Chester asked, knowing that his grandfather was already up in age when the war began.

His grandfather looked sad for a few minutes, and then he answered slowly. "No, I never did." He said it with finality. He was thinking about the Fugitive Slave Act that from 1850 to 1861 had allowed US marshals to return captured slaves to their masters. When that law was passed, he was forty-four years old. He knew of one runaway returned to Jade long before the passing of that law. Calvin stood watching an aging Preston, suffering from the relentless onslaught of his illness, instructing his overseer to relentlessly whip the runaway within an inch of his life. Calvin was twenty-four years old.

"What's wrong, Granddad?"

He didn't answer. The incident had reinforced Naomi's feelings about attempting to escape. "What did I tell you?" Naomi said triumphantly. "See what happened to that young man? Do you think I could withstand that happening to you? It would kill me. It would literally put me in my grave."

When he turned to look at her, there was naked pain in her eyes. Thereafter, for a long time there was no mention of attempts to escape Jade.

He recalled shortly thereafter all eyes being dry in the slave quarters when news came about the death of Preston McDermott. Suddenly Calvin was returned to the present and the questioning eyes of his grandson.

"What you are thinking about, Granddad?"

Again, he puffed on his pipe. Should he talk about Sarah? Maybe he should. He remained silent for a few minutes longer, reviewing his youth. So very long ago.

"Old Lady McDermott was the only white person I can honestly say I knew as good and kind. Maybe it was being in bed most of the time. It sure ain't because all who weren't from the South liked black folks." He paused. "She was from the east—Connecticut—came south when she married Raleigh McDermott Sr. I heard some of the old slaves talking about it. That was way before I was born, when he was at Driscoll. He was a young man then. They're dead and gone now, some that came with him to clear the land and kept on at Jade. Most of them had stories—mostly bad—about those swamps.

"The fall from her horse caused Rebecca McDermott a lot of pain. The doctor said she would never walk again and needed a lot of attention. Mama told me they had hired a full-time nurse, but it was too expensive. Without one she couldn't return home. So, Mama was brought to Jade to be Old Lady McDermott's private nurse. Sometimes Mama had to take care of her for days at a time, but after each sick spell she seemed good as new—except she couldn't walk. On those days, she would have a chore for me, and that was when she would call me in for my reading and writing lessons. Mostly it was Mama giving me the lessons, but always in the ole lady's room and never, ever anyplace else. Old Man McDermott knew it but never said anything. I kept quiet, too. Never told a soul, just like Mama told me. That old lady would always call me in at high noon." He laughed. "I'd be glad too She wanted Old Man McDermott to figure out a way to free me, but he never did. The only way you could get your freedom in the state of Georgia was for it to be in the will of the owner, and you had to be released in a free state."

"Why didn't he put it in his will?" asked his grandson.

"I'm not sure." Then he rushed ahead. "Anyway, he never did. At the end of the Fugitive Slave Act, 1861," Calvin explained, "the Civil War started. When the war was over and even before it started, I was not so young." He paused. *For a slave I was old*, he thought. Grueling toil! Lot of slaves were old at fifty. "I would have been long gone as a young man if it hadn't been for Naomi Beckford, your grandmother, war or *no* war." *Or dead*, he thought. He knew of a few from Jade dead. Trying to escape to freedom.

He did not discuss with his grandson just what had transpired because then he would have had to tell him that his oldest sons were raised as slaves until their early teens. Hale was twelve, and he received some personal consolation that Camilla, four at the time, held only vague remembrances. *Life and time*, he thought. It reminded him of wringing out clothes until they were no longer dripping wet—at least that was what you thought until water yet seeped from the cloth, from life. There were no easy answers, none that were not painful.

"Even though Neville McDermott never came home, he kept in touch with his family, and believe it or not, the McDermotts were a close family, except for Preston. That demon was close to nobody. Anyway, through the grapevine Neville found out what plantation had bought Mama, and he told his father. It was a horrible situation because she was working in the rice fields in Savannah. Mama told me she was not doing so good. She thought she was going to die in those rice fields."

Chester listened intently as his grandfather recalled these memories. For Calvin Beckford, these recollections were a form of therapy, a method of release. However, one memory was particularly different, and he faltered regarding where to begin. He puffed thoughtfully.

Chester's grandfather talked to him plainly, without pretense, and he was glad that he was old enough to appreciate what he was telling him.

"Chester, remember as a young boy how it was necessary for you to grow up fast in this country?"

The young man nodded.

"How it was your responsibility to know what can happen to you in this place, on this very soil. You reached manhood even while still a youngster? Do you understand what I am saying to you?"

"Yes, sir."

"In this country, people—black people—are not allowed to be children. Only occupy children's bodies to one day become grown and, as the Bible says, put away all childish things. I know you laughed and played but never forgot the responsibility of being mature, right?"

Chester nodded in agreement with his grandfather because his father, Hale Beckford, had always emphasized this, most likely because Calvin Beckford had told him the same thing.

"In this country you are not allowed to be any other way. When a person hides behind sheets to do their dirt, they're not only evil. Not only are they cowards, but lower than horse shit." He kept rocking, puffing, rocking, and puffing. "Did your father tell you there have been lynchings in this county?"

"No," Chester admitted, "he didn't."

"If those trees out yonder could talk, a lot of things would be told. A few were used to string up men—two that I personally know about. This took place after the Civil War and in this county, just like a lot of things."

"Why is that?"

"Why? Because they could, that's why. Why? Because the victims were black is why. Because they lost the war is why. Mad because they no longer had free labor is why. Mad because they had to get up off their lazy asses and work is why. So, they worked out a system. They brought in sharecropping so they could still have free labor by cheating and lying and committing all the evil as always. It was business as usual."

Calvin took a long puff from his pipe, pondered, stopped rocking for a moment, and then resumed. The darkness had stolen its space like a burglar, and the nocturnal noises completed the transformation.

For a few minutes Chester and his grandfather sat and listened, sharing the sounds of the night. Some sounds Chester could identify, whereas others he could not; he refused to disrupt the old man's mood to ask about them.

After taking another puff on his pipe, Calvin spoke. "Chester," he said.

"Yes, sir."

Chester's grandfather was in a strange mood indeed and sat rocking for a long time, smoking his pipe as always. "There is always something in this life you should be willing to die for."

The words sent a chill through Chester's body as he considered his young life and thought about just what he might be willing to die for. It was a very uncomfortable feeling.

"Now, what that is will be up to you. Oh, I know you allow nobody to mistreat your family. When you have a family of your own, you'll know what that means." He paused, knowing that there was a young lady from church his grandson was seeing. "That should be understood without question, but there is something even beyond that which a man will die for. When the time comes, you alone will know what that is. Life sometimes is mean, cruel—doesn't give an inch. Fear nothing but God until the day you die. Struggle as best you can. Do whatever it takes to be in control of as much of life as possible. I know that living in this hellhole called America can be very hard sometimes. I'm an old man and know how hard life can be for men—and women too. If you can keep from it, try to never let life beat you down. This land is in the family. When your father is gone it will still be here. That's very good. Remember, land is something that is not like a crop. Not like apples or oranges or those peach, pecan, and fig trees out there." He pointed with his pipe, took another puff.

"Each year, trees bear more fruit for you to pick, but this earth only has a certain amount of space, no matter how many people live on it. Land is what people have been fighting over since this world stood! Of course, there are certain conditions Now, sometimes water takes over with floods that go away, and again you have dry land. At other times the water will claim that dry land, forcing people to find another home.

Nature is always to be respected. That's different from people taking over other people's land by driving them off it with wars just to own it or even what lies beneath it. People fight and sometimes die to own land with its gold and diamonds and everything else. Let me tell you, boy, that no one is any greedier than these devils. They lie, kill, steal, and it appears they always have. This will be your space, and if possible, let no man take your space. Hear me, boy?"

"Yes, sir."

"One other thing," he said. "I know you were not fortunate enough to have gone a long way in school, but even if it starts with your grandchildren, start it! Make sure they are educated. I know sometimes no matter how hard you try, there are mishaps, and land can be taken. Knowledge," he said, gently tapping his grandson's temple with his roughened forefinger, "cannot be stolen away and is in there forever Remember that."

That was the last conversation Chester had with his eighty-one-year-old grandfather. The next morning when his mother approached the foot of Calvin's bed, her father-in-law was already gone. A short time later, as his grandfather lay in the church prepared for burial, Chester was saddened, but at least his grandfather was still there. After the funeral, he occupied no space above ground and the repast was over. Then the house held a stealthy silence. His permanent absence shaped a void that lasted for a very long time. Chester's deep-seated grief over the loss of his grandfather never completely left his heart. For the first few mornings following the burial, Chester envisioned finding him flat on his back, arms folded across his chest, sound asleep as always. He remembered once telling his grandfather that he slept like a dead person. His grandfather promptly replied with laughter that perhaps he was practicing. He was an old man, and everybody is dead a lot longer than alive. While he worked in the fields, Chester's thoughts would wander back to conversations with that old man. At night sleep did not come easily. Often, he stared at his grandfather's rocking chair, visualizing the old man sitting there smoking and rocking with that wonderful twinkle in his eye. The few times when he mentioned Sarah, his favorite mule, Suzie, and a few other things that in old age he yet held dear. Chester also reflected on the coldness of his grandfather's eyes and his stony demeanor whenever talking about the hardships of life. This wonderful person had great stories to tell with every detail in place, never repeating the same one twice. Chester was grateful to have had such an experience. The spirit of his grandfather was so intense that he could practically grasp his presence. The overwhelming memory of those wonderful conversations would often warm his soul, temporarily bring him peace. His father, realizing the depth of his grief, began trying to assuage it with other stories that his grandfather had never gotten around to telling him, ones that were upbeat with intent to make him laugh. When this approach proved futile, Hale consoled his son by sharing the fact that he missed him just as much. After all, biologically, he was closer. His grief encompassed also the loss of his brothers who paid the ultimate sacrifice, leaving him behind to forever alone endure the aftermath of the tragedy.

Months later, Hale Beckford satisfied his son's curiosity regarding Sarah; in his hand he placed Naomi's letter. For hours afterward Chester sat on the porch pondering its sadness.

Another curiosity was also satisfied. For years the images of two crude coffins containing the remains of his uncles at a closed casket funeral would invade his memory bank. His father finally told him that the two men that had been lynched on their property had been his uncles. He couldn't shake the overpowering chill for an instant. It was an intermittent experience that he would have—spontaneously invasive—for months. Both revelations added depth to the chronicle of Calvin Beckford.

When Raleigh IV heard of Calvin Beckford's death, he smiled to himself. The old man had outlived all those old codgers, even those he could not identify. He wondered what Beckford's reaction would have been had he known the background of Marshal Getties. Not that it mattered now, but Raleigh IV had gotten wind that he had met his violent demise during one of the many bloody Indian wars fought out West, bringing closure to the life of Calvin Beckford.

# Chapter Four

I n 1931, Chester Beckford met Jennifer Travis, née Allen, who, having been married twice, retained the last name of her second husband. She was living in the next county with her family of sharecroppers. Chester spotted her at an evening church social. His pastor had invited the entire congregation from a neighboring county for an evening of song, fellowship, and a little preaching.

At forty years of age, Jennifer's only accomplishments were two failed marriages accompanied by the misfortune of no surviving children. During her first marriage she suffered a miscarriage and gave birth to a son, named Rufus. The father abandoned them both. He trekked west as Jennifer survived the stillborn birth of their second son. When Rufus was six years old, she then married Daniel Travis, and had two daughters. At ages two and four, suffering from the lack of proper living conditions and medical care, both Travis girls succumbed to severe influenza. Despondent over the dreadful loss of his daughters and expressing a lack of enthusiasm in being a stepfather to Rufus, Daniel fled to Chicago, with the promise that "once settled in" he would send for them. Jennifer's mother often suggested that perhaps he had difficulty managing to "settle in." Then Rufus, at nineteen years old, had his life tragically shortened by head trauma—the fatal kick of a mule.

Jennifer's mother often encouraged her to discard life's unpleasant experiences. She warned, focus on the beauty of life or bitterness will surely set in. The effort to remain optimistic involved daily prayer not to repeat past mistakes and to be ever hopeful for a brighter future. However, Jennifer had to face the fact that she was no longer a young woman. In fact, she was keenly aware that the same cosmic clock that sifted away her youth was now poised to chisel away a portion of her middle age. It was Jennifer Travis's desire to experience at least a few of the material things during her earthly existence. In case opportunity knocked, she strove to look her very best. To support this, she kept her one possession, a treadle sewing machine, active whenever possible.

It was their fourth meeting, and Chester liked what he saw. A few weeks ago, at the church social, Jennifer had worn a simple white cotton dress. Twice after that, he had hitched a horse to the wagon to visit her in surroundings significantly shabby enough to make her a sharp contrast. For his first visit she wore a simple pale blue dress. The second time she wore a soft yellow that hugged her beautiful hips. For each occasion, she stood, diffident and withdrawn, watching for him in front of the Allen family's drab dwelling. At his suggestion the next visit was to his home. For the occasion she wore a pale-yellow skirt and a white top accented by a simple brooch. Jennifer was a tall woman. Pretty legs, he mused, with beautiful eyes sparkling with liveliness. As always, her only makeup was a spare touch of color on her kissable lips. The consistent Georgia heat dictated moderation was best.

"How long have you lived with your family?" he asked quietly.

They were strolling back toward the house from the small mixed orchard of peach, pecan, and fig trees. Seeing figs up close satisfied her curiosity to see a fig tree up close. The grouping of trees created a loose boundary between the Beckford and McDermott properties. McDermott land seemed to stretch into the distance as far as the eye could see. Immediately she identified the vast configuration of plants that would soon transform most of both properties into a sea of whiteness—cotton! Earlier he had casually informed her of the Beckford's one thousand acres of farmland, plus an additional five hundred acres of woods. He was more concerned about her impression of him and the significant amount of personal-life information he had shared with her, although he thought it best not to appear anxious.

"Since mah son was killed," she finally said in reply to his earlier inquiry. She paused before adding, "As ya can tell, my family is sharecroppahs." *That didn't come out right*, she thought. Well, how else could she say it? For sure the Allen clan had made too many moves, always vowing each one to be their last. "We jus' moved to this farm las' year," she said softly.

"There's a lot of that all over," Chester replied casually. "It's honest work." He smiled. "Sometimes it's hard work for the pay, but you do what you have to do."

*Sometimes no pay*, she thought. She could still hear her mother offering one of her lectures with a bit of final advice several weeks ago as the family dressed for church that Sunday. At first Jennifer had planned to stay behind.

"You never know what you might find," her mother had said to generate some sort of enthusiasm. Understandably, she was despondent over the recent death of Rufus. "Jen baby, you're not over the hill yet."

"So you have no children, is that right?" Chester asked.

"Tha's right." She was momentarily sorrowful. "All mah chil'ren gone," she stated quietly.

They were now strolling about the yard defined by grass and shrubbery; large stones attractively bordered the outer parameters. A mass of petunias and impatiens in vibrant colors nestled close to the soft gray frame house.

"My second wife planted those a few years before she passed," Chester explained. "She was quite the gardener. She loved flowers, and I try to keep them watered as much as possible."

"They look healthy," Jennifer said. She turned to him upon reaching the stoop, before entering the house for the first time. "Did ya say ya have a young baby?"

"Yes, he's not quite a year old," he answered, noticing her pretty legs as again the wind teased her skirt, causing it to billow; not a few times her slender fingers coaxed it back in place.

"What's his name?"

"Ned," he replied. "Presently, he stays with his grandmother, Nettie's mother."

"That was ya third wife, right?"

He nodded.

"She was young enough to have chil'ren?"

"Yes," he responded, candidly confirming what she had heard elsewhere. "Yes, she was twenty-two. The doctor said she had what they call postpartum complications."

"I see." Jennifer attempted to push the thought from her mind, but it kept resurfacing. With a twenty-two-year-old woman, it was a wonder he hadn't had complications of some sort.

He had told her during their last talk that provided they got married, his desire was to have his son come live with them. She had contemplated this proposition as if trying on an unfamiliar but attractive fashion. He was the most prominent man in both counties. *Lucinda*, she thought, *I sho wish you was here.* Then there was her mother's candid input: "One thing is for certain—you gonna have to tell the man somethin' soon because you runnin' outta clothes to wear."

Jennifer continued to weigh the good against the bad as he gave her a tour of the home. It was a large piece of land with decent living quarters. The house sat quietly overlooking land. The previous structure had burned to the ground from a lit lantern placed too close to the curtains. His second wife had died a few years earlier. He related this information to her as she slowly walked through the house without his interference. Jennifer decided that after all these wives the place still needed the updated touch of a woman. Did he say Nettie was twenty-two?

In her mind's eye Jennifer could envision a very attractive home. She moved slowly from room to room, three in all. There were two bedrooms. The kitchen and dining area was a shared space. She decided the home to be adequate.

"All six sons are now out of the nest—so to speak—and have been for a long time," he explained and then laughed. "Anyway, I decided to build a comfortable but smaller place."

She turned to him, smiling her approval while thinking about the comments that had filtered back from the church sisters, rumors whirring like the wings of a helicopter:

*When did she start seeing Chester Beckford?*

*Well, I knew about his first wife. Chile, she was somethin'.*

*Wasn't she the mother of his first three sons?*

*Yeah, but run off to Memphis to get away from farm life!*

*The second wife was okay, but from what I heard, not the best.*

*For sho' she wasn't. I don't think she was much good at keepin' house.*

"After my first wife, my second wife became the stepmother to my three boys and gave me three more," he stated with pride. "I married Nettie a few years after her death." With an uncomfortable laugh he added, "Then along came little Ned in less than a year."

She didn't comment. *You kept two of the wives busy*, she thought, *and the other didn't live long enough.*

"I need a wife," he said with candor, hoping not to sound too pushy, "to be a mother to my little Ned. I always took care of my sons. I don't want little Ned to be the exception."

"I understan'," she said quietly.

All six of his adult sons still resided on the land. In both directions the landscape was dotted with relatively decent living quarters. Gray frame houses in almost perfect alignment with their father's home. Beautiful magnolia trees, a sprinkle of blossoming cherry trees, and an intermingling of large shrubs flanked their homes presenting a landscape of postcard perfection.

It was known that the Beckfords grew their own food and sometimes sold produce at their farm. They slaughtered and cured their own meat, a legacy from Calvin Beckford. He learned the skill as a slave.

Chester Beckford, his sons, and their male offspring were responsible for planting a substantial amount of the crops. Since his sons and their offspring had taken over most of the planting, harvesting, farm chores, and the like, he had more time on his hands. Beckford was getting old and felt he had more than earned the right to stay close to the land without working it.

The women were mainly responsible, categorically, for "female duties"—washing, cooking, keeping house, canning, and so on. The youth were assigned chores such as feeding the livestock, cleaning the animals' surroundings, gathering eggs and other light duties. All lived very busy but relatively comfortable lives and thereafter buried in a small, well-kept cemetery. Strangely, it was not on their land, but instead on the grounds at the rear of the church they attended, which, in years past, the Beckfords had helped erect.

It was well known that the Beckfords lived in isolation. That none had ever sharecropped was stated as a simple fact. There was no intention to speak disparagingly of her own family; she did not take offense to the comment. Through observation she made one confirmation: that their homes were situated within a compound. Not that it mattered, but their land was the closest to Macon. Even though she still had a few questions, she decided to observe closely and allow revelations to naturally unfold as time passed.

The pastor of her church knew Chester well, deciding that a good word was in order. He informed her that Chester Beckford used to work twelve to fourteen hours a day; he was a good and kind man. Consequently, while Chester gave her an oral history about his wives, children, grandchildren, and love for the land, he unknowingly confirmed the information volunteered by the reverend.

After several weeks of these long conversations, her mother initiated a constructive talk, encouraging her to "move things along."

"Jennifer, you're beyond a storybook romance because ya been that route—twice! Be thankful that ya turned his head. One thing ya can count on, ya won't be pickin' cotton, livin' like a vagabond, travelin' from pillar to post. He's sixty-three so it's for sho he ain't lookin' for a flamin' bed of fire."

"He's father to a one-year-old," she gently reminded her mother with a smile.

"Well, he won't be lookin' fo' the same from you," her mother responded reassuringly. "Make up your mind, now," she continued, "before the little fella starts grade school."

Finally, she received the anxiously awaited letter from her sister, Lucinda, in her familiar, laboriously scrawled handwriting:

*Jen,*

*I tend to make it plain. C. J. and I are near the same age and until not long ago struggled, struggled, struggled to make ends met. I still slave in some white folk kitchen and he worked the stockyard until a year ago. I know you didn't forget why C. J. and me came to Chicago. We had no land and was sharecropping day in day out. You will be able to live off the land. You had two young husbands who left you alone to bring up Rufus, and now you got nobody, no Rufus and none of the others you birthed. You been found by someone who can make sure you pick no more cotton for the rest of your days and worry about how to live.*

*Be happy.*

*Lucinda*

It was the reinforcement Jennifer needed to finalize her decision. Thus, a morning wedding was held in Chester's backyard with his pastor performing the ceremony. Except for little Ned, all the sons, along with their wives and a generous number of their offspring, attended the wedding of the patriarch. They came in brogans and overalls, crowned in straw hats, with the men dressed for the field. Immediately afterward, Chester paid the preacher and then followed the men—at least ceremoniously—to the cotton fields. The women and youngsters resumed their farm chores. Jennifer went inside the house to straighten up and prepare afternoon and evening meals for her new husband. The very next day, little Ned was deposited in the lap of his new mother.

In biblical terms, it was over a month before Chester knew Jennifer. Standing at the stove several months later, preparing a late breakfast, the first familiar flutter of life caught her off-guard. A visit to the only black general practitioner in the area (his office was in the next county) confirmed that the sporadic visits of her monthly cycle were not because of menopause. Even though Jennifer was younger than Sarah in scripture, their good fortune reminded her of that biblical couple.

During the next few months, Jennifer, now familiar with her surroundings, began adding a woman's touch. She made curtains for the kitchen and the bedrooms and gowns for little Ned and the unborn baby. She also made clothes for little Ned to wear during the day and from Sears& Roebuck ordered a few additional necessities—cookware, a set of attractive dishes, and silverware. While sitting in the evenings before dark on what was soon to be an unstable front porch, she began to crochet a spread for the iron bed she shared with her new husband. Observing this, he made extra trips into town to keep her supplied with yarn. Two and a half months later the bed had a handsome spread to match the color of the curtains.

After Estelle was born, an elated Chester, having long ago resigned to never having a daughter, lavished everything on her. When she was six years old, he taught her to ride Pacer, the oldest but gentlest of the three horses on the farm. She adored that horse and, standing on a tall stool that her father had made for her, often brushed his black coat until it glistened.

Time surged on. Chester, an excellent carpenter, decided that his nine-year-old daughter should stop sharing a bedroom with her brother. Each day, after making certain all was running smoothly, he would return early from the fields. School was out for the summer, and he deemed carpentry to be an appropriate summer project for his youngest son. It was also time to make life more comfortable for his fourth wife by building a new front porch for relaxing and gazing at the stars.

The daily training sessions involving constant hammering and sawing and nailing accelerated the carpentry apprenticeship of the eleven-year-old. The undertaking was quite extensive, but having the entire summer gave his youngest son the necessary hours to gain confidence in this invaluable skill. He proved to be a good student who learned fast, so his father kindly turned down the offered assistance of his grown sons until near the end of the project. By the time some of the older brothers joined them to finish the heavier construction tasks, young Ned had absorbed most of what he had been taught and felt pride in his capabilities. With the welcome aid of two of the older sons, they completed a new front porch, new steps for the back door, and the much-needed bedroom for Estelle, expanding the house to four rooms.

During this period, the fact that he was needed for the house projects made Ned feel rather special, but most of all relieved. One chore he hated above all others was cleaning up after the animals, especially pigs! He considered them nasty, ugly animals even if their meat was tasty. The farm was gradually becoming smaller than in past years, and so his absence was not burdensome.

The schoolhouse (grades first through sixth during the week) converted to church on Sundays. During the school term, the various Beckford children did their chores early before going to school and completed them in the evenings before supper. Afterward they romped joyously in the evening sun. As night crept in to replace the sunset, individual family members went to their separate homes. Ned and Estelle bathed in the large tin tub containing heated well water, dutifully said their prayers, and then went to bed to prepare for a repeat-day.

So, life within the Beckford clan continued to be comfortable while outside their farm a serious transition was taking place. Laws that had begun in the late 1800s were set rigidly fixed as newly enacted legislation in the South created an extension of the Black Codes. No longer was Jim Crow a minstrel show featuring a white man as a stage caricature in blackface dancing a jig. The carryover from the nineteenth century was a legal cancer invading at least a segment of the nation to further increase the suffering already inflicted on America's black population.

All public facilities were legally closed to black citizens—public parks, restaurants, hotels, and so on. "Colored" drinking fountains began to ubiquitously appear. On trains, there existed separate railway cars for blacks. Only the segregated balcony of the movie theaters was open to blacks. In fact, the entire country adopted many of these practices that had been enacted into law in the South.

Many blacks considered the specific policy prohibiting the "mixing of the races" extremely laughable, especially after centuries of white men cohabiting with slave women, evidenced by the country's numerous descendants in "racial gradation"— mulattos, quadroons, octoroons, and so on; the "corrective" legislation warranted mocking.

Paranoia ran rampant as more than four hundred state laws were passed throughout the South. Lynchings became common, grotesquely sensationalized in print media photographs documenting a sinister malevolence continuing, unchecked, for over eight decades.

# Chapter Five

They were cash poor. Chester couldn't wrap his mind around such a circumstance. Yes, they had always lived off the land but, prior to present conditions, consistently had extra money after purchasing necessities for the farm. In the past, a significant amount had been provided to supplement scholarships obtained by the Beckford youth. The amount was relatively less for those who needed to jumpstart their endeavors but deferred their college education. Most headed North, but a few ventured East or even West. These arrangements for the Beckford youth had been ongoing for quite some time.

One primary challenge facing the dwindling Beckford clan was the fact that they no longer grew cotton for the mill. There were, of course, still vegetable crops to sell, and it was surmised that perhaps within a reasonable amount of time—ten to fifteen years—lumber could become a lucrative commodity. However, things had to be kept in proper perspective. Therefore, such futuristic projections were placed on hold.

The current problem had begun when the mill's new owners decided, without explanation, to purchase cotton exclusively from the white cotton farmers. McDermott land now lay dormant and unused void of explanation: what had caused their loss of the mill. For several years the Beckfords had grown cotton only on their land and sold it in town or on the broader, competitive open market. It yielded a mere pittance compared to what they had been used to receiving.

Chester Beckford felt profound regret that at this juncture in his life his word was no longer his bond. For his last two offspring, Estelle and Ned, there was not enough money to give them the promised two years of college bestowed by the others. He hoped they would understand.

At the same time, he was confronted with his own mortality. He was becoming feeble, and a "busy day" in most cases involved piddling and puttering about. More than occasional forgetfulness was the primary reason he was forced to hand over the finances to Nathan, causing Chester to reflect on interaction with his own father. Longevity had spared Hale Beckford. In fact, he had died two days after his sixty-eighth birthday. Chester was barely fifty years old.

Hindsight now perfected his comprehension of old age. He felt like his entire life was unraveling before him. With uneasy regret, he dared backtrack to examine his journey. He bitterly acknowledged that mapping a better route was reserved only for the young.

These days Nathan, his firstborn, was sometimes short and curt. Chester reviewed the behavior of a son who had always wanted to offer abrupt remarks even as he begrudgingly followed orders. As a young man Nathan had never given him any lip. In retrospect, Chester realized there were times when he had bitten his tongue instead. Those were the days when he relied heavily on Nathan. He ignored any slights during their day-to-day interaction. Accompanied by a few field hands who were paid sparingly until harvest time, they worked the land relentlessly. Times were hard then.

Chester tried as best he could to recall whether he had reacted in kind to his own father, Hale Beckford, but honestly evaluated his daily exchanges with him as always respectful. However, the bitter reality was that what goes around does not always come around in kind, especially since in each life conditions and circumstances are often quite different.

For example, the marriage of his own mother and father, Hale, had lasted until his death.

Two of Chester's six sons had never married. Looking back, the father evaluated some of his own actions. Never had he encouraged Rue and Isaac to marry, as he himself had done four times. *Field hands! Workers!* The words stabbed his thoughts. This surprising intrusion caused unpleasant emotions. Maybe, in hindsight, although he had not said it or consciously thought it, he had intimated with unintentional selfishness that the land was their mate. It would never caress them but could possibly compensate by affording them, not love, but consistent sustenance and pride of ownership.

"I don't understand what you're doing, Dad," Nathan had said with candor soon after Jennifer Travis became his fourth wife. It was said tactfully to avoid bruised feelings or dealing with suppressed animosities. Jennifer never knew, but times became stressful and taut as a thread between him and his six grown sons. The fact that four of his offspring had children and grandchildren of their own drove home the most shattering truth: he was too old for these shenanigans. For quite some time this made him feel lost and in fragile disarray. Together father and sons did manage to struggle through.

Someone had to take care of little Ned, so what else could he have done to resolve the dilemma? Of course, his previous relationship and then marriage had been initiated by Nettie. Embarking on a final interlude with youth, an old man had been foolishly flattered by the attention of someone so young. He realized too late that this was a young woman's desperate attempt to escape at all costs her father's verbal and physical abuse. Not once did it occur to him what the ultimate consequence might be—Nettie dying and leaving behind an infant! Well, just what was his way out? He married Jennifer. And then, although it was unplanned and completely unexpected, Estelle entered their lives. How could such a pleasurable surprise be wrong? Good Lord, his only daughter!

So many more memories began bombarding him. There was more than ample time for reflection.

"Take a bath, boy!"

"In the morning. I'm tired." That was Rue. No time to waste, in the fields from dawn to sunset.

Straw hats. Rough hands! More than anything else "Wear gloves, boy," he'd said. *Like I do*, he'd finished in silence. *And don't say you never noticed.*

*Rue* responded with sardonic laughter. "After all these years, now you tell me." It was well known that Rue never cared about his appearance, anyway. Tired! Overworked!

Both his single sons had women in their lives at various times, but things somehow never blossomed into meaningful, steadfast attachments.

Sun-baked and weather-beaten. They drank corn liquor. Danced in overalls and brogans. Country! That was those Beckford men, especially Rue.

"Not that one," said one of the young women at church that Rue had his eye on.

One of the older, wiser sisters had pointed out with encouragement, "Plenty of land!"

"So what?" A sharp retort uttered by the young woman.

Both single sons had gone through an extensive period of isolation from their brothers, busy raising their families. Both were confronted with a failure to blend and belong.

"Okay, okay, so she doesn't want you. Choose someone else," Chester had advised Isaac.

"You didn't have to," Isaac snapped back in anger.

The relentless calendar moved forward, even lunged ahead to produce saddened stains in the lives of sons who had become lonely and old as well. Not Chester Beckford, though, never that. Indian blood, some said, which caused all six foot four of him to stand straight as an arrow, even as he aged. Well, perhaps the years did subtly alter his stature. Never seemed to make a difference. Others marveled at the fact that he was yet good-looking, producing an aura of charisma.

His oldest children had been raised without their mother, Chester admitted, although refusing to allow guilt to color what had transpired. Nathan had turned out all right. In fact, all three had known the love of a good, kind stepmother, even after she gave birth to three more. Very cautiously he permitted his mind to wander further, then recoiled in a miserable retreat. Other chapters of his life were evaluated with closer scrutiny. Life, he thought, reflecting on his disturbing past, was often brutally uncompromising and equally unkind. Of course, he had to admit that during one's life the fond memories had to be created with perhaps a bit of luck, some help from your Creator, and at least a touch of foresight. Only then could one look back with a smile. However, in his old age he was contrite. He longed for more gratifying endings to the many negatives of his past.

Ned was troubled during these days. Whenever his father asked him if everything was okay, he always said that things were just fine. He offered a guarded smile, wandering off to dutifully tend to the chores. Those who should have been cousins were instead great-nieces and great-nephews (his peers!). Quietly they stole away to Spelman or Clark or Hampton or other institutions. A few simply fled life on the farm. The flashbacks always reminded him of a horrible event that had forever altered the tranquil life on the farm. It was this event, he thought, that had caused most of the inhabitants to be spooked and accept only the retreat—**leave**!

⁓

Ned had noticed that the talk of his going off to college began to subside. He graduated from high school a few months ago. The recent turn of events quelled his enthusiasm, particularly after he walked up on that disquieting conversation. Finally, after being burdened for days about what he heard, he revealed his despondency to Estelle. Both decided it best that they not get caught up in an uneasy existence of wondering where exactly they fit in.

It had happened on a Friday afternoon after all the ripened fruit and vegetables had been picked to sell in the morning (on-site) at their farm stand. Without question, selling vegetables financially yielded much less than the sale of cotton. Nathan's arrangements were always so attractive, and Ned liked his oldest brother's ideas not only about running the farm, but also about numerous other things. They talked often, building a congeniality that bridged the generation gap.

He was troubled after accidentally overhearing that conversation in the barn. Hushed tones were spoken, and although he couldn't pinpoint one voice, he instantly identified the other distinctive voice as belonging to Nathan, who did most of the talking.

"Man, we should be through with raising children. What I mean is we should have no brothers or sisters young enough to be our *grand*children. I know they want to go to college, but ain't no money for that now. It should be behind us anyway," he said defensively. "Man, we done seen about all our children and helped with the grandchildren! It isn't fair to have children that you no longer provide for. Old men should never have children. I'm not saying that Dad should have to work, but that he should have planned better. Now is the time that all of us, including him, should be able to live off the land and not have to worry about educating anybody."

"You're right about that," agreed the mystery voice. "You know, we could get by with the money that's left since there's enough to carry us through the winter. We have enough feed for the livestock and enough food and everything to tide us over. College! Can you believe it?" There was a pause. "Let alone Nettie, even Jennifer—older, all right, but still young enough to be our sister."

"You know," Nathan continued, "Dad wanted to take some of the money I saved for Prentiss and give it to Ned." He paused. "I know Prentiss is getting a little more than the rest, but he's studying law, and that takes longer. We were going to do the same for Tillie, remember?"

Ned's heart was in his mouth at the mention of Matilda. He wondered if Tillie had ever become a doctor. It had been so long since anybody had heard from her. He listened for the rest.

"Yeah, I do," the mystery voice answered. "What did you say to him?" It was spoken just above a whisper. Ned had to strain to hear it.

"I said I couldn't do it, but he knew it wasn't right anyway." He paused. "He knew it," Nathan repeated angrily. "Like I said, old men shouldn't have children. It's a time to mosey along without worries.

Just live on what was done in your productive times. We all know Dad hasn't worked in years."

There was no answer, a long silence. The only sound was movement. With the discussion over, they had resumed their work.

Now Ned knew why the planning for him to further his education had ceased. Of course, whenever he and Nathan had talked about it, Ned was always the one to bring it up, but Nathan had been consistently in full agreement—that is, until this past summer. *A hypocrite*, Ned thought, attempting to quell his brimming anger.

When Nathan's last grandchild, Prentiss, had gone off to Morehouse, he'd sheepishly bade farewell to Ned, who was also, astonishingly, his great-uncle. As they parted, Ned wondered just what exactly had been said and slowly began to assemble the pieces of the puzzle. At first, it was perplexing when Nathan suddenly stopped helping him plan to attend at least *two* years of college. Now Ned finally understood the sadness in his father's eyes whenever the subject was education.

Nettie. Ned purposely repeated her name to himself on the way back to the house. Sure, he knew who Nettie was. His mother who died during his birth. Years ago, together his father and Jennifer, his stepmother, had explained in detail.

Well, at least he knew the other voice was neither Rue nor Isaac. He saw both single brothers working in the fields before he approached the barn. It had to be Jesse, Gabriel, or Bart. The mystery that would remain unsolved. What he had overheard strengthened his emotional resolve about leaving Georgia. He never knew Nathan felt that way. They had such a very good relationship, and he had always been so kind.

Things were taking place too fast. There was no time to prepare for one event before there was another. Chester Beckford had just celebrated his eightieth birthday a few days prior with cake and homemade ice cream. He now sat on the back porch waiting for Essie and Ned, who had gone riding on Pacer and his offspring, Gypsy. Lightning flashed across the sky, trailed by a boisterous boom of thunder. He needed to talk to those two. He wanted to explain his regret of the present circumstances created by the lack of money and relatives, young like themselves, leaving the farm. He hated breaking promises. He would explain to them that if he had a choice, his promise was still his bond.

Spontaneously, a hard downpour began, often described as Georgia rain. Scuffling to his feet as quickly as possible to avoid getting drenched, he opened the screen door, stumbling into the kitchen clutching his chest. The fall to the floor positioned him on his back, looking up into the horrified eyes of sweet Jen and his two youngest children. Both were thoroughly soaked, hurrying inside just as he mouthed the words, "I'm sorry."

❧

"Granddad was a very good person," said one of great-grandchildren who had spurted in from college to contribute to the eulogy. All attended the funeral, with some offering a few words of praise as others remained silent. "He was extremely generous and always there to listen to our problems," the great-grandchild continued. "Most people listen, but they don't hear you. Granddad heard you and assisted you in solving the problem. I will always remember that. However, I think everyone deserves to die without having to worry about the ones they leave behind. Granddad, may you rest in peace. All of us are going to be just fine."

Ned assessed the "all" expression as a joke. *Just fine,* he thought, bitterly shaking his head. Experiencing grief with the passing of his father, he could not quell the feelings of anger and despair. He and Estelle left in the lurch. He battled these mixed emotions aware that no one prepares to just up and die. He knew his father had meant well. Truthfully, both were born during his later years. A recent discovery— some resented their presence. It was never an issue until the old man became vulnerable. Age had a way of doing that to anyone surviving long enough. Well, he thought, we're here for now, and that's that.

Jennifer considered the union with Chester as her best marriage. She longed for the arms of that strong, old man. She could still hear him as he sought around under the covers of their large iron bed, saying, "Where are you, little bit? I can hardly find ya." She would laugh and snuggle close against his back, spoon fashion. Of course, he always said it in jest. Although relatively slender, she was in no way diminutive. Yes, it had been a good marriage. Never did she think losing him would be this hard. His permanent absence made her realize just how much she had loved Chester, and her bereavement equaled that love. Her pastor had been right. He was a good man. He had been a good husband. During their relatively short time together, age was never a factor.

Possibly Pacer was even more grief-stricken than the rest of the Beckford clan. He dropped dead exactly a month later.

☙

Ned, at nineteen, growing into adulthood and increasingly more dissatisfied, decided there had to be a better way of living. It seemed that since the death of Chester Beckford he had been permanently relegated to handling all the worst chores—cleaning the chicken coop, the barn, and that god-awful pig pen—Unequivocally, it sealed his disgust with farm life. Nasty, filthy animals were swine! Very appropriate name that the Bible had given them.

The death of Chester made the status of Estelle and Ned even more prevalent. An occasional occurrence of great-grandchildren visiting their great-grandparents dramatized the fact that they indeed represented Chester's last hoorah. Both wondered how many people were in such a preposterous situation. Most of their classmates had grandparents the age of their brothers and parents the age of their brothers' *offspring*, who were Ned and Estelle's own nieces and nephews, although a full generation older. The great-grandchildren, siblings or cousins to each other, were Ned and Estelle's great-great nephews and great-great nieces! They pondered their positions in this familial quilt and decided that they were the excess pieces.

Estelle was in deep thought. Ned was two years old when she was born, and Chester Beckford was an incredible sixty-three years of age. At his death, when she was seventeen, he was a mind-boggling eighty. Although some of the time she did think about her mother being in her late fifties, she could easily be mistaken for mid-forties. Still in all, she was a contemporary of Ned and Estelle's brothers!

They plotted their escape and chose Chicago, as had many of their unrelated predecessors. The remoteness of anywhere north made it seem like a distant land and the trip more like a voyage than a bus ride. They began to devise a plan to monetarily support their flight, but Jennifer wisely intervened with a plan of her own. She did not want her children living independently in a big city like Chicago, so she wrote a letter to her sister Lucinda and, without delay, received her prompt response, welcoming Ned. It was agreed that Estelle would follow immediately after graduation. Even though the financial supplement from the small cotton crop had been seriously reduced, Jennifer insisted on giving Ned her portion. She always kept money underneath her mattress from selling vegetables at their farm stand. Her stepson would be supplied with a decent amount to begin his life in the North.

❧

It was a council of old men; the self-appointed lead councilor was Nathan. ( "The Old Men" was the private name Chester's youngest children used for their aged brothers.) Ned and Estelle sat in a somewhat hostile camp, exuberantly spilling over like cups too full to explain their future goals to their senior siblings. The older brothers listened unemotionally to what they considered foreign expressions about the two striking out on their own. For them there was no existence outside of their agrarian experience.

It became an effort for Ned to hide his disgust, especially when addressing Nathan. How dare he be against him leaving! *Of course*, he thought. *I'm the shit cleaner, from the chicken coop to the pig sty to the barn.*

Since his dad's death, a few great-great-grandchildren had been there periodically to handle chores. In all fairness they weren't yet in their teens, didn't live here, and justifiably allowed to be selective. *These men are my father's first two sets of offspring*, he thought. For the first time he envisioned the generation gap partitioning the young from the old.

"Why is it that you young folks always think that the grass is greener on the other side?" asked Nathan, the oldest and the least flexible. He was the same way with his children and grandchildren. They always complained about how hard it was to convince him to try anything new and how difficult it was to persuade him to even buy new clothes. Until recently he owned only two suits, alternating them for church on Sunday. Finally, his wife intervened. He now owned four.

"Do you realize that a few years back Chicago had the biggest race riot this country ever saw?" piped up Jesse, the youngest of the Old Men.

"I know about that, and it was 1919, not just a few years ago," Ned replied immediately. He was more than glad to correct him, although he didn't want to express any animosity. Nathan looked slightly taken aback at Ned's quick response but said nothing. The others simply stared at them both, as if a time machine had instantaneously dropped them in their midst from light-years away.

Estelle broke the awkward silence with a partial truth. "We want to get away from separate water fountains. We want to sit on the main floor when we go to the movies. We want to be able to shop in the stores like everyone else." *To fit in somewhere!* It was a sentiment Estelle and Ned had discussed in private. "Everyone else" meant their white counterparts who were free to try on clothes before purchasing them. (It was rumored, although not documented, that similar incidents had occurred in one of Chicago's prominent stores.)

"What about college? I thought you wanted to go to college," said Rue. He truly did not wish them to leave, although he never offered to help Ned with all the distasteful chores. Things had surely changed since the death of their father.

"We do, but not here," Ned replied. He and his mother had discussed at length what had been happening since his father's death. With continued tenderness she had warned him to bide his time, keep the peace. This instantly caused Jason, fondly called Bo, to more than cross her mind. The incident had taken place about four years ago and caused a drastic family breach never fully healed.

"Why not?" insisted Nathan, exaggerating his shock. "There's Spelman and Morehouse in Atlanta. What's wrong with those two colleges?"

"Is there any money?" Ned said pointedly, suppressing his anger.

Nathan didn't offer a reply. He instantly rendered a perplexed expression instead, then looked away.

*Hypocrite!* Ned thought. *How dare you.* "Besides," Ned added, "outside school there are these same white folks."

Ned had asked the question point-blank. There was no money left for education, an ongoing problem over the past several years. During summer break those in college now had a new arrangement, working outside the farm to afford extra money for the next semester. Previously there had always been extra money from cotton grown for the mill. Nathan and the others had held several private discussions regarding what was to be done about furthering the education of Estelle and Ned. The result was always the same: the family couldn't afford it. The topic was placed on permanent lockdown.

"You live with these same white folks up north, too," Gabriel said quietly.

*Guilt*, Ned thought. *All of you feel guilty.* He wondered exactly what had been said about him and Estelle other than what he had heard.

"Who do you think allowed the South to exist?" Nathan asked. "There are northern crackers and southern crackers. North, south, east, or west, white folks are white folks."

Ned could not help thinking that this continuous grasping for straws was a cover-up to please Jennifer.

"Okay, okay," said Ned, more than slightly perturbed. "Do you know why we don't have trouble with these dogs? You want me to tell you why? It's because we stay to ourselves and don't go anywhere. It's because they know how this family has been perceived as the crazy niggers ever since Calvin Beckford." He steered clear of the conversation regarding Bo. "We own all this land, and there is still a reasonable number of us, so they don't bother us. Great-Granddaddy Calvin and his sons were and still are like legends. If we went into town more and were around these rednecks more, we would have a lot of trouble, believe me. They would try to stir up *mess* even now. Most of the McDermotts that these rednecks feared because of their power and influence and our attachment to them—descendants of their ex-slaves!—have . passed on. That and plus, *plus*, Kane and the rest of those knuckle draggers—troublemakers!—are also gone. There is no one else left to keep up a lot of… of… crap!" He had groped for a word less profane than the one on the tip of his tongue. "Who knows when there will be a new bunch while we continue to dwindle?" He paused to allow comment, which was not forthcoming, and then continued. "I don't want my children to grow up in this mess," he blurted angrily. *Not with you, either* he thought silently.

"That can happen anywhere in this country," argued Nathan in his calm but firm way. He was the self-appointed spokesman for the council, which sat mostly in rigid silence as their younger siblings were subjected to ongoing interrogation.

"Boy, this is the United States," said Gabriel quietly. "Did you ever hear about what happened in Greenwood? Nothing was done about that, nothing, and Oklahoma is not actually considered the South."

Ned knew what Gabriel was referring to: the atrocity of Black Wall Street in Tulsa, Oklahoma. "It sure ain't north," he scoffed. He really wanted to say: *Why don't all of you shut the hell up and stop all the pretending?* But the conversation that had taken place in that barn was a mystery to remain eternally unsolved.

"It's southwest," he continued, "just like Texas. Matter of fact, it's bordered by Texas, and they had slaves in both Texas *and* Oklahoma," he added triumphantly.

"Boy, that ain't nothin'," said Nathan as he again joined the conversation. "They had slaves in the North—Pennsylvania, Rhode Island, and the other states too—so if you think Chicago is going to be so much better, think again. You just goin' *up* south, that's all. It's about the same all over this whole country. Ain't got a thing to do with geography."

Ned had wanted to have it out with Nathan, but Estelle and their mother had decided that some things were better left unsaid. Wisely, Jennifer considered it unfair to put all the blame on Nathan.

Circumstances suggested that they had made the decision as a group. Times were not as prosperous, and Jennifer intuitively knew that the older sons felt that children their father sired in his late years were not their responsibility. As she had told her children, one thousand acres was a lot of land fifty or even twenty years earlier. Money went further even though a lot of folks occupied the space. This was a different time. In the end, she was depressed by the turn of events, but considered their leaving to be for the best.

Jennifer listened to the discussion becoming mildly heated with remarks that were moving the loved ones toward a potential breach. She perceived the danger of cleavage in the family and interceded. For one thing, she was fearful of Ned exposing what he had heard. She pleaded their case to her contemporary stepsons.

"Y'all, listen, Ned and Estelle want a change, that's all, 'n' should be allowed to have it. They's young and need a fresh start." She paused. "They's already decided, so let'em be," she said gently.

She told their older siblings they would be staying with her sister, their aunt Lucinda, and there was no need for concern because neither of them would be living alone.

When Chester was seventy, before Ned was old enough to lend a hand, he had employed a teenage field hand from the next county who attended their church. Jennifer had recently approached him one Sunday after service, and he had gratefully consented to return to their farm. He was now married with a young child, and the family survived as sharecroppers in a little shack on one of the smaller farms. Jennifer proposed that the family share her home free of charge in exchange for working the land and helping her grow produce. Some produce would be sold, and some retained for themselves. It was an attractive offer. The young man accepted. This released her children to live their lives without worrying about her. As a woman growing old, she rejected the northern way of life. Besides, she wanted to be close to the land and her widow's inheritance just in case the land was sold. She could then pass her share on to her children. She often thought of Chester's account of the conversation he'd had with his grandfather, Calvin Beckford, before his death. The sons of that man paid the ultimate price. She knew beyond any doubt that this turn of events would have caused that old man profound heartache, Fervently, she prayed for a pleasant outcome that would one day satisfy the spirit of Calvin Beckford.

This turn of events brought her life full circle. Nevertheless, she understood her children's reasons for leaving and recognized that restlessness was a trait of youth and a sign of the times; so many young people were leaving the South. She wondered whether, if her life had begun in this era, new places and new adventures would have lured her as well.

# PART TWO

# TRANSITION

(1950–1982)

# Chapter Six

Chicago! It was often called Chi-Town, City of the Big Shoulders, and—the label that Uncle C. J. loved—the Windy City. Ned and Estelle arrived in Chicago within six months of each other to reside with Aunt Lucinda and Uncle C. J., leaving behind in Georgia scrutiny of the Old Men. Quite often, their older siblings, Jennifer, and the farm were topics of discussion with their aunt and uncle, who made several calls to Georgia in attempts to coax Jennifer north. The offer was always gently rejected. She considered herself too old to become a Chicago transplant.

In January 1950, when Ned arrived, he obtained employment as a janitor for the Board of Education with Uncle C. J. He often teased his wife, a few years older and now retired, about her senior status. In jest, she would suggest that he was envious of having to wait his turn; he agreed that she was right.

July of the same year, Estelle arrived, and for her a job was procured with Lucinda's previous employer. Even though Estelle was hired as a domestic, Lucinda cheerfully assured her niece that this job was only a 'tide-over.' She would retire from such a mediocre position. She pointed out that she herself had recently retired with a modest pension combined with an additional monthly benefit from Social Security. The latter had been wisely withheld from her paycheck by that same well-heeled couple who had exhibited enough concern to ensure that, once retired, their former employee would be assured a decent lifestyle. For that she daily thanked God.

Estelle and Ned's monthly contributions from their moderate wages impressed their aunt and uncle. Jennifer had taught her children well. They insisted on paying rent, contributed toward groceries and utilities, and consistently helped keep the large flat clean. Lucinda often noted this in her correspondence to her only sibling, continuously asking that she come to Chicago—at least for a visit. As further enticement, Lucinda described the large, roomy, three-bedroom flat and its full bath (plus a half bath—the powder room!). It contrasted with the communal bath she and C. J. endured during Jennifer's only trip to the city. However, that previous condition represented a step up from what existed in Georgia, then and now.

Estelle was euphoric over the giant leap from an outhouse to indoor plumbing. It had been the same for Ned six months earlier. For the first few weeks Estelle sometimes flushed the toilet without using it just to assure herself of her personal upgrade. Letters home didn't elaborate on this because never did she wish to be mistaken as no longer appreciative of the provisions that had existed on the farm.

Cousin Booker, C. J. and Lucinda's only child, lived on the second floor. He and his wife, Bobbi, attended a celebratory welcome dinner prepared by Lucinda in Estelle's honor. Six months prior, Ned's arrival had been celebrated in the same fashion.

As nineteen fifty segued into 1951, Estelle completed her first six months in Chicago. Still a farmer's daughter, she decided to remain in Chicago, gradually becoming acclimated to riding the rapid transit and the CTA in general. Walking on concrete was yet strange as was shopping for fruits and vegetables. A select few of the latter were grown in the designated corner of Lucinda and C. J.'s considerably large backyard. There was mental comparison to the large sprawling garden in Georgia—separate from the plowed fields, the peach orchard, fig trees, and the fields of cotton. Even her Georgia strawberry patch, which she had cultivated annually from the age of six, would singularly rival all of what was grown in the urban garden of her aunt and uncle's backyard. Estelle missed the watermelon and cantaloupe, but especially the peaches. Intermittently, an urge to return home nagged at her. She thought of Nathan and all the older siblings—the Old Men—with subdued fondness. Never had it occurred to her that she would miss home so much. If she thought her return would truly be welcomed even the separate water fountains, the segregated balconies of the movie houses, and above all, the degradation suffered by black men, could not have kept her away. With the death of Chester Beckford another segment of Beckford family unity had also been buried.

As a new Chicago resident, she dwelled in ambiguous limbo. Still, she decided to deal with these facts, stay put, and begin her college education.

The night of August 4, 1952, Policy King Ted Roe was assassinated. His death ended the ongoing struggle with the syndicate which had attempted for more than thirty years to wrest the lucrative racket—Policy—from the black community.

C. J. was among the thousands of mourners in attendance at Roe's funeral. Chicago, the last stronghold, had now fallen the way of New York City, Youngstown, and other major cities. (Years later, Policy or numbers, would evolve into what would eventually become known as the lottery, and placed under government control.)

The sad news circulated within the black community as a very heavy loss. When Estelle arrived home from work, she found an upset Uncle C. J. She discovered that at one time he had been heavily engaged in that lucrative racket. It was how he and Lucinda had acquired the two-flat dwelling they now occupied and another attractive three-flat building, two streets over.

Uncle C. J. explained to his niece what had happened and why. In fact, all four of them—Ned, Estelle, Aunt Lucinda, and Uncle C. J.—sat around the living room right before the funeral discussing Policy and its positive influence on the black community. It would end now that Roe was dead.

Even for a few days following the funeral, there was a lot of activity at the Owens residence. C. J. Owens was reunited with some of the Policy sidekicks he had not seen for years. Lasting friends made during that period also had attended the funeral and stopped by as well. The dining room was full of food and drink. Eventually, all gravitated to the living room to sit around, relating tale after tale about the old days when Policy was huge in the black community. Both Ned and Estelle were intrigued, listened intently, while C. J. and his friends discussed the operation at length.

As days passed, such therapeutic release became no longer needed. Policy's heyday had to be allowed its proper burial along with its slain king. Never again did Ned and Estelle hear their uncle discuss his turbulent past life in such detail.

Even as normalcy slowly returned to the large flat, Lucinda proudly revealed to her niece that, thanks to God protecting C. J. during those dangerous times, both buildings were mortgage-free. She revealed the constant distress she had endured and the numerous letters she'd written to Jennifer about her husband. A much younger, relentless C. J. had been heavily involved in that dangerous operation. He learned the streets fast enough to maintain a methodically determined "do or die" stance. Stubborn determination allowed him to defy the odds, challenging an uncertain future. Lucinda continuously sought solace in her sister, simultaneously pleading with God to keep him safe from harm.

After his tumultuous, precarious years in that illegitimate venture were over, C. J. once admitted to his wife that a couple of times he had looked death dead in the eye. She did not pressure him for further elaboration. With great tenacity he had prevailed. They had raised their son, Booker, and now lived in relative comfort. In a few years his employment would provide a comfortable retirement. Lucinda once told her niece in confidence, she could now close her eyes at night without watching the clock, and an empty pillow.

Estelle continued to faithfully attend Loop Junior College, remained steadfastly engaged in corresponding with her mother, and worked as a domestic. Finally, she received notice from the post office: her test score was satisfactory. She would be notified when there was an opening.

That the couple had no grandchildren, Estelle considered unfortunate. She inquisitively asked Lucinda why, certain that they would embrace becoming grandparents. "I don't know, baby," Lucinda said. Estelle thought of her own mother, who had married into a family that provided her with immediate motherhood to Ned, an infant at the time. The additional bonus was becoming an instant grandparent to Chester's numerous grandchildren. Estelle tried to minimize thoughts of home. Always, she recalled the conversation overheard by Ned, still marveling at the years the Old Men had managed to skillfully conceal their real feelings.

Estelle and Ned continued to live with Aunt Lucinda and Uncle C. J. and their brown boxer, Bumstead, who dutifully and punctually delivered Estelle's house slippers. "That dog really is taken with you!" commented Lucinda. He would get them and drop them at her feet whenever she entered the apartment. He reminded her so much of back home and her own dog, deceased long ago. Some memories were becoming more distant as day-to-day city living defined her more recent way of life.

Then it happened fast, with lightning speed. Along came Mason Ingram. Pepper's Lounge provided the stage as the blues were belted out loud and raw—live! As unfamiliar nightlife unfolded around her, there he was, well dressed and attractive, introducing himself with his Mississippi accent still mostly intact.

The first time he came to the house to take her out for the evening, she introduced him to her aunt and uncle. C. J. quickly and alertly sized him up, decided with wise skepticism that he was all wrong for Estelle. This is what he told Lucinda when she asked why he did not like the young man. C. J. pointed out that he was not so young, candidly stating he would disrupt Estelle's life. He and Lucinda agreed that Estelle was a grown woman, respectable in every way; they could not forbid her to keep company with Mason. As the pair left the apartment for their first date and walked to Mason's car parked at the curb, C. J. observed from the front living room window that he drove a Buick. He drove a

Buick as well. You are what you drive, he often said. At this time, C. J. no further analyzed Mason—at least not aloud, to his wife. He however held the same mindset whenever Estelle left the house with Mason. He continued to behave as a gentleman in every way, wisely bringing her home at a decent hour. Consistently, he was extra kind to her aunt, but cautiously courteous to her uncle, who steadfastly wished his niece finally moved on.

In passing months, serious discussion began because Estelle continued to date Mason Ingram. Estelle was Lucinda's blood relative. C. J. wanted to intervene, so Lucinda wrote to Jennifer to ask her advice. What did she think about the two of them having a talk with Estelle to perhaps suggested that she not date this man? Jennifer wrote back that she was against that approach for her daughter. She had discussed with Estelle many times about life, especially regarding men. She was confident in the upbringing she had provided.

One night, after she had been dating Mason Ingram for approximately four months, Estelle was uncharacteristically late getting in. Her uncle was up waiting for her, inconspicuously seated on the living room sofa. Even though it was rather late, it was a Saturday. C. J. never retired early on weekends. He was leisurely listening to jazz, his favorite music, and reading the *Chicago Defender*. It wasn't really a "read" at all, but mostly pictures with brief captions and comments here and there. However, he did support it and the *Pittsburgh Courier*. Those two papers and the printed pages of the *Chicago Daily News* kept him abreast of what was going on in this country. (March 2, 1978, the *Chicago Daily News* would go out of business with its feisty headline stating: **So long, Chicago**. At its closure it could boast an impressive 102 years of circulation.)

Finally, Estelle arrived, accompanied by Mason, who, leaning in the doorway, seemed surprised to see C. J. He spoke, hesitated, and then opted not to come in as Estelle bade him Good Night. It was an awkward moment in which he became tentative, decided against a good-bye kiss. His exit was abrupt. C. J. heard him murmur that he would see her after class on Monday.

Quietly locking the door, Estelle followed the tantalizing mixture of pleasant smells coming from the kitchen to say hello to her aunt busily packing into containers and refrigerating the prepared Sunday dinner. When Estelle offered her assistance, Lucinda replied that she was through except for the chicken. She volunteered to fry it when they arrived home from church the following day. C. J. loved the way Estelle fried chicken.

She entered the living room, and her uncle invited her to join him. "Sit for a few minutes," he said kindly. She seated herself in an adjacent chair. C. J. loved Estelle. He had told Lucinda more than once the young woman had so much potential.

"How are you doing in school?" he asked.

"Very well," she replied quietly.

"And you will have completed two years of college by the end of this term, is that right?"

"Yes," she replied proudly. She had gone to night school even during the summer to accelerate her transfer to a four-year university.

"Very good," he replied encouragingly. "Education always helps. I finished my last year of high school after I came to Chicago and then took a few night courses, but that's about it." He paused. "What about Mason—is he going to school?" C. J. already knew the answer.

"No," she said sheepishly and with apprehension. "He works at the mill in Gary."

"What is his position? Does he discuss his work at all?" C. J. asked.

"No," she quietly replied, "he doesn't."

"Ask him about his work." He paused. "Chicago is a big place, honey. He's the first one you've dated. See other guys."

She promised that she would. Later in her room, she did her homework for Monday and then lay in bed staring at the ceiling and thinking, somberly visualizing Mason standing in the lobby of Loop Junior College consistently waiting for her every evening as she came out of class. After some time, Doretha, wisely reading what was happening, had gently suggested: "Estelle, you should begin to discourage him, and move on," but omitted an additional comment. Instead, she simply smiled and left it at that. They had become good friends and often met in a coffee shop not far from the school to have a light meal before attending class.

Estelle considered Doretha's advice worthy, but after the fact. She anxiously watched the calendar, hoping and praying as the month came and left; her misery deepened. It had been only one time, she told herself, just that once. She had just momentarily lost focus and allowed herself to be overtaken by her emotions. Now she was near tears from worry.

☙

The Owens' living room was a large, beautiful room with rich ivory walls. The color theme was burgundy and vibrant gold. Multicolored throw pillows nestled the corners of the burgundy-colored sofa and matching armchairs. Large, mahogany end tables flanked the sofa, with a matching cocktail table centered in front of it. One matching mahogany table was centered between the two armchairs. Carpeting and drapes in soft gold completed the tasteful décor of the beautiful room. On the mantel was a large clock and a small gallery of family photos tastefully arranged on both sides.

A serious family discussion was taking place. Lucinda sat on the sofa directly in front of the cocktail table with a look of deep concern and compassion. C. J. was absentmindedly seated on the arm of the sofa. If the walls could talk, they would have revealed Lucinda's favorite good-natured comment: *Mr. Owens, I keep asking you if a few of your retirement checks are to be donated toward new living room furniture."* Almost immediately he would take a seat in his favorite spot, one of the sofa's matching armchairs. Furniture wasn't the topic today.

"I cannot have a child out of wedlock." Estelle's eyes told the tale. They were red, the lids puffy. "None of the women in our family has had a child without being married."

"Okay," Ned responded calmly, "so you will be the first."

The tears began flowing again, and C. J. discreetly signaled to Ned. His response was a disgusted sigh as he appeared extremely perturbed. He stood near the fireplace, leaning against the mantel.

Lucinda often commented to Jennifer about the Beckford men whenever she visited Georgia. "Fullbacks," she would comment to her sister, "and their gridiron is the land."

All were big, dark, handsome men, robust from hard work. Ned was of the younger generation. Never enduring farm life extensively, his frame was large but less robust. He continued leaning against the mantel in the same position. He had met this son of a bitch a few times. Never liked him. Finally, her crying subsided, and he offered his opinion.

"I know what happened," he said quietly. "You are the nicest lady he ever dated." All the explosive comments had already been expressed in the privacy of her bedroom; one was repeated now, but this time with a shrug. "You're pregnant, so what?"

That statement brought more tears, causing her to rise from her seat and take flight. C. J. stopped her.

"Estelle, Estelle. Doll, you're not the first woman to have a child and not marry the man," he said, gently taking her into his arms to comfort her. "The sun will rise in the morning."

"Estelle, honey, don't cry so," Lucinda added, remaining seated. For days, she had tried to break through to her niece; "I'm on the brink of laryngitis," she exaggerated earlier to her husband. "Baby, you'll make yourself ill," Aunt Lucinda said consolingly. "Come on, now. Settle down."

"Being an unwed mother is not that bad, Estelle," explained C. J., gently coaxing her to the nearest armchair. "Especially when you're about to marry wrong. Lucinda and I have talked about it." He leaned over her as, restlessly, she barely remained seated. "Don't be ashamed to the point of deciding solely based on a mistake to compound your error. I'm sure your mother will understand. You can stay here with us and raise the little one when it comes. It could work out for the best. Lucinda is no longer working and could babysit for you." He turned to Lucinda, nodding vigorously; there was an earlier positive discussion. "She would love it since so far she has no grandchildren of her own."

"I would," Lucinda added quietly. She paused. "Estelle, you continue to tell us you want to marry him, so why are you so unhappy?"

"I have to," Estelle said. She sounded desperate. "I have to marry him."

Her aunt looked disturbed but offered no comment. *It's a pity that none of us are getting through to this young woman*, she thought.

Ned had not left his position. He watched, attempting to calm himself. Earlier in his sister's bedroom, nearly incensed, he had chastised her for not being smart enough to sidestep the ditch. Oh, had the tears ever flowed! This was a way for the sorry bastard to claim her and upward mobility.

"Estelle," Ned said once she had become more composed. "So, you marry this guy. He's not marriage material, okay?" He paused. "Don't give the—" He sighed, shaking his head in disgust. "He's not going to make a very good husband," he finished. "He's not that bright. Know what I mean? What kind of life do you think you're going to have married to the likes of him?"

"But I can't have a child without being married to the father," she said. Fresh tears were flowing.

She thought of her mother, Jennifer Allen Beckford. Three marriages. Never once suffering the shame of becoming pregnant before marriage. Although she was abandoned twice because of wrong marriages, all Jennifer Allen's children possessed the legitimate names of their fathers—Peoples, Travis, and Beckford, respectively.

*You should have thought about that*, Ned thought, *before the fact, not after.* Oh, hell! He was seething. He wanted to hit something. In fact, he wanted to beat the motherf—he stopped the thought before finishing the silent expletive. Estelle stayed on him about cursing. His defense was that sometimes nothing else sufficed.

It was during one of her rare Saturday nights out with her friend Doretha that she had met Mason Ingram. She was "country green," and it stood out like a sore thumb. She had learned how to dress by perusing the fashion magazines and taking suggestions from Doretha, a first-generation Chicagoan whose family had migrated north in the late thirties.

When Estelle and Mason began dating on weekends, he dazzled her with the South Side nightlife—Sixty-Third Street, the Sutherland a couple of times, even Club De Lisa once. Always, he managed to have her home at a reasonable hour, her personally selected curfew. She was forever conscious of her mother's advice regarding city life. She remembered her mother telephoning more than once with that frequent reminder: *Nice young ladies don't stay out too late.* Then he began to pick her up after school and drive both her and Doretha home. However, Doretha gradually eased away, leaving the two of them alone. Finally, after their third month of dating, he coaxed her to visit his Drexel studio apartment. It was neat and clean.

The relationship was a roller coaster speeding downhill. A reckless automobile race with failing brakes. Approximately four months into their courtship, Country Green knew the total male anatomy.

Now, facing her pregnancy, Estelle was in a state of depression' Lucinda telegrammed her sister about the upcoming wedding even though Estelle stated miserably that her mother did not have to come for the ceremony. Jennifer arrived on the eve of the wedding. Prentiss, who had always been extra fond of Jennifer Beckford, volunteered to chauffeur her to Chicago in his father's late model Chrysler.

Mother and daughter sat side by side on the large bed in closed-door conversation; the anticipated Georgia visit would now be postponed. It was the first time they had seen each other since Estelle came north. Jennifer, still mildly shocked, deduced that her daughter's introduction to adulthood had not been as pleasant as it should have been. Never had she seen Estelle in such agony. She longed to help her in any way she could.

"Do ya want to talk 'bout it?" Jennifer paused. "Do ya think maybe ya shouldn't wed this man?"

"I have to," Estelle said miserably.

"I won't think any less of ya if ya don't, Essie," Jennifer said in quiet honesty as she lovingly embraced her daughter. Now she regretted that she had not come earlier, but instead had abstractly, from a distance, addressed the circumstances. Such remote evaluation and correspondence could not substitute for the in-depth, face-to-face conversation that mother and daughter had engaged in during Estelle's adolescence. Why had she postponed her visit that Lucinda had urged time and time again?

Essie. Only her parents called her that. Verbalizing the problem only made it worse, segmented it as a sordid chapter in the family annals. Removing the bandage to expose the pus of an infected wound. She was becoming familiar with wearing a new emotion named contrition. It was becoming her constant companion. She began to sob, thoroughly ashamed.

*I must marry him*, she thought. *There is no choice.*

Minutes before the wedding ceremony, Uncle C. J., dissatisfied with all of it, watched her from across the room, He wished he had monitored her comings and goings. *That was what you do to children*, he admonished himself. She was almost nineteen when she arrived in Chicago, twenty-one when she began dating Mason Ingram. Young. An adult, nevertheless. She never went anywhere but to work, school, back home, and church on Sundays. Finally, she had decided to have fun weekends as Aunt Lucinda and Uncle C.J had suggested. Doretha suggested that she needed a break from textbooks and the like for a change.

A few weeks earlier, before knowing exactly what had taken place but with close observation, C. J. had told his wife he feared that Estelle had gotten herself in a pickle. He felt even worse when he was not proven wrong. She was such a nice young woman, soft-spoken with grace, charm, elegance, and poise. He told his wife that she was marrying beneath her. He was incensed because of it.

Lucinda purchased a small wedding cake. Compliments of C. J., there was expensive champagne. Immediately before the ceremony, in the privacy of Estelle's bedroom, Lucinda placed a string of pearls around her niece's neck, representing something borrowed. After the ceremony she would give the necklace to the young woman. A matching set of small genuine pearl earrings from her mother served as something new. Nothing represented something old except the bride's disposition. She envisioned herself leaving her body shrouded in mournful black.

Estelle was adamant about not exchanging vows in a church, so the ceremony took place in the living room of C. J. and Lucinda's home.

Their pastor officiated what resembled the last rites. Forever canceled was her dream of a white, floor-length gown accompanied by all the fanfare. In a ceremony finalized with a simple wedding band for the bride, Estelle Beckford became Mrs. Mason Ingram.

Crying had become a much too familiar experience as tears again threatened to surface. She struggled, suppressed the urge, when her brother Ned came over to hug her. Discreetly he placed money in the pocket of her eggshell-white suit. Congratulations, he thought, in reference to Mason Ingram.

"Cheer up," he whispered before releasing her. "Everything will be okay."

Nelson Ingram, Mason's brother, stood across the room assessing Estelle, miserably retreating to the sofa. Different, he mused, from anyone his brother had ever dated. Nelson, smiling to himself, suspected only one reason for this wedding. Well, now Mason would have no choice but to become responsible and sensible with his money, to cease trying to impress with his appearance. Well, this time it had worked!

Nelson approached Mason. "You ran the stop sign, fella," he teased with soft, amused laughter. Mason withheld a quick, angry response.

Moments later, Estelle sat observing her new husband's siblings to pass judgment on them and herself as well. She watched everyone mingle. Her mother offered an upbeat smile, beckoning for her to join them. Nodded her response and remaining seated. She did not feel married and didn't want to. For certain, her new in-laws did not treat her as such. Cold! This was her assessment of them all, Mason's brothers—Luther, divorced, and Nelson with his wife, Deidre, the sister, Hattie. Positively no warmth whatsoever. Prior to the short ceremony, they had simply squeezed her hand when introduced. *Not even a welcoming hug*, she thought, feeling ambiguous frustration. Well, in all fairness, Deidre had hesitated before taking her cue from her husband. Last in line, Hattie had not broken from the bland, emotionless greeting extended by the other three. Ned, following suit, was deliberate about where he stood.

Families were supposed to welcome a new person as her mother did Mason. Estelle wondered how often they gathered to celebrate holidays or engaged in family get-togethers. The short courtship highlighted all the wrongs. She had married into a family before meeting any of them. A definite no-no.

Her self-imposed solitude continued. As a spectator, she sat sadly observing the lack of affection the Ingram family displayed even for each other. When they were children in Mississippi, she asked herself, was there any positive interaction? Were they so scuffling poor that they didn't have time to love each other? Why had she not insisted on meeting them prior to the wedding? Well, the grandparents as well as the parents were deceased—she knew that much. Prior to the wedding, she had asked to meet his relatives. He was reluctant, but she persisted. Therefore, the siblings were invited to the ceremony. She surmised only curiosity prompted attendance.

Prentiss appeared disengaged from it all. Her sense of shame allowed very little interaction with him. What would be shared upon his return to Georgia?

Unable to shed the shame of her circumstances in becoming a married woman, she was relieved that Doretha had honored her timid request not to attend the ceremony. Her friend had delivered her wedding gift, after class, concealed in a plastic bag. The thoughtful gesture symbolized conclusiveness. Tears welled in the corners of Estelle's eyes. No more talks before class. No more carefree chats over coffee. She could still hear the consoling yet tremulous voice of her friend. She too realized the gravity of what was taking place. Change forever moved one forward with constant persistence, with or without consent.

*You failed to plan*, said that quiet inner voice, *so you planned to fail.* In haste she purged the thought that prompted such overwhelming emotion. Just then, Mason joined her on the sofa to confirm that the train carrying her dreams had left the station without her; she was traveling in an opposite and less secure direction. She kept telling herself it shouldn't be this way as in silence they sat, side by side, while the new husband stole glimpses of his new bride. *Get over it*, counseled an uncompromising inner voice. *At least he married you!*

☙

There she stood in the lobby, gazing at the familiar first-floor entrance of the building where she no longer lived. Should she let herself in or perhaps ring the bell? Deciding to use her key this one last time, she quietly let herself in. Timidly she followed the sound of activity coming from the kitchen to be cheerfully greeted by her aunt and uncle. Glad to see her, they encouraged her to join them. Prentiss, seated at the table, also extended a warm greeting.

"Join us," said C. J. invitingly. He was still in his bathrobe although dressed for church from the waist down, which he did quite often.

"Let me make you a cup of tea," said her aunt, immediately rising to pull out a chair at the large kitchen table.

"I ate breakfast already," she answered with a sad smile. These days it seemed as though she was stumbling through life in a stupor. She stood awkwardly gazing out at the people around the table, not knowing exactly what to do or say. She felt absolutely lost.

"You can still have a cup of tea," Prentiss said kindly with a smile. He wanted to draw her into conversation. He wanted to tell her that having to get married didn't make her a pariah.

Her aunt sensed the tension. "You mother is in the bedroom, sweetheart," she said gently to provide Estelle a comfortable exit from the kitchen.

Overpowered by emotion, she escaped to lightly tap on the door of a room that only hours ago was hers. The voice from inside bade her entry, and moments later, mother and daughter stood face-to-face greeting each other. Jennifer waited, silently urging her daughter to begin a conversation. Oh, such a fragile moment. It was the very first time Jennifer was cognizant of the size of her little Essie. She recalled Chester speaking about his own mother: "You know, Jen, I think Essie's going to be small just like her grandmother."

She welcomed her daughter into her arms. The young woman expressed her pain with deep sobbing. She expressed heartbreaking sorrow over this turn of events. How she longed to be peering through a window or standing on the sideline, in sympathy for the life of someone else.

Later, for what seemed an eternity both sat on one side of the large bed. There were no more tears, just somber calm. Still without words Estelle somberly looked about the room. *Strange*, she thought, *all my belongings have been removed from this room. My dreams are unfulfilled.* Many nights she had lain in this very bed, planning her future. In the blink of an eye…! This was what her mother had meant, constantly warning her to be ever vigilant, ever alert.

"Are you going to be all right?" her mother softly asked just above a whisper. "I can stay a few more days, if you want."

"No," she answered. "I'm okay." *Just go*, she thought, *before I break down all over again.*

Finally, they stood in the cold lobby. Prentiss put their luggage in the trunk, then scurried inside the car from the cold. Patiently he waited at the steering wheel, observing mother and daughter embrace. They bid each other farewell in the cold space of that building.

"Essie, let me know if you need anything." Jennifer Beckford offered an encouraging smile. She hesitated as Estelle again became teary-eyed. She waited for her little Essie to speak, hugged her one last time. Momentarily, she lingered, waiting, and then was gone into the winter morning chill.

Uncle C. J. had earlier cleared the snow from the sidewalk and a narrow path in the parkway because Jennifer was without boots. "Been so long, you forgot it snows in Chicago?" C. J. had teased after shoveling a pathway for his sister-in-law.

Forlornly, Estelle watched as her mother slipped into the passenger seat as the great-grandson of Jennifer's late husband held open the car door. Just before quickly sliding back under the steering wheel, he waved good-bye to his great-aunt. Earlier, Prentiss had explained his need to get back to school. In a few days he had exams to complete for the remainder of his senior year. He would start law school in the fall. *Law school*, she thought, fighting back a tinge of bitterness. *Imagine that!* Briefly, she dared wonder if any of that money could possibly have gone to her or perhaps Ned.

Jennifer's smile was visible from the car window as she waved one last time. The car pulled away from the curb. Estelle gazed piteously after the gray Chrysler until it became lost in traffic. *My great-nephew,* she thought, *was a few years older, not younger!* Who would believe it? Her life was in reverse order. She stood there in the cold lobby, newly married, feeling very weary, aged beyond her youth.

Earlier, Mason dropped her off, mentioning something about her needing to visit her mother without him. Never would he admit the emotional heaviness and discomfort he felt about what had transpired in the last twenty-four hours. He would always remember her fear of being pregnant—without a husband! The ultimate sin. Kept emphasizing that her mother and her mother's mother before her had never, ever been pregnant without a husband. He wondered what that was all about because he had wanted to marry her. He simply had not thought it through clearly enough to realize the breadth of it all.

Lucinda hastily ushered her niece inside, remarking that in her condition she should avoid getting chilled. The niece silently followed her aunt to the kitchen. She sat down as a freshly brewed cup of tea was placed before her. Gingerly, as if needing permission, she stole glimpses of the large kitchen. It held so many happy memories. Both women at the breakfast table sat quietly sipping their tea. After tea, Estelle remained seated, not knowing what to say or do, feeling out of sorts, lost, and sad. She listened to Uncle C. J., familiar with his routine, as he stirred about in the bedroom. He had taken off his robe and was completing his attire from the waist up, as he did most Sundays.

She rejected a second cup of tea. Lucinda wanted to offer the young woman words of wisdom to take into her new marriage. These days the young woman's spirit was as fragile as fine China. Gingerly and ever so slowly, as tears crept into the corners of her lovely eyes, Estelle laid the keys to the apartment on the table. Painfully, she was severing the last thread to her previous life. Lucinda, smiling kindly, picked them up from the table, handing them back to her.

"Keep them, honey," she said gently, almost in a whisper. "Estelle, just remember prayer changes things."

℃

Their daughter's first name was Clarissa, after Mason's grandmother. Her middle name, Lucinda, was in honor of Estelle's aunt. The first six months of their marriage existed in his studio apartment. Three weeks before the baby was born, they had moved into a relatively decent one-bedroom apartment on Drexel. Estelle wondered why he had not acquired at least a two-bedroom apartment. Even so, she had suggested that they should start saving toward purchasing a house. This had received no comment from her husband. Admittedly, he had not thought that far ahead.

Estelle managed to complete her semester at junior college. When Clarissa was three months old, in February 1954, the post office finally notified her that she was to start work. Under the current circumstances, the news held no pleasure. She hated the necessity of not working toward her degree. She was surprised when Mason resentfully exclaimed, he didn't see the need to get all that education in the first place "just to toss mail." She had informed him shortly after they met that she was awaiting notice of her test results from the post office. Strange, she thought, that sort of negativity never surfaced during their short courtship.

Why now was she constantly taunted, she asked herself, with persistent memory of warnings and instructions given to her as a young girl? They bombarded her thoughts like weeds in a flower bed. "Estelle, honey, never, ever lay down wit' a man that ya don't wish to marry." She could still hear her mother warning: "I really think it best that ya marry'im first." Her mother could draw from her own marital experiences. She had become successful only after her third try, as she explained to her daughter more than once. Now Estelle's sobering thought was that at least each time her mother had become pregnant, she was *already* married.

To further frustrate things, Estelle became pregnant for a second time. Despondent and angry that her precautionary dependence on his use of condoms proved futile caused his response to be even more infuriating.

"It slipped off," he said. "Besides," he told her, "I got no feeling when I use'em."

Clarissa and Jeffrey were born exactly a year apart.

"It's up to the woman," Lucinda gently reprimanded her niece.

Lucinda's physician referred Estelle to a gynecologist. He fit her for a diaphragm. Her woes became even lighter during the early sixties when she segued into an oral contraceptive.

Gradually, Estelle discovered many troubling things about Mason Ingram. In particular, he didn't read well. When she offered to help him, he became almost angry. She found it puzzling that a man with such potential and keen perception about many things could be so shortsighted about something so fundamentally important. He shared very little about his family background. She recalled Doretha suggesting that she discourage Mason Ingram and move on. Her friend had no way of knowing the advice had come too late. Uncle C. J., now a church deacon, had a favorite expression, "*bass ackwards*," cleverly phrased for his present lifestyle. Thinking back on the many conversations she'd had with Aunt Lucinda made her smile. She often referred to her husband as "that man of mine." His past was the reason they lived so well in the present.

Their two children were getting older; they needed a bigger place. Clarissa relinquished her crib for her seven-month-old brother that had outgrown his bassinette. Little Clarissa was becoming known as Clare. (Jeffrey would grow up calling her Rissie.) She presently slept on a folding bed in the living room between the wall and sofa to prevent her from falling to the floor. Still, they had not begun to save for a house. Estelle contacted the real estate office, which confirmed there were two-bedroom apartments available. She suggested acquiring one of those apartments, then save toward owning a home! The idea of opposite sex siblings sharing the same bedroom was unacceptable.

One Saturday C. J. paid them a surprise visit. Feeling extreme intimidation, Mason was always in his best behavior whenever her uncle stopped by which secretly amused Estelle. She admired her uncle. His persona indicated a past quite different from his present life, which included a deacon at his church.

Much to Mason's surprise, her uncle had come specifically to discuss a proposition with him. They sat facing each other on the living room sofa.

Booker and Bobbi were buying a house, C. J. explained. The second-floor apartment, identical to his first-floor flat—three bedrooms and one and one-half baths—was becoming vacant. He was offering it to Mason and his niece. He quoted a price to Mason and asked whether he found it reasonable. Mason replied that he did.

A while back, Mason had put in for the evening shift at the mill, which paid the night differential. Request granted; he would begin the following week. Now he could be absent evenings without needing an excuse, and the extra money would not be missed. He could recapture some of his past freedom. He missed being able to occasionally unwind by stopping off to have a drink with some of the guys from the mill before coming home. Of course, he never told Estelle that he, not the mill, had initiated this change in his schedule.

The following Monday there was a knock on the door. When Estelle answered the door, there stood C. J. Laughing at the surprised expression on her face. He kissed her on the cheek and entered the small apartment.

"Don't look so surprised," he said in a hushed voice. "I knew the children would be asleep." He paused and added jokingly, "It's not your bedtime too, is it?"

"No." She laughed.

They sat on the sofa in the small apartment talking softly so as not to disturb the children.

"So, here's the deal, doll," he said with a wink. "Don't look so surprised. You know me. I always have more up my sleeve than just my arm." He paused. "We are going to build you a nest egg, okay? I am going to take the money from that husband of yours and open an account for you." He held up his hand. "Let me finish. Lu and I have discussed this thoroughly. We're not charging you rent, but instead establishing a savings account for you and the children, okay?"

"Uncle C. J.," she began in protest, "we should pay something."

"Don't go looking a gift horse in the mouth," he advised with mild firmness. "Just help yourself get ahead so that if anything happens, you can take care of yourself. You got these two little ones to think about."

Privately, C. J. still felt partially responsible for what he considered his niece's stumble. Although he was aware that Estelle was an adult and therefore responsible, he had told Lucinda more than once that he should have intervened. He felt the least he could do was favorably act on his regret.

One discussion about it with Lucinda had resulted in one of his rare outbursts of anger. He should have intervened, he shouted, and kept her from marrying that son of a bitch. He had immediately apologized to his wife, who simply turned away in amusement.

⁋

A family of her own, Estelle Beckford Ingram was back on South Parkway. She had always liked the building and the street. The positive arrangement that lacked nothing but ownership.

Like clockwork, the account was opened. As agreed, all bank statements were addressed to C. J. and Lucinda Owens; monthly enclosed statements bore the name of Estelle Beckford Ingram. Wisely, nothing came directly to Estelle.

"I don't want to have to hurt that man," C. J. had said with a sardonic laugh.

Estelle knew beyond any doubt that Uncle C. J. would never have any problems with her husband. She continued to find it amusing that Mason was so intimidated by her uncle.

Lucinda insisted on keeping the children, but adamant about accepting no money. This made it easier for Estelle to work without the little ones having to leave the building in the mornings. She too felt that something should have been said about her dating Mason. Humbled by the generosity of them both, Estelle marveled, *I am surrounded by angels.* Daily she thanked God for her good fortune. She no longer had to daily deposit the children with outsiders or worry about them during work hours. The bonus was extra minutes of needed early morning rest.

When not purchasing things for their flat, the children, or personal necessities and limited frivolities, she periodically added what would have been the babysitting money to the windfall. From time to time, Estelle expressed her appreciation to her aunt and uncle in the form of gifts. On weekends, she insisted on running errands for Aunt Lu, now moderately arthritic.

Lucinda, still without grandchildren of her own, fussed over Clare and Jeffrey. She spoiled them incessantly with baked cakes and cookies, made certain they had books and toys. Some had belonged to Booker as a youngster.

Often during nice weather, Estelle and Ned would spend enjoyable and uneventful evenings in the backyard with Uncle C. J. and Lucinda while Clarissa and Jeffrey played. Celeste, Ned's girlfriend, often joined them. Estelle teased him about getting serious. She observed that he had stopped dating anyone else, unaware that Celeste had been in the mix since before her wedding to Mason. With pride in his academic progress, Ned expressed pride in becoming a college graduate within the year. Estelle could not help feeling more than mildly envious. The important factor: choices. Jennifer Travis Beckford had constantly spoken to them both of life's choices. Was it that life demanded your attention to the slip-ups or were they highlighted for future reference?

Meanwhile, Mason was feeling boxed in on all sides. People were either smarter, more educated or both. He had never finished grade school severely limiting his childhood. Laboring in the fields from the age of nine, he had helped his father on that small Mississippi dirt farm. Both he and his brothers saved themselves from becoming third-generation sharecroppers by fleeing to Chicago.

Estelle was familiar with sharecroppers because for years they had worked off and on for her father. Instead of scheming and imposing blatantly unfair treatment, her generous father had always been mindful of their struggles. Often, he allowed at least one or two a couple of acres to work and from their profits subtracted only what was fair. He was always cognizant of the shenanigans that took place on other farms at the hands of whites. Once Jennifer revealed to her children that she too had come from a long line of sharecroppers. placing emphasis on the fact that it wasn't the start of the journey, but its end.

As Estelle considered her husband's bitterness, she determined it to be the crutch that caused him to hobble mentally. Mason's father had needed his oldest son's full support on the farm. Poor health dictated no other alternative. Mason's admission of only a sixth-grade education, sporadically snatched here and there, turned out to be even less. Finally, he revealed to his wife that "I was out of school a lot more than in." Once he approached twelve years of age, academic pursuits were totally discarded. At age sixteen, to escape a life of thankless, backbreaking toil, he then fled to Chicago. As he related all this to her, she saw this as the beauty of a teenager who had struck out on his own and survived. When she said this aloud, he shut down and never told her what he had done before obtaining the job in the mill, except that he was a World War II veteran. She scolded herself for speaking up too quickly, canceling a more in-depth view into his past. Although she knew her positive appraisal of the situation was the very thing he did not want to hear, she refused to support his self-pity.

Two beautiful children allowed her to reconcile her regret over marrying Mason, a bitter, rigid man. She couldn't say where it all would end. She wrote in a letter to her mother, for the sake of the children, she would try to make the best of it. She had grown up with a father and would try not to deprive her son and daughter of the same. Though she still held a certain attraction to Mason, it could not be equated with love. If she could get past that barrier of negativity, perhaps they could build a life together. Admittedly, a substantial segment of his character was less than likable.

Periodically when the children were out of the house, Estelle would attempt to have a discussion with their father about becoming more diplomatic. One time she started with a tactful but more forceful comment about his method of conveying a message, any message.

"Mason, you need to temper your truths with something positive," Estelle said quietly, "especially for Jeffrey's sake. Your son is going to become a man and needs to be left room to maneuver, to manipulate the system. Why do you insist on leaving him no choice whatsoever with his back against the wall?"

"Stelle," he answered, "his back *is* against the wall. He's gonna be a black man, 'n' there's no way 'round it."

"Education becomes the key—"

"Educated like you, huh?" he replied derisively. "You work at the post office, woman."

She was incensed to the point of deliberately sleeping on the couch for two weeks, during which time there was very little conversation between them. Finally, Mason succumbed and offered a genuine apology.

Nevertheless, instead of establishing a meaningful relationship with his son, Mason substituted macho toys like GI Joe and toy guns. Although tolerant, Estelle suggested educational toys such as Erector Sets and games to stimulate the thought process. Soon Jeffrey would be seven years old. Mason became livid whenever Estelle offered these suggestions or personally took the initiative to provide the necessary stimuli for their son. *You're ashamed because you cannot read well*, she thought, *and therefore cannot follow the instructions or even decipher the pictures provided. Mason*, she wanted to say, *do what's necessary for your son's sake.* He became sullen if she asked Ned to provide help for Jeffrey. However, he knew if he pushed, the stubbornness of the woman he'd married could match his.

"Since you will not allow me to help you, Mason," Estelle quietly suggested one day, "take a few classes so that you learn to read well."

"Where'd that come from?" he answered defensively.

"Help yourself, Mason," she replied. "The only wrong about not knowing is not correcting it. All of us are lacking in something, but knowledge is the equalizer for most shortcomings. It nourishes the soul. Aside from allowing a person to gain financial security, it makes a person feel good about him- or herself. Knowledge," she said, "is carried into the grave. Pride is a demon, Mason. It is ego, what the reverend calls Easing God Out. You're a veteran and could have gone to school under the GI Bill. One less suit, one less silk tie, one less pair of expensive shoes would have allowed you to feel less inadequate."

"I pulled you, okay?" A triumphant reply.

Finally, she was beginning to understand the psyche of the man she married. He was more correct than she cared to admit that one slip-up had cost her. Because of his lack of education, he focused on improving the external and not the internal self. Nevertheless, his words stung. Inwardly she admitted that she had yielded to carnal temptation. What did that say about her? Doretha simply laughed when she truthfully expressed feelings of self-reproach. In fact, amused, she had dismissed them.

"You never had sex before, Estelle. You were an adult, but green, a twenty-one-year-old virgin. The body decided it wanted to be turned on, but the heart reneged. When I told you to let him move on, that is exactly what I was referring to. I should have been more explicit a little sooner." She laughed. "Don't look so surprised. Had I known you as well as I do now, I would have told you—with the necessary precautions, of course—to sleep with the guy, then move on. Obviously, you were not promiscuous. It did not take rocket science to figure out that the man, the *wrong* man, wanted you and that you wanted him—at least physically. What you needed was a fling, that's all. Plain and simple." Again, her friend laughed. "Perhaps you needed just one so that in the future you would be less naïve. The man took you to all the right places—the Trianon, McKee's, the Parkway Ballroom—you name it! He was out of nice money just to keep you interested. Still, in all, had you gotten him out of your system, you and I would have been lockstep, cap and gown, together." She paused. "Don't think for one minute that Mason doesn't know it." Doretha instantly read Estelle's expression. "Oh no! There would have been no repercussions, that is for certain. Don't forget who your uncle is, okay?"

Doretha had visited Estelle at her aunt and uncle's flat more than a few times; she liked them immensely. Doretha's astute observation presently drew laughter from them both.

Estelle was curious. "How many flings did you have before marriage?"

Doretha held up two fingers. "And then I met Miles and got married. By then I had finished my undergrad. I met Miles in grad school. As a matter of fact, his mind is what I love most."

The conversation momentarily made Estelle's spirits drop. Her thoughts drifted to "what if," a futile question. Quickly she dismissed it.

Estelle had attended their wedding. Miles was a nerd and not extremely attractive. He was drawn to Doretha's perky prettiness and wit, and the two were captivated with each other enough to exchange marriage vows. They lived in a lovely home on the far south side with three great children. He was a chemist, and the only black Estelle knew of employed by a pharmaceutical. She and Doretha remained good friends. Doretha always said: "A step up is not a step away."

"Estelle. Don't look so sad," she said consolingly more than once, offering genuine encouragement. "Under the circumstances, marriage was the right decision. All children need their father. Don't worry, you will finish school. It's in your DNA," she finished cheerfully.

Still, Estelle hated Mason's disdain for education even if it hid the deeper problem of doubts about measuring up. His additional argument was that education by no means led to escaping what he labeled "the black life" in the United States. Besides, he often argued that only sissies kept their head in books, though she knew this point of view merely massaged feelings of inadequacy. Nevertheless, she was still perturbed by his attitude. Jeffrey's personality already exhibited a trace of willfulness. Additionally, like most youth, he was impressionable. It was "Dad said this" or "Dad said that." Sometimes she ignored the remarks. At other times she tactfully snuffed out the ideas as potentially harmful.

Mason challenged her at the table one evening as they were finishing dinner. Thankfully, the children had already eaten, completed their homework, and gone to bed. He begrudgingly acknowledged that she was much more educated than he was, but still cleaning up behind white folks before she started tossing mail. *Tossing mail,* she thought. His statements, reflections of his own personal feelings of incompetence, were never meant to uplift.

Estelle abhorred arguments. She said nothing else. However, his remark did motivate her to take another post office exam. In 1959, after being on the list for quite some time, she moved up. Years later she would pinpoint that incident as the initial wedge between them. As the years passed, the divide would significantly widen. Other than the fact that he was a good provider, the most prominent reason they remained together was the children, especially Jeffrey. She believed that every son needed his father. She willed herself not to evaluate her life according to what-ifs or what could have been. The druthers, as Doretha called them. The most positive benefit in personal acknowledgment of negatives in her personal history was as a future reference for improvement.

# Chapter Seven

Their marriage chugged along like a slow locomotive. With the accumulation of money in the bank, Estelle no longer talked about purchasing a home. She privately perused the statements monthly in the flat of her aunt and uncle. The statements further fortified her confidence, nudging away the nagging guilt about Mason's total unawareness. In fact, the financial increases strengthened her; she was finding her voice.

It was Saturday and a beautiful summer evening in July. The children were still outside playing with their neighborhood friends, as they often did until almost dusk. Estelle decided this was an ideal time for the much-needed talk with her husband.

"Everyone has an inner spirit, Mason. You are simply suffocating the spirit of your son. He needs to know life can be good if he chooses to aim high. Born black is no excuse."

"Like you did?" he asked directly, with a tinge of sarcasm. Unaware of the statement being a direct reflection on himself.

"No, not like me, Mason," she replied angrily. "I didn't reach my goal because I married you to give our daughter a name. Not quitting while I was ahead, I still attempted to make a go of it. I gave you a son deserving more attention from his father than he's getting."

The silence thundered. In response to the mounting awkwardness, Estelle incoherently mumbled about the need to wash the dishes and sweep up, exiting the room.

Standing at the sink washing dishes, she listened as the laughter of the other neighborhood children combined with the familiar voices of Clare and Jeffrey filtered through the open windows. Being reminded of why she had not completed her education always aroused mixed feelings, which most of the time she managed to control. Thoughts of how she usually held her tongue now surfaced to cause her deep, penetrating anxiety. *I will not apologize*, she vowed adamantly, *not this time,* wrestling with the idea of bedtime and having to share that space. She vowed tonight she would not capitulate as always, accepting directness absent of foreplay. *Not tonight*, she thought. Her thoughts returned to how much Jeffrey needed his father. Except for Calvin, born as a slave, none of the Beckford men had grown up without their father. Internally, she was almost screaming. Again, in anger, she recklessly dared to revisit the juncture in her life which delivered her to this space with this man and two children. The "trick of the enemy" had taken charge. Immediately that phrase invoked an amused smile' That term, "the trick of the enemy," was one of Jennifer Travis Beckford's favorites.

She thought of Doretha. She now taught fourth grade! She had completed her master's degree in education even though she had a husband and three children! They two were so suited to each other. The key factor was Miles's unwavering and unselfish support. They were what her preacher often described as "equally yoked."

What was it her mother had constantly stressed? "Be careful who you allow to father your children, for their sake as well as your own." But despite all else, she loved her children, wanted the best for them. At this time, she dared not concern herself with that fundamental truth.

"Jeffrey," she often said in defense of Mason, "your father has had a hard time. He assesses life differently. He's bitter, that's all." *As many black men justifiably are*, she thought silently.

Lost in thought, her back stiff, she finished washing the dishes. She heard footsteps approaching the kitchen. Suddenly he was behind her, grabbing her by the shoulders, almost causing her to drop the plate she was drying. He whirled her around to face him.

"Think it through, Mason," she said, and for once her anger matched his. "Hit me, and we are finished. I mean it, so think it through very carefully. You're always ready to lash out. Always combative. Be so very careful."

He released her and backed away. At that moment C. J.'s presence directly downstairs didn't enter the equation for her. However, she was certain it did for Mason. In a moment of desperation, she wished he would strike her to propel into motion what perhaps might be the best result. The recklessness soon ebbed and died away. The quiet storm remained.

"I'm goin' out," he said roughly.

"That is a good thing." She measured her furious reply as her eyes, steady and unwavering, met his.

He seemed shocked, in disbelief. Shortly thereafter he swiftly sidestepped his children in the doorway as they were coming in.

"See you later," he said to them both as he hurried out, not waiting for a response.

Later that evening, after the children were in bed, with Mason still absent, Estelle sat in the living room taking mental inventory of the positive qualities of the man. He was very clean. She never had to pick up after him. He always wore nice colognes and was impeccably dressed. No, he couldn't afford to buy as many clothes as before because of familial obligations, but he never wore work clothes as street wear; he changed into them on the job, retaining a week's supply at work with alternates at the laundry. *Only concerned about the outer self*, she thought. *He should turn his attention inward. A lot could be accomplished.*

Because he now worked the evening shift, he ate a good meal before leaving home and carried an evening snack. From the very beginning, because she desired and needed to work, hiring and paying a babysitter for Clare and Jeffrey and getting them to and from the sitter had always been Estelle's responsibility, though the need was thankfully short-lived.

His actions had spoken loud and clear. Suddenly it was as bright as a neon sign, and she got it! Mason Ingram was still attempting to live the life of a single man even though he had a family; he wanted to have his cake and eat it too. However, she had always known that he did not regret marrying her.

Not a television enthusiast, he often listened to the radio and then left it on while away from the apartment. For a long time, whenever she opened the door to the apartment and heard the radio, Estelle assumed that he was inside. After experiencing so many of his absences, she was surprised whenever she did find him there.

Mason was not as talkative as when they were dating. He now kept a hidden agenda. Even when she asked, he seldom talked about his job or discussed what he did at the apartment whenever she and the children were away. Every day, he left for work before she arrived home, even though his shift did not start until four. That gave him ample free time before his work hours began. On weekends, whenever he left and then returned to find her and the children there, he was cordial. Never offering an account of where he had been, only inquiring about dinner instead. He was never willing to help with any household chores except taking out the trash. He was not handy around the house as Uncle C. J. was for Aunt Lu or as Ned for Celeste. Most of all, he seldom showed affection toward Clarissa or Jeffrey. She could understand to a certain degree his not bonding with his daughter, but not bonding with his son was less comprehensible or acceptable. She wanted him to bond with both, but particularly Jeffrey.

Jeffrey's best friend was Noah Daniels; He and Noah had connected from the very beginning during their days in kindergarten. As they grew older, they often studied together, exchanged books, and spent some of their weekends together. So, one Saturday, with Estelle's permission, Noah's parents took Jeffrey along with Noah and his two sisters to the Field Museum. The following Saturday, they invited him along again when they went to the Shedd Aquarium. Jeffrey had such a grand time that he talked about it for weeks. It piqued his interest in finding his own niche in life.

Mason did not like Noah and made remarks about how he always had books with him. Obviously, he was one of the better students. Mason's input became even more ludicrous when he stated that sissies and pansies kept their heads in books.

Jeffrey, totally dumbfounded by such a statement, reacted with confusion and anger. Noah and the newest inclusion, Dudley, were the brightest and nicest. Jeffrey was honored that they had chosen him for their friend. They were his detour from what had been a road to nowhere. Of course, some of the other less scholarly boys poked fun, labelling them stuck-up. Noah had been taught by his father that "gray matter matters." He was a high school math teacher working on his doctorate. Noah had to hit the books and stay a cut above the curve, as he put it, by learning as much as possible. Noah's mother worked for the Internal Revenue Service.

One weekend, Noah and Dudley came to the house; Mason answered the door and turned them away instead of inviting them in to wait on Jeffrey. He would be back momentarily. When Clare pointed out his action, he told her to stay out of it. Her only regret was that her mother was not within hearing range. It was this incident that caused her to begin seeing her father in a much different light.

There was never much conversation between Clare and her father, mostly because she wanted to discuss things he was unwilling to talk about—what his parents were like; why his brothers and sister never visited even though they lived in the same city; why there were only family pictures of the Beckford family and none of his. Of late, conversation between them had become minimal because Clare was at a loss regarding what to ask next. Every so often, Estelle would see her stealing stares at her father and looking away before he became aware.

Estelle decided Jeffrey needed a challenge. After all, he was eight years old. When he opened the bag and saw a box with a picture of a plane on it, she explained that he would have to assemble it himself. The picture on the front of the box displayed the completed model. Her intent was to promote mind stimulation in conjunction with gross motor skills.

"That ain't gonna help him build a plane," Mason argued.

"Of course not, Mason," she said quietly, "but he needs such mind stimulation. It should have started even before now." Jeffrey was getting older. She didn't fully elaborate on her reasoning for fear of creating discord in the presence of the children.

"When could he ever build a plane in this country, woman? During World War II, they didn't even want black men to fly planes."

It was now 1962, and the war had been over for seventeen years.

"But they did finally let them, Mason," she rebutted impatiently, thinking of the Tuskegee airmen, "even if it was in a segregated squadron."

That was Mason: negative, irritable, unchanging. Without a reasonable comeback, he became sullen, offering no immediate answer. In fact, his response was to leave the house. "Win the argument or become absent for a while" was his new approach since she had found her voice.

She continued to be baffled by her husband's knowledge (so out of character) on many subjects. Sure, he had mulled over self-improvement and thought about going back to school to read better, to improve himself. It was a steep, mountainous climb. Once he edgily discussed this with a mill buddy while they were having an after-work drink at a bar. His buddy offered a practical solution: go back to school, learn to read better, but Mason replied that it was too hard.

This drew a confused frown from his buddy, who promptly replied, with irritation, "Okay then. Let your wife handle it."

Uncomfortable with the answer, Mason never again approached the subject with anyone.

One Saturday afternoon Estelle felt the urgent need to discuss the matter. Jeffrey would soon be nine and time was becoming a crucial factor. After a certain point, it would be next to impossible to keep the communication gap from growing beyond repair. In any kind of relationship, communication was always the key factor. She flashed back to the dynamic that had existed between her father and his oldest son, Nathan. She often wondered why they never actually talked to each other. Her father's firstborn. She suspected something irreparable must have happened long before she was born. She had never given it much thought until just now. She recalled interaction between them being guarded, curt, nonflowing. Growing up, she had been incapable of analyzing the problem. However, her current frame of reference brought new objectivity. She could now define it. Being the youngest of all her siblings and the only girl had placed her even farther out of the loop than Ned, the youngest male sibling. She wanted to deal with the issue in her own family while it was fresh in her brain. She entered the apartment ready to have that discussion.

This was one of the many times she came into the apartment from running errands to find her husband absent and, as usual, the radio playing. *Another missed opportunity*, she thought. There she was home alone. To the kitchen on this sunny Saturday afternoon to prepare dinner. It was her weekend off! That meant a great dinner with everything freshly prepared.

Clare was at a matinee movie with her friend Nadine, accompanied by Nadine's mother. Jeffrey had been close to ecstatic when his uncle Ned walked in impromptu earlier in the day and said, "Okay, young guy, get your coat and let's go." Ned had slipped Estelle a wink as he said: "We're going to hang out. This had Jeffrey smiling all the way out the door. Her brother had mentioned something about Celeste and their daughter, Druscilla, having an all-day affair at the beauty shop. Now that Ned had written his thesis. He was about to obtain his MBA. Almost there, on cruise control.

It was 1963. The Civil Rights struggle daily unfolded on television, visiting America. Mason deplored this ongoing turmoil in the South. Cameras documented blacks demonstrating in the streets. Birmingham, Alabama. Under the instruction of Bull Connor, even child demonstrators, being assaulted—water hoses, billy clubs, police dogs. Mason never left the North out of the equation.

"These bastards up here are evil too." Mason never allowed anyone to forget. "There are places in this city just as bad as Miss'ippi." He paused. "Speakin' of Miss'ippi, Emmett Till was only fo'teen," he told nine-year-old Jeffrey, "when he was took from his relatives' home 'n' lynched. That was in 1955. You was nothin' but a baby."

"Why?" asked Jeffrey.

"Claimed he whistled at some white woman. Can ya believe it? Only fo'teen," he repeated.

Estelle felt a momentary chill as the past came hurling forward bringing Bo center stage. Forcing away those thoughts, she silently exited the living room to check on the cornbread for the evening dinner.

"It's the black life," Mason concluded, "no matter where you go."

In retrospect, Jeffrey would assess that era as one in which the North gleefully reported on those numerous incidents that they themselves were guilty of in various ways. In particular, he remained disturbed with history books omitting black achievement. Jeffrey loved the big screen but despised Hollywood's obsession with relegating black actors to demeaning roles of either buffoonery or subservience. Also disturbing was Mason's comments about black life even though they were mostly justified.

The more inquisitive Jeffrey became, the more alienated Mason felt, although he was too stubborn to admit it. This evolution in Jeffrey meant that Mason was being left behind, imprisoned in his own ignorance. The key to unlocking the cell and becoming a free man was to be willing to accept assistance from his wife or stop sleeping late and take classes during the day. His ego wouldn't allow him to let her in, and he lacked the motivation to seek outside help.

During that year there was a small exodus of families purchasing homes farther south, including Noah and Dudley's families. Their departure created a sudden intellectual void in the life of young Jeffrey. The three of them, with periodic input from a few other classmates, had posed as a united front against the bullies and bad influences at their school. Other students were scholarly too, but most were not in his age group.

The trio—Dudley, Noah, and Jeffrey— made a pact to keep in touch. It lasted for a while. They got together on weekends, and occasionally the parents of Dudley or Noah would invite Jeffrey over. Even though Mason did not approve, Estelle overruled him. After these arguments, he would sulk for a few hours and then angrily leave the house. Estelle relished the few hours of peace without his negative input during any given conversation.

The micro-fraternity would study together or hang out at the home of either Noah or Dudley. Jeffrey never invited them to his home because he considered the setting all wrong. (He was beginning to find some of his father's mannerisms and comments embarrassing.) Gradually, Noah and Dudley both found new interests and new friends. The three of them still telephoned each other, but substantial changes took place. Jeffrey felt the loss since he was the one left behind. For some time, he attempted to maintain relationships with both young men. However, whenever he telephoned them, there was only limited conversation, especially with Noah. At the insistence of his father, Noah was now enrolled in private school. This meant additional homework and less spare time.

With Noah and Dudley no longer at his school Jeffrey was now in the fourth grade. He still sought knowledge, but not as forcefully as in the past. Equally intelligent and motivated classmates are there "if you seek them out," Ms. Ballenger, Jeffrey's fourth-grade teacher suggested. The ones he chose seemed to have their circle of friends and were less willing to include him.

His grades were slipping. A segment of his classmates—the troublemakers at school—and the negative sessions with Mason were beginning to contaminate his will to learn. His resistance to all the negativity was beginning to lower.

Ms. Ballinger informed Jeffrey that excellence was not the beaten path. Choose the road less traveled even without the intellectual support previously provided by both Noah and Dudley. Yes, even though he would receive ridicule from some of the unmotivated students, he needed to recognize this as their way of stroking their self-esteem. She stayed away from targeting certain students but told him in general terms that there were students unwilling to cultivate the skills needed to accomplish academic success. She volunteered as much support as possible for as long as she remained his teacher. She tactfully told him he needed to turn away from negativity wherever he found it. She knew that was becoming a difficult task if it resided where you lived. She had taught school for a long time and recognized all the signs.

He was one of the students she had given a booklist for extra reading. Among the authors were James Baldwin, Ralph Ellison, and Charles Dickens. His first selection was Dickens's *A Tale of Two Cities*.

To steer clear of Mason's ridicule, Jeffrey read the book only during the week while his father was at work. At first, he was unenthusiastic, but as he began to turn the pages, he became intrigued and mentally crept inside that fantastic book, dwelling there, page after page. When he orally reviewed what he had read, Ms. Ballenger expressed her pleasure. Next, he read Ralph Ellison's *Invisible Man* and gave an oral report. Aside from the book's maturity, Ms. Ballenger wished she had omitted it from the list because Jeffrey mentioned his father a couple of times while critiquing Ellison's powerful narrative. Certain passages supported his father's point of view regarding black people within American society. Still, she knew he was a bright student with great potential. She hoped he would not allow Ellison's overall objective to negatively slant his young mind. For certain students, she often wished she could keep a constant vigil.

These days, Jeffrey now went to the library alone or with one nice young man named David. He seemed to be suppressing his brainy side for fear of others poking fun, particularly his speech. David used very good English.

☙

How long had it been since Jeffrey had heard from Noah? Three months maybe, or perhaps longer? His friend was so excited when he called that he was close to breathlessness. Noah's father had not long ago completed his dissertation and received his doctorate from the University of Chicago. He had submitted his résumé to institutions on the East Coast and West Coast and was now accepted in the mathematics department at a university in the Los Angeles area. They were moving there over the summer so that the family could become acclimated before school began in the fall. Beside himself with delight, Noah was calling to say good-bye with a promise to stay in touch. They said their "goodbyes" and hung up. Immediately there was another telephone call. Jeffrey picked up, and Noah exclaimed that he had forgotten to invite him over to spend the next weekend; he said that he had also telephoned Dudley so that the three of them could get together for a farewell party.

Noah's mother intercepted the telephone conversation between the two youngsters, pleasantly asking to speak to Estelle, and the two mothers exchanged pleasantries as Jeffrey listened intently, following the gist of the conversation. Estelle graciously gave consent for her son to join the festivities.

Somehow this news lowered Jeffrey's future expectations. He was glad for Noah but sorry for himself. Noah was leaving for the West Coast, which for Jeffrey represented the final bell.

Estelle could not recall Jeffrey crying since he was a toddler. Embarrassed by his own emotions, he went to his room and softly closed the door. When she quietly tapped, he did not answer. Respectful of his privacy, she waited for an hour or so and tried again and this time was invited in. The devastated look on his face stirred in her a very deep sadness.

"Jeffrey," she said quietly, "go to the party, sweetheart. It will probably be a lot of fun."

"It just means I'm staying here, and he is moving even farther away."

"But sometimes friendship doesn't know distance or time and endures regardless of all circumstances," replied his mother. "Life always presents challenges, Jeffrey, but the way we approach them is what matters. You don't know what can happen. The two of you can correspond and keep in touch that way, periodically call each other, and travel to see each other as well."

He sat up on the side of his bed but did not respond right away. He was quiet for a long time. "I should go, huh?"

"Yes," she said and smiled encouragingly. "You three were very good friends. Just think, Dudley will still be in town, and the two of you can still get together."

Jeffrey did not answer. Noah had been the glue that held the threesome together.

The weekend farewell party came and fled quickly into Sunday evening, to be remembered as enjoyable. Noah's father drove Jeffrey home and waited in the car as Noah came in with Jeffrey to extend his good-bye to the family. There was only a slight decrease in his level of excitement. Estelle was happy for Noah as he explained that their departure was to take place in the middle of the week. The moving van was already traveling ahead making other stops along the way. His father had decided to drive so that the family could see some of the country; their arrival was scheduled to coincide with the delivery of their furniture to the new address.

Estelle smiled, recognizing through Noah's phrasing that he was repeating his father's words.

Following his friend's departure, a somber calm that equaled Jeffrey's mood enveloped the apartment. Slowly he unpacked his overnight bag.

"So," Estelle pressed inquisitively, "did you have a good time?"

"It was nice," he answered, leaving the room with clothes for the hamper. Upon his return, he shook his head with a defeated expression.

"Jeffrey, what is it?"

"I don't know," he said dismally. There was a long pause before he finally spoke again as if sorting his thoughts. "Why do you think some people have so much more in life than others?" He stored his overnight bag in the closet and sat beside his mother on his bed. "What I mean is why do you think some people are rich, others are poor, some are educated, and others are uneducated?"

"Jeffrey," she explained kindly, "as for education, that's a choice, an individual choice." She sighed thoughtfully. "Many people inherit wealth—the Kennedys, the Rockefellers, the Carnegies, the Hiltons, just to name a few." She paused. "The wealth," she continued, "began with a family member that paid the price to provide a legacy—the inheritance of money and power—for their descendants."

"But my ancestors were once slaves, right?"

"Yes," she said, "you're right." She paused. "The country was founded under those conditions and other complicated circumstances," she continued slowly.

Her mind drifted to many of the conditions and cruelties that had been inflicted on black people—the lynchings, and the Black Codes that had worsened under Jim Crow. She deliberately omitted that white people, no matter what their status, always inherited privilege and entitlement because they were members of the Caucasian race. All were part of the European melting pot.

"But what does that mean?" he asked, resuming their discussion.

"It means the scale is not balanced, that you have to run faster and be smarter, but you can also achieve success."

"I have to run faster because I'm black," he said, "right?"

"To a certain extent, Jeffrey," she said. "But that doesn't mean that you can't achieve success." She paused. "But you need to hit the books, young man, and work hard."

"Mom," he said, "I read white people's books all the time, and they don't mention anything about black people doing anything. I read the books you and Ned give me too, and there are a lot of things we have done." He paused. "Because of Charles Drew, there are blood banks all over this country, but in school we don't learn about that. If you don't get what is in those books at school about white people, you fail." He paused. "It's not right. It's not fair."

"Jeffrey," warned his mother, "that means you need to acquire two sets of knowledge, one inside the classroom and one on your own."

"Why?" he exclaimed in exasperation.

"Because, young man, you will be twice as smart. You need good grades to be able to go to college."

Jeffrey sat on the side of his bed for a long time, pensive. He seemed far away for a moment. He looked at her as she continued to sit beside him, smiled, and then looked away. "Life is not fair, is it?" he said.

"In what way?" she asked, probing his thought process.

"Why should I have to work harder than anybody else?"

"Working hard," she said firmly, "translates to good grades and moving upward in life."

He did not speak for a very long time. Patiently she sat with him, sharing his silence. As she waited, she became briefly lost in thoughts of her own. There was so much she wanted for her children. What if she had postponed marriage? Quickly she put aside that question.

"Mom," he said, having sorted out what he wanted to say, "What made you marry Dad?"

"Two individuals who met," she answered slowly, "were attracted to each other enough to marry."

"But did you *love* Dad?"

"Yes," she said. "Why do you ask?"

"I don't know. It just seems that you and Dad never talk and laugh with each other and have fun." She sensed that he wanted to add something else but stopped short of doing so. "Dudley's parents are always talking to each other," he continued. Then he paused and laughed. "Noah's parents like to joke around. One time I saw him pat her on the behind, but I don't think he knew I saw it. They were in the kitchen, and I was taking my empty glass to the sink."

*A very intelligent, aware young man*, she thought. The entanglement of her marriage to Mason Ingram involved two young people who needed both their parents, even without the love that should exist between two individuals before they have offspring. For the first time she willed herself against regretting her marriage to Mason Ingram. Though she sometimes wished that she had sent him on his way before the birth of Clarissa Lucinda, that very act would have determined that Clarissa did not have the name of her father and canceled Jeffrey. And so, no, she couldn't wish for that because she loved her children equally—differently yet equally.

૭૭

It was a few months later that the earth shifted and jolted Estelle to attention. Caught up in the rigors of everyday living, she had recently failed to notice changes on the first floor involving her extended family. Despite still visiting Aunt Lu almost daily, she had not noticed subtle indications of the bigger picture until Clare mentioned what was happening with Aunt Lu. It was more than just her arthritis. These days Jeffrey and Clare, nine and ten, respectively, required only Aunt Lu's watchful eye until Estelle came for them each day. Sometimes Estelle would stay for an hour or so, and the two would sit at the kitchen table drinking tea and talking while the children finished their homework and slipped in that limited period of television. During the week, once they were inside their own flat, there was very little television. Other times, when Estelle was tired, she would just come in for a brief chat with her aunt, collect the children, and head upstairs. On those days, however, if they needed Uncle Ned to help with any difficult homework, such as math, they would go with their mother to their own flat for a brief visit. Then they returned to Aunt Lu's to wait for Uncle Ned to arrive. When they were finished, Ned would sometimes spend time visiting with his aunt. He still missed living with Aunt Lu for various reasons even though his marriage to Celeste was satisfying.

Clare, a very insightful youngster, began to talk about how Auntie Lu slept a lot nowadays. She told her mother that Uncle C. J. sometimes did all the cleaning and often ordered food for all of them. Estelle knew that C. J. was never one to cook. At the same time, Estelle noticed that these days C. J. was no longer his cheerful self. He had anxiously anticipated his retirement, but now that it was here, there were no signs of contentment. For the last few months, she had been able to tell that he was worried. Concerned as a family member, she inquired about what exactly was going on.

"Lu has cancer," he said. She had always known that C. J. loved Lucinda, but now the depth of his love could be measured by his level of utter despair. He sounded near tears, which frightened her because C. J. was a tough individual. "She has surgery next week," he said almost in a whisper.

"Uncle C. J.," she said softly, and lovingly placed her arm about his shoulders, "she's going to be all right."

Her uncle didn't answer. Instead, he looked away. Never in all his life had he been confronted with anything so potentially devastating. He wanted desperately to force it away. Not all those years of involvement with Policy while dodging the police, sleeping in hiding, and even landing in jail a few times. Never had he experienced such a feeling of defeat and raw fear. This thing he faced now mocked, cornered, and surrounded him. Death had always been its name.

℃

Aunt Lu looked like she was asleep. The small South Side church was filled with people; flowers flanked the casket. Lucinda Allen Owens, a big woman, had lasted exactly one year from the oncologist's diagnosis and on her deathbed weighed slightly over 116 pounds. The bilateral mastectomy followed by a combination of radiation and chemotherapy had failed.

People were viewing the body and then offering their condolences to the bereaved, mainly C. J., Booker, and Jennifer, Lucinda's only sibling. Other more distant relatives were there as well.

Confronting Jennifer were bothersome, nagging thoughts of her refusal to visit the city under more joyful circumstances. It was difficult to suppress thoughts of all the letters Lucinda had written asking her to come. So many missed opportunities to seize more of those joyous occasions ultimately melting away into family albums as smiles, a kiss, or an embrace. Occasions documenting the lives of loved ones that once walked the earth. Still the site of their numerous family gatherings remained in Georgia as Lucinda continued her photographic documentary. Otherwise, there would have been only mental files for those who chose not to forget.

Repeatedly, Jennifer told herself that it was her personal dislike of cities that had kept her away. She remained averse to such a simple compromise after "the days of struggle" for C. J. and Lucinda were a thing of the past. Nevertheless, the Georgia outhouse and all the other inconveniences had never once deterred Lucinda. The disturbing reflections caused Jennifer to weep even more regretfully. She yearned for the return of happier times.

To Jennifer, urban progress created a hostile environment by covering the soil with concrete. God's beautiful living room should be carpeted with grass, enhanced by flowers and various plants. Land grew food and decreased dependency! His umbrellas were the trees, she always said, to shade you from the sun or to provide a breeze to fan you when you were hot or to protect you from the rain. Of course, man-made fans did help, but that solitary relief was only for the individual using it.

To Jennifer, the cold bricks and mortar, labeled progress, took away nature's enveloping warmth. Cities seemed a mass of confusion, with people going to and fro, attempting to make a living that never seemed large enough. Black people who migrated north seeking better opportunities often ended up eking out an existence, occupying tenements or other equally deplorable environments. Even other living things—the squirrels, the birds, even the ants—scampered about as though they did not know what onslaught had taken place to force them to seek livable space wherever they could find it.

Ten-year-old Jeffrey sat quietly between his grandmother and Uncle Ned. From his youthful perspective everything was changing much too fast. Noah was in California, Dudley was predictably no longer communicative unless Jeffrey telephoned him, and he could no longer talk to Auntie Lu. He considered it so unnatural that someone could appear to be sleeping but you couldn't wake them up. He imagined Auntie Lu getting up any minute to bake cookies or instruct him to get ice cream from the freezer. He could envision her rising to render a loving smile to them all.

"Uncle Ned, exactly what is death?"

"Proof that you once lived," his uncle answered slowly and thoughtfully.

Ned was going to miss that beautiful human being. Although he had been married now for over five years, he often stopped by to see her and would miss their long visits.

He wanted to tell his nephew not to feel at a loss because even adults never make the adjustment to the tremendous chasm created by the loss of a loved one. Death was always alien and forever the invader with its uncompromising method of constantly terminating lives. Somehow, he believed this was God's way of making people bond with each other, never allowing anyone to take even a second for granted. Mortality encouraged expressions of love between human beings momentarily, in the present.

"But Uncle Ned, why do people have to die?" Clarissa asked.

"Clare, everything comes with a price. Death is the price for having lived."

She considered it an awful price to pay. Why did God have to make anything die, especially people? Bumstead had died a few years back, but he was a dog. Even though she liked him very much, his death had been more acceptable.

After the interment ceremony, most returned to the church basement for the repast. It was well attended by the acquaintances and good friends the couple had accumulated over the years. There was a significant number of people whom neither C. J. nor Lucinda had seen in ages, as well as buddies from C. J.'s past. He did hear from them periodically. A few were friends from Lucinda's first years in the Windy City. Lending their staunch support to C. J. was that intimate group who, through it all, had maintained a consistent, unbroken connection with the couple.

*He seems lost*, Estelle thought with concern as she observed her uncle. She secretly vowed to look after him. Make sure he functioned as normally as possible. Grieving was hard, especially when you lived alone. She would try her best to keep him from spending too much time in that lonesome flat, grieving, residing with the ghost of Lucinda. She would be everywhere he looked and on whatever he touched. Estelle wished she could invite him to be with them all the time.

Weeks passed; with keen observation, Estelle suspected Booker's concern for his father to be less than sufficient. At first, he regularly visited his father, three or four times per week. Time progressed. The visits were gradually reduced to once on weekends. As requested, she dutifully telephoned her cousin a couple of evenings per week to keep him abreast of how his father was doing. Eventually Booker's weekend visits became pit stops; oddly, Bobbi ceased to come with him. Although they lived in the suburbs, Booker worked in the city. Therefore, Estelle felt he could easily stop by on his way home, as Ned often did.

Mason continued to work the evening shift. Two or three evenings per week Estelle invited her uncle to have dinner with her and the children. He always came, consistently subdued and withdrawn. Disturbingly, as the months passed, her uncle continued exhibiting the same level of grief as Estelle continued to hope for gradual improvement.

Understandably, near the first anniversary of Aunt Lu's death, Uncle C. J. was very sad. Estelle thought that Booker should have been more caring because Lucinda had been his mother. Had he forgotten that fact? That day she had coaxed her uncle to a home-cooked meal.

Much later, the dishes were washed and put away. The children were in bed. This was her weekend off. Thank God for privacy, she thought, so that she could talk to this dear man. The apartment was quiet, the television purposely off as they sat together on the living room sofa.

"Uncle C. J.," she suggested softly, "why don't you take a vacation to the Bahamas or somewhere here in the States? Just get away for a while."

"Estelle, where would I go alone?" He paused. "Before Lu got sick, we had decided to start traveling. First, we were going to take a trip to Florida to see an old buddy of mine." He smiled sadly as he recollected his past life. "He left this town quite a few years before Roe was shot, as if he knew time was not on our side." There was another brief pause. "Lu and I even discussed visiting some of the islands." He shook his head and sighed. "Then about a year and a half into my retirement she started ailing and went to the doctor. We got the news, and well, you know the rest." He wore such a defeated expression.

"But you have friends," Estelle encouraged. "Get with some of them and go out, take trips, do things."

Her uncle offered a sorrowful smile.

☙

Small talk followed the greetings when Cousin Booker dutifully responded to Cousin Estelle's request to stop by. He asked polite questions about the family news—about Clare and Jeffrey, Cousin Ned (whom he seldom saw), Aunt Jen, and all the others in Georgia. She offered him coffee, tea, and then something stronger. He declined all. He seemed in a hurry but did manage to seat himself on the arm of her living room sofa. This much-needed discussion was important, so she managed to conceal her irritation.

"Booker," Estelle said quietly, "I'm worried about your father."

"Why?" he asked calmly.

"He's so alone," she replied. She paused. "Perhaps some weekends you could invite him out to your place?" She paused. "I know you told me to keep an eye on him and give you a weekly report, which I have been doing. Booker, your father is alone. He's lonely."

"Estelle," he responded, "Dad knows he's welcome to visit me at any time. Anytime," he repeated.

"But don't you think it would be nice if the invitation came from you?" She smiled. "What I mean is, extend the invitation…" She trailed off, thought for a moment, and then slowly continued. "I am sure since he is your father, he is always welcome, but perhaps you could come by—don't have him drive out—pick him up on your way home on a Friday. Bring him back before going to work on a Monday morning." She paused again. "It's just a suggestion, Booker."

"Estelle," he answered, "do you realize what time I would have to get up to do that? I'm due at work by 8:00 a.m. I live quite a distance from the city."

*That's by choice*, she thought, but she didn't allow his answer to be a deterrent. She had been very patient. For the last eight months the two of them had skirted around this issue during their weekly telephone conversations.

"Don't you think it would give him less time to mourn, Booker? You mother has been dead for a year, and he's still grieving as though she died yesterday. That's because he spends too much time in that apartment by himself."

Booker didn't answer but just kept sitting on the arm of her sofa, dangling one leg. He appeared mildly annoyed. Finally, he went into his coat pocket to retrieve a cigarette, gesturing to his host for permission, which she granted. Why not? She lived with a human chimney. Booker sighed, momentarily lost in thought. He lit his cigarette.

"I realize that you're not privy to this information," he said. He paused, contemplating whether to continue, then rushed ahead. "When I was growing up, my dad, my *father*, C. J. Owens, was never a dad, a father. A fantastic provider, but never home, okay? Dad was a rough guy, a hustler, a street guy when I was growing up, heavily involved in the Policy racket. The only time I would see him—that's if I wanted to say hello or visit him—was early mornings before he went to bed, and I was getting ready for school. When I returned home from school, he was either still asleep or had started his day." He sat smoking for what seemed a long time. "And I do mean *his* day, which was certain to last all night." Looking lost in thought, a sad expression crossed his face. Quickly he retrieved the ashtray from the end table to tap the long tail of ash from his cigarette.

"But Booker," Estelle said, softly pleading her uncle's case, "he educated you. He gave you a good start in life. You have a college degree. Where would you be if he hadn't given you such a great start?" The reminder was presented as a question although a simple truth. "Don't you think you owe him something for that?"

He sat smoking as though he had revealed too much. Again, Booker was momentarily lost in thought. He looked at his cousin, heaving a weary sigh, and smiled sadly.

"Estelle," he finally replied, "I am doing the best I can." He sighed heavily again, as if burdened. "When my father and I get together, we say very little to each other. It would be the same way wherever, whenever, okay?"

When Booker left, Estelle wept for them both. Life, she thought, was sometimes like a dusty rug stored in the attic, underneath cobwebs to never be disturbed.

Uncle C. J. began to stay to himself more and more, seldom ventured from the house for anything other than a few groceries and his newspapers. Oh, his beloved newspapers! He loved reading them even more than watching the news on television because, he always said, the news was covered better in print. As for his lapses into voluntary seclusion, many times Estelle knocked softly on the door after ringing the bell with no response. She would then go upstairs to her flat, telephoning with persistence until he answered.

"Uncle C. J.," she would often say in her most cheerful tone, "you have to stay on this side, know what I mean?"

"I know, doll," he would say quietly. "Doll" made her smile. It was his favorite expression of endearment. Vivid recall captured the times Uncle C. J. would walk up behind his wife washing dishes or standing at the stove cooking. He stood as close as possible to embrace her, kiss the nape of her neck saying ever so softly, "Hey, doll." An intimate expression of deep love.

He avoided visiting weekends when Mason was there. Such interactions were uneasy for them both, with Uncle C. J. attempting to be cordial and Mason feeling discomfort, never knowing what to say. So, dinner invitations were scheduled for weekday evenings only.

"Uncle C. J.," Estelle would insist, "you must come to dinner. Yes, is the answer."

He would show up casually dressed—he had beautiful casual wear—looking very dapper indeed. Except on Sundays, he never wore a suit and tie, which he described as being "choked up." She would tease and wink, stating truthfully that he was still a sight for sore eyes, and that would make him smile; C. J. was still ruggedly handsome, lean, and clean-shaven.

Fried chicken was regularly on the menu; C. J. had always loved her fried chicken. He loved greens and told her more than once that her mustard and turnip greens came close to duplicating those of his late Lucinda. That made her proud because no one could cook greens like Lucinda. As much as Estelle hated washing them, she would do so on weekends, cook them, withhold a portion for their family meal, freezing the rest to heat up for one of those scheduled occasions with C. J. The entrée was sometimes a beef roast with side dishes of greens and candied yams, always served with cornbread. Occasionally the candied yams would be alternated with potato salad or mashed potatoes and gravy. These times brought C. J. temporary reminiscent cheer of happier days. Inevitably, in solitude, he departed to his lonely flat. Always it was her fervent desire that he arrive at his flat sleepy enough to avoid lonely reflection.

When Mason would venture out on Saturday afternoons with some of his mill buddies, often Estelle would call her uncle and show up at his door with the children in tow. He would greet them all with a broad smile, becoming used to them remaining an integral part of his life. Estelle continued to clean his apartment every weekend. Jeffrey was a precocious youngster with whom Uncle C. J. enjoyed jovial bantering; he loved teasing witty Clare.

C. J. was a neat individual. The flat was never actually dirty, just dusty, never requiring more than an hour to clean, including the one and a half baths. After she vacuumed, dusted, and straightened up, the two of them would have a chat while the children watched TV. By now, she realized he was resolved to everything left undisturbed. Estelle hated his refusal to get rid of his dead wife's clothing. He courted her ghost.

One Saturday, when she had finished cleaning up, C. J. made a request. He was somewhat upbeat, or at least pretending to be. The subject was serious.

"I'm forgetful these days, doll," he said, flashing those beautiful white teeth. "I want you to arrange for your statements to go to a post office box. Okay?"

She was taken aback and mildly protested, as if trying to thwart some unforeseen doom.

"Estelle," he insisted quietly, "I want you and the children to be all right. It's a nice little nest egg for a rainy day, and I want things to be bang-up, okay?"

"Okay," she answered quietly. *Bang-up*, she repeated silently to herself and smiled. Uncle C. J., she thought fondly. There weren't many like him.

"And doll," he said earnestly, "thanks for being such a splendid niece."

She embraced him warmly for a long time, and one quick, tight squeeze for emphasis before she released him. She prayed that he and Booker had mended that fence. When she left his apartment, she felt such deep sorrow for them both.

The very next week, she took care of the mail situation as instructed. From then on, her statements were retrieved from a post office box, then stored them in a metal box at Doretha's home. Doretha had volunteered to keep the statements at her home because Estelle had mentioned her plan to obtain a safe-deposit box, which her friend considered an unnecessary expense. The conspiracy continued as promptly the monthly statement now appeared in her friend's mailbox, decreasing long chats over the phone. There were more personal visits in Doretha's kitchen or at her dining room table over hot tea or a glass of wine.

ℇ

It was Jennifer Beckford's fourth visit to Chicago with Greyhound as her chauffeur. She tried to no avail to rid herself of blame for not visiting Lucinda and C. J. more during happier times. In misery, she watched as her brother-in-law's casket was lowered into the cold earth. The wailing wind chorused the death knell.

Most were walking away. Oblivious to Booker's eyes watching her, Estelle lingered at the grave site for a few quiet moments, praying that the soul of this beautiful man be at rest. His wife stopped him from approaching her, gently coaxing him to return to the black limousine that had brought the family. Somehow the numbing cold did not penetrate as Estelle stood there with the wind whipping the hem of her full-length wool coat. She surmised the stage being set for winter to act as the backdrop for all unpleasantness in the family.

"Mama," said Clare. It was a plea. "It's cold." She was shivering. "Come on, Mama, let's go." She paused; her voice took on a tremor. "Mama, don't cry… Come on, let's go."

Together they left the grave site with Clare gently but firmly holding her mother's arm, as if she needed to be guided away from C. J. Owens's final resting place.

*She will someday understand*, Estelle thought. *In life there are few people that can touch you deep inside, reach your very core. When that happens, it remains with you forever. Good-bye, dear man. I will never forget you no matter how long I live. Please, please rest in peace.*

During this visit, Jennifer shared her granddaughter's bedroom, and they bonded—Jennifer Allen Beckford and Clarissa Lucinda Ingram. Because of this, Jennifer Beckford decided to stay longer than planned, and other than the funeral, it was an enjoyable stay. Not overcoming her past apprehensions but vowing to make more visits to Chicago so that she and her grandchildren could become close. Ned endorsed this as a very good idea.

They sat around the dining room table after dessert on Jennifer's last day. It was Saturday; she was leaving in the morning. Ned had driven in to return Jennifer, who had spent the evening with his family; Druscilla and Celeste had ridden in with them.

The family had touched on many topics. Now the subject was the splintering of their family all over the country. In every nook and cranny, Ned said.

"One day," Ned said, "I am going to find out what makes this family the way it is."

"Please let me know when ya find out," Jennifer said, "'I been tryin' fo' a long time."

"It seems that certain families—sometimes, not always, okay? They gravitate toward other families with the same dysfunctions that exist in their own." He turned toward Jennifer. "Mama, how many times have you visited Chicago?"

"I don't know," she said as she toyed with her napkin, surprised that the inference was directed at her.

"This is your fourth time, Mama," he told her accurately, "only your fourth time! Why is that?"

She sighed heavily as if weighed down. "It's so big 'n'… " She trailed off.

"No," he said. "Uh-uh, that's not it. It goes beyond that. Aunt Lucinda told me she tried to get you to visit Chicago for years. Every time you always had an excuse—even since I've been here."

Ned saw sadness cloud his mother's eyes, relenting momentarily as Celeste's eyes met his. Druscilla was very quiet, exhibiting a slight frown.

"Okay," he continued, sidestepping his initial approach, "let's make a family pact to change this formula. From now on, we are going to visit each other at least every couple of years."

"We could start next year," Estelle said enthusiastically. "We do need to change this scenario, really."

Mason had eaten dinner with the family and managed to ease away. Estelle excused herself momentarily to discover him now in the bedroom changing clothes to go out with his mill buddies. *If just once,* she thought, *he would join in.*

"Estelle," Ned said upon her return, "do we know where any of the younger Beckfords are? The ones near our age?"

She shrugged helplessly. "Last year when we were in Georgia to attend Rue's funeral, I saw a few that I didn't recognize." She smiled sadly. "The next day when I went to a church member's house—where they were staying—they had already left."

❧

The next weekend, after dinner, when Estelle and Ned were visiting his home, he brought up what he thought might have kept Jennifer Beckford away from Chicago all these years. He had given this a lot of thought, never voicing his theory before now.

"I wonder if Mama was ashamed that she didn't have what Aunt Lucinda had."

"I've thought about that," Estelle said slowly. "Frankly, I cannot for the life of me see how any mother can stay away from her only living child as she does me. I mean—"

Ned held up his hand to thwart her explanation. "Hey, I know exactly where you're coming from. She raised me from a year old, but you are her only living biological child."

Estelle nodded slowly.

"There's something wrong with that picture," Ned continued. "Aunt Lucinda visited Mama throughout the years. We were there. I remember her visiting all the time."

Estelle nodded again.

"We all knew Lucinda Owens." He paused, shaking his head in fond memory of that wonderful human being. "Estelle," he said quietly, "do you think Mama was jealous because of her hard knocks in life, that she didn't accomplish what her sister did?"

"But Aunt Lu was willing to share what she had with her," she replied. "Families," she said thoughtfully, slowly fingering the edge of the dining room tablecloth.

With that they moved on.

❧

Being the shrewd, calculating individual he had always been, shortly after Lucinda's death, C. J. arranged with the bank, overseen by his lawyer, upon his death to immediately stop all deposits to the Estelle Ingram account. His lawyer was also instructed never to reveal this arrangement to his son. Estelle placed the money from the account in a certificate of deposit. Unless she made additional deposits, accumulation of interest would now be the only growth. She was grateful for this handsome amount of money that otherwise would never have been saved.

Another surprise. She had to be present for the reading of the will. C. J. and Lucinda evidently had been very thrifty, accumulating an impressive bank account. Never enjoying grandchildren of their own, the will was read that great-nieces and great-nephew, Clarissa, Druscilla, and Jeffrey, upon graduation from high school, would each inherit the amount of five thousand dollars toward a college education. If they decided not to attend college, their inheritance would not be received until age twenty-one. Booker Carlton Owens inherited all the properties and the sum of fifty thousand dollars. Estelle did not fail to notice with that news the sparkle that flashed in Bobbi's eyes.

Booker was anxious to establish a more affluent lifestyle as quickly as possible. Now that he had possession of both buildings, he decided to sell, never considering the second building as lucrative rental property. In addition to their combined incomes, this building, with full occupancy, could render financial security for years. However, the goal of her cousin and his wife was to purchase a more upscale home in a suburban community. Estelle thought that decision unwise, tactfully pointing this out to her cousin. He didn't respond, so she let it go. After all, it was part of his inheritance and therefore his choice.

Cousin Booker gave them one year to find an apartment. He asked Mason what his father had charged for rent; Mason told him. A few days later Booker telephoned again to speak to Mason. He had inquired about rent for an apartment that size, he said, and the going rate was more than they were paying. Booker reset their rent at a price only a fraction below the going rate. *Greed!* was Estelle's angry summarization. For once, she and Mason agreed. She telephoned her mother just arriving back in Georgia. She was not in the least bit surprised.

By early summer Booker was getting antsy, anxious to sell. Estelle gave him what she named her "periodic progress report." To no avail, she and Mason had looked for reasonable three-bedroom apartments so that the children could have their own bedrooms. Exposing their ignorance of current rental rates, Mason complained about the cost. Estelle complained about both the locations and cost. Better locations cost even more. If they were going to stick to the plan to purchase a home when their one-year lease was up, a three-bedroom apartment would be economically unfeasible. Reluctantly, Estelle settled for a two-bedroom apartment. The one stipulation—that they stay in that apartment for one year only. Since Mason was a World War II veteran, they could get a VA loan and move into a house. The inevitable time had arrived. He consented, and it was settled.

To jumpstart the savings for the house, Estelle withdrew and transferred to a separate account a substantial amount of the personal deposits she had made over the years. Every two weeks, she added to this account deposits from her paycheck combined with a portion of the grocery money that Mason gave her every payday. Estelle had always been responsible for the utilities, and Mason paid the rent.

Her plan was to save for at least six months. Then she and Mason would start looking for something to buy, preferably within the city limits, as Ned had suggested. They had only one car. Ned and Celeste, enjoying suburban living owned two.

☙

*Well, how about that, Booker*, Estelle thought mildly perturbed, *you can sell in less than a year*. Their South Shore apartment was on the third floor. Mattresses now stood along the walls. Bed frames lay on the floor. Headboards rested together. The living room furniture was in its rightful space even though not in the desirable arrangement. Garment bags of clothing occupied closets.

Clare, thirteen, and Jeffrey, twelve, were viewing their home for the first time in the next year. Only the bedrooms appeared as large as Estelle remembered. In retrospect, Estelle was mildly irritated that she had allowed Mason to rush the process. Because he was not the most patient person, she now wondered whether there had been an oversight on her part. Her memory of the living room envisioned a larger space. Both work schedules allowed only weekends to view apartments. They had been looking for quite some time before they found a two-bedroom apartment with a second bedroom large enough to adequately accommodate both Clare and Jeffrey.

The galley kitchen (long and rectangular without windows) was narrower than Estelle remembered. The breakfast set was not a comfortable fit. Dissatisfied with the misfit, she decided the one alternative—keep one of the four chairs against the wall when not in use. What did her mother always say? "You never miss your water until ..." *Oh well,* she thought as she listened to the children complaining about only one full bath and no half-bath that Aunt Lu had always called the powder room.

Suddenly Estelle had an idea. Without comment, Jeffrey and Mason followed her lead. They moved the breakfast set to its newly assigned space in the living room. Surprisingly, it didn't look too out of place. She would enhance it with a tablecloth. All approved of the small revision because at least meals would not have to be served in that narrow, windowless kitchen! As she observed her husband and son, she longed for them to bond. Well, one thing was certain. The lack of space assured their stay here would be short-lived. Finally, she would finally get her wish—their own home!

The large dining room buffet and the china cabinet were going to storage with the rest of the dining room furniture. There was no place for her good set of china. Quietly, Estelle stored the large box, unpacked, against the wall in the back of her bedroom closet. Her crystal and sterling silver as well.

*Change,* she thought, *the one guaranteed constant.* She thought of Booker and Bobbi. Greedy people! Because he was a blood relative, she refused to let her mind drift to the futile "what-ifs." Promptly she flashed back to Nathan and that entire situation. No what-ifs were allowed to surface there, either.

In Jeffrey and Clare's room, two handsome screens extended slightly beyond the foot of their beds as clever partitions. A matching chest of drawers sat at the foot of each bed, leaving ample space for opening the drawers. However, the dressers simply would not fit! Then there was the closet. Large, but not like the walk-in to which they were accustomed. More significantly, they had to share it. Mason told them both they didn't have so many clothes they couldn't share a closet. That statement caused a wry smile from Jeffrey. *Ah, Mason*—he could always bring you down a peg or two. Compliments of Illinois Bell, the telephone was on Tuesday of the following week. As promised, Estelle contacted Doretha. Her excess furniture—two dressers and dining room furniture—still hampered the use of the living room. Her friend protested Estelle's plan to transport it to storage, instead insisting she bring it to her basement. Of course, it wasn't an imposition, she exclaimed almost indignantly. A year would pass like the blink of an eye! Thus, Estelle counted her blessings.

Meanwhile, she explained to Clare and Jeffrey the need to conserve. There would be meals of beans and rice (three, sometimes four, times per month); greens with candied yams and cornbread, which they didn't mind, even if they were served with only a small portion of roast beef (with the remainder frozen for an additional meal); cabbage, potatoes, and cornbread served with fried chicken. That too was okay. Greens, beans, green beans, and even black-eyed peas, the children could accept, but did they have to have liver? Ugh! To punctuate his disgust, Jeffrey would eat rice with gravy and onions, and a tossed salad. That outlaw of the meat family was omitted.

"It needs to be hanging all alone in the meat locker with horror stories written about it," he said one night.

Clare lay in her bed laughing with the very attractive screen partitions separating them. It was Jeffrey's nature to exaggerate his dislikes. Although she sometimes labeled him a rebel, in this instance she agreed totally. She couldn't see how liver could possibly be categorized as a meat! She recalled reading that liver and other internal organs of animals could contribute to gout if eaten too often.

"So," she asked, "what about the cow itself?"

"Well," Jeffrey answered, "we cannot alienate cattle. The steak, short ribs, and roasts are very tasty."

Strangely, that weekend the entire family visited Seventy-First Street. It felt awkward that Mason joined them. Jeffrey could not possibly imagine what had caused his participation. They discovered that there were two theaters, an ice cream parlor, nice shops, and a certain ambience representing decent maintenance—clean streets with all the amenities yet intact. Furthermore, Jeffrey and Clare discovered all of this with the most family unity they had ever experienced. Their father never accompanied them to church, to the museums, to picnics, or to Aunt Doretha's. (Clare and Jeffrey had addressed Estelle's closest friend as "Aunt" and her husband as "Uncle" since they were old enough to talk.)

"I give it less than five years before you goin' to see the change." Mason's prediction touring their new neighborhood put a damper on the family's enjoyment of simple togetherness.

"Good grief," exclaimed Jeffrey when out of hearing range of their father as they made their way back to their apartment; Clare responded with laughter.

"What you two laughin' 'bout?" their father inquired.

"A private joke," responded Jeffrey, slipping a wink to Clare, who smiled, offered no comment.

Later, Clare and Jeffrey talked about how their father loved to rain on any pleasure or potentially pleasant circumstance. Most likely he was correct, but couldn't they live in the now and let the future unfold on its own? After all, by then they would be living somewhere else, right?

Meanwhile, Clare and Jeffrey had transferred to a new school. Clare quickly became acclimated. Jeffrey did not. (Their mother explained this to be a temporary necessity until they moved into their home.) Additionally, Jeffrey felt the sudden weight of nostalgia and emotions over the fact that he now had no way to communicate with Noah. The relationship carried important weight because Noah, a friend since kindergarten, was his first true friend. Almost three weeks had passed before Noah eventually returned one of Jeffrey's phone calls. When he did call, Noah told Jeffrey that the house his family now occupied had been a temporary rental and that his parents had finally bought a house close to his father's university. In fact, they would be moving in a week or so. Sounding agitated and seemingly distracted, he promised to keep in touch. Another three weeks passed, and Jeffrey assumed they had moved, but he telephoned again anyway, to inform Noah that he too had moved. The number had been disconnected. The result was that neither boy had the address or telephone number of the other, a disruption Jeffrey hoped was only temporary.

"How long that boy been gone?" Mason asked apathetically when overhearing a discussion about Noah between Jeffrey and Clare. Jeffrey considered the interjection rude. He didn't dare utter the retort right on the tip of his tongue as his angry thoughts ran haywire.

To further add to his frustration, his seventh-grade teacher, Ms. Taft, was a no-nonsense, rigid, unsympathetic warden who was forever peering over each student's shoulder, especially his. At least it seemed that way to him. Most of all, she did not like him. Of course, she did not actually say she disliked him, but that he was not applying himself: "You mentally tread on your academic potential"—her exact words! She seemed more than willing to hand out demerits for even the smallest mistakes, or at least that was how he interpreted the red marks on his returned papers. After class, he once deliberately stayed behind to inquire about so many red marks, privately labelling them assaults.

"If you want less red, do more work," she told him. "You are a very bright student, Jeffrey Ingram, so do the work."

"You ought to be glad that she cares enough, Jeffrey," his mother told him when he related the comment verbatim right after school that day. "Do you know how many of them do not care, but simply get a paycheck?"

He placed his books on the chest of drawers at the foot of his bed. He and Clare usually did most of their homework at the table in the living room after their evening meal. It was Friday, without weekend assignments. Instead, there were ongoing projects due the following week.

"You need to stop mentally treading on your academic potential, Jeffrey Ingram," Jeffrey spontaneously said, mimicking Ms. Taft's voice and diction.

Estelle suppressed her laughter. Jeffrey could be very funny, but this was not the time to encourage it. "As you should," she said quietly.

"So, you are siding with her," he said, dramatically raising his eyebrows.

Estelle considered him blessed with all the innate talent to develop into a very good actor if he were to choose that path.

"It isn't cool to be smart, right?" She agreed with Ms. Taft's observation. "You downplay your brainy capabilities just to fit in."

Both were sitting on the side of his bed. There wasn't enough space for a chair in the room. Moving was worth anticipating, she thought, her thoughts momentarily wandering to what she'd titled the Booker Project. He had telephoned her this week "just to touch base," he said. The call was to let her know he had moved into a new home in a Southwest suburb. Her first thought had been *Retreat from the city, get away from black folks—who will follow!* She'd quickly dispelled the thought, recognizing that her anger was tinged with envy.

Jeffrey didn't answer but pondered his mother's words and his feelings while she was lost in her own thoughts. Uncle Ned was still working on his master's degree. Jeffrey's mother had explained that his thesis needed revisions and therefore was taking more time than he had previously thought it would. It permitted less time for tutoring his nephew in math or even spending leisure time with him, for that matter.

"Just work harder; become more motivated, Jeffrey!" his uncle had said.

As his mother had stated more than once, "It isn't a permanent condition."

Then there was Mason. Well, he remained in his own personal time warp, continuing to talk about things that held no current relevance. *Mason,* Jeffrey often thought after one of their "back in the day" discussions, *you are becoming mingled gray. Don't you think you need to at least discuss relevant topics?* Other than for a history exam, who cared about World War II at this late date? Who cared about what had happened on a farm in Mississippi so long ago when Mason was a young boy, especially since the story excluded any information about his family?

Jeffrey felt much closer to Uncle Ned. His uncle had always been the one to spend time with him—baseball games at Comiskey Park, an occasional Bears game at Soldier Field. Sometimes it was simply a visit with the family. Most of the time Ned's visits occurred during Mason's absence. Ned never said as much, but his actions clearly stated his dislike of Mason. Jeffrey never asked him why because he too found his father not very likable.

"Jeffrey," his mother said, drawing his attention back to their conversation, knowing he had a way of maneuvering away from a conversation that was not to his liking. "That's it, isn't it? It isn't cool to be smart, right?" she repeated.

"Remember David from my old school?" said Jeffrey. "I brought him to the house a few times."

She nodded, fleetingly sorrowful. The two of them had never bonded quite the way he had with his previous friend, Noah. She realized Noah was his first true friend. They had met in kindergarten, but she did not know exactly how to guide him to a place where he could learn to let go and move on.

"Some of the guys at school made fun of his speech all the time," Jeffrey explained. "I mean, almost every day."

"And?" she replied. "How did he react?" She remembered David with the perfect diction; she'd evaluated him as a nice young man.

"He didn't. He moved away to another school." He paused. "I think they were going to move anyway, but that did help."

"Everybody can't afford the luxury of running, Jeffrey." She paused. "Sometimes you have to take a stand."

"To do what?" he asked.

"Be the best you can be," she answered. "Take the least traveled path."

"Dad says it doesn't matter because—"

"I know," she replied gently but firmly to discourage that direction of dialogue. "We are discussing you, not your father," she continued ever so softly. "You are the son, Jeffrey Ingram, not Mason Ingram, the father."

This act of referencing his father was becoming his method of deflecting all responsibility. When he was younger, he'd done it out of innocence, but now because of his lack of motivation, it was becoming part of his maturing repertoire. "What was your dad like?" Jeffrey asked.

"I was my father's very last child, the only girl," she said.

Even though she had told her children many things about Georgia, the land, and her parents, never was there any discussion about age. So far, she had taken them to the farm only twice; it was after her mother had indoor plumbing installed. Both, especially Jeffrey, had constantly complained about the isolation of the farm and the lack of young people. Both times Mason had decided to stay behind, claiming he couldn't get the time off. Estelle had to admit that she'd savored the temporary separation.

Jeffrey recalled gazing at the photo of this old man in their family album. Before his mother identified him, Jeffrey thought he was her grandfather. The age difference between Gran Jennie and Granddad Chester was obvious from the photos.

"How old was he when he died?"

"He was eighty," she replied.

"How old is Dad?"

"Your father is in his forties."

"Closer to fifty, though, right?"

"Well, he has a few years left."

"So, he's forty-eight?"

A stir in the living room with footsteps came closer. Clare stuck her head inside the doorway of the room she shared with Jeffrey. Estelle knew her schoolbooks had been deposited on the living room table. Always they were moved each evening to perform her task of setting the table for dinner.

"This is where you are!" Clare said cheerfully. She was late, she explained, because she had to go back to her locker for a forgotten book she needed to read. The book report was due next week.

Later, the apartment was quiet. Mason was at work, so Estelle lay alone in bed, thinking back to the conversation with Jeffrey. He was developing the skill of guiding a conversation in a direction that allowed him to then take it over. Eventually, once perfected, this practice would enable him to avoid many meaningful discussions throughout his life, a potential detriment. Mason bullied; his son was acquiring the skill of manipulation. *Hard and soft, coarse and smooth* she thought, comparing father and son. Just before drifting to sleep, she decided that since this was her weekend off, they still needed to have that talk.

❦

Seventy-First Street. The Ingram family sat quietly at a table of the ice cream parlor eating banana splits. It was Estelle's family treat every alternate Saturday during her weekend off. As Jeffrey often commented, it was one of the few things the family did together. *Mason*, Jeffrey thought, *no traditional banana split for you.* He continued stealing glances at his father lifting the top to expose his three separate mounds of vanilla ice cream under traditional toppings of chocolate, strawberry, and pineapple toppings. Like a ritual, first his father ate each maraschino cherry atop the whipped cream covered with nuts. Jeffrey smiled to himself, thinking that this limited family togetherness should be captured in a photo. Blown up, displayed on a billboard in the black community. The caption underneath should read: "SPEND QUALITY TIME WITH YOUR FAMILY."

"Jeffrey," his mother asked, "who was that young man that waved at you?"

He wore a coat like Jeffrey's in the exact same color—midnight blue. Upon passing the plate glass window, he had waved to Jeffrey as he stood patiently with his mother waiting for their order0s. Briefly, he'd seemed to hesitate, as if wanted to come inside. Estelle had noticed the striking resemblance; they could almost pass for brothers. If Mason possessed a sense of humor—God, how she wished! She could tease him with a question about extramarital activity. It could make for a great private joke between the two of them. It was the exact type of banter that would take place between Aunt Lu and Uncle C. J. How she missed those two. They were so well suited for each other and had so much fun together.

"That's Simpson," Jeffrey explained. "He's in my class. He's from New Jersey and lives with his grandmother."

"His first name is Reginald," added Clare, "and he's always in trouble."

"Not all the time," Jeffrey countered.

"Okay, most of the time."

Jeffrey shrugged, kept eating. He then turned his attention to his father. "Hey, Dad, why don't you like any other ice cream but vanilla?" Boy! He wanted to address him by his given name.

"Don't know," he replied. "Guess it tastes better."

"But with a banana split?"

"Yeah, with a banana split."

*How do you know, Mason,* he asked in silence, *if you never try any other kind?*

Later, the apartment was quiet. Estelle listened to distant noise from the street below. Jeffrey was in the bedroom he shared with his sister. The door was slightly ajar, so she peeked in to hear his even breathing. *He needs to make new friends,* she thought. The screens hid him from view. The books that he had brought home lay, undisturbed, on the chest of drawers at the foot of his bed.

How she missed that building and the people who had owned it. The one familiar feature in this apartment was the high ceilings. For once, the entire family completely agreed on something—the move couldn't possibly happen soon enough.

Clare, now in the eighth grade, had gone to the library with one of her classmates. Mason had gone to meet some of his mill buddies and was not due back for a few hours. Finally, he had begun to account for his whereabouts. He appeared mildly awkward the first time which had caused her to suppress the smile flirting with the corners of her mouth.

She and the children had spent the entire Saturday with Doretha's family. Estelle decided they should spend the night. (Of course, it had been a deliberate move on her part; she had taken overnight necessities and a change of clothing for them all.) When she finally reached Mason to state that she and the children wouldn't be home until the next day, he was taken aback, practically speechless. He was rather disgruntled the following day. She made no apologies and stated pointedly, "At least you knew where I was and for how long." Weeks later, she and Doretha had a good laugh about it during one of their phone conversations. Her friend's opinion was that the favorable result indicated it should have happened a lot sooner.

Now momentarily lost in thought, she absently perused the cover of a novel she intended to read when Jeffrey joined her on the living room sofa. He looked positively bored; she knew it was because he still hung out with no one. There was not much hanging out for a twelve-year-old. Still, there were matinee movies, the library, telephone conversations, and a few other activities. Clare maintained a friendship she'd had since first grade—Nadine Jamison. However, Estelle also knew Clare would have developed other friendships had that one not worked out so well. Nadine was her closest friend. They did not see each other that often but kept in contact by phone calls gently monitored by their mothers. The young lady Clare often studied with was merely a classmate; they spent no other time together.

Estelle categorized her son's situation as a little peculiar for a person so young. Okay, so he no longer heard from Noah, but he needed to strike up other friendships. How could she approach the topic of how people can often be on your path for only a short while? She wondered if he realized that perhaps Noah had been on his path simply to awaken and challenge certain capabilities. The character flaw she hoped he would outgrow was his inability to shake things off and move on.

She smiled at her son. He was Mason's son all right, even though the Beckford genes were dominant. She thought with pride that he was going to be a handsome man someday, a Beckford. She wanted his good looks to be complemented by a strong character that would guide him toward academic achievement. Therefore, the finer things in life.

"Have you done your homework?"

"It's not homework, but a book to read for next week's book report."
He was mildly irritable, a mood that often accompanies boredom. "We
don't have homework over the weekend, Mom."

She ignored his mood, which she knew would soon pass. "So, don't
you think you need to get started?"

"I read some of it, but then I got sleepy." He yawned and smiled
at his mother. He seemed to be contemplating a line of discussion but
then just sighed.

"If you are bored, we can play checkers or gin," she suggested,
attempting to steer him away from turning on the television. That
square box was gradually becoming the American cure-all.

"No," he said, suddenly laughed. "Noah and his sisters used to
play gin rummy all the time. Most of the time Monica won." A pause.
"Monica was funny. She used to make all kinds of facial expressions,
especially when she thought she was about to lose. Noah always talked
about what a poor loser she was."

"I know you miss Noah, Jeffrey," she said gently. "But you can make
new friends, you know."

"I know," he agreed, rising to leave the sofa. "I guess I'll read some
more, if I don't fall asleep again."

She wanted to resume their previous conversation but hated to
disturb the pleasantness of the afternoon. Plus, she didn't want to be
a nag. She would wait until he brought home a few more test scores
for math. His grade in English had gone from an A- to a B. Still above
average, but his math was worse, a C-. She hoped his grades wouldn't
spiral any farther downward.

She left the living room and headed into the kitchen to check the
spaghetti sauce. It had simmered long enough for their evening dinner.
Tomorrow's menu would be pot roast, mustard and turnip greens,
and baked cornbread. Other than church, she intended to have an
uneventful, lazy Sunday evening to be fresh for work on Monday.

# CHAPTER EIGHT

Slowly, Jeffrey climbed into his uncle's car. It was a Friday, and Mason was still at work. Estelle had threatened hysteria when the desk sergeant telephoned to notify her that Jeffrey was at the police station with several other boys.

His thesis was now completed, and graduation set for spring, Ned was again visiting regularly. Coincidentally, he had telephoned just after Estelle received the call from the police. Discovering what had transpired, he had told his distraught sister to calm down.

With Jeffrey in the car, he stepped into a telephone booth outside the police station. "Okay, Estelle, we're going to make a stop, so I'll bring him home a little later. I want to talk to him, okay?... Estelle, don't go on so; he's fine... No, he's fine, so don't worry." He thought of something else to say, decided to let it go. "Just don't worry, all right?" Assisted by the streetlight, he could see his nephew anxiously watching him through the automobile's passenger window. "Listen," he finished, "we won't be that long, okay? See you a little later."

A brief pause as he dropped more coins into the slot. "I'm running late," he explained to Celeste. "No, everything is fine… I'll explain when I get home."

Jeffrey watched him as he slipped under the steering wheel. Neither of them had spoken a word since leaving the police station. Ned marveled at the fact that until this evening he had never experienced the interior of a police station.

They stopped at Harold's Chicken for takeout orders. Ned drove to the lakefront at Sixty-Third Street. Both listened to the steady purr of the motor to keep the car warm, looking out over the Lake Michigan shore. In a few months boats would be docked there. Having lived not that far from the Ocmulgee River, Ned in his youth discovered that water was peaceful. Chicago benefited from both Lake Michigan and the Chicago River. It was that uniqueness that he truly loved about this city.

Ned ate the chicken and fries, pushed aside the warm slaw, returning it to the bag for disposal. His unspoken complaint was, as always, that they should package it separately. Jeffrey picked at his chicken, still relatively warm. Normally it was one of his favorite foods. Circumstances made it tasteless.

"Do you realize how many seconds it takes to ruin your entire life, Jeffrey?" Ned deliberately snapped his finger close to his nephew's ear. "Just like that," he said. Briefly, he thought of Mason, as he had several times in the past. What had happened in that man's life to make him so negative and therefore so bitter? A fleeting thought he purged. "Do you realize that?"

"But I didn't do anything."

"Were you there?"

Jeffrey nodded, not sure if he should explain in detail.

"Then you did it. That makes you an accomplice."

His eyes welled up with tears as he looked down on his meal. He heaved a heavy sigh. "What do you think is going to happen?"

"Well," Ned said, "for one thing you're going to need a lawyer. It seems that those little thieves have been at it for quite some time. Since you are implicated, you've caused an expense your parents don't need with plans to move in the fall. Public defenders are often unreliable since they are appointed by the courts. They're known not to work as hard to defend their clients—even though they are paid regardless of the outcome." Ned realized that more objectivity and fair-mindedness was necessary. "Well, it's not *all* their fault since most of them are still gaining experience. I understand their caseload to be quite heavy. Many can't afford to hire a lawyer."

Jeffrey looked at the half-moon over Lake Michigan. It appeared cold, gloomy, and partly frozen, an accurate reflection of his emotions.

"What possessed you to even be present while all this breaking into cars was going on?"

Jeffrey remained silent because he had only been there for that last garage break-in, the one time he had been late getting home from school. The people were supposed to be at work, so who had seen them? Clare was already home when he got there, questioned him about lately "hanging around Simpson so much." It was the one evening that Estelle had worked a little late.

"Jeffrey, what were you thinking?" his uncle asked. "And for whom were *they* stealing car radios and tape decks, for crying out loud?"

"I don't know, but I didn't steal anything," Jeffrey said. He knew for certain that Simpson was involved, as were a few of the others, including Leonard Skaggs. He couldn't tell, though, because that would get him into deeper trouble.

"But you were there, so that makes you equally guilty."

He wanted to explain that he was there only that last time but instead remained silent. He had often heard that Leonard Skaggs was mean; the crowd he ran with was even meaner.

There were so many things Ned wanted to say to his nephew and some that he couldn't. The lack of proper male guidance loomed as a major factor. His uncle wanted to ask him what he and his father discussed when together. How did he tactfully approach that subject? He would never know why in life the scale was often tipped so unfairly. Although the lack made him love Druscilla no less, he had always wanted a son. He had no intention of ever telling Celeste this, though. Her gynecologist had told them that she was still able to bear more children, but so far it appeared that she was destined to conceive only once. Life included no guarantees, often unfolding as if conditions and circumstances were simply up for grabs. The wife of a friend had conceived four times, all girls! He thought: *What the hell?*

"Where did he go—what did you say his name was?" he now asked his nephew. "Simpson?"

"I don't know." Jeffrey shrugged helplessly. "He just slipped away." Jeffrey recalled the two of them walking together, as they sometimes did, while casually chatting on the way home from school. Then suddenly Simpson vanished like the blink of an eye. There he stood all alone as the police approached him. At the police station he was identified as one of the boys who had broken into two cars.

The ride to the station felt strange, and it was the first time he had ever been in the company of Leonard Skaggs. "He's dumb," his sister had previously said of the teenager. Often, he appeared sullen and very intimidating. A grade behind Jeffrey, soon he would be passed on to the seventh grade—if he did not quit first.

"Since he ran," Uncle Ned asked, "and you fit the description of what witnesses say they saw, you were tagged?"

"But I didn't—"

"Jeffrey, you are beginning to sound like a parrot practicing the phrase he knows best. I repeat, you were there. Do I make myself clear?"

Jeffrey nodded. He started to speak up but held back. His uncle's impatience was now bordering on anger, which was a side of him Jeffrey had never witnessed.

"And eat your food before it gets stone cold." Nothing tasted worse than cold fries.

"I'm not hungry," replied Jeffrey miserably as he returned his food to the brown paper bag.

"In life, Jeffrey, there are always pitfalls that must be avoided at all costs. You must be aware. No matter how difficult, take the high road. Sometimes that means you travel alone, be *lonely*, even ridiculed. Do you understand what I am saying to you?"

Ned thought of his own childhood in which these challenges had never existed, although others were equally harsh. He thought of that

Georgia farm and how he and Estelle had existed in gradually increasing isolation as all the other young relatives left to head for higher education or places with better conditions away from farm life.

"Furthermore, do not nod your head."

"Yes," Jeffrey replied, recalling that Mrs. Ballenger had given him that same advice.

"Where does Simpson stay?"

"I don't know. I know he lives a few blocks from me with his grandmother, but I think she works nights until about nine or so."

"Just great," Ned said. "Meanwhile, her grandson is doing God knows what." He paused. "Did you tell the police he was the one they were looking for?"

"Yes, but the others never said anything. So, the police believed the witnesses, that it was me."

*That sounds about right*, Ned thought. If the others incriminated the little bastard, he could probably make things more toxic for the rest of them in a hurry. Ned wondered just how long they had been involved and for whom they were working. He didn't believe Jeffrey was totally in the dark. Ned surmised that it seemed as though a decision had been made by the other little criminals not to reveal Simpson's intricate involvement. It would have meant implicating Simpson and bringing him back from wherever he was to stand trial with the rest, causing even further incrimination for all. It appeared the agreement was to leave the little son of a bitch out of the loop.

There was more he wanted to say, questions he wanted to ask. He would let this small talk suffice for now and delay delving further for a later time, when and if he had more information.

It was very late when Estelle stood in the hallway looking down as her brother and son finally climbed the stairs. Jeffrey felt a lump in his throat as he looked at his mother. There was no Mason, but Clare was there communicating with her eyes. Never had he seen his mother in such a state. He could tell she had been crying. Temporarily, he felt sheer relief, although he wondered exactly what to expect when Mason discovered what had happened. Obviously, he had stopped for drinks with his mill buddies. A common occurrence on Fridays.

A month later, a bench trial took place in a large and mostly empty courtroom. No one was in attendance except for the parents and lawyers of all involved. Nothing like the movie court scenes he had seen as the judge, supported by twelve jurors, wielded his gavel. The judge looked extremely detached, commenting about his docket. The bailiff read aloud the case number and the names of the defendants. His voice echoed throughout the large facility.

The mother of Leonard Skaggs was a heavy-set, dark-skinned lady with bad skin. She seemed extremely unfriendly, or perhaps just cautious. Several other kids Jeffrey recognized—he didn't know them well, but they were on speaking terms—were also accompanied by both parents. Two with only their mothers. Mason was there with Estelle. Jeffrey was keenly aware of the one and only person conspicuously missing: Reginald Simpson. That caused a mixed reaction of anger and panic in Jeffrey. He kept stealing glimpses of the other defendants. *You are guilty and so is Simpson*, he wanted to say. *You know I didn't do any of it.*

In the end, Jeffrey's lawyer managed to have his case thrown out. It was a close call. Later, he learned about the sentence for Leonard Skaggs simply because he was no longer at school. Because of multiple run-ins with the law, he had been sent away. Where was Simpson? Evaporated into thin air!

Jeffrey told Uncle Ned a few weeks later about what had happened to Skaggs.

"Well," Ned muttered with a tinge of sarcasm, "his curriculum has been assigned."

Jeffrey felt bitter, resentful, angry, and confused, but still didn't offer what he knew. Yes, he had been at the wrong place at the wrong time, but how had Reginald Simpson gotten off scot-free? *Because you were afraid to speak up*, that quiet inner voice scolded.

Weeks later, Estelle discovered the whereabouts of Reginald Simpson. She had asked around out of curiosity, and the information meandered its way through various people, like a bad cold to finally reached her. He had returned to New Jersey to live with his mother and new stepfather. Reginald's grandmother referred to the new stepfather as "a good man who will provide the necessary stern hand." That last tidbit had been volunteered by one of the church members who knew the grandmother very well. The information? Obtained without anyone ever mentioning Jeffrey by name.

"Just be careful, Jeffrey," Estelle later told him quietly.

*I had to go to court,* he thought angrily, *and Reginald gets to leave town and start all over again.*

Uncle Ned sternly instructed Jeffrey to express gratitude to his mother for spending the money to provide him with legal counsel. Jeffrey did so with some reluctance, and in return, his mother made certain that he knew she was still far from pleased.

His grades fell even further because he couldn't shake the fact that he had been in front of a judge and Simpson had gotten away scot-free. Meanwhile, the incident seemed to heighten Ms. Taft's impatience somewhat. Perhaps a reevaluation of him as not so nice after all? "Bring your grades up, Jeffrey, or suffer the consequences."

Once more his parents were summoned. "I can't take off from work again," Mason said when Estelle told him. "We movin' in the fall, right?"

Estelle only nodded in quiet disgust. She then decided to pursue it. "Mason," she said, "why do you always manage to find a way out of tight spots?"

"Stelle," he answered, "I can't take off from work, okay? I can't take off," he repeated. "During this time, we short at the mill. I can't get time off."

There was a second meeting in which Ms. Taft conferred with both her wayward pupil and his mother. A plan to salvage the student's floundering grades.

If he could manage at least a C in both math and English, Jeffrey could pass to the eighth grade. He had six weeks to accomplish this feat. Ms. Taft even said that she was totally receptive to extra projects to help his cause, suggesting that perhaps he hand in book reports to satisfy his faltering grade in English and do extra math papers to enhance those scores.

"Are you up to it, young man?" asked Ms. Taft.

"I guess so," he answered glumly.

"You have to be," she said with quiet firmness.

"Jeffrey, you have to improve your grades," his mother pleaded as they walked home that evening from his school.

His response was only a blank stare.

"Your Uncle Ned would be happy to help with the math," she offered. "Do you know that Ms. Taft is being generous because she sees potential? You must fight for it, Jeffrey. Don't you realize that?"

He nodded, unable to speak because it felt like his tongue was stuck to his palate. Why was life so unfair? The court incident overshadowed his every action. It hurt his ability to concentrate. The guilty party, or at least one of them, had made a clean getaway. That infuriated him. To steer clear of the same fate as Leonard Skaggs, the others had remained quiet. Even as he tried tediously to focus on his grades, preoccupation with the unfair events stubbornly warred against his efforts.

Estelle devised a plan that would be suitable for all concerned. A change of scenery would do her children good as they became better acquainted with their grandmother. She hoped that Jeffrey would listen to her closely because she was a very wise woman. *You didn't!* She reminded herself, saddened by that thought. Yes, she decided with finality, both grandchildren would spend the summer in Georgia. She and Mason had been shown a few nice houses already, but the absence of the children for the entire summer would free their weekends for house hunting. The children would return in time for enrollment in a new school for the fall term. It was the perfect solution.

Both Clare and Jeffrey were as excited as their grandmother about their upcoming visit. Estelle called Ned to include Druscilla in the visit to Georgia as part of the family agreement. but Druscilla didn't want to join her cousins. Secretly Clare was relieved, and her excitement remained high about visiting Gran Jennie.

Jeffrey's excitement plummeted when he saw his report card. Fuming, he stalked to his side of the room. With a fixed stare and for a very long time, he looked at the D's, but mostly F's, in vertical alignment ending with the inevitable recommendation: he was to repeat the seventh grade. His inability to focus had continued as his grade in

English remained dismal. Efforts in math spiraled further downward like confetti, leaving him stuck.

This was the state in which his mother found him. Gingerly, he handed over the report card and was further incensed that she showed no surprise.

"Ms. Taft wrote to me of her decision a few days ago, Jeffrey," she said. She sighed. She didn't bring up his obvious inability to even attempt to prevent this. *He has the summer and different surroundings ahead of him*, she thought. She hoped perhaps upon his return he would be in a better frame of mind.

Jeffrey braced for the onslaught from Mason that never came. Mason, running late, said nothing on his way to work but "see you later." Jeffrey wondered what was going on with him.

It was the most detrimental flaw in her son's character, Estelle thought. It was this inability to shake off bad experiences. Even at such a young age, it nipped at his heels, dogged him.

"Move on," his mother had encouraged more than once, just as she was now. "Jeffrey, get over it," she was pleading in a tone so beseeching that for a moment he thought she might cry.

"Mom," he said. "Okay, don't get so worked up."

Too much Mason, Estelle decided. The other prominent factor was Jeffrey's lack of motivation. What was the cure? She had tried everything, including exposure to things more positive, to counter all the negativity Mason constantly espoused. There were trips to the suburbs to visit with Uncle Ned and his family, trips to the museums, Navy Pier, trips downtown and, occasionally, a long drive outside the city. (The trade-off for her use of the car was that Mason got a weekly Saturday night out with buddies without a time restriction.) These countryside excursions did have a positive, surreal effect on both children, but impacted Clare more residually than Jeffrey. She would mention it for weeks. In the city, except for patches of greenery provided by parks and individual properties, tall buildings walled you in. City living sabotaged a person's bond with sprawling, vibrantly green landscapes.

"You've not always lived in the city, Mason," Estelle would say whenever petitioning for a family weekend picnic in the country. "Or have you forgotten?" Twice she had suggested Indiana Dunes State Park or just a roadside affair in some enticingly scenic area where they could spread a blanket and eat out in the open. He was never receptive to the idea.

There were moments when she longed for a family getaway to somewhere like the farm where she'd grown up. Would her children like spending time on a farm? Perhaps once they were settled in their own home, the children could continue to spend some summers there. During her vacation she could join them in that peaceful setting. Even with Mason most likely staying behind, it would indeed be a worthy treat for the children, even for her. Suddenly she was toying with the idea of purchasing a car of her own. In her home she now spoke without reservation, emboldened by the secret knowledge of the money she had set aside. Plus, she had learned early in her marriage to Mason that assertion was a must. What would be her stance without the money? Certainly, it now accrued more slowly, but nevertheless the growth was steady. She realized that Uncle C. J.'s intention was to prepare her to leave Mason. Thus, to correct a less than desirable marital arrangement to a man who had never met his approval. What had he once told her in anger? "Doll, I wish you could have had a clean, swift pillow talk with that bastard and then moved on, know what I mean?" She smiled over the bittersweet memory. She recalled assuring that sweet man to stop feeling guilty; he was not to blame.

❧

Georgia: it was too quiet for Jeffrey. Additionally, come nightfall it was too dark. Strange sounds to which he was unaccustomed. The hoot of an owl, strange bird sounds. "Crows, baby," his grandmother explained. "So many crickets," he complained. "There had to be more crickets than usual," evoked amused laughter from relatives.

"You have crows *and* crickets in Chicago," said one of the relatives. "But they compete with all the other sounds. Wake up early in the morning before all the other activity starts, and if you listen, you can hear birds chirping."

"How do you know?" questioned another relative.

"A long time ago I visited Chicago during the summer." It had occurred long before Clare and Jeffrey were born.

On nights when the moon shone brightly, Jeffrey was always reminded by Gran Jennie of God's nightlight—the moon! Night's tiny assistants. Stars! That is how his grandmother explained it.

"The firmament," said Cousin Prentiss one night as they looked up in the sky. Jeffrey mentally stored that word so as not to forget it. *Firmament*, he repeated several times to himself.

Too dark, Jeffrey decided. No streetlights. Even with the moon and the stars, you could place your hand before you in the dark without it materializing until your eyes made the adjustment. Too much open space, he concluded.

Preoccupation with the fact that he was to repeat the seventh grade kept him from fully appreciating what otherwise would have been a very rewarding experience in his young life. During his entire visit with his grandmother, he felt trapped in a translucent bubble, isolated even as he interacted with others. Therefore, Jeffrey never experienced total pleasure vacationing in Georgia. He decided it would have been better to discover his punishment upon his return. He suffered within his space, attempting as best he could to shut out what awaited him— repeating the seventh grade!

"Used to be cotton as far as the eye could see," commented Gran Jennie. She cautioned them both not to venture beyond a certain point. Unlike "back in the day," when there were many more individuals living on the land, some of it now lay untended. Home to wildlife such as snakes, coons, and opossums. "Gone wild as befo'," she explained. "Back to nature. Even we return to it, so to speak, when we die. Only the soul lives on." After a pause, she returned to her previous line of thought. "We even planted fo' free on McDermott land 'cause the crop—cotton!— was fo' the mill. Those were good days. If a cash advance was necessary to purchase cotton seeds, it was took from profits. McDermott considered it fair since the Beckfords amassed a generous amount of money from the cotton crop. Before that, during slavery, no one got paid but white folk."

Clare thought she detected underlying bitterness when her grandmother mentioned injustices endured for centuries by black people.

Presently, it was a different era, a separate time. Only a few animals—chickens, a few pigs, and no large animals such as cattle or horses—now existed on the Beckford farm. Therefore, a select segment of the land produced only what was necessary for the sustenance of Gran and the few sharecroppers who lived in the other houses, beginning to show age and wear. Some had already been torn down because, Jennifer had said at the time, "they looked so bad." Afterward, that land, together with the McDermott land, had been cleared of the unruly, wild vegetation that had taken over. The immediate area where Jennifer and the others lived had been cleared by Stuart McDermott as a kind of compensation to the Beckfords for the money no longer coming in from the mill. "But it doesn't happen often enough," Jennifer had complained. At the time the clearing took place approximately four times per year, and one of those times gave them access to the peach orchard and the fig trees, adjacent to a segment of land that continued to be farmed. Then, after several years of saving from produce sold in town, Jennifer had been able to purchase a reconditioned tractor to keep things "neat and tidy" independent of the McDermott generosity. McDermott had been mildly taken aback when it happened, but he only smiled in recognition of the self-reliance that he had always identified with Jennifer Beckford. This upgrade also helped to bring the sharecroppers into the twentieth century, speaking volumes about the continued generous provisions made for the existing sharecroppers on land still inhabited by Chester Beckford's widow.

Prentiss had begun to complain to Gran Jen, as he called her, about her living arrangements. He wanted her to shut the place down, come live with him and his family. It was okay to let the sharecroppers eke out subsistence for themselves and their motley crew. "They have families, Prentiss, families!" she corrected him. But she did not have to stay there with them, he sternly protested. They weren't related to her, but he was! Leave the place and them with it, he constantly suggested; let it tide them over until it is eventually sold. (His wife constantly complained about the situation and therefore agreed with her husband.)

Finally, she relented, and arrangements were made for her to leave the land that she secretly loved to move in with Prentiss and their family within the next year or so. She thanked God daily that she had met Chester. The remaining family, especially Prentiss, completely ignored the fact that she was unrelated to them by blood. She often reviewed her life and God's mysterious and marvelous way of sorting every detail for the good of all. She couldn't have planned a better outcome.

"Hens lay eggs, honey," Gran Jennie was now explaining as she entered the chicken coop to gather eggs with her two grandchildren traipsing close behind. It was the middle of their second week visiting with their grandmother. Neither Clare nor Jeffrey had ever before seen chickens lay eggs. They did not actually see the hens laying the eggs now either, but they witnessed the evidence as their grandmother gently gathered them from their nests.

"What do the roosters do besides crow?" Jeffrey asked.

"Roosters are needed so that the hens can bring us chicks."

Mason covered this topic when Jeffrey was close to ten years old, keeping it factual without elaboration. Now Jeffrey was thirteen. He and his classmates approached the subject of sex differently, in an arguably less positive or proper way. *Lucky roosters*, he thought. *They can walk about all day without a care in the world.* Immediately his alert grandmother knew what he was thinking; his smile exposed his thoughts.

"But men, 'specially black men, can't live like dat," said Gran in her cautious wisdom to counter what she considered negative thoughts. "It was the way of plantation livin' when slaves no longah was brung from Africa. Can't be havin' sex without carin' and lovin'." She paused, and her eyes met his with piercing directness. "Understan', Jeffrey?"

He nodded, but she pressed for an oral reply until she received it. He heard her voice from what seemed a distance away. Gran, a serious individual, hoped to influence her grandson as well as her granddaughter about the importance of life's lessons while on God's earth.

Years later Clare would reflect fondly on that summer, age fourteen, as the one special vacation that she would always cherish.

"Clare, what do ya do to have a beautiful flowah garden?" her grandmother asked one evening as they sat together on the open porch. Jennifer was seated in her rocking chair, and Clare sat on the top step watching the sky as it turned dark. The moon was dim. The stars remained hidden, refusing to produce their sparkle. The summer breeze fanned cool and gentle, indicating that rain was on its way. The only light keeping them from sitting in almost total darkness came from the kitchen. Clare thought about her answer.

"What do you do," her grandmother asked again, "when you help me in my garden? What is the enemy of the'tunias and the'patiens, the roses? What do we have to do to'em?"

Now Clare knew the answer. "The weeds!" she exclaimed. "We have to keep the weeds away."

"Right!" her grandmother exclaimed, joining Clare on the steps and hugging her. "In life the weeds are the bad thoughts, the bad choices, or the wrong people. In life, Clarissa, yo' very own flowah garden is kept beautiful with good, fine ideas that lead to good decisions and by surroundin' yoself with positive people. Often the road is hard, but cling to that foundation. Yo' foundation is yo' mind, honey, and it is up to you to make it strong and good to have a good life. The mind is the key to ev'thing. It's like the soil that grows things. If ya work on the foundation, you'll have a mighty fine garden. Don't forget that no matter where ya go."

"What about the real flower garden, Gran?"

Her grandmother laughed. "God gave us all those plants fo' entertainmnt, fo' decoration, so his living room won't be so plain."

She always talked about God's living room. Jennifer Allen Beckford had no scientific explanations. She wasn't educated like Cousin Prentiss. He talked about the balance of nature and the necessity of trees and plants. He explained why humans couldn't cut down all the trees, causing an ecological imbalance. There was the mention of photosynthesis, the necessity for trees and plants, humans' waste, and the workings that provided the necessary oxygen for the earth. When Jeffrey asked him to explain, Prentiss casually told him to look it up. Additionally, he said, gallons of water could be contained in one single tree and prevented a lot of the earth's potential flooding. At other times when there were floods and mudslides, these "natural disasters" were often not natural at all, but man-made. Therefore, it would be avoidable if people had taken heed and adhered to nature's laws.

❧

It was a beautiful vacation, and Clare had loved every precious moment. Somehow, she sensed that Jeffrey, robbed by persistent preoccupation, had not. In reflection, Clare often wished Jeffrey had allowed their grandmother's words regarding the mental flower garden to impact him the same way because she had told them both the very same thing.

"Dad," Jeffrey said, wanting to test what Gran Jennie had told him. "Have you ever heard of a mental flower garden?"

"What?" He frowned. He was at home on one of his rare Saturday evenings. Even Estelle was mildly surprised by his presence.

"A mental flower garden," Jeffrey repeated. "Gran Jennie said it's your mind, keeping away the bad thoughts by mentally planting a beautiful garden as a good way to be positive and"—

His father cut him off. In fact, he laughed. "That's crazy talk from a silly old woman."

Estelle spoke up immediately with considerable anger. "My mother is a lot of things, but silly is not one of them."

Her reaction surprised even Mason. One of the few times he offered no tart response.

Through the years, including while she was in college, Clare would hold steadfast to Gran Jennie's advice. Frequently she would turn down invitations to parties. She had to spend time studying for a test or writing a paper that was due instead. Eventually she began to date, and even though she had a small wardrobe, mostly from a North Side thrift shop, it was cleverly coordinated and fashionable enough to sustain her. She would have loved during these times to be able to utilize her craft. Sewing! But time was limited. However, during her long educational journey, through good times and bad, she would work on maintaining that strong foundation, her mental garden. It would keep her going and ultimately pull her through.

# Chapter Nine

They needed a bigger house but couldn't afford it. Well, perhaps they could, but revealing how would have opened Pandora's Box causing insurmountable disruption. Then again, the maintenance of a larger house still would have been steep. One convenience they had previously enjoyed when living on South Parkway was theirs once more—they had one and one-half baths again! The master bedroom was medium-sized. The other two bedrooms were, no matter how you evaluated them, smaller than Estelle would have liked. She smiled when she thought of Jeffrey's exaggerated analysis. "Tiny!" She momentarily lingered on that thought. Her son was such a drama king, to the point of generating amusement. She hoped that one day he could capitalize on that gift.

She thought about a few of the homes she'd been shown in a remote south suburb. Each had a master bedroom—the real McCoy with a private bath, and a matching price tag. Her broker, a friendly elderly woman near retirement had made a generous living from the business of selling real estate. She suggested that Estelle tour a few homes that could possibly be in her future within the next five years. Her name was

Florence, and she had immediately taken a liking to Estelle, showing her a couple of these homes in the "serious price range." Doretha's terminology when Estelle told her about these spacious homes.

Briefly dreaming, then back to earth. She and Mason secured a VA mortgage, in partnership with the bank, for a modest house within the city limits. After the movers delivered the remainder of the furniture from Doretha's basement, no matter how strategically they arranged it, the space was somewhat cramped. Separated from it for a year, Estelle did not recall her living room furniture being quite so large. Good furniture couldn't be disposed of even though the designated space didn't comfortably accommodate it. *Now*, said that small voice from within, *you have money you cannot spend without explaining exactly where it came from.*

"We ain't rich, Stelle," stated Mason. She heard the finality in his voice. "We jus' have to make do."

The chest of drawers and dressers for both the children left no space for the promise—large, oversized chairs. She purchased a chair for each room that was a compatible fit. "Small" was Jeffrey's comment. Inwardly Clare grimaced.

To add to Estelle's distress, Mason was not himself. It had become more noticeable and could no longer be ignored. His night sweats were becoming progressively worse, and he got up frequently during the night. He was more withdrawn than before and slept fitfully. Lately, the disturbances often caused her to retreat to the living room sofa, though she managed each time to return to their bedroom before the children woke up. The stark realization that a house was not automatically a home. So, the question was: what was this journey called life?

Finally, without preamble, she said to Mason, "You need to see a doctor."

He pushed back. "Ah don't need no doctah."

They were against the wall. Estelle wished she could take the children and back away from this situation that had been prevailing her for years. Neither of her children liked the South, plus her mother had resolved her living circumstances. She was moving to Macon to live with Prentiss and his family. Furthermore, she recalled the relief on her children's faces as they alighted from the Greyhound bus. Visiting Gran Jennie had been fine. The beauty, the open space, and the clean air were enjoyable, but they didn't want to live there. Well, what about living somewhere else without Mason? The words "in sickness and in health" intercepted her thoughts. She was reminded that it was she, not Mason, who had wanted the responsibility of a house.

He was dressing to go to work when she said again, "Mason, see a doctor." The tone was threatening, words delivered with such finality that he dared not test the outcome.

"You're diabetic," said the doctor. No empathy, just professional diagnosis. "You have diabetes mellitus, Type 1," he said. "If the person is not born with the condition, this type usually develops at a much younger age." He paused. "I wish I could put you on the insulin pill, but you will have to take injections. Does anyone in your family have diabetes?" When there was no prompt response, he surged ahead. "Had you waited a little longer, you most likely would have risked having a stroke or even worse. It is possible that you could have become… well … comatose." He added the last comment to get his patient's attention because Mason's behavior indicated denial.

"Coma…" Mason was tinkering with enunciation.

"Comatose," the doctor repeated. "Out—like in death, but on a ventilator; alive without knowledge of it."

"My father, I think…" Mason spoke with uncertainty, dumbfounded. He sat in front of the doctor as if in a daze. He needed to ask Nelson what their father had died from. He vaguely recalled his Uncle Morris having a medical condition beginning at a young age. He then asked, "How long?"

"I don't know. It depends on—"

"No," he said, "fo' the shots."

"Injections?" the doctor asked.

Mason nodded.

"Mr. Ingram, it's for life, for the remainder of your life." He paused. "So how did your father die?"

"He died at the plow," Mason answered in reference to his father. "They say he had untreated… I'm not sho'."

To Estelle the information felt like a personal attack. All these years he had never mentioned that he was absent when his father died. Or was this secondhand information?

Later, while riding back to the house from the doctor's office, she asked him. "Mason, were you there when your father died?"

"No, Stelle," he said defensively. "Years later, my brother tol' me."

"Mason, do you mean to tell me you didn't attend your own father's funeral?"

He did not answer but continued to drive, as he left the Westside VA Hospital to merge with the traffic on the Eisenhower Expressway. For the first time in his adult life, Mason Ingram was at a loss for words. No curt remark was forthcoming as an unfamiliar emotion suddenly filled him. It felt like his necktie had been knotted too tightly. It was fear.

&

After almost five months, Jeffrey's complaining about the low ceilings continued. He said they made the house hot. Their mother admitted this with mild irritation—yes, the ceilings were low, not like the high ceilings to which they were accustomed—but the air conditioning alleviated that discomfort.

It was a nice ranch-style house with a front picture window surrounded by a somewhat spacious yard, at a decent address, approximately two blocks east of Halsted.

Low ceilings caused claustrophobia, crowded your brain, asserted Jeffrey outside their mother's hearing range. He wondered if padded cells were similar. He had Clare in stitches even though she considered his analysis a bit ungrateful, especially toward their mother. Only a straitjacket was missing, he continued. Finally, he would need electric shock treatments to bring him back from the brink of mental instability. Meanwhile, Clare sat cross-legged at the foot of his bed, as usual, shaking her head but remaining silent.

"Jeffrey," Clare now exclaimed, suppressing her outburst of laughter, "you're absolutely crazy."

"Exactly," he said. "They bought this place so they could finish the job before having me picked up and carted off to the real place. This is my period of initiation."

"And what about me?" she questioned.

"You?" he said with a playful wink. "Oh, you're here to humor me, distract me, so I don't run away. Cause an all-out search to keep me from becoming a danger to society." Becoming serious, he momentarily paused. "Mom wanted a house bad, huh?"

"Jeffrey, really, it's not that bad."

"Well," he said, finally relenting, "the rooms are decent size, but not as big as the rooms at Uncle C. J.'s and Aunt Lucinda's."

"Well, not quite," she agreed slowly, "but I think it's hard to find houses with rooms that big unless you pay a lot for them."

He shrugged. "You're probably right." He paused and then lowered his voice to just above a whisper. "And what is wrong with Mason lately?" He had begun to call his father by his given name in private conversation with his sister.

"What do you mean?" She was searching to see if they were on the same page.

"He gets up a lot to wee-wee. Lately, I think it's not quite as bad, but still, it's a lot."

Clare shook her head, suppressing her laughter as she cupped her hand over her mouth. "Jeffrey!" she exclaimed. "Wee-wee?"

"Okay, then, he pisses a lot," he said, and Clare again shook her head. "Well, I was trying to be nice, but you wouldn't let me."

"It's what you wanted to say all along, Jeffrey Ingram."

"Well, I know he's in the bathroom a lot at night. Haven't you noticed?"

She nodded slowly.

"Mom has to know, don't you think?"

Again, she nodded slowly, feeling a twinge of sorrow.

❦

At least the Illinois Beckfords were adhering to the family pact. Estelle had just gotten off the phone with her mother; Jennifer Travis Beckford had lapsed back into her usual stance on visiting Chicago. Estelle dutifully informed Ned that next week there would only be his family and hers for Thanksgiving dinner. He wasn't surprised.

Clare sat at the kitchen table polishing the sterling silver for the occasion. She loved this time of year but wished their family was larger like that of Aunt Doretha and Uncle Miles; they had huge family gatherings. Papa's family was nowhere to be found on holidays. She recalled that her mother had reached out several times. However, it seemed their absence brought their father relief.

"Clare," Estelle said as they prepared, "I hope you marry into a loving family. On this earth family and a few friends is all you have throughout life."

"Mama," she said softly, "you've told me a thousand times."

"All right then, this is one thousand one. Whoever you marry, get to know his family, especially his parents. Believe me, it will provide a blueprint regarding his upbringing, so choose carefully." She paused at the kitchen sink as she washed the china. "I have nothing against marrying a man without a formal education, but make sure he doesn't have a lot of insecurities because of it." She stopped her task entirely and turned to face her daughter. "Clare, I want you to get it and never *forg*et it."

"Mama," she said with a smile, "I will remember, believe me."

"See that you do, young lady." She paused. "And make certain you protect yourself at all times—and I do mean each and every time—against STDs and pregnancy."

Clare continued to polish the sterling silver as her mother turned back to cleaning the china.

"Believe me, life is hard enough," Estelle said. Then she stopped again and turned toward her daughter, smiling. "Guess who's coming for Thanksgiving dinner?"

"Tell me."

"Doretha and Miles, and they're bringing the children!" she exclaimed.

"What happened?" Clare asked with excitement.

"They wanted to do something different. Their Christmas is going to be a large, combined family get-together."

So, Clare realized, this was the reason her mother was so upbeat. Often, she watched her mother while helping her with house cleaning, when shopping for groceries, and even as they prepared meals together, regularly she appeared stressed. She attempted to help alleviate her mother's sustained despondency in any way she could. Clare was pleased that she was so happy.

Clare had suggested to her brother more than once, "Let's not complain, Jeffrey. If not for Papa, then let's do it for Mama." He would always agree, and finally the comments about his dislikes pertaining to their home discontinued. Instead, he resumed his preoccupation with repeating the seventh grade. These days, even though he still thought about Noah, wondered what kind of life he led, appearing before the judge had canceled all interest in a renewed friendship.

"What are you thinking about?" Clare had asked during their last conversation, knowing that he often nursed even a potential crisis.

"Nothing much," he said. *California, imagine!* Jeffrey thought. What had his grandmother told him when he'd mentioned Noah one time too many? "Jeffrey, ya never lose a friend, not a true friend, but gain a lesson. Life has many lessons that ya on this earth to learn from people placed on ya path fo' that purpose. It is God's way of makin' each of us better human beings, that's if each time we understan' why these people are on our journey. Sometimes it is fo' a short period of time, and at other times it is fo' a long period, or even a lifetime of learnin'. Like your mother and father or, when ya get older, the person that becomes ya wife. These become lifelong lessons of love and sharin'. Understan', Jeffrey?"

He remembered nodding, but at the time he hadn't wanted to be reminded of his mother and father. Their relationship appeared too complicated and sad.

☙

Estelle stirred and opened her eyes and was startled to see Jeffrey standing by her bed. "Jeffrey? What is it? What's the matter?"

He heaved a heavy sigh. He was in his third month of the new school year. This time his teacher, Ms. Tully, was an unconcerned, older individual. She had labored long and, now tired, seemed less concerned about her students than about her paycheck. Retirement was close, and she was looking forward to it.

Estelle reached for the nightlight.

"Mom, leave it off," he said as he slid down the wall to sit on the floor, hugging his knees. He wanted to talk before Mason came home from work, and she ended up on the living room sofa. He wanted to ask why she often slept on the sofa, but first things first.

She complied by not switching on the light. "Tell me what's wrong."

"I am repeating the seventh grade."

The preoccupation continued. As usual, her son treated each problem, large or small, as a monumental project. He nursed and fed it like a mother does her infant. She hoped he did not detect her impatience, but it was late for him to still be holding on to this.

"I hate repeating the seventh grade. Why did you let them hold me back?"

"They—Ms. Taft—said it would help you. She said it was for your own good. And" she added firmly, "you weren't keeping up with your studies, Jeffrey. Remember how I tried several times to get you to improve your grades?" She paused, but a response wasn't forthcoming. "You know that!"

"Now I'm a year behind," he said, as if ignoring her explanation. "That put me behind." He sighed again. "I hate that. Everyone will probably know I flunked the seventh grade."

"How, Jeffrey, if you don't tell them? You're just paranoid, that's all. No one will know unless you tell them."

She sensed he wanted to say something else, but she didn't know quite how to draw him out. He was blaming her for not supporting him against Ms. Taft, but she knew he was picking at a sore that was part of a deeper wound.

"Jeffrey, you must learn that life presents a series of problems. You must be the problem solver. In fact, you should avoid as many of those problems as possible. Since you are now thirteen and I am your parent, I am here to help you with both avoiding and solving as many problems as necessary. Do you understand?"

He nodded slowly. He had almost forgotten that Gran Jennie was her mother, so of course all that stuff about learning lessons had also been taught to her. That close call with the law and then not passing—it was too much. Repeating the seventh grade, a review of the same subjects was extremely monotonous! He was beginning to think it didn't matter anyway, like Mason always said.

Estelle telephoned her brother. "If it's not too much to ask, please come talk to your nephew. He's out of school starting Monday for Thanksgiving break. I don't want this same conversation over the holidays because I'm about worn to a frazzle."

Increasingly colder weather was preparing them for a hard winter, Chicago-style. When Ned arrived, Estelle let him in the back entrance. They conversed briefly, and then it was to the dining room to have that promised talk with his nephew.

Making certain not to disturb the beautiful lace tablecloth, Ned sat with Jeffrey at the dining room table. The living room and dining room furniture were familiar that Ned recalled being absent in their South Shore apartment. His sister was trying hard to make this place into a home. It was shaping up nicely. He recognized the seascape painting from the flat on South Parkway that hung over the mantel, and now above the living room sofa. There was no fireplace in the new home! He tried not to tarry on the memories of those two dear souls whom he would forever miss terribly. Finally, the china once packed away out of sight was again decoratively shelved in the china cabinet. From the walls hung creative, tasteful art. The curio cabinet, a treasured piece of furniture from Aunt Lu, had been converted to shelve select artifacts, not the traditional ornaments Estelle described as dust catchers. All her efforts exemplified class. He wondered if Mason was even appreciative of the vast differences between himself and the woman he had managed to marry only because of a careless mistake.

There were probably countless marriages held together by such a slender thread. Of course, he knew his sister loved her children and would consider neither one a mistake. Circumstances such as these were an example of the conflicting ambiguities of life.

Ned wanted to suggest to his nephew that they converse in the living room. The move would alter the moment and focus compromised.

"How are your classes going?" Ned asked his nephew.

Jeffrey was glum, practically uncommunicative. Ned categorized this characteristic in his nephew as one held mostly by older individuals. He wanted to be fair, withhold judgment.

Jeffrey heaved a sigh. "Okay, I guess… All this stuff, I've had it already." He sighed again. "It was bad enough that I had to be in front of a judge for something I didn't do, but…" He trailed off without finishing.

"Evidently it didn't stick because your grades indicated otherwise," Ned said none too kindly and then paused. "Okay, Jeffrey?" He looked directly at his nephew, thinking that a stern hand that only a father could provide was indeed lacking. Additionally, a couple of times while visiting, he had noticed a physical difference in Mason, as if he might be sick. He would have to ask his sister about that.

"You are victimizing yourself, guy. Don't cling to the negatives; rise above them. While I was growing up, my mother, *your* grandmother, always talked about life's challenges—bridges, she called them—and how you must keep your mind on the positive no matter what." He paused again, thinking that a review of one subject was indeed redundant, but perhaps one last attempt would bring closure. "First of all, Simpson's back in New Jersey. Second, didn't you tell me you used to laugh and joke with that guy. Be around him because you thought it was a big deal because the two of you looked so much alike? Some of your classmates teased you about it, right?"

"But he never visited me," Jeffrey replied defensively, "and I didn't visit him." Another person who had been taught by Gran, thought Jeffrey, with the same ideas. He needed another point of view. This was like talking to his mother all over again. There had to be another perspective apart from that of his mother and uncle. He already knew what Mason would have to say. He was tired of hearing about "the black life." Then again, these days Mason didn't talk much about anything.

"But you socialized with him on the way home, sometimes on the way to school."

Jeffrey remained silent and sullen.

"Jeffrey, is that right?"

He sighed and nodded slowly. "But I don't see anything wrong with being friendly. I mean, we weren't friends, just nice to each other."

"There's a way of being friendly yet keeping a person at a distance. You are kind, cordial, but not to the point that it can be defined as socializing. You're going to have to move on, okay?"

Admittedly, Jeffrey was far removed from that court and judge, but repeating the seventh grade had made him doubly angry. He continued telling himself that he was not the guilty party, but the victim. He told his uncle the same thing.

"Jeffrey," said Ned, growing impatient, "you are riding that horse to its death. Listen," he explained, "life is challenging you. There is a lesson you must learn. Repeat the seventh grade and do it with tenacity, vigor, and enthusiasm. This will teach you discipline, Jeffrey, which you need." He held up his hand. "Just listen. Your reward will be more knowledge and a brighter, stronger mind. Get it?" He paused. "Do you understand?"

He wondered if Estelle should leave the son of a bitch, if that would help at all, because this young man was becoming his father's son. Then again, what the hell? Leave now, after the fact, with the house and all? The suggestion should have come beforehand, not now. Then again, some of the blame for these correctible shortcomings had to be shouldered by Jeffrey Ingram himself. He was indeed a willful young man.

"Jeffrey, I need an answer. Otherwise, this is like talking to the walls. Do you want to be considered unreachable, Jeffrey?" *Like your father?* Ned thought.

The young man sighed deeply. "I get it," he said with great effort. "No, I don't want to be considered unreachable."

*Okay, out with it,* Ned decided. "I don't care who tells you education will not make a difference. Nothing is farther from the truth. Why do you think the courts in this country enacted a law making it illegal for your ancestors to be taught to read and write? You will have to work hard—in fact, *harder.* Let me tell you, young man, the white man's dumbest are absorbed by their smartest. Not all of them are used to or even familiar with the existence of Chantilly lace and Waterford crystal. There are those that aspire to be Wall Street brokers and super rich, but plenty are as poor as sharecroppers. Don't think for a minute the welfare system was invented to take care of us."

℘

That year passed, and Jeffrey, now fourteen, moved on to the eighth grade, but he continued to worry about another fact. Instead of one grade ahead of him as before, Clare was now *two* grades ahead of him in school—the tenth grade! A sophomore! His irritation over having to repeat the seventh grade was like wearing wool clothing in hot weather. It stifled his enthusiasm to learn. He didn't work to achieve anything above a C. For the first time Estelle became angry. His uncle had talked to him; she had talked to him. Both continued to expose him to books and music and art and all they could think of to make him become well-rounded. Ned continued to take him to ballgames, for long drives. Clare never joined them. She considered these encounters a male thing.

Meanwhile, Mason focused on his physical struggles. He was having a difficult time as the word "diabetes" churned ominously round and round in his brain as if riding a carousel. It prompted him to telephone Nelson. Mason's assumption of their father dying of diabetes was laid to rest.

"No, no, no, Mason. He had a heart attack."

"Do ya know for sho'?"

"Mason," his brother replied impatiently, "of course I know for sure Dad didn't die of diabetes."

"I was jus' wonderin' because—"

"I was there, remember?"

Their strained exchange ended with a frustrated Nelson hanging up.

Finally, Mason's attitude dictated that his doctor become brutally honest. "Mr. Ingram, it doesn't matter if you don't recall what family member had the disease. You are a diabetic."

"Forevah? I must use the needle forevah?"

"Yes, you will always need insulin *injections*," the doctor said. "Oral medication isn't strong enough." He paused. "Mr. Ingram? You need to stop smoking; you really do. I suggest no smoking or drinking." He was dealing with an unusually stubborn individual. "If you are disciplined and stay under the care of a physician, you will do reasonably well."

A few days later, Jeffrey and Clare approached their mother, and Jeffrey asked, "What is wrong" stopping himself in the nick of time "with Dad?"

Estelle, surprised by her own approach to this family dilemma, hesitantly sat her children down and told them exactly what was going on with their father. Both were astounded. Clare had heard of the disease, recalling her study partner at school saying something about her grandfather being a diabetic. He took pills instead of injections. Jeffrey couldn't remember ever hearing about diabetes. And no, their mother told them, he wasn't going to die. However, for the rest of his life he had to take insulin injections and adhere to a strict diet.

"I kept telling you there was something wrong with Mason," said Jeffrey to Clare a few days later.

Clare calmly agreed, but she felt bad for her mother. Of late, Clare didn't approve of Jeffrey's selection of friends. She suppressed a deep urgency to discuss this with her mother, opting not to jeopardize the good rapport with her brother.

"How much longer do you think Mason will be able to work?" Jeffrey asked.

She was sure he had given the situation plenty of thought. Her brother's approach to any given situation never ceased to astonish Clare. He had a habit of analyzing the aspects of situations that were of the least concern to most people their age. She considered this discussion eerie for someone so young.

"Jeffrey," she said, practically flabbergasted, "where did that come from? What makes you think Papa won't be able to work?"

"I don't know," he answered. "I heard Mom tell him the other day that he needs to take his injections on time. He sneaks to take them, you know—either to the bathroom or in his bedroom—because he doesn't want anyone to see him. I think he's ashamed of it."

"Eventually he'll probably be okay with it." It was more a wish than anything else.

"Think so? I don't."

❦

The excitement about living in a house was a distant memory for Jeffrey. When school began this fall, he would be a freshman in high school and fifteen years of age a few months thereafter. A one-family dwelling isolated on its own piece of land was a lot of work, especially when roles were not shared, but instead totally reversed. It was the son who was stuck with a lawn to mow and snow to shovel. Why hadn't Mom taken Mason at his word? Here they were, after the fact. Not wanting to own a house was probably the one solitary thing on which he and his father were in complete agreement.

He remembered his mother almost immediately having a fence installed. It kept the next-door neighbors' Doberman out of their yard, "pissin' and shittin'," to use Mason's crude terminology. "Another reason I never wanted a house!" Mason said to his wife. She deliberately ignored him.

Jeffrey had begun to think that the one positive aspect of Mason's disease was that it made him argue less. Except for the incident when Ned had gathered some of his friends to help him build his sister a patio over the objection of Mason, living under the Ingram roof during this time had been more pleasant. However, this change was short-lived. At first there were little quips of sarcasm, like the quick jabs from a prize fighter. There was no drinking for Mason like before (at least not of the serious type). This meant no more boys' night out. He made the decision to transfer back to days, only to be told there were no openings.

Days were the preferred schedule of most workers, and seldom was there an opening. "Are you sure?" his foreman had asked when he first requested the evening shift. "It's hard to transfer back," he'd warned. Mason decided the evening shift bearable enough because the drive had become routine—before the Diabetes! However, now he had to concentrate on remaining alert. The commute made him sleepy on the way home, a vivid reminder of the changes in his body caused by this disease.

There were also other changes, some more noticeable than others. His significant weight loss began to correct itself as his body adjusted to its condition. Gradual weight gain menaced his midsection resulting from regular beer consumption. More noticeable was the rapid graying of his hair. Something less acceptable was occurring with regularity, becoming embarrassing. Now approaching fifty, he told himself it was his age. With candor his doctor pulled the rug from under that theory. Understandably, the aging process did cause mild changes in virility. This was, however, drastic and the direct result of his chronic condition. Attempts and repeated failures aggravated the situation, causing his wife to choose the couch more regularly rather than the bed they shared. This infuriated him.

Jeffrey was aware of many of his father's physical changes. Monitoring them for some time while making comparisons he inferred to Clare, their mother looked basically the same.

"It has been a few years since Papa developed diabetes," Clare replied matter-of-factly. "There's nothing wrong with Mama."

"Nothing but Mason," Jeffrey replied.

He never revealed to Clare his constant eavesdropping and wondered whether his mother would frown upon this behavior if she knew. After one prominent incident he discovered just how detrimental eavesdropping could be.

"I know you feel stuck with me, Stelle."

It was one of the few times he'd been able to make out his father's words. Affixing his ear as close as possible to the wall, he listened intently. Never hearing her response, he assumed she had made none.

"You only stayed wit me 'cause of Jeff. I know that. Clare would never have kept us together. I know that." He paused. "Only Jeff made you stay."

"Every son needs his father, Mason."

"But that's why ya stayed, right?"

"A son needs his father, Mason," she repeated.

It was quiet for a little while. He was about to steal back to his bed when his mother spoke again.

"Mason, stop it," she said in an angry, low voice. "Just go to sleep."

"You shoulda knocked him in the head," he replied. An angry, frustrated voice rose above a whisper. "Why didn't ya?"

"Stop talking nonsense, Mason. Foolish, irresponsible nonsense."

His parents' bedroom door opened, closed softly. He was beginning to appreciate and admire his mother's poise, her natural elegance and grace. That demeanor also meant that she could be like a freezer compartment.

Waiting a few minutes, he then ever so quietly checked the living room sofa. Sure enough, there she was with her trusty pillow and throw. Otherwise, it was always in the same spot—draped over the back of the sofa.

His mother had begun learning to knit a few years back when the church offered weekly classes. Prior to learning this craft, she would sit resting her eyes with a book in her lap. Desperate for an alternative to excessive reading, her proficiency in the craft grew. Several months passed when she introduced a beautifully knitted, multicolored throw. She simply flung it, neatly folded, over the back of the sofa. "First come, first served," she announced. Clare titled this chosen craft "Select Therapy." Both agreed: What a life!

As a young girl, Estelle Beckford had learned crocheting and sewing from Jennifer, but neither held her interest like knitting. When she started knitting, concentration to avoid dropping stitches was difficult for a painstaking period. The instructor demonstrated with a crochet hook the skill of correcting a dropped stitch. Estelle's persistence conquered the problem. Occasionally, she would sew a few simple garments for Clare. Discovering her daughter's interest led to her learning the art of sewing. She then returned to the craft that interested her most—knitting!

It was an alternate Saturday and their mother's weekend off. An extra special breakfast! She stood at the kitchen counter making pancake batter. The aroma of bacon frying in the oven (the only way she ever fried bacon) filled the room. Estelle, looking unrested, taut as a drum. Tension lurked, rendering an edginess to the quiet. Other than morning greetings no one spoke.

Jeffrey always rearranged his lawn-mowing schedule to evenings on the weekends his mother was home. Usually on these Saturday mornings, his favorite pastime was watching cartoons. This morning, he sat staring at the television screen, seeing nothing as his brain kept repeating his father's disturbing words: *You shoulda knocked him in the head.*

The absent family member was sticking to his routine. In the bathroom taking his injection with the door closed. He emerged afterward from his ritual, facing his family like a drug addict being fingered by narks before being placed under arrest. He had spent a long time adjusting to his condition. Finally, he had settled in. This disease's assault on his manhood was still painful for him, pinching terribly like the wrong-size shoe. Complicating and further aggravating his predicament was the unwillingness of his wife to be, if unloving, at least more understanding.

Earlier, he had eaten an early morning snack after ascertaining that his wife was camped on the living room sofa. Now, entering the kitchen for the second time, went to the refrigerator to pour a glass of water. He then sat down at the table. Trouble stirred. Clare knew it, Estelle expected it. Jeffrey still sat in front of the television, stewing. Clare always knew when something was wrong. She made an innocent comment. No response, so she let him be.

Jeffrey intuitively left the television just as his father suddenly rose from his seat. The entire bowl of pancake batter taken from the counter slammed to the floor.

"I don't want pancakes, woman!" he yelled.

"Mason, I was making them for Clare and Jeffrey!" his wife exclaimed. *This man*, she thought. *Good heaven!*

In stature, Jeffrey was now taller than Mason (a fact Ned often made mention of to his sister). Armed with what he'd overheard, Jeffrey glared at his father, breaking his stare only long enough to look down at the mess he had just created. Batter, mingled with bits of glass, was strewn over the freshly mopped floor, spattering the oven door, speckled the closest wall. Back to temper tantrums, are we?" Jeffrey asked before thinking.

Mason was utterly enraged. "Boy, don't talk to me like ya crazy!"

At the precise moment Mason swung at Jeffrey, Estelle anxiously stepped between them. The blow landed on her temple, practically knocking her down.

Chaos ensued. There was yelling and screaming from everyone, even Clare got involved. She and a tearful Estelle separated Jeffrey from Mason. Mason slipped on the batter, hit the floor. Finally, after a few minutes, bedlam subsided, but the morning was ruined. In fact, the weekend was ruined. Slipping and sliding, Mason awkwardly picked himself up to flee the scene.

The bathroom door slammed to remain closed for a very long time as the others listened to running water. Mason finally emerged; his pants clumsily clutched in one hand. Hurriedly he disappeared behind a closed bedroom door. Minutes later he rushed out dressed, tightly holding a bag in one hand and mumbling something about going to the cleaners.

Suffering the rare emotion of embarrassment, Estelle gingerly treated the small facial bruise near her hairline with a small ice pack so that there would be no telltale mark. Jeffrey kept asking if she was hurt. Kindly, she brushed him aside, seeming almost withdrawn because of the display in front her two children. It appeared as if overnight, time was transitioning them into young adulthood.

Estelle, Clare, and a furious Jeffrey cleaned up the kitchen. *What a mess! A mess! In every possible way*, Jeffrey thought. The three of them worked diligently for over an hour, even wiping bits of debris from the kitchen cabinets. No one talked.

Desperately needing to stay busy, Estelle threw out the charred bacon and made more batter, this time in a plastic bowl. She opened a new package of bacon and again placed the strips in the oven on a baking sheet. Jeffrey returned to the television, only to switch it off.

Later, the pancakes and bacon were eaten at the breakfast table in silence; All three avoided any conversation.

*So*, thought Jeffrey, *the real Mason finally returns with that nasty disposition no longer dormant. It's as well as ever.*

Hours later, in the early evening, Jeffrey was mowing the lawn when he heard his father's voice, "Jeff," loud, above the drone of the lawn mower as he held the kitchen door open. "I wanna talk to ya."

"Can it wait until I'm done?" he answered with a trifle of impatience, hoping his voice didn't give him away.

His father hesitated for a moment, turning away slightly, nodded, then called out the affirmation as he closed the door.

"You know he mows the lawn evenings when all the family is home," Estelle said gently.

She was fully aware that her son revised his schedule, without fail, every weekend she was home. After breakfast Estelle and her children would enjoy sitting around the kitchen table, discussing a variety of issues. Jeffrey mowed the lawn Friday after school or Saturday evening.

Mason had already apologized to his wife for the ugly incident, awkwardly explaining that he had never meant to hit her. Estelle was still upset about Jeffrey's outburst and, in turn, Mason's aggression toward his son. He had yet to make amends. Anxiously, she hoped nothing was brewing.

"You shouldn't have been lashing out at him either, Mason," she said, allowing that to be her only statement about the incident as she dried the dishes. Troubling was what had triggered their son's comment? Estelle often privately pondered the fact that this man seldom, if ever, interacted favorably with either of his children.

Clare's offer to clean up the breakfast dishes, or even to help, was gently declined by her mother, a queue to immediately exit the kitchen.

"Mason," Estelle said as calmly as possible, "for once, talk to Jeffrey."

"About what?" he replied defensively.

As *if you don't already know*, she thought. "Let him know you are proud that he is your son, Mason." There was silence. "For once, *talk* to him. After all, he is your son." What did it take to reach this man? "Didn't your father ever tell you and your bothers that he was proud that all of you were his sons?"

"Not really. He was in the field from dawn to dusk. All of us were doin' the same thing, workin'. There was no time ta' spare."

*Good grief,* Estelle thought. At that moment she felt helpless. After all these years of marriage, talking to this man was yet a struggle. Rightly or wrongly, she considered Mason's state of constant borderline anger to be partly the cause of his diabetes. She recalled her mother repeatedly reminding her to stay as calm as possible in any situation.

Outside, Jeffrey assessed his youth as not so pleasant. His parents, especially his mother, wouldn't permit a part-time job. "Let's wait until you're sixteen, Jeffrey," his mother had explained. He sensed there would be push-back to permitting it even then. She wanted him to take more interest in his grades and told him so. From then on, she had given him an allowance. They had become coconspirators as it appeared weekly on his dresser with only the very end of the bills visible from beneath his clock radio.

It was dusk when Jeffrey walked slowly back to the house from the garage after storing the lawn mower and the half-full gas can. *Since when have we talked? You complain, Mason,* he thought, *I listen.* Often his father mentioned his own childhood, but only in measured degrees of unpleasantness. Jeffrey wondered whether any part of Mason's childhood had been enjoyable, wishing he knew Uncle Nelson well enough so they could discuss it.

As always, the back storm door squeaked. Mason looked up, expectantly, waiting for his son to sit at the table while he finished his evening snack. Jeffrey complied. They sat facing each other in silence. Estelle was putting away the dishes, slowly, hoping there would be no shouting. *No,* her demeanor said when her husband looked her way, *I am not leaving the kitchen.*

*Okay, then,* Mason thought. *Here it is.* "Jeff, don't evah talk ta' me like that again, ya' hear?"

Jeffrey offered a guarded nod, not trusting his voice as the words he'd overheard that night remained front and center in his brain.

"Answer me, Jeff," he said.

*Answer,* his mother silently pleaded with her eyes as she and her son made eye contact.

"Okay," he answered.

"Don't use dat tone with me, either." He paused. "What's eatin' ya' anyways?"

They continued staring at each other, father and son. The wasted years between them.

*Mason,* Estelle thought, *you don't even know how to talk to your own son. The two of you have never had a conversation.*

Suddenly the words knifed the air, sharp and treacherous. "Why did you tell Mom she should have knocked me in the head? Why did you say that?"

Mason recoiled, momentarily speechless. The words stung. "Boy, I was talkin' to ya' mama, not you." He sputtered the words in shame, thinly disguised as muted ire.

"It was about me, though," Jeffrey said as he stood up. He always became animated when angry.

Estelle put away the last dish and came to the table. "Jeffrey," she said quietly to stabilize the dialogue, "sit down."

"Stay out of it, Stelle."

"Mason, please lower your voice." She paused and gently placed her hand on her son's shoulder. Jeffrey was a head taller; the Beckford genes were becoming dominant. "Sit down, Jeffrey."

"Stay out of it, Stelle!" Mason repeated.

"Stop yelling, Mason," she said with quiet firmness.

Jeffrey complied and again sat at the table facing his father, repeating the question. "Why did you say it?"

"You had to be listenin' hard to hear that."

"Why did you say it?"

*Mason,* her eyes pleaded, although she remained silent. *Tell him you didn't mean it,* she wanted to say and attempted to convey with her eyes; *tell him that you were upset with me.*

"Stelle, just leave us be."

"When you stop raising your voice," she said quietly.

"I still want to know why you said it," Jeffrey said for a final time, despite knowing he would never get the answer he deserved. *I will never know this man*, he thought. *He goes to work, comes home, eats here, sleeps in the bed beside my mother, and is my biological father. Still, I don't know him. He prefers it that way. I know Uncle Ned better than I will ever know Mason.* At that moment he felt very lonely and decided he would never again be able to address him as "Dad" or "Pop." "Mason" sounded right. In fact, he considered it fitting.

Mason never answered his son's question, but instead in deliberate deflection turned to Estelle. "Is you leavin', Stelle?"

"When you stop being so angry," she replied firmly, "but not until then."

*Tell him you didn't mean it*, she wanted to say as she stood beside the table. Saying it aloud would have caused something close to chaos. *Later*, she thought, *"I'll tell your son why you said it. I was the target; you were angry with me. I won't tell him everything, but at least that much.*

For a long time, the two of them, father and son, sat at the table across from each other, only sharing the space with no more words between them. Finally, Mason mumbled something about going to bed and got up from the table. Moments later he could be heard stirring about in the bedroom. *He's restless*, she thought, *and will be the entire night.* The living room for sure.

Jeffrey continued to sit for a little while. When she joined him, sitting down in the same spot his father had just occupied, he seemed bewildered.

She began to talk softly in muted tones. "He was angry with me," she explained quietly, just above a whisper.

The moment was awkward. Words did not come out naturally or easily. She faltered, not sure how to explain; it was embarrassing because of the intimacy of the incident.

"I know, Mom," he said quietly. "I heard the entire conversation. I just wanted him to tell me why he said it, you know?"

"I know," she said.

She wished she could elaborate and move beyond her uneasiness; she wanted to ask exactly how he had heard the conversation. Had he been standing by the door, or was the wall between their bedrooms thin enough to hear without strain? She didn't want to accuse or question her son. She could hear Mason continuing to stir about in the bedroom. *All because he hates to say he is sorry*, she thought. *He hates to be placed in a position of weakness, which makes him just that—WEAK!* A missed opportunity to rescue something, anything. This house, this man, this marriage, she lamented. All except her children. They were the one good thing.

‽

One Saturday evening when Jeffrey answered the phone, it was Nelson Ingram telephoning his brother again. The uncle offered a brief but cordial greeting to his unknown nephew, who simply passed the receiver to his father. That was the way it was. Intermittent conversations for months to glean as much information as possible about this unwanted affliction. Nelson had been rummaging around in his memory bank for remnants of information that might be valuable.

"Come to think of it, Uncle Morris was a diabetic," Nelson said. Uncle Morris, their father's brother, had died when all of them were very young. This vague information had slipped Nelson's mind until just now.

"Who else in the family?" Mason inquired.

"How would I know who else in the family—if anybody—has it? You're older than I am, Mason," replied Nelson on the verge of agitation.

It was true. Mason was two years older.

"Anyway, I remembered," Nelson said, "and just thought you should know."

After exchanging just a few more words, they hung up. With that small segment of the Ingram family history completed, it was silence on both ends just like before.

"After all this time," Jeffrey later said to Clare in his bedroom, "he still wants to know why he has diabetes. He has it, okay? End of story."

They were in conference at their favorite meeting spot, his bedroom, during one of the final weeks of summer. Jeffrey often teased his sister because she always positioned herself, legs crossed, at the foot of his bed. He told her all she needed was to clasp her hands for meditation.

"Jeffrey," Clare inquired, "why so quiet?"

He had spent the entire Saturday with his uncle and was unusually pensive. He had finally discussed what he'd labeled the "kitchen incident" with his uncle. Strangely, his uncle said very little, which meant he wanted to say a lot. He knew that about his uncle. His father had been the topic of conversation between them only a few times, and each time his uncle had said very little. Jeffrey had so many things to consider in his young life. He didn't like school. He was tired of studying about white folks and their accomplishments. Biology could be an escape, but he never studied his textbook well enough to fully grasp the subject. Yes, Uncle Ned and his mother had told him about black people's accomplishments in this country, and he had read quite a few books that both his mother and uncle had given him. Outside the printed pages of select books, who else talked about the genius of black people?

"Rissie," he said, "do you know that a black man by the name of Charles B. Brooks invented the street sweeper?"

She was leisurely flipping the pages of *Vogue* magazine. Like most young girls, Clare was maturing with an interest in the latest fashions. "No," she said.

"How many drivers stop at the red light and are aware that a black man created the traffic signal? They stop, the light changes to green, and off they go."

"What's his name?" she said, looking up from her book.

"Garrett A. Morgan," Jeffrey answered. "And the third rail was invented by Granville C. Woods, another black man. I'll bet that people riding the subway or elevated train never give it a thought."

"Why would they, Jeffrey?" Clare asked quietly. "They're simply riding to a destination."

"Rissie," he said with slight impatience, "are you listening to me?"

"Yes," she answered. She stopped turning the pages and became thoughtful. "If we learned about them in school like we know about Thomas Edison…"

"Exactly," Jeffrey said as he sat up on the side of his bed. He snapped his finger. "Guess what? Lewis Latimer was the one that helped Edison invent the lightbulb. Edison's carbon filament would burn for only a few minutes while Lewis Latimer's carbon filament burned for hours! Who gets credit for the entire lightbulb? Thomas Edison, okay? Latimer's name is never mentioned. All over this country the name connected to electricity is Thomas Edison. Edison. Edison. Thomas Edison!" He sighed, shaking his head. "So many things in this country have been invented by black people, and we get no credit whatsoever."

"Jeffrey don't get so upset," replied Clare, closing her book.

"It doesn't upset you to read about all the accomplishments of white people and nothing about us?"

"Yes," she said, "but you can't get so upset, Jeffrey."

"It would be different if we were lazy without a brain in our head." He sighed and then paused to retrieve from his bedside the book on black inventors. He scanned a page. "Okay, Alexander Miles patented an electric elevator in 1887 with automatic doors to close off the shaft, and this made the elevator safer, Rissie. Do you ever hear his name when they mention elevators? No! Otis is always the name associated with elevators."

"Jeffrey, why don't you study harder in school and get good grades?"

He returned the book to the floor next to his bed. He was very angry and didn't know how to relieve the emotion. "Rissie," he finally responded, "I am tired of studying about what white folks have done on this earth as if black people have no knowledge."

"But you know that is not true," Clare responded gently. "You haven't forgotten that laws were enacted and enforced by this government to make certain we were *not* taught to read and write."

"And?" he said.

She hated it when her brother was in such a mood. She wished he would make friends. She wished he would work harder in school.

"Jeffrey, whites that made the laws knew that black people were not dumb. They know that now." She paused. "Why don't you study harder subjects like math and biology? Jeffrey, you are smart! Your aptitude in math is better than mine."

"I'm tired."

"Jeffrey," Clare said, laughing, "you're a year younger than me." She shook her head. "You're too young to be tired."

"Mama and Uncle Ned give me all these books about black people's accomplishments. What good are they?"

"You are armed with the information, Jeffrey Ingram! You know who you are so that you can be more confident."

"Do you know who invented air conditioning?"

"No," she said, "who?"

"Frederick McKinley Jones. When white folks try to stay cool, it's too bad they don't know that."

"Neither do most black people," she answered, but she didn't laugh. She wanted her brother to make friends, get out of the house. Do something. Anything. "You are exceptionally bright, Jeffrey," she said, "so why don't you put it to good use?"

"Don't you want the world to know the accomplishments of black people?"

"Yes," she replied, "and if or when I have children, I will make sure they know as much about our history as I possibly can, just like Mama and Uncle Ned are doing now." She smiled.

"Each one, teach one, like Uncle Ned always says, right?"

"Right," Clare agreed.

"How long do you think that will take?"

"It wouldn't take long at all if all black people worked at it. Not enough are interested in getting involved. I don't read as much about it as you do, but I do find the information interesting."

"All we have is Black History Month," Jeffrey complained, "when they mention you know who."

"George Washington Carver, Booker T. Washington, and Harriet Tubman," the siblings said in unison and then fell back on Jeffrey's bed in uproarious laughter.

The deafening quiet that followed transported Jeffrey to deeper thought.

"Did you enjoy being with Uncle Ned?" Clare asked, wanting to avoid another heavy subject. "Did Druscilla do anything mean?"

Even though Jeffrey was tactful with his cousin, sometimes they exchanged unkind words. However, Ned no longer had to intervene; the age factor had kicked in. They were now young adults capable of settling their own disputes.

"No," Jeffrey answered. "Since you didn't come along, we didn't go to the house, but instead did things here in the city. We even took a ride and talked, rode almost to the Michigan State Line. When we got back in town, Uncle Ned drove over to South Shore Drive because he'd almost forgotten to deliver something to Aunt Celeste's sister. You know she lives over there." Clare nodded as Jeffrey paused and laughed. "Uncle Ned told me to wait downstairs. He could use me as an excuse not to stay. It wouldn't be a lie that I was waiting downstairs in the lobby." He laughed again. "And then the strangest thing happened. You couldn't guess who walked in while I was in the lobby. Of all people," he said, "in walks Noah Daniels."

Clare was astounded. "You're kidding! They moved back to Chicago?"

"No, no," he quickly replied. "He was in town visiting his grandmother. She lives on South Shore Drive in the *same* building."

"She no longer lives on Cottage Grove?"

"No, because I think—from what I was told—after their grandfather died, it got to be too much upkeep and all, so she sold her house and moved to an apartment." He paused. "Her lease is just for another year, and then she is moving to California. She's Noah's father's mother. He wants her to leave Chicago to be near them."

"Was he by himself?"

"His sister Monica was with him. She was the one who gave me all the information about their grandmother. She spotted me first and came running over to me. 'Jeffrey,' she said, 'is that you?' She hugged me." He thought about her for a minute. He was noticing girls and considered her very pretty. And boy, she sure smelled good! Of course, he didn't share that with Clare. Even before he had begun to pay attention to the opposite sex, he considered Monica better-looking than most. For a few minutes, he was silent, thinking, reviewing the incident, inwardly debating whether he wished to continue. He then surged ahead. "She had more to say than he did. He was friendly, but she did most of the talking. First, about their grandmother and her moving and all, then about California and her first year at UCLA." He stared into space and then gave a rather disgusted sigh. "He has changed."

"In what way?" she said.

"He's different."

"Taller, heavier, looks older, what?" she asked.

"He is taller, but so am I, and both of us are heavier, but I don't mean like that." He paused. "But I still would have recognized him and his sister because they haven't changed that much, you know?"

She nodded.

"I'm a little taller than Noah." He had to admit that he took pride in the fact that he was not going to be medium height like the Ingram men. "But that's not what I am talking about. He is different, that's all."

"Jeffrey, he probably considers you different too," Clare said thoughtfully. "Both of you are older. Don't forget, he left our neighborhood even before he moved to California."

"I'm aware of that, Rissie," he replied reluctantly, as if he now regretted bringing up the incident. "I met Noah in kindergarten, remember?"

She nodded.

"But I don't know him anymore," he continued. "I think—no, I don't think—I *know* he has changed…" He stopped and thought for a moment. "Rissie, have you ever known anybody that was once a friend, and then you didn't see them for a long time? When you do see each other again, you wonder what happened because you no longer seem to …" He shrugged. "I can't explain it."

"I know. You couldn't pick up from where you left off," she said, "like I do with Nadine. I've known her since first grade. Even though we talk on the phone all the time, I can go for months without seeing her. When we do see each other, we just continue from our last visit."

"That's it. We were once friends, but I got the strangest feeling that we will never be friends again." There was such a complex mix of thoughts and feelings stirring around in his head. "I dropped him a card once after we moved to South Shore, and it never returned."

"Do you think he got it? Maybe you should have asked him if he got it."

"Well, it never came back, and Mom said that if it never returned, it was forwarded to his new address. He was moving into a house when we moved to the apartment, remember?"

She nodded again.

"He got it; I know he did."

Clare wished her brother would make friends more easily. She could transition in and out of encounters with classmates that often left her with no desire to delve beneath that superficial layer. She had study partners who were nothing more, nothing less. There were lunch buddies with whom she discussed trivia, but never engaged in anything meaty. Sometimes she needed a good laugh, and there was one classmate who was so jovial, just loads of fun, but she was a gossip. They would share an innocent joke or two, but that was that until the next time. When she needed a friend with whom to have an earnest heart-to-heart, she called Nadine. Presently, she reflected on their phone calls and smiled. Both mothers monitored their conversations—but never in a nagging way—because they always had so much to talk about. Whenever anyone else telephoned Clare, her mother never poked her smiling face inside the doorway.

Not quite sure how guys treated friends they considered more than casual acquaintances, Clare had hoped Jeffrey and Noah would experience that kind of relationship. Then Noah moved to the West Coast. Okay, so it was not destined to be. Her brother needed to chalk up the friendship to an experience that was good while it lasted. She wondered why Jeffrey considered every life experience that ended contrary to his liking to be a crisis. She often told him, "Jeffrey, come on, it's not that bad. Your limbs are still intact. You're not in a cast or suffering from third-degree burns, know what I mean?" Inwardly, she was saying, *Get over it!* Knowing that this would have an uncaring ring, she never once sounded the bell.

"Jeffrey," she now said tactfully, "I think Noah has moved on, and you should do the same. He probably will always remember what you two had at the time and was glad to have the brief encounter today. He probably has no interest in long-distance friendships. Some people are like that, and all their experiences are hands-on. They want to be able to literally reach out and touch for it to have constant meaning. Besides, it requires effort to maintain anything special with a person that you don't see on a regular basis, especially from a long distance. Plus, this is the first time you've seen each other in quite some time."

"Anyway, then Uncle Ned came down," Jeffrey continued. "I introduced him to them, and we all said good-bye. We left, and they headed toward the elevator."

He recalled Uncle Ned asking, "So that's the infamous Noah?" He had nodded his reply.

Meanwhile, he didn't answer his sister, but instead reclined with his hands resting behind his head, gazed at the ceiling. He thought of what had occurred since Noah moved to California—his run-in with the law and failing the seventh grade. He decided to dismiss Noah as part of his past. He remained in that position and Clare in hers. For what seemed a long time, neither of them spoke.

"Well," he said, "perhaps I will spend the rest of the summer mowing and counting the blades of grass."

Both laughed. Then she reviewed the comment, deciding that her brother was too young to be bored. Nevertheless, he was.

Jeffrey was slightly upset when at the dinner table that evening Clare brought up the incident, causing their mother to react with raised brow. Later when she questioned him about Noah, he was reluctant to discuss him.

"He looks a little different," he offered.

"Aren't you glad that you saw him? That he's doing all right?" She paused. "And that you're doing all right as well?"

"Think so?" he asked.

She knew he was referencing himself, finding the reply rather disturbing. "Yes," she replied, "I think so. What exactly is wrong with your life?" She paused, but he didn't reply. "Jeffrey, you cannot always believe the grass is greener on the other side. I'm positive that Noah's life has challenges, things that are not to his liking." She remembered the card just then. "Did you ask him if he received your card?"

"No," he said, "the conversation didn't go that well with him. His sister was doing most of the talking. I thought it would sound rather silly. It was so long ago. What would I say? 'Did you get that card I sent you a few years back?'" He heaved an aggravated sigh. "I'm sure he got it." He paused. "Things have happened since I saw him last. I was in trouble—well, at least almost—and then failed the seventh grade. There is nothing good about that."

"Jeffrey," she responded firmly, "you cannot continue to worry about the past. You must move on." When he didn't answer, she continued. "If you had asked about the card, your curiosity would have been satisfied. You wouldn't have to forever question if he received it. Sometimes mail does get lost, but I would say that most of the time when it isn't returned, it is received.

"The world is a big place, Jeffrey. Number one, forget about the past. Let it become a positive lesson for the future. Make new friends. It's not that hard. I'm sure there are some nice young men at your school. Get your grades up so that you can get involved in after-school activities. What are your interests—track, basketball, football, an instrument? It's still not too late." A few years ago, Estelle had attempted to get him involved in sports or music or both. "You will be in high school in the fall, and there are lots of things you can become involved in."

"It's just as well about Noah," he said. Jeffrey had an uncanny knack for ignoring whatever he didn't care to discuss. Depending on her mood, Estelle sometimes found it irritating, like now. "I'm still a year behind," he answered.

"Jeffrey," she replied none too kindly, "let that go. You are going to have to release it." She paused to control her impatience. "You are still not keeping up your grades, okay? You could have nothing on your report card below a B, yet you refuse to study." *As Clare does,* she thought, but caught herself before she uttered it. Sibling rivalry had not been an issue in their family yet, and she took pride in that fact. Unaware of Jeffrey's constant eavesdropping, she believed that she handled—at least most of the time—what was between her and Mason tactfully. Their problems didn't negatively affect the children.

Jeffrey sighed. Should he or should he not bring it up? He wanted to know. He rubbed the corner of his eye. He wished he had gained this knowledge without eavesdropping. Still, he needed to know. "I need to ask you something," he said quietly. There was a long pause, and he looked at her with a forlorn expression.

"Jeffrey," she urged quietly, "go ahead and ask me."

"I don't know," he said, heaving a troubled sigh. "You might get mad."

She offered a tolerant smile. She could never give birth to another individual like this person if she tried. "Jeffrey, just ask me," she coaxed gently. "I can't tell you what you need to know unless you ask."

"Would you and Dad be together if I was never born?"

Taken aback, she gave him a wide stare. "What on earth makes you ask me that?"

"Would you?" he demanded quietly. "Just… would you?"

"Where is this coming from, Jeffrey?" There was an element of anxiousness in her voice. What else had he heard? "I told you your father made that statement because he was angry with me, that's all. He was angry with me," she repeated.

"Okay," he answered.

She wondered if it would ever be resolved, if he would ever forget. *No*, she thought, *he will never forget*. She wished her son had thicker skin. His father, who was comparably smaller in stature, was of a rougher temperament. Jeffrey, his son, had a sensitive and gentle nature as he grew into a Beckford in height as well as size. Father and son were such contradictions and opposites of each other, she thought. The son had so much potential but attempts to convey this to him met with so much negativity. In a rash moment, she considered leaving Mason. The thought dissipated just as quickly. She was trapped with sickness, the house… Now she had a few bills. She could still hear Doretha urging her to spend some of the money from what was now a serious bank account. "Money is mercurial, Estelle, unless you are a Rockefeller or one of the Hiltons," her friend had advised. She took only the advice to return to school. Once a week she took a class toward her long-overdue degree. No longer would she permit this circumstance to thwart that goal as she continued to hold on to the money. A support system that reinforced her position in this loveless marriage.

On several occasions Estelle had talked to Ned about Jeffrey's relationship with his father and the incidents that made their coexistence a strained one. These days Jeffrey and Mason exchanged very few words, avoiding each other as much as possible. If only Mason knew how to apologize. Their son dramatized each incident more than a little, but she had to admit that this one was major. No child wants to feel unwanted.

"You have never been close to your children, especially Jeffrey," she said in their bedroom one Saturday evening. "The two of you don't even talk. You don't even make the effort, Mason. He's your son."

"I nevah asked fo' a son. Jus' happened."

"What a cold thing to say," she said. She watched him for a long time. His eyes avoided hers while he continued to dress, looking uncomfortable. He was going out with some of his mill buddies. "Our entire life together just happened," she spat angrily.

He looked up from putting on his shoes. He had tried to stay out of the bars. Even though he couldn't drink much, he liked the atmosphere. He started to answer, but she dismissed him by turning her back and leaving the bedroom.

# Chapter Ten

His new friends were the rough boys; some had long records of truancy. Others frequently had run-ins with the law. He felt like his mother watched him from the shadows of his mind, so he cautioned himself not to follow suit by skipping school. Therefore, his bad behavior was kept to a minimum. Although the forged notes would work periodically, he knew he couldn't make a habit of it. Pangs of anger were sharp whenever he thought about Mason's outburst. He had repeatedly tried to force it from his thoughts, yet it remained lodged rigidly in place. Sometimes he lingered in the dark places of his mind to picture himself as a blank, totally nonexistent. It was at these times he allowed himself to ask: *What if I had never been*? If there were only Clare, would his mother have stayed with Mason? He once divulged this to Rissie. It was the first time he witnessed his sister lose her temper. Her anger was jolted awake by a deep, inner fright, spontaneous and surging, like a voltage connected to an emotional switch.

Their parents weren't home when the conversation happened. The house was quiet except for their voices as they engaged in early evening small talk before homework. His words knifed into that calm.

"I guess it would have been better if I had never been born," he said. "Then you and Mom could leave Mason."

Clare erupted. "Jeffrey," she shouted, almost leaping from the foot of his bed, "you're spending too much time by yourself or with those numbskulls you hang with!"

She had mentioned his choice of friends several times before, even though she would never tell their mother. She had enough on her plate. She was working hard at her job and, in addition, completing her bachelor's degree. Prior to deciding about classes, their mother had queried them both about the arrangement. It would cause her to be absent more than usual and take away some of the quality time they spent together. Both had assured her that they would be just fine.

"I don't know what you think about most of the time," Clare finished heatedly, "but this is the most stupid idea yet."

Stalking from his bedroom, his sister moved about their home for the next few days with guarded caution, engaging in only limited conversation with him. Clare had discussed her intuitive fear with no one, not even her best friend Nadine.

It had never happened before, so Clare's outburst surprised Jeffrey. He felt so alone during this period. She continued helping their mother with household chores as always but did homework in her room instead of at the dining room table. *She's avoiding me*, he thought miserably. Sometimes he would listen and hear her quietly moving about in the private haven of her bedroom. A few times he heard their mother call her for a phone call. (Phones were no longer in their bedrooms: Mason's orders.) He waited, emotionally dejected, with intense anticipation. Sadly, he stared at the vacancy at the foot of his bed each time she passed his room to and from her own.

Finally, he willed himself to apologize creating an almost immediate reunion. Initially, the conversation faltered, but he nudged it forward by managing to say something comical. Her melodious laughter caused them both to relax. Like magic, all the tension melted away like ice in heat. He loved that about Rissie. Had she totally forgotten? Probably not, but she easily forgave. If their mother noticed what had transpired between them, she never let on. She went about her usual routine. All except Mason had homework, although only two produced favorable results. As for Mason, well, he never paid that much attention to them anyway.

☙

Jeffrey remained entangled in his own personal war. A good percentage of his anger was directed at himself. Enough was left for his father and, even though unjustified, his mother as well. After running into Noah that past summer, with finality that segment of his life was jetted to the past.

The crowd he now hung with was not a studious lot. Their personalities suited his lack of motivation. The words of his father would sporadically crash into his thoughts—*You shoulda knocked him in the head*—when least expected. It sometimes disturbed any short-lived tranquility to cause an emotional carousel. The words were often reviewed in private, but never discussed with anyone.

Uncle Ned continually told him, "Life is what you make it." Whenever he mentioned his father to his uncle—and several times he did try—the latter engaged in a verbal cha-cha. Encouraging statements about positive steps such as getting better grades, staying focused, and on and on. Not once did he comment about Mason, and somehow Jeffrey wished his uncle could become an ally in that respect. The result was unfavorable because his uncle's statements began to sound rhetorical. It was understandable that his mother was too involved to be objective; she was married to the man. Plus, her saying anything against Mason would be like dropping a pebble in a pond. Disquieting and far-reaching effects in the house with low ceilings that the four of them inhabited. However, the fact that his mother now slept on the couch a lot more than before was silent testimony of her discontent. He found comfort in this act, easing away most of the anger he harbored against her. It made her his totally unaware ally.

"What do you want Uncle Ned to say?" his sister once replied. "He's not going to say anything about Papa. You shouldn't want him to, really. He does spend time with you which means he supports you. That is a good thing." *That is a good thing.* It was his sister's favorite phrase, especially for ending discussion of a subject.

*You are lucky to have Uncle Ned to fill the void*, Clare thought. She did not want to elaborate further complicating a difficult situation.

Lately, Jeffrey had been examining a myriad of past incidents, which at times presented him with an influx of doubt and confusion. In particular, he reflected on an incident occurring years ago. He had come inside the South Parkway building for a few minutes. Often when playing outside, he would go to Aunt Lu's when he wanted a drink of water. This time he had climbed the stairs to the second floor. He then halted in the small hallway that led into their apartment, overhearing his parents mention his name in the middle of their discussion.

"Can't you for once not elaborate on the bad. Simply explain to him the possibilities. He's only nine years old. The country is changing, Mason." It was the early sixties. "We are amid history. Books are going to be written about this era."

His mother was referring to the civil rights era being documented on television, in the print media, and on talk shows with Malcolm X and Dr. King.

"Ya see how they nevah, evah have both of them on at the same time, don't ya? Ain't nothin' gonna change that much. Ever since I been here and my father and his father's father, it's the same-o, same-o."

"It won't always be this way, Mason," his mother replied. "Children, *our* children, are living in a new day. They must be taught optimism so that their minds are receptive to what can be accomplished if they think big and aim high. How do you think W. E. B. Dubois became the first black person to receive a doctorate from Harvard?"

&

"By the time they found out he wasn't a dark white man, he'd already graduated." His laughter was cynical. "Who do you think helped get Garvey deported? I'll tell ya: W. E. B. Dubois, that's who."

"He was not the only one," she replied. "There were other leaders of that day who envied Garvey's well-deserved status within the black community. Marcus Garvey gave Black America hope and instilled pride."

"Stelle, you think this country is gonna evah help black people? They didn't bring us to this country to help us, Stelle. We were brought here to work, and they runnin' outta jobs real fast now that they pay us."

In the present, Jeffrey watched his parents at the dinner table while all four of them ate in silence. It was his mother's weekend off, and she had dressed the table with fine china, silverware, and a meal with all the trimmings. That was Mom. Years later he would wonder if Mason ever knew how lucky he was. As a young boy he couldn't imagine all households eating in silence like theirs did most of the time. He thought mealtimes, especially on a weekend with all the family present, should be a time to have lively discussions. At least that was how Uncle Ned and Aunt Celeste, and his cousin ate their meals. Well, perhaps Druscilla was not that nice to him when her parents were not present, but she was very well behaved when they were.

When the three of them spent the night (Mason never accompanied them) with Aunt Doretha and Uncle Miles, it was the same way. After the dishes were washed and put away and the kitchen swept, conversation shifted to the living room. The children eventually had to retire relatively early. Then the adult conversation became less guarded and took on a new flavor. Periodically the volume fluctuated from high to very low, hushed, and muted exchanges would be followed by joyful laughter; these were discussions never held in the presence of children.

Before he pieced it together, Jeffrey was always in a state of wonderment about what had brought his parents together. He considered them an odd couple like a jigsaw puzzle with missing pieces.

Jeffrey thought about how things had always been when he was growing up. He had to admit that his mother had at least tried. She took them to the library, and later when they were older, he and Clare went together. His mother wanted to make the aquarium, museums, and zoos family outings, but Mason wasn't interested. In the end it was just the three of them, or often Aunt Doretha and her children, a few years younger, joined them. His mother always managed to make these weekend getaways fun affairs.

Mason liked movies all right, but the ones he chose were not for family enjoyment, especially children. He cared nothing about family games—Monopoly, dominoes, checkers, or Scrabble—and he definitely steered clear of chess. Uncle Ned loved chess and was pretty good at it too. Well, at least he always won when playing him.

Jeffrey must have been about twelve when he began to develop a keen awareness of how much his father knew about the world and history. Every so often Mason would make an unusually knowledgeable comment. Jeffrey would always have to remind himself: *He was overseas during World War II, remember?* It was even more baffling that when Mason spent a rare evening watching television, he insulted his own intelligence by limiting his viewing to Westerns. Whenever he deviated from that pattern to watch the news, it was to complain about how bad things were in the United States. Always Jeffrey's cue to leave the room. You couldn't hear the news peacefully anyway because Mason steadily talked throughout the entire newscast.

At these times he wished for a pal, someone he could relate to. However, at school he didn't gravitate toward the brainy kids. Why? Well, he wasn't in the loop because of his lack of ambition. Granted, he was in some classes with them, but he wasn't excelling in any of them— biology, math, world history. World history made him angry. Whenever they included Africa, it was always indicted (Uncle Ned's analysis) as the "dark continent." He often wondered whether things would have been different if he, Dudley, and Noah had remained friends, and not been separated by life's changes. It was a question never to be answered.

Now that he was in his teen years, Jeffrey's observation of Mason was more critical. It was weird how this man dissected the layers of this racial landscape called America with black people, in every category, always and forever behind the eight ball. Never was education an advantage to anyone black. Admittedly, education didn't interest Jeffrey all that much either, but for entirely different reasons.

Years later some would label the 1960s as the Turbulent Sixties. On November 22, 1964, in Dallas, Texas, President Kennedy was assassinated. The next fatality was in New York on February 21, 1965, when the life of Malcolm X was ended by an assassin's bullet. On

April 4, 1968, in Memphis, Tennessee, at the Lorraine Hotel, the life of Martin Luther King Jr. was cut short. Robert Kennedy sent a plane to Memphis to transport Coretta and her dead husband back home to Montgomery. Exactly two months and one day later June 5, in Los Angeles, California, Robert Kennedy met the same fate.

Jeffrey recalled a classmate reading an unusually mature essay in class. He would forever believe her mother helped her write it, especially the last few sentences in reference to America:

> "Snuffed out was the potential for America to forge a mature, peaceful path toward becoming a kinder nation. It can be historically depicted as a nation that dwells in a glass house and throws not stones, but boulders. It exhausts its promise, its potential, by consistently killing off its best and brightest—JFK, Malcolm, Martin, and Bobby, respectively. Did the universe shut down. Did it tire of sending them in a steady stream? Perhaps future great ones have begun to self-abort in the wombs of their mothers as if to say, "I dare not lest I too be slaughtered."

Meanwhile, what were Mason's comments? He had very little to say until April 4, 1968, when King was assassinated.

"Well, they showin' ya' what they think of civil rights, and the man of peace and love," he muttered angrily as he slammed the door on his way out.

Jeffrey continued to be cautious with his uncle, unable to muster the candor or the nerve to ask him exactly what he thought of Mason, to just lay it on the line. It was a tug of war or perhaps a game of Simon Says. Naturally, his uncle was Simon, and he remained the rebellious student. He needed a critical analysis from someone else about Mason to evaluate whether Mason's point of view was right or wrong.

He had taken this Mason thing apart by analyzing it, examining it, mentally spreading it out, and then refocusing to conclude: *To hell with it!*

"What are you going to do?" Clare asked. She was terrified. Their mother was in class and wouldn't be home until after ten. Mason was at work.

Jeffrey continued to sit on the side of his bed staring at nothing. What had he gotten himself into this time?

"Jeffrey, what are you going to do?" asked Clare for the second time, fearful of what would happen if the police came. "Why were you with that little twit, anyway?"

"Rissie," he said he was going to stop to see Darien. I never thought he was going to pull anything like that, really." He heaved a ragged sigh. "I had no clue."

The slightest sound had him on edge and Clare as well. How she wished their mother was home.

"Darien isn't always there with her mother, is she?" Clare frowned thoughtfully. Jeffrey seemed unfocused, didn't answer. "But doesn't she sometimes go to the drugstore to walk home with her mother?"

"Yes, Rissie," he answered, "on her late night, on Thursdays."

"Today is Thursday," she confirmed quietly. "But you should have been home already, okay?" Clare was fuming. "I told you a long time ago about these addle-brained misfits."

He felt numb as he slowly took off his jacket and hung it in the closet. He felt as if his legs wouldn't make it back to his bed. He had never known such fear in his entire life. His heart pounded so loudly in his chest that he wondered if his sister could hear it. He sat on the side of his bed with his hands between his legs, nervously biting his lips, breathing hard.

"I know," he finally said as a tremor stole into his voice. "But I didn't do anything."

*That sounds familiar*, thought Clare furiously, *just like last time, and you got six months' probation.* "Mama is going to be so upset," she warned. "What did Darien's mother say?"

"I don't know because when Kendall pulled a gun, I left. I never went inside." He shook his head miserably. "Rissie, he pulled a gun on Darien's mother."

"I don't get it, Jeffrey," said Clare as she joined him on the bed. "Why must you deal with the misfits?"

"Rissie," he exclaimed in self-defense, "I didn't know he was going to do anything like that!"

"From what you told me, he never gets to class on time. He never has his assignment. Why do you want to be with people like that?" She released an exasperated sigh. "You can't learn anything from him," she said between clenched teeth, "because he knows nothing worth knowing."

For the next few days, neither Jeffrey nor Clare mentioned the incident to their mother or even to each other. Whenever Jeffrey and Kendall saw each other at school, they passed each other as if tiptoeing on hot coals. Afraid to ask Kendall what had happened, Jeffrey began to think perhaps it had blown over, and he was in the clear. Each night, he lay in bed hoping Kendall had lost his nerve while attempting to discern what could possibly be the worst-case scenario. Frantically, he shoved it from his mind.

For the rest of his life Jeffrey would remember the amount of money involved: $958.13.

It turned out to be a teenage web of confusion: Jeffrey was smitten with pretty Darien; he didn't know she liked Kendall. And Kendall? Well, he liked Kate, Darien's best friend, who said she wouldn't give "the little small-time thug a glimpse."

Common knowledge was that the drugstore was open late Thursdays. What Darien blabbed to Kendall was not: Mr. Dupree had designated the office in the back as the place to count all monies. Positively no deviation was permitted. However, Kendall's mother counted the money at the cash register and not as instructed, in that hideous backroom.

It appeared that all had blown over when, a few days later, Darien was at Jeffrey's locker, a substantial distance from her own, exclaiming she was late for class. She asked Jeffrey to allow her to hang her coat with his until after class, promising to secure the combination lock. Immediately he agreed; the classmate he shared the locker with was absent today. Jeffrey took from his locker the necessary book needed to complete his assignment. Maybe he should start doing things Rissie's way. He went to class.

Darien did lock Jeffrey's locker, but not before stashing in his jacket pocket an object wrapped in a small brown paper bag. Then she hastened to her own locker and arrived in class apologizing profusely for her lateness, claiming she had stopped at the school library and lost track of time.

When the police extracted a frightened Jeffrey Ingram from his class, they already had the gun from his locker. It was true that he had been with Kendall Lisle (aka Pearls) when Kendall went to the drugstore. Jeffrey told the police he realized what was occurring once his classmate stepped inside the doorway. He never entered with him. Instead, he left. Vera Caruthers had already identified Kendall Lisle who implicated Jeffrey. The gun was discovered in Jeffrey's locker. The police connected the dots. Jeffrey's story about not knowing Lisle's intentions was considered a little flimsy. Darien's mother, Vera Caruthers, did identify Jeffrey Ingram as being there. She also validated that he truly had run away.

Mr. Dupree, the drugstore pharmacist and owner, brought his own lawyer to the separate bench trials to make certain that not only was Lisle incarcerated; he wanted Ingram jailed as well. Kendall Lisle's lone fingerprint was identified on the gun because he had panicked during his amateur heist. The scarf was allowed to slip away, causing his fingerprint to be on the trigger.

All the Ingram family and Uncle Ned were present for the last courtroom session. Dread was so thick in the courtroom you could reach out and touch it. The judge was prepared to hear Jeffrey's plea. Mr. Dupree was accompanied by counsel to ensure jail time for both young men. Kendall Lisle had a record and was sentenced to ten years for armed robbery. A plea was entered for Jeffrey Ingram by his lawyer.

"If you plead guilty, you will get a lighter sentence," his counsel advised. Because he was considered an accessory offender, Jeffrey's sentence had been plea-bargained from five years down to three. The lawyer Estelle hired came highly recommended for a costly price.

"How do you plead?" the judge asked.

Meanwhile, Ned had left his seat. He said something to his nephew's lawyer, exchanged glares with Mr. Dupree. Ned's unwavering stare caused Mr. Dupree, unnerved, to look away. Again, Ned leaned over to say something to the lawyer; Jeffrey listened intently. Ned then resumed his seat beside a very distressed Estelle.

"This motherfucker," Ned softly said to Estelle, nodding toward Dupree, "wants Jeffrey to go away for *more* time." He paused with a heavy sigh. "We cannot in midstream get another lawyer. At this late date you'll be out of way too much money with no guarantee that he'll get less time." Ned paused again, in deep thought. "I see no way out of Jeffrey being convicted," Ned said, deeply disturbed. "Can you believe that this son of a bitch is hell-bent on Jeffrey serving time?" He paused. "He won't stop until he gets a conviction."

"What do you suggest?" Estelle asked miserably.

Ned placed a consoling arm about her shoulders. Sighed once more, shaking his head in disgust. "Sis, I don't see him getting less than the three years."

She began crying again. Mason sat as motionless as a statue; he said nothing. He had been quiet throughout the entire ordeal but, surprisingly, never missed any of the three court dates.

"How do you plead?" the judge asked for the second time.

Ned nodded to his nephew and the lawyer, who then conferred with Jeffrey. The family waited as counsel answered the judge.

"He pleads guilty, your honor."

"Young man," the judge advised Jeffrey, "when released you will be older and, I hope, much wiser. Try choosing your friends more carefully so that you never again appear before me or any other judge." She paused. "Your sentence has been reduced to three years."

Estelle wept quietly. Clare bowed her head as if whispering a silent prayer. Ned tensed. Mason continued to sit motionless.

Jeffrey hugged his mother, Uncle Ned, and Rissie good-bye, one by one. "Good-bye, Mason," he murmured almost inaudibly, his eyes averted. Just before the guards ushered him away, he thought: *Finally, I've been knocked in the head!* His brain kept continuously churning the same thought.

To Mason Ingram the events felt like a personal assault. He sought refuge from his own contrition. A myriad of emotions pummeled him from all sides, imprisoning him within all the wasted years. For the first time since the birth of that infant who had grown into a young teenage man, he thought of times gone by. Lost. vanished. He had been reluctant to cradle the boy in his arms as an infant. He could still hear Estelle asking, as she smiled sadly, "Don't you want to hold him, Mason?" He couldn't recall exactly what he had said. Never did he pick him up, as he lay in his bassinette, only a few days old. He had never in all fifteen years of Jeffrey's life held him in his arms. He had to come to terms with the fact that he had never attempted to get acquainted with his son. What had Jeffrey just called him? Mason! He called him Mason! He felt as if he'd been gut-punched.

Jeffrey Ingram did not look back. Accompanied by two courtroom guards, Jeffrey Ingram disappeared as the doors closed.

# Chapter Eleven

Clare attempted to keep the line of communication open during Jeffrey's absence. In fact, her letters were informative to keep him current about life at home. Clare mentioned their mother was in the home stretch with her degree but avoided mentioning to Jeffrey she had just begun her first year of college. *That would really be a putdown*, she thought.

When writing Jeffrey, she cherry-picked the topics. It always took several letters to get one reply. It was like pumping that well in Gran Jennie's front yard. Suddenly there would be a rush of water. "It's stubbuhn," she would say. "But it still works." One time Clare suggested that she and their mother come to see him. His reply was short, frosty, direct. It was the only prompt reply ever received.

*Rissie,*

*Don't encourage Mom to make the trip here. If you do, the blame falls on you, Rissie. For sure, I will not honor your visit.*

She didn't share the reply with her mother. In fact, she read and immediately destroyed it. When their mother did consider driving down, Clare gently discouraged it. Her mother never questioned her change of heart. Although Estelle didn't tell her, whenever she wrote to Jeffrey she felt like a nag, burdened with a mother's concern expressed in her letters. She couldn't resist telling him how to conduct himself to avoid additional trouble that would inevitably extend his sentence. She expressed how very much she loved him, wanted the best for him, was regretful of this outcome, and so on. At those times, Jeffrey would relay any message to his mother by responding to Clare only, further frustrating the circumstance.

Estelle insisted on paying the balance of the tuition that Clare's scholarship did not cover, to allow her the enjoyment of being a full-time student. She had suggested working a part-time job. No, work later, her mother had advised cheerfully, but not now. Simply get the swing of being a student, she told her. For now, avoid using your inheritance from Uncle C. J. and Aunt Lucinda.

These days Mason was miserable. His condition worsened. He now experienced an increased burning sensation on the soles of his feet. Driving had become difficult. He couldn't feel his foot on the gas pedal. The first time, he was on the expressway, driving home from work. In heavy traffic, semis in front and behind. His heart lurched as forced to the shoulder of the highway, he couldn't gauge his speed without constantly watching the speedometer. Soon thereafter there were occasions when he had to be driven home by coworkers. As time progressed, this became a frequent necessity.

"Mr. Ingram, exercise, walk. More movement, all right? And one more thing," the doctor sternly instructed, "absolutely no drinking!" He paused to see whether his patient was mentally digesting the seriousness of what was happening to his body. "You have been told this time and time again."

What made the situation even more difficult was that Mason was coming home late at night from an eight-hour shift. Most people were in bed getting a good night's rest for work during daytime. Clare, without early morning classes this first semester, dutifully stayed awake to greet him. The designated driver simply dropped the keys in his hand, bidding them both "good night". This frequent inconvenience resulted in someone's car being left in the parking lot overnight. That person was driven home and to work the next day as well.

Clare hated these times because her father was at his lowest depth, angry and unreachable, expectant of impending problems not discussed with his daughter or his wife. His dark mood overshadowed any positive communication; he was dead tired. An unagreeable body refused to comply with the doctor's advice of exercise.

The calendar pushed time forward. Jeffrey was due back in civilian life in four months. Clare wondered just how much he had changed. With caution, like stealing snippets of the milder scenes of a scary movie, she began peeking in on the most entertaining memories of Jeffrey. Physically, before he went away, he was becoming a Beckford. Was he still comical? His letters were succinct responses without one inkling of humor. She prayed that this experience had made him instead of bitter, wiser. Venturing any further was to tread near an emotional precipice.

Meanwhile, Mason Ingram suffered mood swings feeling both dread and sorrow regarding his son's return with constant worry regarding his own condition. Mason inwardly disguised feelings about his son by keeping that courtroom scene fresh in his memory, shouldering none of the blame for their difficult relationship.

Combined anger and contrition were exacerbating the graver effects of his disease. On a few occasions, remembering what he considered the unsympathetic instructions of his doctor, he forced himself to walk to the store for cigarettes. He envisioned the man standing formidably in his white coat watching his every step. Walking made the bottom of his feet tingle with an additional burning sensation. This problem was a constant complaint to his doctor. Poor circulation, the doctor explained. Keep walking, the condition will improve. Mason had neither the energy nor will. Solution: an ample supply of smokes before entering the house.

Estelle was only weeks from the finish line to complete her degree. Clare dutifully supported her by daily straightening up and preparing her father's snack for work and meals whenever her mother was absent or pressed for time. Mini meals were placed in the refrigerator in clear view to offset her father's sour temperament possessing the erratic sway of a malfunctioning pendulum.

Mason targeted his wife whenever possible. Her reason for sleeping in her son's room was twofold: she avoided contact with Mason and fulfilled the need to be as close to Jeffrey as possible. Nothing in his room was disturbed other than the bed, which she left fully made each morning. At least for the time being, she was no longer on the couch. Clare considered that a good thing.

Jeffrey's homecoming should have been a joyous occasion for everyone. The best China, polished flatware, and cloth napkins set the table. Crystal water glasses taken from the cupboard and washed completed the dining scene. Estelle attempted to quell her overjoyed feelings.

Upon first arriving home, Jeffrey was that emotional thirteen-year-old in Georgia. Encapsulated in that same translucent but inescapable film, he stared out at all of them. Of course, it was nerves then, nerves now. Except for Mason, moving about behind a closed bedroom door, the family was all there. Smiles from friendly faces attempted to engage him as he managed to return only an uneasy smile.

Jeffrey looked around at his mom, sweet Rissie, Uncle Ned, Aunt Celeste, and—was this for real? Even Druscilla! He wanted to inquire about Mason. He couldn't say "Papa"—that was what Rissie called him—or even "Dad." His better judgment told him this wasn't the occasion to call him by his given name again. Strange, he thought. Mason never emerged from his room during the entire family gathering. Once during the evening, Druscilla offered a less than positive comment regarding his absence, but it went unanswered. *Yes, Druscilla, everyone heard you!*

After Ned, Celeste, and Druscilla had left for home, the dishes were washed and stored in the cabinets. The remaining food was put away, the house quiet.

Jeffrey was more than pleased that he and his uncle were now at eye-level. Based on the measurements he'd provided her, his mother had sent to him what she described in the note accompanying the box as Welcome Home Attire: boxer shorts, one pair of pants, a shirt, and a cardigan sweater.

*Life*, he thought, as later he sat on the patio looking up at the sky. He witnessed stars. Well, it was an exceptionally clear night. He shouldn't be surprised; he had seen stars within the city limits before. Uncle Ned often said they didn't go anywhere, but readily appeared when travelling away from tall buildings obscuring the construction persistently attempting to kiss the sky. *The Tower of Babel in a modern setting*, Uncle Ned had once said with a laugh free of sanctimony. Tonight, stars glittered with the bonus of a full moon shining brightly. The word "firmament" spontaneously popped into his brain, along with the laughter of Cousin Prentiss. Peculiar how the smallest things were never forgotten. Momentarily he was again thirteen years old, caught up in unhappiness over failing seventh grade. Sadly, he recalled his inability to enjoy that Georgia vacation.

"You're smoking now?"

The question sounded more like a complaint coming from the doorway as the screen door squeaked shut. His mother stepped out onto the patio to join him at the table. The kitchen light prevented total darkness. The alley light was still out. She had telephoned twice within the past week.

Mildly startled, he nodded. He had so many questions. In her letters, his mother never mentioned that Mason had lost a leg, so when did it happen? He recalled that Clare did intimate that there had been changes, not what exactly. She mentioned that his leg was in bad shape. Mason's right leg had been amputated just below the knee. His mother did mention that she was close to completing college. When did she finish? Was Mason avoiding him, or did he always hibernate in his bedroom?

In all fairness whenever his mother or sister wrote to him, and the entire correspondence was not upbeat, he didn't respond right away. He was to blame for some withheld information.

An extra two months had been spent inside because of fighting with four months of parole to be completed on the outside. Someone had lied on him and for it he beat his ass. He knew this additional stress weighed heavily on his mother. To her it meant the lack of a clean slate necessary for picking up the fragments of his life to start fresh. Although he had written a brief explanation of what had taken place, she now wanted a more thorough one. Still, he was brief, repeating what he'd already written in the letter. Her reaction was an expression of sorrow.

Estelle smiled in the darkness as she thoughtfully focused on his physical height and size, questioning his mental fortitude. She didn't consider being kind and gentle anything but positive, but his ongoing inability to shrug away the negative was a deficit. She decided that he was Mason's son, so he couldn't totally be a Beckford. Three and one-half years of negative influence didn't help matters, either. Well, on the positive side, at least four months were to be completed on the outside.

"What were you fighting about?" she asked quietly.

No answer.

"And you still have six months of parole? I mean four." A quick correction. She cautioned herself. *It was already reviewed when we were driving home from the bus depot. Mason was no longer driving,* she had explained. She started to ask about his arrangements concerning school. *Just stop it!* She could hear herself beginning to sound like a nag.

"We should shop for clothing." She attempted to sound cheerful. She felt sad. What would become of this young man, her son? She told herself he was much too young to have lost that great sense of humor. She hoped it would return in time. For now, he was pensive, almost taciturn. Communication with Jeffrey had never been easy. However, before at times it had been pleasant, even as he skirted, maneuvered around issues, skillfully manipulated conversations. That element of his character had yet to surface. She prayed that he didn't become negative and bitter. His personality could easily embrace the transformation.

"Where's Rissie?" he asked quietly before lighting another cigarette.

"Probably in her room studying. I think she has an exam tomorrow." She paused, wanting to warn him against smoking too much but instead remarked, "We need to buy you new clothes. I'm off tomorrow." She paused. "Okay?"

For some reason his parole, no matter how short, made her hesitant to allow him to go alone. She wanted to ask how he felt about his predicament. Thought better of it, deciding that some things were best left unexplored.

"Okay," he answered.

*Two smokers under the same roof,* she thought. Already she avoided her bedroom as much as possible. Clare consistently kept her door closed, mildly complaining about the smell. Low ceilings made it linger. It was worse during the winter months with the windows mostly closed. Although both women were glad to have Jeffrey home again, they detested that he had picked up such a distasteful habit.

"You need a few suits too, Jeffrey," his mother suggested gently while they were shopping the next day. Proudly, she stole glimpses of this handsome young person about to enter manhood. As Clare had commented, he would make any mother proud.

"Why?" he asked quietly.

"Church," she answered matter-of-factly, withholding judgment on the subject. "A few ties too."

"We can pick them up later," he said calmly. He was certain many of the people at church knew where he had been all this time. He wanted none of it. "This is enough for now."

She didn't respond. Besides, she'd had to force the issue even before he'd gone away. In that respect, he was more like Mason. That father-son relationship was even more strained than before. Whenever they were in each other's presence, they said very little to each other. They were in the ring, wary, cagey, waiting to see who would throw the first blow. Both were very much aware of the last words between them, which still reared up defiantly in their minds. *Talk to each other,* she wanted to tell them. *Mason,* she wanted to say, *you are the father. Talk to your son. Coax him across the threshold. Do something! Anything! End the stalemate.*

It was late afternoon when they entered the house with packages. Casual clothing had been purchased—Jeans, slacks, a few more cardigan sweaters, two pullovers, shirts, a pair of sneakers, even a nice pair of dress shoes. Of course, they'd had to buy underwear as well—socks, T-shirts, boxer shorts. She regretted that he had reached almost full physical maturity while away, denying her the privilege of witnessing it.

Reluctantly, she had followed Ned's advice to use some of the money left by Uncle C. J., even though it was specifically intended to further his education. Her secret stash had been hit hard. Although, as her brother commented, it had not kept Jeffrey from serving time. Hiring one of Chicago's best Jewish lawyers had kept Jeffrey's sentence from being longer. Initially, when the lawyer was hired Estelle and Mason paid the retainer. She had mailed the larger balance owed without Mason's knowledge.

Presently, she left her son's room—or more accurately, surrendered—as he began to fill his vacant drawers and closet. In the short hallway, she sidestepped the boxes full of clothes he could no longer wear, making a mental note to donate the mild obstruction to either Goodwill or the Salvation Army. She dreaded having to sleep with Mason or on the sofa as before.

In the weeks that followed, Jeffrey seemed out of sorts, not knowing exactly what to do. A few of the neighbors recognized him and waved their greetings. His parole officer had a job waiting for him, washing dishes in a fast-food restaurant; he hated it. Just as before, he was soon caught up in the old routine of mowing the lawn and emptying the trash, with one seriously significant void.

"Forget that you were gone for a while and go back to school," Ned advised one evening. He had stopped by to chat, which initially seemed a lot like old times. It was a Friday evening, and Jeffrey was coming from the garage after putting away the lawn mower. The air was filled with the fresh scent of cut grass. His mother was home because she had driven Mason to the doctor for his checkup.

"That parole officer," his uncle continued, "has to know you need to resume your education."

His nephew had been home almost three months, and it was nearing the middle of summer. He had one more month of parole. Ned hated that Jeffrey had lacked interest in following through with the correspondence courses. Ned had taken the initiative to go to Jeffrey's school and talk to the counselor. She had readily provided all the required information. Jeffrey had completed none of the necessary paperwork to get it started. Sure, it would have been a lot of hard work, but would have placed him in a more advantageous place. Ned desperately wanted to pick up from where they'd left off even though the years had caused a barrier. Jeffrey was harder to reach. Perhaps just a push in the right direction would help.

"Finish school. Okay, Jeffrey?"

His nephew gave no response.

"Get on with your life."

"That's easy for you to say," Jeffrey replied. "You have an MBA. Uncle Ned, I can't sit in class with kids so much younger than me. I'll be nineteen on my next birthday," he exclaimed.

"Then go to night school," Ned suggested. "Do whatever it takes but do it."

Ned's reply prompted anger or maybe it was his tone. Before answering he should have thought it through.

"Education is not going to give me back the years I lost," he said.

For a lifetime Jeffrey would never forget the look his uncle gave him. Never had he witnessed this Uncle Ned who gazed at him a long time before finally responding.

"You know, you're too much like your father for your own good."

It was the one-time Ned wished that words could be retracted. The years of separation had created a barrier of awkwardness. He realized that recapturing the closeness they had once shared was going to take time. This was a fragile period. Making a statement like that guaranteed alienation. This was a young man, not fifteen like when he went away. The uncle-nephew camaraderie had been disrupted, incapable of withstanding such a raw truth.

"I didn't mean that as a putdown," began Ned apologetically. *Now the cat is out of the bag*, that still voice chided. "What I meant was…" He trailed off. "Jeffrey," he said as his nephew stormed from the backyard into the house, slamming the screen door behind him, which gave a loud screech. Ned followed right behind him but didn't catch up before

Jeffrey softly closed his bedroom door. It stung more than if he had slammed it.

After tapping lightly, Ned waited for a response. He knocked again. No response. He wanted to knock a third time, thought against it. *These things can fester*, he thought.

"What's wrong?" Estelle whispered anxiously as she hurried from the kitchen, dish towel in hand.

Ned turned to Estelle, witnessed his own naked expression of sorrow immediately mirrored on his sister's face.

"What happened?" she asked.

He followed her into the kitchen and silently helped her put away the stack of dishes. Together they entered the living room to sit on the sofa, her sanctuary, facing each other. She had resumed sleeping there. The alternative was not working.

He sighed, shaking his head. The first time since leaving Georgia he had felt such overwhelming defeat. This time, after all these years, he recognized sorrowfully he had assumed the role of Nathan; Jeffrey was his younger self. At least, he told himself, he had encountered Nathan's true feelings accidentally.

"What did you say?"

He was overtaken by embarrassment as he shook his head, offering a sad smile. "Something I shouldn't have." He heaved a miserable sigh. "That he was too much like his father."

Both were quiet for a very long time. Never since leaving the farm had Ned been swept up in such an emotional struggle. For the very first time he thought about how he adamantly refused to attend Nathan's funeral even though Estelle had pleaded with him to go with her. He now dreaded the thought of Jeffrey, years later, doing the same. Presently, it was no consolation that he had indeed attended the funerals of all the other Old Men who were the last to be buried near the land. The Old Men's offspring, Ned and Estelle's nieces and nephews (astonishingly old enough to be their parents), were scattered in graveyards assigned by their spouses. These were arrangements encouraged by their children—Estelle and Ned's great-nieces and great-nephews. It was almost unimaginable that they too, mostly, had passed on. Ned thought about those closest to him in age, his great-nieces and great-nephews (the grandchildren of the Old Men), scattered both north and south, a few going east and even one or two out west. Except for Prentiss, the only interaction between most family members was at funerals, and a few who had opted out of higher education. These chose to work the land, but without the agricultural knowledge necessary to bring the place into the twentieth century. What about the others for which the land had yielded financial assistance for their education and prosperity. They never contributed annually toward the property taxes, as did both he and Estelle. Their display of gratitude were abandonment and negligence. Years ago, they had divorced themselves from both the desire and the responsibility.

Bo! The memory was like a jolt. He was Nathan's oldest grandson. "Bo" was a nickname. That awful event involving him had started it all. He couldn't possibly be blamed for the turn of events, yet it had brought about bad times for everybody. Ned could still hear the dogs barking as those bastards searched the entire property looking for him and, at gunpoint, entered every house. Later, it had often reminded him of Emmitt Till, as he thought about what might have happened if they had been able to find him. For some strange reason the sheriff called off the hunt. Afterward Chester and Nathan were livid, blaming Bo's sister, Matilda Bethanie, fondly called Tillie. Of course, the feelings during that time were anything but fond for poor Tillie.

Ned pushed away these thoughts. He had hated those times and even to this day was still attempting to void his memory of that horrific event. The episode had soured the atmosphere and catapulted farm life toward a chaotic outcome. It was only the grace of God that no one lost their life. That sole fact differentiated the incident from the legendary bleak period in which Calvin Beckford's sons were killed. Compounded were the effects of Jim Crow and all the other atrocities that raged in the South and elsewhere. Life on that farm lost its appeal for most of its inhabitants. The family dwindled steadily as only remnants of the former prosperity remained. The Old Men remained until each, one by one, was no more. They were the last to be buried near the land—in the small cemetery behind their church. Finally, in that same cemetery, the graves of Jule and Medgar had been moved to a resting place near their father and mother, Calvin and Maude Beckford.

"Ned, what are you thinking about?"

"Nathan," he replied. *Well,* he told himself, *Nathan and, quite naturally, all the rest.* He didn't wish to hash that out as they had on several occasions before, with Estelle always winning the debate. Instead, he said, "It's like history repeating itself, you know?"

"If it's any consolation, these days I too have a hard time communicating with Jeffrey." *Even before, too,* she reminded herself. "And history won't repeat itself."

It was getting late, and Ned still had to drive home. He wished he could talk to Jeffrey before leaving.

"Ned," his sister gently offered, "I'll talk to him. It will be okay, really. It will." She paused. "Go home before it gets even later, before Celeste starts to worry."

After her brother left, Estelle sat alone on the sofa. *Fall will be here soon,* she thought. Shadows fell across the living room, yet she didn't switch on a lamp or draw the drapes. In contemplation, she continued to stare out the living room window, watching a few neighbors stirring about, going to and fro, guided by the streetlights. Except for the muted sounds of Mason moving about behind the closed bedroom door with the radio playing low, the house was quiet. No sound came from Jeffrey's room. Well, tomorrow was another day. She finally reached out and switched on the table lamp and closed the drapes. She hoped Clare was going to emerge from behind her shut bedroom door. *She must be tired,* she thought. (Regarding Mason, Estelle never forgot the fact that Clare helped in every way she knew how to make her load lighter.) She was working so hard. *Slow down—don't try to go too fast,* she wanted to tell her daughter. *It gets better,* she wanted to promise, *not easier, but better.*

As for Mason, things had not been the same since he lost his leg, and he said very little to anyone. His sullen demeanor was also directed at Estelle. *Sharing our bed must be minimal for my mental wellbeing,* she wanted to tell her husband.

*At last,* Ned thought without empathy when Estelle talked to him about Mason, *something has shut him up.* He hoped at least there was some relief for Estelle. For years, he had honestly attempted to express goodwill toward his brother-in-law but found it extremely difficult. Prior to surgery, on Mason's best day he still could find a method of disagreeability without saying a word. His sister was a good candidate for canonization on this side of the grave for remaining married to the man all these years. However, they bought the house, then he became ill. The rest was history.

The surgery had taken place only six weeks prior to Jeffrey's homecoming. These days his wheelchair was used specifically for meals. Otherwise, he would hobble on crutches to the bathroom and bathe with the assistance of the nurse. Until a few weeks ago, she had come in the mornings. She left with mild complaints about her disgruntled patient. A new nurse would start in a few days. During the interim Mason did the best he could. *Papa,* Clare wanted to say, *I think Jeffrey would help if you allowed him to. You're the father, so reach out to him.*

Estelle, waiting for an opening, had yet to resume working the dayshift. "You could help him bathe, you know," Doretha once offered with a wink. Estelle said nothing in response; the look she gave her friend said it all. When she began to weep and then sob uncontrollably, Doretha apologized profusely in startled recognition that: No, she could not help him bathe.

On weekends or evenings when the house was empty, Mason would often spend time in the living room looking out or, whenever the weather permitted, on the patio. A few of his mill buddies faithfully continued to visit periodically.

Estelle supposed that Jeffrey being in the house made Mason feel even more ill at ease. She knew beyond a doubt that he had never forgotten the unfavorable courtroom departure. The loss of his leg added to his feelings of vulnerability.

A few hours later, she was startled to awaken, eerily, and find Jeffrey sitting there in the beginning haze of dawn, calmly watching her.

"This is where you were when I left," he said quietly.

He smiled and started to say something else but hesitated. "Mom, I cannot remember any time in my life when you were happy, when we were a…" he faltered, shrugged, and then in exasperation rushed ahead. "When we were a family."

*Even then he knew*, she thought, wishing that it was only a recent discovery. Now fully awake, she was confronted with words that forced momentary retrospect into the crevices of her life. In hindsight, she dared to rummage through the whys and what-ifs, choices that possibly could have rearranged her life. It was like becoming a reluctant understudy after not getting the starring role. She yearned to compensate for past mistakes enabling her to grasp even a small amount of present satisfaction. Well, it had been a struggle, finally she did have her degree. That was a good thing. She smiled to herself. She was annexing one of Clare's favorite phrases, or perhaps vice-versa?

"I'm okay, Jeffrey." She stood up from that same end of the couch beginning to sag slightly from overuse. She had begun to look at new furniture before Mason stopped working. Early retirement had cut his full pension; he was still too young to apply for Social Security. One advantage was his GI status which made all medical care a Veterans Administration expense.

She folded the sheets and the blanket, placed both on top of the pillow. The pile on the floor tucked discreetly out of sight was stored behind the end of the sofa.

"Don't you think you owe your uncle an apology?"

"For what?" he answered.

"Jeffrey, you know your uncle has always supported you. Always."

"There were many times, when I was younger, when I wondered if he disliked Mason. Finally, I can be sure of it. I now know he considers me a lot like him, which means that part of me he doesn't like."

"I think he said it to motivate you, not as a putdown." Just then, she registered what her son had said. Mildly shocked, she frowned with measured displeasure. "Jeffrey," she cautioned just above a whisper, "you shouldn't call your father by his name."

Jeffrey flashed back to the scene in the courtroom. Again, witnessed the look of confusion and pained dismay on Mason's face.

Peripherally, Estelle glimpsed Mason coming from the bathroom on his crutches. Had he heard Jeffrey? She hoped not as she listened to the bedroom door close softly behind him. She knew better than anyone that he sometimes allowed things to smolder before reacting.

๛

The honeymoon was over. During the summer Clare, now working days, had taken two evening classes not included in the calendar school year. In a few weeks she would again resume her regular school-year schedule and work evenings to pay for the required books. Jeffrey continued his unbroken schedule on what he described (at least to Clare) as his "penny-ante gig."

During the next few days Estelle kept telling Jeffrey, as gently as possible, he needed to finish school, hoping she wasn't beginning to sound like a nag. "Life is not going to be pleasant without it, Jeffrey" she found herself saying. *I do sound like a nag,* she thought, *but there's no way around it unless he responds with favorable action.*

"Mom, I have to work during the day."

"That's true, but you can go to school in the evenings... I did it." *Estelle,* she chided herself, *that was college, okay? Not high school!*

She had been thinking about the money from C. J. She had turned the decision over time and time again, deciding that the "contract" was already broken. She considered it settled. Who knew better than she that things didn't always turn out with pristine perfection as planned?

"Uncle C. J. left money."

Not yet twenty-one meant he needed her signature to spend any of it.Detached, he nodded his response.

"There should be more than enough money to finish by going to night school, Jeffrey," she continued. "And you need to register now so that you can be tested to see where you are."

Jeffrey complied, unaware that his mother was keeping his uncle abreast of where things stood. Ned stopped by a few times. Although cordial, Jeffrey offered very little conversation. Meanwhile, Estelle decided to work on that from her end.

It was like old times, at least as much as their schedules allowed. Whereas before their meetings had taken place every evening in Jeffrey's bedroom, now they happened only a couple of times per week. Clare was so thrilled that her brother had finally recaptured his wittiness and great sense of humor. Both soldiered through and sidestepped discussion of the lost years, focusing instead on the present and the most memorable positive incidents from their childhood. There was a sense of serenity in their conversations, along with poignant snippets of frolic and joy, too. Looking back, Jeffrey finally had to admit that his mother had given them priceless childhood memories of what indeed had been good times. For him, these conversations led the way back. Now he was reclaiming his person as Clare gently coaxed him every step of the way with her uncanny recollections of the smallest details. Triggered were his recalls of shared gaiety from their youth.

Jeffrey was also losing that defensive edge with Uncle Ned, who was more than relieved that his nephew was not harboring a grudge. Now they were discovering each other on a new level as they eased into mature interaction, testing the untapped camaraderie that could be shared by an older man and a younger male about to enter adulthood. Whenever Jeffrey had free time (and this was not often because of work and night school), they would take long rides just like they used to when he was a young boy. Now they were exploring an untraveled path of friendship welcomed by both.

His weekly day off at the restaurant was usually during one of their slowest days, Tuesday or Wednesday. Once a month, he had a treasured Sunday off, and this one pleasantly coincided with Estelle's weekend off to make it even more special. The house was quiet. Admitting that it smelled so much like smoke, he opted to smoke outdoors. He insisted to Clare the aftereffects of a California wildfire surely loitered in Mason's bedroom; this drew laughter. She was happy that overdramatization was still part of his character. In defense of their mother sleeping on the sofa, he said that otherwise she could lose her way groping through the dense haze attempting to find the bed. By now Mason should be a casualty of smoke inhalation. Clare had missed her brother so much.

Inwardly Jeffrey wondered what the doctor was saying to this man about practically being a human chimney. It was more than he himself indulged. It certainly increased the effects of Mason's disease. Of course, Jeffrey's speculation was right on target. The doctor had repeatedly advised against smoking as well as any drinking. Mason had begun to also sneak the hard stuff when his mill buddies came to visit. However, cognizant of his serious, chronic condition and Estelle's disapproving looks, that was kept to a minimum.

Jeffrey's decision to smoke outdoors meant he needed a jacket as summer ebbed into fall, then a heavy coat as the season became crisp. Winter became so frigid that even the heavy coat was not enough. He resorted to smoking in the cooler environment of their unfinished basement. No furniture dictated that he would stand, leaning against the concrete wall. He decided that Old Man Winter was the perfect name for the season. It was indeed a cantankerous, mean-spirited old man who never gave an inch which perfectly described Mason Ingram.

He could yet hear with stark clarity his mother, before his incarceration, talking of her renovation plans for the space, with expert input from Uncle Ned. Jeffrey wondered just how much she'd had to spend to lighten his sentence because that pharmacist was adamant that not just Kendall, but *both* go to jail. No sentence and only probation? Oh, definitely not, even if he was not the one who'd held the gun! The bastard had fortified his stance by bringing his own lawyer. Other than the judge, Jeffrey's lawyer and the one belonging to Dupree, he was the only other white person present. Okay, Dupree's lawyer argued in support of his hard-nosed client, so Jeffrey Ingram had run away, but the complicit intention was still there.

Learn from your mistakes, his mother advised whenever he received her letters, accompanied by Clare's cards or letters. There was never a word from Mason. Could Mason write? He had long known that his father couldn't read well.

He had always been perplexed by his parents. They were misfit, like cereal without milk, riding a horse without a saddle, spring without birds and flowers, summer without sunshine, thunder without lightning. The comparisons were endless.

Presently, the men were home alone while the women attended church. From the basement Jeffrey could hear Mason's wheelchair rolling about. He was in the kitchen retrieving his early afternoon snack from the refrigerator. It was more convenient to simply roll the wheelchair up to the table than to hobble around and awkwardly maneuver his body into a regular chair. However, this made it difficult for anyone else to freely move about in the kitchen. During these times Jeffrey would have breakfast at the dining room table.

When he was finished smoking, Jeffrey made certain the cigarette was thoroughly out before clearing all the debris from the ashtray to the wastebasket. He then waited to hear the wheels of his father's chair return him to his bedroom. Father and son avoided each other as much as possible. Back upstairs, he switched on the television. Before, he had tried to convince himself that it was only Mason, but in all honesty, he was part of the problem as well. There was an occasional morning greeting. Otherwise, they had only brief, necessary verbal exchanges.

Clare and Estelle entered the house through the kitchen, instantly ushering in liveliness and cheer. Clare poked her head around the corner to greet him with a smile. "You should have come with us," she said brightly.

He merely smiled at his response to discourage any words from his mother, who had commented more than a few times about his need for Sunday attire. In his mind's eye he could envision the elders scrutinizing him—maybe not all, but most.

He became lost in thought and didn't realize that he had dozed off until he woke up to the smiling face of Rissie. His disoriented look caused laughter. She gave him a playful slap on the shoulder. "Dinner is served, sir."

The table was beautifully set. What did his mother always say? Learn to dine with the finest so that you don't reach for the wrong water glass. Before he had become older and critically analyzed the situation, it used to always make him wonder how on God's green earth she had ended up married to a mill hand.

"Pass the bread," Mason said.

Jeffrey, the closest to it, complied ever so slowly, wanting to say, *Mason, you need to add "please"—at least occasionally.* Could he recall the man using good manners, ever?

As usual, the family meal was eaten in silence. It made him think about other households (perhaps even on the same block) who, unlike the Ingram family, talked at length during meals. Even within their family, conversing during a meal had been routine with Uncle C. J. and Aunt Lucinda. Uncle Ned and Aunt Celeste always laughed and talked while eating. Sometimes Druscilla interjected a comment.

"Jeffrey, what do you want for Christmas?" Clare asked to break the silence.

*Hooray*, he thought. *Warm weather*, he wanted to reply. "Nothing special," he answered. "You?"

"I need a pair of gloves," she said matter-of-factly.

"I would like a colorful scarf to go with my black coat," said Estelle, with a wink at Jeffrey.

"Papa?" asked Clare. "What about you?"

"Quiet at the dinnah table," he replied.

"Why is that?" questioned Jeffrey impassively. He offered a steady, benign gaze.

The father was rather taken aback and seemed to struggle to find a logical reply. "'Cause I don't feel like talkin'."

"Really?" answered Jeffrey. "And what if we do?" he asked with quiet firmness.

He had been given over three years to finally, in his mind, satisfactorily work it out. *At last*, he told himself, *I get it. Just for once, Mason*, he thought, *join the family! For once forget that you only have this woman as your wife because she got pregnant! That is what's eating at you, isn't it? Had I been knocked in the head, there would be no reason for Mom to be with you. She and Rissie would be long gone. I was the adhesive that turned the circumstance to "stuck with you." And then you got sick and, I might add, are not getting any younger.*

For Clare the siren went off. "Let's just finish our meal," she said with anxious quickness. It was almost a plea directed toward Jeffrey. "We can talk later."

Silence returned, but this time accompanied by agitation and tension. Estelle had lost her appetite and gently pushed her plate away; yet remained seated. Both her children finished their meal in silence.

"Does anyone care for dessert?" Estelle asked with an effort to sound cheerful. She had baked a German chocolate cake. "I made your favorite," she said to her son, smiling.

She breathed a sigh of relief as she and Clare began to clear the table. Gently she eased the dishes from Jeffrey's hands.

"That's okay," she said just above a whisper. "Clare and I can handle it." He was no stranger to what he had always overdramatized as "kitchen toil."

"I'll have cake later," he replied, returning her smile. He strolled off to the living room. Perhaps he could still catch part of an afternoon football game.

Mason backed his wheelchair away from the table and moments later closed the bedroom door behind him.

Suddenly the bedroom door opened again. "Jeff," Mason called, "come here."

*Now what?* he thought. The man needed to learn manners. *Mason,* he wanted to again ask, *do you ever use "please" or "thank you"?* He rose slowly from the sofa and walked to the door, and so did an alerted Estelle.

"Not you, Stelle," Mason said. He was still in his wheelchair. "I called Jeff."

She didn't leave but instead became the human barrier between her son and his father.

"Go on now, Stelle," Mason said in a lowered yet gruff voice. She didn't move.

"Mom," Jeffrey said quietly, "it's okay." He placed his hands on her shoulders and gently guided her aside. She hesitated momentarily and then returned to the kitchen.

"Didn't I hear ya call me by my name not long ago?"

"When?" asked Jeffrey calmly. He was aware of precisely when.

"You did it befo' ya went away. And yeah, I heard ya do it again the othah day. Ya don't call me by my name, understan', Jeff?" He paused. "Answer me, Jeff."

*Answer him,* instructed that inner voice. He nodded quietly with a steady gaze. He noticed that his father's hair was no longer salt-and-pepper, but totally gray. He wondered how much man's ever-present underlying smoldering contributed to the taxing toll of the disease to accelerate the aging process.

"Answer me, boy," Mason said in a rough tone.

"Okay," he replied quietly.

"I'm yo' father, boy," he said. "I'm not Mason to ya, okay?"

*Really,* he thought, *you don't say?* "Okay," he said and turned away to go back to the living room.

From the kitchen, Estelle was thinking, *Mason, let it go.*

The troubled man sat in the doorway for quite some time, staring at the spot where this young man, the son he hardly knew, just moments ago stood facing him. Beating back thoughts of why they were never better acquainted, he slowly backed his wheelchair into the bedroom and closed the door; from the kitchen Estelle breathed a sigh.

# Chapter Twelve

I t was inevitable. Just as Estelle had sadly anticipated, the drawers and closet were empty, and of course his suitcase was gone. Six months away from the heralded, celebrated twenty-one! Freedom from the house with the low ceilings. Somehow, she knew he would never again live here. The clock radio and the television were undisturbed. A pair of sneakers still sat in the corner of the room. One set of slightly soiled pajamas, neatly folded, lay on the made bed. A sorrowful smile played at the corners of her mouth as she picked up the pajamas to drop them in the hamper. They would be washed, then deposited in one of the empty drawers. He would never again wear them. *He remembered,* she thought. She had trained both her children to never travel to their destination with dirty clothes or return with any that were unwashed unless separated from the clean ones. She felt no need to check the bank account that she had released to him only a few weeks ago. Replenishing what had been spent, she had added a bonus, mentally recapturing that perplexed expression on his face. Just spend it wisely, she said. STAY IN SCHOOL! Her unspoken but fervent wish.

Clare was despondent for a little while, recalling that her brother had been pensive those last few days. Now that he was gone, she gazed at her favorite spot at the foot of his bed. The last time they'd sat there together. She never thought that it would be their final such meeting, at least at this juncture.

"No," Estelle said, as if reading her thoughts, "you couldn't have talked him into staying."

As usual, she was doing the weekly laundry in their chilly basement while Clare kept her company. They had recently purchased a card table and chairs. She was seated on one of the chairs, wrapped in the quilt from her closet shelf. Estelle folded the laundry, placing the piles from the card table into the large laundry basket.

"I wonder if he went to California," Clare said. Just a few days prior he had been humming "California Dreaming."

"If I recall, the Mamas and the Papas were only *dreaming* of California," her mother replied with mild sarcasm. It was now 1975, and Jose Feliciano had popularized his rendition in the late 1960s.

Estelle felt a very heavy sadness as she mourned the youth of her son who continued to live in a time warp. His inability to release old haunts, hurts, and wrongs was a character flaw that, so far, he had refused to attempt to overcome. Still, it was her hope that one day happiness would caress her son, even ensnare him. *Clear the way, Jeffrey. At least try to release the clutter and then invite in gladness to dwell for a while. Dispel what cannot be changed, Jeffrey*, she thought. *Create space. Stop crowding out your joy.*

"Mama, what are you thinking?" asked Clare as she looked up from her *Vogue* magazine. She loved the cleverly coordinated hues, the fashionable flare, the sophisticated chic captured in the vibrant, colorful photographs.

"What do you want for dinner?" Estelle answered. "I thought I would broil some halibut. I could make potato salad. We could have coleslaw, or what about spinach or even both?"

Clare nodded agreeably, volunteering, "I'll make the slaw." She went back to the magazine, cognizant of her mother's evasiveness.

*Where do the years go?* Clare thought forlornly. She could still hear Jeffrey recently saying empathetically, "Rissie, it's hard to pursue an education without interruptions unless you don't have to think about money." *But, Jeffrey,* she had thought at the time, *it isn't that difficult to at least finish high school!* She had reluctantly decided to take a full-time job and become a part-time student. Her scholarship had run its course; she had stretched it as far as she possibly could to complete two years. Now, a junior, she still attended DePaul University on a part-time basis, thankful for her inheritance from Uncle C. J. Even so, next semester she would need at least a small student loan.

A few weeks after Jeffrey's departure, there was fantastic news: Estelle was offered that long-awaited promotion. After completing her degree, she took the test. Almost a year had passed, and now the person who headed one of the branch offices was retiring; she was chosen as his replacement. There was only one aspect that she did not like: it was on the southeast side of town, deep in the heart of South Shore.

Dear, sweet Uncle C. J. He had done everything humanly possible to make sure things were "bang-up," always and forever one of his favorite expressions. *Such a wonderful man,* Estelle thought, looking at the bank statement that Doretha had handed to her. It was still a reasonable amount of money, but it was on the verge of approaching the low five figures. It had been a handsome sum for a very long time. Before any more spending, she wanted to close the account on a positive note. She needed to live closer to her new job, and Doretha suggested that she buy another house and move. When she mentioned that this might arouse suspicion, Doretha broke into amused laughter.

"How would he know? You have the equity in the home you are now living in, and you can take out a loan for the rest of the down payment and then pay it off discreetly. I know just the person to handle the loan transaction. Case solved." She grabbed her friend's hand. "Estelle," she said gently, "do this, and you'll feel much better about life, I promise." She hesitated before asking, "What about Jeffrey? Have you heard from him?"

"I have, but only briefly. He sent a postcard. He's in Minnesota."

Estelle now regretted her decision to allow him early control over his inheritance from Uncle C. J. The tension between Jeffrey and his father never eased, although the potential surely did exist if only the father had been mature enough to initiate a truce.

Doretha faintly raised an eyebrow and asked, "Why Minnesota? They have more snow than we do, and if you can imagine, it's even colder." She remembered Jeffrey's complaints about winter from the time he was very young.

"He worked at the restaurant with a young man named Craig who was from Minnesota," Estelle explained. "The friend returned home. Jeffrey said he needed the change, so he went with him."

When he had mentioned this plan to Estelle, she had suppressed the comment that he needed to finish school more than anything else. At last! He finally had another real friend. Craig had been to their home several times, and she'd liked him instantly.

"Don't regret releasing the money to him early, okay? Besides, he would have left anyway. Whenever he calls, don't alienate him to the point that he stops keeping in touch."

"Yes, Mommy," she responded. Doretha laughed.

Strangely, Mason didn't have much to say when she told him about her promotion. He said even less about the likelihood of selling their home to purchase something closer to her new job. She couldn't tell whether he was receptive or not. In fact, he was so withdrawn that she thought perhaps his diabetes was giving him a bad day.

She hadn't felt this good in years. When she told Clare about her decision, her daughter was elated. They were leaving the house with the low ceilings! Estelle and Clare went house hunting together, and for the first time Estelle felt she had been given a new lease on life.

They found something! Two dormers, one in the front and one in the back. Not all on one floor as before, but there was a first-floor bedroom. That would be for Mason. While Clare was visiting Nadine one Saturday afternoon, Estelle and the realtor took Mason to see the place. He went on crutches, remained sullen as the agent guided them through the house. It was Estelle's second tour. During the drive back home, Mason didn't utter one word.

He gave his opinion the very next day. "So now you wanna kick me to the curb."

She didn't respond.

"It's okay, right, since we ain't doin' nothin' as man and wife?"

"Mason," she said quietly, "you are not able to climb stairs, you know that."

"You real glad 'bout that, ain't ya?" He paused. "So why would ya pick somethin' with a second flo', huh? Tell me that, will ya?"

For the price, the house was spacious and sunny *and* came with high ceilings, she told him. It was a steal in the heart of South Shore. It even had a fireplace! Although it was not all brick, there was an impressive amount of masonry with the remainder of the house attractively sided. Clare absolutely loved it. Well, Mason was not going to dampen her spirits. It was settled. They were moving. Period! She experienced a fleeting pang of sadness when she thought about how Jeffrey would love the place. The bedroom on the first floor was a bit smaller than the other three on the second floor, but there was a full bath adjacent to the first-floor bedroom. Off from the kitchen there was even a powder room and the bathroom on the second floor was large. Wow! What a find. It had been on the market for only three weeks, which meant she had lucked out. To strengthen her chances, Estelle bid an extra two thousand. The realtor was a friend of an acquaintance who attended her church. *My dear, beautiful Uncle C. J.*, she thought, *bless you, bless you, and bless you—a thousand times, bless you!* Wherever he was, she was sure he was smiling.

However, her promotion meant no more nightshift. The permanent part-time nurse was set to begin in two weeks; she was there until noon for five days per week. What could they do about Mason being home alone for the rest of the day? Clare had just started her job and now attended school in the evenings. What to do, what to do?

"He's somewhat ambulatory, Mama," Clare said assuredly. "He needs a part-time nurse during the day to help him take a bath, but other than that, I think he can manage until one of us gets home. And he's been taking his injections by himself for years. He won't be home alone at night, so I think he will be okay."

Estelle had calculated carefully. Added to a significant amount from her personal stash, the equity from the home they lived in would complete the necessary down payment. It left her with a comfortable mortgage. The remaining four-figure bank account would still hold more than enough to purchase living room furniture. On the other hand, she could make just a small down payment on the furniture. Her promotion would afford her the option of making monthly payments toward the balance, even more logical than dissolving all her savings and starting anew. She was so excited and grateful that for once things were on the upswing.

It was a Saturday morning. She was in the kitchen making breakfast when Mason rolled his wheelchair to a dead stop just a few feet from the stove. "I ain't signin' a thing. Not one thing." With that he turned abruptly, wheeled himself back to the bedroom, closing the door with a reverberating thud. The words sent a chill down her spine, like drips of ice water, leaving her speechless. It was three days before the closing.

A few hours later, when she finally contacted her broker, she was offered a suggestion, which Estelle relayed to Mason.

He exploded. "What, a quitclaim? Woman, ya gone mad or somethin'?"

The deposit she'd given to the agent included earnest money. Everything more than earnest money was retrievable. Reclaiming earnest money meant going to arbitration. The broker did as Estelle requested. She personally informed her of the outcome and could hear the disappointment in her voice. The property would have to go back on the market. The young agent had worked hard on her first sale. Estelle didn't have the heart to try for the earnest money.

She told Doretha even before she broke the news to Clare. When she told Clare, she saw an element of her daughter's personality she'd never witnessed before. She didn't utter a word, but she exhibited a rigid coldness. When would her mother have one thing that she truly wanted? Well, she knew the answer to that. It made her uneasy, and quickly, she purged the thought.

The loan was returned, untouched, the agent retained the earnest money. Estelle resumed life as usual. She daily drove to her new location, still counting her blessings, ever thankful that she at least had received her degree, and the big promotion with a sizable raise.

To boost her injured morale, she decided to do a little decorating. The living room received a fresh coat of paint, eliminating, at least temporarily, some of the residual effects of cigarette smoke. She also ordered new living room drapes as well as new furniture, which this time comfortably filled the space. These actions did lift her spirits somewhat. Clare approved immensely; Mason made no comment, pro or con.

Meanwhile, Mason was battling more challenges. The doctor talked to both during Mason's next visit, explaining why he was losing some of the sight in his left eye. The fact that the doctor informed them as a couple, instead of telling him privately, infuriated Mason. This anger was compounded by the doctor's questioning of both Mason and Estelle regarding timely insulin injections. This placed her at an embarrassing loss for words.

Estelle asked toward the end of the drive back home, "Are you taking your injections when they're scheduled? I pick up your prescriptions without delay."

"What do ya care, Stelle, huh? Tell me what? Answer me, huh? Just let me outta the car," he said as she approached the curb, before she could drive to the alley to park in the garage.

"Mason, be calm," she said quietly. Awkwardly, he struggled to turn in the car and retrieve his crutches from the backseat. Patiently, she held the passenger door open, hoping there would be no scene for their nosy neighbors to witness. She was positive that some of them were viewing the entire episode from their windows. The doctor had been advising him for quite some time to get a prosthetic fitting, each time his response was adamant refusal.

"Mr. Ingram, once you make the adjustment, you can advance from crutches to a cane."

However, Mason Ingram was not receptive to that possibility. The doctor once informed Estelle of professional counseling; she smiled knowingly. Although his physician never commented beyond his medical expertise, his warm, sympathetic smile communicated to Estelle that he understood.

As the months stubbornly trudged on her elation regarding minor upgrades had fluttered and died. Intermittently, Jeffrey telephoned or sent a postcard; during one telephone conversation she asked him what was wrong with letter writing. Both Estelle and Clare wanted to drive to Minnesota for a visit, but he always gave a noncommittal response and a nervous laugh. Several times he told Estelle that he didn't know how long he would reside there, which she relayed to Clare. Estelle was always careful not to mention his father because whenever she had done so in the past, for a period Jeffrey's calls were noticeably brief. The fact that Jeffrey never asked about his father spoke volumes. She continued to follow Doretha's advice to keep the conversations very upbeat, despite missing him terribly and longing for him to come home. It was whenever Mason Ingram was having a bad day that her feelings toward her son were a mixture of anger and troubled anxiety. She thought: *You should be here helping.* She quickly suppressed these emotions because otherwise such feelings would surely emanate from her during their phone conversations. Besides, she knew the truth: never would Mason allow Jeffrey to help him in any way. Jeffrey's postcards and brief phone calls always asked about Clare, which always came during her absence. Jeffrey didn't tell his mother that his inheritance was dwindling. He now worked odd jobs to stretch it. Part of one winter and entirely another had been spent in this place; it was time to move on. He was always evasive whenever she asked when he was coming home. Finally, he said: "Mom, I will never again live in that house." He paused. "Besides," he said in an upbeat manner, "the ceilings are too low now for sure. I'm a big guy now."

They joked about the fact that physically he truly was a Beckford. She did not allow herself to think about his mental frailties reinforced by old wounds permitted to govern his actions and therefore his life. She once told her friend Doretha how very difficult it was following her advice. Her tone remained pleasant and tenderly engaging when they spoke. Mother and son continued to converse positively while geography kept them apart.

Meanwhile, after contemplating the change for quite some time, she had decided that no longer would Jeffrey's closet or drawers remain empty.

"What the hell ya doin', Stelle?" Mason asked upon entering their bedroom.

"What does it look like?" she said matter-of-factly as she stripped the closet and drawers of the remainder of her belongings. For months she had been leaving some of her things in the vacant room, such as her coat when she came home from work and her usher uniform from church. Some of her freshly laundered underwear had begun filling the drawers when brought up from the basement. For months her fragrances and pieces of her jewelry had been finding their way to Jeffrey's dresser. She also had begun to make use of his television and radio. She might not have a new house, but she would garner some semblance of freedom. Yes, inside this very house that she no longer wanted, she would carve out a niche that permitted her to maintain her sanity and the essence of her being.

☙

It was spring when her mother telephoned. The fact that she was so elated meant good news. "Speak to someone you know," she told her daughter excitedly. It was Jeffrey. He had found his way from Minnesota to Georgia.

☙

The envelope was on the kitchen table, opened. He sat before it in his wheelchair, looking incensed. The bank had made a mistake. Somehow Doretha's address had been overlooked, and the correspondence mailed to the alternate address.

Her heart was in her throat. She started to explain, but he cut her off.

"I already know what it is. I ain't completely dumb. I know how to read a bank statement. I ain't educated like you, but I'm not stupid."

"How dare you open my mail!" she replied with an anger that equaled his.

"How ya have that kinda money in the bank, huh? It ain't the bank we use. Well, at least it ain't the one I use." He paused. "So, tell me, who ya fuckin', huh? You puttin' out to somebody fo' that kind of money." He paused. "I know ya doin' somethin' with somebody 'cause it sho' ain't me. So that's why you wanted me on the first flo', right?" He paused. "You ain't talkin', right? I gotta give it to ya, you is good, that's for sho'."

He couldn't come up with a more feasible theory even though he claimed that he knew. For years she had been saving the money, *his* money, and yet that conclusion didn't occur to him. She withheld the fact that there had once been considerably more. Never would he know he had paid for the patio, paid twice for Jeffrey's lawyer, and even helped pay for the living room furniture. That money rendered her a certain amount of independence in a loveless marriage. He knew, yet he didn't know. She thought of how Doretha had always said that he wouldn't figure it out in a thousand years. He still did not actually know, and Estelle did not bother to explain. She permitted her husband, Mason Ingram, to continue believing her to be unfaithful. She allowed him to constantly label her a whore, a bitch, a cunt, a two-timing bitch, though he was careful to spew these verbal assaults only during Clare's absence.

"You and ya goddamn degree. You think that makes ya special, huh? Slut. Bitch."

Now, not only was school occupying Clare's time, but sometimes on weekends she also dated, and often got in late.

When Mason began to come to Estelle's bedroom to argue and hurl an even more scurrilous barrage of insults, she called a locksmith. He showed up punctually the very next day. Clare let him in. Mason obstructed his path, blocking the bedroom entrance with his wheelchair.

"This mah house. No locks on dohs around' heah."

When Estelle got in from work, Clare related what had happened. Estelle said nothing. She simply entered Mason's bedroom and closed the door behind her. Surprised, he sat up in bed.

"Mason," she said quietly, "I intend to honor my vows. You are not well, and I will stay the course."

"You not honorin' ya vows," he retorted. "Why did ya leave our bed, Stelle?" he asked in frustration. "A man and his wife should always sleep together."

"Why should we sleep together? It's frustrating." She paused and gave him a thoughtful look. "You know, you have never considered foreplay—that preliminary stage of lovemaking. You selfishly have sex. Although it's the farthest from the truth, I guess you think a woman is always ready. Perhaps if you had worked at satisfying as well as being satisfied ," she didn't finish, but was certain the message was clear. "I was twenty-one at the time and had never before had sex…," she continued "but, well, even after years with the same man a woman learns. Had you ever been considerate and engaged in making love, not just sex, maybe we might have been able to explore possibilities to create something pleasurable for us both…" *That's right*, she thought, *you can no longer just walk away in a huff, so you've devised another method of shutting out what you don't want to hear.* Mason was no longer sitting up. Lying down under the covers, he had turned his back.

"The locksmith will be back tomorrow," Estelle finished quietly, "and I will be here to let him in." She opened the door and closed it softly behind her.

The locksmith returned the next day, this time during the evening, with Estelle there to greet him; Mason never left his room the entire time.

Installation of that lock caused an uncanny, hushed calm to blanket the house like a down comforter. It was a divorce decree without a judge. It represented boundaries, a finality more than words on paper ever could.

She checked to make sure he had taken his injection; their eyes met just as she was closing his bedroom door. It was at that moment that he began to privately inventory his life. There was a void where fond memories should have been, where bonding should have taken place with his children, where cherished good times and fond thoughts should have filled his memories. Looking over his life felt like viewing a lengthy, depressing documentary.

For a moment before she closed Mason's door, Estelle thought he was going to speak. Instead, he said nothing.

Mason, in the still of the night, reminisced about the first time he saw her in Pepper's Lounge, soft and a beautiful brown. Nice legs and hips, beautiful almond-shaped eyes. Clare had his hue, with a richer underlying copper glow, and her mother's eyes. In fact, Estelle was still a good-looking woman. Time and their differences had wedged them apart. Could he have tried to change so that she was drawn closer? Could he have made her love him so that when his illness changed his body…? He backed off the thought, deciding probably not. He met a woman, a woman he admired and wanted for himself, but as Nelson told him, he did not think it through. She got pregnant. He was glad. Nelson interjected with candor she was so very different from those he had dated in the past.

Did he have any regrets? No need for that. He'd gotten what he wanted, but he hadn't been able to enhance the partnership to create something fruitful and lasting. Therefore, the marital union soured, causing difficulty sharing the same house, let alone the same bed. A marriage entangled with children, bills, sickness, and all else that marriage entails for better or worse. Nelson was right—he didn't think it through! There he was in one room, all alone. She was miles apart, in the very next room, and equally alone. It felt like another lifetime. These thoughts continued until finally he drifted off to dream of passion and fulfillment in a body that granted ecstasy only while he slept.

She didn't lock the door that night but instead lay listening for any sound from his room. Earlier, she had checked his door; it remained unopened. She even eased the door open to check further; he was sound asleep.As she lay in her bed awake, she mentally catalogued and labeled the main events of their life together. What could she have done differently—or even what could they both have done, together—to salvage a pleasant existence as husband and wife. Therefore, create a better environment for themselves and their children? Those two individuals were now young adults with their futures ahead of them. She prayed that they would live great lives with few drastic mistakes, choosing compatible mates forging positive relationships, secure marriages. A good marriage, she repeatedly told both children, only happens if both work at it. The primary ingredients: love for each other, communication, and the willingness to compromise. From that point you trust trial and error.

"Since ya got so much money, you and ya man can pay the mortgage," Mason told her a few weeks later while eating at the kitchen table. He had given this some serious thought.

"It's a joint bank account, Mason," she reminded him, not managing to hide the triumphant edge in her voice. "If you want separate accounts, we need to decide who pays what. There are the utilities, the mortgage, and your nurse that comes five mornings each week. Your insurance will only pay for three days, and the other two we share equally. I will gladly pay the mortgage, but only on one condition: if you are willing to sign a quitclaim."

"Back ta that again!" he yelled. "You crazy, ya know that?"

She continued to sweep the kitchen floor as he rolled his wheelchair from the kitchen to his bedroom. He never again brought up the subject.

Mason Ingram lasted another year and forty-five days. The meanness had dissipated, leaving no tenacious fortitude to feed his will to survive.

While planning the funeral the day after Mason's death, Estelle realized, *He's going to miss his father's funeral.* When she anxiously telephoned Georgia, her mother informed her that Jeffrey had been gone for over a week. Fear clutched her heart like a vice.

"Estelle, honey, it's goin' ta be fine. He's okay. I jus' know it."

It was almost two weeks later when Ned came through the door with Jeffrey in tow. Jeffrey had telephoned his Uncle Ned to learn that he'd missed his father's funeral by two days. The two Beckford men were practically the same height. As if she was walking backward in time, the younger man's appearance presented her with poignant, bittersweet memories. He possessed the same eyes and mouth and practically the same deep brown complexion as someone else.

Nevertheless, it was one of the most joyous times of Estelle's adult life. She made dinner with Clare home in time to assist her and set the table with the finest china and crystal. The four of them—Uncle Ned,

Estelle, Jeffrey, and Clare—conversed and laughed. It was the merriest occasion ever in that house with the low ceilings.

When dinner was over and they had pushed back their plates, Estelle spoke first. "Ned," she asked, "who does Jeffrey favor?"

"You know who," he answered, smiling. "He's almost the spitting image of Bo."

In unison Jeffrey and Clare asked, "Who's Bo?"

Jason Beckford, nicknamed Bo, was Nathan's oldest grandson and had long ago been forced to leave Georgia under haunting, horrendous circumstances.

"A relative," Ned said. "We'll talk about it sometime."

Hastily, Estelle left the table and came back with Mason's obituary. "I tried to get in touch with you, but your grandmother said you were gone." She paused. "I had no way…"

"Mom, it's okay," he said consolingly as he stared at the picture of a younger man. He started reading the obituary, only to resume once more staring at the picture. He didn't mention that he had looked around Georgia for over a week before leaving the state. He had discovered Georgia to be beautiful. He wished he could thank Uncle C. J. for leaving him that money. For certain, in his opinion, he had made good use of it.

He continued to gaze at the person looking back at him. He was in uniform, a man in his youth, who had gone on to become his father. Now he would never know this father, who had transitioned into the void without sharing any real family history with any of them. Estelle had requested this photograph from his brother. "Any picture, Nelson," she'd said, "any one at all of him as an adult."

Gran Jennie cautioned him when he was leaving Georgia. "Jeffrey," she warned, "a rollin' stone gathehs no moss—don't forgit it."

He said he wouldn't and then decided to spend a few days in California browsing plush sections of Los Angeles—Marina Del Rey and Beverly Hills. He had always imagined Rodeo Drive as longer. He realized as he looked at the window displays of the fashionable shops, many resembling North Michigan Avenue, that there was nothing on that short street that he could afford. He wondered if that would ever change. Well, for certain not now.

He had become recklessly wayward, spending on anything and everything that didn't include furthering his education. By the time he was done, he had visited six states—Minnesota, Georgia, Tennessee, New Jersey, New York, and California. Had he not decided to travel to California, a trip that was sporadic and unplanned, he would not have missed his father's funeral.

Now, reading his father's obituary, he assessed it as the shortest one he had ever read. *No input,* he thought, *so no output. Like father, like—no way!* he thought in fleeting panic. That was surely not the way he wanted to leave this planet. The obituary listed Mason's brothers and one sister simply because his mother knew their names. Sure, she'd had to ask Nelson just as she had for all the other pertinent information, which included their parents' names, Mason's birthplace, what year he was inducted in and mustered out of the Army, and so on. To date, her conversations with Nelson were the most extensive interaction that had ever taken place between their family and any of Mason's family members during Estelle's entire marriage to Mason Ingram.

Never while his father was living had Jeffrey heard that his Uncle Morris had earned a degree in chemistry. Yet he died helping his older brother, Mason's sharecropping father, on that Mississippi dirt farm. Had his diabetes killed him at the young age of twenty-nine? His death had occurred in the 1920s, so most likely he couldn't get a job in his chosen field, but could he have possibly taught the subject at one of the black universities? What happened? These were questions that would never be answered unless Uncle Nelson voluntarily gave them the information. According to Nelson, he was six when Uncle Morris died; Mason was eight.

The funeral had been small, with all the Ingram siblings and their spouses present, together with Mason's mill buddies, who had also been his drinking buddies, including even those who had ceased stopping by. The service was held at Estelle's church; her pastor preached the funeral. Out of respect for Estelle, some of her fellow church members were there. A man who had never gone to church was given a church homecoming. Doretha and Miles were there to support her.

"It's always a homecoming," Doretha quietly reminded her. "All that leave the planet go *home*, so to speak, even if they never attended church."

Estelle wondered if perhaps they became lost spirits, lost in death as in life. It was not a pleasant thought, so she offered a silent prayer for his soul.

# Chapter Thirteen

As a man whose accumulation of wrong decisions had sealed his fate, he was exactly where life's journey could deliver him. Hungry and with his hands deep in his pockets, he walked down West Forty-Seventh Street. He needed a job with decent pay that would sustain him. He didn't want to, but he needed to call Rissie again. Where was she? And where was his mom?

Uncle Ned had warned him not to venture out on his own. His response was he wanted to be independent. He would never forget that conversation.

"For a period, at one time or another, each and every one of us is dependent on somebody," Uncle Ned said. "Stop living in the past," he had cautioned. "So-what if your father told your mother that she should have knocked you in the head? Know one thing: everyone that makes it to this planet is supposed to be here. Jeffrey, all that are not supposed to be here are 'knocked in the head' by nature or by God—for sure, a higher power. Call it what you will, but they don't survive because of a miscarriage, are stillborn, or whatever. Now, the abortions performed by clinics, those are another story. I can't speak about that." He paused.

"Your mother would never do such a thing. You've been on this earth for close to twenty-four years. Are you going to allow the past to forever govern your life? Besides, I'd be willing to bet your father said that in anger." He shrugged. "Get over it, move on. Besides, it was a private conversation not meant for you to hear, okay?"

In retrospect, Jeffrey recalled that there had been a brief expression of shame on his uncle's face. The conversation with his uncle (a few months ago) did cause him to reflect on the fact that his mother had said practically the same thing. He remembered how she had remained ill at ease and provided as little explanation as possible. He smiled to himself as he thought of another conversation with his uncle who he considered very wise.

"Now why on this earth, Jeffrey, would I discuss my dislike of the father with the son? I am your uncle. The seed that fertilized that egg inside your mother, my sister, came from that man, good or bad. That's how you got to this planet. I'm here to support you in any way possible."

Jeffrey now realized his mother had added additional money to his inheritance almost in desperation, as a way of encouraging him to get his GED and begin a college education. However, during his stay in Minneapolis with some of that money, Craig and two other fellows had traveled for a weekend trip to the boardwalk of Atlantic City (that wooden walkway reminded him of his uncle's herringbone tweed jacket). Then, haphazardly, the four decided to visit New York City for a few days. While there, he sent his mother a postcard featuring a picture of the Statue of Liberty. No access to a helicopter, he wrote, so couldn't see chains hidden from view. Both Ned and his mother had educated him regarding the misconception regarding the Lady bearing the torch.

Gran Jennie was living with Prentiss and his family. Upon Jeffrey's arrival in Georgia, Prentiss insisted that he stay for as long as he wanted. During his visit, Jeffrey took a day trip with Prentiss and his wife and children to Chattanooga, Tennessee. They took the Incline Railway to the top of Lookout Mountain and then rode the elevator down 1,500 feet inside the mountain to see Ruby Falls. It was cold inside that mountain. All had been advised to take a jacket on that very hot summer day. Along the way, the tour guide gave a description of the cavernous sights—stalactites (hanging down) and stalagmites (jutting up from the mountain's floor). Prentiss and his wife had visited Ruby Falls before, but neither Jeffrey nor their two children had ever witnessed such a spectacular wonder. A good thing that his mind captured the beauty of Ruby Falls—water cascading down inside that mountain in all its magnificence. Disappointingly, the developed pictures contained a blur where such a breathtaking sight should have been.

Now Jeffrey had to focus. Chicago. The temperature had dropped. He needed his warmer winter coat, left with a friend who lived too far away.

How long, he thought, would it take him to catch up with the rest of the world. The past was nipping at his heels. There were so many unanswered questions. The answer to some only when his future unfolded. *What future?* That inner voice interjected an impromptu jeer. *Don't know what future*, he thought miserably. His life was wretched. He couldn't even get laid. Nobody wanted a broke nig—Hell, nobody wanted a broke man no matter who he was. He clenched the last ten-dollar bill. He still needed to eat. It would be the first time in nearly two days. There was nothing more pathetic than a poor, uneducated, black man. Had he followed Uncle Ned's advice, he would at least have his GED! Suddenly the words he often saw on billboards flashed across his subconscious in neon proportions: *A mind is a terrible thing waste*. His sixth-grade teacher, Ms. Taft, gazed at him with regret and disappointment. Failing seventh grade had caused so much negativity. "You're a smart young man, Jeffrey," she had said encouragingly. "If only you would choose a different group of friends and work harder you could go far." He was impressionable, hated ridicule. Not cool to hang out with kids who always had their heads in a book. Often being smart was lonely. Absent was the support of Noah and Dudley. Reflections brought regret. Were the most accomplished ever lonely? Daniel Hale Williams, Charles Drew, Carter G. Woodson; the list grew long. Hindsight was a motherfucker. No need to think about that now. The life you led delivered you to the address of the justified harvest. *Ego*, he thought. What had Uncle Ned said about pride and his mother too? Ego: Easing God Out.

One could argue that even when you sowed bountifully, circumstances and situations could still lead to a meager harvest indefinitely. Those were the stages in life that Gran Jennie called bridges. Mason had never counseled him as he should have. He could have taken the advice of Uncle Ned who had supported him as much as possible.

Momentarily, he pushed these thoughts aside. It was getting late. Colder. He was homeless! A label to which he was yet unaccustomed. He had slept on the rapid transit for one night and reluctantly considered a repeat. *Go ahead*, that inner voice said, *call your uncle.* He was so ashamed, too ashamed to call his uncle. His uncle's voice, in his head, a constant warning. "Stop acting like a turtle." "Quit rambling." "Stay put." "Get yourself together." "Seize control of your life." Sternly cautioning: "Life is a cosmic photo-shoot in rapid pace."

Jeffrey smiled sadly to himself. A turtle, he thought wryly, the one creature nature had designed to be able to stop wherever he desired and retreat inside his shell—*voila!*—Home!

The sound of the train ride, metal against metal, echoed in his brain with every step he took. He was fearful of seeing Rissie on the train. She took the A train. Cautiously, he took the B train. Just in case he did end up on the same train as his sister, he could be back on the street before she was due to board. He was certain that her schedule had not changed. Which car did she ride in most of the time for her daily commute? Unless the train was late, she boarded at Seventy-Ninth, Monday through Friday, seven thirty.

"I'm sorry, Mr. Ingram," she'd said. "I've got to have the room. You haven't paid rent in almost three weeks." The voice of the landlady who owned the rooming house where he had been staying. She required the first week's rent in advance. Thereafter, rent was due Monday of each week.

The owner told none of his staff that he was stretched financially. In the blink of an eye a new owner had taken over the place. Transformed it, retaining only one waitress. His dishwashing job folded! The money stash had run out. Why did he wait so late to let them know? Now he couldn't reach either his mom or Rissie.

Still had a little change! For the third time telephoned Estelle again, then Rissie. No answer. He placed the change back in his pocket. No need to leave a message on the answering machine for either of them. Nervously, he quelled the feeling of panic attempting to surface. Where were they? He could hear his mother teasing about no longer having low ceilings to entice him to visit. Finally! In her new home for about six months, much closer to her job.

He left the telephone booth, continued to walk in the cold. The temperature plummeted—Chicago style! Sinatra's "My Kind of Town" played in his head. It was late! By now Rissie should have been home. Naked vulnerability visited. He thought back to the time Reginald Simpson had abandoned him and there he stood, all alone. *Get your act together, buddy!* That inner voice was louder than ever before.

Gingerly, he entered the hot dog stand on the corner, ordered a dog and fries. Paying the short-order cook who also served as cashier, he stood in the small eating section. Ate as slowly as possible, drank the water he had requested. Periodically, he stopped eating to rub his hands together. He needed to get warm. It was going to be another night of riding the train. Where was his mom? That metal against metal echoed in his brain like the repetitive words of a scratched record. It was the repetitive voice of his mother: *Stay put! Stay put! Stay put!*

He was cold. He thought about walking to the apartment of a buddy who didn't live far from here. Pride prevented it. He was more of an acquaintance than a friend.

He stalled for time. Unless he was going to call Rissie for the fourth time, he had to use his one alternative. He walked toward the train hurriedly. It was too cold to go to Fifty-Fifth to catch the B train. Anxious and shivering, he made it as far as the Forty-Seventh Street platform. He needed a place to clean up so that he could again look for a job. He remembered his mother asking him whether he had any of the five thousand dollars left. Read the disgust on her face when he told her, No. "And you still don't have your GED?" It was a plea. The red sign of the A train rolled closer, slowed to a halt. Very few people were on the train. One man, eating a hamburger and fries, plugged in, listened to his radio. A few others were sprinkled about, enduring the ride to their stop. In the subway, at Roosevelt, he thought switching to the B train would be easy.

The CTA rapid transit (known as the 'L) has in the center of each car, on both sides of the aisle, a row of seats positioned in opposite direction of each other. The heaviest concentration of riders, seated and standing, occupy this section. (Often the train is crowded enough for a person to overlook someone they know until it reaches the subway. At this point, riders are exiting in great numbers.) In every individual car there is one right-angled seat (against the car wall) directly behind the very last seat of this center group of seats facing forward. Jeffrey settled his weary body there and closed his eyes.

That nightmarish echo of metal against metal— *Stay put! Stay put! Stay put!* It was the last thing he heard as he drifted off to sleep. He was a young boy again, running, running, running through the field of high grass beyond Gran Jennie's house. She waved to him but said nothing. Uncle Ned, building a fence, turned, smiled, then waved. Cousin Druscilla was rocking her newborn baby who wouldn't stop crying. Suddenly Clare, in a burst of hearty laughter, was running toward him, calling his name. He seemed to be receding farther into the distance, even as he tried desperately to reach out to her. Then the scene was severed. He was hurled through time and space. Landing in Chicago, playing in the flat on South Parkway. Surrounded by all her dishes, Clare was preoccupied with her dolls. He was busy with macho toys that Mason had bought him. She smiled, reached over, touched him. Then began shaking him, gently at first and then firmly. Opening his eyes, he stared into the face of his sister. She was crying.

"What are you doing, Jeffrey? Why are you sleeping on the 'L?"

Only momentarily disoriented, he focused. Dressed for work, she looked so pretty in her good black coat, red scarf, and black hat. He couldn't believe he had been asleep for so long. It was the middle of rush hour.

Some of the people exiting the train at the Monroe/Madison stop watched them in a curious yet detached sort of way. The train jerked forward before moving smoothly on. "Washington. The next stop is

Washington," the conductor called. "Change here for the West Side trains."

Moments later, people hurried from the train at Washington; some descended the stairs to the tunnel leading to the West Side trains. Clare's stop was Washington. Her distracted state caused her to miss her exit. Some passengers began to watch them with curious interest. The train lurched forward.

"Lake Street. Change for elevated trains. Lake Street."

"I didn't see you until some of the crowd cleared," she said almost apologetically, visibly distraught. (She didn't add that had she *not* been about to seat herself directly in front of where he was lying down asleep, she would never have seen him.) The conductor brought his head back inside, electronically closed the doors, and raised the window.

"Fullerton. The next stop is Fullerton."

They were leaving the Loop behind. The train accelerated, moving further north, bypassing Grand, a B stop. Regaining focus, she said, "We need to get off at the next stop."

They disembarked at Fullerton, descended the stairs, crossing the street in the merciless Chicago wind to ascend the steps of the other stairwell to head back south. They seemed to stand on that platform forever. Jeffrey turned his back to the wind. For a moment he was reminded of Minnesota. No, he decided, that was a different type of cold. There were no winds as vicious as those in this city. When the train arrived, the siblings sat down together in the closest seats. Neither spoke. Both mentally processed the seriousness of what was happening. Clare had regained some of her composure. Though still upset, she was over the initial shock of seeing her brother sleeping on the rapid transit. Back in the tunnel the train traveled in reverse order. As they approached Washington, Clare reached inside her purse, retrieved her house keys and money that he pressed in his hand.

"Go to the apartment and stay there until I get home." She was crying again. "Don't you dare leave until I…" Her voice trailed off as she reached inside her purse for something to wipe her eyes. "Oh damn!" she said quietly. Fresh tears impaired her vision.

"Don't cry, Sis."

"Jeffrey…" She didn't finish, but instead heaved a weary sigh, miserably shaking her head. At Washington without saying another word, Clare briefly glanced back while exiting the train. She was still crying.

No longer rush hour, the wait for the seventy-Ninth Street bus was long. Jeffrey's lightweight jacket was no match for the pitiless Chicago winter. Finally, the bus pulled up, and feeling like breaking glass he boarded the bus to ride the blocks to her street. He hurriedly walked the few blocks to her apartment. Once inside, he found it just as homey, clean, and attractive as his last brief visit. Since earning her degree, she had been living on her own for the last year.

While bathing, he evaluated his life. He sat in the tub soaking and thinking of what to do next. He had just turned twenty-four a few weeks ago, and his life was a train wreck. He wondered just how long it would take to get it on track. How long would it take him to cultivate some type of existence that resembled life? Somehow, someway, he had to seize control of his destiny. Life's hourglass that Gran always talked about was kicking his ass.

He washed his underwear and shirt in the bathtub, wrung out as much water as possible to place them on the radiator to dry. Draping himself with the blanket taken from the foot of Clare's bed, he sat in front of the small TV screen. Barely registering anything, he watched the soap opera scenes play out. He had heard you could literally not tune in for weeks, months in fact, but remain current when watching again. In that respect TV was an idiot box, but he just wanted to hear voices and will himself not to think.

Several hours later, his shirt and underwear were dry. He put on the boxer shorts, ironed his shirt. He checked his pants. They were somewhat soiled, but black, so the stains were less noticeable. When fully dressed, he put on the men's cologne, neatly placed and to one side of Clare's dresser, undisturbed, from his last visit.

He waited for her all day. Everything was so neat and clean that there was nothing in her apartment to do other than listen to music, watch TV, or read. Clare always kept a generous assortment of magazines and books on a wide range of subjects. Perhaps he could make dinner for her.

In the freezer compartment was ground beef, and in her crisper, lettuce and one small tomato. In the cabinet was a box of spaghetti, small but enough for two people. There was a can of tomato sauce, and vinegar and oil for the salad.

That evening, when he heard a soft knock on the door, he briefly wondered who was coming to visit his sister, momentarily forgetting he had her keys. When he opened the door, there stood Rissie, grinning broadly and happy to see him.

"Something smells good," she said. "What's for dinner, sir?"

"Spaghetti with meat sauce and a salad," he replied, tenderly kissing her cheek.

Later, when they had eaten and washed the dishes, he told her what was going on in his life. Clare's heart ached for her brother. Choices were made in life, either by you or someone else more in control, often making the road back close to impossible. He had never finished high school because he'd spent three years and two months behind bars, and then the aimless rambling without purpose. Back in Chicago for almost seventeen months—although closer than before—still no GED.

"Where's Mom?" he finally asked.

"In Cancun with Max," she replied.

"Max?"

"Oh, that's right, you don't know him. They started seeing each other about a year ago." *It began a short while after you first returned from traipsing about the country*, she thought. "He's a nice guy, really."

Clare knew Estelle had met him during that fiasco that had occurred while Mason was still alive. She had inadvertently spotted his business card on her mother's dresser, where it remained, untouched, for practically six months. He was the loan officer at the bank, Jared Maxwell.

Estelle had admitted the mutual attraction to her friend Doretha even before Mason's death, but she had understandably rejected acting on it. Mason's choice "endearments" would have then been accurate indeed.

Approximately six months after Mason's death Aunt Doretha had given the suitor her friend's number without Estelle's permission, meeting with Clare's wholehearted approval. Her mother had refused his phone calls, flowers, and dinner invitations for some time; however, her excuse being that that she was busy with work and focused on finding a house close to her job.

"Mom, he seems to be a nice guy," she had encouraged. *Don't let your past spoil your future*, she wanted to say—and was prepared to say, if necessary, though respectfully, of course.

She had wanted to tell her mother that experiences in the land of the living could be quite enjoyable. *You've been away for a long time, but you're back now.* Clare thought that perhaps her mother did end up having a heart-to-heart with Aunt Doretha because she finally stopped refusing his advances.

"You'll meet him," she presently told her brother. "They are due back this weekend."

At Clare's it was peaceful. Jeffrey didn't mind sleeping on the couch. It was nicer than a lot of living conditions he had endured; so that he could save money and travel cheaply, some of the motels had not been the best. Most of all, here everything was clean, without all the foul smells he'd encountered while bumming around the country.

*So, Mom has a friend*, he thought. He couldn't help wondering what he was like.

That night, he slept on the couch converted to a bed. Awaking the next morning, he realized he hadn't enjoyed such sound sleep for a long time. That day, with money borrowed from Clare, Jeffrey ventured out. His plan was to retrieve his clothes, including his warmer coat, from his friend, and then go job hunting, but not before seeking the help of his former parole officer. He was relatively glad to see him. At first when Jeffrey walked into his office, the older man didn't recognize him. How long had it been, almost six years? After a few minutes of chatting Jeffrey had brought the officer completely up to date on his life. Much to Jeffrey's chagrin, he was yet qualified for the same menial employment he had held in the past—chump-change teenager gigs, busing tables or washing dishes. And so, he went to the restaurant west of State Street. Yes, the job was still open. If he wanted it, he could start working the same day. His plight weighed on him heavily. How long would it take for him to get out of this rut? That inner voice chided: *You didn't even finish high school. Why not?*

*Gran Jennie* always said a cloudy sky did not stop the constant sunrise or sunset somewhere on God's earth. He felt the urge to run again, but if he wasn't careful twenty-five could happen in a flash. The biggest factor keeping him in place was that he had no money to get himself anywhere. He now regretted the mistake of, as his mother said, "All that foolish squandering." How he loathed admitting that she was right.

He was unaware that Doretha, meanwhile, gently chided his mother during their long discussions: "Estelle, he feels bad enough already. Try to be patient."

Jeffrey continued working the restaurant job. Several times he promised his mother he would stop by. He didn't want to face what he considered her harsh scrutiny.

"Jeffrey, you need to get back in school," she complained most of the time. She was anxious for him. Time was galloping! He would look around in a few years and, over and out, no more twenties! She didn't mention that his uncle had already shared with his sister the new nickname for his nephew. She disapproved but withheld any comment. Turtle, Ned called him—whenever pulling up stakes, he didn't need to call a van; he could just get up and go.

At first her suggestion that he go back to school was a casual one made periodically, but then it became anxiously consistent. He had spent all the money with nothing whatever to show for it. Of course, she never said this directly, but Jeffrey knew she was thinking it.

"I thought you said you wanted to stop running and settle down long enough to make a life for yourself?" said Rissie. They sat in her small apartment with the TV off. They needed to have this heart-to-heart. ( "Maybe you can talk to him," Estelle had suggested tremulously. "I've tried over and over again, but I guess I'm too close to the situation.")

"I got the promotion I was after," she said. "Now I can graduate from this kitchenette apartment." She informed him that she had scheduled all her apartment hunting for after-work hours, so she was gone the night he telephoned. She told the good news with subdued joy, and then totally sobered to direct her focus on the present dilemma.

"Jeffrey," she said ever so gently, but with firmness, "you have no choice. You are going to have to try. Otherwise, life is going to leave you behind."

It was a painful conversation for both of us.

"I'm uneducated, prepared for only menial labor."

"That's true," she agreed quietly, "but you can change that."

"It will take forever," he countered.

"No," she answered simply. "The journey begins with the first step." She paused. "You start by acquiring your GED and," she added encouragingly, "you're close."

"How can I rise above what I have become? I have a record as a felon, without stealing anything or even holding a gun. I have been all over this entire city looking for decent-paying work. What major company is going to hire me? I've been home this time for a while and still cannot make enough money to have a decent place." He looked around her small but cozy apartment, and now she was moving to a larger one.

"We can live together, Jeffrey, at least until you are established."

*Bridges*, he thought and could immediately hear Gran Jennie. Why had he not allowed her words to direct his path long before now? He thought of her wisdom: Bridges in life, she had told him, are not like the ones you drive your car across or that you walk over. Sometimes you're on one of life's bridges for years to strengthen you for the next phase. You can't see the other side, but you must keep that mental picture of what it will be like when you get there. Until you are delivered to your blessing you must mentally tend to that flower garden. It strengthens you and lets you never lose hope. "The bridges are the challenges in life, baby," she had said, "but you just keep plantin' those flowers."

"Sis, I am a grown man," he said, returning to the present. "I shouldn't have to live with you."

"I found a very nice one-bedroom apartment, and my sofa converts to a bed," she said cheerfully. She wanted to guide him away from living with their mother. She had moved out because their mother needed her space. Clare wanted to allow her to enjoy her relationship with Max. And maybe, just maybe… She kept positive thoughts.

Her brother would not fare well living with their mother. Estelle would continue trying extra hard to correct what had been wrong for a very long time. He had returned to Chicago over a year and a half ago. They argued constantly as she attempted to correct his past as he, in turn, rebuffed her efforts. He attempted to do it without being too offensive, but it was hard to watch. Although her approach had become weary and impatient, she was not wrong.

"Live with me until we can make things right, Jeffrey, just until then," Clare urged.

He smiled sadly as they sat across from each other at her small kitchen table. "When will that be, Rissie?" He laughed bitterly. "Do you realize how long it would take me to establish myself if I decided to go back to school, to go on to college? Do you know that certain professions do not allow felons?" he exclaimed in exasperation. "There is a list of occupations. Once there was a close call with the law, then I messed up, and…" He trailed off. Suddenly, the raw, raunchy melody of Muddy Waters' "Rollin' Stone" coursed through his brain.

Clare turned quiet and didn't answer. Uncle Ned was working on that with a lawyer friend. She didn't want to get Jeffrey's hopes up.

The haunting mental picture of Ms. Ballenger's deep disappointment and Ms. Taft's crisp insight never grew dim for Jeffrey. He could still see Ms. Ballenger shaking her head in despair and Ms. Taft offering her cutting glances, accompanied by sterner words. He had finally arrived at the exact place they had predicted.

Two people Ms. Taft had simply not liked were Kendall Lisle and Leonard Scaggs because both had habits and characteristics belonging in a dumpster. He had wanted to tell Ms. Taft so many times for so long that that incident was not his fault.

"Jeffrey, you have to start somewhere," Clare now pleaded, but with a firm tone. "Try, Jeffrey. What other choice do you have? Surely you know you can no longer run here and there and everywhere." She smiled sadly. "I know," she said, "Langston Hughes was known as the itinerant poet. However, Hughes was an educated man. Plus, this is a different time, becoming progressively more difficult as time moves on. I'm not even sure that Hughes's lifestyle would work as well now. Even then, his travels weren't always under the best conditions."

Jeffrey simply stared at her across the table. He regretted his life was a mess. Although everything she said was true, it felt like in front of him on the road back, there was a very tall, inescapable wrought iron fence impossible to climb, with a keyless gate. He thought about his father. Perhaps this was why Mason had never possessed the motivation for self-improvement.

"Sis," he said, "I am in a wasteland with all the bad choices. Where I am the land is barren; there is no beauty." *At least I have my memories*, he told himself, but he had to admit that, although pleasant, they would not financially sustain him. "But to cross the desert of my existence to get to that oasis where you are would be like riding a camel through an extended desert storm without enough water."

"Don't talk like that, Jeffrey."

"I can't even afford a decent suit," he said quietly.

Clare wondered what would have happened if their mother had left their father. What if Mason had not gotten ill? What! What! What! She wondered in exasperation. However, Uncle Ned had always supported his sister and her children, despite Jeffrey's willfulness a good percentage of the time. What would their life have been like if Mason had stayed healthy and their mother had left with them to fend for herself? That vein of thought was futile, period.

"There are secondhand shops—some very nice ones—until you can afford something new," she said encouragingly.

She was very familiar with most, especially on the North Side, having browsed for years and selectively chosen from their racks. Recently she had relaxed her rigid thriftiness to enjoy purchasing clothes that were new. This recent promotion had moved her into a comfortable income bracket, but her wardrobe selections, although stylish, remained pragmatic. She had even resumed a limited amount of sewing.

Suddenly she rose from her seat to come and kneel before him. She placed her hands on his knees. Somehow, someway, she had to reach him. He was back and needed to settle down. There had to be a way to break through.

He stared down at her as she looked up at him.

"Jeffrey, you have no choice but to try. Life has you boxed in unless you try. Don't be like Mason, Jeffrey. He refused to expand and grow because of pigheadedness and foolish pride, and he died bitter and broken. That wasteland you claim is in your mind, Jeffrey. You must change your thinking."

He started to protest.

"Hear me out. Widen your view of life from where you are. Try planting flowers in that wasteland. You know how Gran Jennie always says that your mind controls all things, to grow your *own* flowers mentally to have the right kind of environment?"

He nodded; their grandmother had said the same thing during those eight months he had recently stayed with her.

"Please plant flowers, Jeffrey. Replace all the negatives with flowers." Tears were trickling down her face. She reached up and placed her hands on his shoulders. "And let me help you. We can do it together."

Suddenly Jeffrey was weeping too. For a long time, they remained in that position, gazing at each other through their tears.

For the first time in his life, he felt that circumstances called for a celebration. For seven months now, he'd had a meaningful job counseling the wayward teen. His former parole officer had been excited about acquiring a five-year government grant for the work. The monetary reward held promise for the future of youth who otherwise might never have the opportunity. Jeffrey welcomed supplementing that income by working part-time in a clothing store. He began to dress better. He took Clare's advice to start a small bank account.

Meanwhile, thanks to Uncle Ned, his record had been expunged, so he was free! When he was given this news, there were no words to describe his feeling of indebtedness to his uncle. Estelle practically cried with joy. The lawyer informed his uncle the evidence had never been solid, suspect at best.

The same former parole officer, who had always seen potential in Jeffrey, worked with him on acquiring his GED and starting his first year of night school. Carrying a full load, he triumphantly completed his first year of collegiate studies. He worked hard, voicing his determination not to lose time, shoving aside what Mason had always claimed: "You ain't got nothin' but time." So, he put in the same level of work the following year to receive his associate degree, allowing him to enter a four-year university the subsequent fall. He was proud of his accomplishments. Clare too was proud of all he had accomplished in a relatively short period of time. Also, she is equally proud of herself for finishing the last year of grad school.

The potential had always been there in Jeffrey. Clare said this often, which caused his spirits to soar. The following summer he intended to again visit Gran Jennie; he called her often.

Whenever Jennifer spoke to her daughter, she never disclosed how often she talked to Jeffrey knowing it would make her feel a sense of rejection. She knew that Jeffrey deeply loved his mother but found a relationship with her difficult. *In due time*, she thought. She prayed repeatedly that he would come in due course.

❧

Things were settling down; Jeffrey's life was on track. As he sat at the breakfast bar with his sister he looked around at her home. She really had a nice place. He was ecstatic. Over the weekend he would be moving into his own apartment, a studio with a bed that let out from the wall. The transition sufficiently indicated he had finally achieved his independence.

"Sis," he said, "I'm finally going to have a life. I owe you."

"I want to share your first million, thank you very much," she teased as she grabbed her coat. He followed her out into the hallway, she locked the apartment door. Together they descended the stairs from the second floor and entered the street to catch the bus to the 'L. They rode the train together as far as Forty-Seventh. Exiting the train, Jeffrey waved good-bye.

On her way home that evening, Clare picked up an inexpensive red wine to go with the victory dinner she was planning. It would be something quick but delicious. Goodness, that man loved pasta! And so, the menu was pasta with a delicious sauce, broiled lamb chops, and a garden salad.

At home cooking dinner she thought she heard the faint sound of gunshots. *It would be nice*, she thought as she added the spaghetti to the boiling water, *if all the black community could be tranquil, with an aura of genuine wellness, like other communities. Or was it that those stories never made the news?* Well, one day, she hopefully told herself. Almost an hour later, the tossed salad was in the refrigerator, the lamb chops were in the warm oven, and the sauce and spaghetti were away from the burners. Dinner was ready. She sat down with the newspaper crossword puzzle to wait for Jeffrey; often he was slightly late. He was going to do well in life, and she couldn't be happier.

When the doorbell rang, she buzzed him in, thinking that he must have forgotten his key that morning. When she went to meet him at the door, two uniformed cops stood there instead.

"Is this the Ingram residence?"

❦

Except for his winter coat, all his worldly possessions would fit neatly into a large shopping bag. There were two lightweight summer jackets; three pairs of boxer shorts; three T-shirts; two pairs of slacks, one black and the other gray; two pairs of jeans; four tank tops; and a half dozen pairs of socks. On top she placed the shaving kit that he had used daily. He had stopped smoking a couple of times, but the lighter was still on the kitchen table. She dropped it in the bag.

Everything had been a blur since she identified the body. *Gun shots*, she told herself. Was that what she'd heard? The very same gunshots? Clare engaged in self-interrogation for hours as she sat at her mother's kitchen table and even later in the guestroom. Once during the night, she heard her mother's footsteps on the kitchen floor and started to get up to join her. The familiar footsteps just as quickly left the kitchen and became muffled as Estelle returned to her carpeted bedroom, so Clare climbed back into bed. It was going to be a very long night.

*I'm finally going to have a life.* An unfulfilled projection reverberating through the corridors of time.

It was too bad, she thought in a surge of renewed anger, that Mason had not lived to see how his cynical view of the world, corrected too late, had impacted the life of his son, Too bad he had died before being able to look down on his son stone cold in a coffin, stunningly handsome and, thanks to Uncle Ned, impeccably dressed. In fact, he was wearing a suit fresh off the racks of Brooks Brothers, complete with a silk tie and matching pocket square, something he'd never been able to do during his short life. His face was unmarked; all the shots had been to the body. The police said it was a robbery. Once she stared into the apathetic, dead-fish eyes of the detective assigned to the case, she knew she could never be certain. She doubted that there would be any serious, in-depth follow-up. She bitterly surmised his sentiment to be "Another nigger gone!" It was a rash thought in a time of deep, gut-wrenching grief.

Well, gone were all his money and that beautiful watch, an expensive gift from Estelle after he finished his first year of college. Clare recalled that their mother had been beside herself with joy. Clare lamented miserably, when would this small element in the black community stop killing over trivia? Yes, trivia! When would they ever learn that life, all life, even black life, is the most important thing on the planet? When would they know that?

*The Lord giveth and the Lord taketh away.*

*Blessed be the name of the Lord.*

*Amen*

Last words uttered at the graveside by their pastor. Clare kept telling herself it was much too soon. She dropped a lone white rose on his coffin to watch it slowly descend to its final resting place. Other words were spoken, but none as significant. Death for the young held such irrevocable cruelty, as if being stalked by a greedy, crazed predator.

Clare stood at the gravesite a long time. Only then could she finally come to grips with what had burdened her for years. As teenagers, Clare could never envision the two of them sharing memories, raising families, and growing old together. There were times when she longed for Jeffrey to embrace life with gusto, move forward and shake off all past negatives. Instead, he wore each one as a millstone inevitably outweighing everything positive.

A deeply grief-stricken Craig had driven from Minnesota to pay last respects to his friend. Prentiss telephoned to tell them that the news had aged Gran ten years. She had grown old and too weak to attend the funeral of her only grandson; this hurt her deeply. He said she cried herself to sleep, as overnight, very cautiously, he watched her thinking: *always physical frailty forever accompanies the old.*

# PART THREE

# FAMILY

**(1983–Twenty-First Century)**

# Chapter Fourteen

It was Friday, the day before Christmas Eve. Just a few hours earlier Clare Ingram had been released from the hospital with the greatest Christmas present ever. She silently mouthed the word "benign" with almost reverent appreciation. There was no cancer in the lymph nodes or the lump that had been removed from her breast. She considered the permanent scar from the lumpectomy a small price to pay. Even before Dr. Wilson reached her gurney in recovery, his smile said it all; she thanked God for allowing her to land on solid ground.

Everything was happening so fast. She still wanted to give the bridal shower for her best friend, Nadine, who eloped the first time. Her dear friend's second marriage was tomorrow, Christmas Eve. The shower was scheduled for that afternoon, just hours before the ceremony. Dr. Wilson's instructions were "Have the affair if you agree to take it easy."

Clare was familiar with Nadine's college friends, and she had consulted one of her former high school classmates, Frieda, to identify closest high school friends and help plan the entire event. Aware of Clare's recent hospitalization, Frieda answered her clarion call. She even brought additional assistance, her twelve-year-old son.

The three brought yuletide cheer to Clare's living room. Generous amounts of holly and sprigs of pine decorated the mantle. Tinsel, lights, and ornaments adorned the Christmas tree centered in the living room window. Temporarily joining the celebration were a pair of gilded wedding bells cleverly displayed from the chandelier with gold paper streamers in celebration of the upcoming nuptials of Nadine Jamison and Cornell Bennett.

Finally, at ten o'clock that night, Clare, Frieda, and Frieda's twelve-year-old toasted their accomplishments with a glass of eggnog. Clare had discreetly spiked both Frieda's and her own.

The next morning, Christmas Eve, Clare approvingly examined her dining room table, covered with her finest lace tablecloth. Within the hour, she was due at Jazz for her appointment with her hair stylist. She cheerfully hummed "Deck the Hall" as she locked her door. At last, the spirit of Christmas was permitting her to join the annual cheer with everyone else. Her heart sang. She could fly over Chicago without wings, singing joyously about her victory.

At eleven fifteen Clare returned home with a beautifully coifed head. While preparing to host the event she listened to the four messages on her answering machine.

Nadine: "I'll be a little late. What is so urgent anyway? Girlfriend, it had better be good since you've interrupted my shopping day."

Karl: "Hey, small frame, just checking in. Pick you up at nine this evening. Glad you're okay." He was not attending Nadine's wedding ceremony. It had always been obvious that she wanted her best friend to move on.

While Clare was in the hospital, a dozen red roses had been delivered, accompanied by a card that read, "I'm missing you like crazy. See you soon." His flight from Florida had arrived late the previous night. Clare hoped his mom was much better. He had dutifully complied with his sister's request to be with her to discuss their mother's medical status with her doctor.

Her mother: "Oh, that's right, sweetheart. I forgot this is your glad hair day. Give me a call when you get in."

The fourth message: a pause and then a soft click. Her curiosity was brief. Preoccupied, she dismissed it.

She called quickly telephoned her mother, briefly describe the beautifully decorated room. Of course, she and Max would see it when he came to take away the nuptial decorum. All other decorations would remain undisturbed. Clare simply loved this time of year!

"I'll save food for you both," she promised just before hanging up.

Punctually, at 12:00 p.m., the catering service arrived, efficiently arranging the luncheon on her dining room table. The sizable check she had handed over was worth every penny for her oldest and dearest friend.

They had been friends since grade school. In review of the years when she and Nadine were practically the same height, it seemed as though Nadine went to sleep one night with her pituitary gland in overdrive. When both awakened as teenagers, they remained on the same mental plane, but never again were they physically eye-level.

Clare had instructed Nadine not to arrive before one fifteen in the afternoon, under the They had been friends since grade school. guise that she had to run a few errands on her way from Jazz. At twelve forty-five Frieda arrived. They chatted for about ten minutes over a glass of wine, and then the doorbell rang almost nonstop until Clare's living room was full, with nobody missing but the guest of honor. As planned, Clare was the self-designated lookout. When she spotted Nadine's car, she gave the signal to the lively group to conceal themselves in her bedroom.

Nadine entered the foyer, took off her coat, and slipped into the trusty house slippers that she always kept just inside Clare's closet. She mildly scolded Clare for declining to join her on the trip to downtown Chicago for her once-a-month therapy—shopping!

Then as they entered the beautifully decorated living room, the other women suddenly streamed from Clare's bedroom to all at once yell, "Surprise!"

Nadine was in a state of pleasant shock. On a rare occasion of tears, she embraced and kissed Clare. Tearfully, she began to move around the room, hugging some, kissing others, warmly grabbing hands, overwhelmed with deep joy and gratitude that people cared enough.

It was a fun event with gifts ranging from ridiculous to hilarious. Most were beautiful accompanied by something outlandish or bizarre. One of her church friends gave her a vibrator accompanied by a beautiful flowing white negligee. Concerning the vibrator, the card read, "Just in case Cornell has postnuptial jitters and that essential part of his anatomy becomes inept." The friend and church member personally delivered a verbal afterthought. "Nadine, don't you dare tell Bartholomew I gave this to you." Everyone laughed. (The Reverend Bartholomew James was their pastor.) From a teacher friend she received an explicit how-to guide for lovemaking to share with Cornell. Suggestion: "For teaching outside the classroom," Beautifully gift-wrapped were a bathing suit and matching wrap. Another fun gift was a rubber duck, quacking when squeezed. The card read, "Dear Nadine, nothing spoils a duck but… This is a reminder that when the honeymoon is over, in some instances the less said, the better." Nadine did not share the note inside the next card as she did with the others. It was from Clare. No other friend knew Nadine as well. Penned in tactful jest, it was firm yet gentle counseling. Nadine knew her friend had paid a small fortune for the breathtaking red camisole with matching brassiere and panties. All the presents were thoughtful additions to her trousseau.

Finally, they engaged in playing a word game. A six-letter word clue: one thing rarely found on a honeymoon? Answer: a virgin. The combined laughter, merry gestures, antics, and animated dialogue made for an afternoon of crazy frolic that Nadine would always treasure.

The party ended with poignant memories—unforgettable good-byes, best wishes, and warm embraces to be forever cherished. Some of these women Nadine had not seen in years, most not since high school, and some she would probably never see again in life. All had cared enough to come and wish her well for the future.

Minutes later, Nadine and Clare sat at her dining room table quietly reviewing the lovely afternoon.

"Who was the girl in the red top and jeans?" asked Clare. "She was of medium height and"—

"Oh, that's Vivian!" Nadine replied. "She and I want to Dunbar together. She got pregnant in her last year of high school and married her childhood sweetheart. I hadn't seen her since we were in our twenties. I ran into her once in Woolworth's on Michigan, and we exchanged phone numbers. That's how we kept in touch all these years." Nadine was pensive for a moment. "Life is sometimes so strange. I remember that Vivian always wanted to become a singer—she had a beautiful voice. She always invited me to her church musicals because she was and still is her choir's soloist and lead singer. Funny how I never took the time to attend, but still, we call each other frequently."

She sipped her glass of wine, collecting her thoughts as she delved into the past. "Remember the girl with the very long hair, medium brown, rather tall?"

Clare nodded.

"She was a hot mama when in high school, a real party animal. I don't know what happened to make her change, but she went to college, then law school, and now practices criminal law. No one ever thought she would do anything. That just goes to show you."

"You never know," Clare agreed.

They were silent for a while, just sipping their wine and sharing closeness.

"Nadine," Clare said softly, "be kind to Cornell, okay?"

"I love Cornell," she replied.

Ever so gently, Clare placed her hand over Nadine's. The fidgeting with the tablecloth ceased. "Don't be so caustic with him, okay? Cornell is not as educated as you, but he's a good man."

"I know that" her friend said earnestly. "We have discussed our differences, and Cornell knows I don't consider that an issue."

Tactfully, Clare moved on. "Girl, just think, Christmas Day, you will be waking up to a honeymoon in the Big Apple. I don't want you two to wait until New Year's Eve to leave the hotel room."

Nadine laughed. "Don't worry. We have a great itinerary. We're even taking in a couple of Broadway plays."

"Nadine," Clare said, alerted to the time on her wall clock, "I think you had better be on your way home. I don't want Cornell to be standing at the altar thinking he's been jilted."

Clare helped her friend carry her many gifts to the car. They parted with plans to meet at the church in approximately four hours. Wedding vows were to be exchanged at seven o'clock.

જી

Only the front of the church was well lit in the large South Side church to accommodate the small wedding. The flowers were yellow calla lilies and purple irises. Nadine's suit was almost the color of irises. Cornell Bennett looked handsome in his black tuxedo, as did his best man, who was also his brother. Clare, the maid of honor, wore a soft yellow suit, complementing her skin tone.

Nadine's siblings did not see why their sister had to have a Christmas Eve wedding in the first place. One even told her so. One month prior, her entire immediate family had been summoned to her living room and quietly informed of her desire to have a Christmas Eve wedding. It was also her desire—and Cornell's—to spend their honeymoon in New York City. Hotel reservations had been made six months in advance for the occasion. They would take an overnight flight to allow a Merry Christmas honeymoon in the Big Apple. They would also welcome 1984 with a multitude in Times Square. Nadine had always wanted to personally witness the countdown and the dropping of that famous Waterford crystal ball; when she watched the festivities on television, it always looked like the throngs of people were having such a grand time. In response to the family pushback, she had asked: Why was an hour of time during the afternoon of Christmas Eve too much to ask? If they chose not to attend her wedding, that would be quite acceptable. Everybody in the family knew Nadine well. So, in the end, Nadine's family, the Jamisons, filed in to occupy the front pew and part of the second. Clare, cognizant of the limited time, but as her maid of honor, stood with her. Although seated near but separate of Nadine's family, was Estelle. Traditional seating on separate sides of the church was ignored. Cornell's few family members were positioned on the same side directly behind the Jamison family.

The wedding ceremony began at seven o'clock. Except for customary attire worn by the groom and best man, tradition was completely abandoned. The wedding was without fanfare because both had been there before. For Nadine, there was nothing old. She was wearing something new simply because she needed the appropriate suit and shoes. There was nothing borrowed and not one thing blue. The entire wedding ceremony: very informal and exact, lasting all of fifteen minutes was over by seven fifteen. Limousine service to the airport was a wedding gift provided by Cornell's brother. Thus, the transportation waited at the curb to whisk the newlyweds to O'Hare in time for their flight.

Nadine's mother, who had sat quietly the month before as the rest of the family debated the issue of a Christmas Eve wedding, now wondered, why all the fuss? It was over with minimal disruption of a day mostly spent with family.

With the ceremony over, some family members got into their individual cars and went home, others sped away to spend the evening together. Everyone's next-day Christmas celebrations went on with minimal disruption.

Back at home by eight, Clare waited for Karl who picked her up at nine sharp, and they went to a movie. (He always spent Christmas day with his girls and Clare wondered if his estranged wife was included.) Anyway, they exchanged gifts—he received a pair of leather gloves from her, and she a pair of beautiful pajamas from him. Somehow it turned out to be the strangest date ever to be discussed later.

The entire Christmas Day was spent with Max and Estelle. Mother and daughter exchanged gifts like always. Clare received the set of bathroom rugs she wanted. She gave her mother a new kitchen clock to replace her old one. Max had given Estelle a very expensive bathrobe. She gave him a wallet.

With her best friend in New York enjoying her honeymoon and Christmas only a fond memory, Clare arrived at her office on Monday to find a note on her desk asking her to call Dr. Wilson. It was only eight fifteen. His nurse was not due in the office for another fifteen minutes, she thought while dialing the number. Her doctor picked up the first ring.

"Thank you for your promptness, Ms. Ingram," he said. As always, he sounded as smooth as silk, so perhaps it was of no importance.

"Is anything wrong?" she asked hesitantly.

"Ms. Ingram, how soon can you come see me?"

She began to worry, but she remembered what Estelle always told her about coming to hasty conclusions. "As long as I can clear it with my boss, I can be there within the hour."

"Thank you, Ms. Ingram. I will see you then."

She had coincidentally driven to work that day as she did on rare occasions with errands to run after work. After clearing the departure with her director, Grant Stafford, she quickly made her way across Michigan Avenue and to The Outer Drive, heading south to Dr. Wilson's office in the heart of the city, right off Hyde Park Boulevard. She despised Hyde Park's parking limitations. Already beginning to worry, her anxious mood was exacerbated by the experience of driving around for over ten minutes to find a parking space.

Dr. Wilson and four other surgeons, all affiliated with the University of Chicago Hospitals, were located on the top floor of the building. Noting that the waiting room was already full Clare added her name to the list as the receptionist instructed. She was nervously skimming a magazine when the nurse called her name; Dr. Wilson was going to see her immediately.

He came from behind his desk to shake her hand as she stepped into the room. "Good morning, Ms. Ingram. Be seated, please," he said softly as he perused her chart.

"Dr. Wilson, is anything wrong?" She was still standing.

Again, he said very gently, "Please be seated, Ms. Ingram."

Only when she sat down in the chair opposite his did he look up. "Ms. Ingram, the pathologist reexamined the slides from your biopsy once more and discovered there were microscopic strains of carcinoma." He paused. "Your tumor is what is known as *in situ* carcinoma."

She felt herself going numb and her body freezing up. She was speechless as her gaze remained fixed on him. Exactly what was he saying?

"Ms. Ingram?"

"I'm sorry, Dr. Wilson." She was allowing this nightmare to settle in her brain. "But you said I was fine, that there was no cancer." She raised her hand to her mouth, muffling a sob.

For a moment Dr. Wilson looked helpless. "I know, Ms. Ingram," he said with sincere empathy. "I know this cannot be a good feeling, but when the slides were reviewed for the second time, Pathology looked closer and…" He held up his hands helplessly, not knowing what else to say. "I tried to contact you Saturday because I was in the office a little while, but when you didn't answer, I figured it was just as well—why not allow you a pleasant weekend."

So, he was the one who had called and hung up. She began weeping. Tears streamed down her face as she sat there, and she made no effort to take tissue from her purse.

Dr. Wilson quickly pulled tissue from the box on his credenza and leaned over to aid her in drying her eyes. She eased the tissue from his hand, tried to blot away the tears stubbornly refusing to stop.

How long did he allow her to sit there? It seemed like an eternity although it could only have been a few minutes at the most. She turned to him, more composed, but filled with dread. He was talking, but she had not heard a word.

"I'm sorry, what were you saying?"

"We have sent your slides to a team of oncologists to tell us exactly what kind of surgery to perform."

She began to sob again; it was becoming increasingly more real.

Dr. Wilson hurried to the door and called one of the nurses inside his office. "Get Ms. Ingram a mild sedative," he instructed softly. Moments later she was kindly refused it.

"I'll be all right," she assured them. It was like a bad dream.

"Are you driving, Ms. Ingram?" Dr. Wilson asked quietly.

"Yes," she replied hoarsely. Her eyelids were beginning to feel slightly puffy.

"Is there anyone I can call to come and drive you home?"

"No," she said sadly. Nadine was on her honeymoon. Estelle was at work.

"I'll go have coffee until I gain my bearings," she said calmly. There was a restaurant within walking distance. "Then I'm certain I can drive myself home."

Dr. Wilson moved his chair closer until he sat directly opposite her and could look into her eyes. I don't know how you feel and cannot make that claim, but there is a positive side to this." He stopped momentarily. He usually maintained a professional detachment when interacting with his patients. That demeanor had been temporarily discarded.

"Think of it this way, Ms. Ingram. What if Pathology had not been moved by something, a higher power, intuition, a gut feeling—whatever you want to name it—to review your slides and then a couple of years, five years, would have passed? What then, my dear?"

She stared at him through her pain.

"Do you follow me?"

She nodded sadly. She remembered something he had said earlier. "You said something about 'in situ' carcinoma?" she asked tremulously.

He was glad she was beginning to focus. "It means that the cancer is encapsulated and has not spread."

She paused to think. "What if just that part of the breast, the actual site of the tumor, is removed—what then?"

Dr. Wilson, a surgeon but an oncologist as well, gently refused to discuss the procedure prematurely. He had thoroughly reviewed her medical history, which revealed breast cancer on both sides of her family, the significance of which some oncologists debated. However, he remained tactfully silent because his policy was never to discuss any procedure that was not solely his decision.

"That is why an oncology team has been consulted," he said kindly. "They will determine what is to be done." He patted her consolingly on the shoulder as he rose from his chair. "Sit here for a while, Ms. Ingram," he advised. "Relax—at least for now."

He stepped toward the door—there were two other rooms in his private suite of offices—and just before opening it turned and smiled encouragingly. "I'll be in touch in about three to four days."

She heard him greet a patient as he closed the door behind him, faintly heard activity beyond the shut door. Approximately thirty minutes later she calmly rose from her chair, put on her coat. Her better judgment told her not to drive. Suddenly she decided who could probably drive her home.

Karl Pugh began looking around as soon as he entered the restaurant to soon spot her sitting in a corner booth, drinking her coffee as she waited patiently. The waitress came over just after he joined her; he ordered the same with cream and sugar. She had caught him in the office making last-minute calls to some of his clients. Karl was an insurance agent and could always be reached in his branch office until late morning.

"Clare, I don't know what to say," he said after she gave him the news. He was astounded, and even a forced expression of consolation. Comfort simply would not come. "Life can sure deal from the bottom of the deck," he finally muttered grimly.

Somewhat disappointed by his handling of the news, Clare didn't respond as both finished their coffee in silence.

"I'll leave my car here and take you home," he said.

Clare nodded her consent.

"I'll call the office and have Dexter meet me at your house so that I can come back and pick up my car." He walked to the pay phone located in the far corner of the restaurant and returned a few minutes later. "Okay, he's going to meet me at your house." He left a small tip on the table and paid the cashier.

Moments later, Karl was merging left into the middle lane of the drive while Clare gazed out at Lake Michigan. Complementing Karl's temperament, it lapped angrily at the shore of the lake. There was only the constant, quiet purr of the car engine amid an awkward silence. Blanketed in her misery, Clare sat there dejectedly searching for something to say; twenty minutes later, they were on Jeffrey Boulevard, and she still hadn't found the words. Minutes later, Karl parked her car at the curb and pressed the keys in her palm. Dexter, already parked out front, waved to her from behind the steering wheel.

Karl followed her to her door, where she stood on her stoop with the car keys in her pocket and the house keys clutched in her hand. Hesitant, he stood at the bottom of her steps looking up. "I'll call you this evening." Suddenly he mounted the short flight of steps, two at a time, and planted a hurried kiss on the side of her mouth. "I promise I will call you," he said.

Nodding somberly, she let herself in. She didn't look back, but instead closed and locked the door behind her. Walking through the living room that just days ago had held such laughter and gaiety, she desperately longed to recapture that emotion. As a potter molds clay, she longed to smooth away all the sadness and pain to exist in a suspended animation until this tribulation was over. There was no escape.

*The Lord is my shepherd. I shall not want.*

The words nagged her troubled mind. *Oh, but I do want*, she thought. *I want to be free of this monster.*

She recalled that even on Saturday night Karl had chosen the movie. She couldn't make up her mind, so both watched without much interest. Usually, they shared a large bucket of popcorn with separate beverages. This time they watched the movie in silence without refreshments; she subdued, and he in deep in thought. He seemed to want to say something, but he never got around to it. They left the theater, headed north to his apartment. Tere was not one single parking spot less than two blocks away on the crowded streets. Parking was always difficult on the North Side. In the past, he had vowed several times to rent parking space in his building, but he'd never followed through, mentioning something about being on the waiting list. They walked the two and half blocks in the blistering cold to his building where, once inside, he seemed a trifle more cheerful. They rode the elevator up to the tenth floor, walking down the long corridor to his corner apartment, neat and clean as always. Since he usually spent weekends at her place, it had been several months since she had been there. She noticed a few changes: a new spread on the bed, a new living room sofa, carpeting that looked fresh and extra clean, and the spare bedroom no longer used as a study. He explained the desire to get workout equipment and stop leaving the apartment so early to go to the gym and possibly economize. She agreed that it was a good plan, and they stayed up for a while to watch television. He discussed his trip to Florida, his mother's illness, the fact that she was dying of congestive heart failure. The angioplasty had made her healthy for only a short period of time. He and his sister met with their mother's cardiologist who explained to Karl what both she and his mother already knew—that she could go at any time.

Never did he express gladness that she was alright. Never did they even briefly discuss her stay in the hospital. He examined the incision on her left breast and uttered a brief expression of relief that the surgery was favorable, ending the discussion.

Once during their three-and-a-half-year relationship he had talked about divorcing his estranged wife and marrying Clare, but lately the subject had become a dead issue. Karl had two preteen daughters whom she had never met. However, she had seen a few pictures of them and their mother. All three were of average attractiveness with pleasant smiles.

She now sat at her kitchen table. She had telephoned Grant, informing him she was unable to return to work. She would explain the next day.

Who was there to love her, she thought sadly, to care for her, to give her that male support when situations like this arose and threatened to make her feel less than beautiful? Karl had always adored her body. She had perfectly formed small breasts—a B cup in fact—with great uplift. "A beautiful mouthful," he called them. For a short time, Clare and her cousin Druscilla had attempted a loose friendship while Nadine was away in Seattle. Druscilla used to tease her about her perfect little duet of guards standing at attention in full salute. Clare had once read about a woman who had undergone a bilateral mastectomy. Opting not to undergo reconstructive surgery, she was as flat as the average man, perhaps even flatter than some. Her husband never again entered the bedroom until she was under the covers. The mere thought made Clare suddenly feel like a caged animal with a trap in front of the door.

*There's no hiding place down here.*

*There's no hiding place down here.*

The rest of the words would not come. Her memory failed her. Who sang that song? She couldn't remember if a choir sang it or perhaps a quartet. She felt so tired, as if she could sleep a week or a month, or even bed down for as long as Rip Van Winkle. She yearned for that possible scenario. She thought, *Wake me when it's over!* In the bedroom, she hung her coat and jacket in the closet. Still in her street clothes, she slowly crawled onto the neatly made bed, reached for the throw that she kept at its foot, and drifted off to sleep. Her last thought before she drifted off to sleep was "the end is the beginning."

Disoriented, Clare raised her head and looked at the phone ringing with urgency, and on perhaps the fourth or fifth ring, she grasped it right before the interception of the answering machine.

"Clare?"

It was Estelle, calling for their once-a-day connection. Clare always telephoned from the office on her mother's days off. On the other hand, Estelle often waited until her daughter got home from work to phone.

"Are you alright?"

Clare looked at the clock radio on the dresser. As she focused, she realized she had been asleep for a long time. Was it after five? "I'm…" her voice trailed off. Momentarily composed, she fought off the distress that was coming in waves. "I must have gone to sleep," she said through suppressed tears.

"You don't sound right. Today I called your office, and they said you left not long after you came in."

Clare couldn't hold back the sobbing, and Estelle heard the muffled sounds even as Clare attempted to conceal her grief.

"Oh, sweetheart, what is it? Whatever it is, I'll be there in about ten minutes. I'm leaving now."

Fifteen minutes later the doorbell rang, and Clare, clasping the front of her bathrobe, greeted her mother. As they sat on the living room sofa facing each other, somehow Estelle knew even before Clare began to tell her about her visit with Dr. Wilson.

Estelle did not say so, but she was thinking of Mason. Mason had escaped the dreaded cancer that plagued his family members, especially the women. It was one of Mason's many "secrets" that she had discovered from Nelson after his death, pertinent information that Estelle had passed on to her daughter. And of course, there was also what Aunt Lu had gone through. Nevertheless, diabetes had assaulted Mason's body as much as any cancer could, but she would not reveal that thought to her daughter, thinking how cold and unfeeling it would sound. *Some escape*, she thought.

This dreadful disease existed on both sides of their family, but oncologists had been known to say that this sometimes meant nothing because some were known to have cancer even when no one else in their family had the disease. She could not think of anything soothing to say to lift her daughter's spirits. Words at a time like this were frivolous no matter how sincere, but she knew she would be in deep prayer that the surgeon's scalpel would rid her daughter's body of this demon.

Clare sat there looking so beaten, staring at her hands until they became a blur. She was crying again. "I know it sounds so utterly useless and full of self-pity, but why me?"

"Well, if it's any consolation at all," Estelle offered with gentle empathy, "just thank God, they didn't miss it."

Clare wanted to rest, but after Estelle left, she remained wide awake. For the next four days she did manage to go to work. Her assistant and Grant noticed that there was something wrong, but even though subdued, she was pleasant. She never heard from Karl until that Friday evening. She was about to change into something comfortable when the phone rang. There was absolutely no preamble; he sounded extremely tense.

"Clare, we need to talk."

"I haven't heard from you since you drove me home on Monday," she replied, ignoring the statement. "What could possibly be so urgent now?"

"That's precisely what I need to talk to you about."

She relented when he informed her that he was near her house, at a pay phone, and would be there in about three minutes.

The doorbell rang about five minutes later. She was still in her street clothes and jewelry, and while removing her watch and earrings, she let him in. He appeared so harried. She didn't offer to take his coat, so he hung it in the foyer closet and followed her into the living room.

"Okay, you have my undivided attention," she said with an edge of mild sarcasm.

He didn't sit down but stood a few minutes, took a few steps, wearily rubbed his forehead, paused, and then stood looking at her as if not knowing the best approach. "It's Sherry—my wife," he finally said. He began placing the floor. "She is threatening to take me to court for nonsupport." He paused. "I'm in a bind, Clare; I'll never catch up. I'm too far behind, so…" He stopped pacing, looked at her, and shook his head.

"Let me say it for you," she offered calmly. "The decision is house play for the third, fourth, or however many times. From my observation, your apartment now has a spare bedroom for your two daughters, the reason your computer equipment occupies your bedroom. Harm's way is avoided by this family reunion. How am I doing, Karl, or did I omit something?"

"What do you expect me to do, Clare?" he asked beseechingly.

She didn't answer for a few minutes. "The truth is all of you are now a family again. They've already moved in, right? Karl, my news is so awful that it sends you scurrying back to a situation you once said was—to use your phrase—highly improbable?"

He looked at her in disbelief. "How can you say such a thing to me?"

"Cut the drama, Karl. How can I not say it?" She was tired and worried. She felt a thousand years old. She heaved a ragged sigh as her head began to throb. "Is there anything else that you must tell me?" She needed to slip into more comfortable clothing and told him so.

"I never wanted us to end like this, Clare."

"But as long as we end, isn't that it?"

Suddenly he sat down on the edge of the sofa facing her. "I wanted to be there for you, Clare. I just cannot handle sickness very well. First my mother, now you—honestly, I can't." He seemed genuinely contrite. "Clare, I—"

She raised her hands as if warding off a blow and moved to the other end of the sofa. *I'm not sick in the true sense of the word*, she thought with disgust. She looked at him for a long time, and he at her. Three years were now filtering into a black hole.

"Now that you have said your good-bye," she said coldly, "Just leave."

That her voice held such contempt surprised even her. He sat there for a few minutes as if capturing a mental snapshot of her to carry with him, got up from the sofa to retrieve his coat from the foyer. She heard the door close softly behind him. Only then did she move from her seated position to secure the lock.

# Chapter Fifteen

D r. Wilson looked so different in his surgical garb. His voice was cheerful when he greeted her as she nervously nodded her response. She could see only eyes, but he seemed to be smiling. In a matter of seconds, the team's professional efficiency donned her for the occasion—a cap for her head, surgical shoes, and the exchange to a surgical gown. His team, all dressed for the OR, moved her to the operating table where she stared up at the light directly above her, looming large and unfriendly. Dr. Wilson gave her hand a reassuring squeeze, gently moving aside as one of the surgical nurses attempted to find a suitable vein in Clare's right hand for the third time. The anesthesiologist took over, located the vein to skillfully tape the IV needle in place. No patient should be upset immediately before surgery. Necessary mechanics were there to monitor the heartbeat and blood pressure.

The last thing Clare heard was the gentle voice of the anesthesiologist making a promise, as he injected a substance into her IV. "Miss Ingram, you're going to have the best high ever."

She drifted off, thinking, *I have never had a drug-induced high outside this hospital. What a way to start a new year.*

She awakened to what seemed a madhouse. Nurses moved quickly, charts in their hands, conversing in medical jargon, in constant movement, pausing only to query patients regarding their discomfort level, busily viewing monitors, taking blood pressures and temperatures. Clare listened to other patients' soft moans to beckon any available nurse.

"Miss Ingram?"

Her eyes were open, but she was still woozy from the anesthetic. She felt suspended somewhere between semi-sleep and wakefulness. She raised her right hand. The much dreaded necessary IV was still with her. She wondered when they would devise a new method of getting nourishment and drugs into the body before, during, and after surgery. The IV needle was causing a dull ache in her right hand.

"Hi, Miss Ingram," said a Filipino nurse standing beside her gurney. She offered a friendly smile. "How do you feel? Okay?"

"Okay," she repeated. The voice did not sound like her own. "You're in recovery, Miss Ingram."

*Where else,* she thought, *unless I'm in an asylum…* Fully awake now, Clare slowly positioning her head to look up, her eyes focused on the elevated machine monitoring her heartbeat.

"Are you in pain? I can inject medication directly into your IV."

"Not much," she answered. "I'm a little woozy, but otherwise I'm not feeling too bad."

"Good, you will stay here for another hour or so and then be transported to your room, okay?"

She nodded as the nurse moved away from her to another patient who had just been delivered, generating a new flurry of activity. *Such a busy place,* she thought.

Clare raised her right hand and brought it over to her left side to confirm what she already knew. She wept as she lay in recovery, thinking miserably, *I will never be the same again, ever.* She wiped the tears from her face with the palm of her hand, mindful of the IV. Through a blur she looked over to see Dr. Wilson approaching her and tried to put on a brave face but failed.

"I talked to your mother and your uncle, Ms. Ingram." He rested his hand lightly on her shoulder. "The surgery went well," he said encouragingly. "We were very successful. Pathology did not find a trace of cancer throughout the remainder of your breast or any of the lymph nodes."

"Thank you," she managed to say, turning away as she began to cry quietly. *It took some of me with it,* she thought.

"I will see you tomorrow during morning rounds." It seemed he started to say something more, then paused and instead said, "I'll see you then."

He turned and left. Clare's eyes focused on his back as he moved farther and farther away until the double doors closed behind him. Ninety minutes later, she arrived back in her room to be greeted by her mother and Uncle Ned. The orderly and an accompanying nurse transferred her from the gurney to her freshly made bed.

She was grateful for the presence of the family, wanting to express her gratitude for their support. The words would not come. With her good arm she managed a hug for each one, even though the IV made it somewhat awkward.

"Hey, little lady," Uncle Ned said warmly. He smiled encouragingly as he leaned over and kissed her cheek.

"How do you feel?" questioned Estelle.

"Not too bad." Inside she could wail to the melancholy tune of a string choir.

She experienced nausea for the rest of the day, so attempts to eat that afternoon and evening proved unsuccessful. Her wound ached, and there was numbness in the upper left arm.

Her mother and Uncle Ned stayed until the end of visiting hours. When they had to leave, Estelle kissed her goodbye, promising to return the next day. Uncle Ned briefly lagged.

"Hang in there, little lady," he whispered. "I'll see you tomorrow."

He kissed her forehead. Her spirits so low her best response was a nod, Struggling, she held back the tears, acknowledging her mother's departing wave from the doorway as Uncle Ned left her bedside to join his sister.

The drapes were open to reveal winter busily adorning the city in white. Still cognizant of the IV in her right hand and the surgical wound on her left side, Clare lay on her back staring at the ceiling and reviewing her life. While other classmates married and raised families, she had spent most of her twenties attending college. It had been long, arduous, and hard-won. During those years marriage was less attractive. Many people she knew began their education but then dropped out never to finish. They got married, the babies started coming, and priorities were juggled as they dealt with individual choices. A few of her female classmates' lives were even less attractive. Marriages failed or never happened, and they struggled to raise their children alone without the support of the fathers for one reason or another, often confronted with multiple challenges.

She reviewed her offers of marriage, rejected in fear of being snared by the same entrapments—life without enough education and additional disruptions because of children to support. Now as she approached her thirty-first birthday, there was not a prospect in sight. She wanted children, but with a responsible father, and then to have this happen was overwhelming. She was weeping again and slightly startled when Dr. Wilson entered her room with the stealth of a burglar. Dressed in street attire, he came into full view at the foot of her bed. He had not waited until morning but instead now pulled her chart and began reading.

"Sorry to disturb you, Ms. Ingram," he said kindly.

"I wasn't sleeping," she said, attempting to smile, though she was again unsuccessful.

"How are you feeling?"

"Okay, I guess," she said quietly. Hospitals were not made to give a person rest; they merely cured the underlying problem, with convalescence beginning in the comfort of your own home.

"The nurse said you were nauseous most of the day; is that right?"

"It is," she answered quietly.

He read for a minute, flipped the page, read some more, and then jotted down something before returning the chart to the foot of her bed.

"You will no longer need the IV once you can keep your food down." He told her to get a good night's rest and promised to return in the morning.

☙

From just inside the doorway, she briefly watched as her friend lay sleeping. She had gifts in her tote bag, including the most current magazines—*Ebony* and *People*, as well as *Elle* and *Vogue* because her little friend loved fashion. Various fruits and today's newspaper were also in the bag. In her free arm she held a bouquet of flowers ordered from the florist and delivered to her home yesterday; she had immediately refrigerated them to bring with her today. As planned, she arrived early, seven thirty, even though visiting hours began at eight. Stopping at the nurses' station, she told them she was Clare's sister from out of town. That was sufficient.

Even while sleeping, her friend looked exhausted. She sent a silent prayer to the only power you could contact in times like these. *Enough already*, she silently pleaded. *Give this little person a break.* Quietly entering the room, she placed the tote bag on the floor and laid the flowers on the nightstand. In a little while she would summon the nurse for a vase and put them in water. She had just sat down and started to make herself comfortable when Clare stirred. When fully awake, Clare saw her visitor, offering the best smile possible.

"Hello," she said.

"Hello yourself," Nadine said.

Words couldn't explain how glad Clare was to see Nadine. When did she come into the room? When in unfamiliar surroundings, Clare usually woke up to the slightest sound.

"When did you get back in town?"

"Yesterday morning. Cornell and I were having such a wonderful time that we extended our stay. Just before I left New York, I called a couple of times but couldn't reach you. When I got home, I called your house several times again and got only the machine, so then I called your mom."

Smiling sadly, she asked "How was New York?"

"You know that city never sleeps." She laughed. "Cornell and I often hated to go to bed for fear we would miss something." She left her seat to place her hand gently on her friend's shoulder. "I'm so sorry," she said. "I thought everything was fine."

"So did I," Clare said, "and then Dr. Wilson called." Tears formed in the corners of her eyes. "I…" Faltering, she briefly closed her eyes to fight back the tears.

"There are some good times ahead, sweetheart. You must believe that because it is true."

"I know," she answered quietly. She searched deep inside as the billows continuously rolled in her life. She was a ship without sails, being tossed from one place to the next.

"When you get out of here, we are going on a shopping spree, and I will not take no for an answer." Nadine was glad to see that statement brought a genuine smile to Clare's lips. "Then we'll hang out. You need a healthy dose of therapy, and there is none like shopping."

Clare was queen for a day. Nadine's all-day visit started a small entourage. As she made her departure that evening, Uncle Ned came, bringing fruit and flowers. Estelle came with Max, who brought her a game of checkers—to be played, he teased, when she felt up to getting a good spanking. Her Reach to Recovery representative visited for the first time, keeping her visit short with a promise to return the next day, gently demanding that she have a wonderful evening.

When the telephone rang, Estelle picked it up. She looked over at Clare, who was talking to Max and Uncle Ned. For the first time there was laughter as her daughter joined her Uncle Ned and Max in debating who would win the Super Bowl. Football was Clare's favorite sport, and Estelle wanted this dose of cheer to be extended.

Estelle jotted down the message, placed it on the bedside table, and then again sat on Max's knee. The evening head nurse, Frances, was bending the rules that allowed only two visitors at one time. She was glad to see this young lady with such moral support as she went through this ordeal; one telephone call to housekeeping brought another chair. She further encouraged the visit by leaving the door only slightly ajar.

It was a nice day, and when it ended, Clare was again left alone in the privacy of her room, grateful to have at least these most recent pleasant memories to hold onto. After a while, as she lay in the dark listening to all the activity in the corridor—the voices, the hustling and bustling as people moved about—Clare found it difficult to envision her life returning to normal.

The next morning began with the arrival of a dozen beautiful long-stemmed yellow roses, accompanied by a note:

> *I'm deeply sorry that I couldn't be there for you. I wish you the best.*
>
> *Karl*

She gazed at the yellow roses. *So now*, Clare thought, *he wants to be friends, does he?* She felt a tinge of bitterness over the three-year investment, an irretrievable waste. Somehow, she had never doubted that he would stand by her if she needed him. She dropped the card in the wastebasket near her bed and rang the nurse.

When the day nurse, Janet, responded, she asked her to give the flowers to someone who had not received any flowers or plants. Looking rather puzzled, the nurse took the unwrapped flowers from the room.

"Coming in," said a cheerful voice from the doorway.

Clare looked up to see a blonde, attractive woman of medium height. At first Clare did not recognize her, but then the years slipped away.

"Sharla," Clare exclaimed as she identified the recognizable laughter. "Sharla Kantor!"

The friend came to her bedside smiling, carrying a shopping bag. Bubbly as always, but with a bittersweet edge, she placed the bag on the floor, leaned over, and laid her cheek against Clare's.

"I called last night," she said. "I talked to your mother a few minutes."

Clare remembered her mother taking a call the night before. "I remember someone calling," Clare said, "but I haven't looked at my messages. They have been poking and probing all morning." Dr. Wilson's residents and nurses had been dutifully carrying out his instructions.

"Not to worry!" Sharla replied as she thoughtfully gazed at Clare. "I have been back three months and kept putting off calling you." She paused. "Clare, what happened?"

She was reluctant and did not answer right away. "I've had breast cancer surgery."

"Is everything okay?"

Sharla seemed alarmed but remained calm. Nobody could ever read Sharla. It was the one dimension of this woman that used to baffle Clare. She could genuinely dislike someone and still talk to them without expressing a trace of animosity.

"They were successful," Clare said.

"Good," Sharla replied, visibly relieved, "that's all that matters."

Clare electronically raised the head of the bed so that she was in a sitting position. Sharla fluffed her pillow and again placed it behind her head. Then she took off her coat and draped it over the back of the chair.

"Oh!" she said. She leaned over Marshall Field's bag. "I brought you a pair of pajamas and a robe."

"Sharla," Clare said, "that wasn't necessary."

"Of course not," she replied simply, playfully wrinkling her nose.

The same old Sharla. That antic dissolved time. They were again attending DePaul, sitting in their most frequented State Street restaurant, having a salad before class. When splurging, they had dinner—or at least when Sharla was splurging. She came from money. Once, when she had come into town for a visit from California, they had met on Seventy-First Street. Clare had forewarned her about the transformation. Still there were disturbing pangs of nostalgia recalling. the vanishing Jewish neighborhood from another era. She wanted to enjoy a banana split. Clare told her candidly Seventy-First Street underwent tremendous change. There was no ice cream parlor any longer and both theaters were gone. "Transition," Clare tactfully summarized, recalling her father's prediction.

Avoiding the issue of race allowed great visits. However, picking at a wound that was attempting to heal, Sharla continued trying to remember on Seventy-First Street what block previously housed the ice cream parlor, ruining most ed their time together. Wishing to move the conversation forward, Clare refused to join discussing the "once-beautiful South Shore." Begrudgingly, Clare had to admit Seventy-First Street looked nothing like before the 1970s, when whites, supported by a robust tax base, still resided in the area. Begrudgingly, Clare admitted Seventy-First Street looked nothing like before the 1970s, when whites, supported by a robust tax base, still resided in the area.

Aside from that incident, Sharla was bubbly and energetic Sometimes they would leave school on Fridays to sit in a restaurant along State Street or Wabash, talking for hours, with Sharla becoming upset if she decided not to join her. Nevertheless, Clare's pride coupled with adherence to a strict budget often influenced her decision to flatly decline. A pastime for Sharla was to Clare an unnecessarily frivolous indulgence. Those were the lean years.

During the Ingram's family year in that third-floor apartment on Crandon, in the evenings (Mason was always at work) they often walked along Seventy-First or to Jackson Park to escape their hot apartment and the steady, monotonous drone of a window fan. (Mason considered a window air conditioner a waste since they were moving to a house with central air.) Often, they sat in Jackson Park, enjoying the evening breeze from the lake. She and Sharla did not know each other then. The Kantor family were most likely suburbanites by then, as were so many other families of the former South Shore Jewish community. Racial demographics shifted almost overnight, permitting the real estate agencies a frenzied financial feast.

When Clare and Sharla became acquainted, Sharla's family was living in Skokie. During the week, she lived with North Side relatives to avoid the daily commute. However, right before her junior year, Sharla left DePaul. Her hurried good-bye note was scrawled on a sheet of lined paper at the end of her sophomore term. Once, at the insistence of Estelle— "That young woman telephones you all the time." she exclaimed— Clare relented to return one of Sharla's calls. An unfamiliar voice answered the phone; introducing herself as Sharla's mother, promising to relay the message. Sharla called back the very next evening, explaining that she had been accepted at UCLA and finishing school in California. Clare had wondered with fleeting curiosity what was it like, without even a hitch, to simply pick up and continue your life.

Through the years that followed letters became fewer with long lapses into one-way correspondence from Sharla, which for a time stopped altogether. Clare accepted the blame for not encouraging what had potential for something rewarding, finally deciding they lived in different worlds, anyway. Out of the blue Sharla mailed her a postcard from San Francisco with a brief up-to-date synopsis of her life. It arrived at her mother's address. Estelle dropped it off.

*Hi, Clare!*

> *I was going through my address book and ran across yours, wondering (I didn't know for sure) if you still lived in the same place. I hope these few lines find you well. After graduating UCLA, southern California lost its mystique. However, so has Frisco for that matter, but I'm hanging on. The gay world is well represented, with the heterosexual community still intact. Even if not for me, Othere are children. I have a job that I am thinking of vacating because of circumstances. I'm in need of more interesting scenery, but just haven't decided exactly my destination. Anyway, let me hear from you sometime.*

*Always,*

*Sharla*

As a seeming afterthought, at the bottom Sharla had quickly scrawled her phone number. Clare did call, but almost four months later. The man who answered introduced himself as the ex-husband informing her that her friend had moved out east.

However, here in the hospital room, this blonde woman was the same Sharla, still full of laughter and energy. She now sat down and scooted her chair close to the bed. "I visited Seventy-First Street a few weeks ago as one of the old haunts, you know." Apparently, Sharla had momentarily forgotten that this subject had been hashed out before—and snuffed out.

"Excuse my redundancy, Sharla," Clare replied quietly but candidly, "but isn't this a frustrating revisit?" *Here we go again*, she thought. Clare, painfully aware of the political and economic ramifications that always impacted the incoming black community, was unwilling to again unlock the vault to that discussion.

"When do you get out of the hospital?" Sharla asked quietly.

"I think I should be out by the weekend."

"Clare, why did you stop writing to me?"

"I wrote," she answered unconvincingly. She recalled Estelle telling her, "That woman stays in touch with you no matter what, so I guess I'd better not move." She would then simply drop the mail on Clare's small kitchenette table.

Had Sharla been black Clare knew she would have gladly opened to explain that she had been confronted with many obstacles while attending college. There was her father's illness, her attempt to help her brother, and other financial circumstances. She was not about to discuss any of it with this extremely affluent Caucasian woman.

"I was having problems," she said quietly, "many problems." She paused. "But I have been writing to you since then for quite some time."

It was true. Clare had experienced a nascent change of heart. She had begun to feel good about herself since acquiring her master's degree, coupled with a very impressive promotion. At the time she was proud to be buying a home, evaluating her upwardly mobile status in life as placing her on comparable footing. Surprising even herself, she had contacted Sharla's mother for her address, which was readily given. *She gets around*, Clare had thought when jotting down the New York address; it was a suburb and not Manhattan as before. Sharla's was pleasantly surprised to hear from her. From then until now communication has remained uninterrupted, either by phone or by mail.

Sharla started to say something but then held back. Her former husband had commented on her donation of overkill to every subject. She had to admit it was a flaw that needed correction.

Clare filled the void. "By the way, who were you married to in California?"

"Some jock who didn't want children," she replied.

"Really, did he tell you this before or after you were married?"

"Before and after." She sighed, shrugged. "He definitely did not want to become a parent."

"Sharla, you of all people should know you never marry with a plan to change your spouse. Make certain you both are on the same page before marriage." She paused, laughing. "He wasn't staging a retreat in delayed search of his sexual identity, was he?"

"Quite the contrary, he was screwing anything with a vagina."

The remainder of their visit was pleasant. Sharla gave Clare an update on her life.

"My mother is now divorced. Dad left her for someone with less wear. Since I'm single again and was tired of the major rat race, I came back to lend moral support."

"How young?" was Clare's question.

"Two decades. I won't be surprised if he ends up with heart failure."

They both laughed. They visited for a while longer, and after two hours or so, Sharla departed, so as not to tire her.

*Sharla Kantor*, Clare mused. It had turned out to be a pleasant afternoon. Clare would keep her promise and contact her when she left the hospital. Their resumed friendship was off to a good start.

Nadine called to check on her, and so did her mother and Uncle Ned. It was perfectly fine if they postponed their visit until the following day. She hung up the phone with too much time on her hands.

Thoughts of Jeffrey suddenly surfaced. Although yet sad there were no tears. She still mourned his life with potential never realized.

Prentiss, always noble, strong, and the lawyer in the family, not a few times had paid the taxes with the financial assistance of the relatives from the North, Estelle and Ned. They had assisted their mother with this burden while others adjacent to the problem excused themselves as financially unable. Those granted the most opted for the least responsibility. Wisdom dictated that at designated intervals, approximately 150 of the 500 acres of the forestry's valuable lumber be cleared for additional income. This strategy had allowed Prentiss to avoid involving a significant amount of his own assets until the last three years, when it became progressively necessary to supplement the taxes with the assistance of his relatives from the North. After all, as Cousin Prentiss had said more than once, the Creator was in control of trees; they grew on His or Her appointed schedule. Prior to deciding to have the land sold to developers, Prentiss met with all the necessary relatives. He asked them to waive the right of ownership unless they could repay him for their share of the owed back taxes. It was a shrewd move because he knew some were not able and others unwilling to raise the accumulated monies. He wondered what assessment Granddad Nathan would make of this if he were still living. Regardless, circumstances dictated that he and only a handful of the others, including Ned and Estelle, were the rightful heirs. Jennifer had always acted responsibly. With money earned from the sharecroppers, her burden was lighter. Also, she was due a widow's share because she had been married to Prentiss's great-grandfather, Chester Beckford. To reinforce this, Chester Beckford had left a will.

While attending her grandmother's funeral, the literal meaning of land weighed heavily on Clare so powerfully it almost brought her to tears when gazing out over the 1,500 acres. It had been in the hands of the Beckford clan for over a century. While visiting her grandmother as a young girl she had not been impacted by what ownership was all about. The patriarch, Calvin Beckford, no longer there to refresh their memories, most likely was shaking his fist from the grave. The fact was that the desire and skill for farming had been lost as the younger generations began to desert the land and inevitably force its sale. Only a few wanted to keep it, but their monetary contributions for upkeep or the taxes were not forthcoming. They had not assisted Prentiss Beckford with paying the accumulative taxes. Although her mother and uncle, who had once known how to farm also left, their contributions were paid annually.

The few weeping willow trees seemed foreign as their branches flailed in the soft summer breeze like a sad ballet. Weeds gnarled like the arthritic hands of an old man surrounded the fruit trees that no one dared pick. The developers had waited patiently to purchase the land for at least five years.

Prentiss honored his great-grandfather's will. The others would not know the exact amount owed to Estelle and Ned. *You never offered a cent,* he wanted to say to all who crowded the small church, *even though a few of you were right here! You saw what was happening.*

After Jeffrey's death Gran Jennie, old and frail, lasted only three weeks. She was ninety-one. Following the trip to Georgia, two weeks after their arrival back in Chicago, Estelle telephoned Clare: come discuss something important. Upon arriving, her mother had a check for her in an amount so generous she wanted to refuse it, but Estelle was very firm. "You need to get on with your life. Get things you need and some of the things you want."

"What about you, Mama?" Clare said with concern.

Estelle smiled and hugged her daughter. This was not a celebration or a holiday or one of those other rare occasions when she displayed affection. Now that Mason was gone, she was slowly transitioning, relearning demonstrative displays of warmth and affection, like a person who has not been fully ambulatory for quite some time begins to assuredly walk again.

"Take it," she said with tears at the corners of her eyes. "Your grandmother left me and Ned her share, and I realize she meant some of it to be passed on to you and Jeffrey, if he were here. Clare, you cannot begin to know just how much of a blessing you were to me during that bout with Mason's diabetes. I was at my wit's end. Without you I do not know what I would have done." She paused. "So, I am passing this amount on to you because you have been a good daughter, the best, never complaining, always there. I knew Mason very well, and it could not have been pleasant. Take it, finish school, do something wonderful for yourself.

"As you know, your father had a pension, and as his widow I receive it each month. It pays the mortgage. My degree affords me a good living, and I am keeping enough of the inheritance to do a few things to the house," she said. "You enjoy that money," she added.

Clare finished paying for her graduate degree; she was barely twenty-eight. She then purchased a house, a three-bedroom bungalow with one and one-half baths. The small foyer was adequate; a fireplace enhanced the living room. There was a full dining room, a full-size basement (unfinished) with a walk-in attic. Not elaborate by any means, but a nice house. Uncle Ned helped her select a neutral porcelain tile with an interesting design for the kitchen floor. He also helped her tile the bathroom. She protested when Uncle Ned wanted to help even more. Instead, she hired a professional painter to spruce up the bedrooms. and the foyer. She further updated the kitchen with new cabinet doors, deciding that the countertops would suffice until a later time. Thankful for her good fortune because of her mother's generosity, she was doing very well. The next year, at the age of twenty-nine, she tested her luck even more. With her master's degree, she applied for a new position and got it. Grant Stafford, her boss, had steadily promoted her even as an undergrad.

Clare would forever hold Gran Jennie's memory close while planting those mental flowers throughout her entire life. *Gran*, she thought during this time, *wherever you are, I made it!*

❧

Symmetry was a thing of the past; balance had to be purchased. She had researched breast reconstruction and learned that unless both were reconstructed simultaneously, it was almost impossible to make them identical. (Although nature often made one breast larger than the other, it was with invisible subtlety.) She sat in the comfort of her living room looking through a catalog addressed to her. It stung that there was no longer a need. Her initial reason for subscribing was the great panties with matching brassieres featuring great variety and unique styles. She gazed longingly at the beautiful women with their full, healthy busts. She had wanted to have the reconstruction surgery along with the mastectomy, but Estelle had suggested that she follow the doctor's advice because they were using the delay as a precautionary measure.

Three years was a lengthy span of time, but she had reluctantly relented, especially after her mother agreed with the doctors. With the help of her Reach to Recovery representative, one of the volunteers who traveled from hospital to hospital to talk to women who'd recently had breast surgery, she had discovered a manufacturer that allowed her to maintain her fashion stride. It was mandatory that the representative was to undergo breast surgery. Thankfully, her representative was a well-groomed lady from head to toe.

"Honey, it is necessary that you look great after this ordeal," she had announced in her most cheerful yet professional tone before Clare left the hospital, "so order from here." She had handed her a small catalog. There were other manufacturers also, but their bras were matronly and rather plain. This manufacturer's bras were beautiful. Of course, they couldn't provide cleavage, but their attractiveness did allow you to feel good about your appearance. If you paid the price, which was a small fortune, a separate category of brassieres had a prosthesis built into them. There was the silicone prosthesis too, also expensive, in what was at that time termed "skin tone," which Clare found laughable. She disapprovingly shook her head. *Whose skin tones?* Even though the prosthesis would be well hidden inside the bra, both Clare and her representative had scoffed and laughed in unison upon reading the description. (A few years later, an inclusive skin tone would be introduced for darker hues.)

If someone had told Clare this experience would be part of her future, she would have wanted to know what sensitivity classes they had been attending. In her other life, certain types of bras had been made to go with certain clothing. In the foreseeable future, a left prosthesis would now have to be temporarily included in all her bras, no matter how beautiful, and therefore, for her certain fashions were automatically out.

Even though it pained her deeply, examining her nude appearance in front of her full-length closet mirror had become a daily ritual. She could not force herself to discontinue the daily practice of standing sideways in the mirror to view her body from the right side, recalling how she had looked before the surgery. It meant ignoring the fact that the picture still revealed the yet visible imperfection. It was at these times she cried for her body. She cried for her inability to keep select garments she had once worn. In the past, if a dress was cut in a way that wouldn't allow a bra—cut lower under the arm or in the back—she went without one. She owned four such dresses, so she donated them to a charity organization.

"Give your cousin a call," Ned had said to his daughter. "Stop by to cheer her up, make her feel better." Well, so much for that.

She could still picture Druscilla recently sitting in her living room on the sofa, before the biopsy, making an authoritative prediction. "When you are older, it is usually cancer."

Estelle had gazed at her niece, dumbfounded. "Druscilla," she replied none too gently. "Clare is only thirty years old. What on God's earth are you talking about? I guess it will be your turn in four years, when you cross the threshold to join your elderly cousin."

The statement had left Clare positively devastated. The conversation then became awkward, sending Druscilla rushing off with an embarrassing explanation about having to run errands. Nothing could ever negate their bloodline, but they would never bond.

Clare looked at other women on the streets now and, as they walked by, wondered which, if any, had been under the knife. If so, what were their feelings about that surgical experience? Were they as uncomfortable with their bodies as she was with hers? Did they mourn their loss as she mourned hers? Did they feel like they'd lost part of their glory? To exacerbate her ongoing distress, America was a country that glorified the buxom female. The big screen celebrated some of the most endowed bosoms, such as those of Jayne Mansfield, Sophia Loren, Jane Russell, and Raquel Welch, to name a few. In the world of paratroopers, there was a parachute malfunction named a Mae West because it resembled her well-endowed chest. Of course, all these women possessed other star qualities, yet emphasis was placed on that part of their anatomy and helped to accelerate their careers. In some instances, this feature was dominant over and above their acting capabilities. Some women who could not boast that abundance naturally were known to undergo breast implants or other forms of endowment. The phrase "breast man" indicated the bigger the better. In the past Clare had found the phrase amusing, but now it stung.

Since exercise had always been part of her daily routine, she was now even more consistent. She would get up early, go to the lower level of her home, turn on an exercise tape, work out for twenty to thirty minutes, take her shower, and then prepare for work. She maintained a neat waistline, great legs, and a firm butt. For moral support, she stayed in touch weekly with her Reach to Recovery representative. Clare struggled to become comfortable with her appearance when not fully dressed in the comfort of her home, but so far it had not been successful. Even so, Nadine encouraged, she needed to get on with her life.

❧

The reflection in the mirror was stunning, to say the least. She ignored her lower body, still in tights, as she focused only on the dress. The sweater, cold denim, and full-length shearling coat she'd worn here were hanging on the wall hook in the small fitting room; the coat had been a delayed treat to herself upon completing grad school and paying off all her student loans. It was early February, and this winter was—in Nadine's words—in the trenches. Taking a deep breath, Clare engaged in scrutiny. No one would even suspect. Except for the exquisite shoulder detail, it was a simple white winter dress. As she analyzed her reflection in the mirror, she decided that even in the past this dress would be included in her collection. She found herself constantly comparing then with now, a habit she had to suppress with frequency.

She had been out of the hospital for only three months, and there were no male suitors of interest. She had been seeing a man she had recently met by the name of Bernard, but she could not see that leading to anything exciting. He was a shoe salesman (in The Loop) that she had met one day while buying shoes. They struck up a casual acquaintance. However, she remained insistent on permitting no emotional inroads. Once he had asked for her work phone number so that perhaps they could sometimes meet for lunch, but she never complied with the request and even now decided to return his call later.

Of course, it would be nice to have something brand new hanging in her closet, waiting for the right occasion, but she knew that occasion would not include Bernard. This was her third and final purchase for the day. Nadine had bought her two beautiful skirts, but Clare firmly insisted on buying coordinating jackets later. *Nadine* thought, *I cannot buy happiness, but I will work at securing it in every other way despite my loss.* Then, to the only one who could help her, she silently prayed, *please help me work it out.* In the full-length mirror, Nadine's reflection was behind her, smiling encouragingly.

"You look stunning, really," she said as she watched Clare continue to scrutinize the one-piece dress with modified dolman sleeves and shoulder detail. The shoulder detail was what caught her eye.

"All you need is a simple pump, and you'll be a knockout."

"I think I'll buy it," Clare said.

"No," Nadine disagreed with a smile, "you are not allowed to rain on my parade."

Just then, the saleslady knocked politely and peeked in. "How are we doing?" She smiled. "My, you look great."

"That's what I told her," Nadine agreed. "We'll take it." She was not going to give Clare a chance to change her mind.

"When you're ready, I'm Wynona," the woman informed them and disappeared.

Since the operation, Clare had been having mood swings. The pendulum swayed between mildly happy and sad and often got stuck on sad. To date the old Clare had not readily surfaced, but Nadine was determined to resurrect her.

Thirty minutes later, the two of them sat in a restaurant booth on South Wabash, perusing their menus. Packages surrounded them.

"I'm buying lunch," Clare announced pleasantly as the waitress approached their table.

# Chapter Sixteen

It was 1984, and a hot mid-July Thursday in Chicago. Harold Washington had been in office since April 29, 1983. As two of the frustrated electorate who had voted to elect the first black mayor of the city, Clare and Nadine often discussed what was becoming a national spectacle. Both ignored the articles written in the newspapers and seldom watched the evening news. Clare told her mother she could practically hear Harold Washington's gavel in her sleep as he attempted to bring order to the rowdy Chicago City Council meetings. These obstructionists would become nationally known as the infamous Vrdolyak 29.

After hurrying home from work to change into more comfortable clothing and grab her grocery list from the kitchen countertop, Clare then made the short drive to the supermarket. As always, she started in the produce section. She made all her selections for salads and fruits and decided to also pick up a few avocados. It was near the weekend, and sometimes she avoided cooking, especially during hot weather.

"Excuse me," said a handsome gentleman. "How do you choose the right ones for guacamole?"

"Well, you have to select those that are pretty soft." Clare smiled as she bagged her choices. She tested a few that were softer and handed them to him. "Do you need another one?"

"I don't think so," he replied as he dropped them into the empty plastic bag. "Thank you."

"You're welcome," she replied pleasantly.

"What are you doing with the ones you chose?"

"They make great sandwiches," she answered, "but they must be a little firmer than those used to make guacamole. You toast your bread—at least I do—spread a little mayonnaise on the toast, add lettuce and tomato, and you have an excellent lunch."

"Sounds interesting. And what do you have with it?"

"Just something to drink," Clare replied. "I only have them on weekends for lunch if I don't want to cook."

"What do they taste like in a sandwich?" He was suddenly curious.

"To me avocados are an acquired taste," she replied with a smile.

"Maybe I'll try one sometime," he said. "And thanks again for your help."

"You're welcome," Clare said.

Pushing her cart from produce, she thought, *He's a handsome gentleman, but I'll bet he's not single.*

She could sense his eyes following her as she moved away to another section of the store. In her periphery she could see him looking at her as he continued to make his selections. She wondered if she measured up. Certainly, for her he measured up.

Again, she caught him looking at her in the cereal aisle. He paused but then continued with his shopping in another section of the store. *Oh darn*, she thought.

In the condiments aisle she was checking items off her list as she plucked each one from the shelf and placed it in her shopping cart. There was one that she knew she could not reach, but she tried anyway since she saw no one to ask. From behind her, a male voice said, "Let me get that for you." He did and handed it to her.

When she turned to thank him, she saw that it was the same gentleman from the produce section.

"You're welcome," he replied and moved on.

⁊

She resumed her shopping, working to focus on only the items listed, which was difficult since she had eaten only a sandwich at her desk during lunch hour, routinely her largest meal of the day. As always, she was comparing prices and bargain hunting for certain items, which was time-consuming. In the snack aisle she contemplated buying a few items not on her list but instead just checked off the listed popcorn and dry-roasted peanuts once they were in her cart.

She discreetly glimpsed him briefly watching her at the far end of the aisle as she continued to peruse her list, hoping he would approach her and strike up another conversation.

Pushing her cart to the meat counter, Clare took a number only to find the handsome gentleman already there. She smiled to herself and thought that life would be very interesting with him in it. Then again, she liked tall men but not when their size was intimidating. Whenever she made such comments, Estelle was always amused because her Uncle Ned was that size, as Jeffrey had been. In fact, all the Beckford men were of similar size and build. Clare guessed this man weighed close to two hundred pounds. He had such beautiful broad shoulders! *That is a lot of man*, she thought, attempting to keep her scrutiny as inconspicuous as possible, stealing discreet glimpses as he made his selections. He must prefer fish, she thought, because he was purchasing four different kinds; he selected only one other kind of meat.

Turning from the counter, he nodded in recognition, and she did the same. Placing his packages in his cart, he moved on just as the butcher was calling her number.

In the detergent aisle, as she checked her list, she decided that laundry detergent would be cheaper elsewhere, so she circled that and a few other items, such as paper goods and dishwashing detergent, to be picked up later at one of the discount stores.

"Are you following me?"

She looked up, and there he was again, taking a box of laundry detergent from the shelf. He was flirting.

"And if I am?" Clare replied to his question, flashing her prettiest smile.

*Such a beautiful complexion*, she thought, wondering exactly who the lucky one was.

"I don't mind," he said with a boyish shrug.

As she pushed her cart down the aisle, sensing he was watching her, she was thankful to be wearing one of her nicest white tank tops and white denim shorts. Not a few complimented her neat waistline and pretty legs.

Discreetly, from her periphery, she spotted him at the end of the cosmetic aisle and knew he was watching her as she selected, then checked it off her list. She wished she could send a message telepathically. What would she say? Perhaps something like: "I enjoyed the brief moments we had and wish they could be extended long enough for us to become acquainted." It seemed that he was finished with his shopping and was pushing his cart to the shortest checkout line.

Grady Mayfield opened the trunk of his car and slowly put his groceries away and then entertained an idea. He thought, *why not?* When he looked around the parking lot he saw someone who resembled her, but this particular lady had on beige shorts and was a few inches taller. His interest was wearing white denim shorts. Since this approach was out of his realm, he didn't want to appear too obvious. He closed the trunk of his car and, to kill time, slowly deposited the cart at the nearest rack in the parking lot. He caught a glimpse of her just as she came through the automatic doors and started pushing her cart toward the next row of parked cars. Getting in his car, he drove toward her, arriving at her car at almost the exact moment she opened her trunk to deposit her groceries. He stopped and emerged from his vehicle, leaving the hazards flashing.

"Let me help you," he said. Looking down at her, he smiled.

She appeared startled until she looked up and recognized him; she then thanked him.

When the last of her packages were in the trunk, with the cart put away, he offered a congenial smile. "Let me introduce myself—I'm Grady Mayfield," he said. He held out his hand.

Hers, well-manicured with clear nail polish, was small and soft with slender fingers. She gave a warm handshake, and he noticed there was no wedding ring.

"Clare Ingram," she replied with a smile.

Suddenly it mattered. "Are you married, Clare?"

"No, I'm not. Are you?" She could just faintly smell his fragrance. My, he smelled good, and she liked that. To her there was nothing more appealing about a man.

"Not at the present time." He gave a chuckle.

She possessed a beautiful white smile, pretty eyes with long lashes, and high cheekbones. He had never before dated a petite woman but had appreciated them from a distance. He suddenly felt awkward, which in turn seemed to make her a little more forward. She went into her purse to retrieve a business card.

"Here's my work number." She smiled as she handed him the card, and in exchange he offered his own.

Both said their farewells, got in their cars, and drove away.

He called her the next afternoon, wanting to follow through before he changed his mind and lapsed back into his familiar pattern. "What does a pretty little girl like you do on weekends?" he said right away.

She was taken aback even though Grace, her administrative assistant, had come to her office door to alert her that she was putting through to her private line someone named Mr. Mayfield with a great voice. Clare had not expected that he would call so quickly. Perhaps this was an indication that he wasn't playing games like men usually did, particularly when they were that attractive. They would hold on to the number a few days before making the call, to suggest nonchalance.

"I don't know," she replied. "I presume the same things big girls do."

She could tell her smile was coming through because his voice became more relaxed and very warm. "Could you keep a lonesome gentleman company this Saturday?"

He thought of Helen, with whom he usually spent his Saturday evenings. She was in Detroit this weekend visiting her daughter, Bridgette.

"What does the lonesome gentleman have in mind?" she asked. She could not possibly imagine him being lonesome.

"How does dinner and a movie sound?"

"Sounds just fine," she replied.

"Say around seven o'clock?"

"Perfect."

"One more thing," he said. "I need your home address."

She gave him the address, and in exchange, he gave her his home telephone number.

"Just in case something comes up and you can't make it," he said.

She smiled. That he had given her his home number meant that he was probably not married or involved in "housekeeping," Nadine's term for live-in arrangements. They each wished the other a pleasant evening and hung up, and once again Grace was at her door.

"Is he as good-looking as he sounds?" she asked.

"He's very attractive," Clare answered quietly and smiled.

❧

"I'm going to be nosy and ask where you were Saturday night, Clare Ingram?" Nadine said. "I called you twice, girlfriend. Let me guess, you were out with Bernard, weren't you?"

"No, I wasn't, and you couldn't possibly guess," she said with a smile. "I had a real date. His name is Grady Mayfield."

Are you and Bernard not on real dates? Girl, you sound so bubbly and alive, so you'd better start talking, right now."

"I met him in a grocery store, can you imagine?"

"A grocery store—well, that's different. What does this Grady Mayfield look like?"

"I would say handsome," Clare said, "but not the type I usually date. You know me, I like them rather tall but slim. This man must weigh close to two hundred pounds, muscular, and a looker, my dear."

"Is Grady an SBM?" This was Nadine's acronym for "single black men"—in the strictest sense, one who lived alone.

"I think so," Clare said with laughter. "I have his home and office phone numbers, but time will tell."

"This is a good thing," said Nadine, borrowing her friend's favorite phrase. It was the first time Clare had been this upbeat since her surgery, and Nadine hoped it would add some spice to her life. "When do you see him again?"

"He said he would call me."

"Tell me, what did you do?"

"We did nothing out of the ordinary—just went to dinner and a movie. Nadine, the man is so classy, and I cannot get over the fact that I met him in a grocery store." She paused. "He is the first man I've met in years that I find myself attracted to, but I have a feeling that he is not totally unattached as no man that attractive is, especially in the black community."

"Well, cross that bridge when you come to it. If the female isn't occupying any part of his livable space, you can work on filling the vacancy legally, okay?"

"You're moving too fast." Clare laughed. "I have only been out with the man once."

"You had to start somewhere, girlfriend. Keep me posted."

Grady called her that next week, on a Tuesday, while she was at lunch with some of the other managers. The message was on her desk when she returned, so she dialed the number and was told that he was with a client. They never made contact for the rest of the day, which caused her to regret having missed his call.

When she arrived home, Bernard telephoned and asked if she was free Saturday, but she told him she would have to let him know. Admittedly, she favored the new over the old.

For the next few days Clare did not hear from Grady Mayfield. Now more than ever, she wished she had not missed his last call. She did not want to seem anxious, though, so she did not dial his number again. Friday came and went. Calling Bernard to beg off for Saturday meant an evening alone. Sunday, she attended church and ate dinner with her mother's and. Max. She often wondered why her mother did not marry the man because he was a constant in her life. Estelle had previously told her daughter they were quite happy with things the way they were.

Clare was starting to suspect that Mr. Mayfield was attached and had just happened to be free that weekend. When Bernard called her during the middle of the next week and asked her out for that Saturday, she relented and made a date for a movie. With Bernard, the choice was either dinner or a movie; his finances would not allow both. He was a nice guy, but his financial circumstances kept him in a bind. Both she and Nadine agreed that the pickings were slim in the black community. Even though she was now married and not pondering the problem personally anymore, as a concerned friend Nadine objectively discussed this circumstance with Clare. She wanted this person who had caused Clare to sparkle to hang around until something else could materialize.

Clare's Saturday date was an early one because Bernard, who moonlighted as a security guard late evenings during the week, was doing a Saturday midnight shift for one of the other guards.

As she was showering Sunday morning, in preparation for eleven o'clock service, a telephone call was intercepted by her answering machine. She heard the ringing and guessed it was probably Nadine because she always telephoned her on Sunday mornings, usually as she was having her morning coffee and preparing for church.

As always, before leaving the bathroom, Clare put on her underwear, pantyhose, and makeup. She then went in her bedroom to retrieve the recent message.

"Hello," the voice said. "I guess I missed you. This is Grady Mayfield. Just thought by chance you might like to join me for breakfast. Perhaps we can do it some other time. Give me a call."

Her heart lurched and she stood by the machine. After calming herself, she slowly dialed his number, and he answered.

"Good morning," she said.

"Good morning yourself. I thought I had missed you," Grady said, chuckling softly.

"I was in the shower," she replied.

"So are you available for breakfast?"

She wanted to tell him she was busy, but she couldn't bring herself to say it. "As a matter of fact, I am," she heard herself saying. "What time?"

"Well, I am ready to go now, so what do you say?"

"By the time you get here, I'll be ready."

"I can come collect you in the next half hour, okay?" He paused. "I know you ladies. I am casual, so you can be the same."

"Okay," she replied. "I'll be ready."

As soon as she hung up, she found herself wishing she could remain as unemotional about this man as she could with Bernard. How awful, she thought, and then again, how appropriate. She had not known anyone she really liked since her college days. *Well*, she thought matter-of-factly, *I guess I am going to miss church this morning.*

A black Lincoln pulled up roughly a half hour later. She watched from her living room bay window as he emerged from the car. She wondered where he lived. His business card showed his office address to be a few blocks outside Hyde Park. The doorbell rang just as she picked up her purse and was grabbing a sweater. She always carried one because air conditioning gave her a chill. She opened the door, and there he stood with his white smile, keys in hand, as he waited for her to lock up.

Once they were in the car he asked, "What kind of breakfast food do you like?"

"Pancakes," she replied. "Sometimes omelets."

"A little girl like you?" he teased, and then he flashed that white smile, which each time erased five years; she guessed him to be fortyish. "Well, there's a nice restaurant on Cicero. We can go there, or if you have a preference…"

"No, that's fine."

"You said you like omelets, and they have good ones. Their menu also includes pancakes."

"You want me to waive the pancakes?" she teased. "Not good for my figure, is that it?"

"Not at all," he said, chuckling. He liked this little lady; she was different. "There is a nice place on Lincoln Highway if you would rather go there instead."

"No, your first suggestion is perfect."

The restaurant was large with booths near the windows and the walls and tables positioned in the middle of the floor; the hostess led them to one of the booths located away from the windows. Living on the southeast side she seldom ventured west of State Street, but instead frequented River Oaks and some of the restaurants in the southeastern vicinity. After their meal they drank their coffee and talked. She noticed that he wore an expensive watch and had large, beautiful hands.

"Tell me something about yourself," he said. "What do you like to do, what kind of music do you like, where do you go when you go out?"

"Well," she replied, "do you want these all at one time or in increments so that we can alternate?"

He chuckled. He found her quite likable and very different. She was pretty and poised and possessed a sense of humor. He took a drink of his coffee. "In increments, if you prefer." He smiled, enjoying being with her.

"I'm not the nightlife type, although I do like to go out occasionally. I like to take long walks. Although I have not been on one for a long time, I also like bike rides." She paused and decided to dash the increments and give a succinct profile of her interests. "I like gardening because I love to see things grow, inside and outside. I like to sew, which is a rather waning art." She sighed thoughtfully. "I like to read, especially about the African continent and other faraway places. One day I would love to travel, which so far has been postponed." She flashed a pretty smile. "It took me a long time to finish my education, which is in education, but that's another story."

"Have you ever been married?" he asked.

"No," she said simply. "Have you?"

"Yes, twice," he replied, holding up two fingers.

The waitress was making her rounds serving coffee, and he motioned for a refill. He was promptly served, but Clare declined, already finishing her third cup.

"So what else can you tell me?" she asked. "Do you have any children from either marriage?"

"One son," he replied, "from the first."

"How old is he?"

"Almost Nineteen and in his sophomore year of college," he answered.

Suddenly his pager sounded. Retrieving a retractable pen and small notepad from his shirt pocket, he jotted down the number that appeared. He had purposely left that cumbersome cell phone in the car. "I'm going to have to find a pay phone," he said quietly.

When he returned to the booth, he sat down for a few more minutes so as not to seem rushed. "I have had a great breakfast and enjoyed your company," he said, smiling. "We will have to do this again."

"Likewise, and we will," she said.

With that, he took her home.

"We have had two dates," she told Nadine later, "and I really like him, but I think he is a busy man and an attached one."

"Come on, girlfriend, don't read complications into an uncomplicated situation. Just keep dating him, and you will find out everything worth knowing." She paused. "Clare, my dear, roll with the flow."

"I am," she replied.

"No, you're not. You are trying to create drama. Relax, girlfriend. Don't create drama without cause, since life presents enough on its own," she said, "and that plaque reads, No Help Wanted."

"You're absolutely right."

"But did you have a good time?"

"A great time," Clare said.

"I haven't heard you sound this good since you left that hospital room. If nothing else, he is causing you to sparkle, and that is a good thing." Nadine paused. "When do you hear from him again?"

"He said he would call me."

"And Clare, count on it—he will—because it sounds as if you are adding some spice to his life too."

❧

Clare had evaluated reasons for Grant's promotion of another employee before being informed of this individual's strong background in finance. The need of a higher income was the reason Clare refused to teach school even though both degrees were in education. For a single woman, education was a profession that did not provide a secure living unless you could teach at the college level with a doctorate. Nadine, who held a doctorate, recently had been promoted to principal at her high school and sometimes contemplated teaching at the college level.

There was an opening for a regional director coming up, Grant said, that was tailored for her and would put her in charge of mortgage loans in this part of the country. To strengthen her skills outside of English education she had recently taken courses to improve her math skills. She was in a high five-figure income range, but was shooting for six figures, a goal she could realize as a regional director. Though there had been proposals of marriage in her past, there was no guarantee that there would be any in her future. She was already at the max for contributions to her 401K, and now she wanted to invest in other strategies. To accomplish this, she needed to expand her take-home pay. Suddenly her thoughts were interrupted by a call on her private line.

"You know, you have only once given me a call. Don't you like me enough?" he teased. It was Grady Mayfield.

"Oh," she replied to the familiar voice, "but I do." His question made her feel as warm as a caress.

"Okay then," he teased, "you will have to stop abusing me."

That comment generated mutual laughter. Only a man with self-confidence could tease about something so personal.

"I will," she agreed.

"Let me hear from you," he said. "I need to hear that beautiful voice of yours from time to time, okay?"

"Absolutely," she replied.

"Have a good afternoon," he said and hung up.

He was a different kind of gentleman, she decided.

That was on a Friday afternoon, but she did not hear from him that entire weekend. She began to wonder what exactly he did with most of his weekends. Where did he go, and with whom? He wasn't mysterious but hard to evaluate. She did not know exactly what to make of him, but one thing was for certain: she was deeply attracted.

She had a conversation with Nadine to see what she gleaned from it.

"I don't know," Nadine said, "but I know he likes you. Otherwise, he wouldn't care whether you feel the same way." She paused. "Not to worry, he is going to step it up, believe me."

"We've only had two dates, and he is definitely taking his own sweet time about whatever his intentions are."

"Girlfriend, roll with the flow; all will be revealed."

That weekend Clare went out with Bernard, but she now found it difficult to maintain their relationship because although she encouraged nothing more, she knew for him their casual dating was no longer enough. Soon she would have to stop seeing him.

As she sat in her office one day the following week, she decided to dial Grady Mayfield's number, and he answered.

"Now," he said, teasing her, "was that hard?"

She laughed. *This man is a character*, she thought. "No," she said, "not at all."

"That business partner of mine is at my office door beckoning. Such an impatient fellow. Hold on." After a minute of silence, he was back. "Listen, tomorrow I am going to pick up this conversation from where we left off. I am glad you called me, Clare, and you have a great evening."

"You too," she replied. *A busy man*, she thought, and hard to figure out.

He did call the very next day, but she was in a meeting. Upon her return to the office, she called back, only to be informed that he was not in.

When she arrived home from work that evening, there was a message from Bernard.

She was taking off her work clothes when the telephone rang. *Bernard again*, she thought. When she answered, she found she was wrong.

"I tried to call you before you left work," he said, chuckling. "You don't tarry, do you?" He paused. "This is Grady."

"No, I don't. And how are you?" She felt almost giddy. He certainly did have that effect on her, awakening an emotion that had lain dormant since her mid-twenties.

"Not bad, but I will feel better if you come out and keep me company."

She wanted so much to act nonchalant but discarded the thought. "I guess I could do that," she said, smiling. "So should I meet you or "

"Oh, so the guard dog was put up last time?" He paused. "Well, you're pretty enough to have one."

She laughed. Goodness, this man was a character. "Thanks, and no," she said, "there's nothing like that."

"So when can I pick you up?"

"Give me an hour."

"Okay," he agreed, "it's now six ten and I will pick you up shortly after seven."

Somehow, she wanted to seize control of where this was going because everything was too sporadic. She liked him so much, but she needed more stability, something that didn't keep her so off-balance. Nothing this haphazard could be categorized as meaningful.

After a quick shower, she scurried around to get ready. She changed into fresh underwear and knee-highs to wear with her slacks, put on fresh makeup, added a touch of fragrance, took something from the closet to slip into quickly, and changed her jewelry, and when the doorbell rang, there he stood, greeting her with that beautiful white smile, casually dangling his keys.

He stepped into the foyer, looking down at her. She was pretty and petite. He had not liked anyone this much for a very long time.

It was almost the last of September, and the changeable Chicago weather prompted her to reach the foyer closet and pull from it a coordinating jacket to match the slacks she wore.

"I'm always cold," she admitted.

"Good that you are bringing it because we might sit on the lakefront."

A few minutes later, they were in his car, entering Outer Drive headed north, but going only as far as Hyde Park. He parked the car in the back of Harper's Court.

"Have you eaten yet today?" he asked.

"I have," she said. "My largest meal is at lunchtime."

"I usually don't eat this late, either, but I was with clients all day and had only coffee, orange juice, and an apple. Do you mind if we eat in Hyde Park?"

"No," she said, "not at all."

"The reason I wanted to catch you before you scampered from work," he explained, "was because I was downtown and wanted us to have dinner somewhere."

"I'm sorry about that."

"Don't be. I'll catch you next time."

He ate a full meal while she had only a dessert with coffee.

"So," he said after dinner, "you are not fond of lounges; you like to sew, bike ride, grow plants, and read; and you would love to travel. Is that right?" He paused. "And you have a degree in education."

"Two, in fact," she replied with a smile. "You remember everything I told you?" Her eyes sparkled. "I'm impressed that you remember all of it."

"Of course, I remember," he said. "Don't you remember what I told you about myself? I'm going to be disappointed if you don't because I only told you a few things due to the interruption." He winked. "So, make me happy."

As if there was a personal switch, her body grew warm. She smiled. "Let me see. You have been married twice and have a son who is a sophomore in college." She paused. "Oh, and your son is by your first wife."

"Good, now I know you at least think I'm worth some of your time."

She shook her head in amazement at this man who had walked into her life. He had such a great personality.

"No?" He was teasing her, referring to her shaking her head.

"Yes," she said hurriedly "you are. Goodness, you are a character."

"Is that good or bad?"

"It's perfectly okay." She laughed. "I don't think I have ever met anyone quite like you. Where do you live?"

"Here, in Hyde Park," he replied. "I've lived here ever since my second divorce."

"How long ago was that?"

"Since my very early thirties," he replied.

"So, you've been a bachelor for quite some time." She assumed he was no longer in his thirties.

"This is very true. And without any live-in arrangements or entanglements whatsoever," he added with emphasis.

She decided to not venture any further into that arena but found the information valuable. She was relieved that he had voluntarily divulged his exact marital status. At last, she knew at least one full-fledged, eligible bachelor existed in the black community, and she had met him. She remained silent for a moment as she drank her coffee.

"Could I ask you a question?" she said.

He nodded his consent.

"Why were you shopping for groceries so far from your neighborhood?"

"I was showing a property in the area, so why not?" he answered.

He looked closely. She had the prettiest eyes. He loved the shape of them and those long lashes. Flawless skin, deep chocolate brown with a copper undertone. He wondered why she was not at least engaged, but her availability was not a phenomenon, given that eligible black men were not that plentiful. Plus, he was also aware that a significant percentage of upwardly mobile black men tended to gravitate toward, if not white females, those of a lighter hue. Still, in all, she should have some choices out there. He noticed that she wore very little makeup. His attraction was strong, and he wondered whether she was dating anyone. If so, who and whether she was serious about the guy. Perhaps she had the same sort of arrangement that he had with Helen, the kind that would never lead to marriage.

Once again, they were in his car. He turned the dial to a jazz station on his radio, commenting that it was his favorite music. They were cruising down Lake Park, leaving Hyde Park behind to enter the Outer Drive at Forty-Seventh. He folded the arm rest away and took her hand. How long had it been since he'd felt this way about anyone? He was going to have to take it slow with this little lady.

"Come closer," he said softly.

She did but left a reasonable amount of space between them. He drove farther north, around Fullerton, until he found a suitable parking spot where they could leave the car to simply walk and talk. They walked only for a short distance before heading back to the car. The lake was getting choppy, and she looked cold even though she was wearing a jacket.

"Are you cold, little girl?" he asked quietly.

"I'm comfortable."

"Now, where were we? Oh yes, what kind of music do you like?"

"You're not going to laugh or think condescending thoughts?"

"Try me," he answered.

"The blues," she replied emphatically. "I also like a few of the so-called classical pieces and jazz and R&B, but blues is my favorite music. Muddy Waters and Albert King most of all."

"I like the blues too."

"You do?"

"Sure," he said. "Pop had blues on the stereo during our entire childhood." He chuckled. "Weekends, if he wasn't watching baseball—my father loves baseball—he had the stereo going constantly with the ones you named and John Lee Hooker, Little Walter, Elmore James, Jimmy Reed, even Chester Burnett, the Howlin' Wolf himself." He paused and laughed. "My mother turns her nose up at Wolf."

"And so do I," she said. "Ugh, I cannot stand Howlin' Wolf."

"Snob," he teased. "When we were growing up, Mom listened to big band jazz—Count Basie and Duke Ellington, and she loved Billy Eckstine and Nat King Cole. She was crazy about Billie Holiday, Sarah Vaughn, Ella, and Satchmo." (Satchmo was a popular, fond nickname for Louis Armstrong.) "Mom liked the blues sometimes, but Pop is still a classic blues man."

He had been leisurely leaning against the side of the car, but now he stood and spontaneously lifted her to its hood. A gentle kiss stirred an involuntary response in her, as if an automatic switch had suddenly raised her body temperature.

"You taste delicious," he whispered as he kissed her again, cupping her face with those nice hands, this time sensually probing and exploring with his tongue. Tenderly he kissed the inside of her wrist and then gently held her hand. "Is Clare short for something else?"

"Clarissa," she said, steadying herself after the reaction he had caused, which was making it difficult to concentrate. "But my preference is Clare. The only place Clarissa exists is on my birth certificate and other legal documents."

She did not mention that her deceased grandmother had called her Clarissa, and when she was younger, so had her mother whenever voicing displeasure.

"I heard that," he said and chuckled. "I guess the little lady doesn't wish to be called by her christened name. Well, I'm Grady Collier Mayfield on everything legal and to all who know me."

"One person used to call me Rissie," she said. "My brother Jeffrey. He was killed in 1981."

"Sorry to hear that. How old was he?"

"It happened right after his twenty-seventh birthday," she said, momentarily sorrowful.

He noticed that her mood shifted briefly to sadness, but just as quickly the melancholy vanished into a smile.

He lifted her down from the hood of the car to the grassy mound and opened the car door, noticing that the top of her head was barely above his shoulder.

ജ

Nadine was exuberant. "Girlfriend, I just love it. I think this is going to go far. I feel good about this one."

"I still say I suspect that he's attached," countered Clare.

"One thing is obvious: Mr. Mayfield isn't on a leash. You would be surprised about some women, especially in the black community. I guess it's because there is such an eligible male drought. Whoever she is, she stays put while he's at play."

"First of all, I don't think that would work with him. He specifically told me, point-blank, that he is a bachelor without any live-in arrangement of any kind."

"That sounds good. He wanted you to know that he is a bona fide, single black man, an SBM." Nadine paused. "The relationship is still young, and I suspect it will get better. You just keep me posted."

# Chapter Seventeen

Throughout his entire adult life, Grady Mayfield's main goal had been amassing wealth. During his first marriage, at twenty-three years of age, he fathered a son. This led to an even keener focus on gaining affluence.

Grady had graduated from college at age twenty-one with a degree in business. He achieved this by choosing the proper electives and taking courses during the summer months that he could transfer to satisfy his business focus. Since real estate was his field of choice, he opted not to spend the additional two years in college to acquire an MBA. So, after completing an internship with a company during his last year of college and then graduating, he secured employment with another downtown real estate firm. Grady's maternal uncle, Maurice Cambridge, questioned his motives. He wanted to know why Grady was working for someone else when he should be in business for himself. Grady explained that since the internship had been for only a few months during the summer, it had been a limited experience, and he wanted to acquire knowledge regarding day-to-day operations. So, his uncle advised him to pay very close attention—quickly!—and he would "cut him some slack."

In a very short time, he acquired his broker's license and was eager to get started. He could have simply passed the real estate exam to become an agent. However, securing such independence strengthened his goals. Additionally, the firm's management had already selected its preferred cast of characters—all of them white—ignoring the fact that Grady's educational background was stronger. These agents were steered to the most lucrative ventures, such as commercial sales and housing deals in plush northern suburbs that commanded hefty commissions. His uncle counseled him to play their game, sell what they offered, rapidly save as much money as possible, and then move on.

One person in the office befriended him. Harvey Cohen was a part-time associate broker with the firm. He reviewed with Grady all the intricacies of the trade—home foreclosures, real estate auctions, title searches, shared listings, the value of being licensed in more than one state, out-of-state sales, and commercial sales. He also encouraged Grady to ask any questions that he might have.

Cohen also intimated that he was a stockbroker by profession, and real estate was secondary for him. He told Grady to contact him whenever he was in a position to invest in the market and that if he was permitted to handle Grady's portfolio, there was a substantial fortune to be made in the stock market; a combination of real estate and various stock investments would make him financially secure. Keeping that card in a safe place and maintaining a close connection with Cohen, Grady shrewdly calculated a five-year projection for launching such an undertaking.

In 1966, as Grady approached twenty-three years of age, with some money saved, he went into business for himself. He made one mistake. He met Olivia and became involved in a courtship when he should have been devoting every minute to furthering his enterprise. She was a few years older, traveling in the fast lane, and not exceptionally pretty but still extremely attractive, and she knew her way around, or so he thought. Grady soon discovered why she urgently wanted to become Mrs. Mayfield. Approximately seven months after the wedding, little

Kevin was born. Grady had failed to heed the warning of his father, Joseph Mayfield, which was the same for all his sons: "Boy, always use that life jacket. It keeps you in total control."

∾

The truth was that Grady loved having a son but would have chosen just to pay child support without the additional responsibility of a wife. However, Joseph and Rachel Mayfield would have frowned on that arrangement because all Mayfield children had legitimate last names.

So as not to place everything on hold and slow things down, Grady discussed with his uncle the possibility of securing additional properties in his name—Maurice Cambridge—and having them converted in the future, and his uncle gladly consented to this arrangement. He made these plans during his second year of marriage because, prematurely, he was entertaining the idea of a legal separation. He had second thoughts about seeking the separation and didn't follow through. He knew Olivia would surely seize the opportunity to accuse him of abandonment, which could possibly be supported by the courts. Even so, he kept his plan in place to secure properties without transparency.

Many times, he arrived home dog-tired, seeking nothing more than a shower and the warmth of a bed without intimacy, which infuriated Olivia. She would lapse into the one-character flaw that infuriated Grady the most—she sulked, a shortcoming that spotlighted her immaturity whereas one of his strongest attributes was communication. Even as a boy he had despised those who lacked the ability to properly engage in discussion to achieve a reasonable outcome in a situation. More and more, she began to threaten to take Kevin and leave. Consequently, when Kevin turned three, Grady decided that the building where they resided could be debt-free within another year; he worked diligently to meet that deadline. His plan was to file for divorce when Kevin turned six years old and would be attending school all day.

During his marriage to Olivia, he had repeatedly explained that periods of absence, often for extended lengths of time, were necessary. He persistently stressed how the first five years of any business were the most crucial and asked her to be patient. Often, he had to leave home, impromptu, to show a house to a client, to work weekends. Olivia was constantly left home alone with their son, and this caused constant arguing and bickering in the relatively new marriage, thus creating a negative environment for their young son. Because of these circumstances, Grady decided to postpone purchasing any other properties, at least with transparency.

Their building contained three flats, each consisting of six rooms. He, Olivia, and little Kevin occupied the first floor. The second- and third-floor occupancy would bring Olivia an income. Looking ahead, he also renovated the basement, paying close attention to the building codes regarding ingress and egress. When the final lease was signed for the basement apartment, commonly called a garden apartment, the building had full occupancy. It was Grady's plan to file for divorce when Kevin turned six years old, when he attended school all day.

Another of Grady's prominent attributes was his ability to quickly regain focus after each distraction, which baffled both Olivia and, later, his second wife. He remained unwavering and unrelenting as he plodded steadily toward his goal even though he was fully cognizant of neglecting home, the one aspect of his life he would always regret. His final analysis, when reflected on his marriage to Olivia later, would be that it accomplished two things: it provided little Kevin with his rightful name and avoided critical scrutiny of his parents.

In 1967, during his second year in business, Grady had contacted his Uncle Maurice for an updated listing of tradesmen. From that listing he met Bradley West. As real estate brokers, they had compared notes only to discover similar experiences with corporate America, though for Bradley the experience had been longer. Several years older, Bradley had worked his way through college as a licensed electrician.

Bradley West also knew some stages of renovation. Starting at the age of twelve, Grady had learned home remodeling through working with Uncle Maurice on weekends and during summer breaks. Because of their wealth of individual skills, Grady and Bradley complemented each other and made the decision to go into business together.

The listing provided by Uncle Maurice proved to be invaluable to these young men in every area—electricians, brick layers, drywall professionals, roofers, and plumbers. It allowed Grady and Bradley to assemble a crew of men and begin their rehab venture. Some of these properties were purchased at auctions. Often for the sake of expediency, only one of them attended an auction while the other stayed on-site to keep working and oversee their crew. You had to know exactly when and where the auctions were being held and be prepared to pay cash. Both Grady and Bradley agreed that loans for these properties were never to be considered.

Additionally, Uncle Maurice counseled these young entrepreneurs to also have a list of those hired to work by the day in addition to their main crew, who were always paid weekly. With these two groups, they could rehab the houses rather quickly to go on the market for sale. Near the end of the job, they cut expenses by sending the crew to the next site, and together completed the remaining minor renovations. This suggestion from Uncle Maurice, based on his wealth of experience, proved to be very sound advice.

It was understood that their crew would work other jobs during the dry spells, jobs secured through the networking of associates and the business connections of Uncle Maurice.

In preparation for the inspectors, both knew exactly what to look for to ascertain everything was up to code when completing a project. Often Uncle Maurice, who sometimes wanted to get out of the house, would go with them to add a third pair of eyes. They were always thorough, leaving the inspectors without complaints. They ran a tight ship, and the two young men always inspected behind each other on every job, often twice. However, it never hurt to add Uncle Maurice's sharp eye to their arsenal.

As partners, their profits had to be evenly divided, but there was a considerable reduction to their equally shared overhead expenses. As an additional source of income, they decided to hire a person with some real estate background to perform tax searches for properties with unpaid taxes. Often the owners met the deadline and came up with the cash plus the interest owed which, according to the value of the property, frequently was a handsome amount. Of course, there were other times when the owners did not meet the deadline. These homes could be purchased by just paying the delinquent taxes. Purchasing them was worth the hassle only if renovation expenses could be kept to a minimum. So, pooling their monies, Grady and Bradley embarked on this enterprise with great enthusiasm, always mindful of the necessary, constant cash flow. The primary lesson Uncle Maurice had taught Grady at a young age regarding self-employment was that cash flow (liquid assets) was a must.

It was a struggle, especially when a neighborhood was in transition. Uncle Maurice called the white realtors, contractors, and developers "The Boys." They wanted to share on their terms only, manipulating the most lucrative outcomes for themselves. Both young men were shrewd, as Uncle Maurice had been, and they covered all bases. Therefore, they made sure that tradesmen, especially the plumbers, electricians, and roofers, were licensed whenever purchasing properties for renovation. Thus, avoiding complications when the properties were ready for the inspectors.

After a couple of years, they were making a reasonable profit. Often, they worked around the clock, relieved that there was no nine to five. They were young and valiantly endured the pressures of chasing "that mean green," a Bradley West description.

In 1970, Grady was drafted for a stint in Vietnam. He was twenty-seven. Bradley empathized with his friend. He had already paid his dues in Vietnam, seldom mentioning the distasteful topic. He was yet resentful of being drafted to fight a senseless war. Reinforcement of his stance was the disastrous and nasty Chicago drama televised worldwide—the Democratic Convention of 1968.

His scheduled five-year plan to launch his investment plan began in his fourth year before he left for Viet Nam. Harvey Cohen cautiously invested his new client's money.

Fortunately, during Grady's two-year absence, Uncle Maurice had voluntarily come out of retirement to assist Bradley West to keep things going smoothly. His interim participation brought a level of security to Bradley's business, guaranteeing an unbroken partnership for his nephew upon his return.

Grady returned from Vietnam in 1972 and once again secured his broker's license. Though small, diversified monthly investments began; he was on his way. Kevin was now seven years old. Grady filed for divorce.

During all of Grady's marital problems, not once did Joseph Mayfield ever utter "I told you so" to his youngest son. Instead, it was Grady who not a few times mentioned to his father that he should have listened. Always the diplomat with all his children, Joseph Mayfield commented to his son that at least his own personal benefit from the now-dissolved union was the enjoyment and blessing of another grandchild.

Joseph Mayfield had never liked Olivia and, unaware of the pregnancy, had warned Grady against marrying "that type"—in the "fast lane," aesthetically endowed (or so she thought, a private conclusion), and so on. She was unaware of the inner self as most important in nurturing outer beauty! She possessed what he called the Baroness Syndrome. He often observed but never mentioned that during their entire marriage, whenever Grady, Olivia, and little Kevin attended a family gathering, not once did she ever offer to help the other women with any chores. This warranted and received their full resentment. Joseph told his son Olivia's problem was she possessed the limited capacity to love only herself. Nevertheless, Joseph was always kind to his daughter-in-law He had taught all his children that rule: if you dislike a person, extra kindness is the solution that kills the tendency to be cruel. Because of this, Olivia never knew that she was the only daughter-in-law that Joseph Mayfield genuinely disliked.

The divorce was a nasty and bitter one, which Olivia wanted to convert into battles regarding their son. Procuring an excellent lawyer allowed Grady to protect his rights as Kevin's father. As part of the divorce settlement, Grady Mayfield relinquished to Olivia total ownership of the property they had previously owned together. The judge complimented Olivia as a very young landlady, financially capable for herself supported by a sizable income even without working full-time.

Parental rights as a father also included visitation on alternate weekends, a month during the summer, alternate holidays, notification of all school activities to be provided by whichever school Kevin attended. (The courts granted Grady total financial responsibility for his son's livelihood and education from kindergarten through college.)

At the time of the divorce, Grady and his business partner, Bradley West, owned two six-unit buildings together. However, on paper these properties were owned by Bradley West and Maurice Cambridge.

There was also a third property, a small court building they were purchasing, approximately six months after Grady's return from Vietnam; there was a problem. They had made the down payment from their liquid assets; but also needed a bank loan materializing slower than anticipated. Although Bradley and Grady's offer was more lucrative, the owner was being pressured by another real estate agency. At the beginning, the owners accepted their offer. However, Grady and Bradley had been negotiating with their bank's loan officer for over a month, then two months. Each time, the bank requested more information with the owners becoming impatient. At one point, their bank requested proof of exactly how much cash flow they had and how it was consistently maintained. This prompted their decision to take their accountant with them. As Meghan, their astute accountant, was gathering all the necessary information, Grady was becoming somewhat agitated. Meanwhile, to ward off other buyers and ensure the owners stayed with them, the down payment was increased and accepted by their bank. Finally, the deal was sealed. That incident did cause them to change banks!

A sudden distraction fluttered into the life of Grady Mayfield like a spring blossom, floating on a breeze, possessing a melodious, cultured voice. She was graceful and full of warmth and passion. Ethel was tall and willowy without the excessively polished veneer of Olivia but possessing her own unique attractiveness and an underlying air of subtle sophistication. The marriage lasted eight months.

Brad had recently married Maggie, and they were happy. Viewing this arrangement with a tinge of envy, Grady also wanted in out of the cold. Now thirty years of age, he felt it was time to act on a partnership that did not involve a ledger sheet. Even Rolanda was mildly shocked by his serious approach to the relationship.

"Lover, she doesn't look like she wants to cook and clean," said Rolanda who had been in Ethel's company on several occasions. "I think you need to pass on this one. I detect a resemblance somewhere." Despite Rolanda's advice, Grady and Ethel got married. After eight months, the union was terminated with Grady returning to single life.

Ethel knew, Bradley argued, that at any other less vulnerable time, Grady would have been unattainable. In reflection, Bradley was right. Had they waited, no wedding! She had stubbornly petitioned for marriage, not wanting to wait for a more opportune time. Afterward Ethel had walked away confused and hurt. In her frustration she settled for nothing more than her freedom, which, relieved, Grady had immediately rendered. After this second marriage, he vowed never again to jump into matrimony that quickly. As Bradley put it—and Grady agreed—sheer luck had allowed him to escape the second marriage without any financial disturbances.

Bradley also told him that his vulnerability was accentuated because of the problems they had just endured during their business transactions from which he needed a recess. Bradley said that could have accomplished that by spending time on one of the islands—Jamaica or the Bahamas—without the marriage license. However, the suggestion came after the fact.

So, now that Grady had resumed the life of a bachelor, his sister Rolanda, a single young woman four years out of college and working on her first *good* job (her own description), offered her assistance. Now engaged, she promptly established her "tour of duty" for at least a year. She could be there only as her schedule allowed, though, because the man of her choice, a good man, needed TLC. Her brother welcomed it with enthusiasm. Often, she would call to see if he was eating on the run (i.e., fast food), her label for the killer diet. "Eating too much from that menu will make the body rebel," she always advised. Thus, she began to consistently ring his second- floor apartment bell, volunteering to make dinner. Since she shared an apartment with a former classmate, Grady attempted to persuade her to move in with him. She graciously refused, explaining such an arrangement would cramp her style. So, he did as she suggested and had an extra key made. Each evening, she let herself in, straightened up the place and cooked, enough for both, but never moved in. Before each departure, she would leave him a funny note; Rolanda was comical, and each one of those whacky, crazy notes evoked laughter.

The best times were the short days when a job was near completion, and she was still there when he arrived home. Even though most of the time he was tired, he was immediately rejuvenated upon entering the apartment filled with the aroma of good food and the smell of freshly cleaned surroundings. An additional bonus was his sister's magnificent smile.

Sometimes he wondered where he would be if he had married a mature woman willing to work with him as Maggie accommodated Bradley. That was one genuine lady, a gem, who loved Bradley. In fact, they loved each other and, for a while, lived together in Maggie's home inherited from her deceased parents.

Often Grady reviewed the fact that he had ignored his father's warnings about his rash involvement with Olivia or her type. In retrospect, he was satisfied that even though upset with his father at the time, he'd never displayed it. Now he scoffed at his own youthful stubbornness and false sense of sophistication but, overall, years that earned him immeasurable maturity.

Grady and Bradley were now discussing at length getting out of the rehab business that was becoming time-consuming, less profitable. They were getting older, and their goal had always been to own a real estate office.

During Grady's absence, Uncle Maurice influenced Bradley's personal enterprises; he now owned two liquor stores and held part ownership in a health club. All three were yielding lucrative returns, so Bradley could comfortably finance his end. Grady needed more cash to avoid disturbing his investments.

As part owner, Grady already held a twenty percent interest in a moderately large strip mall; two other investors held equal amounts.

The fourth partner, Harvey Cohen, owned the controlling share of 40 percent. This investment yielded Grady handsome quarterly returns.

Uncle Maurice informed his nephew of a contractor that he had known for years who was developing land in a South suburb. He was having problems with the realtor tentatively contracted to work with him to sell the properties. There was an unresolved misunderstanding and, thus, the stalemate. Maurice seized this opportunity for his nephew, knowing this was the cure he needed to get his life solidly back on track. The commission was a little less than Grady would have liked; however, since the development was considerably large, he accepted.

So, after a period of two and one-half years the development, which consisted of thirty homes, held the status of full occupancy. This put Grady solidly in the black. He now reimbursed his uncle for monies owed plus a 'thank you' bonus for all properties temporarily held in his name. Legally, the name of Grady Collier Mayfield was restored to those properties.

At this juncture, Uncle Maurice mentioned to Grady that he too should engage in personal enterprises that would afford him a consistent cash flow. He suggested car washes to achieve that goal.

"People," his uncle explained, "love to keep their ride together. There are plenty of young guys, some high school age and those even older, looking for a side hustle. Computerize the operation so that the cash flow remains intact. Hire a bright, young lady as a cashier; the computer will do all the calculations, so her part involves no figuring. This prevents the opening of the cash register for anything other to complete a transaction just like the operations at the large grocery store chains. Get your car washed a couple of times a week to stay in touch with the operation. This is multi-purposeful: it lets them be aware that you might show up at any time; you keep your ride clean; at the same time, you monitor how your business is progressing. While there, randomly check the statements provided by the computerized printouts and, quarterly, have your accountant record all sales.

Grady purchased two such enterprises, granting maintenance of a larger cash flow. Under the shrewd guidance of Harvey Cohen, he also increased his diversified investments in the stock market.

In 1975, at thirty-two years of age, Grady and his partner, Bradley West, could now open their real estate office. All necessary was the right person to run it. They agreed on equal ownership and hired a middle-aged woman, Ursula Jackson, as office manager. Ursula, a former broker, was seasoned in all aspects of real estate with an impressive résumé. Since she had once endured the rigors of business ownership with all its headaches, she sought only a comfortable income and accepted the position. Because there could be only one broker for the office, Bradley volunteered without hesitation to be the associate, with monetary compensation to authenticate his equal partnership with Grady Mayfield. She aided them in bringing in top-notch agents, and "when the dust settled," Bradley's analysis, the result was an office smoothly run without the partner having to involve themselves with any paperwork other than signing off as necessary. This allowed them to focus on their personal enterprises and larger real estate deals.

Grady also decided that this was the appropriate time for a change of address. Bradley wished he would consider renting (for a lot less money) one of the apartments in one of the buildings they owned. Instead, he chose the heart of the city—Hyde Park—ideal since their recently opened office was nearby. For their office, all other available commercial spaces were either farther south, west or a less attractive area of the city. By car, Grady was no more than twenty minutes from the office.

Chicago was the city of Grady Mayfield's birth, and he loved it. Some of his friends and colleagues complained to him about Chicago being the most segregated northern city even as they kept in step with their white counterparts' desperate scurry to the suburbs. His reply, to loosely paraphrase Malcolm X, was Canada is geographically north of us, which makes the location of the entire United States south! He had always found the North Side less appealing because, among other drawbacks, it was too congested. Besides, in Hyde Park he was privileged to have a unique ambience considered ideal—because of the University of Chicago, it possessed features within the city limits that resembled suburban living. The one other place on Chicago's South Side that provided this atmosphere was Beverly. He listened patiently to those who debated the North Side as more beautiful, with less crime, etcetera, He listened, but stayed put.

So, his current address was Hyde Park; Beverly was more conducive to family living. At this juncture the final decision could remain pending; there was ample time to decide. Granted, the property in both locations was steep, but if you wanted to reside in the city and have a beautiful environment, Grady considered these the two most ideal spots on the South Side to raise a family, and he was mainly a South Side guy. His current apartment was on the fifteenth floor at the north end of Regents Park, offering a breathtaking view of Lake Shore Drive and the magnificent lakefront.

When Kevin spent his first weekend at the apartment, he was so impressed with the view that he sat in the window and gazed, mesmerized, for long periods of time at the Drive below, snaking its way alongside the shore of Lake Michigan. Displaying the picturesque Chicago skyline as a backdrop, it provided the highest order of scenic splendor.

In the past, Kevin often wasn't able to attend scheduled Mayfield family gatherings because whenever possible, Olivia schemed, due to sheer meanness, to keep him from attending. Of course, if the get-together coincidentally fell on one of Kevin's court-scheduled weekends with his father, her efforts were totally futile. Otherwise, these events were not part of the court settlement. This made his son miserable because he loved attending Mayfield family gatherings, lively and full of fun. The additional bonus was the center of attention because of his frequent absence. However, Grady kept reminding him that a time would come when such decisions would be entirely his. Not once did Grady make negative comments to Kevin regarding his mother. Just as his father had promised, Kevin now, as a legal adult, made these decisions independent of both parents.

Through the years Grady and Harvey Cohen became relatively good friends. Sometimes, when Grady had business downtown, they met for an early dinner in the Loop because Cohen, who lived in Wilmette, commuted daily by train. For a while, Cohen had maintained an apartment on the North Side. Once his wife decided against it, the apartment was sublet to a single friend, who eventually purchased the place when the building converted to condominiums. Even now this generated a smile from Grady because Cohen's wife knew him well: formerly, she had been the other woman.

Grady often reflected on his own two failed marriages and considered his unwavering obsession with making money as the culprit, but hindsight made him evaluate the situation more closely. He identified rash decisions as the main nemesis in both instances. Pop had always told him, "Positive results come from sound decisions." Now financially secure and still young enough to live in comfort with the woman of his choice and provide a life of quality for them both, he chalked up his previous two mistakes as past experiences to fine-tune his judgment. He hoped he could make his next marriage—his third—a lasting one. He had always loved children and wanted more before he became too old to enjoy them.

It was nineteen eighty-four. Grady with his friend and business partner, Bradley West, of seventeen years owned a total of fifteen rental properties, including three small court buildings and a few commercial properties. All were managed by their agency, conveniently located on the outer parameters of Hyde Park. The buildings had been purchased with equal investments from each of them and the monthly income from these properties divided evenly except when real estate sales were finalized. Grady would take the broker's share, but personally reimburse Bradley from the rental properties subtracted from his own balance. Only Ursula was responsible for these ledgers.

Through the years physical fitness had always been a must for Grady Mayfield. He both jogged and worked out in the gym to maintain good health as well as look good both to himself and to the opposite sex. In the company of women, he was charming and attentive, possessing all the admirable social graces. Optimistic and expecting a more positive outcome, some women would date him for a considerable amount of time. He would date a woman for a year or two, sometimes seeing her frequently and at other times seldom. At this point in life, his preference was still bachelorhood, so that he could remain focused on his main priority—making money without the distractions of a wife. It was a focus that persisted well into his mid-thirties. Of course, he also had female acquaintances, including genuine friends, with whom he was not intimate because of his business dealings with them. Grady had always made a point of keeping business separate from pleasure. He might stop by to visit and talk or take them out for dinner or a drink because, overall, Grady was a man who enjoyed the company of women.

In recent years, an issue had arisen in his intimate relationships that had not been there before. Older now, and the fact that he made no commitments to any one woman sometimes became a deficit, altering his attractiveness to those who wanted steadfastness and dependability in their lives. When younger, this was part of his mystique and appeal. Now the more pragmatic females terminated the relationship after a reasonable amount of time had passed, in favor of the company of someone more reliable. Of course, there were also a few in search of matrimony. Still others were looking for someone to take them out, and in return, they would permit him to share their bed on his terms. However, Grady found many of these options unattractive and, most of all, unsafe. He wisely kept his sexual prowess to a minimum.

His sister Mabel introduced him to Helen. At that juncture in his life, the fact that she was considerably older and more amenable to an arrangement without the hassle of total permanency (marriage) was attractive. Deceptively youthful in appearance, Helen was also a very stylish woman possessing an element of elegance that made her quite attractive. Their relationship did provide stability and still granted him the freedom of being single.

Lately, he could be in a room full of people with a female on his arm, with or without whom there was amorous involvement, feeling isolated. On holidays when with his family—he had a large one—no longer did he feel gay and carefree as he did in younger years. He was discovering the simple togetherness with those he loved less satisfying. These events were never attended to by Helen although he had been involved with her for a long time. Their relationship would never go any further and therefore suggest the wrong message.

Whenever he observed his brothers and sisters interacting with their mates and offspring, having fun or just being together and sharing the moment, a jolt of loneliness would, without warning, catch him off-guard.

On weekends, while jogging in Washington Park or on the lakefront, he would see parents with their children, especially men with their sons. He deeply sensed that his son Kevin had missed out on the uninterrupted, day-to-day rapport that makes adults fondly reminisce about their childhood. He himself held great memories from his youth. In blatant contrast to his two failures, his parents' marriage spanned more than fifty years. A significant percentage of his son's relationship with him had been determined by the courts, including alternate weekend visits, summer vacations, and negotiated arrangements around special occasions, casting an additional negative connotation on the time spent away from Kevin. That he received formal invitations to Kevin's school functions emphasized the separateness of their lives. Often, he felt like any outsider as he, based on that court-assigned schedule, grabbed bits and pieces of Kevin's life. However, the alternative could not possibly have been more suitable, bringing about even more damage than did their present circumstance. Termination of that marriage while his son was still young was a far better decision for all involved. What he had financially accomplished over the years would never have been possible, either. That would have impacted on his son's future as well.

Grady was not getting any younger. Often his thoughts were centered on family life—backyard barbecues and lazy Sunday afternoons and the laughter of playing children. Secretly, his desire for a family was more pronounced during the holidays, especially Thanksgiving and Christmas, the most significant time of year for family gatherings. For some time, he had experienced discomfort as the only one to arrive and leave alone. He had to decide exactly when that would change.

# Chapter Eighteen

Saturday, and office hours were from nine until one o'clock. Except for Grady everyone was gone. At two-thirty he locked the office door, deciding not to go home. Forty minutes later, he was pulling up in the driveway of a typical suburban home; this one belonged to his sister, Rolanda. They were getting a preview of November, just a few days away, on this exceptionally cold day in October. Emerging from his car, he heard the steady drone of a nearby lawn mower. Keisha spotted him from across the street in the small playground where she was on the slide playing with the other children, all in heavy jackets. She stopped immediately and, after checking traffic, crossed the street and ran toward him as he stood beside his car.

"Uncle Grady!" she yelled excitedly.

"My, you're getting to be a big girl."

He scooped her up in his arms. As soon as the words slipped out, he wondered why the potholes for adults always remained the same. He had mentioned that fact to Rolanda when attending the summer picnic. Although he didn't get a chance to visit frequently, he telephoned often.

Jada, the oldest, and the reason Keisha was allowed in the playground, now crossed the street. "Hi, Uncle Grady," she said as she approached him.

He waved, and when she reached them in the driveway, he said, "Hey, Jada. Where is your mother?" Leaning down, he kissed her on the side of the face, and she returned the gesture. The family station wagon was parked to one side in the garage.

"She's inside," Jada said.

The three of them, his nieces leading him by the hands like a captured runaway, headed up the driveway, entering the house through the garage.

"Mama, Uncle Grady is here!" Keisha called out from the kitchen. Sometimes the kitchen was as far as Grady got if he didn't have much time, but today he allowed them to lead him from kitchen through the dining room and deposit him on the living room sofa.

Jada dashed from the room. Moments later, Rolanda followed Jada from the basement with a basket of clean laundry deposited at the kitchen island. With a broad smile, she went to greet her brother, who sat quietly thumbing through the latest *Jet* magazine taken from the cocktail table.

"What brings you out here?" She sat beside him planting a kiss on his cheek as he grabbed her hand. The Mayfields were a loving family, and when they greeted each other, there were always hugs, kisses, and handholding.

"Decided to pay you a visit," he said, smiling fondly.

"No lady friend with you today, lover?" questioned his sister.

She was the only family member who knew most of the women he dated because sometimes when paying her a visit he would bring along a female friend. However, he had brought Helen only once. None accompanied him to any family gatherings.

"No, I'm by myself today," he said. "Where's Stan?"

"Don't you hear that lawn mower out there?"

Grady left the couch, walked through the kitchen, parted the sliding glass doors to step on the deck. He waited until Stan was guiding the lawn mower in his direction before attempting to get his attention, certain that his brother-in-law was relieved the season for lawn mowing was ending.

Jada voluntarily ran down the steps of the deck to trot alongside her father, pointed up. Releasing the handle to shut off the lawn mower, Stan looked up to greet him with a wave.

"Hey, sport," Grady responded.

They talked briefly; his brother-in-law told him to stick around, he would be done in a few minutes.

Rolanda was in the kitchen at the island on one of the high stools, folding clothes. "Jada, please put the last load of clothes in the dryer."

Dutifully, Jada complied with the request; Keisha remained in the kitchen with her mother and uncle.

Rolanda's entire house was lovely, but he especially loved her large, sunny kitchen with light maple cabinets. A multicolored backsplash enhanced beautiful black granite countertops, streaked with teases of yellow matching the walls and the granite countertop island as well; the swivel stools were black. Bamboo flooring was throughout the house. An attractive inlay centered in front of the fireplace enhanced her large living room. Stan always bragged about Rolanda's exquisite decorating capabilities.

Grady had never paused to examine his marital status as much as now. All his siblings had mates, even Mabel who had no children.

"Where are Danny and Michael?" Grady asked. They were Rolanda's almost inseparable twins.

Keisha was struggling to climb up on one of the two remaining stools. Grady picked her up, sat her on his knee. He kissed her cheek as she offered him a gaping grin; two new front teeth peeped through.

"They're at football practice," his sister replied. "They'll be in around five."

"Little League in the summer. Football in the fall. Basketball in the winter." He smiled. "You keep them busy. I haven't seen them since last Christmas."

During the summer they were heavily committed to baseball. They had a game on the Saturday of the annual family picnic.

"Well, do like Stan said—stick around!"

"Where is your car?"

"In the shop, I pick it up Tuesday." She paused. "How is Helen?" she asked; she knew Helen was his most steady lady friend.

"Fine. I talked to her this morning." He paused. "What's wrong with your car?"

"The regulator went bad." She smiled. "What you been up to, brother dear?

"Making a dollar," he said with a wink. "Hey, when was the family picnic? I can never remember when we have it."

"Every year, the second week in July, just like clockwork."

"It's a long way off then," he said. "This is only the last week of October."

Rolanda thought there was something different about her brother today, a pensive restlessness that caused her to wonder exactly what was going on. He was talking but was not actually engaged in conversation. He seemed bored and preoccupied.

"Exactly, months ago." She paused. "You were there, remember? You're working too hard, brother dear. The months on your calendar are starting to bump into each other."

In July, alone to the annual family picnic, just like he attended every family gathering. She wondered if he would ever marry again because he would be a good catch and not just for financial reasons. He was her brother, sure, but that did not color her objectivity; she honestly knew he was a good man.

Grady extended his stay long enough to visit with his nephews and to eat dinner with the entire family. He then joined them as they gathered around the television to view something that he later couldn't begin to recall.

Transitioning from I-57 to the Dan Ryan and entering Chicago, Grady realized he was experiencing boredom, which felt strange. He had not felt this way in years. During the week he had called Clare a few times, but he had not seen her. He was fighting against getting too involved, although this inner battle was different because Clare was different, the kind of woman a man could marry. He did not want to see Helen this evening but had wanted to spend time with Clare. Why had he hesitated to make a date for the weekend? The reason was clear: He did not want to start planning weekends with her, not just yet. He liked her company but wanted to take it slow. *But* that inner voice warned, *not too slow.* He thought back to their conversation on Thursday, the last time he'd spoken with her. He did not commit to calling her over the weekend, and she did not ask. In all fairness to her, what was transpiring certainly did not fit the description of a meaningful relationship.

It was six thirty in the evening when he entered the apartment to find a message on the answering machine from Helen. He decided not to return her call until tomorrow. Except for the weekend she'd spent in Detroit, during his first date with Clare, this would be the first Saturday in months they had not spent together. During their long relationship, twice before he had gone through a span of time when he saw Helen less than usual, but each time it had passed; she had simply waited it out.

"Your security blanket isn't going anywhere, my man," Bradley had said, his constant tease regarding his relationship with Helen.

*Oh, what the hell,* Grady thought. He dialed Clare's number. When there was no answer, he left a message.

"Hey, little girl, I thought I might reach you early enough on such a cold day, perhaps we could go out for a drink. If you're back before seven, give me a call." There was a pause, a momentary distraction, then he hung up.

Waiting until approximately seven ten for Clare's call, he then left the apartment. Entering the Outer Drive heading north, connected with Dan Ryan, then drove south to his parents' home. He noticed the light in the window as he parked the car. Checked his watch. only seven forty-five. His parents never retired early. He rang the bell, no answer, rang it again.

"You should have used your key," his mother said when she opened the door, giving him a hug, he returned with a kiss. Because his parents were getting old, both he and his sister Mabel had an emergency key. "I was in the bathroom. You know your father can't hear the doorbell."

"Hey, Pop," Grady said when he reached him, warmly grabbing his hand.

Seated in the living room in his favorite chair, a *La-z-boy* recliner, Joseph Mayfield was watching television. Although the volume of his hearing aid was turned up, he failed to hear his son's greeting. (That chair was Joseph's last Christmas present from his children; from then on, both parents received money instead.) His wife always teased him about being "too focused" even when he conversed with her. It was either conversing with her or listening to the television or listening to the radio or the stereo, selectively—one at a time. He was glad to see his youngest son. It had been a long time since Grady had paid them a visit on a Saturday evening.

"I baked a cake today," his mother announced.

"I'm fine," Grady said, draping his jacket on the back of the sofa as he sat down.

"What brings you out this way on a Saturday?" asked Joseph Mayfield.

"Oh, just decided to stop by the home front and see what the old folks are up to," he said. Grady loved teasing his father.

"Watch it, boy."

He called all five sons "boy." He always told them that he was the only one who was entitled to call them "boy." He had sired them and used to change their diapers—before Pampers! During their family gatherings that remark always generated laughter. "I knew you before you knew yourself," he would say, "before you became a reflection in the mirror." That comment always evoked laughter from at least one of them, sometimes all five. That was Pop, and all his sons and daughters knew what a good father he had consistently been. At one time Joseph Mayfield had worked two jobs to provide for eight children. For years their mother, never working outside the home, had taken in sewing.

Rachel Mayfield returned from the kitchen to bring a small serving of cake to Grady's father. "Are you sure you won't have some?"

"Okay, don't mind if I do," Grady said in a sudden change of mind.

He felt out of sorts this evening, admitting to himself that he wished he had made a date with Clare. Schedules created permanency he kept telling himself. *Not yet.*

"Want coffee with it?"

"That would be nice," he said.

They chatted a few minutes longer while Joseph Mayfield finished his cake. Rachel returned the plate to the kitchen.

"Mom," Grady yelled, "I'm going to come in there and eat it."

"I can put them both on a serving tray," she yelled back from the kitchen.

Before long, the three of them were seated around the kitchen table. Both Grady and his mother were having cake and coffee while Joseph looked on.

"Boy," his father said with deliberate directness, "when are you going to get married and settle down?"

"Now, Joe," Rachel protested mildly.

He gently waved her off. "You need a wife and more babies. Who're leaving all that money to, just Kevin? Your brothers and sisters? Your nieces and nephews? You can't leave it to us because we'll be gone."

"Pop," he replied good-naturedly, "everything in due time."

"Time is due now," Joseph answered. His son's response was a smile.

Later, Joseph discreetly watched from the living room window as Grady slowly drove off. Afterward, he positioned the drapes carefully so that his wife wouldn't chide him for disturbing them, but he hadn't wanted to fully open them and make it so obvious that he was watching.

"I worry about that boy," Joseph Mayfield said as he resumed his seat. "Like I said, he needs a family. He'll be in his mid-forties in a few years." He paused. "I can tell, Rae, that the man is lonely."

"Joe, he has a girlfriend. What's her name? Helen?"

"A *lady* friend," he corrected his wife.

Joseph went to the kitchen, his wife following with her empty plate; she had eaten another small serving of cake. There was nobody left at home to help get rid of all those calories, the reason she seldom baked. Like most men, her husband loved sweets, and she was tempted as well. Joseph had high cholesterol, dictating less consumption of cakes and pies although his request for them was constant. After this evening, the remainder of the dessert would go in the freezer for their young-adult grandchildren. Frequently they made unannounced visits, always requesting something sweet.

Rachel placed the dish and fork in the otherwise empty sink. Joseph opened the refrigerator to pour a cold glass of water from the container. She then followed him back to the living room, and again they sat down.

"Helen is old, too old for what he needs."

"She's older," replied Rachel. "I know that much."

"Fifty-three," he said. "I asked the boy. She is fifty-three, so you know why he keeps her, don't ya?"

"I'm sure you'll tell me," She teased.

"You know those are some mean streets out there. He's a vibrant, virile guy. This way he has that stashed for when he wants it."

"Joseph, he might really like her."

"Probably, but it's still true." He paused. "I want him to meet somebody and get married, have some more babies. Rae, he spent most of his young life—other than that stint in Vietnam—most of his twenties, all his thirties, chasing money, *making* money.

"But all that money can't love him at night or give him a back rub. Money is to spend on whatever you need and want. Even if you're super rich, that's all it's good for. You exchange it for whatever you need or want. That's it." He paused. "The one child we raised driven more than all the others to achieve wealth because that's the way he's wired. Now is the time for him to do something for Grady, for his well-being. Find a nice young lady, make himself whole and alive with the love of a woman. Create extensions of himself—more children! Money can't do that. I want that for this boy before he's old and has lost his looks. Then it's guaranteed that all a fine young thing will be marrying him for *is* his money."

"Joe," his wife responded in her own defense, "I also want Grady to marry, but I don't like to pressure him because I want him to marry someone who is different from Olivia and the other one—Ethel—so that's why I don't have that much to say about it."

"I know what you mean, but I doubt if that will happen again. He's older now, more surefooted, and has had time to think and look back over past mistakes. I don't think we have to worry about him doing something that stupid again."

In his monologues, the classy Lou Rawls was known for his vivid depictions of Chicago's brutal winters. It was already unusually cold for the end of October with a promise of ushering in progressively worse months.

Clare had allowed Julia, the older of Bernard's two daughters, to lure her out to spend an afternoon with him and his girls at the Shedd Aquarium. She now found herself strolling from room to room, gazing at all the magnificent species of sea creatures. Tropical fish with all their brilliant colors, a magnificent inspiration for any artist's palette, were her very favorite; she could literally watch them for hours. However, she was not alone, so the entire group continued to travel from room to room, examining the stingrays, intrigued by one who looked like a marvelously large piece of floating inspiration for a fabric designer.

"Clare," Julia said excitedly as it lazily swam near the glass with its identical twin partially hidden beneath a giant rock, "look at that one—it looks like a piece of cloth gliding around."

Clare agreed, discovering that she was having a good time. The affinity that Clare and the ten-year-old felt for each other caused Clare a trace of anxiety because she was not the least bit attracted to the father. Clare had been in their company on several occasions. If only things were different, what a perfect foundation on which to build a relationship. Andrea, four years younger, age six, simply offering a shy smile whenever Clare looked her way. She was not very talkative even with the father, now holding her hand. The four of them intermingled with the rather sparse coat-carrying crowd. As Nadine had suggested just a few months ago, Clare was forcing herself to focus on the present and not allow her thoughts to drift.

Andrea shyly asked of her, "Clare, are you coming to Grandma's with us?"

She discovered that Andrea, less talkative, also liked her. The two girls lived with their mother, spending most weekends with their father at the home he shared with his mother, Bernard's home ever since his divorce. That the girls liked the woman they assumed to be their father's girlfriend was rather unusual, especially since their mother was alive and well. Clare felt a small measure of despondency evaluating what would never transform into something meaningful.

"Dad rented a movie, and we're going to have popcorn," Julia said, squeezing her hand encouragingly. "Come with us."

So, after ending their outing by watching the dolphins perform their act—such smart animals!— they were on the expressway headed to Grandma's house. Clare realized that Bernard's daughters possessed the innocence of children incapable of perceiving the reality of the situation; they presumed their father to be in a positive, serious relationship. However, certain that Bernard's mother read the signs, Clare pleasantly greeted the older woman during the few visits she'd made to her home, with unspoken guidelines for their guarded, subdued interaction.

Later that evening, after popcorn and the movie, in which she successfully feigned interest, Bernard drove her home. Julia wanted to come along for the ride, and inwardly Clare was relieved. As Bernard said his good-bye at her door, Clare quickly let herself in to escape the frigid weather and his brief kiss, which landed in the vicinity of her cold, averted cheek. She returned Julia's wave just before securely locking the inside door as they pulled away.

He was beginning to press for something more; the moment of truth was at hand: she would have to stop dating him. In fact, had today's outing not been a family affair where she could use his daughters as a buffer, the invitation would have been declined. She surmised him sensing the end and goaded Julia into extending the invite.

Once in her bedroom, she saw her answering machine blinking three messages. The first one was from her mother, the second from Nadine. Her heart lurched as the third message started to play. It was from Grady.

Calling on a Saturday? Well, that was unusual! She checked the time on the bedroom clock radio; it was now seven forty-five. The time of the call—approximately six-fifty. She dialed his number, left a message on his answering machine simply. Changing from street clothes into her bathrobe and slippers, she dialed her confidant. Cornell answered the phone, and after they exchanged a few pleasantries, Nadine picked up. As usual, Nadine's first question concerned Grady.

"It's good to be unavailable once in a while," said Nadine. "Now he'll know that you don't have to sit around counting the days, waiting on him to call. Were you with Bernard?"

"And his daughters," she replied. "It's too bad that I don't like him; he's a nice guy."

"Just as well," said Nadine dryly. "He's broke, and if the two of you got married and had children, you would be financially responsible for supporting his second family while he finished rearing and financing the first litter."

"Litter?" questioned Clare with laughter. "That sounds as if we could be in the cat business."

"Well, I'm projecting that you and he would have two or three more in addition to his kids, for the sum of a whole *human* litter, one smaller than exists for cats and dogs. You would be better off if you were—in the cat business, that is," Nadine replied. "Cats have true litters, all born at the same time. If raising pedigrees, you could make extra money."

Earlier, before Clare had received her invitation to the museum with Bernard and his daughters, Nadine had attempted to coax her to North Michigan Avenue. "Oh, I just remembered," Nadine teased. "You rejected my offer, but accepted Bernard's."

"Absolutely," Clare replied, "I was in a warm car. I was not about to freeze my buns traipsing about in this weather. Crossing the Chicago River at Wacker is the worst."

That morning, Clare had reluctantly told her friend that today's weather had teeth and she did not want to be a target. Being cold-natured, Clare sometimes would not venture out during a seriously frigid weekend for anything except church and, if the thermometer dipped too low, she would also be absent from that gathering as well.

After hanging up from idle chitchat with Nadine, she contemplated what to wear to church the next day if she decided to attend. Although Estelle would offer no comment, she disapproved of her daughter missing church. However, even on the brightest, warmest, sunniest day Clare, upon making her departure from the building and heading for home, often felt worse instead of better following the benediction. Furthermore, all that preaching about hell and damnation, getting your crown and wings while much of the congregant screamed and shouted, caused her to question the sincerity of it all. It was her desire to leave church feeling emotionally uplifted, but most of the time it left her in low spirits. Until she and Nadine had honestly discussed this aspect of religion, she had assessed her point of view rather abnormal.

She was also bothered that in this most stable institution of the black community, gay men were numerous congregants. Often, they were handsome, educated professionals. Clare was saddened to think that in the black community, already plagued with a shortage of eligible black men, these men were not potential mates.

She once intimated these thoughts to her mother, commenting also on how amazing it was that the same sermons could be preached year after year. She also remarked that most members seemed to accept it all without question, even though a hefty number of books from the Bible (known as the Apocrypha) were missing. The ones retained included passages frequently not making much sense. Realizing such comments made her mother uneasy, Clare no longer explored the subject of religion with her. The candor between her and Nadine was so uncompromising that it would certainly cause the church sisters, including her mother, to recoil and cringe with dread, even fear. What she wanted to know was whether any of them ever took a good look around to observe that a significant percentage of the bodies filling the pews were women and those striving to be. A disturbingly large number of the heterosexual males stayed home, as did her now-deceased father even when fully ambulatory. His then-healthy legs had transported him to places considered more appealing. She had once asked her mother why their family did not attend church services together. Estelle had simply dismissed the question by stating that Mason did not like sitting that long—least of all in church! Clare had wanted to protest that he sat at home for hours.

Ultimately, she privately questioned how her mother had managed to stay with her father all those years. He was cynical, rather dull, and uneducated, lacking incentive for self-improvement, never becoming an adequate role model for Jeffrey. Until overtaken by his illness, Mason had one favorable quality: he never missed going to work. The two-paycheck family was no longer a phenomenon in the United States but necessary. Aside from that fact, her father for years endured an illness that left her mother no feasible alternative.

Wandering aimlessly into the living room, Clare picked up the remote to surf the TV channels only to discover nothing of interest. How had she arrived at this juncture in her life? Well, she had already reviewed the outcome countless times and knew the answer well.

Monday morning, she was back at work, and did not hear from Mr. Mayfield again until that Wednesday.

"Ms. Ingram," he said when her assistant transferred him, "we missed each other's call over the weekend, so I think it is best that I make my bid early."

"I agree," she answered. "I guess you were lost somewhere in Chicago until now," she replied, keeping it light as Nadine had suggested.

They planned for that Friday to meet in the lobby of her office building.

Two days later, she entered the large lobby from the elevator and began to look around. As if materializing out of nowhere there he stood in a beautiful tan cashmere overcoat with a chocolate scarf peeping out from underneath. She offered a pleasant smile. She was very glad to see him but tried not to let it show too much.

"I'd almost forgotten what you look like," she teased.

"I remember you, little girl," he countered. "Come on, I'm double-parked."

A few of her inquisitive coworkers pointedly bid her good night. One suggested, with emphasis, a wonderful weekend. She knew that on the following Monday they would attempt to incorporate her into the office gossip, but so far, she had managed to keep her life outside the office private.

"Have you been waiting long?" Clare asked.

"No, but I gave myself a minute or two," he replied as they approached the street. "I didn't want to be left in your lobby because you definitely do not waste any time leaving this place." He chuckled. "I'm surprised I don't have to put your skateboard in the trunk."

There were times, Monday through Thursday, when she did stay late, and there were other times when she took work home. She decided not to defend herself and instead simply responded with a good-natured smile.

Once they were in the car and heading east, she looked out at a few of her coworkers who were bracing the Chicago wind, exacerbated by the Chicago River, as they walked across the bridge headed for Union Station. Most in her office were suburbanites.

"Commuters," Grady said and chuckled. "I'd be willing to bet that years from now they will be clamoring to get back to the city. Commuting is no fun."

"What makes you say that?" Clare replied.

"You know the history of your neck of the woods, right?"

"Yes," she said.

"Okay. And you also know why they left?"

"To become suburbanites, be less urban, and of course get away from us," she replied and laughed. "It only takes a few of us to contaminate the entire neighborhood."

She thought again of how often she and Sharla had clashed over this issue. How many times had Sharla lamented the transformation of South Shore, and how often had she mentioned her family moving from the South Side of Chicago to Skokie, the more secure Jewish enclave?

They continued to travel east, approaching Wabash Avenue. "Do you like Chinese food?" he asked.

She said she did, and so they took Wabash and headed south toward Chinatown.

"And so goes the chess game," Grady said, resuming their previous conversation. "It isn't a rarity that this occurs like clockwork every couple of generations. In this city everything twenty to thirty minutes from the Loop will again be reclaimed, starting with all the public housing, which sits on prime property. In many cases they will displace three generations of those who rent at the mercy of the city of Chicago, thus sending them to the hinterland." He paused. "It will be like South

Africa's Bantu stands, where many blacks live in deplorable conditions while the privileged white population in control of the country's wealth occupies the cities. And then the existing amenities in select suburbs will dry up."

"What about the homeowners?" Clare interjected.

"Well, there are various methods of targeting homeowners. Remember, these people have done their homework and can rely heavily on the projections of a national, very accurate demographic study that has been in the works for years. For instance, there are ideal properties in these targeted communities that can be converted into condominiums—warehouses, apartment buildings—plus vacant land that can be developed into expensive living quarters, and expensive high-rises, which are more ideal because they hold more people and require less space. Robert Taylor public housing was decent enough when first built, but it is hard to maintain that kind of model for the poor unless you continuously screen who is coming in, which is what is implemented for the expensive high-rises. Of course, that is a lengthy story and well documented. High-rises are ideal, consistently popular residences for affluent singles, with all the guarded security intact. This is also an attractive place to live for some who are married but have no desire for grass and all the upkeep confronting anyone that owns a one-family dwelling."

This made Clare immediately think of Mason, who would have enthusiastically embraced that lifestyle, but his less affluent status could not support it.

"With the necessary renovations to attract their targeted market, they then have a starting point to exploit the situation. These luxury and semi luxury properties cause an increase in real estate taxes for the entire community, including homeowners, because of the concentration of wealth in a relatively small space. Then there are the more lucrative properties, the ones closest to the lake, creating a situation capable of forcing out all who are not of a select caliber."

"You mean black people," she interjected.

"Don't sound so somber. Remember, there are more poor whites than poor blacks, but their community, because of its wealth, can absorb many of their poor. Of course, that is another story altogether. In our community there are some who can afford to stay and who are possibly relieved regarding the ones that cannot. That group welcomes the transition as a long time coming, but upgrades and property maintenance can be pricey. And so, ultimately, this well-thought-out scheme ensnares those who can't keep up. This is where it gets thorny because this group is in the majority. It takes a while—oh, say, approximately ten to fifteen years, sometimes sooner—but eventually the entire neighborhood becomes very upscale. The unfortunate homeowners without the necessary means to remain—for property upkeep, increased taxes, et cetera—are forced to sell. This is the kicker. Because of the condition of the property, it will be bought from them for far below market value, and they will not be able to afford to purchase anything within the desirable proximity, and therefore, they'll have to move farther away to a neighborhood much less upscale, or to some of the less affluent suburbs. This is always the ulterior motive and repeated nationwide. Once the house is sold—most likely to a realtor who is involved in development of a more, well, let's say, robust environment—it can then be upgraded and sold for two to three times what was paid the former owner, which is the ulterior motive for the disruption: money! They make a killing. On the South Side, it is the reclaiming of their former neighborhoods, the reasons all those coach houses ever existed in the first place. And so the scramble—better known as gentrification—continues." He paused. "You do know about the Golden Rule, right?"

"Not 'do unto others'…" she began.

"No," he said with a chuckle. "It's he who has the gold makes the rule."

"You make it sound so grim," she replied.

"It can be, pretty lady, but enough of that," he said as they entered Chinatown.

Soon they had eaten their meal and were on their third cup of tea, which was not an impressive amount because the cups were typically small. The optional chopsticks for both were placed to one side, unused.

These people had managed to transport a small piece of China to America, she thought, and then pass it on from generation to generation, inviting other countrymen to come and join them. Thus, expansion of Chinatown was always in progression. It was such a unique culture, even though down through the generations some had lost their native tongue. She had attended DePaul with a few Chinese Americans who admitted they could neither speak nor write Mandarin, the official language of China. She liked the ambience and the paintings expressed in cool, quiet colors. She realized, as she scanned her surroundings, that the intricate details of the Far East were indeed unique, and this was only a glimpse of the largest country in Asia. She had read briefly about the Great Wall of China. She had been told by a black history professor that there had once existed a black dynasty in China, although the name escaped her. *I am in a foreign land*, she thought, *on American soil*; this caused a brief tinge of sadness.

"A penny for your thoughts," he said.

"I was thinking," she answered, a sad smile on her face, "that every ethnic group but ours has brought their culture with them to this country and successfully integrated it into the broader scheme. One political figure in Chicago always comments that because of our forced immigration, we alone are without country and currency."

"Remember this," he gently said: "Even though they tried with all their might to brutally beat it out of us and did manage to stifle it in many other ways, our music—ragtime, rhythm and blues, jazz, gospel—reigns as the only genuine American music and is celebrated worldwide, so some of our culture did survive through it all."

"You're right," she conceded thoughtfully. "I almost forgot about that."

"There were atrocities such as Rosewood, Black Wall Street, the Black Codes, Jim Crow, lynchings, Emmitt Till, and countless other gruesome events, rightfully defined as raw terrorism waged on American soil. Our music has influenced the world, so we did manage to salvage something very significant."

He paused when the waitress returned to ask if they wanted another refill of tea. Both declined, and Grady asked for the check.

---

"There was a restrictive covenant here in Chicago from 1916 to 1948," he said once he had the check, and they were alone again. "Did you know that?"

"No, I didn't, but it sounds right," she said. "Since to this day there are still neighborhoods where blacks are yet not welcome. I remember Marquette Park where Dr. King exposed how segregated Chicago was and still is."

"I used to go to Rush Street every once in a while," he said, "back in the sixties, and late one night a friend and I decided to enter this one club, only to be promptly stopped at the door and informed that admittance was 'for members only.'"

"Great tactic and a very convenient way to exclude the unwanted," she replied.

"Exactly," he said, chuckling ever so softly. "Chicago. Still in all, I love this city and have been blessed because it has paid me well. However, that friend now lives in one of the more affluent northern suburbs. I still see him from time to time. He's married with teenagers, and we often meet for a drink and have what I consider meaningful discussions."

As they left Chinatown, Clare silently bid farewell to the persistence of a culture that insisted on blending with rather than adapting to Western civilization. Entering the Dan Ryan, she attempted to imagine China itself on a grander scale and knew it could be a vacation of great educational value.

They merged with the traffic on the expressway traveling south, and she happened to glimpse the dashboard clock. She was amazed at how she lost track of time whenever she was with this man. He was very interesting, and they always found so much to talk about.

"We could take the Outer Drive," she suggested as they traveled south.

"Oh, so you are trying to get rid of me?" he teased. How he did like this little lady, so much. He found himself wanting to be involved even more, although he cautioned himself to take it slow.

"No, no," she answered quickly.

"Let's take the long route." He turned on the radio, which was tuned to the same jazz station as before. "I'd like to make a stop if you don't mind."

"Not at all," she replied.

❧

Clare and Nadine were having a lengthy discussion at Clare's kitchen table, and as was inevitable, the topic had turned to Grady Mayfield.

"We stopped by to see an old friend who just moved back to Chicago from California," Clare explained, recalling the last part of her date with Grady.

"This is encouraging," replied Nadine. She laughed softly. "Where does he live?"

"Southwest, near Beverly," she replied. "And why are you laughing?" Clare took a sip of her coffee. It was Saturday evening, and they had been shopping because, as always, Nadine wanted something new. This Saturday, Nadine had purchased just two pairs of lovely but expensive shoes. Clare had placed emphasis on "expensive," and Nadine had laughed, telling her not to be vulgar. Cornell was playing poker with friends this evening, so Nadine was in no hurry to get home.

"This is getting to be very interesting," Nadine said. "Next, it will be family."

"Not so fast," Clare protested mildly.

"No, I am being very practical. When men reach that age, they do a lot of procrastinating and soul searching, they enter a stage of cold feet, and then they spring it on you. That's what happened to me with Cornell, and one day out of the blue, he simply asked me if I was free to go house hunting."

"House hunting?"

"Yes, that was his proposal. When I asked him if he thought I wanted to do any kind of housekeeping without the nuptials, he simply stated that his intentions were honorable and told me to set the date, and that was that."

"And then it took you two almost a year to find a house that you liked."

"We were in no hurry. Cornell had a nice place in Lake Meadows," Nadine replied. "It sufficed until we found what we wanted. Plus, we were determined not to adhere to the norm and move in the vicinity of Old Orchard, if you know what I mean."

✧

It was Sunday morning and Clare had just hung up on talking to Nadine. The telephone rang once again. *She always does this*, she thought with a smile. Often, they could have a lengthy discussion as they had this morning, causing her to miss the eight o'clock church service. They would hang up and, a few minutes later, Nadine would call right back. "And one more thing," she would say. Clare picked up, smiling expectantly.

"So, you're not at church; you're home." It was Grady.

Her heart almost skipped a beat.

"Hello? Clare?"

"So how have you been?" she asked, not forgetting what her social coach, Nadine, had told her.

"I've been good. How about you?"

She paused briefly before answering. "I've been fine."

She had been contemplating going to the eleven o'clock church service. Talking to Nadine had made her miss the early one.

"Come out and play," he said. "Let's do brunch."

"May I ask where?" She wanted to know how to dress.

"Sure, a champagne brunch in Itasca." He paused. "Ever been there?"

"No, I haven't."

She wished she could play hard to get, but she liked him too much. They agreed that he would pick her up in an hour, at ten fifteen. She hung up slowly, thinking about how he kept her off-balance; she hadn't heard from him for over a week. He hadn't initially seemed like a man who played games, and she still couldn't be certain. She thought of their first date—planned, unhurried, genuine, the kind to which she was accustomed. Since then, everything had been spontaneous, impromptu, sporadic, and not her style for a meaningful relationship. It was like being a novice mountain climber unsure of where to securely plant your feet next. She wasn't certain that he had in mind or where it would lead. She liked him so much but tried to remind herself that part of the attraction might be the scarcity of eligible bachelors in the black community, especially of his caliber. On the other hand, her genuinely deep attraction would still make him a favorable choice.

*Well, there will be no church today*, she said to herself as she returned her red suit to the closet. What should she wear? She reached toward the back of the closet. The dress had been hung there waiting for the right occasion since March.

Her makeup, which she always wore sparingly, was fine. She changed from red to white underwear, kept on her skin-tone pantyhose, and slipped into that simple winter white dress with the shoulder detail. After stepping into her black suede pumps, she put on her white gold pendant adorned with small diamonds and matching earrings. The pendant had been a gift after her surgery from Uncle Ned, and the earrings had come from Max at the same time. Most likely they had made the purchases together. It was the most expensive set of jewelry she owned. She gave herself a quick once-over and found that her appearance met her approval.

The newspaper was still unopened on the living room floor beside her favorite chair. She sat down to wait but did not pick up the paper after all. The anticipation of seeing him was great. Oh, how she wished she didn't find him so attractive!

At ten twenty, the doorbell rang. She had not heard him drive up. When she opened the door, there he stood with his car keys in his hand, flashing that boyish grin and those beautiful white teeth.

"Ready?" He winked at her and hurriedly stepped inside out of the cold. He had left his overcoat in the car. "You look ready—you look gorgeous."

"Thank you. You're looking great yourself." She could tell the suit, as always, was expensive, as were the shoes.

She reached in the closet to get her coat, and he helped her slip into it. She left it unbuttoned, draping her silk, rectangular scarf over it. Even though it was only approaching the last of November, this was still Chicago. However, she didn't want to be too warm during the drive.

She turned to face him and stood expectantly, waiting for him to open the door, which he did. Suddenly, with his hand still on the doorknob, he leaned over and gave her a light but lingering kiss, arousing a response deep within her. As always, he smelled so good.

"I needed a proper hello," he said softly.

In the car on the way to the brunch, he talked with her about his business for the first time. He then talked about his favorite pastime, live entertainment, which he enjoyed whenever he could work it into his schedule. He talked about all the things he liked to do. He liked the simple things in life, including baseball games, which he had watched as a child with his father either in the Comiskey Park stadium or often on television. In the winter on Sundays, his only day of leisure, he loved to watch football, especially the Pittsburgh Steelers or the San Francisco Forty-49ers. His favorite games were played on New Year's Day and gave him an idea of which college players were going pro. He liked plays, select movies, and, like her, long walks. He loved visiting museums, browsing the art fairs, and at least once every summer, strolling around Navy Pier. He liked a limited amount of nightlife, especially on Fridays because he usually worked late, until nine or so, and he could stop off on his way home to watch people have a good time. When he was much younger, he had danced quite a bit, but now he was a spectator, except for an occasional slow dance. He loved music, his favorite genres being jazz and some blues artists of course, as they had discussed before. Although classical music was not totally unfamiliar, his was formally introduced while attending college. Still, he appreciated only select operas, arias, concertos, and symphonies. As for art appreciation, he liked black art and artifacts best even though art critics analyzed them as primitive. That in some circles this art was categorized as crude and simple did not matter to him. His analysis was that primitive meant nothing came before it.

When they arrived at the restaurant and she saw the buffets, the ostentatious display of food struck her as almost brazenly profane, and she thought that she now knew why so much of the country was hungry. One table had nothing but seafood, another only salads and fruits and vegetables, another breakfast food—eggs, bacon, ham, and so on. Throughout their meal, champagne was poured. She drank hers slowly, observing people as they came and went to and from the tables, filling their plates. *America! The Promised Land!* She wondered what was done with all the leftovers, which could benefit the homeless shelters throughout Chicago. This silk-stocking suburb with a wealthy tax base flourished with all the trappings of, if not opulent, vast comfort.

She ate from a plate filled with a fair amount of food as she enjoyed the entertainment provided by the male singer at the piano bar, who played excellently and sang old standards. When they left, it was a little before two o'clock, and she thanked him for a wonderful time.

They were cruising on the Dan Ryan when he invited her to come home with him. Well, it was about time she saw where he lived, she thought, and a few minutes later, they were on Lake Shore Drive headed toward Hyde Park. They exited the Drive at Forty-Seventh Street, and minutes later they pulled into his reserved indoor parking space. As they entered the complex, he started toward the mailbox and then postponed the action to instead guide her to the bank of north elevators. She was observant and secretly amused; the fact that he had hesitated was a dead giveaway. It was Sunday, not a mail delivery day, so she surmised he had not been home for any length of time this weekend. Where had he been over the weekend and with whom? She had mixed emotions and felt like her suspicions were confirmed: there was another woman somewhere.

Once inside his apartment, she found herself in the environment of a true bachelor, and although it was neat and clean, it was without fuss. His living room furniture was expensive chocolate brown leather, and the carpeting was tan, which she considered a nice combination.

"Would you care for anything to drink? Perhaps a soda?" he suggested as he hung her coat in the closet.

"Yes, I'd like a soda, but water first."

Earlier while traveling to brunch, and being a good listener, she hadn't revealed that she too was an ardent football fan. She told him now, and he was pleasantly surprised. Because they had come in during half-time of The Bears and the Detroit Lions game, they watched the second half. On another channel there was a later game, but he suggested music, and she agreed. So he put on some music—first a Coltrane album, just part of it, and then the Crusaders, whom she revealed as one of her favorite groups; part of an album by Rashaan Roland Kirk; and finally, Stanley Turrentine, because Clare said he was her very favorite. She loved what she described as that lonely city sax for which he was famous. It was beautiful, haunting in fact, and changed the mood for them both.

He had dated her enough to begin to focus on her—the fragrance she wore, her emotions of surprise or joy. He'd seen sadness briefly too, just that once, when she mentioned the death of her brother. So far, he had never witnessed her anger. He liked to watch her walk; her gait, to those who did not know her, might make her appear haughty or aloof. And he loved her laugh. Lately he'd caught himself thinking about her more often. Suddenly an image of her would break his concentration in the middle of a business day, and he would pause, entertain the emotion that came with that image, and then attempt to move on. Sometimes he was successful. If not, he gave in to the urge that accompanied the pleasant intrusion, especially on a day of leisure like Sunday, which resulted in a request to see her, like today. He was beginning to spend more time with her. He felt an urge to plan things they could do together yet had not acted on it.

They were sitting on the spacious leather sofa listening to Turrentine. She was talking, offering an innocent comment about the music, when he reached out and gently pulled her into his arms and kissed her, deeply, just barely allowing her to finish her sentence. He had wanted to do that ever since the brief kiss in her foyer. He kissed her again, forcing his tongue inside her mouth with passionate exploring, to which she responded. Suddenly they were engaged in more than just kissing. Her heartbeat quickened, and the desire that came over her was overwhelming. When she felt his hand on her back unzipping her dress, she pulled away.

Foremost, there was no commitment, no substance to these impromptu encounters. His casualness and nonchalant inconsistency made her uncomfortable. Her rationale for continuing this seesaw arrangement was that maybe, just maybe, if she was patient, something more meaningful would manifest. However, her better judgment dictated that she is not drawn into an arrangement that would place her in a precarious position.

"You're toying with me," she said quietly. "You see me and then stay away for a week. You see me and then stay away for nearly two weeks. Out of the blue you call again. I don't know what you want or what you expect." She looked almost bewildered. "I…" She stopped and shrugged, slowly shaking her head as if to clear the confusion. She didn't say that she cared so much and that she wanted to know if she could expect the same feelings from him. "I don't know where this is going," she concluded helplessly. She felt such disturbingly mixed emotions. What if he did not find her so appealing once he knew about her surgery? That added another dimension to her distress and caused such a profound feeling of anxiety.

"Could you please take me home?" she asked somberly.

She suddenly felt so defeated by his lack of commitment to any sort of schedule that would at least establish consistency. Meanwhile, the results of her surgery remained constant. She hated having to wait to receive reconstructive surgery. Then again, even that would not be hers, but something rebuilt as a replacement for the original. Her struggle with this part of her life and her body had not ever gone away. It remained a cloud over her private life.

"Sure," he responded agreeably to her request.

He got his coat and hers. Remembering her scarf, he returned to the closet to retrieve it from the hanger and then helped her on with both. He slipped into his own overcoat without his suit coat, which remained in the closet where he had hung it earlier.

Once inside the car, he drove in his shirtsleeves, and they rode all the way to her house in silence. The radio was tuned to the same jazz station; music was softly playing as they pulled up in front of her house. She wondered if she would ever see him again, if maybe he was a game player after all and wanted to remain unattached without commitment. She recalled his statement: without any live-in arrangements or entanglements whatsoever" was how he had phrased it. Some men with his attractiveness—with a lucrative business and most likely not super wealthy, but well-off—remained single because they did not want responsibility or because they simply preferred variety and had no interest in a monogamous relationship. Many thoughts coursed through her brain.

As they pulled up to her house, the movement of the curtain at the double window next door momentarily caught Clare's attention because it had happened before. *Mr. Willaby*, she thought in mild irritation, *you need a life.*

Turning off the motor, Grady turned toward her with one arm on the steering wheel. He did not want such a beautiful day to end badly. "How did you put it— 'toying with you'? Clare, I am not *toying* with you."

"What then?" she asked as her eyes met his, unwavering and steady.

He was silent for a moment. "Let's plan to do something Saturday," he said. A promise made to Helen attempted to surge forward from the back of his mind, but he thwarted it. At this particular juncture with Clare, he didn't want there to be any lapse of time. "We could go to a play, take in a movie, whatever you like—what do you say?"

Since their first date, this would be only their second outing together that was not a sporadic, last-minute undertaking. "Okay," she said quietly.

He examined her face with the aid of the streetlight. She was so different. He loved to watch the expressions in those beautiful eyes, which he was gradually learning to read. Suppressing the urge to reach out and touch her, he instead remained in the same position with his arm over the steering wheel. "Decide what you want to do, and then give me a call."

"Okay," she agreed.

Removing his arm from the steering wheel, he reached into the backseat to grab his overcoat. He helped her from the car and didn't let go of her hand until they were at her door. When finally, she stood securely in her doorway, he did not ask to come in or make a move to kiss her.

"Call me," he said, and turned to quickly descend the short flight of stairs.

From her living room bay window, she watched his car move slowly away from her block and then, like a grand panther, lurch to gather speed. He slowed down slightly to turn the corner and was gone.

Closing the drapes, she slipped out of her coat to hang it and her scarf in the foyer closet. Usually after coming in, she immediately took off her street clothes so that she could get comfortable. Instead, she sat in her favorite chair fully dressed and gazed for a long time at the unread Sunday paper, without focusing on it. She was thinking of how high her spirits had been when she talked with Nadine that morning and about today's church service that she hadn't attended. One phone call, and the entire day had become unscheduled and unplanned. On seldom occasions that was fine, but it was becoming a regular occurrence, sending her into fluctuating mood swings of despondency and anxiousness. What if he began dating her consistently and consequently, inevitably, she told him about her surgery? What would happen then? Would he run like Karl? She had known Karl for more than three years, and he had chosen to recoil into the arms of a wife he had previously been planning to divorce. A sudden reprimand intercepted her thoughts: *You don't have the confidence you once had, and you need to reclaim it! Know that this man won't flinch if he cares about you. What did Gran Jennie say about bridges? You must envision the other side, so think good thoughts.*

However, the cause of her melancholy was twofold. There were all the telltale signs that he was seeing someone else, someone scheduled in his life and consistently on his weekly agenda. She also had been seeing someone else, but Bernard had never been under consideration for anything permanent.

Who would have thought that she would go grocery shopping and meet someone like Grady Mayfield? Now she had known him since the middle of July—a little over four precarious months. She never knew when he would call or want to see her. Sometimes he would call to just say hello, but this always occurred during work hours. He would simply say that he was calling to see how she was doing or that he was thinking about her. Or he would say something funny and prompt laughter from them both. Often her anticipation would be so intense whenever the telephone rang, but then the call would not be from him. When he did call, she was like a delighted schoolgirl fighting hard to remain composed. He would always begin without preamble, briefly talk about a few insignificant things, and then bid her good-bye—just like that—and hang up. He might call her again at home during the weekend to ask her out, unplanned, spontaneously, relatively late at night, or early in the evening, but only twice was it for a Saturday. That their dates took place on either Fridays or Sundays was the only consistency in their otherwise sporadic dating. This made her extremely cognizant of Saturdays being reserved for someone he saw on a regular basis. Often, she longed for the days when her suitors were numerous, to add additional spice to the pursuit, ever so aware that choices and opportunities decreased with age.

Bernard was a nice enough guy but lacked panache, which was hard to pull off without financial resources. It wasn't just that; there were other factors. He was also a divorcé living with his mother as he supported his two children who resided with their mother, his ex-wife. He was not a man with any skills beyond his liberal arts bachelor's degree. The courts had granted the mother of his two daughters a house in the suburbs along with the newer car and, finally, generous child support. More than once he had mentioned his inability to afford a place of his own on the salary from his day and evening jobs. Being sensitive to his lack of financial stability, they engaged in a routine of rigid, economical dating that seldom made romance blossom. They spent quiet evenings at the movies or Sundays with their children at the museum or the zoo. In the summertime they attended free concerts in Grant Park or took long walks on the lakefront and, finally, spent evenings at her home because he could not afford privacy of his own. This made their adult relationship seem like a high school courtship and restricted entertainment to her living room.

She thought about another time, a younger time, when she was in college. It was a time when she had her pick of eligible men. Curtis was a schoolteacher. Donald was a premed student. Byron, several years older, had been married once, though, he always stated, "without children, thank the Lord, Jehovah, Allah, Buddha, and all the others!"

With Byron, what had been said in jest was reflective of his feelings generally: he wanted no children. This allowed her to be forever satisfied with rejecting his marriage proposal. He owned his own home and several properties in the city, south and west. Through the grapevine she'd heard that he had married again, sold all his properties, and moved back to his hometown of Tallahassee, Florida. She recalled that he lived well. She was positive that he had purchased a beautiful spread in Florida for him and his wife to share, which was the Byron way— without children!

Curtis never had an opportunity to propose marriage because Clare's preference had become Donald, whose tentative plan to attend medical school gradually became fact. This would have pushed the nuptial date at least six years into the future. At that point in time, marriage was only a remote interest for her anyway because her focus was education. Since she was attending college year-round, she had never anticipated that it would take her as long as it did to finish, but various interruptions slowed her plans. However, the strain on their relationship had already begun. Looking back, she was unable to pinpoint exactly when they had begun to drift apart. She was plagued by financial problems throughout the years she spent acquiring her education.

Now as she sat in her living room in tranquil solitude, only the ticking of the clock on the mantle could be heard as she examined the path she had stubbornly chosen. Yes, she had achieved her goal of being educated. She was also very single.

ℇ

Where Helen was concerned, this was new for Grady, and he knew he had to handle it with at least reasonable tactfulness. True, occasionally, he did spend Saturdays away from her, but never before had there been anything of this nature. In his younger days, he had struggled to be truthful without coming off as cold, a flaw in his otherwise charming and kind demeanor. Maturity had allowed him to refine his personality and tone down that particular trait, making him less indifferent and uncaring. However, if he was not careful, sometimes the tendency still surfaced and rose above that fine-tuned veneer it had taken him years to perfect.

So far, he has been considerate and respectful. While at her place for the night, he continued to procrastinate, unsure of exactly how he was going to delicately break a promise without specifics, what he deemed a soft lie. It was after his shower and a couple cups of coffee, while he was getting dressed, that he finally told her. She wanted to know why and continued to press, gently of course, for the reason for the change in plans. Her persistence in reminding him that the trip had been scheduled for over a month was causing him mild irritation; he had purchased their roundtrip tickets. Grady hated avoidable arguments, and he was not going to tell her why.

He stood in the doorway of her condo, car keys in his hand. Her face held a peculiar expression, but she did not speak harshly. "This is the first time you haven't kept a promise," she said with hurt surprise. "Bridgette is expecting both of us to come, Grady."

Grady had met Bridgette a few years back before her move to Detroit to work for Ford. "The airfare is paid, so take a friend if you wish." The words slipped out before he thought about them, and his inner voice chided, *Hey, careful! Now that's cold.*

"I apologize for that, Helen," he said quietly, "but I cannot go with you." He paused. "I can, however, take you to the airport and pick you up. How's that?"

She was hurt. He could hear it in her voice and see it in her face. He could tell that at first, she'd thought he was joking because he often teased her, though not about things so fragile. This was an unfamiliar side of the man she had grown to love and respect.

"I can take a limousine."

"Helen, come on," he coaxed gently. "Let me take you to the airport and pick you up. I want to."

"I'll take a limousine," she said just above a whisper.

They seldom argued, and this conversation was headed there, so he relented. "Let's do something when you get back," he said. He started to say that perhaps next weekend they could plan something, but then he thought better of it.

*You have never been into game playing,* that inner counsel cautioned. *You've known Helen for a long time, and the two of you have always had a good relationship. Most of your Saturdays are spent with her, and now things are changing. It's probably best that you say nothing until she returns from Detroit.*

She was now sitting at her breakfast table having her last cup of coffee before getting ready to go to the hospital. Helen had been a registered nurse for over twenty-five years. He hesitated and then left the doorway to walk back to the table and deliver a kiss to her cheek. *You're not kissing your mother,* he reminded himself. He brushed her lips lightly. "I'll call you later."

Except for those two previous and relatively brief intervals when he'd spent less time with Helen, she had been the steadiest woman in his life for a long time.

"You know you keep Helen because she's older and can't stick you with any crumb snatchers," Bradley had teased. "She's that dependable 'significant other' without being a wife. She's your security blanket, my man, that smooth groove. There are things in these streets these days that don't turn you loose."

He had agreed with his friend and business partner and could yet hear his own chuckle to somewhat dilute the seriousness of the conversation. *Smooth groove* thought Grady. Bradley had said more than once that his ties to Helen were like spinning your tires, a smooth groove—an icy ditch. His favorite description of her was "security blanket."

Helen was now approaching her mid-fifties but looked younger. No one would ever believe she was a day over forty-five. With her statuesque elegance, she fit the description of the type of women Grady had always dated. Helen in turn loved showing Grady off to her friends at the parties and social gatherings that they sometimes attended. Possessing a cool and reserved persona, she resembled his first wife, Olivia, but was more dignified, without the fast-track pizzazz.

Clare called him at the office Wednesday morning just before he was due to leave to go to a closing, to discuss what was to be their second planned date. She suggested that they attend Nadine and Cornell's housewarming, if that was okay with him. No, he did not object at all, he said. At last, he would be able to link that name to a live person. The affair was being held Saturday evening, she said. He was to pick her up at seven.

∾

The house was nestled in a plush south suburban cul-de-sac. He commented on the odd time of year for a housewarming, but Clare assured him it would be fine because Nadine knew legions of people. Nadine had brought up the possibility of a winter housewarming to Clare about a month ago, and Clare had reassured her that it was not written in stone they had to be given during the warmer months. When they parked in the driveway, Grady was impressed. The house was made of light stone and had magnificent curb appeal that could be detected even in this weather—what Bradley West called "lure." When Clare directed him to pull up in a particular unoccupied spot in the driveway, he knew it was reserved for them because other cars were parked everywhere. Their hostess greeted them before they pressed the bell, opening the door with a cheerful smile and quickly ushering them inside. Grady placed the large gift from Clare on the foyer floor. Immediately one of Nadine's friends greeted them and whisked the gift away to put it with the

others.

"Nadine Bennett, Grady Mayfield," said Clare.

Finally, he met Nadine who was nothing like he expected. Her handshake was strong, and she had the sincerest smile. They hit it off immediately.

Cornell walked up as they were taking off their coats and kissed Clare on the cheek.

Cornell Bennett, meet Grady Mayfield," Clare said.

The two men shook hands. The four of them briefly engaged in idle chat, and then Cornell whisked Grady away to mingle with the crowd.

A mutual acquaintance of both Nadine and Clare came up to them just as they were emerging from the foyer, and another guest joined the small circle at the same time, exclaiming, "Such a beautiful the house!" It was, and there were wall-to-wall people inside it.

Nadine gave Clare the grand tour. The fireplace was solid ivory marble with beige stone cascading from the ceiling to the floor. The house featured all the trappings common to homes on the high-end scale, which this one certainly was: the large master bedroom with an adjoining sitting room; a private bathroom in Italian porcelain with a corner whirlpool tub, a separate shower, and double face bowls enhanced with granite countertops; vaulted ceilings; granite countertops in the kitchen; a balcony enhanced by a skylight overlooking the great room below; and on the first floor, near the side door, a mudroom. Nadine's tour then took them to the back of the house, off the dining room, where there was a large, enclosed, heated patio. A beautiful red hibiscus plant caught Clare's eye, and she saw that there were other tropical plants too, causing this to instantly become Clare's favorite place in the entire house. There was also a deck with an attached screened gazebo, the perfect hideaway for gatherings on warm summer nights. It was a striking deep sage green, complementing the light stone of the house. Nadine commented to Clare that she and Grady would have to come back during the midsummer months when the yard was in full bloom. This summer show had been part of the broker's sales pitch, presented in photos when he showed them the house that fall, when only mums and weigela shrubs (known to bloom from late spring to frost) had been in showy display. This garden was one of the most beautiful for blocks, Nadine explained, because the previous owner was a horticulturist.

When Nadine was still looking at houses, she would call Clare and walk her through each house she toured, and when Cornell could not go with her, Clare did. House hunting had been difficult because Nadine was determined not to move north. Finally, in late fall, she had stepped into what she considered the ideal property, and they had moved in quickly before being overtaken by cold weather. This inconvenience had caused a late start in planning the color schemes, purchasing the furnishings, selecting the drapes, and so on.

Someone presently waved from across the living room to Clare just as one of Nadine's guests said she still wanted to take the much-anticipated tour, so Nadine and Clare temporarily parted. Upon her return, Nadine observed Grady meandering through the crowd with Cornell, drinks in hand as they stopped to join others, drinking and conversing. Clare was mingling with some of the ladies and a few of the male guests. Nadine smiled to herself as she watched Grady with Cornell, intermittently stopping to converse with guests. Now, she just wanted to observe Clare and Grady as a couple. Later Nadine commented to Clare that she had failed to mention brother man's flawless, golden-brown complexion; his eyes discreetly followed Clare around the room as she interacted with some of the people she knew. Women were giving Grady the eye because he was indeed an attractive man. Nadine was curious about the rest of the Mayfield clan.

She watched Clare toy with her drink. She used to tease Clare about her drinking habits, how she could sip one drink for an entire evening. Finally, having made their rounds, Grady and Cornell approached the area where Clare was standing with some of the other guests. Grady joined Clare, and as he did, she looked up at him in the most alluring way. Nadine could always tell when Clare was deeply attracted to a man because she was noticeably shy, as she was now. Yes, things were getting interesting to say the least.

# Chapter Nineteen

Clare still could not come to grips with the effects that her bout with cancer had on her, how she couldn't escape feeling in limbo. She couldn't shake the sense of being emotionally afloat, like being the new swimmer on the team who wore the life jacket.

She and Nadine were walking north down Michigan avenue after leaving Marshall Field and stopping on Wabash for lunch. Clare's current silence stemmed from a dress that had caught her eye at Field's. She enthusiastically tried it on, but it was cut slightly too low on the side-front, revealing just a tiny bit of the surgical scar that the bra did not conceal. Smiling sadly, she silently returned the beautiful dress to the attending salesclerk. Her expression said it all, even as that inner voice was encouraging her to seize control of her new existence instead of hovering timidly in the shadows. She felt that her mood was placing a cloud of somberness over their entire shopping excursion; neither woman had any packages.

They crossed the bridge at East Wacker with the famous Chicago River flowing beneath it and entered the Magnificent Mile of North

Michigan Avenue. In her attempts to calm her melancholy mood and avoid thinking, Clare diverted her attention to the buildings. To the left facing Michigan Avenue was the Beaux Arts Wrigley Building and Tribune Tower. Immediately west of those was the formidably huge Merchandise Mart, opposite the Hyatt Regency. Both faced the river but were separated by the Magnificent Mile.

As they passed the home of the peacock, the NBC building, Clare thought about how much tourists loved this section of Michigan Avenue. They oohed and aahed, frantically snapping pictures. They would start their sightseeing tours either across the bridge opposite East Wacker, traveling north, or around Oak Street, trekking south. Either way, from all over the United States and abroad they would visit and then return home to proudly share with friends and family their trip to the Windy City, captured in photographs.

Those not familiar with Wacker Drive often found it to be somewhat confusing, as she had when much younger. Not only did it run east and west along the Chicago River, but it *bridged* the Chicago River as well, traveling parallel to LaSalle, north and south. To make matters even more confusing, there was also a Lower Wacker that traveled in amazing proximity to the road above.

Further along, Clare and Nadine intermittently paused to engage in window shopping. Burberry was a very upscale store, with rigidly classic fashions such as the London Fog trench coat and other standard apparel. Seldom did they enter any of these ground-level enterprises unless something in the display windows got their attention. Of course, there were other stores further along the avenue. There was Saks Fifth Avenue, which they did enter from time to time, but they never got past the fragrance counters. Also, there was Neiman-Marcus, which some, in jest, labeled "Needless Markup."

During the summer, Clare always observed who was impeccably attired and who didn't adhere to chic. However, today it was cold, and everyone was appropriately armored to combat the dip in the Chicago thermometer; some even wore fur coats. Both Clare and Nadine were wearing their shearling. On this evening the sun was descending aggressively, and the temperature encouraged them to step briskly.

"Want to go in Crate and Barrel?" asked Nadine mostly to break the silence. Clare nodded her approval, and they crossed to the west side of the street to browse the store but found nothing of interest. They exited and continued walking toward Water Tower Place, always their ultimate destination, even though often they left the shopping center without additional packages.

"I'm sorry," Clare said.

Nadine frowned. "For what?" she asked.

"I'm not very good company."

Clare's previous mood had again returned as they continued their stroll down Michigan. When they reached the intersection at Chicago Avenue, they crossed to the east side of the street to briefly tarry in the small park across from Water Tower Place, named after the adjacent landmark, the Old Water Tower.

"I feel like this most powerful deity," she now explained to Nadine, "is in full control and calling me out to the front of the line to mete out this punishment just because it can. I feel so helpless, as if I'm waning, ebbing away slowly. The doctor says that I am cured, but I don't feel whole because part of me is missing; part of me was taken in order to get rid of what could kill me."

Nadine tenderly grabbed the hand of her dearest friend. "I long for the restoration of the confident Clare, that old Clare who had her share of beaus and suitors. I realize that this is a different time, but I still want the resurrection of that old Clare. I detest what this disease has done to you. Clare, you are a beautiful human being. There is a hesitation in you regarding all things personal, especially where men are involved. I see that certain anxiety persistently managing to surface in various ways, and I want the old Clare to take center stage and push out this imposter. As I have said before," Nadine continued quietly, "I could not begin to know what you are going through, Clare, and don't profess to, but I beseech you to try doubting yourself less. Enjoy life for the moment; live in the present. Try living for now."

"I wish I could be different," Clare said over the noise of the traffic, the people, and the distracting aggravation of the pigeons, often fed by those who frequented the small park. They solicitously waddled about in proximity. *When do they ever go away?* she thought. "I try, honestly; I do try," she said. She shook her head helplessly. "It's an entirely new way of life, in every respect," she said quietly. "It's been almost a year, and I cannot get used to it. Maybe if I didn't have to wait on the breast reconstruction… I guess…" She shrugged helplessly. "I don't know."

She never told anyone that her ongoing melancholy was influenced by Grady Mayfield, that she was preoccupied with the probability of having to tell him her secret and her fear of his reaction to it.

"Clare, I hope that I don't sound cruel, but you have to try harder to be happy. Try to be comfortable in your skin beyond this disease, which you must convince yourself is behind you. I notice how whenever a man looks your way, you look in the opposite direction, and you used to love indulging in innocent flirtation. You have not been deposited on the shelf, sweetheart. You are still a beautiful woman worthy of a man's affection. You cannot continue this attitude, especially now, because I don't think Grady is going anywhere." Nadine didn't know how she knew this, but she knew. "I know you still think about your experience with Karl. He was an ass, and you must not allow the way he acted to color what you can have with someone else. Know this: the fact that you are still here, cancer-free, is proof that God has bigger and brighter plans for your life, my friend. Embrace life's new lease," encouraged Nadine, "and ask that higher power to lead you to those new beginnings that he has in store. Promise me." She pressed for a response. "Promise me."

"Okay," she replied quietly, "I will work on a better attitude."

"Right on," replied her friend, smiling. "Now let's continue shopping."

They struck out across the park to enter Water Tower Place for what turned out to be the balance of a fun afternoon.

◌

Having skipped her routinely large lunch, Clare now sat in the mezzanine eatery of Water Tower Place, awaiting the arrival of Sharla Kantor. She observed people as they got on and off the escalator, and each time she saw the head of a blonde, she paid close attention. Suddenly she heard a familiar voice, and turning her head, she saw the smiling face of Sharla.

"Where were you?" Clare asked cheerfully.

"On the other side where I reserved a table for us," Sharla replied. She had left her coat to reserve their table, but with her she carried a package. "I've been watching for you and decided to get up and do a search. Come on."

"What did you buy?" Clare inquired, pointing to the Lord& Taylor bag as she followed Sharla to their table.

"My mother celebrates another birthday in a week. She's practically a yuletide baby. I bought her favorite fragrance to give to her now so that the two celebrations won't coincide." The approaching holiday was only three weeks away.

"I didn't know you celebrated Christmas, Sharla," she said.

"Only my father is Jewish," she answered kindly and smiled. "It's a mixed marriage, dear. Remember?"

Clare had forgotten. She smiled apologetically. "Now I remember," she said.

"Anyway," Sharla continued, "she's almost out of her favorite and needs cheering up. She's beginning to exhibit symptoms of throwaway-itis." She placed her package inconspicuously to the side of her seat underneath her coat; Clare placed her coat on the back of her chair.

Most of the restaurants were open-counter walk-ups. You could make your selections and even observe them while preparing your order.

"What are you eating?" asked Sharla.

"Stir-fry—I love their stir-fry."

"Oh, you're just so disciplined, as always," Sharla teased. "I'm having something fattening."

"We'll meet back here," Clare said as she headed for the stir-fry counter.

About twenty minutes later, Clare came back balancing a tray of stir-fry with chicken and her drink. Sharla was already eating her spaghetti with meatballs and a small, tossed salad. They sat quietly eating their meals, drinking their beverages, and observing the people.

"So," said Sharla after a while, "what are you doing this weekend?"

"I have nothing planned, at least not yet" Clare replied.

She attempted to banish thoughts of Grady since she had no idea when he was going to ask her out again. Disappointingly, he had lapsed back into the sporadic dating pattern of Fridays or Sundays, which meant that the housewarming affair had changed nothing. He did call more often, but that was usually when she was at work. When she mentioned this to Nadine, her friend countered those doubts by encouraging her to hang in there and, in reference to conversation, to keep it light and upbeat. "Thus far," she told Nadine, "I'm always well wined and dined at least." She had to admit that with him dates were never dull although their inconsistency upset her emotional equilibrium.

As much as Clare longed to discuss Grady with someone other than Nadine, she did not trust Sharla to be the appropriate confidant. Perhaps she should discuss him with Estelle and then insert her sentiments about Max. It would be a suitable approach to exploring why those two had not married.

Constantly mindful of cultural differences between herself and Sharla, Clare always kept her contributions to the conversations on the surface. In contrast, this woman from her college days shared very personal information without the least inhibition.

As Sharla talked, Clare thought about the shopping spree she'd taken with Nadine the past weekend. For her, this time of year included a few insignificant Christmas gifts, including fun gifts for her favorite students and a party of cake and punch for all (her favorite students were those with potential who needed motivation to continue their upward mobility climb toward success). Clare believed Nadine's incessant shopping, however, to be a needed diversion. Missing from her life were children she wanted desperately but couldn't have. She and Cornell were considering adoption, but that had the potential to become a thorny issue. Cornell's daughter, Kimberly, would need to be prepared for such an undertaking. *Enough with the distractions!* Clare thought.

"What are you doing this weekend?" she now asked Sharla. She was willing to stay in the present and avoid the mental drift, which she frequently engaged in during time spent with Sharla, when she was avoiding in-depth discussions.

"A girlfriend of mine is pregnant," Sharla said, "and a mutual friend is throwing her a baby shower. This couple has been trying to get pregnant for almost eleven years."

It was evident that she was beginning to get back in the mix since her arrival from the Big Apple, even though she was starting to complain that she wasn't meeting guys. Sharla, like Nadine, had a far-reaching circle of acquaintances. She intimated that there was one single fellow at work who was always asking her out, but her policy was never to mix business with pleasure.

"And anything else?" Clare questioned.

"Taking my mother out to dinner," she said, "even though I'm a poor substitute for what she's missing." She paused. "Do you know that although I have been back for over a year and continue to leave messages at my dad's office, he has only called me twice? I guess he's ashamed, as he should be. He and the love of his current life have set up housekeeping on this side of wedlock. My mother found out through the grapevine."

"You make it sound like the poor woman is expecting," Clare said, laughing, and then she forced her mood to match Sharla's soberness. "Sometimes people simply grow apart; it happens."

"Are you talking about the mother that used to be married to the father or the father who still has a daughter?"

"That sounds like a riddle," Clare said. "I'm talking about your mother and father of course."

"Well," she answered, "I think he did what a lot of older men do—traded in the older model for something younger and considered more beautiful, a younger, sexier, sleeker body, like buying a new car."

"Umm," Clare mused, "I think that is bound to play out eventually because there is going to come a time when his depreciation is far outpacing hers, unless the bank account remains substantial. Not to mention how he will have to extend his own personal warranty by looking comparably good with his clothes off. That means frequent tune-ups. Does he exercise?"

"Oh, you are still so very pragmatic, Clare Ingram," she replied. "Yes, he does, but I don't know if it's on a regular basis like he used to back when I was still at home." She paused. "Anyway, his head is in the clouds."

"My grandmother used to call that being in heaven with your feet hanging out."

This caused a mild eruption of laughter from Sharla. "I have never heard that one before," she said as she regained her composure.

Her reaction prompted a smile from Clare, who knew the expression as cultural. In fact, her mother and grandmother had often used the phrase.

"Does she talk about it?" Clare asked moments later. "Your mother?"

"No," she replied, "just that one time, and from then on, mum's been the word."

"Does she have any outside interests with girlfriends? That always helps. Maybe she and some of her friends should take a vacation because a change of scenery is always helpful. A cruise would be nice."

"The same Clare," Sharla commented, thinking how she still deciphered and worked with the pieces so that they were a perfect fit.

"Have you done your Christmas shopping yet?"

"No," Sharla answered. "How about you?"

"Just a few things," Clare answered. "My family is small, so the gifts are few." She thought of Grady. Should she or should she not purchase a gift for him?

Overall, the evening with Sharla was pleasant. They finished their meal and afterward talked for approximately an hour. When they concluded their friendly time together, as always, Clare was privy to a lot more information about Sharla's affairs than she had shared about her own. Outside of Nadine, her closest and dearest friend, Clare had mostly acquaintances and had to admit that she was a very private person. Somehow, though, she did want this friendship with Sharla to be one of substance, but to date she had not been able to bring herself to share anything personal about herself with this woman, this Caucasian woman, who genuinely befriended her. There was a mutual respect and admiration, as there had always been. However, she felt that now they had reached a fork in the road in their relationship. Both had matured beyond DePaul, where they had been considerably younger. So, to maintain something lasting, Clare would have to become more open, as Sharla had always been willing to do. Otherwise, the scale would remain tilted, and they would drift apart.

*Next time*, she thought, as they parted on State Street and went their separate ways. Sharla of course was taking the commuter train to the suburbs, and Clare's means of transportation was the CTA.

❧

Before the close of business for the Christmas holiday, Grady had caused a mild flurry of activity at her office when the delivery man approached her door with one of the largest, most magnificent poinsettias all had ever seen with an innovative (special order) arrangement of surrounding plants and a card that read:

> *Hey, Little Girl,*
>
> *This is to keep things growing long after Christmas is over. Call me when it arrives.*
>
> *Grady*

Grace, her assistant, had stuck her head in the doorway, smiling brightly. "My dear," she had exclaimed with laughter, "that is nothing less than a poinsettia bush surrounded by a miniature nursery!"

Clare had smiled as Grace quickly disappeared from her doorway. She had to admit it was a gorgeous plant in the center of other healthy, luscious plants. It belonged on the floor instead of her credenza, but she liked the idea of it gracing her office as a small tree. It was one that she did not have to adorn and wished had been sent to her home instead. Placed in her living room bay window, it would spare her the mild agitation of being upstaged by her neighbors.

Her attempt to telephone Grady to thank him was not successful. Someone named Ursula cheerfully informed her that he was out of the office but had promised to be back before closing time. When Clare returned to her office following her company's large Christmas party that had taken place on another floor, he was still not back, and the same Ursula apologized and said his return was taking longer than expected. Their office was closing for the holidays. Before hanging up, two women exchanged happy holiday wishes.

⁊

In two days, it would be Christmas again, Clare thought, as she assisted Estelle in decorating her tree. Although each year Clare only placed a "Merry Christmas" wreath in her own bay window with a few decorative lights, she annually came to her mother's home to assist her in creating a full array of holiday cheer. Of course, Max was there, and the three of them were enjoying eggnog spiked heavily with brandy. When Estelle began the refills, Clare protested that she wanted only eggnog this time, thank you very much.

"Lapsing into a teetotaler?" Max teased.

"Temporarily," she replied, handing another ornament to Estelle. "Mama is heavy-handed with the booze."

"It's the yuletide season," Estelle replied in good-natured protest.

Clare recalled that even when she and Jeffrey were children, their mother had made certain there was hard candy, plenty of various nuts, Christmas cookies, and cakes, but especially a fruit cake, pies, and a tree. The gifts did not appear until Christmas morning, based on the assumption that they were left by that roly-poly man dressed in red. Even though Mason had disagreed with his children believing in Santa Claus, he relented because their mother was adamantly against omitting that part of her children's formative years.

It was during Clare and Jeffrey's absence, of course, that Estelle had told Mason sternly that all children should entertain fantasies as part of the joy of childhood. Each of us should nourish the child inside, she believed. In some respects, we should guard it and never allow it to grow up, never allow the adult in us to rationalize it away. It was that childlike aspect that allowed adults to create programs like *Sesame Street* and cartoon characters for the world to enjoy. Childhood memories can sustain a person through various difficulties, enabling them to delve into their mental file of happy times and withdraw the beauty necessary to get through life's inevitable bad times. This was a good portion of what was wrong with Mason, Estelle thought. He clung to too many bad memories, which nullified his ability to be either an understanding adult or a good parent. And yes, their children would have Santa Claus!

❧

At the time the decision had angered Mason, but he knew whenever his wife's ire matched his own, he would lose.

In the present, Max was there for Estelle, as always, and it baffled Clare that they were not yet married. Why on God's good earth did she not marry the man? Clare speculated that he had asked, perhaps more than once. He never missed any special occasion, and they always attended church together. Estelle, an usher at her church with a small congregation, ribbed him about being a "benchwarmer" and not joining her church to become a participant, which he easily defended. No, he was not a member, but simply attended in support of her membership, and to bring silence to her potentially mounting dissatisfaction, he gently reminded her that when the plate was passed, his contributions were, with consistency, substantial. He knew and did not mind that she was a devout Baptist "sister," but he had always belonged to an ecumenical church and, even though he was seldom in attendance, continued to give it his financial support.

Now was the time for the final adornment to be placed at the very top of the magnificently trimmed tree. It was a black angel that Estelle had ordered years ago from a catalogue whose store was in Harlem, New York. Max did the honors and afterward called out, "Lights please!" Clare obliged, and they all stepped back and looked. It was a beautiful tree, and the party of three cheered.

When Clare arrived home, there were three messages on her answering machine.

"Merry Christmas," the voice said. Telephone calls from Bernard had almost ceased, and she was mildly shocked to hear from him. "I just thought I would call to see if you would like to have a drink, just for old time's sake. If so, give me a call, and if not, that's okay. Have a great holiday."

"I have been trying to contact you all day," the second voice said. "Please call me as soon as you get this message." The telephone number was not familiar. Was that Nadine? It *was* Nadine. She sounded so different, distraught even, causing Clare to feel fearful. What could possibly be wrong?

Hurriedly, she dialed the number she had taken down. Clare's heart almost skipped a beat when she got what was identified as a nurse's station but held on as instructed and then Nadine was on the phone.

"We're at Mercy Hospital," she was saying miserably. "Could you please come?"

"Of course," she replied anxiously. "Nadine," Clare asked with deep concern, "what's wrong. Are you okay?"

"Yes, I'm fine. I'll explain when you get here," she said.

"I'm on my way right now," Clare said.

Although now preoccupied, she listened to her last message; it was Grady. "Hi. I need to apologize for not calling you earlier. I telephoned your office yesterday, got detained, and didn't call back, but I did get your message. Whenever you get in, call me… Oh if you don't reach me at home, page me." He quickly gave his pager number before hanging up.

Clare, delighted to hear from Grady but deeply concerned about Nadine, hurriedly wrote down his pager information and slipped it into her purse. *Perhaps his intentions are going to become clear*, she thought. So far, it was not clear what Grady Mayfield had in mind. Nadine had predicted that he would step it up. So far, Clare was unsure of exactly when that would occur.

Shortly thereafter Clare was on her way to a place that brought up unpleasant memories, which she fought off. *Same place, different date,* she thought as she pulled into the visitors' parking lot. What could possibly be wrong?

Nadine was waiting for Clare when she emerged from the bank of elevators, and the friends embraced. Cornell was in the waiting room seated next to an older woman whom Nadine introduced as Roxanne Judd, Natalie's mother. Clare hugged Cornell, who looked worried and haggard.

Natalie, Cornell's first wife and the mother of their daughter, Kimberly, was in the ICU because she had run a stop sign and was broadsided by a mail truck from the passenger's side; that she wasn't hit on the driver's side was the sole reason she was still alive. It got even more complicated: Natalie was also high on cocaine. Much to Cornell's dismay and without his knowledge, she had now been abusing drugs for almost two years.

Nadine pulled Clare aside and said quietly, "We've been here for over twelve hours, and they worked on her in the ER nonstop for almost three to stabilize her before they transferred her to ICU," she said.

Clare was initially speechless, almost disoriented from the impact of such news. "Where is Kimberly?" she asked in an almost hushed tone.

Cornell joined them momentarily. "She is with Natalie's sister," he replied just above a whisper, "who was here earlier. She wanted to shield Kim from all this, so she took her home with her. I can't believe this," he said, his disbelief on the verge of anger. "I never knew about any of it."

The mental prompt was like an afterthought. Clare excused herself, and one of the nurses directed her to a bank of telephones located on another floor. Ten minutes later, after contacting Grady to let him know what was happening, she was back. He was home and glad to hear from her. He wanted to come to where she was, if she didn't mind.

Suddenly the doctors and some of the nurses began scurrying in haste to the ICU in response to a code blue. When Roxanne approached the nurses' station, followed by Cornell and Nadine, she was directed back to the waiting room with a promise that one of the doctors would be with them as soon as possible. Nearly an hour later, a doctor approached them with that learned professional demeanor, to prepare them for the possibility of the worst: Natalie's condition was unfavorable and complicated by her drug use.

Roxanne began crying profusely, and Cornell placed a consoling arm about her shoulders. He tried to eject the thought from his mind, but he wondered how long she had known about Natalie's habit. He was positive that she must have known for some time, and he would question her about it later, but now was not the appropriate time.

The hands on the clock dragged as everyone anxiously awaited word from the ICU. Roxanne, upon request, was admitted in to see her daughter, which turned out to be not such a good idea, for when she came back from the room, she was even more grieved than before. She was terribly frightened as she described her daughter's appearance and the tubes everywhere. She pressed the doctor to tell her exactly what to expect, and so he did. Even if she lived, there was the possibility of other problems. Presently, they were trying to stabilize her so that they could operate to repair one of her lungs and a ruptured bladder.

Cornell said that he had to take a walk, and Nadine knew what that meant, that he was smoking again. She thought he had stopped.

When he returned a little later, a smile tugged at the edges of his lips. "Look who I brought with me," he told them. Grady stood beside him.

Grady kissed Nadine on the cheek and then put his arm gently about Clare's shoulders as Cornell introduced him to Natalie's mother. Grady said a few consoling words to her as he shook her hand. The small kindness triggered more emotion, and once more the tears began streaming.

They all needed a little break from this environment. "Let's all go somewhere," Grady suggested, "and have a bite to eat." He paused. "Gladys's is near here, so let's go there."

The meal turned out to be a reprieve that hospital cafeterias could never provide. They talked for a few minutes after the meal was over, and Grady paid the entire bill over the protest of all. Roxanne, becoming anxious, wanted to return to the hospital.

When they got off the elevator and returned to the waiting room, one of the nurses summoned Mrs. Judd to the nurses' station. The doctor was there to inform Roxanne that Natalie had lapsed into a coma. He explained that she was probably in excruciating pain, and things looked grim. Often the only way the body can deal with such extensive pain, he said, is to escape in the only way it knows how; they would know more in the morning. However, a few hours later, there was another code blue, and Natalie died.

Grady jotted down Nadine and Cornell's address. He had never met Natalie and had only just met Roxanne, but he did know Nadine and Cornell, so the least he could do was send flowers and a card. After sorrowful good-byes were said, Cornell and Nadine left to take Roxanne home, and Grady trailed Clare to her residence and parked. He was laughing as she came down the walkway after depositing her car in the garage.

"You drive the same way you leave work," he laughed, "fast!"

"Am I that bad?" she asked.

"Not really," he said, following her inside. "Just kidding, but you don't waste any time."

"Would you like coffee," she asked, gesturing for him to take a seat in the kitchen, "or something stronger?"

"Coffee's fine."

"I called yesterday to thank you for the poinsettia; it's beautiful."

"I got the message, little lady," he assured her. "I returned to the office after hours only to pick up messages since this is the holiday season. We are closed until the first of the year."

He and Bradley had always made it a practice to close the office during this holiday season.

She smiled and, preparing to brew the coffee, retrieved two mugs from the cabinet. This was her first inkling of hope that maybe their relationship was entering a more stable phase after these mercurial, haphazard encounters that had been ongoing for the past five months. Thinking of the possibility gave her a good feeling, but what then? There were still things they had to discuss, and she didn't want to chase him away.

He watched her closely as he hung his jacket on the back of his chair. She was such a classy, little woman, and he could feel himself on the verge of being drawn in, toward forming something meaningful, but something was holding him back. Was his hesitation the result of being single for too long? Was he about to initiate too soon something for which he was unprepared?

That inner voice reminded him of his desire for a home with a wife and additional children, that very lifestyle Pop said he needed. Then there was the unusually early visit with his parents (he always gave them a card with a generous check inside). His gift from them remained under the tree unopened with a promise to pick it up upon his return. As always, it would be something nice, but inexpensive, which was the request of all the Mayfield children.

This year he had been contemplating stepping outside that routine even more. It was further encouraged by Helen without her knowledge. Bridgette practically insisted that her mother come to Detroit for Christmas to meet her new love interest. For the past seven years, on Christmas Day, he had visited and exchanged gifts with Helen, but this sounded serious to Grady and influenced postponement of exchanging gifts between them until after the holidays. Grady, encouraging Helen to go to Detroit, had opted out of the trip because it was a family affair. When it came to family, Grady never broke his standard rule.

He could hear his business partner and friend warning him that time was passing, and he needed to make better use of it. He knew this to be true, but he needed just a little more time to enjoy his space, disentangled, without any deep emotional involvement, even though the attraction was indeed strong.

He left his seat at the table and walked over to where she stood. He lifted her, set her on the counter, away from the cups and brewing coffee, and kissed her long and with deep emotion.

"I am deeply attracted to you, Clare," he said softly.

"As I am to you," she responded, resting her head on his shoulder. What had remained submerged and untapped for so long was surfacing.

Suddenly he said, "What am I going to do with you, little lady?"

She raised her head, taken aback. Where was this coming from? Was he beginning to back off just as they were about to establish something tangible? Perhaps she had previously misread his actions. She made direct eye contact. "What do you want to do with me?"

He looked at her steadily for what seemed a long time and then smiled. *No, no. Don't say it!* "I'm not really sure," he answered quietly with slow, direct deliberation.

It was such naked, unadulterated honesty that she was stung with a penetrating sadness. She felt herself immediately withdrawing to a place that, even though it lacked comfort, kept her safe.

The house was quiet. He had gone into the still of night. As the previous day's waning hours ushered in the dawn of Christmas Eve, Clarissa Lucinda Ingram lay in her bed and, for the first time in memory, cried herself to sleep.

<h1 style="text-align:center">CHAPTER TWENTY</h1>

Having retrieved one ticket from the pair in his dresser drawer, Grady boarded the early flight to Las Vegas the morning of Christmas Eve and sat next to an empty seat. It had been years since he had visited Las Vegas. After four hours, late Christmas Eve morning, he found himself checking in at the MGM Grand and then walking along the Strip. His favorite casino, although he had never reserved a hotel room there, was the famous Caesars Palace, sedate yet subtly flamboyant in its prominence, sprawling and splendorous with its gushing water fountains. It was truly a majestic landmark amid the other nightlife glittering like a sensuous harlot. All alone, there he was, on Christmas Eve, walking the Strip with vivid, neon signs pulsating with solicitous frequency. The entire scene was a desert fantasy land of bright lights suggestively sparkling in brilliant greens, vibrant blues, intense reds, and glowing gold; all continuously beckoned like a wanton siren. Las Vegas was indeed a playground where everything was focused on usurping your last dollar like a seductive and skillful prostitute. Leisurely, Grady visited the casinos, especially Caesars Palace, MGM Grand, the Aladdin, and others along this brightly lit, ostentatious boulevard, each time to stand at another roulette wheel. Without participating, he often observed the rolling of the dice and the revolving wheel to stop on numbers known to be most advantageous to the house. He watched with interest and sometimes even became a disciplined participant. He stopped only briefly at the blackjack tables. He never played poker because he tended to get too absorbed and lose cash unnecessarily. He loved making money, not squandering it foolishly. Gambling can be a fun sport only if you limit your indulgence. How many arrived in Las Vegas with that attitude?

Whenever he and Bradley West visited Las Vegas together, West did very little gambling because his primary interest was live entertainment, which he considered a controlled substance in a land of recklessness; Grady was also was a lover of live entertainment. Bradley West detested slot machines the most, which he considered a definite sucker's game. Of course, to him it was all a desert ploy set in motion by the genius of one gangster (at least that's how the story was told) who had devised such a clever scheme to make money in the middle of sand.

Although Grady never played the slot machines, he did enjoy walking through the casinos and listening to the pull of the levers and the whirring of the wheels and the falling coins as they clanked loudly against the small, individual metal floors of the machines. Once in a great while as coins fell generously, drama ensued as a particular machine came alive, with lights flashing and a siren sounding to announce its winner. There would be enthusiastic cheers in celebration for the lucky one, who most likely was recouping some of his or her previous losses. Nevertheless, reinvigorated, the others resumed feeding those greedy little metal teases in an attempt to change their own luck.

Everything was accommodating—from the watered-down drinks and the attendants making change to the ample supply of patrons' favorite nicotine indulgence. All these amenities were there to make sure that participation continued with no one permanently cashing in.

Never before had he visited Las Vegas at this time of year. Grady felt out of place and this particular time did not catch any of the shows but instead retired to his room early in the morning to sleep late in the day, until after five or so. Then he showered and dressed to eat alone from one of the buffet-style restaurants. He felt out of sorts observing the small groups and entourages as they engaged in jovial conversation, eating and drinking while having a wonderful time. Now he had spent most of Christmas Eve in Las Vegas and awakened on Christmas Day. It felt strange to hear "Merry Christmas" so far away from home. It made him wonder just what had caused him to board the plane alone. Ignoring the hotel shuttles, he did a lot of strolling, stopping in the coffee shops, and striking up conversations with people he encountered, for Grady was a very friendly guy. He thought of his conversation with Nadine. If she learned what had happened, she would probably wonder just what his intentions were after all.

He walked and did a lot of soul searching. He thought of Helen and reviewed precisely where they were in an arrangement that would never lead to marriage but had reached that inevitable fork in the road. He thought of Clare and what she must be doing and feeling on this Christmas Day.

He spent an hour or so browsing the lower-level shops of the MGM Grand but soon tired of that. He was restless and decided too late that it was rather nonsensical to be a solitary visitor to Las Vegas unless you were a hard-core gambler, which he was not. He had never visited Las Vegas alone. He used to visit routinely but always with friends, and in those circumstances, it could be a fun place. The night of his arrival and the next of this Yuletide season, he walked the Strip alone, visiting each of the casinos so large and expansive it took a considerable amount of time just to pass each one. He would enter, become engaged some of the time and only observe at other times, and then exit and walk some more. The food was cheap, as was most everything on the Strip except select memorabilia and the vice that brought you there.

He saw a few children, three to be exact, waiting in the lobby just outside the entrance of Circus Circus. The sight tugged at his heart to such an extent that he gave each of them ten dollars, for which they thanked him politely, though their sad faces revealed bored fatigue. Addicted parents were enough to evoke sympathy from strangers.

After his second night, he made reservations for a morning flight home, willingly paying the penalty for early departure and thus leaving the desert playground—*Enough of this!* he thought—to arrive back in Chicago feeling more grounded, arriving home the early morning after Christmas. When he entered his apartment, the telephone was ringing. He didn't pick up because he knew it was Helen. He wasn't certain if she was still in Detroit or had made it back. This year he had visited only with his parents earlier than usual and gave them a card with a generous check inside as he had for several years. He had told them he was going out of town. He had left his own gift from them, opened, underneath the tree to pick up when he returned.

Lately, feeling out of sorts and restless was the norm for him, and he knew exactly why. To use one of his father's sayings, he hoped he had not "torn his britches" with Clare, the direct cause of deep inner emotions that had not been so profoundly disturbed in years. How did the saying go? *Be careful what you ask for; you just might get it.* However, he had been married twice and did not want to have a third marriage failure. How did he tell her to just bear with him while he worked on making the mental adjustments necessary to rearrange his life? How did you tell any woman that kind of garbage?

A few weeks earlier, Helen had said something about his acting peculiar as of late, which he knew to be true. Perhaps he was subconsciously trying to force her to end it, to break it off. West was genuinely amused when Grady mentioned that possibility. He would never succumb to such a cowardly remedy; it was not his style.

✑

It was 1985, New Year's Day had come and gone, and it was the first day the office was open. He felt an unfamiliar, uneasy awkwardness. Why was he running and backing away, and to where? *Old habits die hard,* he thought. He had been single too long and had settled into that "smooth grove" that Bradley accused him of, a slippery place from which he couldn't pull away without necessary traction. He needed to create it. Bradley West considered this path an aversion to a meaningful relationship, but Grady needed to hear something that he did not already know.

---

Business at the office was slow and would likely remain that way for a few months. The month of January would be spent in the quiet of paperwork and office chitchat. For the next week or so, Grady and Bradley took turns leaving early. Around March business would pick up again. Since salaries were based on commission, some of the agents busied themselves with personal things a few days a week and took turns showing up to make sure there was nothing on their desks. They faithfully attended the weekly Thursday morning meetings. Ursula was paid to run the office and not afford the luxury of such a relaxed schedule, which placed her there every weekday from eight-thirty to five, Saturdays from nine to one.

Clare had not returned a single call, and it was approaching February. He was discovering how much her absence would sting, and he did not like the feeling. Was the verdict in?

Rarely did Grady visit Bradley's office, as he was doing now, seated in the armchair directly in front of his desk. There was limited conversation since Grady's return from Las Vegas. Respecting privacy, Bradley was never one to pry, but the suspense was killing him.

"How did the little lady enjoy Vegas?" Bradley asked as he lit another cigarette.

"You need to stop that nonsense." This was the very reason he seldom visited his office; it always smelled like smoke.

"Well, I don't think it matches your nonsense," he replied candidly. "Answer my question."

"I didn't take her."

"So, you visited the con game in the sand all alone." He put out the cigarette. "What was that all about?"

He didn't mention he had cut his three-day trip short. "I'm just not ready for that type of commitment."

"Wrong answer," Bradley countered. "You are afraid of that type of commitment. Okay, so what's up? Have you retreated to the security blanket?"

"Why do you always call her that?"

"Well, give me a better way to describe what you do with Helen."

Bradley could recall two incidents when Grady had met someone of interest. The first time, he had seen Helen for about three years, and that smooth grove was as slippery as glass, allowing no traction whatsoever. Therefore, he had not acted on his feelings for the other woman but instead had allowed them to subside. The second time, the veer from his usual routine had lasted approximately four months, and then it too was over. He had always dated other women, but not with much serious involvement. Apparently neither of those women had held his interest as solidly as this one, and now Bradley wanted to meet her to see what she offered that the others did not.

"It was a foolish move," Grady now admitted. "I told Clare that I did not know what I wanted from her." He sighed. "Now I am sorry I said it. I know exactly what I want with her but can't commit to it just yet."

"You're getting cold feet," said Bradley. "Okay, then simply spend time with her, genuine time, get to know her. You are sending mixed signals, and that is not progressive." He knew about the Christmas greeting sent to Clare's office and then the canceled plan to surprise her with the trip to Las Vegas. "I'm sure she would, at least for a while, just allow you to date her—you know, along with everything that creates a relationship—although I don't think she would settle for that arrangement indefinitely. What I don't understand is why you are backing away, when you say she is the kind of woman you want, that you are extremely attracted—"

"My intention is not to back away," Grady said, cutting Bradley off, "but to simply slow it down." He paused. "I care for her more than I wish to at this time."

"Really," said Bradley. "Hmm, you don't say?" He offered an amused smile. "What now?"

Grady didn't answer. *When is the right time?* Grady asked himself. He again thought of the discussion he'd had with Nadine a few months earlier when he and Nadine had a heart-to-heart. He confided in her because, other than Estelle, who knew Clare best, he sensed she would not betray that confidence. Of course, it did not start out that way. She had consulted him regarding property in Wisconsin that she and

Cornell were considering purchasing—a small cottage for summer getaways. He had given her solid advice. Afterwards, he invited her to lunch. Their conversation finally got around to Clare, and she had to quell her question about his intentions with her best friend because that would have betrayed a confidence. She knew and never failed to assure Clare that the situation with Grady would change for the better, no matter how angry she became with herself. Nadine was always delighted that, despite their sporadic, impromptu dating, Clare sparkled after each encounter with this man.

They talked for about an hour and a half. Finally, the subject was Clare whom, admittedly, he considered somewhat of a puzzle. "I find that she is attracted to me, but something makes her hesitant."

'Believe me, Grady, she more than just likes you,' Nadine had replied with nothing more than a pleasant smile.

Until recently, he had consistently evaluated what he had with Helen as positive: it was steady, it was stable most of the time, and it conveniently allowed him to avoid being totally committed in any relationship. Gradually that changed. However, he wanted guarantees that life couldn't make.

"When is the right time, my man?" Bradley questioned, and then filled the silence. "Well, this is a sign that you do care," he said. "That's good, know what I mean?"

❧

When Clare looked up from the project she was working on, Grace was standing in her doorway with a wide smile on her face.

"I think you are about to receive another visit from the florist," Grace announced and then stepped aside for the delivery man. It was the same man as before, and he smiled at Clare in recognition as he entered her office. She gestured for him to place the flowers on her credenza next to the poinsettia still in bloom, and he complied. As soon as the delivery man left, Grant appeared in the doorway, grinning mischievously.

"Lately you are one popular lady," he teased. "Do you have one admirer or several?" He held up both hands. "Not that I am saying that is a bad thing." He vanished before she had time to respond.

*Life with all its surprises*, she thought on this early February day. She willed herself to react slowly and continued to work for the next ten minutes or so. *What now?* she thought. She had not seen him for over a month and thought of him often, but she had continued to refuse his phone calls. Still, he managed to keep her teetering emotionally.

Why was it that feelings, matters of the heart, were so hard to control and possessed a will every bit their own? What had she said to Nadine? That she did not want the headache? But Nadine had ignored this.

"Hang in there, Clarissa Lucinda Ingram," Nadine had said, "and allow the entire scenario to play out."

"But that's easier said than done," she had argued, still recalling the answer he had given her about what he wanted, although she had never shared that comment with her best friend.

"Do it anyway," Nadine had replied.

Now she swiveled around in her office chair almost in slow motion and stared at the bouquet peeping over the colorful wrapping paper that partially concealed the protective cellophane. Carefully she stripped both away to expose a full, luscious bouquet of red roses—long-stemmed red roses!—accompanied by bits of baby's breath and healthy fern, plants she absolutely adored. Who was his florist? She examined the name and logo. The flower arrangements for both deliveries were simply magnificent. Easing the card from its holder, she opened it slowly.

*Clare—*

*Please let me out of the doghouse. I promise to be nicer, kinder, and more loving. Please call me.*

*Grady*

She recalled arriving home from Nadine's after spending time there providing moral support for her dearest friend amid a rather chilly camp. Some were still unfairly blaming her for Cornell's divorce from Natalie which was influenced by the fact that Cornell's brother was married to the deceased ex-wife's sister. The sister-in-law had always insisted that Nadine was dating Cornell *before* his divorce from Natalie and therefore at least partly to blame for her drug-dependence. It was untrue. At that time, she didn't know Cornell that well. Clare had presented a quiet united front with her friend until the day of the funeral and afterward decided it was time to sleep in her own bed. Upon her return home, she had found quite a few calls on her answering machine. Sharla had called to wish her a Merry Christmas; Bernard had unexpectedly called to wish her a happy holiday season again; and the remaining calls had been from Grady. For the first time she had not been able to bring herself to dial his number, though—what was the point? And to avoid a mild lecture, she had opted not to tell Nadine that he had called—five times! *What is the point of all this?* she had asked herself. Additionally, he had repeatedly called her at the office, but she had advised her assistant to simply handle the calls as if she was not there. However, each time Grace would relay the message. After the first half dozen or so, she would simply smile in amusement and dutifully place the message on her desk: "Please call Mr. Mayfield."

Now, looking at the roses in her office, Clare wondered exactly where this road was going to lead. Building a relationship, she thought in frustration, was tedious and taxing, mentally and emotionally. It was back to square one. He had backed away just when she was finally beginning to relax and unwind to the point that she felt secure enough to talk to him, to establish a meaningful level of comfort that would enable her to open. She was now unprepared to do so because her courage had ebbed, and she lacked the confidence that he would be receptive. There was nothing to indicate otherwise. *I am still not close to settling into the new me*, she thought despondently, and his response that night had made her even more wary. *The temporary me*, she added as consolation. After all, she would undergo breast reconstruction in a little less than two years.

Yet her attraction to this man had grown stronger, even though she had not seen him for over a month. *Imagine that*, she thought, unable to quell the nervous giddiness she felt while staring at the phone in front of her as if it was a foreign object. *It's just a telephone*, that inner voice prompted sarcastically, *your line of communication, okay? You might as well call the man, Clare. You want to, go ahead and call him. Go on!* Gingerly she picked up the phone and slowly dialed his number, fighting the urge to hang up.

When she asked for him, she was immediately forwarded.

"Hello, Clare," he said quietly.

"Hello yourself," she replied. "Thank you for the roses; they're beautiful."

"Not as beautiful as you are, little girl," he said softly. After a pause he asked, "After work Friday, what do you have planned?"

She found herself briefly hesitating. *Don't you dare!* "Nothing special," she replied quietly.

He wanted to tease her but did not. "I'll pick you up punctually at five sharp, okay?"

"That will be fine; I'll see you then."

She thought it was another planned date, but on a Friday. She had hoped that perhaps the lapse of time would have made a more favorable case for a Saturday. Who was this person who monopolized that one day of the week? It was the same pattern as always, but she was feeling more annoyed by it now. Both Nadine's housewarming and their first date had been on Saturdays, but thereafter, never again. With whom did he spend his Saturdays? She hated the fact that she was looking forward to seeing him in two days—today was Wednesday—but unlike before that certain spark wasn't there now. She couldn't stop wondering exactly why Saturdays were so special and with whom.

∾

For some reason she felt the need to unwrap the gift and lift it from its box for one more inspection, all the while considering whether to give it to him now or keep it for another occasion, such as his birthday or even Father's Day since he was a parent, if their relationship reached that point. She then found herself rewrapping the lead crystal paperweight of a dolphin mounted on a pedestal. After much inner debate, she had purchased it in the spirit of Christmas for Grady. The holiday season and renditions of "Auld Lang Syne" and joyous toasts of champagne ushering in the New Year across the so-called free world were long over. When she saw him on Friday, they would be well into the first week of February. It was so odd how one incident could alter the course of a relationship.

She was still feeling somewhat withdrawn even after their phone call. She was still deeply attracted to him, but that one statement— "I'm not really sure"—had made her cautious and not quite at ease with him as before. Now she would have to continue to wait for the appropriate time to tell him what most did not know about her. They had gone full circle, back to the beginning. If January was included, they had known each other for a precarious, unplanned, topsy-turvy seven months, and nothing of substance had been established. Weird, she thought. What they presently had was intangible and uncertain—reflective of his admitted uncertainty about what he wanted. How receptive would he be to what was considered less beautiful? To the necessary alteration to the part of her body that most men heralded as a woman's glory. Certainly, a woman's hair, totally always exposed, said something about her and enhanced her femininity, while also securing the bottom line of most salons. However, those glorious protrusions, even though they were always at least partially concealed in public, served as the ultimate inspiration in the world of high fashion; breasts were heralded on both the big and small screens of entertainment. And once totally exposed in the bedrooms of America, they became absolute treasures to be adored as luscious objects of sensual pleasure, and the bigger the better.

Ultimately, she tucked the gift away in a dresser drawer and went to work with mixed emotions, mildly anticipating her date that evening with Mr. Mayfield. Although she wanted to see him and be in his company, her mood was not as upbeat as it had been in earlier months. Now she was wondering just how long it would be before she regained enough confidence to make her revelation. She also wondered just how other women in the same or similar situations handled it. She sat at her desk contemplating her circumstance as the clock neared the hour.

The reservation was at another Italian restaurant, this time on Rush Street, the second floor. The food was good. When they were initially seated by the maître d', a friendly and charming man, it was suggested that she try the spinach. She loved spinach and discovered theirs was better than most. They were seated near the window, and she kept looking down to the activity on the street below since it was the start of the weekend in the middle of winter. She had savored not a few cuisines in the company of this man, but so far, they'd visited a soul food restaurant only once, and that was over the Christmas holidays, and on such a sad occasion. However, Italian restaurants such as this one dotted the national landscape from coast to coast. Both Italian cuisine and culture was intricately interwoven into the diverse European ethnic tapestry of America.

It wasn't like Clare to be so quiet. "What do you think of Reagan getting a second term?" Grady asked.

Clare smiled. "I didn't vote for him," she answered simply. "I was hoping that the reaction to electing him for a second term was going to be like the weather we're having."

Reagan's swearing in ceremony had been completed indoors because of the frigid temperature and snowy conditions.

"You don't think he's a good president?" Grady teased. Clare loved politics. *Anything to break this silence*, he thought.

"No," she said simply. "My mother didn't vote for him, either, or told me more than once that she didn't think much of his acting capabilities." She didn't elaborate that her mother also had told her several times *Kings Row* was his best acting role. Estelle was extremely upset that Reagan had won a second term and commented on the election for days. Clare didn't feel like expanding any discussion, which surprised even her.

Presently, Clare thought about how black culture, also an integral part of American life—if not appropriated, as if it belonged to the host society—was strategically downplayed as insignificant or nonexistent.

She thought these things as she sat eating her meal, watching the people on the ground busily engaged in launching their weekend. She again reminded herself that until today she had neither been in Mr. Mayfield's company nor spoken with him for over a month. Admittedly, though, that choice had been hers. At this precise moment it became crystal clear that she was growing tired of their dates scheduled for either Fridays or Sundays, and that she was mildly perturbed that Saturdays were reserved for someone else.

Below on the street, Friday night was being enthusiastically acted out. Quickly it would segue into Saturday, then Sunday, and then it would be back to work, with anxious anticipation of the next weekend; it was the American way.

"Have you watched the council wars lately?" Grady asked.

"I try my best not to," Clare replied. "For the remainder of the mayor's term, I would love for the Vrdolyak 29 to take a long trip as far north as possible, without the proper clothing."

Grady had to chuckle. *Leave it to this little lady*, he thought. He remained aware of her calm reserve, watched her attentively as their evening quietly progressed. Something had been temporarily lost, and he tried to convince himself that he could not quite identify it. Of course he could absolutely, without a doubt, identify it. She was, as always, personable but without the same relaxed ease she usually possessed. She was pleasant, following the direction of the conversation wherever he took it. For the entire evening she hadn't led one topic of discussion, which was unlike her.

Again, Grady needed to break the silence. "Did you watch the Super Bowl?" he asked.

She didn't share with him that she had attended a Super Bowl party at the home of Nadine and Cornell. "I never miss it," she replied quietly.

"Who were you pulling for?"

"The 49ers of course," Clare answered. She ate another forkful of her tiramisu.

Time was passing quickly. "You don't like Marino and the Dolphins?" Grady teased.

"I prefer Joe Montana and the 49ers," she replied, and smiled.

Before leaving Rush Street, he asked if she wanted to stop anywhere for a drink, and she graciously declined. He knew she drank very little, but this would have allowed them to spend just a little more time together before he took her home.

"I enjoyed dinner," she said. Southbound, they entered Lake Shore Drive.

"You did, little lady?" He paused. "I enjoyed your company, but you've been rather quiet. Is anything wrong, Clare?"

"No," she answered softly, "I can't think of anything." She thought of telling him what was on her mind but quickly decided against it, fearing that might initiate a conversation for which she had been almost prepared, but now was not.

"I haven't been quiet," she said kindly instead. "I have talked the entire evening."

They both knew exactly what was wrong, but he knew that she would not approach the subject unless he brought it up; the air needed to be cleared.

"There is conversation, and then there is conversation." He attempted to guide her toward discussing the one incident he knew was bothering her—and him as well. "Unless I strike up a topic, you have been rather reticent all evening."

She did not know exactly how to address the problem. He had exposed a side of his personality that she found unsettling, and she surmised that this significantly contributed to his bachelorhood. That one past incident had overshadowed their evening together.

To him the time seemed much too short as presently they were in front of her home. He cut the motor, deciding that he did not want to go inside, but preferred to remain in what he considered a more neutral setting. As usual, he rested one arm on the steering wheel and drove without his overcoat. He was aware of the soft wedge developing between them and knew that one discussion was necessary before this thing hardened and gradually severed what they had; he wanted to prevent that from happening. He wanted to ask if she had intended to ever return his calls without his persistence but thought better of it because he alone had shifted what they'd previously shared to this tentative place. However, he was certain that their mutual attraction had not diminished in the least. They needed redirection to regain what had previously existed, to allow them both to explore the potential of something more substantial.

With the aid of the streetlight, he watched her, although he could not see many of those beautiful eyes. He had to admit that he had missed those eyes, that melodious laughter, and some of her witty remarks. They had so much fun together, and he wanted to retrieve that great feeling he had when with her. *Okay, Mr. Mayfield*, he thought, *out with it.*

"Clare, the last time we were together, I made a statement that is not true." He paused. "I do want a serious relationship with you, but I need time." He paused again and chose his words carefully. "I've been single a long time and have had no new relationships in years—well, at least none that I seriously cared about." His inner voice taunted him: *Why not be totally honest? Were you seeking any?*

"Are you admitting being involved with someone?"

"Yes, but nothing that will lead to the altar."

A chill was starting to come over the car, so he started the engine once more to heat their space and keep it comfortable. They were amid what Mr. Rawls described in his monologues—a frigid Chicago winter.

"Do you even want a relationship that will lead to the altar?" she asked steadily.

"Yes, eventually," he said and then immediately regretted his answer. *Eventually?* he chided himself. *Damn!* This was proof that he had been single way too long and with Helen for far too long and was becoming too entrenched. He promptly thought of Bradley's "smooth groove" comments.

"Eventually," she repeated slowly, as if turning the word over in her mind. "'Eventually' could mean a long time. I've been seeing you for, although sporadically, six months," she said quietly, purposely omitting January, "and other than four things—that you are a real estate broker, have been married twice, have a son, and live in Hyde Park—I feel like I know nothing else about you. By now…" She coolly trailed off.

He reached over and grabbed her hand and pressed it gently. "That word was the wrong choice because I am not talking about years when I say 'eventually.' Clare, talk to me. Whatever more you want to say, please say it."

It was difficult to put what she wanted to say into words. She gently eased her hand from his, longing to share with him what was really bothering her, to earnestly explain how she felt. Prior to the incident in her kitchen, she had been slowly progressing toward the point that would allow her to open up. Now she did not dare, though she did decide to reveal one aspect of her feelings.

"Well, I was beginning to feel comfortable with you until you told me you were unsure of what you wanted… what you wanted to do with me, that is." She paused, toying with the simple but elegant gold ring on her right ring finger. "It put me in a place that makes me very cautious because I don't know…" She didn't finish her thought.

He sensed it would be this way indefinitely because this beautiful woman who was on the verge of captivating his heart had a difficult time expressing her innermost feelings. He found her witty, charming, and fun to be with but sensed that her upbringing in some respects had lacked the openness and demonstrative expressions of caring and loving that his upbringing had included. Whenever they had discussions regarding her parents, which they had on several occasions, he insightfully gleaned that she had grown up in an atmosphere that included a quality of coldness, especially from her father, Mason Ingram. Again, he took her hand, held it, and pressed gently.

"Talk to me," he encouraged softly.

"I don't know where this is going," she said hesitantly. Her own words instantly sounded familiar to her. Hadn't she uttered that exact sentence while in his apartment? This realization added to her sense that what had transpired between them wasn't meaningful at all to him and that the relationship could be factually described as static. "You were beginning to see me more," she said thoughtfully, "but it was still mostly sporadic and unplanned." She paused to gather her thoughts. "I feel that I am now on even less firm ground since you admit being with someone else. I mean—"

"Not 'with,' Clare. Not *with*." "*You're dealing in semantics*," his inner voice said. "You have seen where I live," he continued, "so you know we don't live together, and I will never marry this person. When I said there are no entanglements, I meant there are no entanglements." *Are you sure, sport?* "I am deeply attracted to you and should never have made that statement, so I apologize."

"Perhaps you should have never made the statement, but only if you honestly didn't mean it. Are you sure of that?" she asked evenly.

"Yes, I'm certain I didn't mean it."

"Then exactly what did you mean?"

"I should have said that I need time."

"Okay, I accept your apology, but time to do what exactly?" It was a direct question.

"To allow us a chance to see what can come of this." He paused. "Two single people that have met and are attracted to each other—just give us a chance."

*So far,* she wanted to say, *it is you who hasn't given us a chance.* "You're not single," she said quietly, "not in the real sense of the word."

"What makes me any less single?" he asked with a slight frown as he continued to hold her hand.

She remained silent but acknowledged that he was right, and she was not being fair. He was what Nadine described as an SBM. From the very start hadn't she mentioned to Nadine that she knew he was unattached but probably not in the strictest sense of the word? But how many men were, especially eligible black men? He was unmarried and lived alone, which correctly defined him as single.

"What makes me any less single?" he again asked gently.

"You're single," she admitted softly.

Both were silent for quite some time, but he never released her hand, not wanting her to become withdrawn and lost in thought as she had been all evening—at the restaurant, during the drive home, and once they were parked, until he'd initiated the topic of discussion. She added such interest to his life, and yes, he wanted her to become an essential part of it.

"Where are you?" he asked gently.

"I'm right here."

Her response was evasive. Again, she thoughtfully reviewed how far the relationship had come and decided that since they had ceased to advance toward anything meaningful, and he had backed away; it was still in the beginning stages. She recalled Nadine's statement about older men and how they dealt with serious involvement— the procrastination and soul searching, and so on. Since there was no one else of importance in her life, perhaps there was time, and she had to admit that she was even more deeply attracted to this man than before.

"Clare, I want us to see more of each other, okay?"

"I think we had begun to see more of each other," she said quietly, "but then you backed away."

"Will you give me a chance to change that? Let's really see where this will take us."

"Okay," she agreed softly, seeming to be miles away. "We'll see what happens."

She looked at him with the aid of the streetlight; the shadow over the dashboard and leather seat created a soft barrier between them. She diverted her attention to her thoughts, two. Who was the other woman in his life? And where would all this lead? But she decided not to pursue that latter topic until another time, when or if the two of them established something meaningful. In life there were no guarantees, and who would know that better than she? For once, she was using Nadine's terminology: she would roll with the flow.

*Enough of this,* he thought, and folded away the armrest as he slid over to embrace her, kissing her warmly. He had wanted to do this all evening, and from her response, he guessed so had she. This beautiful woman made him feel so good and alive. He kissed her again, deep and probing, and then gently pulled her onto his lap.

"I really care for you, Clare Ingram," he said, kissing her again.

"I care for you too," she replied, "a lot." With one arm around his neck, she returned his long, ardent kiss. Suddenly she laughed heartily. "We are necking in a parked car like two teenagers."

Now they both were laughing; he had sought out and finally recaptured the Clare to whom he had grown accustomed.

# Chapter Twenty-One

Grady had called as promised, and she now entered the lounge feeling ill at ease because it was close to midnight. She understood he had sent a cab for her instead of picking her up himself because he knew she would suggest they go somewhere other than a lounge. *Devious man*, she thought as she smiled to herself. She had hoped he would be near the entrance so that nobody could presume she was searching. At precisely that moment she recalled a book she had read years ago, *Looking for Mr. Goodbar*, about a schoolteacher who frequented the bars picking up men. She would never forget its gory ending.

When she was about three-fourths of the way to the back of the club, she stopped, turned, and retraced her steps to the coat rack near the door. The air conditioning was on full blast, and already feeling a slight chill, she slipped into her lightweight jacket. Before returning to the back of the club to look more carefully for Grady, she momentarily turned her attention to the dance floor. It had been a long time since she'd danced, and everyone out there was having such a marvelous time. Suddenly she remembered why she seldom visited bars. Having just left Craig's chair that morning and not due back for a week, she now stood in the midst of a smoke-filled room. For that same reason, she used to keep her bedroom door closed in the house once owned by the Ingram family.

The bartenders were having a grand time pouring drinks and cajoling with the customers. One of the men seated at the bar near where she was standing turned and asked if she wanted a seat. She rejected the offer with a smile.

Suddenly she sensed the presence of someone close behind her and felt the body lean toward her. "Looking for someone?" he whispered in her ear.

She turned to look up at Grady, and her eyes flashed instant anger that quickly vanished. "Where were you?" she said, smiling to counter the icy edge in her voice.

Motioning toward the back of the club, he gently placed his hands on her shoulders to guide her ahead of him to the back, near the wall. At the end of the bar, a tall, slender man was leisurely leaning against the wall, a drink in one hand. He smiled, placing his cigarette in the ashtray.

"Clare Ingram, Bradley West. Bradley West, Clare Ingram," Grady said as he helped her out of her jacket and placed it over the back of the empty barstool.

"Hello, Bradley." She held out her hand, which he shook but didn't immediately release, instead leaning in to plant a kiss on her cheek.

"Hi, beautiful," he said. "My, are you pretty." Continuing to hold her hand, he stood back to give her the once-over. "And well-packaged too."

Clare felt her face grow warm.

"Are you shy?" he teased. "Grady, she is a precious find. What are you drinking?" he asked.

After leaning in again to hear her reply above the music, he let go of her hand and motioned to one of the bartenders. Soon she was seated at the bar with a whiskey sour, with two handsome gentlemen standing near.

At the mike, the DJ interrupted the music. "Okay, fellas, let's have those seats—too many ladies standing."

There was an immediate response, and then the music resumed playing. Bradley, still near the wall, asked her to dance.

"You don't mind, do you, guy?" he said.

"I'll save your seat," Grady said to Clare as he sat down and ordered himself another shot of bourbon with a water chaser.

So far, their relationship had played out in three stages: the first five months had been sporadic to say the least; the sixth month had been a splintered circumstance; and the seventh, eighth, and ninth months had been a time of contemplation for him and unsettling anxiety and nervous anticipation for her. These last three months had them grounded and on the threshold of a serious relationship. Finally, Saturdays were on the agenda, representing a significant shift. Nadine's encouraging words were coursing through her brain: "He's getting serious, and he won't blink, believe me."

Still, Clare remained tentative and relatively unsure. For lack of a better gauge, she did think of Karl Pugh. She knew better than to ever reveal this comparison to Nadine, who had never liked Pughee, as she consistently referred to him. She had already warned Clare against using him as a measuring stick for anything positive.

For the last month Grady had not spent any part of a weekend with Helen, although he often stopped by during the week and consistently called. He knew that soon he would have to explain what was taking place.

Grady and Clare closed the lounge, which held a three o'clock liquor license on Saturdays (two o'clock on other days). The big car moved through the quiet city streets like a grand prowling cat, passing people yet randomly dispersed along the concrete walkways. The radio was turned low on his favorite station, and its clock registered three-thirty. Folding the armrest away, Grady took her hand, drawing her closer.

"Back there in the club you were angry, weren't you?"

"Well, slightly," she admitted quietly, mildly embarrassed.

"Why?"

"It's probably unjustified, but I don't like entering clubs unescorted, especially at that time of night." Suddenly she felt like such a prude.

"You knew I was there, Clare. Do you think I would pay for a cab to have you meet me if I wasn't going to be there?"

"Well, I didn't see you and got a little annoyed that you were not waiting for me somewhere near the door." She paused, wanting to drop the subject. "I shouldn't have made it an issue, really."

"Clare," he said, "when you are angry with me, never try to hide it. Communication, little lady, is the best thing between two people, so whether you are happy or sad or angry, let me know."

When they arrived at her house, Clare hung their jackets in the foyer and offered to make coffee, but he declined, following her to the sofa instead. The only light in the room was a soft glow from the corner lamp. He began kissing her deeply and was aroused more than ever before. When she felt the passion becoming overpowering, she moved away.

They were facing each other, and there was nowhere she could turn to avoid what was next. He looked perplexed. This was a woman, not a young girl. Granted, he had been involved with Helen for the entire time that they had known each other, but with her for this past month there had been no intimacy. And how long had he been dating Clare? Admittedly, only the last three months could be considered an actual courtship, but the entire span of time they had known each other was one calendar year. The fact that he called her "little girl" was simply because of her petite size, but now she seemed to be literally acting the part.

"This is what adults do, right?" he asked quietly, but without a smile. "Right?" he continued with gentle persistence.

"Right," she agreed quietly. It had been a long time coming, and inevitably, here it was. What now?

"You must know that my feelings have gone past just caring for you. Clare Ingram, I am in love with you," he quietly admitted. His inner voice promptly scolded him. *For the entire time, sport, you've had Helen in the rearview mirror, remember?* He knew that Clare, in her own defense, could justifiably argue that until recently what they'd had was anything but serious, yet he was pressuring her.

"What is making you so hesitant? Boy meets girl and…"

He smiled. How she loved his smile, that boyish grin that each and every time seemed to temporarily erase five years.

"So tell me, what is it? What's the matter?"

Her eyes became sad. He had said the very thing she had wanted to hear—that he loved her—but she was desperate not to lose that element of magic when she told him.

How could she approach this subject that she had discussed with no one other than Nadine? How would he accept her? She sat there hesitantly, becoming increasingly nervous, wanting to talk but unable to say a word. What would the effects of the revelation be if she told him?

He gently squeezed her hand as she looked at him with sadness yet said nothing. He always marveled at the way those lovely eyes communicated what her lips did not.

"Talk to me," he said softly because he sensed that whatever was holding her back was something deeper than he had knowledge of.

"I love you too, Grady. I really do, but I—" She attempted to force the words that needed to be said, but they would not come.

Withdrawing her hand, she wrapped her arms around herself and moved away. She had prematurely convinced herself that if he said he loved her, it would make all the difference, but it did not. That small inner voice goaded her as they sat on the sofa facing each other. *Go ahead, tell him.* She thought of Nadine's encouraging words: "Clare, he has to know. It's something you cannot possibly hide, and he will not blink, believe me." But they did not presently aid her as she steadily gazed at him. Openly she began to weep. She closed her eyes and then opened them again, as if attempting to shut out this scene or to stop the tears from flowing freely. Why couldn't she combat this dread and discomfort? What she was feeling at this moment was just as burdensome as what she'd felt on the day, she left the hospital. Plus, she couldn't shake the memory of Karl's reaction. She felt so utterly lost, as if someone had let her off at the wrong stop, where there were no people and no means of transportation. *Say it, say it! Go on, tell him!*

"Grady, I've had a mastectomy and…" She choked back tears. "I was told to wait three years—and it's now less than two—before undergoing breast reconstruction, just in case…"

God, this was hard. She'd never realized how difficult it would be until this very moment as she looked at him through blurred vision, fearful and full of regret. She thought of all the fun they'd previously had together, the nice places he had taken her, some she had been to before but many she had not. The magic she had clung to for as long as possible now seemed to be falling away like autumn leaves from their branches, to leave her just as emotionally barren. She was so overcome by deep anguish that she hardly felt his gentle embrace as he tenderly pulled her to him and onto his lap, triggering an even deeper emotion; she began to sob.

"This must sound so awful, and I'm sorry," she said as she sobbed against his chest. She clung to him as if afraid of falling. The emotional cliff was indeed high. Tenderly, he continued to hold her in his arms.

Much later, after the tears had ceased, she lay in his arms, somberly apprehensive. She could hear nothing but the ticking of the clock on the mantle. A sudden click of the lamp's timer flooded the room with darkness. For a long time, she tried to read his thoughts, wondering what he could possibly be thinking. Except for the constant ticking of the clock, the room was so quiet it practically vibrated.

Grady was astounded; he found it simply incredible. This was it, the puzzle he had been unable to solve. This was something he had never even considered. For him she had so long held a certain mystique; she was like an ever so subtle maze that he continually sought to unravel. Whenever they were together, she was always warm, engaging, upbeat, and witty, and yet that maze—the only way he could describe it—was always there. Months ago, when he had talked to Nadine, she had never offered even the slightest clue. "She more than likes you, Grady, believe me," was all Nadine had said.

"Next weekend—Saturday," Grady finally said, "I want the two of us to go away together, spend some time really getting to know each other."

He was mentally rearranging his schedule. He would have to move some things further back to a weekday that had been already pushed back once, but he would work it out. Matter-of-factly, he decided that some of it could be delegated to senior agents.

"I want you to pack a bag, and we're going to drive to Indiana or, most likely, Michigan and spend the weekend. Is that okay with you?"

She still didn't trust her voice but managed to nod her consent.

"So I'll pick you up about seven Saturday morning." He reached out and switched on the nearest table lamp, and she sat up from her reclining position on his lap and looked at him, smiling sadly. Again, the tears welled up, and she struggled to hold them back. Her secret was no longer bottled up inside.

"You have nothing to be sorry for, Clare," he said gently. "Nothing you said sounds awful, and please believe that it is of no significance." He gazed fondly into her eyes. "It means nothing." Then he instigated a sudden change of mood. "It's getting late. I'm leaving so you can get some rest." He kissed her gently and gave her a playful wink. "Put me out before I take advantage of you."

She smiled and slipped off his lap. In the foyer he kissed her again and promised to call her later that day.

⁋

They had enjoyed a full, fun day in Michigan. In the hotel bathroom Saturday evening, Clare draped her outer garments over the commode tank and stepped out of her panties. Gingerly, she unhooked her brassiere and, as always, examined the familiar flat scar, deeply saddened by her reflection in the mirror.

She was nervous, and her heart was beating fast. What would he think when he saw it? He had said it meant nothing, but she gazed dubiously at the flat scar where her breast had once been. America was a culture that placed a high premium on women's aesthetic beauty, and one aspect of that was the glorified bosom. Somehow, she yet wished there had been an acceptable alternative. The ultimate decision against immediate breast reconstruction had been hers, but her mother had cautioned her to listen to the advice of the professionals.

Agonizing over this weekend right up until this morning, she had taken a long, hot bath, given herself a facial, and carefully dressed in her most beautiful underwear. She had changed her weekly appointment with Craig from Saturday morning to Friday evening. The salon also had a manicurist whom she used periodically, so she had gotten a manicure and pedicure on Friday evening as well. Pretty hands, she had thought, together with extra smooth, pretty feet. Mixed emotions and anticipation had caused her to rise at five this morning, so she had started her careful packing early. Initially, she had packed pajamas, but she then decided that to be a dumb idea and returned them to the dresser drawer.

Presently she stood gazing at her imperfect reflection in the mirror and took a few deep breaths to make her heart stop racing. That inner voice gently consoled her: *It's going to be all right; stop worrying.* Clare slipped into her bathrobe and collected all her belongings. Timidly, she left her sanctuary.

There he sat on the side of the bed, waiting patiently. Only his muscular upper body, including those wonderfully broad shoulders, was exposed.

"I thought you had climbed out the window and down the fire escape," Grady teased, "and hitchhiked back to Chicago."

He winked at her as she came into the light of the lamp on the nightstand. Placing her clothing on the chair next to it, she offered a tremulous smile. He could tell she was nervous. Taking her hand and drawing her closer, he allowed the bed linen to fall away. He took away her robe and, as it slid to the floor, gazed at the full length of her magnificently toned body. He sensed her increased tension and read her eyes. Aware of her discomfort under the light, he reached over and switched it off. There was plenty of time to deal with that issue in the future. Her body began to relax, and she softened under his touch as he engaged her in foreplay and gently guided her to join him in bed, deliberately stimulating her even more, wanting her to enjoy him as much as he intended to enjoy her. She sighed softly and reacted by caressing and stroking him gently; he was glad that he was pleasing her.

"Little lady," he said softly, "I'm so glad we're here." He caressed her lovingly, marveling at the satin smoothness of her skin, intensely aware of her mounting desire. "I just want to fill you up," he whispered against her mouth.

He continued caressing her tenderly and stroked her inner thighs. She tingled from his touch, warmed to his promise. He kissed her all over and fondled her in the most intimate places with tenderness, gently inducing a reception so intensely sensual that when he did finally enter her, the heat of her enveloped him like a thin layer of warm oil.

It was early morning before they both dozed off, and it was he who awoke first to a semi dark room. His body was conditioned to rising early because of his exercise routine—jogging and working out on weekdays and often on weekends too. He watched her as she slept and thought, *At last.* She turned, and the covers slipped away to reveal a petite woman of a beautiful, deep brown hue with that copper undertone; she had contours in all the right places.

Clare stirred and then woke up, only momentarily disoriented. She turned her head to look at him as he lay on his side with his head propped up on the palm of one hand, watching her. She looked at his muscular body and remembered Nadine's teasing words: "You did not tell me he was such a beautiful specimen, girlfriend. That mocha gold complexion and those beautiful broad shoulders—Lawd have muhcy!"

"Good morning," he said quietly.

"Good morning yourself," she replied, stifling a yawn.

"Still sleepy?" he teased.

She felt her face grow mildly warm as he winked at her. He chuckled, enjoying being with her because she was so refreshingly different from other women he had known.

"Do I know all your secrets?" he asked.

"What else is there to know?" she replied with nervous laughter.

"Oh, I don't know. Perhaps you drove some poor guy insane. I find you as addictive as some of those exotic aphrodisiacs that they say exist in the tropics."

As the morning sunlight began stealing through an opening in the drawn drapes, she pulled the covers up over her nakedness, and he gently took them away.

"Don't do that. Don't ever be ashamed of preserving your life." His steady gaze held hers. "You are surgically correct." He came out of his reclining position and moved over her to tenderly kiss the flat scar. "That's your battle scar, and I thank God for being on your side."

Moments later, he was making love to her again, and she responded passionately, invitingly, to this beautiful man.

It was high noon when they checked out of the Michigan inn. As they approached the Indiana state line, they stopped for lunch and then, traveling back to the highway, merged with westbound traffic.

❧

Back in Chicago, he decided not to take her home just yet but instead headed southwest to Beverly. On a quiet side street, he pulled up in front of a handsome brownstone property with recently cleaned stone and a generous front lawn; it had a welcoming, majestic, calm feel.

"I want to show you something," he said casually, "and would like your opinion."

Once they had ascended the flight of steps, he turned the key in the lock. As they entered the foyer, she was welcomed by a commingling of smells: fresh paint, varnish, and new wood. The foyer opened up into one of the most beautiful and spacious living rooms she had ever seen, further enhanced by a hardwood floor. The fireplace was surrounded by decorative stone that stretched from its mantle to the high ceiling. A bay window was tastefully positioned on each side of the doorway. To one side was a handsome staircase of solid oak.

"We updated the fireplace," he explained. "Uncle Maurice's idea."

"Great idea," she said.

His uncle had given him ideas that could be executed by the crew he'd hired and had even assisted with some of the renovation. "I've almost worn out my favorite chair," Uncle Maurice had commented, relieved to fill the hours of boredom; it hadn't taken him long to discover how monotonous retirement sometimes can be. He gladly seized the opportunity to, as Grady presented it to him, "make a little pocket change," while employing the knowledge of the construction trades that he knew so well.

Clare's body tingled with excitement as she examined the rooms; Grady followed a short distance behind. The dining room was just slightly smaller than the living room, with a huge double window and tray ceiling. *My, this is a gorgeous house,"* she decided as she entered the kitchen and fell in love. It was huge and updated, with recessed lighting and a large oak wood island positioned attractively in its very center, surrounded by matching cabinets; a matching overhead hood was centered over the range. She soon discovered that, except for the bathrooms, all the rooms had hardwood floors. She looked inside the small and attractive half-bath hidden away near the kitchen.

Turning to look up at him, she smiled and forced herself to quell the intense, giddy sensation. "This is a nice house."

"Let me show you the rest of it."

He placed his hands gently on her shoulders as he guided her from behind to another room on the main floor. There were two rooms at the very back of the house, one large and the other slightly smaller, separated by a beautiful double French door. The larger room had a sliding glass outer door, which Grady reached around her to unlock and slide open, and she walked onto a wonderful deck, obviously a new addition.

Earlier in the month, mid-July, his mother had smiled and slightly raised her eyebrows in surprise. "It's new for you to bring a lady friend to the family picnic." He could tell she was pleased. "She's pretty, Grady."

Those thoughts came to mind as he stood in the doorway watching her as she walked around to get the feel of the deck's newness and beauty. Once she was back inside, Grady secured the locks.

"Come, let's go upstairs," he said. Taking her hand, he guided her back through the kitchen, the dining room, and the living room to the staircase leading upstairs. A grand house, a big house, with so much to discover. The updated master bedroom, located at the rear, overlooked the deck below as well as the backyard. It possessed its own very large private bathroom with a separate shower, bathtub, and double face bowls; the commode stood privately to one side. Off from the bedroom, there was even a private sitting room. The other four bedrooms shared two additional bathrooms.

Descending the stairs, they again walked through the living room, and dining room. From the kitchen they descended the four steps to an open and airy English basement. Light splashed through the windows overlooking the back and side yard, the very feature that had sold Grady when considering the property for purchase. Clare noticed that the baseboards and corner moldings had yet to be added to complete the space. There was also another full-size bath, only slightly smaller than the one in the master bedroom. The entire house possessed not one cramped area. The one feature Clare simply adored was that it was very sunny.

"So, you like this house, do you?" he asked, his back to her while securing the front door locks.

"I think it's a beautiful place," she replied.

She willed herself to subdue her emotions, sounding as noncommittal as possible. His words warmed her as his touch had done only hours before. She struggled to reject any potentially unwarranted anticipation. It was better that certain compartments in her mind remain closed for now.

When they finally pulled up in front of her door, it was dark. He sat facing her with one arm on the steering wheel. He winked at her, then smiled. "I never knew a little woman could be such a perfect fit."

She laughed quietly, vividly recalling their earlier passion. "The things you can say," she said, moving closer. "I'm simply a smaller version, that's all."

"Is that right?" he said, kissing her mouth, nuzzling her ear. "Great discovery. I guess you know you're stuck with me now."

"I hope so," she replied. "I enjoyed being with you, Grady." She kissed him. "I always enjoy our time together."

"You'd better, little girl."

It was the chitchat of lovers.

∾

It was Monday evening; Kimberly was in bed. Nadine could hardly wait for Cornell to be off to Monday night bowling with his buddies, so that she and Clare could have some girl talk.

"Okay, Ms. Ingram," she began. "Fill me in with all the details about your weekend. It is the start of something big, right?"

"I guess you could say that. We visited a suburb of Detroit, Michigan, to see an old buddy from his college days. They played football together and were roommates. When Robert—that's his name—first got out of college, he taught seventh- and eighth-grade biology here in Chicago. He moved to Michigan when offered a great job with General Motors." She paused. "Grady played until his senior year. He was injured toward the end of his last season. That came up while they were talking. I simply remained the good listener."

"Sounds like he is making sure you know all about him, and that's a good sign. Girlfriend, you sound so bubbly and alive."

"All the way there," Clare said, smiling, "he entertained me with tapes. You know how I love the blues. Of course, there were other tapes as well. Nadine, we had such a good time driving there and back, discussing a variety of subjects. We arrived about eleven-thirty Saturday morning. I'm certain the trip was planned. We enjoyed a lovely dinner with Robert's family. He has four children—teenagers! His wife is a great cook. We didn't leave until about seven or so that evening. He mentioned that he and Robert get together every couple of years but talk on the phone at least once or twice a month."

"What else did you do?"

"Heading back this way, before entering Indiana, we stayed overnight at a very upscale inn. You cannot possibly guess where he took me when we got back in town." She laughed. "To Beverly to see this magnificent house he and his uncle refurbished. Nadine, it's beautiful!"

"See?" Her smile came through like sun rays. "Girl, that man is smitten with you."

"Well," she replied quietly, "I don't want to read too much into it. He said he wanted my opinion. I told him it's a keeper. It's a beautiful place." She paused. "You know, he's such a kind, thoughtful man, and he's so gentle. We have so much fun together."

"Start coordinating the wedding colors," replied her friend. "It's coming."

"Well," she replied, "we'll see. Anyway, how is Kimberly?"

"Great," replied Nadine. "She has become quite acclimated to being with her dad and me all the time rather than alternate weekends as in the past. I know she misses her mom terribly. Of course, also her old school and friends. All things considered. she has made the transition remarkably well."

"I felt so sorry for Kimberly when she first came to stay with you and Cornell." Clare said. "She looked so lost. I cannot imagine losing your mother that close to Christmas. To make matters even worse, the poor little girl's birthday was only two days earlier!"

"That was some birthday and Christmas present," Nadine said about Natalie's death.

"That's for sure," Clare agreed.

# Chapter Twenty-Two

In Chicago, summer was passing and with it the heat of August gave way to whimsical September. Both men were dressed casually in jeans, as they always were whenever they went out in the field to inspect potential properties. Sometimes they also checked on other enterprises in which they were involved, but it was decided when they first went into partnership that their separate endeavors would remain personal.

"Why don't you go on and ask the little lady to marry you?" asked Bradley. He laughed and shook his head. "You're scared to death." He had seen the house in Beverly before the start of renovation, when he had volunteered to wire the place and voiced his positive opinion of its potential. "I'll bet those neighbors are now wondering who is going to live here."

"They know someone will eventually," Grady had said as he continued to debate whether to sell it.

Grady had purchased the house from a widow. Even before her husband died, with all the doctor bills they had struggled to stay in the house. At one time, when her husband was making large sums of money—he had once owned a Chrysler dealership—it had been the ideal place for a family of six; they had raised their four children in the home.

Grady and his uncle considered the property a great investment because whenever the place was sold, it would bring a handsome profit. Ultimately, the house had remained on the market too long, steadily depreciating in value as the widow stubbornly continued to ask for the listed price. The needed repairs continued to accumulate, and the widow finally realized that she had waited until she had placed herself at a disadvantage. Most potential buyers weren't interested in purchasing the property now because along with the house also came numerous out-of-pocket expenses. It was then that Grady seized the opportunity to negotiate a feasible price with the seller, which was accepted even though it was considerably less than what she would have liked because Grady's offer involved no loans. Both the ability to pay cash and his familiarity with all the real estate jargon allowed Grady to take possession of the deed to the property rather quickly.

After purchase, refurbishment of the place, worked into their daily schedule, had taken the hired crew two years to complete, and Grady paid in increments as the work progressed. To significantly cut the costs of renovation, Grady invested at least a day or so during alternate weeks on his slow days at the agency. Bradley even volunteered his electrical expertise during leisure time, wiring the house free of charge based on one stipulation: Grady had to reside at the address. It was agreed that if the house was sold (yet to be determined), Bradley would be immediately paid for services.

Within the last few months, except for a few finishing touches, the restoration of the house to its former beauty, with some attractive modernization, had been completed. Finally, Grady could appreciate why the widow had tried to avoid sale of the place. Maurice mentioned the beauty of the wood, which no longer existed in the more contemporary properties unless they were extremely pricey. The solid oak wood doors and baseboards (with only a few needed replacements) were completely refurbished to expose their original grandeur. The plastered walls instead of drywall were a plus. There was a solid oak staircase and a spacious foyer with stained glass windows. There was even a laundry chute, omitted in most newer homes. It would remain optional for a buyer, but if Grady decided to keep the property, the chute would be sealed. Even the landscaping, relatively neglected, could easily be restored to its original beauty. It was such a splendid, prime property, but so often did life throw a mean curve, as it had to this family.

Guilt had urged Grady to spend part of the weekend with Helen that Sunday night. He was there for only a few hours and noticed her visible disappointment, but he had just left Clare and knew it was in poor taste to spend the night. "Old habits are hard to break, my friend," joked West, not fully aware of all the circumstances. Grady was weaning himself away gradually and deliberately. He had always respected and cared for Helen, which dictated the slowness of his exit. He knew that soon he would make his final move.

"What else do you have to do to the place?" Bradley asked.

"There are still just a few finishing touches," said Grady. "Lately, I am out there at least a couple of times during the week and sometimes spend a percentage of my weekend there. Uncle Maurice regularly makes appearances too, to make certain someone is consistently visible. An alarm system will be installed next week."

"You still seeing Helen?"

"Not as much," he answered, "not nearly as much."

"When are you going to pop the question to the little lady, get rid of the security blanket?"

Grady smiled. "Security blanket," he repeated, chuckled. His friend liked that term.

"Well, there are no wedding plans, right?" He paused, but Grady did not answer. "That's a no, right?"

"I've been married twice. I desire my third to be the last."

"The second marriage was much too soon, remember? You'd only been back from 'Nam for a little while, among other things."

"I remember," he responded agreeably.

In the house they were currently inspecting, West examined a few of the rusted pipes they'd found in the basement and then the walls, to detect any basement flooding or cracks in the foundation. Sometimes owners thought they could pull a fast one, attempting to camouflage these flaws in various ways. Grady checked the furnace and the date; it was relatively new as the owner had stated. All seemed to check out well, and from the looks of things, none of the questions they'd asked the seller had been answered untruthfully.

"Procrastination, my man, is always a bad thing." Bradley stopped working and turned his full attention to their conversation, leading Grady to do the same. "Let me tell you what I know about money— because perhaps you have never perceived its effect in this way. Yes, it provides all the material possessions you can imagine, but in the real sense you will never possess it the way it can possess you because of your obsession with it. One can forever be caught up in its pursuit to the sacrifice of everything else of more value. I'm not even talking about the priceless value of family or friends per se but needs that personally exist just for your benefit to make life worthwhile. Money can provide every object of comfort imaginable. Never warmth, passion, or love, priceless things you cannot buy. You can love money, but it never loves you in return. The house will never be a home, and the bed will be empty. Helen knows you will never marry her, but if you permit it, she will use all the prime years of your life as she grows old and as you, my man, approach where she is headed. You will continue to evade—yes, evade—the laughter of children, backyard barbecues you insist you want while denying yourself the enjoyment, until it's too late. Listen, Grady. You're a handsome guy, and perhaps will be for quite some time. No matter how good the body looks, it can never defy time. You can backpedal away from marriage until Helen has usurped your best years. Then the wife and children, too young, will be an experience time will never allow you to fully appreciate. For some things we can wait too long, my friend. I care about you, my man. We're business partners, true, but we're also friends. Clare is a lovely lady. Boredom will not exist with Miss Ingram as your partner. Let her go, and you will perhaps be searching for the rest of your life for the same qualities possessed by that little lady. You will waste the prime of your life with that security blanket that offers no security at all, just a way out of personal commitment to anything but making that almighty dollar."

Grady remained silent as they resumed working. Bradley checked the circuit breaker box once more, decided that it needed replacement with a bigger one. He would advise the owner. Suddenly he laughed.

"What's so funny?" Grady asked.

"Just remembering when I popped the question to Maggie. She told me that she was glad that I didn't wait any longer. She was planning to sell the house and move to California. An old boyfriend from her college days had again asked her to marry him. This time she was not turning him down. I realize there are not that many bachelors in the black community that meet the eligibility standards. What I am saying is life can turn on a dime. So do not think that good-looking woman with a lot going for her must wait on you. That is all I am saying, okay, sport?"

"I hear you," Grady replied.

Helen had brought up the recent changes during a recent phone call. "When am I going to see you during the weekend? You're acting strange lately."

"Soon, we'll go to one of our favorite places—perhaps this Saturday."

That he had no desire to see Helen on a regular basis had happened before, but not for so many consecutive weekends. For the first time it felt right. In the past he had erratically missed weekends, but never for extended periods, especially Saturdays. This chapter in his life was gradually ebbing to a close. Lately, when he stopped by it was just to talk and nothing else. He was aware that she was fighting to keep her attitude and demeanor relatively the same, to wait it out. He found that disturbingly regrettable, wishing she was less emotionally involved. He knew her strategy was to remain open and receptive until they resumed where they were previously because, even if for shorter periods of time, this scenario was not new.

Bradley had pushed open Grady's slightly ajar office door at that precise moment and stuck his head in. He could immediately tell who was on the other end of the line. He was about to leave and go back to his own office when Grady beckoned him inside, just as he was hanging up the phone.

"One of our favorite places, is it?" Bradley said, taking a seat in front of Grady's desk.

"Don't you start," Grady had replied with a good-natured chuckle.

It was Clare who increasingly held his focus and a reserved place in his thoughts these days. His defenses were slowly dissolving, and Bradley was finding this moderately steady transition amusing.

"Well, well, I think you are beginning to show signs of shedding the security blanket," he had said several times, to which Grady would always smile without comment.

Time marched on; circumstances shifted. For the next three months, Helen saw Grady only sporadically during weekends, although he called often and stopped by to talk. Sometimes they still had dinner together either at her condo or at a familiar restaurant. Knowing that Grady did not like eating alone, dinner engagements in no way complimented her or their relationship. Things had changed in a more upsetting way too; other than a kiss or a hug, intimacy between them was almost nonexistent. For the time being, she stubbornly refused to explore what that was about. This had happened before, but she had to admit it had never lasted this long.

✧

Bridgette who was visiting her mother for the Christmas holidays. She innocently inquired about what now was approaching an eight-year involvement she privately labeled a "user-friendly" benefit for Mr. Mayfield. She resented her mother for allowing such an extended arrangement of this sort to play out for so long. Years ago, she had hoped her mother would start to step away, shake off the lethargy causing her to stay in a relationship so detrimental to her psyche. Bridgette sensed she was playing the waiting game. Objectively, she did not blame Grady because, young or old, he was still a man. Her older, sophisticated mother should know better. Bridgette somehow intuitively knew that he was now on the fast track to revising his life. Her mother had stubbornly made the decision to stay put. She had cautioned her long ago not to fantasize that he was going to be around for the duration.

"You knew this was going to happen eventually," Bridgette gently but matter-of-factly argued as they discussed his frequent absences, including her mother's last trip—without Mr. Wonderful—to meet her fiancé. They were on their third cup of coffee. It was an unpleasant topic for the mother, but the daughter felt the need to address it. Her mother needed a wake-up call—a 'snap out of it' approach.

"How long did you think it was going to last, Mama? We are talking about a young man with the potential to have more children, to start all over again." She paused. "If you ask me, the two of you had a good run."

"Oh, Bridgette," Helen responded with more than an edge of irritability, "he has never mentioned wanting to marry again."

"That doesn't mean he won't or that he hasn't thought about it."

Bridgette thought back to when she was a very young girl, reveling in the fact that people thought they were sisters. Not once did her mother correct the mistake. It was fun back then, and she appreciated her mother's exceptionally youthful appearance. Now it presented a problem. Helen wanted to cling to youth; it was ebbing away. She was growing old, although ever so subtly, it was beginning to show. The facials, the massages, the tinted, exceptionally stylish coiffures no longer prodded away time. Others couldn't compare then and now, but Bridgette was Helen Moore's daughter and remembered every phase.

"What happened to Dr. Newton?" Bridgette asked. "He liked you. As a matter of fact, he more than liked you." She recalled that the doctor had a paunch, was a little shorter than her regal mother, but a very nice guy and absolutely taken with her. Her mother refused to adhere to her own advice to always be the one loved the most.

"We kind of lost touch," Helen replied evasively.

"No," Bridgette said, "rejection is a better explanation for what happened, don't you think?" She cupped her mug, briefly pursing her lips in thought. "There was also Basil. Surely you remember Basil?"

"I remember," she said, becoming even more uncomfortable, not wanting to recall what had transpired.

Basil was one of the hospital carpenters she had dated for quite some time. He had moved on because her actions indicated her level of interest was below his. After their relationship, he retired to move back to his original home, Belize. He purchased a modest place and during several vacations rehabbed it into something very lovely. He married one of the ladies from his high school days. A mutual friend from the hospital, unaware of what had transpired, received correspondence from him, accompanied by a picture she then innocently shared with Helen. In the background was their attractive home; in the foreground stood Basil and his new wife.

These were suitors from over a decade ago, before Helen had met Mr. Wonderful. Looks, ha! What Bridgette wanted to know was: who gives a damn about looks if your choice means you end up old—and lonely? There was no replacement for the young gentleman, the Mr. Wonderful, not in the least aesthetically challenged. She'd spent time with him a few times while visiting her mother, and she harbored no animosity toward the guy. Inventorying her mother's past wealth of opportunities, she regretted her refusal to cash in. End of story. The Bridgette motto: being too picky is much too tricky. It was one of her favorite phrases, succinct and to the point which she consistently applied it to her own life. She was getting married in May. He was not exceptionally handsome, but he loved her, and she cared a lot for him. Two prominent ingredients for building a stable partnership.

"He was a nice guy," Bridgette said about Basil.

"Well, if I had married him, you would have had to travel quite a distance to see me."

"That would have been okay; I travel to see you now," she said.

Bridgette always motored to Chicago. Helen preferred to fly to Detroit. Whether driving or as a passenger, Helen hated being in a car for over a couple of hours, whereas Bridgette loved to drive and, with girlfriends, had driven cross-country twice.

"Granted, you cannot reach them by car, but some of the islands are relatively closer than travel in the United States," Bridgette noted. "Let's not forget, Cuba is only ninety miles from Florida. And how many miles is Detroit from Chicago?"

Helen went silent before becoming completely enmeshed in this conversation with her daughter. The subject had the potential for extreme distress while critically analyzing last eight years of her life. She did not wish to ponder one especially nagging fact about herself—she did not like older men! She mentally lifted the cover to dare peek at what was inescapable: age.

✌

It was Christmas Day. Grady and Clare were spending the late afternoon with his parents, Joseph and Rachel Mayfield. Clare had briefly conversed with two of Grady's siblings, Jacob and Arthur. Mabel, Rolanda, Quincy, Ruth, and Cambridge had visited their parents earlier to spend time and bring monetary gifts. What do you buy after purchasing gifts for the same people all your life? Since their parents now lived on a fixed income, money inside a beautiful card was considered a very practical gift, avoiding the mistake of repurchasing a former gift or choosing something they didn't need. It also allowed their parents the freedom of options—spend or save, the choice was theirs.

Only the four of them now sat in the living room: Joseph Mayfield in his favorite chair; Rachel Mayfield one end of the sofa closest to her husband. Opposite his parents, Grady and Clare sat, as usual, in the sofa's two matching chairs. She found his parents to be enjoyable and uniquely compatible. She had spent a considerable amount of time becoming acquainted with them during these last few months, and she loved their constant bantering, giving rise to fond memories of Aunt Lu and Uncle C. J.

Nadine seemed uncannily in tune to what was transpiring between her friend and Grady Mayfield, that the relationship was becoming serious while Clare tempered her anticipation. Being in the company of his parents often did suggest a Christmas gift appropriate, but what exactly? Grady recalled that his parents had experienced a power outage a few times in the past years and needed to replace their oil lamp—just in case.

"You think we sometimes don't pay our light bill, do you?" said Joseph Mayfield, looking on as his wife unwrapped the beautiful hurricane lamp. Gorgeous, expensive, and accompanied by a supply of lamp oil.

Clare, initially surprised, was about to graciously refute the comment when she saw the devilish twinkle in Joseph Mayfield's eye. She laughed just as Rachel gave her husband a soft slap on his arm. Under her breath playfully admonishing him to shush.

"Pay no attention to Pop," Grady told Clare with a soft chuckle, familiar with a lifetime of his father's antics.

"It's lovely, sweetheart," Rachel said warmly, placing it and the oil on the closest end table. "And thank you."

"Little bit," Joseph said, "are you going to allow this man to place a ring on your finger?"

Clare was taken aback, secretly pleased by the question. Her eyes grow large with surprise at the abrupt shift in conversation. "No wonder you're such a character," she said, turning to Grady as she again laughed in that melodious way of hers, but with an edge of nervousness from such a direct query.

"Mr. Mayfield—"

"Call me Joe," he said with a warm smile. "Answer my question."

"Do you think she would make me a good partner, Pop?"

"I do indeed," he answered sincerely.

Grady left his chair to kneel in front of her. "I can't go against the wisdom of Pop," he said softly as his eyes met hers, unwavering. "Let's get married."

"I don't know what to say," she answered tremulously. This was so unexpected.

She attempted to control the emotions she was experiencing. Pure elation that made her want to sing, to cry with joy, to dance. Her heart was racing, seemed ready to leap from her chest. *Life*, she thought, *in all its unfolding magnificence.* She felt as if dreaming, but she knew that this real, happening in the living room of Grady's parents.

Joseph and Rachel Mayfield sat calmly looking on, smiling. They'd known about Grady's intentions in advance.

"Say yes," Grady said, gently holding her hand.

"Are you serious?" She was almost breathless.

"As a heartbeat," he answered steadily as he held her gaze. "Marry me."

"I guess… I have to say yes," she said, nervously feeling as if everyone could hear her heart pounding. "Yes, I'll marry you; I *want* to marry you."

He was dressed in casual wear rather than a suit today. From the inside breast pocket of his denim jacket, he retrieved a tiny box. He removed from it a white gold ring with a brilliant diamond to slip it on her left ring finger. She was so overjoyed, near tears as he pulled her close, kissing her gently.

"Amen," Joseph said. He rose from his seat and kissed her on the cheek. "Welcome to the family."

Grady recalled the conversation he'd had with his father at the kitchen table on an earlier visit. "Pop, she's different," he said just before he started regularly bringing her to his parents' home. "And not my usual type—she's petite. As a matter of fact, you met her at the family picnic."

"Oh yes, I remember." His father paused to recall the mental image of Clare Ingram, a shapely, little lady with a deep copper brown complexion. How could he forget her? "That's exactly what you need, something different," Joseph Mayfield answered with deliberate directness, remembering the family royalty—The Baroness—Olivia. Then there was Ethel, but by comparison, she had been insignificant. "If you blinked," he once said to his wife, "you would have missed it."

"I'm going to ask her to marry me," Grady said.

"How long you been seeing her?" his father asked.

"A total of twenty-three months if I make her a June bride," he answered quietly.

"It's about time, before the body starts going south," his father answered. "Nothin' is worse than an old man with a young wife, raising babies."

Grady examined his person for cigarettes.

"And stop smoking, boy," his father said. "Those little bastards have death written all over them."

"I guess I forgot them," he replied, smiling sheepishly.

He had been weaning himself from the habit for about eight months. There were still times, when feeling troubled, nervous, or restless, that he found himself lighting up.

"Just as well," replied his father bluntly. Joseph Mayfield had never smoked.

In the present moment on Christmas Day, Grady carefully masked his amusement as he sat facing Clare, who still wore a startled expression. Caught completely off-guard as the victim of a pleasant conspiracy, still trying to digest it all. Looking completely disoriented in such a positively delightful way but managing to return his smile.

"Still want to stop by your mother's?" he asked once they were in the car pulling away from his parents' home. He couldn't resist the secret enjoyment of the surprise that still filled her pretty eyes. It was his intention was the proposal there in the living room of his parents' home as they looked on, but the coup, spontaneously created by his father. Regardless, she was pricelessly adorable through it all, making it worth every second.

"Yes," she answered, still sounding slightly breathless, which was nerves. "She's expecting us."

In the car on the way to her mother's she was quiet, stealing glances at her new engagement ring. She had not wrapped her mind around what had just happened. He cut the motor when parked in front of her mother's door. They no longer rode with the armrest between them.

"Wait," he said softly as she began to slide over toward the door. "Are you upset in any way?"

"No, no, no," she said. "I'm just… I don't know what to say." She sighed, still mildly flustered, appearing utterly beautiful the entire time. "I never expected you to ask me this way…" She didn't know how to express what had caught her unprepared. "I mean… I don't know what I mean," she finished helplessly.

He could feel her trembling as he slid from underneath the steering wheel to lovingly embrace her. He withheld laughter so as not to spoil this special moment. So pleasantly stunned with surprise there was not one witty remark.

"Are you coming home with me tonight?" he asked softly.

"Yes, of course."

"Clare," he asked, "you're okay with this, right?"

That question caused her to quickly regroup and regain focus. "Grady," she said, "I love you and want very much to marry you."

"That's what I want to hear, little girl." He chuckled softly and kissed her tenderly. "And I love you and have for quite some time, even before I admitted it. You know that don't you?"

She nodded slowly as their eyes met.

He was thinking of the grocery shopping incident when he'd decided to step out of his comfort zone. While he was growing up his father had always told him to be receptive to all things positive: "Always be willing to try new things, boy. You might be pleasantly surprised."

Estelle was ecstatic with joy when they told her the news. Max was absent when they first arrived, but upon his return, he shook Grady's hand for the first time. He then teased Clare about the rock on her finger being a little weighty, generating laughter from them all. While Max was talking to Grady, Estelle slipped a thumbs-up and a triumphant smile to her daughter as she silently thanked God that all the serious talks had paid off.

*I'm going to miss this apartment,* Clare decided hours later gazing down at the cars on the Outer Drive traveling north and south along Lake Michigan with the Chicago skyline as a backdrop. The nighttime view was nothing less than spectacular. She recalled watching this year's Fourth of July fireworks from this very window with friends of hers and Grady's, including Nadine and Cornell. What a splendid affair it had been. She would miss walking across the overpass to the lakefront to stroll leisurely with the man who was now her fiancé. Lost in thought, she did not realize that Grady had seated himself beside her on the sofa until he kissed the nape of her neck.

"Penny for your thoughts," he said quietly, tenderly caressing her.

"Grady," she said when she turned away from the window, "I'm so happy. Really, I am."

"So am I, little lady."

However, in all fairness, there was one specific part of Grady's life needing closure before he could freely move on.

Profound change called for an early dinner engagement. Grady called Helen. If it was at all possible, she should not drive to work; he would pick her up that afternoon. She readily agreed to him picking her up from work and dining early. *Patience is a virtue*, she thought.

They both liked this restaurant, a short distance outside the Loop. It was one of Grady's favorites. Lou Rawls's rendition of an old Sinatra tune, "It Was a Very Good Year," was playing softly from the jukebox. The words taunted and teased very appropriately. Unlike the Sinatra original, sad and melancholy, included an upbeat monologue. However, Grady wanted to avoid becoming known as "old folks," alone with nothing but fish tales to tell, the exact setting his father discouraged for his youngest son.

Helen and Grady had finished dinner and were having coffee. He wanted to keep it friendly and not hurtful.

"Would you like dessert?" he asked.

"No, thank you." Helen replied. She sensed he had something on his mind.

"Rawls and his extemporizing," Grady said with a soft chuckle. At this time, he felt there was a specific irony in the words—an old man, once a player, left with only fish tales and memories. "Have you ever listened to the words of that song?"

"No," she admitted. "I've never paid that much attention."

"I have," he said quietly, "lately—not because of that particular song of course—but at this juncture of my life," he continued, "I've been doing a lot of soul-searching." From the bar Grady had ordered bourbon with a water chaser; he finished his drink.

"What have you discovered?" she asked, feeling slightly uneasy.

"Something I've always known—that time can never be replenished."

"Do you think you've been wasting time?"

"I think if I don't begin to change some of my habits, I will be on my way."

Neither spoke for quite some time.

"Helen, we've known each other for a long time, and I've enjoyed every minute with you. I have never regretted any of the time we've spent together. I will always cherish those times. We will always be friends and— "

"Exactly what are you implying, Grady?"

"I'm not implying anything," he said quietly, "other than we've had a very good relationship, and I want to always fondly remember our time together."

"Sounds more like good-bye," she said quietly with a thoughtful smile. "Grady, are you trying to say good-bye?"

"I would rather that it was farewell. I want us to always be friends."

"Hmm," she said thoughtfully. "Friends?"

"Come on, Helen," Grady said softly. "We *are* friends. We will always be friends."

*Whoa, my man, friends!—from lovers to friends?* That inner voice mocked him. *Do you realize how insensitive Helen considers that comment to be?*

Helen was remembering their first meeting. In college, she and Mabel had struck up a solid rapport, and they had remained in touch in the years after. Of course, Grady was a decade younger than his sister, and Helen was yet a year older than Mabel. Mabel considered her a good match for her brother just to pass time since both were unattached. Besides, Helen had always been extremely youthful. When Mabel first met her, she was genuinely shocked that she was not much younger. In fact, Mabel told Helen, she reminded her of Grady's first wife, Olivia.

One day when Mabel was at Helen's place visiting, and Mabel's car was in the shop, she had given her brother Helen's address so that he could pick her up there. At first, Helen mildly contested; she would gladly take her home. Mabel insisted that it would be better this way because she and Grady were both attending the usual bimonthly family gathering with their parents that night anyway. She mentioned that he hadn't attended for a long time because he was constantly working, and this was a way of making sure he was at least briefly in the mix.

"I'll have him come up if you would like to meet him. Would you?"

Helen consented. Why not? From the pictures she had seen of him—Mabel had shown her family photographs—she considered him very good-looking, like the rest of the family.

They began seeing each other after that and in time became close. I have never regretted any of the time we spent together. As the years passed, she ignored the fact that she had read that wrong. Persistently, he withheld bits and even large pieces of his life, keeping her mostly on the perimeter.

Presently she looked so sad. *So much for back on track*, she thought bitterly. *Derailed!* She felt like she had immediately aged five years when he told her of his decision. She had previously ignored the indications of something materializing as their Saturday schedule became loose, with frequent absences and cancellations. He had lately stopped his daily calls as well, and often he had chosen not to spend the night, instead simply stopping by for an hour or so to talk and then leaving, as if gradually kicking a bad habit. She had convinced herself that she was being pessimistic. When she called his office, he was there as usual whenever he wasn't in the field. However, if she had not heard from him that day, her pride would not let her mention it. She routinely returned home early because she arrived at the hospital daily no later than six forty-five and was on the floor at seven. Her telephone calls to his office had always been frequent, but she was used to hearing from him every single day when she arrived home from work, around four or four-thirty.

Finally, she had received a promotion the month before to administrator at the hospital, which had come with an office of her own and additional responsibilities, including the entire maternity ward. Grady had sent a bouquet of yellow roses in celebration. *Yellow roses are a sign of friendship, okay?* cautioned that inner voice as later she and Grady sat opposite each other toasting her good fortune. How could she have forgotten that in life the one constant is change? Finally, for the first time after a long silence, Grady spoke.

"Helen," he said, "I don't want to begin spinning my wheels." He thought of Bradley's term "smooth groove." *Tell it like it is,* that inner voice cautioned, *you want to stop spinning your wheels.* "I need to move on." He paused. "This is no reflection on you."

---

"You want to move on, Grady?" she said. "To where? To what?" She paused.

In retrospect, she felt she could pinpoint the Detroit incident—when he canceled his plans to visit Bridgette with her—as the moment things had begun to change. She had tried to dispel her earlier worry as pessimism, even though Bridgette had none too delicately forewarned her.

He tried gently to take her hand, but she pulled away.

"You can say what's on your mind," she said with an edge of coldness. This was what Bridgette had wanted to spare her. Never once had she listened.

"Helen, I want a home and more children that I watch grow up. I'm tired of living alone; I want a family. I have a son that his mother and I did not raise together. We now have a wonderful relationship, but I will always feel a certain loss from not being a daily part of his childhood and teen years. Fortunately, he does not hold that against me, However, I scheduled him on my calendar like I do my clients, it was a struggle to make sure we had at least a consistent rapport." He paused. "I will always be thankful that I did not miss the most significant times of his formative years."

Helen looked at him steadily for a long time before she spoke. "Somehow, I never thought you wanted to be married since you have been twice before. I thought that we would always remain as we were … Well, I guess I didn't really give it much thought." *Stupid, you should have. That was his sister Mabel's diary, not his.* "But if you really wanted to be married…" She didn't have the words for what she was feeling.

Another long silence followed. Hadn't her daughter warned her as recently as her last visit that there was no guarantee he would be part of her future? What could she have been thinking? And did she hear him right? He wanted more children. She tried not to sound angry when she replied.

"You knew that could never be when you started seeing me, Grady."

"Helen," he said, "I don't want to diminish what we had in any way. Really. We had great times together."

Suddenly the fact that she had never even once met his son during their entire relationship had tremendously profound meaning. For the first time she was taking a good look at what had transpired during the last seven and a half years of her life. They were chapters with an ongoing plot that she had allowed him to control. She could feel herself becoming defensive, feeling rejected and cast aside. *'Great times together,'* she thought bitterly.

"It isn't your fault," he explained quietly. "None of it is your fault or mine; no one is to blame."

"Have you asked her to marry you?"

"Yes, I have," he said gently as if to take away the sting. He did not look away, hoping his direct honesty was considerate and kind.

The ride north from the restaurant to her place allowed time for sorrow to transform into anger. She was reviewing all the times she had asked to meet his parents. He had simply let the request linger and go away—*oh yes, your fault.* She had wanted to meet his son and told him so, more than once—*again, your fault.* After all these years she knew only Mabel and had met only one other family member, Rolanda. Amazingly, after dating for over seven years, she remained the mysterious Helen to most of his family, even his friends—*your fault, all of it your fault!* The only one she knew well, at least by voice on the phone, was Bradley West, Grady's close friend and business partner.

"That should tell you something, Mama," Bridgette had wisely cautioned several times, especially after he missed the first Detroit visit.

She now reflected on an elderly doctor at work who no less than six months ago had made a few indirect overtures she hadn't encouraged, that she in fact shunned. His wife had died a few years earlier. He wasn't very attractive; she convinced herself that he distinctively smelled of cigar smoke. (Some of the nurses made mention that he sometimes smoked cigars.) The recent marriage to a nurse near Helen's age from another floor was proof that someone, if not Helen Moore, was indeed interested. She dared not entertain what could have been.

Her condominium, purchased a couple of years after she and Grady began dating, was on Sheridan Road. As they neared the bend on Lake Shore Drive leading into Sheridan, she suddenly realized this to be the last time she would see him. She felt like crying. If it killed her, she would not succumb to such drama. As he began to park in front of her building, she asked if he would just let her out of the car and not walk her to the door.

Their farewell was awkward, to say the least. He was at a loss for words. There was no farewell appropriate. Nodding his compliance with her request Grady remained in the car but made certain she entered her building safely. He then gently pulled away, unaware that she watched from the lobby window of her building through an angry and sorrowful blur of tears.

*Out with the old*, she thought bitterly, *in with the new. Mr. Mayfield, have a Happy New Year.*

✂

Clare had telephoned Nadine about her engagement to Grady. On the afternoon of New Year's Eve, the newly engaged couple arrived at the home of Cornell and Nadine Bennett with overnight luggage and a garment bag that held their evening attire. They were looking forward to the camaraderie of celebrating and bringing in a new year with friends and afterward spending the night. Nadine saw Clare's ring with a spontaneous squeal. "Oh my God!".

Later that evening the group traveled to the North Side to a New Year's Eve party thrown by Grady's stockbroker and friend Harvey Cohen. Nadine kept excitedly stealing glimpses of their backseat guests. Cornell, driving the car, teased her not to create a case of stage fright for their chauffeured stars.

Cohen had rented an entire suite at the Hyatt on Wacker. When they arrived, people steadily filed into a well-attended celebration. The four of them made their entrance with Grady in the lead. He held her hand while trying to seek out Cohen. Spotting Grady from where he stood at the portable bar, Cohen promptly made his way through the well-dressed crowd containing only a sprinkling of black faces making it easy to spot the four of them entering the room. A substantial percentage of the guests were clients, and his wife never attended because she hated crowds. Cohen had always told Grady, who attended this bash annually It was good PR. In past years he had taken Helen,

"Well, we do stand out in this crowd. We're guaranteed discovery, no blending," commented Clare when Grady leaned over to hear her above the noisy crowd.

Grady smiled with mild amusement. Well, she was no longer speechless. He still enjoyed the private amusement and would for a long time reflect on what had taken place the previous week in his parents' living room.

Nadine was overjoyed for her friend, and throughout the entire event, as they discreetly exchanged glances, Nadine's subtle smiles clearly stated, *what did I tell you?*

The foursome, Clare Ingram, Grady Mayfield, and Cornell and Nadine Bennett, brought in the New Year jubilantly with whistles and hats, distributed by the catering service. Champagne was constantly being poured throughout the evening, and Nadine—in small sips, for the sake of relative sobriety—several times toasted the newly engaged couple. Countdown was near, merely seconds away. "Six, five, four, three, two, one," cheered the raucous crowd. Safely populating the suite in zealous unison, yelling "Happy New Year!" Whistles and other noisy paraphernalia assisted in the celebration. Cornell and Nadine kissed, as did Grady and Clare, and then the four of them exchanged greetings with each other. Even Cohen himself hurriedly made his way through the crowd to hug Grady and Cornell and kiss Clare and Nadine on the cheek.

Festivities extended into the wee hours to joyously usher in the infancy of 1986, a holiday season forever treasured. Except for the few hours of separation, the day after their official engagement, Clare had spent practically all this holiday season with the man she was going to marry, more time than in all the many months she had known him. Her time off from work coincided with his, and in addition to spending time with his parents and hers, they browsed the Shedd Aquarium and the Field Museum, attended a play, ate out mornings and evenings, and even went to a couple of movies. It was just a fun holiday season, culminating with this celebration of New Year's Eve and New Year's

Day with her friends, Cornell and Nadine Bennett, who now were also his.

She had to admit that she had not had this much fun since her early twenties, and it dawned on her that she had spent a lot of her young years going to school and helping her family. First, she had stayed busy obtaining her bachelor's degree and assisting her mother with her sick father. She then focused on helping Jeffrey and completing graduate school. Soon she would have her thirty-third birthday. As Gran Jennie always commented, "My, where does the time go?"

The foursome slept into the early afternoon. Kimberly had spent the night of New Year's Eve with her grandmother, Roxanne, scheduled to return late on New Year's Day evening,

Finally, the newly engaged couple sat at Cornell and Nadine's dining room table directly across from their state-of-the-art kitchen. Cornell flaunted his culinary skills by preparing omelets and other dishes for their brunch, served with Nadine's contributions of coffee and mimosas. Kindly, Grady teased her about not knowing her way around the kitchen. She good-naturedly agreed. Other than baking, Nadine's cooking skills were limited. Cornell, once an aspiring chef, was indeed more kitchen-savvy. Since Kimberly had become part of their household, Nadine was showing more interest in culinary undertakings, discreetly seeking the expertise of Clare, who assisted with enthusiasm. Nadine's shopping sprees had diminished, as her best friend always knew they would. In the past, Clare had often intimated to her mother, "Mama, it's therapy for the absence of what she wants most—children!"

It was truly a gay and memorable time shared by friends. Clare could not help but reflect on the previous year. This holiday truly was the start of life on the upswing.

# CHAPTER TWENTY-THREE

Spring was approaching in Chicago and a beautiful day for jogging even as a damp chill still penetrated the air as winter stubbornly held on. Father and son kept a steady pace along the lakefront trail near Lake Michigan, with South Lake Shore Drive to their left. The sun shone brightly in a blue sky, providing a magnificent backdrop for the Chicago skyline. During the summer months they jogged as far north as Twenty-Second Street and back, but today it was chilly.

"Let's stop here," Grady suggested. They were almost to Thirty-Fifth.

"Getting tired, old man?" Kevin was in a playful mood. It was a beautiful day, and he felt extraordinarily good. Unless he decided to go to grad school, come June his education would be complete. He was now a senior, and his attitude was "Chicago, here I come."

His father didn't readily smile and wasn't bantering with him as he usually did. Kevin slowed down to keep pace with him. He let him choose a spot on the grass away from the path where they could stand and talk. During the summer months they often sat on the grass.

Grady was mildly exhausted but observed that so was his son. This was his private gauge for measuring his own endurance, and he was satisfied that he was not over the hill just yet. He gazed in the direction of the John Hancock Building looming large, but his thoughts were elsewhere.

"Kevin," he asked, turning to face him, "have I been a good father? What I mean is, do you think you missed out on an awful lot because your mother and I didn't stay together?" He paused. "Take your time and be truthful."

Kevin allowed his mind to travel back through the years. Although he was not in a serious mood, his father was, so he forced himself to mentally adjust. Purposely excluding his father's two-year stint in Vietnam, he comparatively thought about the father-son relationships of his classmates from grammar school through high school. He was positive those were the years that concerned his father. He could honestly say that this man had always been there when he needed him. He thought about the times when just the two of them would hang out on weekends, going to baseball games, browsing the museums, shopping for Christmas presents, sitting around his apartment eating pizza, watching television, or going to the movies. In particular, his father had never forgotten his birthday. If during those times his father had lady friends, and Kevin was sure he did, they were never included. The schedule was kept simple and uncluttered for just the two of them. He held many fond memories of those warm interactions—just father and son sharing quality time. Now he turned his attention back to the present moment with his father and this unexpected moment of open sincerity.

"Yes," Kevin replied truthfully. "You have been a good father, and you were always there for me. You kept our time together uncluttered and reserved for just the two of us. I will always appreciate that."

Grady smiled and accepted his son's answer. "Let's go," he said, and again they began to jog.

Kevin slowed down his pace. He wanted to savor this moment. "Dad?" he said.

Grady broke his stride and turned toward his son, and the younger man stepped forward to hug his father, who returned his embrace.

"I love you, Dad," he said quietly. "You have always been there for me, always."

❧

Now Grady was satisfied. There was another subject that he wanted to explore with his son too, though. They jogged for another twenty minutes, back toward Fifty-First. Again, they stopped to find a spot on the grass where they could stand. After a few quiet, pensive moments, Grady spoke first. "I have decided to marry again. How do you feel about that?"

Kevin was thoughtful. His father had never mentioned even the remote possibility of getting married again. In recent years, from his late teens up until now, Kevin had heard Aunt Ro ask his father several times about a lady named Helen whom he had never met. Once he had thought about asking his father who she was, but the urge had dissipated quickly. If the question his father was now asking had been put to him at a much younger age, when he was still anticipating a reunion between his parents, he might have felt apprehension, even anger. He had matured beyond those emotions.

"Have I met her?"

"Yes, you have."

"Let me guess—is it the lady you brought to the family picnic?" Kevin grinned, remembering the stir of surprise among family members. He would never forget the pleased smile on Grandma Rae's face. When had his father ever brought a woman to any family gathering? "Her name is Clare, right?"

They were facing each other, both now squatting with their elbows resting on their knees.

"Right, we're engaged to be married. Your grandparents already know about it, but I would like to make the announcement to everyone at the family home on Saturday and for you to be there. It's an important day for me."

Kevin was remembering the small woman who had joined them in softball. He could still hear Aunt Ro saying, "We need a shortstop." She had quickly turned to Clare. "Come on, little bit; you're it."

It was a fun time, and Clare had played just as hard as the rest of them. She was a good hitter too. By the end of the day, she had blended in nicely. Grandma Rae told her she was glad to have met her and to be sure to have Grady bring her by the house.

"It's a date," Kevin replied to his father.

A few days later, Grady stopped by his parents' home. Their car was gone, so he used his key, and there, seated on the living room sofa, was Mabel. How had he overlooked her car? He and Clare had missed her on Christmas Day because she had only made a pit stop at their parents' house earlier, on her way to work. The hospital's administrative personnel were short-staffed, so Mabel had volunteered to work the evening shift.

Often Mabel stopped by to see if her parents needed anything. Since they were old school and liked personally paying their utility bills, she dutifully ran these monthly errands for them. Mabel still had some progress to make in accepting Clare and welcoming her into the family. Grady would never forget the thorough visual scrutiny she'd given Clare at the family picnic. When introduced to her, she had been cordial but distant.

"I still call Helen from time to time," Mabel remarked, "and she's talking about moving to Detroit to be near her daughter. She's been applying for administrative positions at hospitals there."

Grady made no comment and continued to drink the soda that Mabel had offered when he first arrived.

"Clare's very pretty," she continued. "I'm surprised that she is so petite. I don't think you have ever dated anybody that small, have you?"

He chuckled as he finished his soda. "In bed, neither height nor size is a factor," he replied. He said it is mainly for shock value and to forcefully terminate this vein of conversation.

"You are almost forty-three years old, Grady. You have been married twice, and it's not necessary for you to marry again."

*So now,* he thought, *you are my self-appointed counselor.* "For that matter, so have you," he replied. Then he cautiously paused because he did not want this to become a blowup. "Mabel," he said, carefully measuring his words, "how can you possibly be the judge of what I need?" He paused again because he was getting angry, and that would spoil what had begun as a friendly chat between siblings. "Why are we having this conversation, anyway? I am not having this family gathering to be granted approval from anyone, but to make sure that all know I am getting married and to whom."

"Helen is a nice lady and—"

"Mabel, don't do this." *It is none of your business,* his cool stare implied. "I do not want to argue with you, okay?… Know what, when Mom and Dad come in, tell them to call me."

"You don't have to leave—"

"Oh, but I do." His chuckle held a slightly icy edge. "Tell them I stopped by."

He could feel her eyes watching him as he descended the stairs. He quickly got in his car and drove off. What he wanted to say would have caused a big blowup. It was a marvel that she and Lawrence were still married at all, let alone presently living under the same roof. The man had to be a candidate for a plaque that read "I Have Traded Peace for the Love of Stress."

Thirty minutes later, he entered his apartment to the steady drone of the vacuum cleaner. Smiling to himself, he stood for a moment in the doorway, watching his fiancée. She was completely unaware of his presence. Softly closing the door behind him, he stayed out of sight as he moved closer and then, reaching around her, switched off the vacuum cleaner. She turned quickly, mildly startled, and then smiled and greeted him with a kiss.

"Leave that for Mrs. James," he said. Mrs. James was a senior citizen from his parents' church who cleaned homes for extra money. He could still hear his mother saying, "This place would be a lot neater if you hired Mrs. James. There are papers and books all over the place." That was a stretch, but he had to admit his apartment had been very orderly since Mrs. James started making her weekly visits.

Clare had followed Grady's professional suggestion to place her house on the market around the end of February. She had lagged slightly, putting it up for sale with his agency near the middle of the first week of March instead. It got an offer in less than nine days, causing her a mixture of relief and mild anxiety. She was unprepared to move in and share an apartment with her future husband so abruptly. Of course, she had spent nights in his apartment for some months now, but never without being able to return to her own home whenever she wished. The first-time homebuyers were excited and liked the house so much they were willing to pay an additional three thousand dollars to outbid the competition. Clare accepted. They chose occupancy within the month, six weeks at the latest, because their apartment lease expired within that time frame. It had been almost a week since Grady had handed her the extra key, and nothing was unpacked.

Grady had welcomed Clare's arrival by generously providing her the hall closet and part of the one in the bedroom they now shared. Her furniture was in storage, and they had selected the pieces to be delivered to their permanent home, but she had not decided what to do with the rest. She was in an awkward place and was handling this interim phase of her new life with great discomfort, like she was walking on a rocky terrain without proper shoes.

Estelle had asked whether Clare wanted to move in with her until the wedding date, but she had hesitantly rejected that arrangement. Her mother had been very candid in stating that she wanted to have her cake and eat it too. "You cannot sell your house and, at the same time, live there until your wedding." And no, her mother had stated, she was not averse to staying with her future husband until she married him. She totally approved of Grady and did not think she could even wish for a more suitable son-in-law.

"Come, talk to me," Grady said.

He led her by the hand to the sofa; they sat facing each other, and he could not help his mild amusement as he watched her. He found this woman who was now a permanent part of his life so very satisfying and interestingly different.

"How can I make you comfortable for these next few months?" he asked quietly.

"I'm comfortable," she replied, but those beautiful eyes betrayed her.

She recalled her second night in the apartment. When the phone rang, Grady was in the shower. She first decided to let his answering machine get it but on the third ring decided to pick up. It was her future sister-in-law, Mabel, and remembering her from the family picnic, Clare attempted to make small talk. However, Mabel's dry response let her know that she hadn't come around yet. Ignoring the effort at small talk, she simply requested that Clare have Grady return her call. Clare had heard about Helen several times from Rolanda, so she knew that Mabel had introduced them to each other years ago. Rolanda had instructed Grady's new fiancée not to worry; no competition was involved. After connecting the dots, Clare had attempted to discuss the Helen subject with Grady. He had brushed it off as insignificant water under the bridge, so she dropped it.

In the present, he gently squeezed her hand. "But you're not completely at ease, not really. So talk to me."

This was the one thing he did not like about this little lady who had stolen his heart. It wasn't that she did not want to discuss things, but his insight was that she often did not know exactly how to phrase her words until she'd had ample time to sort out the thoughts and words in her head. Sometimes it was as if she walked on eggshells. In this respect, he knew that her upbringing played an important role.

"We have to communicate, Clare. Tell me how I can make you feel less vulnerable."

"You think I feel vulnerable?"

"Clare, I know you feel vulnerable." His eyes held hers. "You cannot transition between here and your own home whenever you wish as before and in turn have me spend nights at your place. Temporarily we live here and share the same bed as if already married, and it makes you feel insecure. That's it, right?"

She mildly admonished herself for being Victorian and briefly looked away. Then her eyes again met his. "I never imagined the house would sell so fast," she admitted quietly, absently glancing at the stunningly beautiful engagement ring. "Forgive me for sounding so prudish," she said quietly. She felt like a naïve schoolgirl.

"Honesty isn't being prudish, Clare."

"Things happen. Well, you know Engaged people have been known to live together and then end up never saying 'I do.'" There, she had said it. She sighed again, feeling utterly foolish.

"Would you feel less vulnerable staying with your mother until we're married?"

"No," she protested quickly, as if that was a preposterous idea. "Grady, I'm not a teenager; I'm in my thirties."

"There are women who have never lived with a man who was not their husband," he said matter-of-factly, "even for a short period of time."

He immediately thought of his mother and his youngest sister, Rolanda. Mabel, however, had a premarital live-in arrangement with her present husband, and for a shaky period, whether they would exchange vows had looked uncertain. Grady was not sure, but the family rumor was that his sister Ruth had lived with her future husband in California during their last year of grad school.

Wanting this conversation over and done with, she moved closer to him and, sliding her arms about his waist, laid her head on his shoulder.

"It has nothing to do with you, Grady," she said softly. "It's me." She heaved a sigh. "I'm fine. I'm okay," she said, suddenly lifting her head and again resting it on his shoulder. His fragrance was always nice. She considered it sexy when a man wore a great fragrance. The man she was going to marry was sexy in and out of bed, as she often told him.

"Do not clean the apartment," he said.

She raised her head again, this time to look at him.

"Mrs. James cleans the apartment every Wednesday."

She moved in last Thursday. Now she realized why everything had been so immaculate when she arrived; the day before had been cleaning day.

"Also, I eat out during the week because there are a few special projects that West and I are working on, so I get here too late to eat before seven."

"Why do you have to eat before seven?"

"Because I have a tendency to gain weight no matter how much I exercise," he said, "if I eat full meals after seven." He paused. "Also, Mrs. James will continue to do my laundry until we are officially married. On weekends if you wish to cook, only if you wish, we can eat in. Otherwise, until we are pronounced man and wife, we can always eat out."

He sensed that the feeling of awkwardness would now subside. The next evening proved him right. She had unpacked all her things and put away the empty suitcases, indicating that the conversation had helped after all. *Communication is the key*, he thought, *to all meaningful relationships.*

❧

For years Grady's nickname for her had been Powerhouse. As a child he had gone out of his way to antagonize her, relentlessly describing her as big as a house and equally powerful, especially when she sat on him while daring him to try to move as he continued to tease her. He was next to the youngest of the Mayfield children, and Mabel was the oldest. Because she was a big eater, he often accused her of hand-to-mouth dysfunction. In retort she would always remind him that she used to change his nasty, stinky diapers. Since he could not possibly remember, he asked his mother, who confirmed that indeed she had.

There was one Saturday he could vividly recall to this very day. Their father was home watching a baseball game, and Mabel was, as usual, eating. This time it was chips, and he was taunting her with his usual name-calling. Much to his surprise, though, she completely ignored him, engrossed in reading a piece of mail. Then with a spontaneous burst of energy and an expression of joy, she ran up the stairs excitedly, calling to their mother.

❧

It wasn't easy to distract Joseph Mayfield during a baseball game—he was an avid Sox fan (a true South Sider)—but he had overheard his youngest son, and he left his seat and summoned Grady. "Come sit a spell."

"Who's winning?" Grady asked, attempting small talk as he walked in the room and sat down on the sofa across from his father.

"The Sox are winning," he said. He looked at Grady carefully. "Don't you think you need to cut that out?"

Grady was shocked, not realizing that their father had ever paid their skirmishes that much attention. Instantly ashamed, he played dumb. "Cut what out?"

"Teasing your sister about her weight. You're getting older now. You're almost ten and growing up, and it's no longer cute. She's your older sister. In fact, she is the oldest of all of you and deserves more respect than that. Okay?"

He shrugged awkwardly. "Okay."

Suddenly Mabel burst into the room, totally elated. "I got it!" she exclaimed tearfully. "I got the scholarship."

Their father leapt out of his seat, the ballgame momentarily forgotten, to hug his firstborn. "That's my girl. I knew you could do it."

A few doors down from his parents' bungalow, Grady remained seated in his parked car, biding just a little more time as he replayed these childhood memories. Driving by earlier, he had looked for his parents' car, which was usually parked in front of their home during the day and then deposited in the alley-accessible garage at night.

Stalling for as long as possible, he continued to gaze across the street at the BMW. It was the car's owner who was making a review of all these childhood memories. Somehow, he wished even to this day that he had stopped teasing her on his own. As he thought back, he realized she was the only sibling he had gone out of his way to antagonize, and to date, he couldn't pinpoint why.

His thoughts again began to drift, this time to when she was no longer in high school, but away at a small college in Minnesota on the scholarship she'd obtained with the assistance of her counselor. The bed in the room she shared with Rolanda was now empty, and there was a melancholy calm, a void, during family activities. Joseph Mayfield continued to make use of the stereo, but Mabel's piano playing was sorely missed. There was an empty chair during evening meals and at their weekly family Monopoly games. No longer was her distinctive voice part of the church choir. Communication came in the form of economically brief phone calls and weekly letters addressed to their mother, with greetings to them all. That first spring break, when most college students traveled home, Mabel stayed at school and worked at an off-campus coffee shop in order to purchase items for school that her scholarship did not cover.

Proof of Minnesota's unruly, merciless winters had come when Rachel Mayfield mentioned to Joseph that she was sending thermal underwear for their daughter to wear under her jeans. Mabel had been forewarned about the frigid weather by her counselor, who had attended one of the state's larger schools, the University of Minnesota, but in her excitement, she had forgotten to pack her necessary armor.

Two years passed, and when his oldest sister did finally begin coming home for family holidays, there was a significant change. Slowly she was transforming. She was no longer the overweight teenager because out of necessity her eating habits had improved. She no longer had extra money to buy junk snacks, and the result was sensible eating of all the food groups, which her mother stayed on her about when she was living at home. Her love of sweets—candy, cake, ice cream—and other junk like potato chips, skins, and popcorn with lots of butter gradually faded, and by the time she graduated, she had overcome her battle with such a negative diet. She had become a young woman, statuesque, with a neat waistline, gorgeous skin, and great legs.

While raising their eight children Joseph and Rachel Mayfield ran a tight ship. They could afford only to supplement their children's education, so they pushed each one to get exceptionally good grades to obtain a scholarship. At the time Joseph Mayfield was still working, and Rachel was taking in sewing. Even though some money had been put aside to assist in the education of all their children, college had become considerably more costly than what they had managed to save. When Grady started college, Mabel was married and well established with an advanced degree in nursing, and she consistently and voluntarily assisted him financially with his education. Grady's athletic scholarship included a clause (in small print) stipulating that he had to be an active participant for the entire four years—that is, play football and never for any reason be benched. In his last year, somewhere during the middle of the football season, he was injured, sustaining a ruptured kidney, and therefore was ineligible to play. Later, he made a full recovery, but not in time to fulfill that fine print of his scholarship, so he applied for financial aid. It helped but wasn't enough to allow him to complete the necessary credits for graduation. However, Mabel had money saved and without hesitation paid the required funds. Even when he became financially able, she refused to accept his offer of repayment. For that he would be forever grateful, and he did not want their present relationship to retrogress.

When younger, he had sometimes wondered whether he would have gone pro had it not been for that serious injury. No doubt, he would now be retired from the sport and handsomely rewarded. He had to admit with pride that he had done quite well without it.

Nevertheless, that oldest sibling was bossy and desired an elevated status among all her sisters and brothers; she wanted to remain front and center. Introducing him to Helen had been an innocent, low-key, spur-of-the-moment idea. At the time Grady was dating others. However, he had kept his options open to date whomever he pleased during the entire span of his relationship with Helen. Emotionally, at least for him, the relationship had reached a midlevel status and remained there; there had never been any discussion of marriage. He had always been a man of integrity, and the idea of taking her around his family had caused an inner discomfort because of the implications of such a move. They had attended only one family affair together during the entire relationship, and that was solely because he had to stop by Rolanda's for a specific reason—just why he couldn't now remember—and she and her family were barbecuing in their backyard with a few friends and neighbors. No other family members were present. Therefore, the only family member Helen knew well was Mabel, a friend from graduate school. She knew none of his friends other than Bradley West, and she knew him mostly from conversing with him by phone. She had always remained a private part of Grady's life.

Mabel had known both his previous wives, Olivia and Ethel, as had all the family. Since his second divorce Grady had been single for a long time. Perhaps this was why Mabel had not noticed what was before her very eyes, that her brother was not as content with bachelorhood as she thought. However, his parents, Rolanda, and a few of the other family members had paid exceptionally close attention.

Reluctantly, Grady now used his key to let himself in his parents' home; Mabel was seated on the living room sofa again and looked up from her crossword puzzle when he entered the room.

"Hi," she said, wearing her truce smile. "What's a nine-letter word for 'everlasting'? I tried 'permanent.'"

"Perpetual, maybe," he replied. "Not back yet, huh?"

He kissed her on the cheek, and she responded kindly, continuing with her puzzle. Joseph Mayfield had instilled this positive interaction in all his children. It always worked like magic, just as he had told them it would.

"How can you stay angry with someone after hugging or kissing them?" he asked time and time again. "All the offspring that came from Joseph and Rachel Mayfield were conceived in love, and that must continue. It is written."

*Pop, where is this written?* Grady had wanted to ask, amused. *I want documented evidence.* He never made the remark aloud because anytime his wise father commanded their attention, such an interjection would trivialize and spoil the mood of the moment. Joseph Mayfield had that effect on his family for he was truly the patriarch of the Mayfield clan.

"Dad took Mama to pick up pantyhose," Mabel said, looking up from her puzzle. "Then they said they had to do a little grocery shopping. You know how Dad loves bacon and eggs for breakfast."

He didn't eat them every morning because their mother monitored his intake of both sweets and other foods, and she alternated what he considered more enjoyable with foods that were more conducive to maintaining their health.

"I offered to go for them, but I think they just wanted to get out of the house for a little while."

"It's good for them to leave the house," Grady said. "Retired people should stay active."

In past years all of Rachel's children, with genuine concern, had chided their mother for not learning how to drive a car. Now only her daughters continued to mildly scold her for not obtaining more independence when younger. Joseph Mayfield was never too busy to take his wife wherever she wanted to go. He was from the old school, when men desired more dependency from women, which most often served to stroke the male ego. However, it all seemed to balance out, and their marriage had spanned more than fifty years.

Grady deposited himself in his father's favorite chair.

"The caterer called and said they would be here at seven," Mabel informed him.

"Okay," he answered.

Getting up after only a few minutes, Grady walked in the kitchen and placed a call from the wall phone; she was there. Earlier that day Clare had called his office to inform him that she was leaving work a little early and offered to drive over so that he did not have to make a trip back to Hyde Park. However, he chose to pick her up so that they could avoid separate cars and could ride back to the apartment together.

☙

The dining room was full. Most of Clare's future in-laws were there: Mabel and her husband, Lawrence; Cambridge and his wife and children; Arthur, alone because all his children were away at college and his wife was working late at her downtown office; Quincy and his wife and four children; Ruth, who had recently moved back from California to a northern suburb, and her husband (their two kids had been left behind with a babysitter); Jacob and his wife, who kept stealing glimpses of the future addition to the family, making Clare slightly uneasy; and Rolanda and Stan, who were not strangers to Clare because Grady had taken her to their home more than a few times. Rolanda and Stan too had left their children with a babysitter—the next-door neighbor's very reliable daughter, who was a freshman in junior college.

Clare was now well acquainted with her future father- and mother-in-law. Rachel greeted her warmly, and Joseph Mayfield hugged her, addressing her as "little lady," and the three of them conversed a few minutes before everything began. That significant Christmas evening was one she would forever remember.

As the Mayfield clan continued to file in, she thought, *this is a tall family!* Usually comfortable with her height and size, she herself placed emphasis on that fact. She considered it unusual that both the men and the women in the family were tall. She smiled at the way they all so demonstratively greeted each other with kisses and hugs with mild envy of their displays of affection, almost nonexistent in her family. Except on special occasions such as holidays and birthdays, Uncle Ned and her mother, whom she thought of as close, seldom expressed affection with each other. With the Mayfield clan, affection was routine and wonderful. Kevin, whom Clare vaguely remembered from the family picnic, was the last to arrive. He caused a stir of emotion. Everyone hurried to hug and kiss him and laugh and talk with him. Some family members had not seen him since Christmas.

Finally, she met Uncle Maurice. He and his wife came to speak to their nephew. Both hugged her warmly like they had known her for years. All were so friendly except Mabel. The ice there had yet to thaw; she remained coolly distant and kept studying Clare from across the room.

Amused, Grady watched his oldest sister stealing glimpses of Clare the entire evening. He wanted to suggest that she get acquainted with the little lady because as sure as rain, she was going to become her sister-in-law.

Estelle, Uncle Ned, and Aunt Celeste came in next and sought her out, demonstrably acknowledging that this was indeed a special occasion; they congratulated her with hugs and kisses. Regarding height, Uncle Ned was right at home. As for Celeste and Estelle, they weren't quite as diminutive as Clare.

---

The catering service Grady had hired opened champagne and filled each adult's glass. The children were appeased with champagne glasses filled with fruit punch, garnished with a slice of orange. Everyone gathered around the dining room table, holding their filled glasses, and turned their attention to Grady as he stood to speak.

"I wanted to make sure Pop got a chance to see me—to use his expression— 'settled in,'" Grady said, All the family laughed. "He really thought it was going to be curtains," he said, nodding toward his father. He playfully shook his fist. "But one day I found this little lady while shopping for groceries." He placed his arm around Clare's shoulders, gently pulling her close. "For those who don't know my fiancée, this is Clare Ingram." She greeted all of them, and they in turn did the same, repeating her first name in unison. Grady fondly looked down at his future wife. "I'm going to make this pretty little lady a June bride," he said and held up his glass. "Can we all toast that occasion?"

All toasted the upcoming event. Afterward, everyone began to mingle and enjoy the relaxed and informal occasion; the catering service was efficient for the entire evening in their black-and-white uniforms.

✧

Sweet memories, Grady thought. Well, most anyway. The movers had just left after clearing the apartment to transport everything to the new address. Only select pieces from Clare's furniture had been removed from storage, leaving all that remained to be either sold or donated to charity. Uncle Maurice was meeting the movers at the Beverly address. That man had always been there for Grady, every step of the way. What would he do without him?

Slowly Grady walked through the rooms of the apartment. checking once more to make sure it was considerably clean. He had never lived anywhere and left it dirty.

Clare had left only a few minutes earlier to stay with her mother until the next day. Her trousseau, yet to be packed, was at her mother's, as were the wedding gown and veil, delivered earlier in the week. He had watched her that morning gathering her personal belongings and preparing to leave. She had attempted to hide her level of nervousness which had her almost as breathless as his proposal.

"Are you calm?" he asked, quelling a chuckle.

"What?" she answered defensively. "Oh, stop it, Grady Collier Mayfield!"

Both laughed and embraced. "It's going to be okay," he said, kissing her tenderly.

His mother really admired Estelle and said repeatedly that she had raised a beautiful daughter who was certain to make him an excellent wife.

"Close to this time tomorrow," he teased, "you will no longer be an Ingram." He pulled her close for one last time to give her a long, lingering kiss.

"That's true, as your bachelor hours are now numbered, Mr. Mayfield," she whispered. She longed to extend this carefree joking, but goodness she was nervous!

Her heartbeat quickened, but she managed to pick up her belongings. Together they left the apartment to take the elevator down. Beside her car, they kissed farewell. She was spending the night with her mother; they would see each other no more until the wedding ceremony.

Life was so very interesting. As his father always said, truly a journey on which there were surprises along the way, some of which unfolded according to the path chosen. After his second divorce, Grady had spent most of his eleven years, single, in this apartment. He checked the keys, two sets, and the key to his mailbox, which he now removed from his key ring; picked up the one suitcase and an overnight bag; and exited the empty apartment for the very last time.

Casey, one of the daytime security guards, smiled at Grady in recognition as he submitted the keys. He checked them, making certain they were all there. "So, you're leaving us and moving on," he said pleasantly. He had known him as a long-time tenant.

"That I am," Grady responded with a smile.

"Well, Mr. Mayfield," he answered, shaking his hand, "it was nice knowing you. Good luck in the future."

"Thank you, and I wish you the same," Grady replied.

Grady picked up his suitcase and overnight bag to make his way to the indoor parking. It was twelve noon as he exited his reserved parking space for the final time, smiling thoughtfully. At this time tomorrow Joseph Mayfield would be the happiest man alive. "Boy, you need a wife and more babies," his father had been saying, repeatedly, for at least the last five years. His mother always gently protested. He was spending the night at his parents' home. He wondered what Pop's words of wisdom would be.

When he arrived, there was his father, with a radiant smile on his face, opening the door to usher him inside before he could even ring the bell. Tomorrow was a big day that they would emotionally share. Finally, life was moving in the direction Joseph Mayfield desired for his youngest son.

"I told your mother you should arrive soon, or I was going to call the police to report you missing," Grady's father said as he closed the front door.

"Pop, twenty-four hours," Grady replied in good humor as he put down his bags. "You have to wait at least twenty-four hours."

"Special case," Joseph replied as they hugged each other. "When I told them why, they would understand."

Emerging from the kitchen, his mother beamed happily and kissed his cheek. For the first time he realized just how overjoyed she too was regarding his exit from bachelorhood.

"Your tux is here," she said cheerfully. "They brought it yesterday morning."

"Good," he said.

Joseph Mayfield took the overnight bag, and Grady grabbed the suitcase, following his father upstairs to the guest bedroom. This experience felt strange because he had never spent even one night in this house purchased with mostly his money. The only time he had even seen the entire house was when he was touring it with other siblings. Most of the time while visiting, he never ventured any farther than the kitchen, dining room, or the living room. It gave him a pleasantly odd feeling to enter the room that he would occupy until morning when he left for the church.

"Have you eaten yet?" called his mother from the kitchen.

"No, I haven't," he answered as he descended the stairs. "What's on the menu?"

Soon he was seated at the dining room table with his parents, enjoying a meal of tossed salad, country-style ribs, collard greens, mashed potatoes, cornbread, and sliced tomatoes.

"I baked a cake," she said.

"Special occasion, huh?" Grady teased.

"Better believe it," his father said, "and a long time coming."

"Joe," said Rachel, "don't you start."

Grady laughed good-naturedly. "And what if I was a no-show?" he asked, playfully encouraging his father.

"An all-out news bulletin with your picture, helicopters, the works," answered Joseph Mayfield, "until you were found, boy."

Even his mother had to laugh over that one.

Grady had opted out of the bachelor party Bradley West wanted to throw for him because he had been honored with such a party twice before and preferred to just spend a quiet evening with his parents. Bradley had said he understood but could not resist the temptation to tease him. "I understand, my man. The third time it's not a bachelor party but a reunion." This had drawn laughter from them both.

Grady called Clare twice that evening. She laughed while he teased her about making sure no man was hiding in her mother's closet; just maybe he needed to request careful monitoring by Estelle. During the second call they became serious about how they missed each other and finally said their goodnights until morning.

∽

Nadine finally left the dressing room after making certain she was no longer needed; Clare had to practically push her out the door. A few minutes later, Sharla entered the room all smiles as she presented Clare with a small pair of very expensive, genuine pearl earrings to match her necklace. Clare had previously commented on not wanting to wear her diamond pendant and earrings to prevent her looking like an ice maiden.

Sharla had suggested that she wear her pearl necklace and imitation pearl earrings instead. "Who will know the difference?" Sharla had said. "They will be underneath your veil." Clare had finally welcomed her as a very good friend, and now they engaged in sincere heart-to-heart discussions, even though Nadine remained Clare's ultimate confidant. Clare now allowed Sharla to place on her ears her "something new" giving her a genuine hug. She was glad to have broken with tradition so that despite being divorced, Sharla could participate in her wedding as one of the bridesmaids. Besides, Sharla's marriage had been a brief affair without children. Naturally, Nadine was her matron of honor.

Sharla exited to leave Clare once more alone, lost in thought. Soon Estelle entered the room all smiles. Clare could tell her mother had been crying but knew they were tears of joy. Earlier Estelle had made sure Clare's bridal gown and veil had been delivered to the dressing room. The packed trousseau and the groom's luggage were in the trunk of the limousine parked at the curb. Estelle had inconspicuously exited the room to check on these matters after depositing the nervous bride-to-be in the makeup artist's chair. They had not seen each other again until now.

At last, she was seeing her daughter fully attired, breathtakingly beautiful in her bridal gown and veil, her feet in simple white satin pumps barely peeping out from beneath the floor-length gown. Estelle radiated joy as ever so carefully as she lifted the nervous bride's veil away for the occasion.

"Be happy, Clare," she told her daughter, lovingly hugging her, carefully pressing her cheek against hers, so as not to muss her makeup.

*Mama*, Clare thought, *please don't say anything that will make me cry.* Her stomach was full of nervous butterflies. Getting married was like a dream; she was practically afloat with anticipation of their honeymoon.

Her mother now consistently demonstrated affection; Mason had not won after all. She had been so gracious and loving the eve of the wedding with just the two of them, mother and daughter, together in the quiet of her mother's home. They shared such a wonderful, unforgettable evening as her mother assisted in packing her trousseau.

"You cannot begin to know how I thank God that you found a good man who will be a rock to you, sweetheart," Estelle said now. "Enjoy him in every way possible."

"Thank you, Mama," she whispered. "Thank you." It was all she could manage.

"God bless you, precious. I'll see you at the reception."

After gently repositioning her daughter's veil, Estelle paused in the doorway to capture a mental picture of her one remaining child as a beautiful bride. She had repeated the path of Jennifer Allen Beckford. She thanked God for granting her daughter the ideal version of a wedding that she herself had not experienced. In addition to the photographs taken to capture the memory of this day, she would hold her own everlasting mental picture of this perfect moment.

Suddenly she again stood in thoughtful solitude, reflecting on the first time she saw Grady Mayfield, their courtship that had spanned practically two years, the unforgettable proposal, as Nadine constantly encouraged her to stay the course. For a few seconds she focused on the beautiful engagement ring and then anxiously clasped her trembling hands. She was getting married!

Uncle Ned looked stunning in his tux as he entered the room, promptly and on cue, to walk her down the aisle. "Come on, little lady," he said and smiled. "Let's get you married."

It was a beautiful wedding, not too large, executed with great taste and style. There were four bridesmaids in coral gowns. One of the male escorts was Kevin Mayfield, dapper in his rented ivory tux, the designated color for the men in the wedding party. Nadine, alone as the matron of honor, walked down the aisle in a beautiful full-length yellow gown accented with a coral corsage. Next came two ring bearers—two five-year-old boys from church; one was bearing the bride's ring, the other the groom's band. The flower girl—four-year-old Tracey, the daughter of Grace, Clare's administrative assistant—followed behind them, daintily dropping the coral and yellow rose petals from her basket.

As the pianist began playing the wedding march, Grady stood waiting with his best man, Bradley West. The guests stood on cue; their eyes focused on the entrance of the church. Finally, Clare appeared, wearing a stunning white satin and lace gown that emphasized her neat waistline, her face covered by a sheer veil. Uncle Ned looked grand and dignified as he escorted his niece to stand before the pastor with the man she was about to marry. Grady smiled approvingly, practically undressing her with his eyes as they stood together before the pleased pastor. Clare was so nervous, as if she might float away at any minute to miss the entire event. From behind Grady, best man Bradley gave the bride a broad grin.

The program was printed on ivory stationery, with the edges etched in gold and trimmed in delicate lace. Beneath a sheer overlay of tulle was a poem in gilded print, written by Nadine Jamison, whose lifetime hobby of writing poetry had begun in grade school.

The congregation was now seated; Nadine's poem was read by one of Clare's friends from church.

***Eternal Love***
*by*
*Nadine Jamison*


*I would love you if you were only a voice,*
*Caressing me with a whisper instead of embracing me*
*With the promise of intimacy,*
*To lie under the stars and keep tempo with the tide.*
*Kissing, loving, and making the moon smile.*


*To tread where you have walked,*
*To kiss your footprints left behind in the meadow,*
*To enter the room that once held your presence.*
*For a moment or a day becomes a treasured memory*
*That will defy and withstand infinity.*


*It is the lingering of your smell, the feel of your face.*
*Against mine as we become one,*
*Enrapturing traces of your caress as smooth as velvet,*

Then began the ceremony officiated by the bride's pastor. As Clare recited her vows, for the first time Grady heard her entire christened name, Clarissa Lucinda Ingram. She caught the amused twinkle in his eye when he smiled with one eyebrow slightly raised for a brief second. When it was his turn, there were no surprises.

Next, they exchanged white gold wedding bands; his for her contained a row of sparkling diamonds, and hers for him held one impressive inlaid diamond. The pastor smiled approvingly and then finished the ceremony.

"I now pronounce you husband and wife. You may kiss the bride."

Lifting her veil, Grady swept her up in his arms to kiss her long and ardently while the entire congregation erupted with applause. Briefly, he kissed her again before gently lowering her to her feet, never taking his eyes off her as she looked up at him, simply beaming. Her new husband responded with a playful wink.

Grady had made only one simple request regarding the wedding: that the ceremony end with them jumping the broom—, and so it was, while Clare inwardly beseeched the forgiveness of her great-great-grandfather, Calvin Beckford. Estelle had told Clare more than once that her father, Chester Beckford, had often told her that his grandfather, Calvin Beckford, told him his first official act of freedom was to have his marriage made official by an ordained minister. He had equated 'jumping the broom' with slavery.

Afterward, he leaned down and whispered in her ear, "You better be good to me, little girl."

"I promise," she whispered back.

Hand in hand, they left the church to be greeted outside by rice thrown from both sides of the walkway, which had been covered for the occasion with a long, soft yellow carpet extending all the way to the waiting white limousine, compliments of Bradley and Maggie West. There was a pause as Clare suddenly tossed the bouquet over her shoulder toward the bridesmaids; the recipient was Sharla Kantor.

Clare and her new husband were ushered inside their transportation and whisked off to the reception being held in Bradley and Maggie West's large backyard. The food was being catered, and Max had insisted on generously helping Estelle pay for the wedding of her daughter. A large white tent had been rented and beautifully decorated, remaining true to the wedding theme: coral, ivory, and pale yellow. Any other white was reserved for the bride. God had sanctioned the day to be hot and sunny with a clear blue sky.

Upon arriving at the reception, Grady helped his new bride from the limousine that would later take them to the airport. She scanned the crowd for her family and spotted Uncle Ned, Aunt Celeste, all the Mayfield clan, even Mabel, but no Druscilla. Of course, she wanted to give everyone ample time to arrive, but she sadly sensed that her cousin would not be in attendance.

❧

Both cars, his and hers, had been parked in the garage before they left for their honeymoon. Uncle Maurice, with the assistance of the burglar alarm system, had been around to make sure things remained undisturbed.

People were out mowing and watering their lawns when they first pulled up in front of the house that Clare remembered touring the previous summer. She smiled. Nadine had been right all along. They both emerged from the limousine dressed casually in jeans and colorful tops. Grady paid and generously tipped the driver, who was quickly descending the front steps after placing their luggage on the stoop. Finally, the neighbors' curiosity was satisfied.

Grady looked down at her, smiling, as he unlocked the front door. Some of the neighbors stopped to watch; a few smiled.

"Well, Mrs. Mayfield," he asked. "Shall we?" With that he scooped her up and carried her over the threshold.

The Bahamas with its straw market, the sherbet-colored houses of Paradise Island, and the numerous tourist activities and attractions were behind them now. Married life was set to begin.

They spent their first three months of marriage in a home literally a love nest. Lovemaking took place in the living room, in his study, and of course in bed. Sometimes she initiated it by going to whatever part of the house he was in and enticing him, naked under her robe. Clare, who preferred baths, always invited him to join her, engaging him in torrid foreplay followed by extended lovemaking. Sometimes he coaxed her to retire early or kept her in bed. Often, he tenderly aroused her from sleep in the wee hours or just before sunrise.

As his wife, Grady began to discover a new dimension. She opened to him like a spring flower; she was freer expressing a deeper passion. There were a few Saturdays when he called his office to say he was not coming in. Laughing, West once asked if Grady was very thankful that he had followed his advice. Indeed, he was. She was delicious, as he often told her. He once asked her if she had drugged him because, if so, what a lovely high. She remained conscious of her flat scar, even if it was more of an afterthought now; she consistently preferred to cover herself after intimacy. With gentle firmness he always remained consistently against it.

"I want to totally feel your body against mine," he would always say.

Things started to settle down. Individual schedules for a married couple with separate schedules in various instances. Being a stickler to time, Clare was never late for work. A few times she did take a day off.

Meanwhile, the house continued to come together. Recalling his uncle's foresight, Grady conveniently converted one of the five second-floor bedrooms to a convenient laundry room realizing that Clare would not have complained of a basement laundry room. Life was made much simpler as the laundry chute was permanently sealed.

Uncle Maurice had mentioned the large size of the house to him when he purchased it. The few houses left for sale in the area were notably smaller, but Grady knew he wanted to have ample space for his wide circle of friends. Plus, the Mayfield family was large.

While movers were helping position furniture, Clare became involved with various decorating decisions. Initially, she sought Grady's reluctant input. All decorating decisions were left to her discretion. The basic primer for all the rooms had been deliberately used, allowing her full charge of color choices and any window treatments she desired. Furniture from both his apartment and her house kept purchases of new furniture to a minimum. Decorating was completed in several months.

As of late, shopping was no longer a priority for Nadine, now that she had Kimberly to keep her happily busy. Nevertheless, she and Clare still found time to get together. Nadine teased the new bride about their tropical honeymoon.

"Did you even once leave the ship when you visited the Bahamas? You two stay in bed so much, I'll bet you even bathe together. I am beginning to wonder when you get up to eat."

Clare laughed.

On Clare's first day back at work, Grant called her into his office. He wanted to know whether she was still interested in a regional directorship. She affirmed that indeed she was. Well, he reported, there was one coming up in another four months. The person currently holding the position was retiring, placing her next line for the promotion.

However, Clare and Grady did discuss what they would do if she became pregnant. As previously agreed, Grady's income was enough that she would be a stay-at-home mom. Both had agreed that they did not want their children to spend their early years with babysitters.

It was their fourth month of marriage; something was wrong. She was filled with dread. Should she say something, go to the doctor? What? She lay across the bed with such a feeling of lethargy. These days, soon after arriving home from work, making dinner, cleaning up afterward their evening meal, and cleaning house on weekends, she wanted nothing but rest. Withholding any comment, Grady was very aware.

It was Saturday morning; she didn't hear him come in the bedroom. When he lay down beside her on the spacious bed, facing her, she was slightly startled.

"Hey, little girl," he said, kissing her forehead.

"Hi yourself," she said, placing her arm around his neck.

"What's up with you?" he asked.

"I don't know."

"Don't you think you should find out?" He took a deep breath. "Clare, we both are aware of your medical history, but you cannot create problems without knowing if there is one… Clare, don't be afraid, all right?"

"I'll call Dr. Hudson on Monday." Dr. Hudson had been her primary care physician since she was a teenager.

"Uh-uh," he said, "call today. Isn't he in on Saturdays until one?"

She nodded.

He softened, held her close. "Don't think anything negative, Clare." He relaxed his embrace so he could look into her eyes. "Make the appointment, and I'll go with you."

"I will," she promised and then looked away.

"Gotta go, West is waiting. I'll see you this evening." Slapping her on the bottom, he kissed her full on the lips and got up from the bed.

She lay there for a few more minutes and then got up to call Dr. Hudson's office.

A few days later, her primary care physician entered the exam room smiling. When he told her the results of the tests he'd just run, she stared at him in disbelief. Promptly discarding her oral contraceptive. when they boarded the ship, she'd had no idea.

"But I'm still having my regular menstrual," she said.

He promptly handed her the business card for an obstetrician. reputedly one of the best in the city. "That is probably the reason you are so exceptionally tired. He'll remedy that problem." Dr. Hudson smiled. "Congratulations! You've almost completed your first trimester."

Grady was sitting patiently in the waiting room reading *Sports Illustrated* when Clare and the doctor came out to share the news.

"Are you ready to go to Little League on Saturdays?" Dr. Hudson asked him.

"Girls play baseball too, you know," Clare countered, and both men laughed.

∽

"Well, well, well, this is high cotton," said Joseph Mayfield as he and Rachel entered the home of their youngest son and daughter-in-law for the first time now that all the decorating was finally complete. (Her mother and her in-laws had decided to give the two a sufficient 'settling-in' period.) He stood in the foyer, looked around before turning to wink at Clare. He was fond of the newest addition to their family. He told his son he considered her special.

Rachel Mayfield laughed and playfully hit at her husband. "Oh, hush, Joe," she said, hugging her daughter-in-law.

" 'High cotton' is the label he gives whatever he considers above the norm," Grady explained, laughing at the quizzical expression on Clare's face as she stood beside him.

Joe leaned down to kiss his daughter-in-law on the cheek. "How are you and that little one?" he said.

"We are both doing fine." She was beginning the second trimester of her pregnancy.

After a tour of the house, Rachel mentioned that she would like a cup of tea, so she and her son moved to the large sunny kitchen to visit. Clare remained in the living room, talking with her father-in-law and pursuing an explanation for the expression he had used earlier. She understood Joseph Mayfield was delighted to see his youngest son finally "settled in" and set to become a parent for the second time.

"Papa," she said. This transition to calling Grady's father "Papa" had been a smooth one, and the term felt much more suitable for her father-in-law than it had ever been for Mason. "I have never heard the term 'high cotton,'"

He laughed softly, glad to have such an elegant addition to their family. He had observed during the tour of their home that of all his daughters-in-law, she kept the neatest home. There were elegant touches of what made a house a home—lovely houseplants, a few sprays of flowers from her garden, beautiful paintings and artifacts, and tasteful arrangements of silk flowers. He was certain that she was the one responsible for creating this atmosphere of elegance and incorporating the recognizable furniture from Grady's apartment into it. Never having visited her former home, he couldn't distinguish her furniture from what was new. Everything was immaculate, but with a warm, welcoming charm. Finally, his youngest son had a life. For the first time he felt a surge of peace for Grady, who now had a place to call home.

"I know you've heard the lyrics of the song *Summertime*," Joseph said to his daughter-in-law. Clare nodded that she had. "Well, it talks about easy living, and then there is one line that says, 'The fish are jumping, and the cotton is high.' The song is euphoric, a nostalgic celebration of wealth, the easy living of the cherished Old South. Nothing was easy for us, from can't see to can't see." He laughed. "But a rich daddy and a good-looking mama were the reason the baby could hush and not cry; all was well." He paused. "'High cotton' now means abundant living."

"I know that song well," Clare said.

"It's reminiscent of the antebellum south, plantation living," Joseph continued. "Those chosen lyrics depict the South in its heyday. It describes the lifestyle of white folks who had that valuable product—cotton!—and plenty of free labor to pick it."

Clare agreed with a knowing smile.

"I'm sure you know that right now, to this day, many white people in this country, north as well as south, in their hearts prefer that time period as the most ideal—free wealth for a lot of institutions that now exist only because of centuries of all that unpaid labor."

"I've heard the lyrics many times, never analyzing their meaning. In fact, I love the music, especially Satchmo's version. He and Ella sing it so beautifully."

"Absolutely," he replied, "but whenever you hear that song again, little lady, listen carefully to the lyrics. Detect the nostalgia." After a brief pause and with a warm smile, he said, "Let me tell you a story. In 1876, there was an election between Samuel J. Tilden, the Democrat, and Rutherford B. Hayes, the Republican. Both were running for the presidency. I'm not sure of the exact vote count for either man. Anyway, there was no clear winner. Even back then, there was the Electoral College to elect the president, and as you already know, winning the popular vote doesn't guarantee getting elected, right?"

She nodded with a smile.

"Well, a deal was cut between Tilden and Hayes. Rutherford B. Hayes, the Republican, would be declared the US president in exchange for the Republicans withdrawing the federal troops from the Southern states. Blacks had been under the protection of the Union Army since the end of the Civil War. That agreement between the candidates ensured that business as usual could resume."

"It was called the Compromise of 1877," she said quietly with a tinge of sadness. "I'd forgotten all about that historical turn of events."

"For blacks," he added, "it was also known as the Great Betrayal. You know the rest—Black Codes started even before then. Jim Crow, sharecropping, lynchings, you name it."

As they visited this new home, Joseph Mayfield recalled how Grady had worried about him and Rachel years ago. That area during his youth was a decent area. It had become drug-infested with oppressive living conditions. Thus, Grady had assembled the Mayfield siblings to decide what to do about their parents. Because of familial obligations, two of them could contribute only a mere pittance. Without a moment's hesitation Grady had made up the difference, supplying the most generous portion of the money. Joseph and Rachel Mayfield's residence was now a handsome bungalow in Chatham, free and clear of any expenses except annual taxes and general upkeep. It was known by the whole family as the "family home." Rachel often reminded her husband, "Count your blessings that your son 'chased money,' That's why we are comfortable without a mortgage."

Until Grady found and married Clare, Joseph had remained dissatisfied that he was so restless and driven. With that chapter of Grady's life behind him, his father rejoiced, thanking God for answering his prayer.

Their time together was joyous with a delicious three-course meal, garnishes, wine, and dessert. All was served on beautiful china with crystal glassware, prepared by Clare. Grady's parents could tell that he was so proud of his wife. What Clare did not know was that Rachel attributed her elegance and grace to her mother, Estelle. She often told her husband that she wanted to spend more time getting to know that woman. She had raised a beautiful, loving daughter who made their son happy. He had found his soul mate.

❧

Months later, during the wee hours approaching dawn, the house was silent, enveloped in early morning calm. Both Grady and Clare lay awake. Trying to find a comfortable position, she rested on her side and positioned her body to a slight angle; her head rested on his shoulder. Her only other option was to lie flat on her back. She would be going into labor any day now, and Dr. Blair had suggested that, if possible, Grady stay close to home. Yesterday was his last day in the office.

"You've been exceptionally quiet for the past few days," he said softly. "What are you thinking about?"

He reached under her gown to tenderly caress her very large belly. He was elated that he was going to become a father again, especially with this beautiful little woman as the mother. He thanked God that he had listened to those closest to him constantly encouraging him to take the plunge for a third time.

"Oh," she said, "I've never been pregnant before. I'm thinking about how giving birth will feel, the pain, or…" She sighed. "I guess it's the normal curiosity all women have if it's their first time."

"Are you fearful?" he asked.

"Not really," she answered truthfully.

"I'll be in the delivery room with you," he assured her, tenderly kissing her forehead.

"I know, and that makes me very happy."

❧

At four thirty in the morning there was a flurry of activity, and Brandon Cambridge Mayfield left his mother's womb protesting loudly. Weighing almost eight pounds, his large size caused his mother to undergo an episiotomy. Proud parents gazed down on their son lying between them on the hospital bed, cleaned and wrapped in his receiving blanket. The deep brown little baby boy, almost the color of Clare without the copper undertone, seemed to gaze back at them; instantly he tugged at her heart. He looked so much like Jeffrey. Grady had rejected even the middle name of Collier for their son; Kevin would never know his major role in that decision. In turn, Grady asked if she wanted to name their son after her brother; she also declined. Both settled on Cambridge, his mother's maiden name, as the infant's middle name.

As much as he tried to alleviate it, Grady still harbored some guilt about his first son. Even though he shared most of his innermost thoughts with his wife, that spot in his heart remained unhealed; he told no one. In kind, Clare didn't talk to her husband about the sad memories that she yet held about her brother; it kept her from using his name.

# Chapter Twenty-Four

Estelle was ecstatic when Clare telephoned her to ask if she could babysit her little grandson. Presently, she anxiously stood on the sidewalk in front of her home as Clare parked the car. It was so strangely wonderful to see Clare with baby formula, diapers, and all the necessities for the care of an infant. He was to spend the entire morning with her. Proudly Estelle freed her little grandson from the car seat, tenderly holding him in her arms as she carried him inside. Unless Clare gave her another, he was the only grandchild she would ever have. Estelle thought of her own mother, who had lost all her children through death except her. This little infant, gazing up at her for the first time, reminded her so much of Jeffrey as a newborn; Clare followed close behind with the bag of formula and diapers. It was almost eerie, as if her son was reaching back from the grave, to not be forgotten.

Without a moment's hesitation, Grady had agreed that Brandon should spend more time with his grandmother Estelle. Joseph and Rachel were blessed with not a few grandchildren and the bonus of great-grandchildren, and until little Brandon bonded with Estelle, the three of them could visit the home of his parents as a family.

Clare was due back in the office today. Grant knew her decision even before she seated herself in that comfortable oversize armchair directly in front of his desk.

"I did not want to say this over the phone because I felt that you deserved better than that," she said with a warm smile. This man had consistently promoted her since she first moved to his department from another floor two years into her bachelor's degree. "We've decided that I will remain at home to raise my son. I'll wait until he's in the first grade to go back to work. Since I am blessed with this opportunity, I want to take full advantage of it."

"If you have another one," he teased gently, "it will be even longer before you return to work."

"Very true," she said, but without regret.

Grant smiled. He had always liked Clare Ingram. He thought back to when her office had become, intermittently, almost a floral centerpiece and was glad to have eventually met the man who was the cause of it all. Grant had been invited to the wedding and, much to Clare's surprise, had accepted the invitation, attending with his wife, whom he introduced to Clare and Grady during the reception.

"Well," he said, "for the time being there is no career on the immediate horizon for Clarissa Lucinda Ingram Mayfield."

"You recall hearing the full name?" she asked with laughter.

He nodded and smiled.

At work, human resources knew only her middle initial. *Life and its changes*, she thought. Change was always a certainty. They talked for about twenty minutes longer. Then it was time to bid farewell.

"Well, Mrs. Clare Mayfield," he said with subdued cheerfulness, "if ever you decide that you want to work again for this firm, especially me, all you need to do is call. I promise you, if there are any openings, you will by no means be offered an entry-level position."

"I'm honored to know that" she said.

With that they shook hands. Clare left his office and the familiar building by the Chicago River to commute back to the south side, pick up her son, and return home.

There was another event that would occur later in the year. On November 25, 1987, at 11:00 a.m., Chicago's first black Mayor, Harold Washington, would die of a heart attack. Clare had just put Brandon in his playpen, taking a cake and pies from the oven for Thanksgiving, when Nadine telephoned her to say anxiously, "Turn on the television." When she did, it was like watching a depressing documentary.

∽

When Brandon was a year and a half old, Clare decided that she wanted to have another child, but her second pregnancy was unsuccessful. Following that miscarriage, she told herself that soon she would be thirty-seven, and Grady ten years older. She did not want Brandon to grow up without at least one sibling. She decided that she wanted to try again.

A few months later, she began to keep track of her menstrual cycle. Month after month it was stubbornly punctual. Grady asked if she was sure she wanted to try again. Her reply was, "Definitely." Almost thirteen months passed before she became pregnant for the third time. She was elated. Grady tried to remain subdued but couldn't hide his pleasure. During the fifth month of pregnancy, when she began to spot, the one thing she thanked God for being was being without a job to further complicate circumstances. However, she panicked slightly. Dr. Blair's advice was to remain calm and stay off her feet as much as possible for the next few months. During that crucial period, Brandon was welcomed by the Mayfield grandparents, returning home when she resumed most of her household chores a few months later. This included nothing exceeding light gardening—doctor's orders! When she began spotting again, it was faint. Dr. Blair placed her on a mild medication, instructing her to monitor herself for any excessive bleeding; the spotting ceased.

She was nearly asleep, on her side. This was the second time her only alternative was to lie flat on her back. It was late evening. Her eyes opened when she felt weight on the bed. Grady switched on his table lamp. He had just finished showering. Sometimes on Fridays, after leaving the office, he stopped with Bradley for a few drinks. She had insisted that he get away from the house some evenings. With her persistent coaxing, he had relented this evening, calling a couple of times to check on her.

Because Clare was so close to delivery, Rolanda, temporarily not working, suggested that Brandon visit with his cousins during this time. From his aunt's home the very active four-year-old telephoned his mother each day during the next few months.

Even when at home, Grady had always found it amusing that during his little son's time spent with him, he would slip away momentarily to visit whatever part of the house his mother was in, pop in to say hello, then rejoin him to resume their activity.

"Hey, Pumpkin," Grady now greeted her as he prepared to join her in bed. He had been using this nickname since her seventh month of pregnancy. Pulling on his pajama bottoms, which was all he ever wore, he leaned over to kiss his very pregnant wife. The doctor had said that delivery was only weeks away. After tonight Grady would stay close to home because he did not like spending too much time away from her. It was for this same reason that he had cut short his evening out.

"Hi yourself," she said and yawned. Lately, she stayed tired.

On the way in from the lounge, he briefly stopped by his parents' house. His mother commented that she would be relieved when Clare had the baby. "She's so tired," she told her son.

"Don't you do that to her too many more times either, boy," joked his father.

The comment generated laughter from Grady; his mother, suppressing an amused smile, chided Joseph to be quiet. Grady left after giving his father a good-bye hug and planting a kiss on his mother's cheek.

"What's the matter?" Clare asked sleepily. His bedside lamp remained on as watched her closely.

"Nothing," he said.

He reached under her gown to place his hand on her very large belly, caressing it gently. She had resorted to wearing gowns during the last three months, mildly complaining that thanks to him none of her pajamas were a comfortable fit, refusing to purchase maternity pajamas for a temporary condition. He had chuckled, pointing out that her problem resulted from a joint effort. However, he still marveled at how the female anatomy could transform so remarkably.

"How do you feel? Are you okay?" he asked now.

"I'm pregnant, so I feel pregnant." She yawned again. "Not to worry," she whispered playfully, "you definitely will never have to be subjected to it."

He chuckled. "Really?"

"Trust me," she said.

A few minutes later, she was sound asleep. He lay there watching her, listening to her breathe deeply. Marriage to this woman had changed his life; he honestly felt complete. *What a difference time makes, Dinah,* he thought, slightly altering the well-known lyrics. Switching off the table lamp, he went to sleep.

Like clockwork, little Jennifer Estelle Mayfield, weighing six and a half pounds, entered the world with a whimper, as if not fully aware that she had exited the comfort of her previous home. Upon full realization of that fact, she hollered loudly at the rude interruption, causing the doctors and nurses to laugh.

"Wow, there is nothing wrong with her lungs," commented one of the nurses.

"For a little bundle, we definitely know she's here," said the anesthesiologist.

Finally, once she was cleaned and wrapped in a receiving blanket, the two proud parents gazed down at their daughter. She examined them as well. She had a mess of jet-black hair, her mother's almond-shaped eyes, and the golden-brown complexion of her father.

Clare had asked if he would mind the name she had chosen, since he hadn't offered any suggestions himself. Grady assured her that three Rachel namesakes—one granddaughter and two great-granddaughters—were enough to make sure no one ever forgot Rachel Cambridge Mayfield.

While in labor with Jennifer, Clare had undergone a tubal ligation. "Reproduction at this Mayfield address has been permanently discontinued," she commented a few months later. "Too bad it's not a versatile oven to be used for biscuits or muffins or something short-order."

Grady got a laugh from that one. *Leave it to Clare*, he thought.

So now that there was a complete family of four, Grady and Clare were looking forward to a lovely Christmas celebrated in their own home with their newest addition, little Jennifer. A week before the holiday, Clare was attempting to decorate the tree during Grady's absence. For seven-month-old Jennifer all the shiny ornaments were a constant distraction from her toys. She kept crawling off the blanket, anxious to reach the brightly colored objects. Finally, Clare summoned Brandon away from a game that held his attention, instructing him to play with his baby sister to divert her attention from all the glitter. When this proved unsuccessful, Clare resorted to temporarily placing her in her playpen. Once all the ornaments were on the tree, the excited little girl was again placed on her blanket. Clare simultaneously switched on the tree lights with one hand and snapped the picture with her other, as Brandon firmly held his little sister. For those few seconds her tiny face expressed such delightful awe. She gleefully clapped her little hands in response to the tree's sudden brilliant transformation. All the family would forever cherish that picture as one of the best of her childhood. Clare would forever remember her baby laughter filling the room.

❧

Christmas gifts had been exchanged, the dishes cleaned and put away with dessert served on paper plates with plastic forks. It had been a great evening for the Mayfields, Estelle Beckford Ingram and Max, and Ned and Celeste Beckford. Everyone was having such a grand time. The two families were bonding beautifully (Rachel and Estelle often visited one another by telephone or in person now). The children were in bed, the football game was over. Everyone had gravitated to the dining room table to converse about a smorgasbord of interests. It was then that the conversation drifted in a very new direction.

"Remember ole Geezer?" Ned asked his sister sitting across the table from him.

"How could I forget?" Estelle replied.

Back in Georgia, the pair explained, Geezer was the family's big brown boxer and Estelle's sidekick. They were inseparable; he died when she was eleven.

"At night she always took Geezer to the outhouse with her," Ned said. "He would dutifully stand there in fair weather, rain, or whatever, until she came out."

"Not always," Estelle reminded her brother. "Mama often insisted that I carry that awful bucket to my room, especially on cold nights. Then I'd have to squat. Ugh!"

"Call it what it is," Ned said, "plain and simple! A slop jar!"

Estelle good-naturedly wrinkled her nose, feigning disgust. Rachel smiled with amusement. Grady and Clare looked at each other and laughed uproariously, with everyone else following suit.

"So I'd—you know, in Georgia it doesn't get real cold—anyway, I'd take Geezer, and off I'd go."

"We never had indoor plumbing," Ned explained.

"Never," agreed Estelle, "until we arrived in Chicago." She paused. "Mama had it put in years later, but never while we were there."

Clare raised her eyebrow. "Mama, you never told me that before."

"I know about that," said Rachel matter-of-factly in reference to the South. "Neither did we," she said. "Most of us didn't."

Estelle smiled at Clare. "I'm telling you now. When I got to Chicago, I'd flush Aunt Lucinda's toilet even when I didn't have to use it, just to make sure it was real. Aunt Lu and C. J. even had a half-bath, thank you very much."

"That privy came in handy, though," said Ned, "the night those rednecks came looking for Bo."

"Who is Bo?" asked Clare. Ned had mentioned Bo once before, during that glorious dinner a few days after Mason's funeral, following Jeffrey's return from all his gallivanting.

Clare and Grady were enjoying this exploration of family history, especially Grady, because it was giving him in-depth look into the background of the woman he'd married.

"A relative you never met, but maybe one day you will meet him," responded her uncle. He then continued because he would need too much time to explain a brief history of Jason Beckford, fondly called Bo; his older sister Matilda was called Tillie. He wanted to finish his story.

"They said he talked back to ole Weaver. Remember that? That he had physically assaulted the SOB."

Estelle nodded.

"Those crackers would have strung him up too if they'd found him. When Dad got word they were coming looking for him, he hurried and removed the top from the toilet—our privy was larger than most— placed plywood over the hole, put Bo inside on top of those boards, and then nailed the top back on. We had to go to the bathroom in slop jars until the next night when those bastards gave up looking for him. If they hadn't been led by Sheriff Eades, they never would have come on land belonging to us crazy niggers, either. That's for sure. Sheriff Eades and those crackers together combed the woods—on *our* property, mind you, plus that of the McDermotts—and all the time Bo was right there. They glanced in the privy because they thought he was going to the bathroom or hiding—above ground, you know. Sheriff Eades finally made all of them leave with him since no harm was done. Remember?"

Estelle nodded again.

"But all the time he was right there." Ned looked sad for a moment. "Sons of bitches! Oh, excuse me." Ned never liked swearing in the presence of women. At one time, Estelle had been the exception, but she had reprimanded him countless times.

"Ned don't get yourself all upset," his sister chided gently.

Every time he told the story, he got upset. Later, in 1955, when Emmitt Till was murdered, for a long time Ned continued to gaze at the *Jet* magazine photograph of Till's grotesque remains. Estelle knew he was envisioning what could have happened to Bo had their father not acted swiftly.

"After dark that next night, Bo was snuck from the privy. He was given Pacer to ride out of there. I don't know how far he rode him. Anyway, Pacer knew the way back home and made it back to us, but we never saw Bo again. Somebody said they saw him in Cleveland. Once, after I came north, I drove to Cleveland looking for him."

"I never knew that" Estelle marveled.

"Yeah," he said with a somber nod. "Spent a whole week of my vacation, went everywhere I even thought black folks stayed in that town, took pictures with me to show people. Nobody had seen him, ever. That Weaver was nothing but poor white trash, the ole redneck, lowlife SOB, nothing but a drunk and a wife beater, poorer than dirt, lived in a run-down cabin with no grass around it, scum of the earth."

Ned stopped talking, and everyone at the table could tell he was thinking back. He then smiled and started laughing. "Excuse me," he said, gesturing apologetically toward the women, "but I'll bet Bo never smelled that much shit since."

That drew a roomful of jubilant laughter. They were having so much fun. Then it was Joseph Mayfield's turn to tell a story, one that Grady had never heard in such explicit detail.

"I'm from Alabama," Joseph Mayfield began, "and where we lived there was only one way in and one way out because behind us, a little distance away, was a big quarry. Well, one time some of those crackers thought they were going to have an evening of entertainment messing with some niggers, right? But we got wind of what they were going to do, so all the men climbed up in trees and waited until they rode their horses up in there and shot a few of those bastards. It scared the others so bad that they hightailed it out of there, even deserted their buddies. Well, we frightened away their horses and pulled those rednecks into the quarry. Now, we didn't attempt to kill them, just plugged them enough to scare the hell out of them, flesh wounds mostly, or just grazed the skin, and shot *at* some of the others. We got back up in the trees to watch for a while, and their buddies never came back for them. We went in our houses late that night, sitting watch at the windows, women as well as men." He laughed. "The ones we had pulled to the edge of the quarry. Before daylight, they limped away as fast as they could. After that incident each night for about a week, we took turns at watch in case they came back. They never did. They never told a soul, either. Too ashamed and embarrassed to tell it. Now, they were supposed to strike fear into us, right? Well, that was a very precarious situation because there was only one way in or out—perhaps not like these fancy cul-de-sacs you have up north but providing enough protection to keep down a lot of disturbance. No more trouble on the home front after that."

Now everybody was laughing uncontrollably. Other than what had begun as a sad recollection from Ned, the evening was full of laughter.

# Chapter Twenty-Five

Kevin was approaching him, smiling, in jeans and gym shoes. Usually they jogged a lot earlier, but Kevin had mentioned that he would be tied up that morning. He had not offered an explanation as to why, but because it was raining, Grady hadn't asked for one. The air smelled clean and fresh on this Saturday afternoon. As agreed, they were meeting at their usual spot on the lakefront. Kevin now resided in the same building of his father's bachelorhood days and used the overhead crossing to the lakefront.

"You look like you know something I don't," said his father. "What gives?"

"Mom got married this morning."

"You're kidding!" *After all these years,* he thought.

"No, I left the church about ninety minutes ago." He had gone home to change clothes so that he could hang out with his father. "I stood with her and David."

After they'd been jogging a while, Kevin asked, "Do you know how long she's been seeing him?"

"Who?"

"Dad!" Kevin exclaimed. "We're talking about Mom. Who else?"

"I don't know. Why? Does it bother you, the sudden marriage?"

"No, but it's close to incredible."

Kevin and his girlfriend, whom he'd met in law school, were discussing marriage now too. Grady considered her a nice girl—quiet, rather a bookworm, very attractive, tall like Olivia, but that was the extent of the similarities. He wondered whether the young woman liked her potential mother-in-law and, if so, whether it was mutual. If there was any tension, he was almost certain it was coming from Olivia. Sometimes he had the urge to inquire about such things, but he never did, wanting to stay out of anything concerning Kevin's mother. It seemed like eons ago that he had lived with her. Even after all this time, he was relieved that life's turn of events allowed him to be far removed.

"Why incredible?" Grady asked.

"She's been dating the guy ever since you two split up."

"But wasn't he still married then?" Kevin had mentioned casually a long time ago that his mother was dating some guy who was divorcing his wife.

"Right, but he and his wife had been married in name only for a very long time. He got a divorce about two or three years ago."

"How do you know, Mr. Tabloid?" Grady questioned with a chuckle.

They stopped but continued jogging in place as they faced each other, slowly decreasing their movement. Kevin had the most mischievous expression on his face.

"I know because his daughter used to date a law school buddy of mine. She always talked about her father and mother having separate bedrooms." Kevin laughed. "Small world, isn't it?"

His father did not answer.

"You know why she got married, right?"

"Probably because she got tired of living alone," Grady replied. Kevin did not realize that his father had never liked discussing with him anything so personal about his mother. This conversation was innocent enough, yet Grady felt uneasy.

"Dad!" he exclaimed, flabbergasted. "You're deliberately playing the nut role." He paused. "Think about it: you have been married to Clare for quite some time, okay?"

"This is my second marriage since your mother and I divorced," Grady said with a thoughtful smile. "I was single for years after both divorces."

"Exactly, you weren't even married to Ethel a year. I was young, but I remember. In fact, you never introduced her to me, but I heard her name a couple of times when I was at Grandma's." He was referring to Olivia's mother; Kevin called Grady's mother Granny Rachel. "Mom hoped you two would one day get back together."

It aroused Grady's curiosity to learn that Peaches, as everyone called Olivia's mother, had talked about his marriage to Ethel. Kevin had never mentioned that he even knew her name. "Exactly what did your grandmother say?"

"Nothing much. I overheard Mom and Grandma talking a couple of times about Ethel and you breaking up after such a short marriage. Grandma said she had predicted that the marriage wouldn't last."

"Really?" Grady asked.

"Really, and she was right. I think Mom knows you and Clare are in it for the long haul. When she saw me dressing not only to attend your wedding, but to be in it, she looked rather sad. I knew then that she still loved you."

"Kevin, come on."

"Dad, I'm serious as a heart attack. You stayed single for a long time before you married again."

Grady managed to conceal the awkwardness he was feeling about discussing something this personal with his son. The fact that he and Olivia had not stayed together to raise Kevin still left an emotional void; the nagging remainder of guilt had not gone away. The fact that he and Clare had been married for quite some time and Kevin had two more siblings spoke volumes.

"Kevin, do you feel in any way cheated? I mean—"

"Dad, now come on," Kevin patiently replied. "I thought we both cleared that hurdle."

"I'm merely asking, Kevin," his father quietly replied.

Kevin vaguely recalled being very young and witnessing the screaming, fitful rages of his very emotional mother. Granted, he was quite young when his parents divorced, but he couldn't remember one pleasant time. Then his father was out of the house, in Vietnam, and then he was back. Things settled down, and from then on, he'd seen his father regularly.

"This is absolutely the very last time we are having this conversation, okay?"

His father nodded patiently. Though still father and son, they were no longer boy and man. This was a discussion between two men.

"I remember," Kevin said quietly, "when you no longer lived with us. There was a brief lapse of time when you were absent from my life. I thought I would never see you again, but then just like magic, there you were." He paused. "I was so happy that Grandma was right. You were working things out. Of course, you went to 'Nam for those two years too, but that doesn't count, know what I mean?"

Grady nodded.

Kevin laughed at the expression on his father's face. "Don't look so surprised. Grandma always liked you and told me to always know that I was loved by both."

"Really?"

"Really," Kevin said. "She would always ask about you whenever I came back from a visit. From time to time, she still asks about you."

With that, they resumed jogging, enjoying the togetherness, father and son. It turned out to be a wonderful afternoon. *Wonders never cease,* Grady thought. *So Peaches knew after all.*

At the age of six, Jennifer started attending school all day, and Clare decided to return to work. She checked in with her former employer and discovered that Grant was no longer in the States but an executive director in the overseas office. Apparently, though, someone in human resources made him aware that she was seeking a job in his former office. She was surprised when he called her at home, talked with her for a few minutes, instructing her to apply for one of the two available directorships. He promised to submit his personal recommendation, which he did. Within the week she was hired for one of the open positions.

Grady was impressed and commented that it must be nice to know people with that kind of clout. She sensed that he did not want her to return to work. However, boredom had taken its toll with both children attending school all day. She explained this, but the more they discussed it, the more aggravated she became, and Grady even more so. At first, she was surprised, never having expected that there would be any resistance to a shift in scheduling so that she could work. He kept mentioning that it was not necessary for her to work.

"Why do you have to work, Clare?"

"What else am I going to do now that both children are in school all day? That was our agreement, remember?"

He loved having her home all day, telephoning her during the day just to say hello, occasionally arriving home early to have extra time with the children, chatting with her before dinner. He enjoyed sitting down to early meals together, just the four of them, without the rush and tight push that a working woman's schedule entailed. She had been home for ten long years. Admittedly, he was spoiled, which made him somewhat resistant to changes that would inevitably take place with her working every day. For one thing, the children had to have someone home when they arrived— Jennifer at three, Brandon about a half-hour later. At this point in time, Grady arrived home at approximately five, sometimes. five thirty. For years, he had worked toward this lifestyle. Now he wanted to enjoy the fruits of his labor, uninterrupted, for as long as possible.

"What if I said I would rather that you did *not* work?"

"Grady, give me a good reason why I shouldn't work, just one good reason."

They were headed for an argument. He could tell she was not going to give in. He decided to let it go. If she wanted to work, let her work. She had been planning on returning to work for almost a year and more than once had permitted him a peek at her mindset, as if paving the way, so that there would be no opposition. He dared not say what he was thinking: other than those hard-core, intent-on-a-career females, most would give anything not to have to go to a nine-to-five. Had she paid attention to the latest trend and noticed that whenever possible women were leaving the workforce to return home and raise their children? But of course, he knew better than to say that to Clarissa Lucinda Ingram Mayfield.

Since her company had seven-and-a-half-hour workdays, office hours were eight thirty a.m. to five p.m. with an hour for lunch. She worked out a schedule with her department, permitting her to start at eight, work straight through the allotted hour for lunch, eating in her office as she worked, and then leave work at three thirty. This meant she was out of the house by six thirty in the morning to drive the short distance to the commuter train, arrive home by five and have dinner on the table by six. The schedule did cause some difficulties; she had to comb Jennifer's hair the night before and lay out the next day's clothing for both children for their father to get them ready for school the following day. Also, he had to make breakfast—cold cereal—for them both. He could not freely involve himself in the field during the day whenever he liked, sporadically act on hunches, show up periodically at the car washes as he wished, visit some of the rental properties, and not be as cognizant of time. Clare was always home to greet them both and that meant he would have to do the same.

For Clare this arrangement worked for about five months, and then began the barrage of complaints from her colleagues. Her schedule was inflexible. Sometimes emergencies cropped up that she was not in the office to handle; there was resentment regarding department agendas that had to be planned around her regimented schedule; there were other meetings that she had to leave before they were over. The list was long. Then the executive director of her department, admitting that he was guilty of oversight, informed her it was against the law to work over six hours without a lunch break. Human resources should never have given their permission. She rebutted that this should have been established by human resources beforehand, not after she was hired with that arrangement in place. If she hadn't known better, she would have sworn someone had been conferring with Grady Mayfield. She realized that wasn't possible. Once again, she was a housewife.

Grady and the children were elated, and she felt as if an insurmountable conspiracy had been waged. Helplessly, she felt defeat and anger taking her over. That weekend she decided she needed a day away from her family and spent the entire Saturday with Nadine. Luckily, she had her friend all to herself because Cornell had gone to visit his brother and family, taking Kimberly with him to play with her cousins and to see her aunt, the sister of her deceased mother.

Clare knew from prior years that Cornell's brother had been influenced by his wife and all the derogatory "Nadine tales" down through the years. Always, Cornell avoided placing Nadine in the middle by adhering to a basic rule: Nadine was never to be disrespected.

"You knew Grady was that way before you married him," Nadine was now stating matter-of-factly seated on the rattan sofa with Clare on her heated patio. As they talked, they were surrounded by tropical plants, many of them recommended by Clare.

"You really believe that?" she asked in frustration.

"Clare," Nadine said, "number one, both of you had no time to waste, really. Logically, you wanted children right away. Two, both of you agreed on how long you would be home with the children. You have been home for a decade, Clarissa Lucinda, an entire decade. Now he's spoiled! I'll bet he was hoping that you would never want to go back to work, and with the way you maintain the home for all of you, no wonder. You maintain a clean house, are a great cook, and during the warm season, your yard is gorgeous. I know the in-laws are glad to have you as an addition." She grabbed Clare's hand in a consoling gesture. "Don't look so glum."

"Everybody but Mabel," replied Clare.

"I was mainly referring to his mom and dad." She shrugged. "Well, one rejection isn't bad." She paused, thinking about her own situation. "The only thing he did wrong was not state up-front that he is a man's man. He doesn't like for his wife to work when he can more than provide for her, and for certain he is capable of that."

Clare experienced a wave of anger so strong she could hardly think straight. It ebbed and died as she sighed heavily. During their entire marriage she had never been confronted with anything that made her feel so low in spirits. She loved Grady, he was a good husband. She wanted nothing except a certain amount of independence. Promptly that inner voice asked: *What exactly is it that you think you are missing, and why do you need it?* She was allowed to do what she wanted, when she wanted, so why was she saying that she lacked independence? She was married, true enough, but Grady had never restricted her comings and goings. She did recall a recent incident when she had taken some money out of her annuity to purchase new living room furniture. Afterward, Grady asked why, if she wanted new furniture, she had to go to that extreme—he used that exact word, "extreme." They had a joint bank account, and since it had a high balance, all she had to do was let him know that she was taking it out. He knew why she'd done it, he said: the original sofa and chair belonged to *her*, so she wanted to use what she considered her own money to replace them, which angered him. Her actions, he said, made it clear that she considered that money solely hers. She attempted to explain that was not why she had done it, and besides, he had a lot more money than she ever would. It had become their biggest argument to date.

"All of the money belongs to both of us, Clare. When we got married, there was no prenuptial arrangement. I thought I would leave that sort of thing to those who are filthy rich, which we are not. I thought you realized it is our money, all of it. If we split up tomorrow, don't you realize you would get a wife's share. Since you say I have more money than you, don't you think you would end up with more than you already have?"

The argument had left her feeling low. She hated that they were arguing about money. Also, she disliked his hypothesizing about them splitting up. She had to find a way to explain why she had paid for the furniture from her annuity. The disagreement hadn't ever been fully resolved, making her feel bad.

"Hon," said Nadine kindly, "the guy is rare, okay? For sure, there are not many men out there like him. You must admit he is a good husband."

"He is an excellent husband," Clare agreed, "but I would like a certain amount of independence."

"Independence?" Nadine erupted into amused laughter. "I'll bet if you asked half the women, in fact more than three-fourths of the women—white, black, or other!—if they would like to be fortunate enough to stay at home and raise their children, the answer would be a thunderous, resounding 'yes!' Give the guy a break, Clare. Grady loves you almost to a fault, okay? I have always known that, so just be happy that he does. God forbid the thought, but he would be hard to replace, believe me."

It was almost five o'clock when Clare pulled in the driveway. All of them had been anxiously awaiting her return. It was rare for her to spend a day away from home, especially during the weekend.

Brandon was at the car before anybody, all smiles and relief, as if he thought she had abandoned them; next was Jennifer, with Grady following close behind, smiling. The remnants of winter were still lingering in Chicago, so all were dressed appropriately.

"We're going out to dinner," Grady announced as if offering a subtle truce. It was also a tactful way, she suspected, of saying he didn't want to wait on her to make dinner. Their family evening of dining out had been yesterday, as it was every Friday.

It was late when they returned home; the children went straight to their rooms. Grady and Clare were in the privacy of the sitting room directly off their bedroom. Grady sat down in his favorite chair, which had been separated from the couch in his den; they had made a complete set when in his apartment.

"Come here," he said quietly, and she left her chaise lounge to sit on his lap. He held up both hands with a good-natured smile. "Just asking," he said, "why do you have to work?"

Before responding she looked at him for what seemed a long while, with that benign, calm demeanor of hers. "Because I feel useless," she answered truthfully. "I feel that I am not accomplishing much."

*And my master's degree is collecting dust*, she thought; she didn't say this aloud because she did not want to hear his answer to that one. starting an entirely new debate. *Men*, she thought, *no matter how nice, still want things done their way.* Nadine always said that there was no explanation other than that they were men, period.

"Being a mom is the hardest job you will ever have, so I don't know how you could possibly feel useless," he said. "At this point in time, what is it that you wish to accomplish? We have two children, ages close to seven and eleven, who absolutely adore you and still need you at home. You are great with them. You maintain our home beautifully and efficiently, which is a great accomplishment. I adore you and, frankly, would rather that you did not work. Corporate America is still not conducive to or supportive of a woman working while raising a family. They haven't quite worked that out. There are a few jobs out there that will allow a woman to work from home, but those are not as plentiful and are mentally taxing when available. This is not to start an argument, Clare, but I love having you at home."

He paused as he sensed her withdrawing, as she still did sometimes when she did not want to express her deepest thoughts and feelings, or when she had not quite sorted out precisely what she wanted to say.

"Talk to me," he softly encouraged as he caressed her, pulling her close.

*This man always smells so good*, she thought, as she told him often.

"Clare, don't go away like you do; talk to me." He kissed her tenderly and thought of Olivia. Clare was nothing like his first wife; she never sulked. Her lovely personality drew you in with softness, depth, and warmth. Even when she would quietly withdraw, there was never a barrier through which you couldn't reach her. Kindness was always there. "Communication is always the key, little lady, so talk."

He loved having her home again and wanted things to remain that way as much as possible. He was relieved that all had returned to normal and to once again not have to worry about the children. He cherished being able to call in the middle of the day to simply say hello and chat for a few minutes. There was nothing that could equal those occasional leisure evenings with just the two of them, unhurried and peaceful, while the children were occupied with homework or those times when all of them just sat around being together as a family. This was his third marriage and the only one he could describe as truly enjoyable. He had worked diligently to build the life that he now appreciated, and he wanted it to last as long as possible.

"I want to say something else," she said quietly and smiled. "I wish we would not argue about money, okay?"

"Okay," he answered. "Did it bother you that much?"

"Yes, it did." She kissed his lips lightly.

"Anything else, little lady?" he asked.

She remained seated on his lap, and he knew she was thinking of what she wanted to say next. The way she incrementally sorted things, discussing them the same way had always amused him. The expressions were clear but didn't come in a continuous flow, coming out instead in bits and pieces, and only after being well constructed.

"You're laughing at me, Grady Collier Mayfield."

"No, no, I'm not, but the way you sort things out before you talk about them… it's a different approach, that's all."

"I just want to make sure that I am not misunderstood," she explained.

She was thinking back to her childhood, when every issue her mother discussed with her father turned into an argument. She knew Grady was nothing like her father, but she had been a member of that household for a long time. Then it had been her turn when he was sick with diabetes, and she tried to avoid the potholes that often caused her mother to stumble. She had to avoid getting caught up in his rants so that she could favorably interact with him without the disagreements that made his diabetes worse.

"Where did you go?" he asked softly.

She looked at him and smiled. "I love you, Grady Mayfield," she stated quietly.

"Hey," he said, "I love you too. Is there something bothering you, little girl?" He was slightly concerned.

"I hope we always love each other," she said softly. "I was just thinking, that's all."

"Share your thoughts with me," he coaxed gently.

"They are not pleasant," she warned.

"All the more reason to share," he said attentively. "Talk about them. Please."

"I did not have a pleasant childhood," she said. "My mother for years shut down her warmth, touch, closeness, expressions of love. It was as if she forgot how to show these emotions, even though the death of Mason did somewhat free her. Only the death of her mother, my grandmother, Gran Jennie, allowed her to transform. Mason was a mean, cold man. The two reasons she remained with him were that he was Jeffrey's father, which she felt my brother needed but never had, and money. When she became financially able to leave him, we purchased a house, and diabetes set in with a vengeance.

"Mama constantly discussed with me what qualities to look for in a man, so I did well in that department because she had made all the mistakes already and drilled into me what not to repeat." She paused. "Also, she always possessed the social graces that she'd learned from her mother, my grandmother. I never knew many of my father's immediate family. He never discussed his parents, his grandparents, or anything much that involved family history, so most of it was buried with him." She paused, offered a sad smile. "Sometimes I think about my family as opposed to yours, and the contrast is so disturbing. I love the way your family interacts with each other, the touching, hugging, kissing—it's beautiful. Every time I see all of you together, I get an emotional high. The Mayfield family is so very refreshing."

As she sat there on his lap, she became almost despondent, but then she smiled.

"Well, little lady, you are a Mayfield," Grady said, "so you've made the transition." He kissed her deeply. "And we will always love each other. I know for certain that I will always love you." He paused. "You consider me a good choice for a husband, do you?"

"Of course," she answered simply.

"Don't think for a moment we don't have our differences," he said. "We just work through them. We are by no means perfect and have most of the same problems as other families."

"I realize that" she responded. "But don't you think it is best when you genuinely love each other and express that love?"

"Absolutely," he replied.

She thought of something Nadine had said— "a man's man." She smiled as she held his hand and laced her fingers with his. "Could I ask you a question?"

"Sure, anything," he answered agreeably.

"Do you want me to return to work, ever?"

"Do you want my honest answer?"

"Yes, I do."

"Quite frankly, no, not to a nine-to-five... does that bother you?"

"No," she said, again reclining to rest her head on his shoulder, "not really."

She slipped her arms around his waist. She had to admit that he was such a kind and gentle man. They had a very solid marriage. His answer was truthful. She had thought that it would bother her, but the discussion with Nadine prepared her for his answer. She wondered how her friend had gained such insight. Then again, Nadine and Cornell visited them often, and after all these years of being in Grady's company, she had observed him and knew him, so her analysis was based on a view from up close. Besides, she had always possessed such an uncanny, in-depth insight into people. Perhaps that was why she was suited to her position as a principal. Clare had always thought that Nadine would have been a wonderful psychologist.

Grady was always honest, which was one of his most admirable qualities, and he more than welcomed discussions. *A man's man*, she thought. She decided that the description suited him. There had been one of those in her family. From what she had gathered, Calvin Beckford had been a man's man, and now she was married to one.

It was a few weeks later, a Monday morning and, had it been warmer, Clare would have been involved in gardening. Instead, she sat at the kitchen island making out a grocery list. She always kept the cordless phone close by. Most of the time she did not get phone calls this early, though; it was only a few minutes after eight o'clock.

"I've got an idea for you," Nadine said as soon as Clare answered. "I'm taking a break before the crew gets here with a few little imps' grab bag of mischief." It was rare for her to telephone from work. "Have you thought about teaching at the college level? You do have a master's degree in education, and your area of expertise is English. It would be nice if you could do that a few days a week. You should investigate it." She laughed a little and said, "That would allow you to launch at least a segment of your desperately sought independence, Mrs. Mayfield."

"You have been giving this some serious thought, haven't you?" Clare also laughed. Leave it to Nadine, always trying to help.

"Don't you think it's a good idea?"

It was not only good, but splendid, and Clare thanked her for it. She hadn't considered teaching since studying for her bachelor's degree; she'd done student teaching for a few weeks during her third year while on an extended vacation from work. She had thought teaching was a rewarding profession, but as a single person, she had needed more money than such a job could provide. To make teaching even less enticing, she had received a promotion not long before entering grad school and then another afterward. These upward moves on the ladder had brought an end to her consideration of teaching as a profession.

Grady had specified that he did not want her working a nine-to-five job, so she would test this idea on him. After the children were in bed that night, she presented it to him.

"What would you say if I wanted to teach a few mornings a week?" she asked.

He smiled. "I think that is a good idea."

"You do?" She was a little surprised.

"Yes, I do," he replied. "I see nothing wrong with it, especially since both your degrees are in education."

*A few mornings a week*, he thought, *which meant she would still be home the rest of the day.* He knew he was being selfish, but loved the way she ran their home and took care of their children. They had a great life together, so why disrupt it? "When do you plan to look into it?" he asked.

"This week," she answered.

"Do you still want to take a vacation this year?"

"That would be nice," she said.

They hadn't decided exactly where to vacation, but both knew they wanted to travel somewhere outside the United States. They had contemplated going to Africa, but they wanted Jennifer to be a few years older before they took the trip. Brandon, now eleven, would most likely do fine, but not Jennifer, now seven. Additionally, the cost of a trip to Africa would be extremely high, whereas trips to Europe were much cheaper. They had taken the children to the Wisconsin Dells, and of course, they had already been to Disney World in Orlando. They also had traveled to Chattanooga one year to visit one of Grady's cousins, where they had ridden the Incline up Lookout Mountain to visit Ruby Falls, 1,100 feet down inside the mountain. Clare had never forgotten the story Jeffrey told her about his trip there and how beautiful he thought it was. Jennifer, who was three years old when Clare and Grady took their family, had kept complaining about being cold even though all the family wore sweaters, with hers being the heaviest. Most of the way, Grady had carried her in his arms. For her young age, Jennifer had already traveled quite extensively. Yes, Africa could wait. Any trip outside the country would be educational for the children and even themselves. Clare avoided bringing up the new living room furniture, which had caused their last skirmish, but did tactfully suggest a vacation that would not be too costly and enjoyable for all.

# Chapter Twenty-Six

For over two weeks Nadine had missed their daily chats, and she had given Clare an additional week to become acclimated to the return home. It was midafternoon as they sat at the island of her sunny kitchen perusing vacation photos. Her gift from Clare was a colorful silk scarf purchased in Rome, laid to one side of the counter with other gift memorabilia—refrigerator magnets from Jennifer and Brandon.

"That's the only pyramid in Europe," Clare said when Nadine held up the photo for her to identify. "At least that is what the tour guide said when she pointed it out to us. It's one and one-half stories tall."

"Hmm," Nadine commented, "by comparison, it's teeny tiny." Clare nodded in agreement as Nadine moved on.

"That's the Trevi Fountain," Clare said when Nadine paused on a photo. "Remember the movie *Three Coins in the Fountain*?" When the bus-tour guide called it by name, in passing, there were blank expressions on the faces of Brandon and Jennifer and their few contemporaries. However, Clare had managed a contortionist's maneuver to quickly capture a photograph of it.

"I do indeed," Nadine replied. Having finished going through the thick package of photos, she laid them on the counter, turning her attention to her friend. They had known each other a lifetime, so Nadine had noticed that at times Clare seemed to drift in and out of the conversation. Finally, Nadine asked, "You seem distracted, so what's going on?"

"Nothing. Just getting over jet lag," Clare replied, smiling. "There's nothing like sleeping in your own bed. We had a day layover in Barcelona without enough time to see the Black Madonna. Grady commented that there is a Black Madonna in different countries all over the place—in Europe, that is—yet a white Mary is still the representative for the mother of Jesus worldwide."

"Of course, and so is a white Jesus," Nadine replied quietly. "That's in spite of the pyramid texts and all else indicating the contrary."

"I fell in love with Barcelona, especially Las Ramblas," said Clare, toying with her wedding ring as Nadine observed her closely.

Las Ramblas, the ideal tourists' attraction where various artisans performed, was a wide strip dividing a four-lane thoroughfare. It was, in fact, as wide as some of the city streets in the United States. It was a tourists' tease, luring visitors to venture into the entire city. Clare had become enraptured with the splendor of the water fountains prominently placed at each end of this long walkway.

"The one problem with cruises," Clare continued, "is the time factor."

"That's generally the case with most vacations," Nadine responded.

Clare smiled as she recalled one amusing incident. "The second day we were on the ship, we were strolling on the deck," she said, "and this poor man was resting on a deck chair, merely basking in the midday sun. He was clad in shorts and an open short-sleeved shirt, simply enjoying a quiet afternoon. A little toddler—she was with her parents nearby—anyway, she spotted something shiny and beautiful and decided to pick up her discovery." Clare started laughing as she replayed the incident in her mind. "The poor little girl began to cry because the sunbathing man leapt up in pain—the shiny object she was tugging on was attached to his left nipple."

Nadine now joined her in laughter.

"It was an amusing sight," Clare said. "Of course, not for him, I'm sure. The frightened child began to cry. Her parents, embarrassed, apologized profusely. It was hilarious to say the least."

That funny story brought a cheerful close to their pleasant afternoon.

They were back on track, and breathing a sigh of relief, Grady silently hoped to never have to endure the rigors of another nine-to-five circumstance involving his wife and corporate America. Once more Clare was home to greet Jennifer and Brandon when they came home from school. Gone were the previous morning debates or hassles with the children. Now they gladly ate whatever breakfast their mother prepared for them. For example, during Clare's brief nine-to-five stint, Grady had placed Brandon in charge of their morning meal consisting of cold cereal for himself and his sister Jennifer. Their father would then dole out to them the daily lunch money. Inwardly, Brandon rejoiced to have that entire ordeal in the past.

It was about three weeks after his mother's return home that Brandon earnestly said, "Mom, I'm glad you're home again."

A simple thank-you was all she could manage. Never again would they take her for granted. Clare felt justly rewarded. Now the entire family, including Clare, was grateful for those five and a half months of experiencing the lifestyle affecting the large percentage of families without an option. When she telephoned Nadine regarding this turn of events, her friend was amused.

"I told you, Clare—your family is spoiled! They all know you are a good wife and mother. In a way it is good that Jennifer and Brandon had a brief peek into the lives of most of America. Now that they know what it's like not having a stay-at-home mom, they will appreciate it as an absolute luxury. How are the classes going?"

Clare was teaching at one of the South Side junior colleges and enjoying it more than she'd anticipated. It was an adult education class that Nadine had suggested she accept just to get her feet wet, so to speak.

"I never thought I would enjoy it this much," she said. "Nadine, they are so eager to learn and soak it up like a sponge. I never realized how rewarding teaching can be. Years ago, when I was working full-time, I was self-supporting, without a choice. Well, you know teaching is not the highest-paid profession, especially below the college level. It's a grossly underpaid profession."

"Tell me about it. If I wasn't a principal, I would be dealing with college students. It's not the children as much as their parents—they're worse. That's what bothers me the most."

"You can still do that, you know—teach college!"

"Maybe in about five years." She would entertain the thought after she was no longer living the pleasant experience of having Kimberly at home; she'd think about it when her stepdaughter was out of the nest, which would occur soon—Kim was a high school junior this year. "How does that husband of yours like the Clare that is now the semiprofessional woman in action?"

Clare laughed. "He's very receptive. I think he really approves of me in that setting. I'm home the rest of the day."

೮೨

It was early Friday afternoon, and Clare was at home, visiting with her mother. She taught class on Monday and Wednesday mornings only with the remainder of the week free. Estelle was on her annual early fall vacation from the post office, deciding to spend a day with her daughter. The children were not due home before three, but their grandmother decided to extend her visit to include them.

Clare was thinking back to Estelle's third promotion. She had proudly graduated from college, coaxed by her daughter into walking during commencement with the other much younger students, that the contrast spoke volumes. She had stayed the course. and because of it lived comfortably.

She recalled her mother's very first promotion too, when no longer "tossing mail" (Mason's put-down). The significant occasion had been celebrated, at Clare's insistence, with a small party. She had taken the liberty of personally inviting her mother's longtime friend Doretha, having to gently rebuff her father's negative comments. From the time she was very young, she had silently deplored her father's mean pettiness. Whenever she thought back to her childhood and young adulthood, she wished memories of Mason were more pleasant. Never had he been a very likable person. During Estelle's small celebration, Clare's mild reprimand had angered him. Estelle's climb upward had begun after Mason's diabetes had seized control. However, he had dismissed this promotion, like all the others, as meaningless.

"Jealousy will get you nowhere, Papa," Clare had chided him quietly. So that he could join them in celebrating the occasion, she had offered him a small dish of ice cream and cake (always cognizant of his diabetic condition). Quite naturally he had refused. The combination of the promotion and her speaking up in her mother's defense had him stewing for hours. Not long afterward his leg amputation had become inevitable.

*Enough reflecting on the past!* she told herself. These fruitful times presented an opportunity for her mother to seize happiness now.

"Mama," she asked quietly, "why don't you and Max marry?"

Estelle didn't answer immediately; she appeared to be choosing an appropriate response. Her daughter believed her question to be straightforward enough and wanted a substantial response. Estelle reacted with a sad smile. toyed with her glass of ginger ale as her eyes grew watery. It practically frightened Clare.

"Forgive me, Mama," she pleaded as she grabbed her hand, thinking that she had overstepped her bounds.

"No," Estelle said quietly, tenderly patting her hand. "You had no way of knowing," she continued with forthrightness, "but Max is still married." She paused briefly. Because of the property." She was somber. "If we let them, material things have a way of creating entrapments. We become ensnared by certain lifestyles." She sighed. "She promised to sign a quitclaim to the properties he owns, the ones he had when he married her. His mistake was placing her name on the deeds. In good faith he signed the quitclaim to the home they shared. When he moved out of the house, she discovered I was in the picture and immediately reneged on her promise. Then he didn't file for divorce as planned. He wants his property because it helps support his lifestyle. Under the circumstances, if he decides to get a divorce, he will have to give her half, or even more because there were extensive renovations that she paid for while the marriage was still good. She is a shrewd, devious woman. Clare, she kept every receipt! He never should have allowed her to pay for those renovations. One of the buildings she'll possibly own outright because the upgrades were a little steep, easily cutting deeply into the profits from the sale."

Estelle gave a helpless shrug, sighed. "Max also has a daughter born out of wedlock. She carries his name. He would like to leave her something. The two children he helped raise are from his wife's first marriage. It's a mess, so until all of this is sorted out, we've decided to live together."

"Are you okay with that?" asked Clare.

"I have given it serious thought. We have invested a lot of time in this relationship," she said quietly. For a long time, she did not speak, but then finally gave a slow, deliberate nod. "Yes, I'm okay with that."

Later that evening while cleaning up the kitchen, Clare thought about her mother and Max. After much coaxing, she had convinced her mother to stay for dinner, with Max joining them. It turned out to be a fun evening for all and a special delight for the children.

There was a time when her mother had strictly adhered to the moral dictates of society, only to painfully discover that there wasn't any perfectly neat, comfortable existence outside those bedtime stories read to children. Grady had once remarked that "once upon a time" beginnings followed by perfect "happily ever after" endings were totally nonexistent outside the pages they were written on.

*Life is so unpredictable*, thought Clare, *altering even the most carefully laid plans.* It tilted your world, jarred you emotionally, toyed with your wants and desires, posing a constant challenge. All she wanted was for her mother to be happy. *For once*, she thought, *be happy, Mama. Just be happy.*

❧

She was in her private domain with no one to disrupt or interrupt her misery. How would she endure this again? The same malevolence was appearing for a second time to take what remained of her once-perfect possession. *Why, why, why, why, why?* she miserably screamed inside. *I eat all the right foods—four or five fruits and vegetables a day—exercise, get proper rest, give myself breast exams often. Even get that painful annual mammogram.* Losing her focus, the shears slipped from her gloved hand. She became even more distraught. Would she be as lucky this time? Would the demon invade her lymph nodes this time? *Oh God, please let me get through this. Please help me.* She battled to keep control of her thoughts less they wander onto more perilous terrain. Suddenly she felt the presence of someone, turned to look into the concerned eyes of her husband.

"Clare, what on earth is the matter?" he asked.

With the back of one gloved hand, she wiped her tears, smudging her face. She attempted to remove the dirt with the handkerchief he handed her.

"I was due for my mammogram the following month after our return from vacation, remember?"

He nodded.

"Well, I went to the doctor this afternoon to get the test results." She wiped at the smudge of soil on her face again as he helped guide her hand to remove the rest. "I didn't want to alarm you until I knew for sure." She heaved a ragged, anguished sigh. "I have breast cancer again," she said just above a whisper, as if to stave off what was far too ominous.

She felt so very forlorn, beaten, lost. She closed her eyes, succumbed to her emotions, allowing the tears to stream freely.

"Come here, little girl," he said gently.

Purging the initial shock he felt at her news, he took her in his arms and held her close. She sighed again as she leaned against him, grateful to God.

He thought back to when he'd first met her. She was such a pretty woman, then and now, with those beautiful, almond-shaped eyes of hers. He did not want lose this human being who was so precious to him. He had never loved any woman as much. He swallowed hard, regaining composure to forcefully reject the pang of fear. He intended to be strong enough for them both.

"I'm getting your suit dirty," she said miserably. He had just attended a closing. For those occasions he always wore a suit.

"That's why there are dry cleaners, love," he said quietly.

Her eyes were red and swollen, he noticed, indicating that the crying had been ongoing for quite some time.

"I'm disappointed," he scolded mildly. "You shut me out."

"I didn't mean to," she quickly responded. "I didn't want you to worry needlessly; I wanted to be sure." She looked up at him and then once again rested her head against his chest. "If it's any consolation to you, you are the only one I've told." She clung to him, her arms wrapped tightly about his waist, as fresh tears began to surface.

"Mom?" The anxious screech came from Jennifer as she entered the garden to witness her mother's tear-streaked face. It was the first time she had ever seen her mother in tears; she also began to cry.

Grady released his wife to scoop up their dainty seven-year-old. From the pictures he had seen of Clare at that age, Jennifer was a taller update, possessing the same almond-shaped eyes and similar daintiness. All else—her softened features and golden-brown complexion—identified her as Grady Mayfield's daughter.

"Listen," he said gently, kissing her wet cheek, "go back inside, okay? Your mother and I will be in shortly."

He put her down to again embrace his wife as Jennifer hesitated, watching her mother dry her eyes with her father's handkerchief.

"Want to start getting ready for our night out?" Clare asked her, to gently coax her inside.

"Okay," she said, turning to run up the walkway and onto the deck. She paused for just a moment at the doorway to look back and then disappeared inside.

"Let's go inside," he said once they were alone again, "before Brandon comes out here. We must keep things as normal as possible and discuss this later tonight when they're in bed."

Dinner was on Cicero at their favorite South Side restaurant. They loved the salads, especially the pasta. None of the usual chatter went on between them, even from Brandon, who always had plenty to say. Brandon usually loved watching birthdays celebrated with a small cake, the waitresses' exuberant spiel, and the rhythmic chanting and hand clapping happening now at a nearby table. This evening the usual interest was lost, and instead he kept watching his mother for signs. Of course, Jennifer had told him that their mother was in the garden crying, and Brandon was a son who loved his mother dearly. He wasn't eating very much of his favorite food and engaging in the usual bantering with his father, but instead kept stealing glimpses of his mother as she struggled to be jovial.

"Mom, are you okay?" Brandon finally asked with focused concern.

"Why were you crying?" Jennifer said, still visibly upset.

Clare was about to answer her son with a half-truth when Grady's hands covered hers tenderly—they were in constant movement, as they always were when she was nervous or troubled.

Grady wanted to shift the conversation before it went any farther. "Hey, guys, let's talk about this when we get home," he coaxed softly. "Let's eat before the food gets cold."

Brandon complied by beginning to eat some of his meal; Jennifer followed her older brother's lead. Grady was extremely proud of how well they got along. He recalled the day that four-year-old Brandon had come home from his weekend at his Aunt Ro's, where he'd stayed until Clare and the new family member arrived home from the hospital. After the initial introduction to his infant sibling, Brandon's intermittent visits to check out his sister became routine. He commented that she was always asleep and wanted to know when she was going to stay awake. His parents informed him that he had slept a lot too, as did all newborns. His envy of the focus placed on the new baby was minimal, especially after he and his father talked. As they grew older, he always helped her with her homework when necessary. Every weekend, he spent a few hours with her, although he had friends always stopping by (like his father, Brandon was well liked).

Grady now realized that he and Clare could not discuss this alone but had to include their children. The family arrived home before ten. Brandon, being the inquisitive and intelligent person he was, still wanted an answer. They were in the family room with the television was off.

"Mom," Brandon asked, "what exactly is wrong with you?"

Clare didn't know quite how to explain what was going on without alarming them.

"Your mother is not quite herself, but she is going to be okay." assured their father.

"What's wrong?" Jennifer asked.

Clare's eyes pleaded with Grady. She was too close to the problem.

"Your mother," Grady said tactfully, "needs surgery. It's not life-threatening, but necessary. Let's think good thoughts about it. We all support her, right?"

Both Jennifer and Brandon nodded in agreement.

"We're a family," Grady continued, "and we must always be there for each other through whatever problems occur."

"You're not to worry, okay?" said Clare, speaking for the first time.

Both children nodded in solemn agreement. Weekends, Friday and Saturday, the only evenings they were allowed to stay up late, television did not hold their interest. They went to their rooms early, leaving the house quiet.

Once in their own private quarters, Grady showered and shaved while Clare took a long, hot bath. She lay back in the tub and could not avoid thinking one disturbing thought: once again she would have to be severed from cancer as it revisited to claim more of her body. Both breasts would be something reconstructed. She could still hear the compassionate words of Dr. Blair when she had timidly discussed her inability to nurse her children. "Mrs. Mayfield," the doctor had said, "bonding is possible without breastfeeding."

She attempted to relax. In silent prayer: she prayed for her family; prayed that this would be her last surgery, to forever rid her of this dreadful disease; prayed beseechingly that it was, just like before, not invasive; fervently prayed that her daughter would never have to endure this during her lifetime; prayed for quality life for herself and, if necessary, for minimal chemotherapy and radiation.

"A penny for your thoughts," he said.

The words slightly startled her. She opened her eyes to discover Grady sitting on the side of the tub, a towel around his waist. She leaned slightly forward, and he smiled. He picked up the loofah sponge from the side of the tub and began to gently sponge her back.

"Don't worry," he said quietly. "I realize it's difficult but try not to worry."

"I just want to wake up to your beautiful white smile for many, many years." She looked at him and smiled sadly. She turned toward him, positioned herself on her knees, slid her hand beneath the towel to caress him gently. She needed to feel beautiful. She needed to feel like a woman completely unmarred. "Grady, make love to me."

He allowed the towel to fall to the floor and joined her in the tub, where he began to engage her in prolonged foreplay. They had been married for twelve years. He could not recall any woman he had enjoyed as much as he enjoyed Clare. She clung to him, her passion mounting, as he guided her so that she straddled him, in position to receive him as her eyes filled with tears.

"Grady," she said softly, "I have never loved a man the way I love you. I want to continue loving you for a very long time. I want…" She was weeping as she allowed him to control the tempo of their lovemaking.

"Come on now," he said softly, kissing her tenderly, "let's keep our spirits high. I know it's hard, but tonight let's just enjoy each other." He totally focused on her, watching her intently, knowing she was feeling a heated rush of pleasure whenever her eyes sparkled as they were now. She embraced him ecstatically, lost in the moment, crying out his name as he brought her to full climax while she held his face between her hands, kissing him passionately.

"I love you, Grady, so very much."

"And I love you," he responded. "Just remember I am always there for you—remember that, always."

She felt as if elevated in midair as she was moved from the gurney to the hospital bed. Her eyes were still closed; the anesthetic had worn off. *It is over*, she thought. When she opened her eyes, at her bedside were Grady, Estelle, Rolanda, and beside Rolanda, Mabel, smiling. It was the best of the best. She felt she had finally become a member of the Mayfield family.

In the months that followed, they established a new friendship, diffident at first, exploratory, but a definite effort to reach out by both, to bridge the void that had, until now, spanned Clare's entire engagement and marriage to Grady.

Time moved on, and now Clare had undergone her fifth treatment, always a daylong affair; this time she prayed fervently it would be her last. As always, Grady was there, and she daily thanked God for sending her such a beautiful human being with whom to share her life. Listless and lethargic, suppressing the nausea as best she could, she lay on her side because it provided the most comforting position. *Help me*, she silently prayed to Gran Jennie, to the spirit of that wise old woman who had traveled on to become an ancestor. It was becoming difficult to keep that flower garden beautiful and in bloom. *I need your strength, wherever you are*, she prayed as she lay drifting on a sea of uncertainty.

The awful, metallic taste in her mouth caused the food to lack flavor. In fact, she had not eaten anything this day except a medium bowl of soup that Mabel had prepared.

"You have to eat something," she had encouraged kindly when she brought the half-full bowl of freshly made soup, steaming hot with such a delicious aroma, and positioned it on the bed tray in front of Clare. She had fluffed the pillows for her sister-in-law before bringing the meal. She now sat in the chair beside her bed to keep her company, scanning the newspaper for interesting articles to share with her while she ate slowly. The queasiness temporarily subsided and allowed her to consume most of her meal. She rejected the crackers.

Mabel—who would have thought that she would be such a valiant ally? It made all the difference in the world. Clare liked the fact that they were becoming close. Rolanda, despite Clare's protest, had spent two of her five weeks of vacation in their home to help out and was also supportive of the growing friendship between her oldest sibling and her favorite sister-in-law.

"If you'd give her a chance," she had told Mabel. "You'd discover she's very likable."

Clare decided that the Mayfield clan was special. In some respects, she appreciated all the activity that her illness had generated. Rachel and Joseph came on the weekends. Their schedules often coincided with that of Max and Estelle. Now that Max lived with her mother, it helped shove away some of the sadness Clare felt for the outcome of her mother's life, allowing almost full concentration on getting well. All the support helped Grady and the children tremendously. Everyone joked about the house suddenly transforming to Union Station. All would go home and once again the large dwelling was engulfed in hushed, quiet serenity.

She now felt weight on the bed, and the strong arms of her husband encircled her ever so gently as he lay with her, spoon fashion, tenderly pulling her closer to kiss the nape of her neck.

He couldn't recall such intermittent spontaneity in their home. It would fill with people, then suddenly shift to silence with no activity whatsoever. Under normal conditions, during the evenings and on weekends, their home came alive with the family home from school and work, friends and family stopping by to visit, sometimes spending the weekend. Often, they had out-of-town guests, mostly Grady's friends originally, but now hers as well.

The atmosphere was totally different when Clare was up and about, as she spent her weekends cooking a great deal and moving in and out of rooms all over the house, interacting with him and the children, full of laughter. In the garden, she filled vases with fresh flowers and brought them inside to scent the living and dining rooms. At the start of each day, she sat at the kitchen counter consuming her one vice—coffee! Except for an occasional glass of wine or a mixed drink, Clare neither smoked nor drank. She loved making breakfast on any Saturday morning they decided to eat in. During the week, except for Clare, everyone ate breakfast on the run. However, the family always had their evening meals together.

All activity had temporarily ceased. Other than the sporadic and quiet movements of the Mayfield women, and relatives visiting on weekends, a great percentage of the time the house was like a morgue, lapsing into mourning the illness of its mistress.

In the beginning, immediately following Clare's surgery and her return home, Grady would coax Brandon and Jennifer from the house.

Kevin would swing by and take them to Navy Pier for the day or to the movies or on other outings and then to his apartment to watch rented movies. Sometimes he would play video games with Brandon while Jennifer looked on. It was a source of spectator entertainment for her because she always complained that she wasn't that good because Brandon beat her at every move. Kevin could not keep the two from telephoning home three or four times during their time away, to be assured that their mother was fine and resting comfortably. Sometimes their father would answer. Often it would be their Aunt Mabel or some other relative who was near the phone. They were always told not to worry, try to have a good time. This worked for weeks, but time dragged on. It them anxious, a result of genuine concern coupled with the impatience of youth. On weekends their time was systematically divided between mostly Rolanda and Kevin, and sometimes Estelle and Max or the Mayfield grandparents. Otherwise, when they were at home, it was constant questions and checking in: Did she want to watch television with them? Perhaps she wanted them to read to her? Was she coming downstairs to join them for dinner? She welcomed the attention, but it tired her, and as Grady gently explained to them, the doctor wanted her to rest more. Rolanda joined in more, and both she and Kevin stepped up the entertainment, including them in activities of interest with the two of them and with Rolanda's children. These adventures would last most of the day. They would return home late in the evening, anticipating their mother feeling better, hoping they would find her sitting in the living room or perhaps lounging in her sitting room. They were disappointed that most of the time she was in bed and asleep. They missed her terribly.

Finally, Grady had to fully explain to his children their mother's condition, why she was not making a speedy recovery. Brandon responded with fearful tears. This influenced Jennifer, who followed suit. It was only when their grandfather, Joseph Mayfield, talked to them that they finally became convinced that their mom was not going to die, but resting quietly in bed a lot to be restored to the mother they'd always known. Absolutely! they would have her back again. He counseled them both not to worry. Every detail would be worked out by the one who works out everything by His clock; His time dictates all time, their grandfather told them, which is what the world was running on. Their mother's health was under the jurisdiction of this awesome healer. Have patience, help their mother get well by not constantly disturbing her. I appreciate and cherish the daily amount of time spent with her. Accept the limitations, which would then make it possible for all of them to share many, many good times once more as a family in the future. Thank God for Pop, who possessed what seemed like such endless wisdom, Grady thought.

Grady's father was smiling when he said, "Grady, God is engaging your deep capacity for love and devotion. He is making you stronger and has given you that little woman because he knows that you are necessary in her life as she is in yours. He makes no mistakes. This experience is going to allow you to love each other even more, believe me. It will make all of you—Clare, you, and the children—appreciate each other more than before."

"Hey little girl," he now whispered as he lay behind her. "How do you feel?"

"Not too good," she admitted.

"Just hang in there a little longer, sweetheart," he said, tenderly kissing the nape of her neck again.

"I just want this episode over," she replied with an edge of anxiety.

"I assure you that it will be." He paused since the last thing he wanted to do was disturb her. "Is this making you uncomfortable?"

"Not at all," she assured him. She lovingly caressed his arm, feeling his warmth, starting to experience arousal. The feeling dissipated almost as quickly as it had surfaced; she was so tired.

He had spoken with her oncologist just the day before, when she was still vomiting. "Mr. Mayfield, it won't be long now," the oncologist had explained patiently. "She might not need another treatment. As you know, we discovered significant amounts of carcinoma in several of her lymph nodes as well as her breast, and we must be certain we got everything before we stop treatment. I will let you know the latest results as soon as I have them."

Upon his return from a long walk—he had to do something!—Mabel had blocked the door to the bathroom, where Clare was on her knees, leaning over the commode.

"Grady," Mabel had pleaded gently, embracing him tenderly, "just let her be. She feels awful, disgustedly so."

He had relented, reluctantly heading for his study to make a few delayed phone calls as tears filled his eyes. He felt useless.

On the verge of embarrassment, Clare had timidly begged her sister-in-law to leave her alone with that part of the ordeal, explaining how distasteful succumbing to it was for her. "At all costs," she had exclaimed afterward to her sister-in-law, "I could not possibly become a bulimic. How on earth do they do it—eat and purge daily?"

"I have no idea," Mabel had said with a faint smile.

"The personal hygiene necessary is enough to discourage such an obsession and, might I add, should cause a strong case of self-consciousness," Clare had said.

For the first time that day she had then managed to laugh, shaking her head in dismay. This drew light laughter from her sister-in-law as well.

On his way home from the oncologist's office, Grady had briefly stopped by his parents' home. Rachel Mayfield had commented about Clare's weight loss. "She can't afford to lose too much."

Grady was in complete agreement.

"You too are somewhat small," Joseph Mayfield had jokingly countered. "You just tall, that's all."

"Oh hush." She playfully hit at him as she usually did.

"To the letter," Joseph said to his son, "it's guaranteed she will soon feel better."

"Oh, so now you're Paul Laurence Dunbar?" Rachel said. She was standing beside his chair, and she playfully patted his cheek. All three laughed. Small antics such as these made Grady feel a little more upbeat. His father had a way of keeping things jovial until it was necessary to do otherwise, allowing him to leave for home with a smile on his face.

"Have you tried to eat today?" he now asked his wife.

"A decent size bowl of soup," she replied. "I felt a little nausea coming on, so I didn't want to push it." She did not mention the awful taste that lasted the first few days following each treatment. "I'll try to eat a little more tomorrow. The medication for the nausea is beginning to take effect, so I am keeping food down—finally."

"It's going to be fine, little girl," he said quietly. "We are going to be fine; I promise you."

Later, as it was getting dark, Mabel tapped lightly on the door and hearing no movement from inside the room, quietly entered to draw the drapes. She looked at her brother and sister-in-law lying there together, spoon fashion, sound asleep. Clare was, as was usual for the first three or four days after each treatment, in her pajamas, which Mabel made certain were fresh each day. He was still in his street clothes. She hesitated near the bed, thought better of waking him, and left the room, closing the door softly behind her. She hoped he wouldn't sleep in his clothes all night. Clare's illness was taking its toll on Mabel's brother as well. Since the inception of Clare's illness, he had been keeping his office hours short, sometimes staying home for the entire day at the insistence of Bradley. He checked in on weekends for the sake of appearance more than anything else. Ursula ran the office very efficiently. Very few marriages were as solid. She could only think of two: that of her pastor and his wife and that of their parents, Joseph and Rachel Mayfield. Grady had made the right choice. She recalled her mother scolding her about Clare, telling her to give her a chance, just as Rolanda had suggested, adding that she was a splendid person.

⁓

A week had passed since Clare found relief from her queasiness, lethargy, and all the other physical ailments that accompanied those dreaded chemotherapy treatments. In the middle of her bed, Clare sat with Nadine. Always, toward the end of the month, she began to feel well and to stir about, with the potential to start recuperating. Then she was due to undergo another bout of that awful substance that was supposed to restore her body to fullness and well-being. Additionally, there was daily oral medication to fortify her immune system and aid against the anemic condition caused by the chemo.

At first, she had fought even the thought, but now, after the devastating experience of losing most of her hair, she surrendered to wearing one of the wigs that Mabel had purchased for her. Being a health professional, Mabel had sent a cheerful, young cosmetologist to her home with a beautiful selection of wigs at the beginning of Clare's ordeal. Prior to the woman's arrival, Mabel had telephoned to state that she wasn't trying to make Clare feel bad, but that she knew most people lost their hair while undergoing treatment; she told Clare not to worry about the expense, to select whatever she wanted. The bubbly young lady had encouraged her to choose a couple of them for the sake of glamour and variety.

Presently, she had a pang of self-pity and she struggled to push away, an effort that was only partially successful.

"How are you feeling, sweetie?" asked Nadine with visible concern.

"Bad," she admitted. She spoke in almost a whisper even though she knew the house was completely empty except for the two of them. She hated to admit even to herself how she felt.

It was Saturday afternoon. Mabel was out grocery shopping. Joseph and Rachel had spent most of the morning and some of the afternoon with their son, engaging in a short visit with their daughter-in-law, and then had taken the children home with them to spend the night. Grady was going to pick them up sometime tomorrow. Urged to do so by Nadine, he had gone to the office for a few hours, his first appearance in more than a week.

"Don't try to be strong," her best friend now encouraged as she observed her struggling to fight back the tears. "Cry if you need to; it will never leave this space."

Softly, Clare wept for the children. Yes, she did want this to be over for herself and for Grady, but it was almost devastating the spirit of their children. These days they looked so forlorn and fearful, as if slowly journeying through a horrendous minefield without knowing where to step next.

"Do I look bad?" she asked her best friend entreatingly.

The wig she wore was a pricey one of authentic hair, closely resembling the styles she had always worn. These days climbing from the tub took a great deal of effort. Lately she had opted to shower instead. She always dreaded having to take off the wig. One time she had looked at herself in the bathroom mirror, and her reflection, wan, bald, ashen, uncompromisingly stared right back, making her wince and look away in utter misery and despair. The tears flowed.

"Sometimes I think that perhaps Grady would have been better off—"

"Don't release that to the universe, Clare," Nadine said firmly, cutting her off. "Never, ever repeat that to anybody else—never, ever, not even to yourself." She was adamant. "Okay? And no, you do not look bad. Sweetheart, it's going to get better. You must believe that. You must know that."

"Okay," she replied and sighed, fresh tears spilling from her eyes. "I'm sorry that this is such a down day for me."

"You know you can be any old way you want with me, Clarissa Lucinda Ingram Mayfield." It was a teas0e as Nadine smiled through her own tears. "Life will return to normal and get even better; I just know it will."

It was one of the rare times Clare witnessed tears from Nadine. She could recall only a few other occasions when Nadine had cried. One of those rare occasions was when she was told that she could never bear children.

"I know this will pass," Nadine said encouragingly. Things will be beautiful again for you and your family. Just hang in there. Keep asking that inner spirit to abide there and comfort you like no one else can. Ask that He send His best angel to lift you over the rocks, deliver you out of the valleys. Promise me."

"I promise," she replied sadly. She daily prayed to God and for the strength of Gran Jennie.

For a long time, they sat in the middle of Clare's bed facing each other, legs folded, elbows resting on their knees as they clasped hands in friendship; they looked as if practicing the beginners' position of yoga. Best friends since grammar school. Clare thought about the time she'd visited Nadine while she attended Washington University in Seattle. "Clare, the Pacific Northwest is so very beautiful," Nadine had said. "It rains an awful lot, but it is so very scenic; it will make you feel better."

It was during spring break. Estelle had insisted that she get away. Mason's nurse came four days per week, and Clare's mother had assured her that she would be fine during her absence. Yes, she should visit with her friend. The trip would do her good. Jeffrey was still "seeing America."

Unbeknownst to Clare, Nadine used part of her grant money to pay for Clare's airfare. Nadine worked as a waitress and saved most of her tips. She was thankful that this saving quickly resulted in a generous stash because she needed to replace that grant money, so that she would not have to forestall completing grad school. She realized that had Clare known, she would have flatly rejected the trip.

Clare finally did complete grad school too, insisting that Nadine accompany her on an island cruise. Clare's spontaneous entry into a sweepstakes (with her sights set on the Mustang or $20,000) was the result of an insistent coworker. She won third place and excitedly commented at the time that it was the only time in her entire life she had ever won anything. The prize was a trip for two to Jamaica and the best graduation present ever; they had a grand time. Presently, Clare reviewed their friendship. It was steadfast, long, and in need of no validation.

Once Sharla had come to see her, staying for only a brief period because Clare had undergone a treatment a few days before. From then on, Sharla would often send a bouquet of flowers and, if possible, telephone for a short conversation. If not, she had consoling chats with Grady.

⁊

Grady had never experienced such elation. For the first time in months, he could express overwhelming happiness. She was asleep, and he did not want to disturb her, so he called his father.

"What did I tell you?" his father replied. "Rachel!" he called his wife who was vacuuming. When she came closer, he touched her on the shoulder, motioning her to turn it off.

"Clare is cancer-free," Grady's father exclaimed, overjoyed. "They just got the news from the oncologist."

"She doesn't know yet," Grady said. Months ago, the telephone volume had been turned off in their bedroom so that she would not be disturbed. "I don't want to wake her, but I will tell her as soon as she wakes on her own."

"Thank God," said Rachel, taking over the phone. "Grady, give that little woman a hug and a kiss for us."

When he hung up the phone, Grady wondered if he should call Estelle or allow Clare to break the good news to her mother. He decided that he would do it himself.

Estelle cried when he told her. She was almost speechless. "Thank you so much, Grady, for delivering such good news." Estelle felt such relief. For months she had prayed for her daughter and her beautiful family, prayed that her grandchildren would not lose their mother. And she did not want to lose her daughter; she had already lost her husband and her son. Now her prayer had been answered.

"Did I hear the phone ring?" Clare questioned as she sat up on the side of the bed just as Grady was reentering the room. She knew good news was in the air from the smile on his face. He sat on the bed beside her, placing his arm about her shoulders.

"Baby," he said, letting out a rare laugh, "you are cancer-free."

"I am?" she replied, initially dazed.

Then as the words registered, she screamed jubilantly. They sat together in a tight embrace and then fell on the bed, kissing each other. They lay in each other's arms for quite some time, staring at each other, simply glad to be unleashed to pick up and start anew. He spoke first.

"Little girl," he said softly, "you're in for it."

He recalled all the times within the past months that he had needed her warmth, affection, and passion, while sustained by only memories. He knew she had wanted him too, but her tired body seldom allowed even limited expressions of sensual pleasure as she struggled to get well.

"Am I?" she answered, her voice growing husky, his words washing over her. She had missed him just as much.

"Absolutely, and as soon as possible, we're going to spend a weekend away from everybody, just the two of us." He kissed her deeply whispering, "I love you, Clare."

Perhaps one day he would admit to her his moments of fear over these past months that he might lose her, but not now. He was not going to spoil such a special moment. He was so utterly relieved to have his beautiful partner back.

"I remember the first time I took a good look at you," she said suddenly with quiet laughter. "You were standing at the meat counter. I said to myself, 'That is a lot of man.'" She smiled. "I had dated a few men your height, but never any your size, because I found them rather intimidating."

"Is that right?" He chuckled, amused to be learning something that she had never shared with him. "But your uncle is my size."

"I know, and my mother used to always tease me about that. All the Beckford men are your size." She kissed him. "You are the right size. And you know what? You are a beautiful man and a good husband. I couldn't ask for a better mate."

It wasn't the first time she had expressed her appreciation of him in her life, but he still loved hearing it. He kissed her tenderly, holding her close. There were so many things he wanted to say, but for now just holding her and being with her was sufficient as they enjoyed the peaceful calm of their quiet home, basking in their good fortune.

❧

For the next three days, their residence was a hotel room on the Magnificent Mile. The first day when they showered together, he sensed her discomfort, but ignored it. Meanwhile, he began petitioning her to make the neatly cropped, beautiful natural hair now covering her perfectly shaped head permanent. "Hey," he said with an approving smile, "that's a keeper, Mrs. Mayfield."

The second day, she showered alone. When the water was no longer running and he heard no movement from inside the bathroom, he suspected what was keeping her. He tapped on the bathroom door, slightly ajar, and then gently pushed it open to find her standing in front of the mirror, completely nude, examining her surgical scar, which he deliberately dismissed. Caught in the act, she reacted as if he had just shone a flashlight in her eyes. At that precise moment he grasped the essence of what she was feeling. With the return of the cancer and another mastectomy, the confidence that she had regained after reconstruction of the first breast (postponed until after the birth of their son) was once more gone. Although she had not expressed it, he knew she was again hesitant about her appearance without the armor clothing provided. In fact, unlike before, she was due to undergo breast reconstruction as soon as her body was strong enough.

"Are you trying to stand me up, Mrs. Mayfield?" he asked softly.

Before she could answer, he scooped her up as the towel around his waist fell to the floor.

"We still have a date, little lady, right here," he said, gently placing her in the middle of the bed. Her beautiful eyes widened with mild bewilderment, causing him to chuckle as he pulled the bed covers over them both.

That night they lay together, simply enjoying the intimacy that had been absent for so long, relishing the closeness. No Jennifer tapping on the door. No Brandon dialing the house phone from his study to make some outlandish request to which the answer was always No. Grady now gently fondled and caressed his wife. He still loved her skin, which, as always, was as smooth as satin. She was yet a beautiful woman, despite having to sacrifice her breasts. He wanted to help her discard the negativity and cease agonizing over what she considered her stolen perfection. True, America placed a premium on the magnificent, heralded bosom, but also vying for top billing were other "aesthetically preferred" attributes such as white skin or at least a fair hue, the bluest of eyes, and on and on. Caucasians led the way, even though a significant number of them didn't meet the ideal prototype either. Most of the world willingly endorsed this nonsense.

In fact, it even existed in the Cambridge family Uncle Maurice had mentioned numerous times that when his friend, dark-skinned Joseph Mayfield, asked for the hand in marriage of lovely Rachel Cambridge, it had caused disruption within the light-complexioned Cambridge household. Maurice had stood by his side. Indeed, Maurice always stood by his sister, his friend, and their children. All the Mayfield siblings knew no love or support as strong as Uncle Maurice's, except that of their parents, Rachel and Joseph Mayfield.

"I don't want you to again lapse into that feeling of self-consciousness, little girl." He nuzzled her ear and kissed her deeply. The nightlight was still on. "To me you are beautiful. I love you without symbols of any kind." He kissed her again.

"You don't want me to get breast reconstruction?"

He looked directly into her eyes and held her gaze. "Only if it makes you more comfortable with your body. Otherwise, for me the answer is No," he replied.

"Okay," she answered tremulously.

"Please stop being so self-conscious about it, okay?"

He knew she would not, and that was understandable.

"Okay," she whispered.

With that he leaned over her and kissed the smooth, surgical scar where her right breast once had been. One other time he had done that. The tender act and the poignancy, past and present gave rise to tears. He responded by holding her lovingly and kissing away the wetness on her cheeks.

"Little girl, don't cry," he said softly as he held her in his arms. "Don't cry."

"Grady, I love you so much."

"Then be comfortable with your body. Never be ashamed for my sake. The fact is that if women did not have to nurse their young, as do all mammals, breasts wouldn't even exist." He paused. "I know it's difficult, but try ignoring what America endorses as beauty; do that for me, okay?"

"Okay," she said.

He switched off the nightlight, ushered in complete darkness.

---

The next day the opened drapes revealed a beautiful, bright, sunny Saturday afternoon with people on the streets below, appearing relatively dwarfed in size, engaged in a variety of activities.

Their reservation at one of their favorite restaurants was for six o'clock, so they showered and dressed to dine out for the first time during their stay on the Magnificent Mile. Before the hotel reservations were made, she had declined the dinner cruise on the Chicago River, not wanting to be on water because she yet tended to get a chill. It was the fall season; she was still taking medication for her anemia, although the doctor said she was much better. With this one exception, they had consistently had all their meals within the privacy of their hotel room and were checking out tomorrow before noon to return home.

A year had come and gone. In bed one night Grady said matter-of-factly, "Baby, you are so tired, and you sleep hard. It used to be that when I left the bed or stirred around in the room, in a few minutes you would wake up. You don't anymore. I think the upkeep of this house is working you too hard."

"I'm okay—really, I am."

The next morning, she lingered behind in bed for close to an hour. There had been a time when she was up early in the mornings, before everybody else, brimming with excitement about something planted that had not yet peeped through the soil or a plant that she had purchased and wanted to place in the earth. Gardening had always been her passion, especially early in the morning before the sun brought the heat. More and more, she had begun to skip that time in her garden, hiring a neighborhood teenager to help weed and mulch some evenings.

It was as Grady had suspected all along. Today he was home earlier than usual and found the house quiet when he let himself in. He had spoken with his wife only an hour or so earlier. When he entered the sitting room of their bedroom, she was reclining on the chaise longue, asleep. He sat down on the chaise facing her and tenderly kissed her awake. Immediately she greeted him with a warm hug.

"You are tired," he said gently, kissing her again.

He then got up to hang his suit coat in the closet. Just the week before, Brandon had asked whether his mother was getting sick again, and Grady had confidently informed him that she was not. She possessed an inner spirit that had abided with her for a lifetime. It was that very drive that had allowed her to finish school with a master's degree against all odds. He could identify it because he himself possessed that same spirit, but he knew when to allow it to ebb, and he no longer worked as hard as in the past. At this time, he also wanted her to let it go.

"Come here," he said quietly. She obeyed, and he embraced her tenderly. "What I am going to say doesn't mean that you are inadequate in any way, but I'm observing you, and baby, you are tired. This is a big house."

He remembered stating that fact when they first got married, when he had insisted that they hire a company to give the house a thorough cleaning—including the windows and all the hardwood floors—twice a year, spring and fall.

Although this house had served them well and provided many happy memories, they would inevitably in time sell in favor of something smaller. And for now, they had to make changes to the way it was maintained.

"What it means is that your body has changed, and you might never again have the energy to run this house mostly alone as before, and I don't want you to fight it." He held her away from him, looked down at her upturned face. "I want you to remain healthy and any revisions necessary will be made to keep you with all of us that love you." He was referring to her chemotherapy that had been hard on her body and challenging for the entire family. "We're not super rich, but we're not poor, Clare." He paused. "We can afford it, are you listening to me?"

"Yes," she replied.

She leaned against him, hugged him, and caressed his back. Maybe her life presented unwanted challenges, but she was blessed to share her life with this beautiful man. Sometimes just the thought of him made her heartbeat quicken and her body grow warm.

"So, from now on, the only thing you will pick up heavier than a dust cloth is a kitchen utensil; is that understood?"

"Yes, Mr. Mayfield."

The woman who came twice a week to clean was very thorough, allowing Clare to resume her morning schedule of gardening. This was different from before too, though, because she now had the help of a handyman, elderly and retired. He came faithfully twice a week and welcomed the supplemental income.

# CHAPTER TWENTY-SEVEN

Brandon had just celebrated his sixteenth birthday. At this time, he was experiencing delayed emotions about something else. For him life was presenting challenges he wished would materialize more slowly. For Brandon, life was changing far too rapidly. He wanted to grow into certain phases of his life like one does a larger size of clothing. His favorite teacher was Mr. Tanner. Occasionally they had lengthy discussions on a variety of subjects. Before the fall semester began, Mr. Tanner had decided to return to his native country, the Caribbean Island of Barbados. Over the summer, without warning, one of Brandon's best friends had moved away to another part of the country. Brandon realized it was the decision of his friend's parents. The cute girl from his school that he had been dating decided she wanted to start seeing someone else that she liked more. That really stung him because somehow, he felt that her decision was influenced by her parents. His father jokingly assessed that he just had a bruised ego. His inner struggle ran much deeper, emanating from what he considered a horrific blow. At the time it occurred, he fought back dealing with an emotion he had never experienced. Now, in fact, for the past few weeks Brandon had felt positively numb.

This morning, Grady and Brandon went jogging through the community as they often did. It had become a regular occurrence after the initial incident was resolved several years back—two black males in the neighborhood on a morning jog. Once they were stopped by the police, validated that they were residents of the community; the problem went away. Now they routinely jogged every morning either in the community or quite often with Kevin who had purchased a home in Hyde Park. The two brothers often jogged on the lakefront with their proud father.

This morning Grady noticed that during their jog Brandon was pushing himself. Upon their return home, Brandon quickly raced up the stairs to the bathroom and closed the door. When Grady reached the landing, he heard the shower. After Grady had also showered and dressed, he joined Clare and Jennifer for breakfast. Expecting Brandon—who loved that meal of the day, especially on holidays and weekends—but he was absent. He waited for a few minutes because the family often teased Brandon about his long showers. Finally, he approached his son's room and heard awful sobbing. After tapping lightly on his door, he entered the room, quietly seated himself on the bed beside his son, allowing him time to calm down so that they could converse without the level of turmoil he knew Brandon must be feeling. He had to think of which direction the conversation should take because he too shared this emotion.

Grady thought back, remembering his mother during different stages of his life—when he was a young boy, during his teen years, and eventually during as an adult. He could not recall her absence at any time, and now he would continue life's path without ever again enjoying her physical presence.

Mentally, Grady still stood at the freshly dug grave of Rachel Cambridge Mayfield as the preacher offered her body, encased in that cold coffin, to the earth beneath it. Walking away from the grave site had been the most difficult because then he knew never again would there be anything of her physically above ground. So yes, he more than realized what his son was feeling.

"My mother, your grandmother," Grady said once his son had calmed down, "can travel anywhere and everywhere with you in your heart, in your mind, from photographs and mental pictures, as she will with me. Whenever you wish, you can also visit her gravesite. I know how you must feel, Brandon, because I loved her first and for a very long time. My interaction with her was different from yours because, as my mother, she was the first person I can ever recall bringing into focus as of major importance. Then I saw my father. The same thing has happened to you. You saw your mother first and then, as your father, you saw me. This is the journey that encompasses the beauty of life, Brandon> The new and the old as well as the beginning and the end. We will never fully understand the mysteries and beauties of life's travels as they continue to unfold. Remember how much time your Granny Rachel spent with you during these past few years?"

Brandon nodded solemnly.

"It was because you needed her warmth and her love and her time. For a significant period, your mother's illness prevented her from functioning totally as a parent, so your grandmother was there for you." He paused. "Brandon, there is a power greater than all of us that knew she would not be with you a lot longer. Although Grandmother Estelle was unable to spend as much time with you, Granny Rachel was there. Cherish those memories, Brandon.

"Think of how your grandfather must feel. Just imagine sharing your life with the same person—raising children, enduring life's highs and lows—for over sixty years; suddenly they are gone. Life dictates that eventually children leave home to live their lives, and their parents are the exact way they began, with just each other. Imagine waking up beside that same individual each morning, never sleeping alone for the entire marriage except during childbirth."

"Never," Brandon repeated, seemingly baffled, "not once ever?"

"From what I've been told, not once ever," his father repeated. "So can you imagine how lonely he must be?"

Brandon was sad and pensive but then offered a subdued smile. "Where is he now?"

"Probably in his room," Grady replied quietly. "He was upstairs earlier, but he didn't eat anything." Grady would be forever grateful to Clare for suggesting that his parents sell their home and come live with them. Many things had transpired to indicate that they should no longer live independently. Having them in their home had made a world of difference.

Before, their immediate family had eaten out on Saturday mornings or on the four stools at the kitchen counter. Several years back—Brandon was thirteen and Jennifer nine—Grady's parents had come to live with them. The routine changed. All meals were now served in the dining room so that could all eat together as a family. Those treasured occasions would remain unforgettable.

Brandon got up from the bed, freshly attired. Together they descended the stairs and entered the dining room.

"There's my favorite son," Clare said, smiling fondly from her seated position at the dining room table. Jennifer kept eating, offering only a pleasant smile.

"I'm your only son," Brandon countered pleasantly.

"Exactly," Clare replied softly.

He and his father joined Jennifer and Clare at the table.

Brandon filled up two plates, and before anyone could comment, he explained as he placed everything on a large tray.

"I'm having breakfast downstairs so I can force-feed Granddad."

Off he went with the tray leaving behind laughter.

❧

Father and son drove all over the city—west, north, southeast, and then back southwest—looking at the different types of buildings: two- and three-flat Georgians, Greystones, Tudors, Brownstones, Cape Cod dwellings, and other architectural constructions dispersed throughout the city. Grady placed emphasis on the bungalows.

"Did you know this city can boast of having eighty thousand brick bungalows?"

Brandon was surprised. "Eighty thousand?" he exclaimed.

"Yes. In fact, it has been said that Chicago has the most of any city in this country."

At one point Grady parked the car and pointed. "Whose house does that remind you of?"

The brick was light in color; Brandon looked at the familiar stained-glass windows.

"That one reminds you of whose house?" Grady repeated. He refused to avoid talking about his deceased parents, insisting that Brandon get used to the idea.

"It looks like Gramps and Grandma Rachel's house," Brandon replied, momentarily saddened by the fact that the house was now occupied by a new family. With mental baby steps, he was beginning toy with a few of the many pleasant memories he held of his grandparents, who had tremendously influenced his childhood.

Periodically, after he no longer lived there, Joseph Mayfield would ask Grady to drive him by "just to check on it." Even though he no longer owned it, Joseph Mayfield had still been unable to sever his sentimental ties; he had so many beautiful memories associated with that house. The money from the sale, untouched, remained in his bank account. Grady would then drive his father back to Beverly.

"Dad, spend some of the money," Grady had once suggested to his father.

"On what?" he had replied softly, as if afraid of disturbing old haunts. "What do I need now?"

Just as Mabel had predicted, their father had lasted only a short while after their mother's death. "He grieves nonstop for Mama," she would often say prior to his death.

Grady and Brandon were on the Dan Ryan, heading back south, before Grady spoke to his son again. "Keep in mind that for the most part the employment of the black race is public sector—government jobs. Private-sector employment of black people is less frequent. To make a difference in your own personal life, you must ascertain, being a cut above the rest, that your education and skills acquired in most situations are second to none. Better yet, if at all feasible, decide to work a limited amount of time for corporate America just to obtain the necessary business acumen to become your own boss. It is a fact that you can never get wealthy working for someone else.

"There are a few things I want to say to you. You are beginning to see girls from a different perspective, As I have discussed with you in the past, for the black race plantation days are over, and you are not a stud."

Brandon started to protest.

"Listen, just listen. I know I have told you this before. I am stressing the point again. We have talked about the need to protect yourself against STDs, and siring offspring for which you are not prepared educationally or financially, right?"

Brandon nodded.

"I can never emphasize enough that you need to care about the women that you sleep with, Brandon. That's what I mean when I say you are not a stud on any plantation, and women are not conquests. During slavery, black men and women were not afforded the privilege or the right of caring for each other. Black men at that time were used for impregnating our women to bring forth a human being for toil and production, nothing else. Brandon, care about the women you sleep with. Leave them like you find them. This allows life to remain uncomplicated for both. And Brandon, never, ever discuss with your buddies any woman you sleep with because it privately concerns only two people, you and the woman. Always remember that. Okay, enough said about that, so let's move on.

"Since you are becoming older, there is one prominent factor in life that I always want you to remember. When you open your eyes to a new day, never abuse time. How you use it is the one thing in your complete control. Make it count by using it wisely. Time—God's time—is that constant cosmic clock: it doesn't hurry or slow down but remains eternally steady. You are already aware that you must work for a living, but even then, there are choices. You can choose to be significant even in the workplace. Also, on leisure days it remains your choice to waste a day, keeping in mind that you can never recapture it. Sometimes you need a release from the hassles, the inevitable problems of life. A diversion becomes necessary, a day spent doing fun things. It can be what you consider the best use of your time. Every twenty-four hours, another day arrives, and that universal hourglass never stops sifting your life. Just remember that each day presents you with a choice. It is always your move."

Grady talked to both his children about these matters; Clare did as well. Their children could never accuse their parents of not preparing them for life through travel, education, discussion, and being there for them in every way possible.

໑

Clare could sense something in the air, and the suspense was overwhelming. What was her husband and their thirteen-year-old daughter up to, constantly talking in whispers? Not only that, but intermittently for the past month, they had been in his office on the computer too. Finally, they came to her with exciting news: they had spent the last few months heavily invested in tracking the whereabouts of Dr. Matilda Bethanie Beckford. Clare's eyes widened with disbelief. This was her mother's great-niece; Estelle had often mentioned Matilda (Tillie, they mostly called her) in connection to Matilda's brother Jason, nicknamed Bo. They had found someone who could be her on staff at a prominent hospital in Providence, Rhode Island. This Matilda also had a private practice in obstetrics and gynecology. Promptly telephoning her office, Jennifer had left a message, indicating that it was important for her to call back, hoping that this person could possibly end all her research. The doctor telephoned the very next day. Yes, she was Matilda Bethanie Beckford from Georgia. Yes, Nathan Beckford was her grandfather. At last, the exact location of Tillie had been traced; Jennifer and her father were overjoyed.

Matilda's first question had been about the well-being of Estelle. Jennifer had explained that she was the granddaughter. Her grandmother was doing very well.

For the couple months since then, the two of them had been communicating by e-mail and phone. Jennifer had told Matilda that their communication should remain undisclosed to her grandmother just a little longer because she wanted to have Matilda's trip to Chicago coincide with her grandmother's birthday. Jennifer presumed her relationship to this family member to be second or third cousin since her grandmother, Estelle, had mentioned multiple times that Nathan Beckford, Matilda's grandfather, was her oldest brother.

Jennifer, now thirteen, had other big news for her mother as well: years ago, Matilda had found her brother Bo. He was a retired state trooper in Michigan. Matilda informed Jennifer that he had lived there for many years. She and Bo often e-mailed and telephoned each other and vacationed together on numerous occasions. He had three children, all out of the nest with adult obligations, jobs, and families—all the usual circumstances of most Americans. As for Tillie, she had never married. Even more exciting, when Matilda came to Chicago to surprise Estelle and Ned, Bo was going to come to and bring his wife.

A few days prior to Matilda and Bo's arrival, both Estelle and Ned were casually informed about a cookout to culminate the warm season. Everyone was aware of the randomly cool days that began filtering in after Labor Day, with temperatures that flirted and fluctuated until winter gradually settled into its rightful place. The Mayfield clan and the Beckfords often had this cookout to celebrate the departure of summer. Grady would grill for this occasion, just as he always did during the entire summer season.

Now seventeen, Brandon was astonished and excited by the news and felt pride in his younger sister. She had initiated the entire Internet search and then brought her father in to assist her; the result was that they found Tillie. Their grandmother had often mentioned her with a combination of such fondness and anguish. The latter would cause a somber thoughtfulness to momentarily overtake Estelle, but then she would almost immediately revert to her normal self.

The anticipation of meeting more relatives from his mother's side of the family had caused Brandon to think and talk to his mother more about her family history. The more he learned about it, the more it sounded like something from an epic novel.

Tillie and Bo had gently declined Grady's offer to meet their plane. Instead the plan was to drive from O'Hare in a rented vehicle large enough for family outings.

With Jennifer's help, Clare prepared appetizers with garnishes, a large potato salad, and a gigantic, tossed salad. Jennifer worked tirelessly, in a way that indicated her potential to mature into such a caring young woman. Clare couldn't have been prouder.

Both Jennifer and Grady had gently rejected Clare's suggestion that the welcoming dinner be catered. It would remain a family affair, warm and welcoming, less ostentatious. Both knew that was not Clare's intention, but they thought it best to keep it simple. Since these long-estranged Beckfords were going to be visiting for an entire week, Grady and Clare decided that the extended family, the Mayfield clan, would be included the following Saturday just before Bo and Matilda's Sunday morning departure. That would be a catered affair.

Finally, with everything ready, a surreal hush enveloped the house, interrupted by Matilda's awaited telephone call to Jennifer on her cell phone to announce that they were on their way. As the youngest family member, Jennifer's integral role in such an important event suggested maturity beyond her years.

Ned and Estelle were the only ones still in the dark, exchanging confused glances with each other. There was a certain jubilance in everyone around them, especially in Jennifer. What was going on? And where was the Mayfield clan? They didn't ask but instead remained patient, seated with everyone else. A car was parking in the driveway.

Jennifer was the first one out of the house with the immediate family following; in tow were Ned and Estelle Based on their many conversations and e-mails, Jennifer already knew Matilda. The tall, elegant woman with stylish gray coiffed hair was smiling as she stepped from the SUV. Her eyes sparkled with immediate recognition of the pretty youngster hurrying to greet her. Bo emerged from behind the wheel, his eyes glistening with tears as soon as he saw Ned and Estelle. All were much older and grayed with the passing of time, but recognition was instant. Jennifer graciously stepped aside to witness the poignant, emotional moment as all four of them—Ned, Estelle, Bo, and Tillie—formed a circle. They hugged. fervently kissed each other, almost in reverence, for a long time. Grady, Clare, and Brandon stood with Jennifer to watch a reunion so close to perfection, it would be remembered for a lifetime; the tender, serene moment touched the hearts of all of them.

When the four broke their intimate circle, Estelle rushed over to her granddaughter to clasp her in an embrace and thank her profusely, emotionally overwhelmed by what a wonderful caring human being Clare was raising. She then she pulled her son-in-law to her to express equal gratitude to him. The astounding beauty of what had transpired was that finding Tillie also returned Bo. Ned too hugged and thanked both Jennifer and her father. What could possibly be a more wonderful gift on any day? Clare and Brandon stood together exchanging looks of warmth and awe. Such a beautiful time for everyone. Then, in what seemed like slow motion, a neat little woman quietly emerged from the vehicle. She had purposely avoided disturbing this reunion, this long-awaited pure joy. Bo introduced his wife, Lorna.

It was times such as these that made them thankful for such a large house. Matilda fell in love with the foyer, reminding Clare of Papa, Joseph Mayfield, and his reaction to their entrance when he walked through the door for the first time. She felt a degree of sadness whenever she thought of that dear man. She missed him more than she did her own father. Life was strange, she thought. Two family members, Joseph and Rachel Mayfield, forever gone. Two considered to be permanently estranged were here, alive and well.

The days were precious, passing quickly. There was a daily itinerary prepared by Jennifer and Grady—Navy Pier that Sunday; a cruise on the Chicago River the very next day; the Ninety-Fifth floor of the John Hancock Building that Tuesday. On the fourth day of their visit, it was decided that they should see some other parts of the city. All piled into the SUV, and Grady, with his extensive knowledge of the city, chauffeured their sightseeing tour. First, as far north as Evanston (it was the home of Northwestern University, Grady explained, and Chicago's oldest suburb). The three visitors—Matilda, Bo, and Lorna—fell in love with the Chicago skyline as they traveled along Lake Shore Drive. Grady next took them far west and then southeast—as far as South Shore. In Hyde Park, Grady showed them the building of his bachelorhood days. They walked around Harper's Court and then ate lunch. Once back in the large vehicle, he took them by his office, introduced them to Bradley, Ursula, and agents who were in the office. As they passed the DuSable Museum, Grady drove slowly to point it out and then headed back southwest as far as Hickory Hills. Tillie kept commenting on how very large Chicago was, and Grady replied that their excursions were providing only a brief snapshot. Next time, he said, they would have to come for a longer visit to see more of the city.

Matilda brought a gracious halt to all the "forever moving about," suggesting they simply stay at home and visit for the remainder of their time together.

The four Mayfields—Clare, Grady, Jennifer, and Brandon—looked on as these Beckfords, no longer estranged from each other, spent what seemed like endless hours making up on all those missed years. It was beautiful to watch.

After that first night, Estelle had done as suggested. She returned home to pack some things and stayed at the Mayfield house. She and Tillie shared a room allowing time to catch up. Lorna and Bo occupied the basement quarters. Clare prepared the room next to Grady's study for Max with a comfortable queen-size airbed. Each night when Estelle and Tillie retired to the room they shared, Jennifer excitedly eavesdropped to hear them talking away. It brought her such peace to know that her grandmother was finally reunited with her long-lost Tillie. Well, not really lost, but out of touch.

A few times, Bo decided to go home with Ned, spending the night with him and his family. Certainly, Lorna accompanied him. Each day, both women, Celeste and Lorna, would return with Ned and Bo, smiling, enjoying their husbands' happiness. They couldn't get a word in edgewise, loving every minute of it.

Somehow conversation didn't touch on the Beckford dispute until the latter part of their visit, that Friday evening. The big get-together was scheduled for Saturday. Their departure was Sunday morning. It all fell into place when Bo commented on how unforgiving Nathan Beckford could be. He had been gone for a lot of years. The discussion centered on Bo leaving Georgia in a hurry, and why.

Clare had decided to bring out her best china with all the accessories in celebration of their last intimate family dinner. They drank from expensive crystal glassware, ate with expensive flatware on beautiful china over the protests of Bo, Lorna, and especially Matilda.

"Collards on China!" she exclaimed.

Clare countered with a cheerful "Why not? They were christened long ago." Everybody laughed.

Dinner was soon over, with all the dining finery washed and put away. Now everyone was at the dining room table enjoying coffee in paper cups and dessert on paper plates with plastic forks. Clare suppressed her amusement as she watched Jennifer, who acted so mature, sipping her limited one cup of tea. Brandon enjoyed the same old soda. A few years back, after satisfying his curiosity by tasting coffee and tea, he quickly resorted to his caffeine in the form of Pepsi or Coke.

Ten people were seated at the table. Only the four Beckfords were involved in the conversation as everyone else sat quietly, listening intently to their family history.

"I went to Ohio," said Ned, "looking everywhere for you."

"Bypassed me," said Bo quietly. "I was in Michigan all the time."

Estelle, meanwhile, was rummaging through a myriad of circumstances in her mind. She sifted out the one prominent predicament of the Beckford family: becoming cash poor. As far as she knew, it had never happened before, except perhaps during the Great Depression of the thirties which affected the entire nation. She knew that the stress of those financial circumstances had influenced the way her father, Chester Beckford, died. To this very day she had yet to dispel the feeling of regret arising from thoughts of that rainy evening.

"Tillie," she said, frowning slightly, "were we ever cash poor before?"

"Cash poor," Tillie repeated thoughtfully. She was about to enter an unopened chapter in the Beckford history. She heaved a submissive, thoughtful sigh. then moved on. "I know why we ended up that way," she said suddenly. "My granddad, Nathan, oversaw the money when Great-Granddad got rather feeble. He wasn't senile," she added quickly in reference to Chester Beckford, "but he was less focused and mentally slower. That was when Great-Granddad put Granddad in charge. He wasn't as careful with spending as Great-Granddad had been."

*Oh, so long ago,* Tillie realized as she carefully collected her thoughts. "Raleigh IV, the great-grandson of Old Man McDermott, was the one to create the fine cotton at the textile mill. He inherited the mill from his father, Raleigh III. Raleigh IV's cotton rivaled the very best, except the mills out east. It was superior because it was soft, great for fine cotton dresses and various household needs. It had not always been that way. Then the mill was inherited by Stuart McDermott, the grandson of Raleigh, IV. That happened when I was a premed student.

"The McDermotts were a family of five generations of lawyers," Tillie continued, pausing to put all of it in proper perspective. "Only Stuart's father broke with tradition. Raleigh IV—by then he was getting up in age—had procured the expertise from this young man who had the formula for this very fine cotton but no financial backing to create it. Raleigh IV gave him the backing by hiring him. I can't remember what Granddad said his name was; maybe he never told me. The trouble didn't start until Stuart took over. At the time we were growing cotton for the mill with the other landowners, so we had enough cash to sustain our families and the livestock, plus the education supplements for all who wanted to go to college. As you might not know, the Grangers and the Kanes had always resented our inclusion. At one time they were known as yeoman—farmers. No slavery was involved because they were too poor to own any. The big landowners pushed them into the hinterland and let them grow a little cotton for the mill, but most of it came from us and the other big landowners. At the time we were still growing cotton on McDermott land and some of our own. We had always used a good portion of our land to grow food.

"Then Stuart lost the mill and, as you know, for about two years we also grew cotton for the new owners of the textile mill. That was when we had to lease McDermott land—five thousand acres—to grow the cotton. The lease amount was simply deducted from the money paid to us by the mill. Estelle, when you were about thirteen, the new owners no longer wanted us involved in growing cotton for their mill, but instead employed only the white cotton growers. It was confusing to all but Granddad and Great-Granddad. At that time that Raleigh IV still allowed us to lease the five thousand acres to grow cotton to sell on the open market, but that only lasted two years.

"Granddad told us that for a long time we grew cotton on the McDermott land free so that it wouldn't just lie dormant. It it was benefitting them because we were growing cotton for the mill they still owned. Ned, you were probably about thirteen and Estelle, you were probably eleven when Stuart simply stated, without any other explanation, that he was going to practice law full-time. That mill had been in the family for generations. Stuart McDermott was no longer a mill owner. Instead went off to practice law in both Macon and Atlanta. A lot of his clients were from his grandfather's practice. He kept the house, though. An old woman named Bessie was his housekeeper, but by then Stuart only resided there on weekends. Bessie was the granddaughter of one of the family's former slaves. You know how it was—although slavery was over…" She shook her head. "I'm sure if he paid her anything, it wasn't much. Mostly he just gave her a place to stay, maybe a little money. Maybe, okay?" There were nods around the table. "But that cash poor situation happened when we no longer grew cotton on the *leased* land.

"You don't know this," she said to both Estelle and Ned, "but that's the year I came back to Georgia. I was only there for the summer and going to Meharry that fall."

"I knew about you attending Meharry," Estelle said quietly. That was when all the chaos had begun, she recalled. Most of the youth were scared and began leaving because of what had happened with Bo.

"Yes, but not about what happened with Granddad," Tillie continued. "Since we weren't growing cotton on even the leased land, there was not enough money to give me an additional supplement. I think that's when Granddad wanted me to forget about going to medical school altogether. He said to wait for another year before going to Meharry, but I couldn't. I was afraid that if I did, I would lose my scholarship to someone else. He had helped me to get through premed and said that with the next cash crop—you know, the next cotton crop—I could have some of that money. It wouldn't have been enough because we were no longer growing cotton on the leased land and only on about six hundred acres of our land. Like I stated before, when Great-Granddad handled the money, it went further. To help with my books and additional money I needed, I went to work for the Sturgis family, remember?"

Ned, Estelle, and Bo nodded.

"And Weaver worked as Mrs. Sturgis's gardener and did other odd jobs—as a handyman—inside the house. She was always there when he worked inside her home, so he was of no concern to me. He was always watching me whenever I came, but I wasn't worried about him saying anything to me because Mrs. Sturgis was always there. However, this day, impromptu, she had to go into town. I was there all alone. He was in the yard, and I thought that was where he would stay."

"But he didn't," interjected Bo. "He had come into the house. When I came to pick up Tillie, Mrs. Sturgis was not back yet. Mrs. Sturgis always let me in the back door to wait for Tillie in the kitchen. Tillie let me in, and that rascal had come into the house and followed Sis into the kitchen. When I stepped inside, I blocked his path." He paused. "That's all I did, just blocked his path. I never said one word. He was shocked because he thought she was alone. His excuse was he was thirsty and came in to get a drink of water. I told him, okay, to get his water, but that wasn't it. I came in just the nick of time. Then he became angry, belligerent, threatening, resorting to name calling. Finally, I also became angry. I told him I'd kick his ass. That did it."

"Later on, that night, Sheriff Eades, gun drawn, came to our property," interjected Tillie, "accompanied by Weaver with a head wound. Sheriff Eades needed Weaver to identify his attacker, supposedly Jason. It was a lie—Weaver's wound was self-inflicted; Jason never touched him. The others waited outside, their guns also drawn, with the dogs barking and growling. Sheriff Eades entered each house with Weaver, searching for Jason. Of course, they never found him.

"So," Tillie gently continued, "Granddad was livid. quiet as its kept, so was Great-Granddad. Both were extremely angry with me because they had told me not to work for Mrs. Sturgis in the first place since Weaver worked for her. There were rumors that Weaver had raped a young black girl in Macon years back, but I don't know if it was true. Well, they didn't want me working outside the farm, anyway. They were absolutely, positively furious." She smiled quietly. "You know how they were when any of us worked outside the farm."

Estelle nodded and laughed softly. Then, after a pause, she asked with dismay in her voice, "Even my father was upset?"

"Yes, Great-Granddad was fit to be tied," Tillie said. "When he was a young boy, his father had told him about his brothers—Great-Granddad's uncles—being lynched on our property. He never forgot it. We were not loved in that county. We had too much land and lived way too well. We would have had more trouble than we did if the McDermott property was not such a vast buffer between us and the other landowners. You know, we were closer to Macon than the other properties.

"Great-Granddad had to hide Bo in the privy until late that night," she said sadly.

Ned nodded in agreement, stating that he remembered that entire ordeal.

She shook her head in sorrow. "All I could think about was that he didn't have food or water for all that time." She paused again and looked over at her brother sadly. "Granddad gave Great-Granddad money to give to Jason because he was going to have to leave. It was money that was needed on the farm through the winter months.

"Because of what happened, Jason couldn't come back," Tillie continued. "Although Sherriff Eades and all of the men left our property, some of them still wanted to do something to Jason." She sighed, sorrowfully shook her head. It was quite some time before Tillie spoke again. There was a pained expression on her face.

"After that I left for med school. Every time I wrote a letter to Granddad, he would return it unopened." After all these years, her eyes still filled with tears at the memory. "Before I left, he told me not to come back unless I found Jason and brought him with me. He knew Jason could not come back. I continued to write, but every time he would return my letter, unopened, enclosed in an envelope. Each time on the back of my letter would be the question 'Where is your brother?' Years later—when I could—I hired someone to look for Jason, and they found him. At the time, there was no Internet, none of the modern methods of…"

"Sis, it's okay," Bo said, gently patting her hand. "Stop talking about it."

"But he died," she said with deep sadness, "angry about you leaving, about the circumstance that made you have to leave." She shook her head and gave a sorrowful smile. "You were not found until much later—after he was gone!"

Estelle did not question how much money it was or even whether that was the beginning of the Beckfords being cash poor. She thought about Prentiss and how much assistance he had received. Almost instantly, she abolished the thought, mentally backed away. She dared not enter such a dangerous entrapment. All so very long ago.

Many years had passed; the sting of what had transpired was no more than a dull ache linked to memories in a distant past of muddled confusion. Circumstances were laced with turmoil and forever filed in the cosmic annals of Beckford history, no longer of substantial importance to any of the living.

❧

Jennifer and Brandon sat together on the stoop staring at the photograph of their parents surrounded by friends. Accompanying the photo was a letter to them both. They looked at the picture for a long time before reading the handwritten letter penned by their mother on hotel stationery. Brandon smiled, thinking how strange. Snail mail on hotel stationery! It was amusing that their mother was not text messaging or using her laptop that she dutifully carried everywhere. Brandon looked again at the photo, with Jennifer sitting a step above him peering over his shoulder. Their mother had worn her short natural ever since her last bout with cancer. appearing positively beautiful. *Boy! Scary times,* he thought.

The letter stated that the snapshot had been taken on a street corner in Senegal; in the background stood Uncle Brad and Aunt Maggie, who had been part of Brandon and Jennifer's extended family since childhood as were Uncle Cornell and Aunt Nadine. One thing was for certain: they wouldn't run out of aunts and uncles. The picture had captured what was clearly a moment of joy for the entire group. Only Sharla and her husband, Michael, hadn't made the trip because he couldn't get the time off.

Brandon could still hear his mother questioning their insistence on remaining behind. "You don't want to see the continent of your ancestors?" she had asked one last time, affirming. They would make the trip to the Motherland later.

It was 2009, and Brandon, a recent Stanford graduate, had decided to do his graduate studies closer to home. His focus was international finance, and he had applied to the University of Chicago and the Illinois Institute of Technology. The University of Chicago had accepted his application. Brandon was relieved and grateful that Grady had voluntarily picked up the tab.

Jennifer as well was sticking close to home. The topic came up after they finished reading their mother's letter. "You just want to be a commuter baby and not leave the nest, right?" he teased Jennifer regarding her decision to attend their mother's alma mater.

Her response was to playfully elbow him. He faked teetering from his seated position on the front steps of the stylish bungalow their parents recently purchased, still a Beverly address. The house vaguely reminded them of the former home of their grandparents in Chatham.

"You won't turn into a pumpkin if you go away to school, Jen," Brandon said.

"Are you sure?" she said, feigning worry. "There's no 'once upon a time' narrative with the promise of a prince in my future?"

"Afraid not," he answered.

"I wonder what Grandma is doing," she said.

In 2004, Harvey Cohen had alerted Grady that it was a good time to sell "that lovely home" and still get a decent price. Economic turbulence was brewing. Grady asked how he knew, and Cohen said only, "Don't ask, but do it." After that sale, Grady had waited to capitalize on another business venture.

For several years Grady had stayed in constant contact with a realtor in Macon, Georgia, who finally alerted him to the fact that the developer's big plans had fallen through. After all these years, McDermott land stretched, unused although well kept, toward the horizon. It was now owned by the direct descendant of Neville McDermott, Sybil McDermott Garth, who periodically traveled to the state. Her decision: the McDermott property, all fifteen thousand acres, would be auctioned off; the culprit was the expensive maintenance. The realtor told Grady that Garth's husband was a corporate lawyer established in New York.

Immediately Grady asked Harvey Cohen to travel with him to Georgia. The person in charge of surveying the land gave them—actually, gave Harvey Cohen—what he believed to be the exact location (or close to it) of the original Beckford land. For a nominal fee the realtor was willing to add five hundred acres to the purchase. Grady, although curious, didn't question how Beckford land had once again become McDermott property. He and Harvey made the necessary transaction to purchase the land. Beckford property had increased to two thousand acres.

Upon his return to Chicago, Grady had presented the deeds to Estelle and Ned. He didn't reveal that after opting for a smaller dwelling, he and Clare had taken some of the balance received for their previous beautiful home to redeem Beckford land. In fact, he considered the transaction more than apropos. Long ago Clare had thoroughly familiarized Grady with the Beckford saga. Ned and Estelle were astonished beyond speech; it was almost unbelievable.

After wiring the house so long ago, Bradley welcomed his portion of the sale as "a long time coming." He told Grady that he was investing it wisely; he and Maggie were traveling to the Motherland with the rest of the gang. (Somehow Bradley West had mostly escaped the health ramifications of smoking. He no longer smoked and only confronted with a mild pulmonary condition alleviated by daily medication.)

Estelle considered this good fortune a new lease on life, decided to return to Georgia with Cousin Tillie. At first Bo had what he called "the willies" from looking back. The idea began to positively take root and grow when Ned broke the news: he and Celeste withdrew their bid for the home in Florida. (Florida was Celeste's home state.) She was just as excited as Ned about joining Estelle and Tillie to build on the land. It was becoming a reunion: Bo and Lorna also wished to build there. A twenty-first-century twist—like old times with new beginnings.

Tillie loved computers. She had e-mailed pictures of their newly built house and an electronic invitation. A light taupe stucco structure with deep rich taupe trim. Well planned, right down to the landscaping. Beautiful shrubbery of burgundy, lush evergreens; flowers of deep rose, lavender, and various other vibrant shades. Their grandmother's signature, Brandon and Jennifer agreed, made a bold statement. Tillie and Estelle posed in the backyard with more of that gorgeous garden displayed as a backdrop. Both wore jeans. Their grandmother was crowned in that vintage straw gardening hat that she loved. It looked like happy times. The caption accompanying the picture said, "Two Retirees Enjoying Life."

Brandon and Jennifer planned to visit them before school began in the fall. Although Max was gone, their grandmother seemed happy enough. He had left her well off with a handsome sum of money—stocks and bonds. There were her own retirement benefits as well.

Ned, Tillie, Estelle, and Bo would be forever grateful to Grady, who had always been intrigued with the prospect of purchasing land previously owned by Beckfords. He was glad that he could be instrumental in restoring order so that Calvin Beckford could now rest easy and not spend an eternity shaking his fist.

"Sweetheart, the door is always open. Georgia's not Siberia, you know," Estelle had teased when Brandon protested that she was moving so far away.

"That's comforting," her grandson had countered. "Otherwise, we'd all need thermal underwear."

During her entire relationship with Max, now deceased, his grandmother had always retained the name Ingram. Brandon suspected she and Max were not married. Brandon had queried his mother who confirmed his suspicion. He wondered aloud if his grandmother had spent quality time with Max and had no regrets. His mother promptly replied, "When you visit her, just ask."

Clare had not the slightest doubt that her son would do exactly that. Uncanny indeed that he was so much like his Uncle Jeffrey he would never meet. She would always feel that life had been so very unkind to her brother. She felt he and Brandon would have been fond of each other. Always she had to force herself to discard those kinds of thoughts as futile and wasteful. Still, she couldn't help but feel that it would have been beautiful if the uncle and nephew could have known each other.

Meanwhile, in the present, Brandon sat quietly with his sister. They'd enjoyed such a spectacular day doing nothing much. They had gone for a long walk, visited with their brother Kevin and his wife and family, eaten lunch at one of their favorite restaurants, and then arrived back home.

The sun was in recline, splashing the sky in a palate of reds and orange varieties—farewell hues to embellish the sky at the end of a beautiful day.

"Don't you?" Jennifer said insistently.

"Don't I what?"

"Brandon, you always do that."

"I always do what?"

"Pay no attention when I'm talking to you." She paused good-naturedly. "I was asking—"

"You wondered what Grandma was doing."

She feigned a high-pitched scream—just an octave above a whisper—which always made Brandon laugh. It was something she had done since childhood whenever she became impatient with a situation.

"Then why didn't you answer me?"

"I guess she and Cousin Tillie are enjoying each other's company."

"Don't you find it strange that we have cousins who are older than our grandmother?"

"Things happen," Brandon answered matter-of-factly. "Dad says it all the time: the Beckford family history reads just like an epic novel with only one difference—it's true." He paused. "Since you are going to be the writer in the family, you should pen a novel about the Beckfords. Sit Grandma and Cousin Tillie down one day and turn on the tape recorder. Better yet, expand it into a videotape interview, Turn it into a documentary or a full-fledged movie."

"What do you think I should call it?"

"When the time comes, you will know."

Both got up from the stoop and went inside.